A KENNI LOWRY (
BOOKS 4-6

SIX FEET UNDER
DEAD AS A DOORNAIL
TANGLED UP IN TINSEL

TONYA KAPPES .COM

Southern Hospitality
with a Smidgen
of Homicide

BY
TONYA KAPPES

TONYA KAPPES
WEEKLY NEWSLETTER

Want a behind-the-scenes journey of me as a writer?
The ups and downs, new deals, book sales, giveaways and more? I share it all!

As a special thank you for joining, you'll get an exclusive copy of my crossover short story, *A CHARMING BLEND*. Go to Tonyakappes.com and click on subscribe in the upper right corner to join.

SIX FEET UNDER

A Kenni Lowry Mystery

TONYA KAPPES .COM

Southern Hospitality with a Smidgen of Homicide

Book Four

BY
TONYA KAPPES

DEDICATION

To Eddy:
    ODO NNYEW FIE KWAN

CHAPTER ONE

"Y'all ain't gonna believe this" was the first thing Mama said as Finn Vincent and I moseyed into Ben's Diner. That was something you didn't want to hear out of Mama's mouth at seven in the morning. Or any time, for that matter.

"The clock is wrong?" I asked. "Because I know I'm not seeing you here at seven a.m."

Mama gave me the mom look. She quickly turned her attention to Duke, my fur-deputy bloodhound that went practically everywhere with me.

She bent down and patted him, letting him give her a few kisses. "You're never too old for a whoopin'." She looked up and wagged her finger at me.

The beating and banging coming from the other side of the diner caught my attention. The construction crew was already at it. And so early. I was going to need at least four cups of coffee instead of my usual two if Finn and I were going to be eating here.

"I know why we're here." I motioned between me and Finn, my deputy sheriff and recent boyfriend. Very recent. We were regular morning customers. "But why are you here so early? And looking fresh as a daisy?"

Mama stood up and brushed her hands together.

I looked at her closer and noticed her olive skin was a little too fresh.

Her long brown hair was fixed as if she were heading to a party and her wrinkles were, um, less wrinkly. Maybe it was the beautiful spring morning we were having. The warm sunlight already beating through the windows of the diner projected on her and made her look a little more youthful.

"There is something going on with you." I pointed my finger in a circle around her head. "There's something wrong with her face." I turned to Finn.

Finn looked at me with a very amused expression. It was one of those curious looks that made my heart flip-flop every time he wore it. Over the past few months, we'd explored a relationship outside of the sheriff's office, and I'd have to say that it'd been going slowly but swimmingly.

"We're happy to see you this morning," Finn said, stepping between us and giving Mama a hug. He was using his new southern charm to do exactly that: charm my mama.

His voice was warm and deep, matching the depth of his eyes. His black hair was neatly combed to the side. The first time I'd seen him had been when the Kentucky Reserve Unit was called in to help on Doc Walton's murder investigation. I knew I was in trouble when my physical reaction to his presence was like nothing I'd ever experienced before. Now, a year later, he still had that same hold on me.

"It's refreshing to see your face instead of his," Finn said to Mama and playfully elbowed Ben Harrison, the owner of Ben's Diner, when he walked over to us with a couple of menus tucked up under his arm and three coffees.

He nodded his head towards our usual table up front near the window. Finn, Mama, Duke, and I followed him over.

"One for you." Ben set a coffee down in front of Finn. "Two for you." He sat the other two in front of me before he handed us the menus. "And something for you." Ben tugged a doggy treat out of the pocket of his jeans and gave it to Duke.

"New menus?" I asked, noticing the stained menus that were normally wedged between the salt and pepper shakers were no longer there. "New way of handing out the menus?"

"I was trying to tell you before you rudely interrupted." Mama pushed back over to me. "I'm sorry," she said to Finn. "I raised her better than that."

"Rude," Finn teased me, his smile making my breath catch.

He knew the tension between me and Mama had just started to dissolve in recent months after she'd finally accepted my career choice. I was the sheriff of our town, Cottonwood, Kentucky.

"I was saying that Frank Von Lee is going to be here today!" She bounced on her toes. "In a few short hours," she squealed.

"Really?" I asked a little louder than normal. The construction worker was making a bunch of ruckus banging on a new wood beam on the ceiling of the old building. "So soon? The diner doesn't look like it's completed yet." I turned around in my chair and gave the diner a good onceover.

Ben Harrison had been working hard over the past few months to get the diner camera ready for the Culinary Channel's show Southern Home Cookin', starring the biggest southern culinary chef that'd turned food critic, Frank Von Lee.

"Yes." Mama clapped her hands together. "He's staying at the Tattered Cover Books and Inn right next door. They sure don't give you much notice. Glad I spruced up a bit." She pushed her manicured fingers into her hair to give it a little more volume.

"The diner will look great once they finish getting the beam up today and with a little elbow grease," Ben noted.

"This is it, Kenni." Mama beamed. "Winning that cooking contest last year and having my pot pie featured in the Cottonwood Chronicle has changed my life."

"Not to mention I added your delicious pot pie to our menu," Ben interrupted and pointed to the new menu, where it read "Cottonwood Chicken Pot Pie, homemade by Viv Lowry." He called Mama by her nickname, short for Vivian.

"Mmhmm." Mama's lips were pressed tight as she hummed and nodded, pride all over her face. "That's me." Her shoulders drew up to her ears. Her nose curled, eyes squinted as she smiled. "I've gotten so much recognition." She talked to Finn like he didn't know what was going on.

"You deserve it too." Finn was good at feeding her ego.

"Do I look good?" She craned her neck side to side. "Which is my good side? Left or right?" She rotated some more.

There was definitely something going on with Mama's face. Maybe it was a lot of makeup.

"What?" Mama drew back and looked at me. "Do I have a booger?"

"No, Mama." I rolled my eyes.

"Both sides are beautiful, Viv." Finn was full of malarkey.

"Oh, Finn." Mama giggled and brushed her fingers towards him along with a nose scrunch.

She ran her hand over her hair and down her custom-made apron embroidered with her initials. "Edna is stopping by to do an exclusive interview with me this morning, and I've got to look my best." Edna Easterly was the Chronicle's reporter. Mama's face glowed with pride. "She's going to take some photos of me cooking my famous pot pie. She's going to come back tomorrow too, because that's when Frank is going to try the pot pie. But can you believe he's going to be here in a few short hours? We've been waiting so long for him."

"Frank? Since when are you on a first-name basis?" I asked, lowering my voice since the hammering had stopped.

Ben laughed.

"It's not guaranteed that I'm going to make it on the show." She let out a deep sigh. "There is that diner over in Clay's Ferry he's going to later in the week." She tossed a loose wave of hair. "It's between me and them." She swung her finger back and forth between us. "But you and I both know I'm going to win." She winked.

The construction worker passed us with some wood propped up on his shoulder.

"I'm sorry about the mess. He should be out of here in an hour." Ben let out a deep sigh. "I was hoping to get the whole diner remodeled, but we just ran out of time."

Ben looked exhausted. He had on his normal baseball cap turned backward over his shaggy brown hair. It didn't matter if the president was coming, he wouldn't stray from his normal plaid-shirt-and-jeans look.

"A whistling woman and a crowing hen never come to a very good end." The faint whisper of a familiar voice breezed past my ear.

Duke jumped up and wagged his tail.

"A whistling woman and a crowing hen never come to a very good end,"

I repeated in a hushed tone, looking around to see exactly where the familiar voice of the ghost of my Poppa was coming from.

My stomach dropped. The room tilted slightly and I grabbed the edges of the diner table.

"Hey there, Kenni-bug," Poppa greeted me in a long, low voice, stretching out the greeting. "I'm back."

CHAPTER TWO

"What did you just say?" Mama asked. Her body stiffened.

"A whistling woman and a crowing hen never come to a very good end." My Poppa's ghost did a little jig on his way over to the table with a big grin on his face. He clapped his thick hands in delight.

Duke shimmied and shook with excitement. His nails moved along the diner's tile floor as Poppa danced around.

"Well?" Mama planted her hand on the table and leaned in towards me. "I'm waiting."

"What is Duke doing?" Finn's head tilted to the side.

I cleared my throat and reached over, grabbing Duke by the collar.

"He's probably hungry," I lied, ignoring Mama.

The diner was starting to fill up with the breakfast rush crowd. The way I saw it was that if I did repeat the expression as Mama asked me to do, there were too many people around for her to pitch a fit. Mama would never let anyone see her lose her religion in public, because it wasn't pretty. I'd been on the receiving end of it, and it was nothing I'd wish on my worst enemy.

"I asked you to repeat what you said," Mama demanded through gritted teeth.

"A whistling woman and a crowing hen never come to a very good end," I choked out.

"Where did you hear that?"

"Yeah, before I died, I used to say that to your mama all the time." Poppa had a way of playing little jokes on me since I was the only one who could see and hear him. "Good boy." He patted Duke on the head.

It'd been a little over three years since he died. Elmer Sims had been the sheriff of Cottonwood and my mama's daddy. He was my rock and I looked up to him more than anyone else in this world. Something Mama had a problem with, especially after I went to the police academy and ran for sheriff of Cottonwood, where I was now in my third year of a four-year term.

Thank God the bell over the front door jingled, signaling someone's entrance, because it took the heat off of me. It was Edna, here to do Mama's interview for the Cottonwood Chronicle.

"Mornin', Sheriff." She nodded my way. The bright orange feather hot-glued to the side of her yellow fedora waved in the air with the swoosh of the door closing behind her. "You ready to get this show on the road, Viv?"

Edna stuck her hand in her usual fisherman's vest where she kept all her writing utensils and took out a pen and paper.

She gave a finger wave to Mama and pointed toward the counter before she walked across the diner and sat down on one of the stools next to the regulars. She didn't give anyone but Mama eye contact. She was focused. There wasn't anything that required such media attention that I knew of, if you could call the Cottonwood Chronicle media. Besides the Chronicle, we did have a small radio station in town, WCKK, that played oldies and did a few interviews with citizens in Cottonwood.

"I'm not done with you yet." Mama shook a finger at me. "I'm going to do my interview, but I want an answer when I get back. I've not heard that expression in a long time and I know I've never said it in front of you." Her tongue was sharp. "And don't forget about my class tonight at Lulu's Boutique. I expect you to be there."

Poppa smacked his thigh and doubled over laughing. He stood next to Finn, who was sitting across from me looking at the menu. He'd gotten used to ignoring Mama's and my banter. Only this time, she meant business.

"I won't forget." I confirmed that I would at the cooking class she was offering to the community.

It had been a little over a year ago when the ghost of my Poppa showed up after two simultaneous crimes were committed in Cottonwood. Before that, there hadn't been any crime on my watch since I'd taken office two years prior. It wasn't until I'd accepted the fact that Poppa was my guardian angel deputy from the great beyond that I realized he'd been scaring away any would-be criminals during those first two years of my term. Since then, whenever Poppa showed up, I knew there was some sort of crime about to happen. Though I loved seeing him, it made me feel sick to know the reason he was here.

"What can I get you to eat? Your usual?" Ben asked.

"Coffee is fine." I'd suddenly lost my appetite. There was no way I was going to be able to stomach a thing before talking to Poppa to find out exactly why he was here.

Finn looked up at me and narrowed his eyes.

"You were starving before we got here. What's going on with you?" he asked.

It was cute how his voice held concern when just a few short months ago he probably wouldn't have noticed if I'd not eaten. We'd been spending more and more time together in the off hours since he'd moved in down the street.

"Nothing." I turned my attention to Ben. "The diner looks great. I love how you're replacing the old wood beams with new ones."

"Thanks." He pointed to the old wooden ceiling. "The beams really needed to be redone, and even though Frank Von Lee is only here to taste the pot pie to decide if they will feature it on the show, I thought I'd go ahead and get the work done anyways."

"I don't blame you. Y'all deserve to be recognized for all this amazing southern food." I smiled. "What are you trying to finish in a couple of hours?"

"I got the floors buffed and shined. He's on the last beam now. The menus are done, and all I have left is getting a new pot holder to replace the old one hanging above the kitchen island." Ben rocked back on the heels of his shoes.

"It looks great so far," I assured my friend.

The door between the kitchen and the dining room swung open and smacked up against the wall. The bang got everyone's attention real fast. The chatter among the guests stopped and all eyes watched as the man who emerged from the kitchen stalked over to Ben.

"I can't work in this atmosphere." The man, wearing a white chef jacket, dragged a white cap off of his head. His brown hair was matted down and wet from sweat. "This is not how I imagined this would be. I expected a quiet work environment for perfection. Not destruction. I cannot and will not work in this...this mess!"

Out of the corner of my eye, I saw Poppa ghost himself gone.

"Yes, you will." Ben's face turned crimson with fury. "You're the one who said you'd love to do the job since we knew each other and graduated from culinary school together. You jumped at the chance. You signed a contract. I paid you upfront and you won't make a fool out of this diner or me. You and I both know you need this job, so you aren't going anywhere. Do you understand?" Ben jabbed the man in between his shoulder and collarbone. The man took a step back in a vicious jerk. His eyes narrowed to crinkled slits.

The man stomped off in the direction of the kitchen.

Ben offered us an apology. "I had to hire Mundy to run the diner while I took care of the construction. I can't be everything around here."

Ben Harrison had a couple of locals that helped in the diner here and there, mainly high school kids to bus and clean, but otherwise, it was just him running the entire place. He had done all the cooking up until now.

"This is why I've always been hesitant to hire people." He offered an apologetic smile.

"No worries, man." Finn shrugged it off. "This Frank seems to be a big deal. I'm sure everyone is a little tense today."

My focus was on Ben. I'd known him all my life and I'd never seen him get so angry.

"Now, what is this about you not being hungry?" Ben asked and changed the subject.

"I'm just going to have my coffee for now." I wrapped my hand around one of the white ceramic mugs to warm them from the chill of nerves that were shooting through my body.

"Fine." Finn handed the new menu back to Ben. "I'm going to have the Cottonwood special."

"Great choice." Ben took the menu. "It's a new one, along with the hot brown for supper. You'll have to come back tomorrow during the tasting so the diner will be full when Frank Von Lee is here. I want a good showing, ya know."

"Absolutely," Finn agreed. I nodded too.

"By the looks of this morning, you're going to have standing room only." I was proud of my friend. He'd come a long way from the grilled cheese we'd made in my mama's kitchen when we were in high school and pulling all-nighters studying.

"Two more won't hurt," he said.

After a few more minutes of chitchat, Ben headed back to the cranky new chef, leaving Finn and me alone. Finn waited until Ben walked off to reach across the table and touch my hand. The warmth of his touch made me tingle. My pulse quickened and my tear ducts swelled.

"Are you okay?" he asked. "You look like you're in another world."

Another world? The afterlife. My stomach churned. If only Finn knew about Poppa.

I licked my lips. Was it time I told my real partner about my ghost partner? Before I could say a word, his cell phone buzzed on the table. He pulled his hand off mine and I watched as he picked it up to look at the number.

"I'm sorry." Finn stood up. "I need to take this." A look of irritation washed over his face after he pressed the phone up to his ear and headed out of the diner to talk in private.

I blinked the tears from my eyes and flipped my attention to my mama. Edna's eye was pressed up against her camera, clicking away as Mama posed in the strangest positions with an empty casserole dish, a spatula, and a big ole smile on her face.

Poppa appeared next to Mama. I covered my mouth with my hand and laughed, watching him mimic Mama. It was so good to see him, but I was also waiting for the other shoe to drop when Poppa came and a crime hadn't been reported.

"Sorry about that." Finn stood next to his chair.

"Cottonwood special." Ben sat the plate in front of Finn.

My mouth watered at the sight of the special. The Cottonwood special was goetta sausage, cheddar jack cheese, and sautéed onions baked in a mini cast-iron skillet with a fried egg on top.

"That was my contractor." Finn sat back down. "I'm having the hardest time getting the construction done on the house. This is the second time they've canceled." Finn shook his head.

The house Finn had bought from Lonnie Lemar, my old deputy, had been a rental property for Lonnie. Like most rentals, there was a lot of work that needed to be done after the tenants moved out. Finn decided to put a little addition on the back, connecting the family room and kitchen into one big room.

"They've been doing this addition for months now. I'm going to have to find someone else." He let out a long exhausted sigh. "He said he's too busy to finish the job but still wants to be paid for what they've done."

"Who did you use?" Ben asked and set down a to-go cup of coffee on the table for me. It was so nice to have a good friend who knew exactly what I needed.

"Danny Shane." The local building company consisted of Danny and his three sons. Finn rolled his eyes.

"Yeah. Damn shame, ain't it? His family has spent decades building up their construction business. Danny takes over and they go to hell in a hand basket," Ben said, catching my attention. "I fired him a couple of days ago, and luckily these guys were in here when it happened and they do construction, so I hired them and they're getting it done." Ben shook a finger at me. "You know what, I'm glad I fired him. Someone told me Danny said my food gave him food poisoning. Jerk."

Ben had never been so on edge. It had to be because of the stress of the food critic's visit. After all, it would be his diner that would take the hit, not necessarily Mama. Her ego might be bruised if she wasn't picked. That'd be on me to listen to for years.

"A couple of days ago?" Finn chuckled. "They shouldn't be busy then and should've been able to come by the house."

"Riley," Ben hollered and snapped his wrist in a wave at one of the construction guys to come over. "Finn Vincent, this is Riley Titan. Amazing man who did all this work."

The two men shook hands.

"Riley, Finn is in the same boat I was in with the same contractor. Do you think you can run over to his house on Broadway and take a look at his addition?" Ben asked.

"I'm not going to do this!" the chef screamed from the pass-through window into the diner. He flung the towel off his shoulder and threw it down.

"I'm going to knock him in the head with a rolling pin." Ben's jaw tensed. He turned on a dime and stalked back to the kitchen.

"Is it okay if I head over tonight?" Riley asked.

He was a little overweight and sweat beaded along his forehead under his shaggy head of hair. He looked around thirty and a little too young to be so out of shape.

"After six is great." Finn wrote down his address on a paper napkin. After Riley walked away, Finn said, "I guess I better go visit Danny and settle up on what I owe him."

"Yeah. I better go make my rounds." I looked down at Duke. "Ready, Duke?"

He jumped to his feet, eager to go. He loved going for rides.

"I'll talk to you soon." Finn gave me a kiss goodbye and Duke a good scratch behind his ear before he left.

On my way out the door, I glanced back at Mama. Her lips were flapping a mile a minute as Edna wrote just as fast. Poppa was nowhere to be seen. Even as my foot stepped over the threshold, the sound of pans banging around and yelling came from the kitchen.

"I'm telling you that I'm not going to work in this noise. It hinders my creative flow and I'm not going to do it. Contract or not!" Mundy, the temporary chef, shuffled backwards in front of the pass-through kitchen window.

When I saw Ben practically chasing him, I hurried back through the diner, but not without noticing everyone was either sitting and watching or walking back to see what was going on.

Even Mama's interview had come to a halt. Duke had already made it to the kitchen before I'd even gotten close. It wasn't unusual for my furry sidekick to rush in before me. He'd even taken a bullet for me a few months ago and got a medal from the town because of it.

"All right. Break it up." I pushed through the door to find Mundy jabbing a big sharp knife towards Ben.

Riley was hanging out on top of the ladder with a DeWalt drill in his hand where he'd been hanging the new pot holder over the island. Slowly he eased down each rung and ducked back into the diner. I didn't blame him. The knife Mundy was swinging at Ben could possibly fly out of the crazed man's hand, and who knew where it'd land.

Neither man bothered to look at me. Duke tried to get between them because he knew they couldn't resist a cute dog.

"You will hold up your end of the deal!" Ben screamed back at him. His jaw tensed, his fist balled at his side. I could feel the anger coming from him. Then he released a finger to swipe it across Duke's head because Duke wouldn't stop nudging his leg.

Ben took the tea towel off his shoulder and wound it around his hand as he tried to grab the knife. Duke stuck to him like a booger on a finger. "Duke, shoo."

Ben lifted his leg to try to get Duke to move, but the dog didn't budge. It was like he knew that Ben needed to calm down, just like I knew he had to knock it off.

"All right!" I had to scream over the two men again. "That's it. Break it up." I did that whole cop stance thing with my legs apart and rested my hand on the butt of my gun nestled in my belt holster. "I'm thinking this employment is over or I can take both of you to the office."

Not that I had to go far. My office was just a few doors down in the back room of Cowboy's Catfish. If I did have to haul them down, I really wasn't sure what I'd do with one of them since we only had one cell. There wasn't any way they'd be able to stay in there. They'd for sure kill each other. Another murder wasn't anything I, or Cottonwood, needed.

Mundy looked at me, his nostrils flaring with his deep inhale. His eyes slid over to Ben, who was still leveling a death stare at the poor man. His chest heaved up and down, and his mouth twitched.

Mundy set the knife down on the counter and put his hands in the air.

"I don't want no trouble. I just want to leave," he said to me.

"Fine. If you have any belongings, grab them and we'll wait right here." I was glad to see things come to an end without someone getting a finger chopped off.

"That's my knife." He went to get it, but I made an eh-eh noise to shoo him away. "Chefs carry their own knives. Besides, I wouldn't've wasted a good sharpened knife on the likes of him." The right corner of his lip snarled.

Ben didn't move, even when Duke tried to get him to rub his head. Duke had even gone as far as putting the top of his head in Ben's dangling hand, but Ben was stiff.

The chef didn't take long. He had a cloth bag rolled up in his hands with his knives in it.

"I swear you are dead," Ben said through gritted teeth when the chef walked past him to get out of the diner. "No one in this industry will hire you ever again."

Ben couldn't leave well enough alone.

The chef stopped so they were shoulder to shoulder. His chin glided toward Ben. Their eyes met. I took a step forward, but the chef hocked a big loogie at Ben's feet before he walked out.

The clicks from Edna's fancy camera clicked at rapid speed. She sure did have a front-page story for tomorrow's edition.

"Sonofa..." Ben grumbled. He took off his hat and threw it on the ground.

"What is wrong with you?" I interrupted him. "We've known each other since we were knee-high babies and I've never seen you act like such a loon."

He dragged the toe of his shoe back and forth before he bent down and picked up his hat. Duke saw this as his opportunity to get in a lick since Ben was at his eye level. Ben's hand finally gave in to the very determined bloodhound. Duke stretched out in delight with each scratch of Ben's nails.

He shook his head and dragged his hand up to his hair, raking his fingers through it.

The stress had taken a toll on him. The wrinkles next to his eyes had deepened. The bags under his eyes had darkened.

"It just so happened that Mundy called me yesterday right after I'd made a decision to hire someone while I took the extra time to get the work on the diner completed. No sooner did I get off the phone with him than the Culinary Channel called to let me know Frank was coming today. Mundy was working up at Le Fork where we'd met in school. I called him back and offered him the job with a contract. Sight unseen, he took the job and showed up here today." He threw his hands up in the air. "He was always a great chef. I even made it easy on him by letting him have free creative expression while Viv and I focused on her pot pie."

"Now it's over and we need to move on. I'm sure you'll think of something. You always do." I could tell by the expression on his face that he didn't give two cents what I was saying. "He did seem like a hot head, so maybe it's a good thing he's gone before Frank gets here."

That sounded like a bright side to me.

While Ben had been doing his culinary thing, I was off to the police academy. During that time I rarely kept up with my old friend from high school. I just wanted to get through my training and get out. It wasn't until Poppa died that I'd decided to come back, which was when I'd reconnected with my childhood friends.

"He can go back to Le Fork up in Lexington. Granted, Ben's is a step down from his big restaurant dreams." Ben shook his head. "I knew better. He's ruined every place he's ever gone. I was giving him a shot."

"Some people just don't know a good thing when they see one. Plus, how well can he cook your cornbread?" I tried to offer sympathy with my voice. Southern cooking truly was an art form. Some people thought we just threw things in a fryer. Not true. It was the golden crisp, just enough lard, and the perfect seasonings that made my mouth water with every dish at Ben's.

"What am I going to do with just a few hours left before Frank Von Lee gets here?" Ben asked.

I would've offered my services, but no one in Cottonwood wanted a frozen dinner from the Dixon's Foodtown.

My phone chirped a text. It was from Jolee Fischer, my best friend and Ben's girlfriend.

"I need a friend to talk to. Ben's all nuts and crazy over this Frank thing and we've not spent any time together."

"I think I just solved your chef problem." I quickly texted Jolee, "Where are you?"

She replied, "On my way to park the food truck at Lulu's."

Jolee owned the only food truck in Cottonwood, On The Run. Every day she parked her truck in different locations around the city. Most mornings she parked in front of Lulu's Boutique on the north side of town so the people going to work in town could stop for a quick breakfast sandwich and coffee.

"Can you stop by Ben's Diner first?" I wrote.

"Sure thing."

"What do you mean you think you solved my problem?" Ben asked.

It was a perfect solution. "Think about it. Jolee and you haven't been spending a lot of time together. She would love to help you out. She can get Viola White and Myrna Savage to take over since they were the runners-up against Mama."

It was a brilliant idea.

"It's only two days that Frank will be here." I continued to sell him on the idea. "You know she can cook good food too. And without you watching over her."

"I think this might work." The smiling Ben I'd known all my life appeared before me with a very thankful face. "One more thing. Can you come here this afternoon and do crowd control? According to the latest phone call, Frank wants to come here after he checks in and talk to me and Viv."

"No problem. I'll be back in a few hours." I patted my leg for Duke to come. "Jolee will be here in a minute. You can discuss the situation with her because I've got to do my morning drive-bys."

Duke and I headed out the door. My shoulders were back and I was confident that I'd just kept the peace once again in Cottonwood. Though there was the one little issue that had just showed up. Poppa.

CHAPTER THREE

After doing my morning rounds and stopping to say hello to a few of the citizens walking around, I headed on back to the office to see what was going on there. All seemed to be quiet and I'd not seen hide nor hair of Poppa.

Betty Murphy, my office clerk and dispatch operator, was busy filing and answering the phones. I typed a little report up about what had gone on at Ben's Diner just in case it came back to bite me in the hiney. One aspect of the sheriff's job was to document everything. This would be classified as disturbing the peace.

The dispatch phone rang. Betty scurried over to answer it, probably thankful for the distraction from answering any more of my questions. I flipped Duke a treat from the jar that sat on my desk.

"Dispatch, how can I help you?" Betty asked in her sweet southern drawl. "Why, hello, Viv."

My head jerked up.

I waved my hands in the air and shook my head at Betty. She looked up at me and smiled. "I'm not here," I whispered.

"Why, she sure is here. No, she's not busy at all. Hold on." Betty clicked the hold button. "Sheriff, your mama is on line one."

I eyeballed her.

"I'm not lying to your mama." She didn't look at me. She busied herself with some papers on her desk.

A bigger sigh than normal escaped my body so Betty would know I wasn't happy with her ignoring me.

I picked up the receiver, pushed the button, and said, "Hello, Mama."

"I found out what restaurant he's going to in Clay's Ferry." There was excitement in her voice.

I should've known Mama wasn't going to let it go. She had an itch to find out what diner she was competing against and she scratched it.

"Betty said you weren't busy, so I'm going to head over to the department and get you and take you to lunch," Mama said. "We have a couple more hours until Frank gets here."

There she went calling him Frank again as if she knew him personally.

"Mama, I'm knee deep in paperwork. I need to get it done. Maybe another day." I thought my excuse was a pretty good one for thinking on my feet, which was hard to do when I was talking to her. She always seemed to fluster me.

"We have to go on what you'd call a stakeout." There was an uptick in her tone that I didn't like.

"Stakeout?" I laughed. "No. I'm not going on no stakeout," I assured her.

"Fine. Then how about lunch with your mama." She wasn't going to let it go that I didn't have anything to do. "We can go wherever you want. I'm nervous. I need my daughter."

And there went the guilt she was good at. What was a lunch date with her going to hurt? After all, she'd worked really hard to get the visit from Frank Von Lee. She'd won a local cooking competition between Jolee Fischer's food truck and Ben's Diner. Mama's chicken pot pie won and somehow the Culinary Channel found out and it was all she wrote after that. The least I could do was go eat with her.

"Wherever I want?" I asked. "Is there a catch?"

"Can't a mama take her only daughter out to lunch?" she asked. "After all, later I'm going to be busy with Frank in town and then the filming."

Mama had a big ego. She'd already proclaimed herself the winner of the spot on the Culinary Channel before the contest had even begun.

"All right." There was no sense in arguing with her. Everyone in Cottonwood knew that what Viv Lowry wanted, Viv Lowry got. "I'll even let you pick where we eat."

There was a nigglin' suspicion that Mama was suddenly feeling generous and it was at my expense. But I was willing to play along just to see exactly what she had up her sleeve.

CHAPTER FOUR

I'd decided to leave Duke at the office with Betty. Not that she'd mind. I knew she'd have to get up and take him out, but she liked getting out in the community and talking to the neighbors. It was good as dispatcher to be known in town. Especially with the election coming up. Luckily, I was running unopposed, though that could change on a dime. I didn't put anything past the people of Cottonwood.

I'd made sure everyone in and around Cottonwood stayed happy with the department. Seeing Poppa this morning was wonderful but meant something was stirring in Cottonwood. That was bad. At least, that'd been the pattern before. When he showed up, there was either a murder or a robbery.

Mama pulled up in her big white Escalade. Her eyes barely reached the top of the steering wheel.

"You want me to drive?" I asked, hoping she'd agree, but Mama never let anyone drive. Not even Daddy. Ever. Poor Daddy.

"Nope." Once I was settled in the passenger seat, she flung the gearshift into drive and headed down the alley.

At the stop sign, she dragged her head side to side to look both ways. I noticed the lines on her face were practically gone.

"Mama?" I asked when she leaned way over the steering wheel to see across me. I pushed my back into the leather seat. "What on earth has happened to your face?"

"What on earth are you talking about, Kendrick?" Mama saying my full name was a surefire way of knowing she didn't want to answer the question.

"I don't know." I gripped the door handle when she punched the gas, pulling right out in front of Doolittle Bowman's car on West Walnut Street. She was able to turn the wheel and push the electric window button at the same time. I feared for my life and held on tighter.

"That's my girl. Woo wee!" Poppa yelped from the back.

"Thank you!" Mama screamed and threw her hand out the window as if Doolittle had stopped and graciously let Mama out. Which she didn't.

I looked at the side mirror and Doolittle was giving Mama two kinds of hell. Good thing I wasn't able to read lips because she was giving Mama the business and honking her horn.

"Mama, you pulled out in front of her." I sucked in a deep breath.

"Honey, there was plenty of room. I'm sure she sped up when she saw me pulling out. That's the way them Bowmans are." Mama tilted her chin up as if she'd done nothing wrong.

"That's right, Viv." Poppa proudly stated from the backseat. I refrained from turning around because Mama would think I was looking at Doolittle, whose front bumper was practically kissing Mama's back bumper.

When Mama turned right on Main Street, my mind turned over, trying to think of any restaurants Mama would privy herself to eat in on that side of town.

"Where're we going to eat?" I asked Mama.

"Now don't be going and having a dying duck fit."

"Trigger word," I grumbled, knowing that this was no mother/daughter lunch to just chitchat about life.

"What do you mean trigger word?" Sarcasm dripped in Mama's honey-sweet southern accent.

"Whenever I questioned anything you did when I was at home or there was something I wasn't going to enjoy doing, you'd say 'Kenni, don't be going and having a dying duck fit.'" I tried my best to do her accent and tone.

"That's not how I sound," Mama shot back.

"Pretty darn good if you ask me." Poppa cackled from the back.

I'm not gonna lie, I huffed and puffed a little. A duck fit might have been brewing up in me.

"Tell me what's in that pea-pickin' brain of yours." I was tired of playing games.

"Well..." She dragged the word out.

"Now, Mama," I said through gritted teeth.

"I've decided to take you to a nice little diner over in Clay's Ferry." She pushed the pedal a little faster as she passed the city limits sign on the far end of town.

"Mama, no," I responded. "You're going to your competition."

"Competition?" Mama laughed. "What have I told you all your life, Kendrick Lowry? We are in competition with no one. We are leaders."

"Poor, poor souls." I prayed for the people we were about to encounter. They'd no idea what the wrath of Mama was like.

This was Mama's pattern. Way back when I was five and entered the pig catching contest at our annual festival, she'd made sure she'd scared all the other kids, telling them about biting pigs, so that when it was time for me to run in the muddy area to catch the pig, I was the only contestant. Then in high school when I was running for student council, she'd offered the mothers of the other candidates a place on the Cottonwood Beautification Committee if their child withdrew from the election. But when it came to running for sheriff my first time, she'd done everything in her power to sabotage me, even went as far as putting in Duke as a write-in.

After I won, she'd sort of accepted the fact that I was an adult and making my own choices. Then, a few months ago when retired deputy Lonnie Lemar decided to run against me in the next election, Mama Bear came out and she pinned a Vote for Lowry pin on anything that she could.

Thankfully Lonnie ended up having a few issues in his personal life that gave him back his God-given sense and he pulled out of the race, leaving me with no competition...yet.

That made Mama happy, because even though she didn't like me being sheriff, she liked losing less. So she'd decided to let me put my life on the line for the sake of saying we won.

"What are you babbling about?" Mama's nose curled.

"Fascinating." I leaned closer to Mama as she bounced us up, down, and around the hills of the back roads toward Clay Ferry. "Even when you crinkle your nose, your lines still aren't visible."

"Shush your mouth, Kendrick." Mama pulled her shoulders back. "I figured we'd just go eat lunch. No one will know we're there. It's healthy to go and check out your competition."

I smacked my hands together. Mama jumped. She scowled again.

I took another look at Mama's flawless face. "You've had some work done on your face."

Why hadn't I thought of that earlier?

"What are you talking about?" Mama held the wheel steady as she sped up.

"You know exactly what I'm talking about. Botox? Filler? I bet you're the first person in Cottonwood to get a facelift." I knew I'd get her goat.

"Facelift? No such thing." Mama dragged the pad of her finger up to the corner of her eye and tapped it a little. "I just had a little plumping done so when I go on camera, I'm not all saggy."

"Mama," I gasped. "I can't believe you did this."

"What?" She drew back. "Kenni, it's national TV."

"You've lost your ever-loving mind. Poor Daddy. I hope he makes it through these next couple of days." I shook my head.

I shouldn't have been surprised. It was just like Mama to try to one-up people before they even knew they were one-upped by her. This was her specialty. Her southern manners were spot on. It was too late when you realized Mama was getting her way no matter what.

"Enough of that. What did you think about Ben's today?" Mama was good at changing the subject.

"For starters, I'm not sure why he's gone and done all this work on the diner. Its oddness was what made it so special. Don't get me wrong, your pot pie is phenomenal, but Ben's trying to change everything when really the focus is on you," I said.

"Chef Mundy wasn't nice." Mama's lip twitched. "He said he'd made better pot pie than me and he even tried to make one."

"He did?" My brows furrowed. Mama nodded. "I'm surprised you didn't whack him."

"I almost did. Luckily Ben put him in his place by telling him that the Culinary Channel was there to see me and he was there to cook the rest of the orders. The chef didn't like that." She shrugged. "I'm glad he's gone."

I looked at the speedometer and noted the Clay's Ferry county line was coming up soon.

"I'm glad for Jolee. She said Ben's crazy attitude has really taken a toll on their new relationship. Slow down, Mama," I said. "Their sheriff isn't as nice as me."

"Speaking of sheriff…" She held the wheel with her left hand and reached into her backseat.

"What on earth are you doing?" My tone escalated. "Keep both hands on the wheel."

"Here." She threw a duffle bag of mine next to me on the front seat. "I took the liberty of getting you some regular clothes from your house to put on while we went to lunch. They can't know we're from Cottonwood and your uniform screams it."

"Remind me to take your key away." I unzipped the bag and tugged on the sweater over my uniform shirt. Mama didn't care; she came into my house no matter what time of day it was.

"And put a little lipstick on too. It'll make you feel better." Mama's cure for everything was lipstick.

"I don't feel bad," I said.

"You probably will after you eat this food." Mama pulled into The Little Shack barbeque joint's parking lot.

CHAPTER FIVE

The Little Shack was one of those barbeque joints that you would drive by a few hundred times and wonder how on earth someone could eat in there. The shotgun establishment needed a new siding job or a good scrubbing and a fresh coat of paint. The OPEN sign only blinked the letter P. Even the parking lot needed a good overhaul. The once-concrete pavement was now in chunks.

"Hold on." Mama gripped the wheel and bumped the car up to the front of the door in the handicap parking spot.

Surely she wasn't going to park here, I thought to myself, but then she put the gearshift into park.

"Mama, I don't know exactly what you've done to your face, but it's messed up your eyesight." I jutted my finger toward the faded handicap sign. "Handicap, Mama."

She leaned her body over the front seat and opened the glovebox. She grabbed a handicap hanger and slapped it around the rearview mirror.

"What on earth?" I took a closer look at the tag. The wheelchair was pink. "Is this real?"

I never took a good look at the tags before; I just gave tickets to cars parked in the handicap spots with no tag in the window or on the license plate.

"Of course it's real or I wouldn't have it." She reached behind the seat and grabbed her pocketbook. She started to get out of the car. "I told you that I got a little plumping, so I'm delicate for a couple of weeks. That's all."

I hollered out to her before she got out and had the opportunity to slam the door. "Did plumping make you lose your brain? You're not handicapped."

"Unless they changed it for gender color, that isn't real." Poppa had ghosted himself into Mama's seat and he too took a nice long look at it. "Maybe I'm here because your mama has lost her marbles. It does run in the family."

"You don't think Mama is going to..." I gulped, wondering if Poppa was like the ferryman to the underworld and he was here to collect Mama.

He shrugged.

I jumped out of the car.

"Oh, Mama." I grabbed her and kissed her cheek. "I love you so much. Are you sick?"

"Sick?" She pushed me away. "You seem to be the one with something wrong." She twisted around on the balls of her feet and trotted into The Little Shack with her pocketbook swinging in the crook of her arm. "You need to mind your own P's and Q's."

Poppa took notice too. He made sure he stayed next to her the entire time we were there.

"Take a seat," the woman behind the cash register next to the door hollered out but never looked up.

"Welcome to The Shack," a man from the kitchen window yelled and dinged the bell resting on the ledge.

Mama helped herself to one of the middle picnic tables. There were five picnic tables perpendicular to the door and two running along both sides of the wall to help accommodate the small shotgun of the building.

"Mama, remember, we're just here to taste the food." I nodded, hoping to shut down any thoughts in her head.

"Y'all want a coke or water?" the woman from the register asked.

She'd moseyed over and pulled an ink pen from her messy brown updo.

"Where's your notepad?" Mama asked in a curt way.

"I don't need no notepad." The woman's accent was much more hick than ours.

You'd find that in Kentucky. You could drive two hours north of here and not hear a bit of a southern accent. You could drive two miles south of here and everyone sounded like they were from the far south.

"Hm." Mama pursed her lips. "This doesn't seem all that nice."

The woman let out a long sigh and leaned on her right side with her hip cocked out.

"I'll have a sweet tea." Mama straightened her shoulders as if she were in the front pew of Cottonwood Baptist Church on display for all to see.

"Coke or water," the woman repeated and took the pen, scribbling something on the white paper tablecloth.

"Is it tap or bottled?"

The woman stared down her nose at Mama, none too happy.

"We'll each have a coke," I suggested the best bet. The woman sauntered off in no big hurry to get us the cokes.

"I don't drink coke. I drink tea," Mama protested like a little child.

"She never did like coke," Poppa backed her up.

"If I didn't say coke, she'd have gotten you some toilet water because you are acting as if you are too good to be in here." I curled my fingers together and placed them in front of me, leaning on my forearms. "You've got to go unnoticed. If someone finds out who you are..." Mama's brows furrowed. She didn't get it. I shook my head and tried again. "If they find out that we're here to see your competition, we won't be welcome. Now act normal."

Inwardly I groaned, knowing this was her normal.

"Let's talk about your face." I had to bring it back up. I was in a state of shock over it. "What did you do?"

"I might've had a little work done so I'll look good on camera when they film the segment." Mama lifted her chin and dragged her fingers along her jaw. "A little tightening here." She moved them up to her crow's feet. "A little filler here. Maybe a little plump up here." She tapped her lips.

"Why on earth would you do that?" I questioned. "You are Viv Lowry. You don't need any help."

"Honey, we all need help." Her eyes assessed me. "Tomorrow it will look better and in a week when they film, it'll look natural."

Mama and I sat back enough to give the waitress some room to put the cokes down.

"What do you want?" she asked.

"Where's the menu?" Mama crossed her arms.

"Right down there." The woman pointed to the white paper tablecloth she'd written on that we hadn't paid attention to. "Pulled pork, pulled beef, pulled chicken. All barbeque. French fries, hush puppies, and coleslaw."

Mama curled her nose.

"I guess I'll have the chicken." Not a fan of the menu display, Mama put her finger in the air.

"What's she doing?" Poppa asked with concern. "Tell her to put her finger down."

"One suggestion," Mama started.

"Mama," I warned, but it was too late.

"You could use a little help on your menu writing skills. You are very sloppy and people can't read that. You could also explain what you are doing. I thought you'd contaminated my eating space."

"Is that so?" The woman shifted her eyes from Mama to me.

I smiled an empathetic smile.

"Honey, you're the one with her, not me." The woman had a point.

Mama's tight plumped-up bottom lip dropped.

"I'll have the chicken too. It sounds good." I said and whacked Mama under the table with my foot before Mama had any opportunity to say another word.

"What did you do that for?" Mama yelped and reached down to rub her shin.

"Two chicks!" the waitress called and walked back to the register.

I looked around to see who she was calling out to, but no one seemed to be looking at her or us for that matter. The place was packed and three new people had joined us at our picnic table.

"You eat here before?" Mama questioned the man next to her.

"Best barbeque in the state." The man smiled. "In fact, they are going to be featured on the Culinary Channel."

"Not if I have anything to do with it," Mama grumbled under her breath and turned from the man. The man's brows dipped and he scoffed at Mama. Again, I gave another sympathetic smile.

Whether she knew him or not, he'd said fighting words and Mama was a grudge holder. Shocker.

"I think that stuff," I circled my finger around her face, "has gone into your brain and messed you up. Where are your manners?"

Mama crossed her arms and ignored me by looking around. She couldn't deny it was clean and really kinda cute with the whole barbeque theme that went so well with the picnic décor. My stomach did a flip-flop. If the food was as good as it smelled, Mama's pot pie might be in trouble.

The waitress walked over with a plastic basket filled to the brim with barbequed pulled chicken, crispy hushpuppies, crinkle fries, and creamy coleslaw. My mouth watered.

"Plastic?" Mama was no fan of plastic. She believed in using fine china for everything. Her motto was to use it if you had it.

"This is just one step up from paper." Mama took her plastic fork and rolled it into the chicken. She put her nose down into it and took a big whiff. "Too much barbeque sauce."

There wasn't anything good about it according to Mama. To me, it was delicious, but I didn't dare tell her.

"She likes it." Poppa pointed and smiled at her. "She's doing that bunny nose twitch thing she does when she eats one of those Cadbury Eggs. She loves those."

"You like it, Mama?" I asked. And I wished I hadn't.

"How's it taste?" the waitress asked over my shoulder.

"This is undercooked. Can you get me a new one?" Mama jerked her basket up in the air toward the waitress.

"That's impossible. This has been cooking for a day. It's fresh." The waitress pushed the basket back toward Mama.

"It's undercooked," Mama said a little louder and moved her head left to right as if she were using a horn. "It's slimy."

"It's delicious." I put another forkful in my mouth, trying to drown out Mama.

"It's slimy," Mama said again and pushed back.

"It is not. And you aren't handicapped either." The waitress had a look of disgust on her face and I stuffed mine as full as I could before the next thing happened. "Get out and don't come back."

My eyes followed the length of the woman's arm and down past her finger where she pointed straight for the door. The twirling lights of the tow truck caught my attention. A man stood next to Mama's car.

"What on earth?" Mama jumped up. The coke tipped over and went all over the paper tablecloth.

A few familiar clicks came from the counter where people could mosey up to eat instead of waiting for an open seat at a picnic bench. Behind the big camera lens was a waving feather from a fedora hat. The camera came down slightly; Edna Easterly was staring right at me.

"This ain't good." Poppa's ghost disappeared.

I jumped up after Mama and dropped a couple of twenties on the table before I headed out the door, where she was giving the man from S&S Auto Salvage a mouthful of sass.

"Excuse me." I inserted myself in between him and Mama. "I'm sure we have a misunderstanding here."

"Say, don't I know you?" He snapped his fingers and then shook one at me. "You're that cop that gave us all sorts of trouble."

"I didn't give you trouble. You illegally towed a truck from a crime scene." I reminded him of a murder that'd happened a few months ago. I'd had to get the truck back before they'd made it into a flat piece of steel.

"No." He shook his head. "You gave me trouble and now she's giving me trouble."

The customers in The Little Shack were staring at us from inside, barbeque hanging out of their mouths. Edna was grinning ear to ear, snapping away.

"Just let us go, please," I said in a sweet voice. "We were just trying to grab a bite."

"You're from Cottonwood. That sheriff." The man shuffled to the tow truck and grabbed the heavy chains.

"You're who?" The waitress had stepped out of the diner and stood on the sidewalk, a lit cigarette tucked in the corner of her lip. "Did you say the sheriff?"

"Yep." The chains clanked quite loudly on the ground when he dropped them next to Mama's front tire.

Mama used her shoe to try to push the chain, but it didn't budge.

"Move that chain." Mama demanded. Her key fob pointed at the car, she clicked it several times to unlock the door. "I'm getting in my car."

"You mean to tell me the sheriff is letting this woman use a fake handicap tag?" The cigarette bounced up and down in the woman's mouth. "I'll be darned. I thought I'd seen it all."

"I did no such thing." I started to sweat and got a little nervous. "This is my mama and she had a minor surgery. The doctor gave her the tag."

"I think I read that the sheriff of Cottonwood's mama is competing for that fancy culinary show." The tow truck employee couldn't seem to keep his mouth shut.

"Is that right?" the waitress asked, lowering her eyelids. "Take it away!" the woman instructed him. She tossed the lit cigarette on the ground and used the toe of her shoe to snuff it out before she turned to go back inside.

"I bet she doesn't wash her hands." Mama had no business spitting out more words, but she did.

Poppa was doubled over in laughter. It seemed as though he were thoroughly entertained by his daughter. I ignored him.

"Mama, stay." I put my hand out and tugged off my sweater, exposing my sheriff's uniform. I walked up to the tow truck guy. "Listen, she's old. Can you please just let us go?"

"She's parked illegally." He pointed to the sign that had S&S's number on it. "Violators will be towed."

At least he could read.

"Yeah. But she did get the tag from the doctor." I nodded.

"It's pink. There's no such thing." The man told me something I'd already known, but I was going to ask Dr. Shively about it when I got back to town. She wouldn't give Mama a fake tag.

"You and I both know that things aren't always on the up and up over at S&S." I bit the edge of my lip. I hated to bring politics into it, but Mama left me no choice. "There were a lot of things I forgave and overlooked during that investigation. In fact, I didn't bring charges against you or the company for breaking the crime-scene tape and taking the truck a few months ago and," I hesitated, nodding my head, "the statute of limitations hasn't passed, so I guess I could look into it, have the company shut down until the investigation is over. But then you'd probably have to look for another job." I shrugged.

He gave me a long hard look. He chewed on what I'd said. I could wait him out. I'd learned to be really good at that.

Mama honked the horn and started the car. He glanced up at her and back at me. He bent down and picked up the chains and took a step away from the car.

"Thank you." I curled my lips in a tight grimace and ran around the car and climbed into the passenger side.

"You can get glad in the same britches you got mad in." Mama's jaw was set. "That's all I want to hear about today. I've got to get home and get my ingredients ready for tomorrow."

"Tomorrow?" I asked.

"Yes, silly girl." Mama was giddy and playful. "Frank gets in town today. We have a little get together and tomorrow is the big tasting. Tomorrow is the big day and a fresh pot pie is just what's going to win this for me."

That was Mama. If she didn't want to talk about it, there was no sense in bringing it up. She grabbed her cell phone and jabbed the numbers.

"Hi-do. This here is Viv Lowry and I need an appointment at two please." Mama um-hummed in the phone, agreeing with whoever she'd made an appointment with. I was hoping it was with a shrink because she'd lost her ever-loving mind.

"What was that about?" I asked.

"Kenni, I don't go nosing in your business." She threw the phone in her purse and slammed the gear shift into drive. Who was she trying to fool? Not only was she in my business, she was in everyone's business.

There was no denying the tension in Mama's car on the way back to Cottonwood. I couldn't even bring myself to talk to her for the first fifteen minutes. Not only was I still mad that she'd conned me into going to lunch there, she'd brought me clothes, complained the entire time, and I still had to pay for food I didn't get to finish.

"Did you see Edna Easterly was there?" I felt restless and irritable.

"I hope she got my good side." Mama patted her face.

"Mama." I scolded. "You have got something weird going on in there." I circled her head with my finger. "I think you need to see Dr. Shively about that stuff she stuck in your face."

"I'm fine. I wanted to see my competition. And now I know it's the lack thereof competition. I'm going to win, hands down." She gave a good hard nod.

I didn't say anything the rest of the ride back to the department. The sooner we got back, the sooner I could distance myself from her.

CHAPTER SIX

"There's no resting now," Betty said after I'd gotten back from my awful lunch and flung myself in my office chair. She pointed to the clock. It was only two in the afternoon, but I sure did feel like it was quittin' time.

For a brief moment, I laid my head on the back of my chair with my legs stretched out in front of me and my eyes closed. I was hoping to meditate the lunch away from my mind.

"What now?" I groaned.

"First off, Toots Buford called." She handed me a Post-it with a message from Toots. "She said that there's been some customers parking illegally at the Dixon's Foodtown. Something about pink handicap stickers. She's not the only one who's called. Seems to be a lot of businesses reporting this."

"Pink?" My uh-oh meter went off. There was no way I was going to tell her about Mama's pink one. "Let's give that investigation to Finn."

"Good. Because Ben Harrison called right before you got here and said that Frank Von Lee is in town and coming by the diner in the next half hour. He'd like the sheriff's presence." She looked over the rim of her glasses at me.

Half hour? I glanced up at the clock and that meant he needed me around two p.m.

"Fine," I said with an exhausted sigh, pushing myself up from my chair. "Let's go, Duke."

Within a few seconds, Duke jumped in his usual spot on the passenger seat of my Wagoneer. I reached over and cranked down his window so he could enjoy the beautiful spring day that popped up. There was nothing like the sight of a fresh crop of the Kentucky bluegrass that blanketed Cottonwood. Today the late afternoon sun was hitting it perfectly and sending the fresh fragrance to my soul. The fresh air didn't hurt either. It seemed to clear my head more than anything.

I took a left out of the alley and stopped at the stoplight to take a left to head down Main Street toward Ben's. The Cottonwood Chronicle box sat on the sidewalk on the corner. From the Jeep, I could see that Edna Easterly had made Frank Von Lee's arrival this week's headline. Mama would have her interview posted next week and being on the front of the Chronicle was better than butter on a biscuit for Mama.

I waved to the people crossing the street. The warmer weather brought them out to peruse our small-town boutiques and antique shops.

There was a big crowd gathered in front of Ben's, no doubt due to Edna's article, where I'm sure she spun more tales than a spinning wheel. Edna was a master at taking a couple of words and making up the biggest story you'd ever heard.

I pulled across the street into a parking spot in front of Ruby Smith's antique shop and parked. Surveying the situation before I got out was probably my best bet to assess how I was going to help Ben with the crowd control. The people stood in front of Ben's and along the sidewalk down to the inn. I remembered the cord of rope I kept in the back of the Jeep, grabbed that, and headed on over. Duke was good at keeping everyone's eyes and hands on him while I made a makeshift red-carpet walkway between the buildings with the rope strung from the trees along the sidewalk for our special guest.

The look on Ben's face told me he was appreciative, though I think he'd spent so much time on the diner he'd forgotten about how to treat Frank Von Lee's arrival.

"Here." Ruby walked over and handed over two Oriental rug runners.

"The sheriff's department can borrow them as long as you take them to the cleaners afterward so I can resell them."

"Why, you do have a soft spot," I teased her.

Her brightly painted orange lips snarled as she handed the rugs to me. I stood there and watched her five-foot-nine lanky frame weave through the crowd. You couldn't miss that bright red head of hers. A smile crossed my lips as I unfurled the long rugs and made the perfect runway for our guest.

The crowd had shifted to stand behind the rope. Most of the women in Mama's Sweet Adelines Group—Lulu McClain, Mrs. Kim, Toots Buford, Viola White, Myrna Savage, and Missy Jennings—stood closest to the door. For years they'd bragged on Mama's cooking, but I just figured they were nice compliments with underlying meanings, like our famous saying, bless your heart. It sounded good, but when you shaved back the layers, it was a dagger in the heart and you didn't even know it.

As soon as the doors of The Tattered Cover Books and Inn opened, a collective gasp rose from the crowd. Then there was dead silence as though everyone was holding their breath.

"Good morning." Frank Von Lee took off his top hat and rolled it a few times in front of himself as he took a bow. The man was as bald as a baby's butt, but his handlebar mustache made up for what he didn't have on his head.

He held the top hat against his chest with one hand and a cane in the other. He slowly walked down the runway as though he was at a television premiere and took the time to nod to the people standing behind the rope line. He even stopped for a few photos and gave a few autographs.

He stopped at the diner door and turned around.

"I'm looking forward to sampling the chicken pot pie." His words were very clipped as though there was a period after each one of them.

Ben and Mama stood at the door.

"Goodness gracious." Mama's hand lifted to her chest, and she fingered her pearl necklace as she giggled. "Thank you kindly."

"Look at your mama." Ruby Smith had snuck up behind me. "She's so stinkin' happy. I ain't seen her that happy since the day your daddy asked her to marry him."

"Is that right?" I asked and tilted my head to the right to get a better view

SIX FEET UNDER

of Mama doing her southern thing. She'd curled her hand in the crook of Frank Von Lee's elbow and escorted him right on into the diner, her lips never stopping moving once.

Poor man, I thought. He'd know everything there was to know about Mama, me, and Cottonwood by the time he left their little meeting. He'd probably not even get a word in edgewise.

"What's that look for?" Ruby patted my arm. "Honey, don't be goin' and worryin' about your mama. She's in full control."

"That's what I'm worried about." I took a deep breath. The crowd around me had dispersed and Duke sat by my feet.

What they'd come for had been seen. Frank Von Lee and his arrival was now tomorrow's news as the entire town waited for his decision, which wouldn't be coming for a few days. Heck, he wasn't even going to sample Mama's pot pie until tomorrow, and then he'd be going to Clay's Ferry.

The tension was not only in the air, but on Poppa's face as he stood over Mama in the diner as she sat next to Frank Von Lee.

As much as I tried to forget Poppa's face, I couldn't. Seeing him gave me fearful clarity that he was there for something that was about to happen. I just didn't know what.

CHAPTER SEVEN

The appearance from Frank Von Lee was just that. He'd only spent about twenty minutes in the diner with Mama and Ben before he excused himself back to his hotel.

After that, I'd made my afternoon rounds in the town and stopped to chat with a few neighbors who were hanging out on their porches. After all, it was getting close to the election. I had to make appearances before I headed on home to change my clothes so I wasn't late to Mama's cooking class at Lulu's Boutique. Finn and I had also made plans to see each other after the class.

Mrs. Brown, my neighbor, was more than happy to take care of Duke while I was gone for the night. I wasn't going to be gone long, but I hated to leave him alone when he could enjoy Mrs. Brown as much as she enjoyed him. Of course, Finn had offered, but I couldn't do that to Mrs. Brown.

Lulu's Boutique, owned by Mama's best friend Lulu McClain, was located on the far end of the north side of town. Lulu had purchased the old run-down clapboard cottage-style house and brought it back to life by giving it a new paint job and refinished hardwood floors. She'd even made the upstairs into an efficiency apartment. The boutique was a little knick-knack shop that sold Kentucky branded items, jewelry, and anything that could have a monogram. We Southerners loved our initials. We even printed them on our cars and bath towels.

There was a line of cars pulled up to the curb outside of Lulu's. Some I knew and some I didn't. Before I went in, I swiped some lipstick on and grabbed my cell, sticking it in my back pocket. At least Mama would be happy to see I'd attempted some makeup, and that should keep her satisfied.

When I walked by her car, I looked in to see if the handicap tag was dangling from the arm of the rearview, but it wasn't. I made a mental note to ask Mama about that right off.

Lulu's held different classes for the community. I especially loved the craft classes. Generally they were attended by the same old gossipy women I spent one night a week with at our Euchre game. Even though they drove me crazy, they'd showed up tonight for Mama. That's the way it was around Cottonwood. No matter how cotton-pickin' mad someone got at you, they'd be right by your side in your hour of need.

It warmed my heart to see them gathered around Mama with a big smile on her face when I walked in.

"Your mama sure can tell a story." Jolee walked up and handed me a glass of Mama's sweet tea. "She's got everyone in stitches about her meeting with Frank and his hearty appetite."

"Oh brother." I shook my head and wet my whistle. "She's got you calling him Frank too?"

"She makes it sound like they've been friends for years." Jolee laughed. "I'm excited to see exactly what she puts in her pot pie to make it so good. That's why I'm here. I could just smack myself for letting her be on Ben's team."

She was referring to the cook-off. Jolee got to handpick her contestants to go up against Ben's. Trust me when I say that we were all in shock when Mama came out the winner. And now here we were today.

"That barbeque don't have a leg to stand on compared to my pot pie, right, Kenni?" Mama dragged me into her sordid tale.

Lulu, Myrna, Toots, Ruby, and Viola all turned to look at me, their eyes wide open, waiting on my response.

"I don't know anything about that, Mama." I waved the ladies off. Idle gossip wasn't my glass of sweet tea. "Mama, I wouldn't be going around telling people about our little adventure today," I warned as a bad feeling suddenly washed over me. "It's not very becoming of either of us."

Mama didn't realize that I'd thrown my badge around. Though it wasn't really against the law to remind the tow truck driver how un-businesslike his boss was, it still wasn't the most ethical thing to do. Citizens of Cottonwood held morality in high regard, often forgetting their own mistakes. They'd be quick with their tongues and finger wagging when it came to election time. Though I was currently unopposed, you just never could be too sure.

"Well, we can all take our places." Mama clasped her hands together.

The tables in the back of Lulu's were set up with three workstations each. Mama had already put all the ingredients we needed in little bowls. All except her special ingredient. She said that would be distributed last. Just like Mama to build up the anticipation. She loved that. And loved that it was centered on her.

We all went to our stations. "And lastly," Mama stood up with pride and held the canister with no markings up in the air, "everyone needs to get their tablespoon ready because this is my very special secret."

Mama had made up the cutest four-in-one country blue measuring spoons with her name printed on them. This entire television thing had made her head swell more than usual.

Jolee scooted to the edge of her seat and eagerly grabbed her tablespoon, holding it way out in front of her. Knowing Jolee, she'd figure out the ingredients and try to duplicate them in her own On The Run recipe. That would send Mama off if she did.

"These are cute." Jolee's brows rose to high heaven. "I should probably get something cute like this for the truck," she whispered after Mama gave her the wonky eye.

My phone rang. I gulped and looked up. Mama's glare had turned from Jolee to me. Her moment was stolen by the sound of my phone and it didn't sit well with her.

"Kendrick," Mama shamed me. "That's rude."

"I'm sorry. I've got to take this." I answered when I saw it was the late-night dispatch. Were they calling about Mama's charade from today?

We shared the service with Clay's Ferry dispatch. Neither of our departments needed to be open twenty-four hours a day, so we chipped in and used someone from seven p.m. until eight a.m. to field the calls.

"Sheriff Lowry," I answered.

"Sheriff, there's been an ambulance dispatched to The Tattered Cover Books and Inn. A Dr. Camille Shively called it in," the dispatcher said over the phone. "It's concerning an unresponsive male."

"I'm on my way." The chair clattered to the ground when I stood up in haste. I looked up at Mama, but it wasn't her gaze I met. It was Poppa's. Fear struck the very center of my body. Chills zoomed up my spine like a roller coaster.

"Frank Von Lee is dead." Poppa's words pierced my ears.

"Frank is dead?" The words fell from my mouth.

CHAPTER EIGHT

"Wait." Mama ran beside me, the can of her secret ingredient in her hand. "Did you say 'dead' and 'Frank' in the same sentence?"

"Nope. Didn't say a word." I ran faster to my Wagoneer. The less Mama knew, the better off I was.

"Kendrick Lowry. You said Frank is dead. I might be old, but I'm not hard-of-hearing old." Mama stood at the door of the Wagoneer.

"Gotta go, Mama." I grabbed the old beacon siren from underneath my seat and licked the suction cup, sticking it to the roof of the Jeep. I slid my finger down the side and caught the switch for the siren.

I threw the Jeep in gear, did a U-turn, and put the pedal to the metal. Immediately I dialed Finn and left no room for chitchat. Nothing but, "Meet me at the inn. Frank Von Lee is dead," then I hung up. Within minutes, I was standing with my sheriff's bag tight in my grip in Frank Von Lee's room, where Camille Shively looked a bit disheveled and Poppa was standing next to her over Frank's body, surrounded by EMTs. Finn arrived soon after.

"I've been doing CPR, but he's not coming back." Camille gasped for breath before she went back down to give Frank more CPR while the EMTs were doing chest compressions. "You keep doing compressions and I'll keep breathing."

Her long black hair that was normally neatly parted to the side and hung down to her collarbones in a flawless cascade was pulled back in a messy ponytail. Something she'd obviously done to get it out of the way. She wasn't going to step back and let the EMTs do their job.

"Doctor." One of the EMTs stopped doing the compressions and patted the other to stop too. "Ma'am, I don't think we're going to bring him back."

"Nope. Nope. They aren't." Poppa put his hands in his pants pockets. "This whole situations smells bad enough to knock a dog off a gut wagon."

That was bad, and he didn't mean the smell in the room.

"He's dead. I think you need to call it." I tapped Camille on the shoulder. "Camille." I tapped harder.

"Not on my dime, Kenni," she said through gritted teeth. By the crack in her voice, I knew that she knew he was gone. She glanced at the EMTs. Her pale skin was even whiter. The whites of her eyes were tinted red. "What are you doing? Don't stop."

They stood up, but she was relentless for about three more minutes, going back and forth between doing the compressions and the breathing herself. Finally, she sat back on her heels and put her head in her hands, sobbing.

"Oh, no." A gasp came from the door of the room Frank Von Lee had rented. "Well, this just butters my biscuit."

"Mama." I looked at Finn. "Please take her out of here and call Max Bogus for me."

Finn rushed over and grabbed Mama. Mama didn't like it one bit.

Max Bogus had a dual job as our county coroner and the undertaker of Cottonwood's only funeral home. He'd come and make an initial report before taking the body to do a final autopsy.

"Kenni."

I looked at Poppa when he said my name. He was pointing to the small brown desk that sat in front of the window.

I walked over to the desk and let Camille collect herself.

"This is why you're here," I muttered.

"That pot pie looks familiar." Poppa pointed to the plate. Next to it was an empty glass. "If I'm not mistaken, that's a plate from Ben's Diner."

"Sheriff," one of the EMTs called. "Is there anything else you need us for?"

I turned around, shaking my head.

"No. Thank you for all you've done. I got it from here." I turned back to the window and peeled the curtain away from the glass. "My deputy called the coroner so he should be here any minute."

"We'll get our report to you," the EMT said before they gathered their equipment and left.

The window looked out over Main Street and I could see news had spread fast. There was already a crowd lined up around the ambulance and the Jeep.

"This is the first patient I've ever lost." Camille's voice broke the silence and the stillness that death always seemed to bring.

"And to be a famous man to boot." Poppa shrugged. "This doesn't look good." He ghosted himself over to Frank's body. "There's a bit of the pot pie stuck on the front of his shirt."

"I'm sorry, Camille." I didn't have the words to comfort her. Dealing with the emotions following death was never easy for me. Though I wanted to cry out and beg that this hadn't happened again on my watch, as sheriff, I had to hide those emotions and do my job. "I am going to need a statement from you."

I placed my bag on the floor and took out the small tape recorder. I felt it was best to have a general conversation with her while I made her more at ease by taking photos of the crime scene after putting the yellow crime-scene tape along the door. I pressed record and got to work.

"I got a phone call on the emergency line. The operator said there was a call from room number three. He'd not given his name to the operator. They said he was slurring his words." Her eyes slid over to look at Frank. She fidgeted.

"Try not to touch anything." I knew it was a strong statement.

"You think this is a murder scene?" She jerked her hand off his body. Frank was getting bluer by the minute.

"I haven't ruled anything out. Do you have any suspicion on a cause of death?" I asked.

"Well, I came in and he was on the bed. Alive." Her words faded into the space around us.

"Kenni, this doesn't look good for your mama. My daughter." There was a sudden fear in Poppa's voice I'd yet to hear since he'd come back as a ghost. "I'm telling you there is something wrong with this pot pie."

What was Frank doing with some of Mama's pot pie? Where'd he get it from? Mama had mentioned that she'd planned on making the pot pie Frank was going to be critiquing in the morning. "Let it sit for a spell. Thickens up the liquid." Mama claimed that was part of her special recipe.

I snapped a few photos of the pot pie as Camille continued to talk into the tape recorder.

"He was alive. Talking. I asked him where he felt sick. He said that he'd been working and felt an onset of nausea. He went to lay down for a bit because of some pain in his stomach. He called 911 when the abdominal pain didn't go away after an hour." She continued to gnaw on the edge of her lip.

I put on a pair of gloves from my bag and used my finger to move around the papers on the desk next to the plate. When I saw one had Mama's name on it, I picked it up.

"He started to sweat and got really confused." Camille's voice was in the background. I wasn't really listening, which was awful to admit, but Frank's written words had caught my attention.

Mrs. Vivian Lowry, though tall in the charming southern way, fell short in my expectations of the chicken pot pie that's staked her claim to fame in her small town of Cottonwood. The chicken was tough. For a pot pie, the number one rule is to pre-cook the chicken barely pale so the baking process will tenderize it to a juicy goodness. Mrs. Lowry claims the crust is where her secret ingredient is hidden away. All I know that's hidden is the big secret she's keeping from patrons of Ben's Diner: using a readymade flour mix from a box. There was nothing special about it. The only part of the pot pie that was even remotely tasty was the larger-than-normal sized vegetables used.

"I continued to tell him who I was and where he was. He got confused and agitated." Camille's voice grew stronger and louder. "That's when he stood up, grabbed his chest, and fell to the ground." She huffed a few times through her nose. "I think I'm going to be sick." She stumbled to the bathroom and let go of anything she'd had in her stomach.

I folded the paper in half and stuck it in my pocket.

"You know it too." Poppa appeared. "Get rid of the evidence."

"There is nothing here that says Mama did him in." I ran my hand down the front pocket of my pants where I'd put the note.

"Kenni, if your mama walked in here and saw that review he was working on, she'd have lost her marbles." Poppa paced back and forth, his hands clasped behind his back. "She's been driving herself nuts since she got word he was coming. I've been with her. She's not slept. She did that thing to her face."

Poppa was right. Mama had been acting out of the ordinary, beyond her usual crazy antics.

"I shouldn't've ignored her behavior like I did." The thought of it made me want to grab the pot pie and throw it in my bag. I reached my hand out to take it.

"Go on. If she did it, there'll be more evidence. This buys us time to think." For the first time, Poppa made me question his honesty in his time as sheriff. But family deserved loyalty.

"I can keep the review and shred it. I can flush the pot pie or throw it in my bag. No one will immediately know he was eating it. Though Max will find it in his belly." I put my fingers on the rim of the plate.

"And it will buy us time," Poppa repeated.

"It'll buy us time to get her a lawyer. A real lawyer, not Wally Lamb." The thought that this town that Mama loved so much was going to turn their backs on her broke me to my core.

"Kenni." Finn rushed into the room.

I jerked my hand away from the pot pie. What on earth had gotten into me? I knew. Poppa had gotten to me.

"Dagnabit!" Poppa ghosted himself away.

"What happened?" He was quickly followed in by Max Bogus. Camille walked out of the bathroom with a washcloth on her head. Finn greeted her with a nod.

My moral compass took over and I slipped the review out of my pocket and underneath the plate. What was I thinking? I wasn't. I sucked in a deep breath, and the smell of death hung in my nostrils.

"Please, can we do this later?" Camille asked. "I'm not feeling well and there's really no more I can do about this situation."

"Kenni, do you care if Dr. Shively leaves?" Finn wasn't going to let her go without my consent since he didn't know what'd taken place before he'd gotten here.

"Sure, I'm fine with it. Please come by the station tomorrow to give a formal statement." I offered a smile. "Camille…" Though we both grew up in Cottonwood, we weren't what I considered good friends, but I cared about her. "I'm really sorry you had to go through this. You did all you could do to help him."

She pursed her lips as if she were holding back tears and nodded a couple of times before she rushed out of the hotel room.

CHAPTER NINE

"Thoughts?" I asked Max Bogus after he'd stepped back out of the room into the hallway.

"I won't know anything for sure until I do an autopsy, but from the sound of Camille's statement, he probably had a heart attack. Given his lifestyle of eating all sorts of fatty foods, not to mention not being in the best shape, it's all the classic signs." Max took a deep inhale.

"Kenni, can I see you?" Finn stuck his head out of the door. His eyes bore into me.

"Kenni! Kenni!" Katy Lee Hart trilled from down the end of the hallway.

"What on earth is she doing here?" I asked and gave Finn the hold-on-a-second gesture.

I met Katy Lee halfway down the hall. How did she do it? I wondered how day in and day out Katy Lee looked fresh as a daisy. For a thicker gal, she walked with more grace and dignity than any thin girl I ever saw. Her silk shirt dress had the sweetest beautiful botanicals with a simple sweet lace collar. She even had a piece of grosgrain ribbon neatly tied as a waist-defining accent. Her cowboy boots made it even cuter.

"Kenni." Katy Lee's eyes dipped in sadness. "I just heard what happened. This is awful."

"Yeah. Say, what are you doing here?" I asked, trying to sound nonchalant.

"Kenni?" Her face contorted. "Frank Von Lee is dead and you want to know why I'm here?"

"You know I can't say anything, so I want to hear something good." I shrugged. "Like what's going on with you?"

"You can't tell me the tiniest bit?" She lifted her fingers an inch apart in front of our faces. "Fine." She seemed to be satisfied at my "no" face. "I've got the annual Shabby Trends summer fashion show today."

Shabby Trends was a clothing line that Katy Lee sold out of her house, kinda like Tupperware, only clothing. It wasn't just any clothing line. They were fancy duds that I rarely wore, but I supported my friend and attended all her parties.

"I sent you an invitation and you did RSVP." Her lips twitched to the side and her eyes glanced past my shoulder toward the crime scene. "I guess you have a valid excuse, though I do have the cutest dress that would go great with your hair color." There was always a piece that Katy picked out for me. Usually the most expensive. "I've held it back for you."

"Thank you. Do you have a full house?" I asked. I'd actually forgotten about the fashion show.

"Yes. And your mama was here earlier." A broad smile crossed her face. "I'm going to pick out some pieces for you and let her buy them. She said she'd pick them up from me at the agency. Now that you have a boyfriend, you need to have some new clothes for dates." She winked.

Katy Lee's family owned Hart Insurance Agency in the strip mall. She was an insurance agent during the day and Shabby Trends consultant the rest of the time.

"Did you send Mama an invitation?" I found it particularly odd she'd invite Mama since Shabby Trends was more of a clothing line for the ages between twenty and fifty and she'd never invited her before. Though Mama insisted she felt my age, she certainly wouldn't dress in Shabby Trends clothing.

"Nope. I figured she knew about it because of you." Katy Lee shook her head. "She was coming down out of the stairway door while I was coming down the hall to set up the fashion show. We practically ran into each other.

Well, she did run into me, as if she were in a rush." She rolled her eyes. "They put us in that old library room. I wish there was another room we could use, but it's the biggest when you move all those old dreary tables out of the way."

"She was coming out of the stairway?" I asked.

Mama never took the stairs. She said they made her sweat, and Mama didn't like the slightest bit of sweating.

"Yes. She seemed upset, so I figured I'd tell her you liked this one particular shirt and she must see it. Anything having to do with you takes her mind off whatever upsets her."

"Do you remember the time?" I asked.

"It was around supper time because my stomach was growling when Nanette served the guests a meatloaf to die for." Katy Lee smacked her lips together, referring to the hotel's owner and manager. "Speaking of food, do you know how your mama's meeting with Frank went?"

"A meeting?" I asked urgently.

"Kenni Lowry, are you okay?" She drew back, staring before she narrowed her eyes and slightly shifted her head to the side, looking at me all side-goggling.

"I'm fine, but Mama didn't have her meeting until tomorrow." My head was all foggy. I felt like I was having an out-of-body experience. Mama had motive and opportunity to kill Frank Von Lee.

"Hmm." Katy Lee pressed her lips together. "I thought I overheard her ask Nanette what room number Frank had." She gave a slight shrug. "Oh well. I probably heard wrong and just assumed they were getting together."

"They did have the initial meeting at Ben's in the early afternoon. Is that what you mean?" I asked.

"No. She was here earlier, but I couldn't say anything to her then because I was packing in all my clothes. But after she ran into me, that's when I talked her into buying you some new clothes," Katy said.

"What time was it that you got here?" I didn't want it to seem so obvious that I was trying to get a timeline for Mama's whereabouts.

Her nose curled and her lip twitched as though she were searching for the time up in her head. "Sometime around four-ish. I think." She waved her hand at me. "You know me. I was so focused on getting set up that I didn't pay much attention to it."

"There you are. People are waiting to fill orders before you close up." Whitney Hart had stopped at the top of the steps that lead up to the rooms. Her hair was pulled back in a low ponytail, her gold earrings dangling. She wore a denim shirt dress with a big braided belt around the waist and a pair of sandals with gold straps. "Kenni, how are you? I heard about that fancy food critic. Shame."

"Hi, Mrs. Hart." I offered a sympathetic smile. The last time I'd directly talked to her was when I had to tell her about Rowdy, her son. He was murdered a while back and I knew this was bringing back some hurtful memories of that time.

"It's a shame." I nodded.

"If it was a heart attack, it's the way to go. Sudden." She placed a hand on Katy Lee. "Come on, your daddy's at home waiting on me."

"Bye, Katy Lee, Mrs. Hart." I waved to them.

The walk back to the room seemed long as I thought of Mama coming to the inn with her pot pie—which seemed like a bribe. If she did ask Nanette his room number and go up there, that put Mama at the scene. Not to mention a good motive to kill him was in the written words he'd put on that piece of paper. Not good for Mama if Frank Von Lee was murdered.

CHAPTER TEN

It took a few snooze buttons, a hot shower, and a couple cups of coffee to get me going the next morning. The investigation into Frank's death had gone late into the night with very little evidence gathered to make it seem like a murder. Finn hadn't called or stopped by. Max Bogus hadn't called. And Poppa wasn't around.

I wasn't sure whether to be happy or worried. Either way, it was a new day and I still had a job to do and a possible murder to solve. The Cottonwood Chronicle was delivered every morning around five a.m. and I couldn't help but think when I saw Mama sitting proudly next to her freshly baked pot pie from her interview at the diner she'd be proud as a peach this morning even though her dreams of being on the television show were dashed.

A little bit of recognition in the Chronicle would make her happy. Or at least temper her mood about the death of Frank Von Lee and her lost chance.

"Duke." I stood with my back up against the counter of my kitchen, my legs crossed at the ankles, a cup of coffee in one hand and the paper in the other.

Duke had just gobbled up the last bits of his kibble and his droopy eyes looked up at me.

"You ready to go bye-bye?" It was the trigger word he knew meant get in the Jeep and get out of here.

His growl and loud bark followed by the prance to the door signaled he was ready to go. I grabbed my cell off the counter along with my sheriff's bag, took the keys from the hook, and headed out the back door.

I'm not going to lie. I looked down the street toward Finn's house to see if he was home. When I didn't see his Dodge Charger, I wondered where he'd gone so early. Come to think of it, I didn't see his car there when I let Duke out before bed, which was around midnight. Maybe he had a lead on the handicap sticker investigation and was checking into those.

"You still have a hankerin' for that boy." Poppa appeared in the passenger seat of the Jeep. Duke jumped to the back.

I pulled the Jeep to a complete stop at the stop sign at the end of the street.

"What are you doing here? Not that I'm not happy to see you, but I figured since I'd not seen you since the inn that you were gone." I was searching for answers that my gut told me I feared most. "I'm guessing Frank's death wasn't accidental."

"You'd be right." Poppa stared at the window. "I guess you better head on over to your mama and daddy's to check on her."

"Is that a mere suggestion or are you telling me to go?" There were two sides to Poppa, his loving family side and his sheriff's side. His voice told me this was his sheriff's side.

"I think you know what's going to come down the line" were Poppa's last words before he ghosted away.

In frustration, I smacked the wheel with the palm of my hand. What good was having a ghost deputy if there were more questions than answers?

I jerked the wheel to the right and headed in the opposite direction of the department, downtown toward my family home. Normally I'd have called Max Bogus by now to see what the initial autopsy had said and what the plans were for Frank's body, but I couldn't bring myself to find out the answers too quickly considering that I already feared the worst.

My childhood home was a modest three-bedroom brick ranch. There was a long covered porch on the front and a nice patio on the back. If you came in through the left side of the house through the garage door, it led into a laundry room with a full bath, traveling into a kitchen nook, passing through the kitchen and into the family room that led to a hall with the three bedrooms and a bath at the end. In the front of the house, through the front door was a small entryway that spilled into the hallway, or you could go left into the living room.

The living room was the fancy room with the expensive furniture that Mama had bought down at Goodlett's Furniture. You couldn't sit in there unless it was Christmas. That's where we opened presents. Mama insisted on having the furniture in the Christmas photos, never mind that my hair was stuck up all over the place and the wrapping paper was strewn all over the floor.

It was also the room where she'd hold court with her Sweet Adelines and whatever other social gatherings she'd have.

I walked up to the front door and knocked. Dad opened the door. I looked up at him. He still towered over me, and for his age, he remained in good physical shape. His brown eyes were tired and sagged a little more than usual. His brown hair was starting to get a little grey in it, but if I dared to say anything, Mama would have him down at Tiny Tina's for a color. I wasn't going to put him through that again.

"You don't want to come in here." He rolled his eyes. "Your mama acts like it's a funeral in here."

Duke shoved his nose in the door and pushed his ninety-pound body into the house.

"He does." I laughed and stepped into the foyer. "What's going on with Mama?"

The corners of Dad's eyes drooped. "She's been up all night. She came home and told me about Frank."

"What did she do all night?" I asked.

"The funny thing is that she did nothing." Dad shrugged. "I waited to see if I needed to call Dr. Shively to get your mama some of them relaxing pills, but she simply grabbed her robe and went to the bathroom where she took a long bath and read one of her romance books while she soaked."

"She didn't say a word?" I thought that was strange.

"Not a single peep." Dad shook his head.

"Stayed up and read all night. You and I both know that ain't like your mama. It all started yesterday afternoon after she said she was taking you to a mother-daughter lunch. What happened on that lunch?" Daddy had a curious look on his face.

"She didn't have any intentions of having any daughter time." I cocked a brow. "She took me to the barbecue restaurant in Clay's Ferry that was going to be her competition."

Dad's face held a blank stare before he closed his eyes for a brief moment.

"That explains the weird cooking talk she did after she came home." He suctioned his tongue on the front of his teeth like he always did when he was thinking.

"What do you mean?" I asked. I had a nigglin' that every single moment of Mama's whereabouts needed to be accounted for.

"She came in, muttered something about needing some creamer for a new recipe, and took off again. She seemed really distant." He shrugged.

"Did she do anything different to the pot pie she'd been making?" I'd questioned the comment he made about creamer because I knew Mama used milk.

"Not a word. She just left, and I didn't see her again until she came in last night when she told me about Frank." He smacked his lips together when we heard movement coming down the hall.

"Kenni." Mama walked into the foyer with a big pair of black sunglasses covering her eyes. "What are you doing here?"

Dad walked away, but not without running a loving hand down Mama's arm.

"Mama." I reached out my arms. She was in a time of need. I bet she'd been crying all night from the news of Frank Von Lee and Dad didn't even notice. "I'm so sorry."

"Are you okay?" I ran a hand down her arm. In the background I could hear Daddy and Duke in the kitchen eating God knows what.

"I'll be fine." Mama brought the back of her finger up to her nose and gave a little sniffle.

"I'd love a cup of coffee," I suggested, since Mama wasn't about to offer me nothing.

"Not today." She sighed a little weepily and turned back around.

"Well, I'm having a cup of coffee." I pushed past her. She jerked around, her glasses falling to the ground. "Mama!" I gasped and drew my hand up to my mouth when I saw her big black and blue eye. "What on earth happened?"

"It's nothing. Act as though you never saw it and you must not speak a word of it," she whispered and scurried off toward her bedroom.

"Daddy. Daddy," I called on my way to the kitchen. I pointed behind me toward the hall. "What in the hell happened to Mom's eye? Did she fall?" I wondered if she'd slipped getting out of the tub.

"I don't know. She wouldn't tell me." He threw a piece of his toast to Duke, who gladly snapped it up.

"She's got a black eye." My jaw dropped. "Dad." I gulped and rushed over to the kitchen table, sitting down next to him. "What happened?"

Dad stood up. "You need to ask her. I think she's lost her cotton-pickin' mind over this television show and now that the chef is dead, she's really gone bonkers. She won't tell me how she got the black eye."

"Dad, how did she get the black eye?" I demanded. "How do you not know? You live with her."

"I told you to ask her. She tells me not to worry about it." He gave me a kiss on the forehead and put his dish in the dishwasher.

My mind swirled back to Frank's written review. I'd seen Mama strike someone with her words and they could do damage, but I'd never seen her get into a physical altercation. Had she with Frank? There were two things that were strange to me. One, Poppa was here and he only came when there was a murder. Two, Mama was at the Inn around the time of the murder and now she has a black eye. Poppa being here told me Frank was murdered. But what did Mama know, if anything, about it?

"Kenni!" Betty's voice pierced my ear through my walkie-talkie and brought me out of my head. "Get over to Max Bogus's right away. It's urgent. He's got some results."

"Results?" Mama poked her head in the room. "Did she say Max Bogus?"

"On my way, Betty." I grabbed Duke by the collar and dragged both of us out of the house as Mama continued to nip at my heels. "Mama," I turned around after I'd gotten Duke in the car, "I don't know what Max wants. I'll let everyone know when I find out."

SIX FEET UNDER

. . .

MAMA GNAWED on the edge of her lip as I left her standing in her driveway when I pulled out.

"I don't like this one bit, Kenni-bug." Poppa ghosted himself next to Duke, holding on to the handle of the Wagoneer as we drove to Max's place with the siren blaring and lights flashing.

"Don't put the cart before the horse. Maybe Max is going to tell us that Frank had a heart attack and all this worry is for nothing." If ever there needed to be a bright side to anything, it was now.

In no time, I parked the Jeep in front of Cottonwood Funeral Home, the only funeral home in our town. The county morgue was in the basement. Like most businesses, the funeral home was in an old Victorian house that'd been remodeled. The old wood floors and dark crown molding were preserved but still gave me the creeps.

A few minutes later, I found Max standing over Frank Von Lee's body in the morgue with his lab coat on, gloves and many gadgets scattered around the small metal table next to him. Frank was hooked up to the lines that were draining him of his blood.

"I came as quick as I could." Out of breath, I stood at the door and looked at the dead body. No matter how many dead bodies I'd seen, it didn't get any easier. I felt a little queasy.

"You aren't going to like what I have to say." When Max looked up, I could see the look in his eyes I'd only been seeing in the last couple of years.

"Frank Von Lee didn't die of a heart attack?" I asked hesitantly.

"He did. But with the help of a little-known poison called Compound 1080. Also known as sodium fluoroacetate. It was found in the preliminary test I ran last night with a blood panel. I also pulled some samples of the food in his stomach and bowels to see if I can pinpoint to source the 1080 was disguised in because the poison has no taste once cooked." Max's eyes did a slow glide from Frank's body to me. "He was murdered."

CHAPTER ELEVEN

"I'm not so stupid." Poppa jabbed his head with his fingertip. "Things are addin' up. And it don't look good for your mama."

"Shhh." I closed my eyes and waved my hand in the air, shaking my head. "Stop!"

"But I thought you'd want to know all the facts as I got them, like we always do." Max's voice was tight as he spoke.

I opened my eyes.

"No. No. Not you," I said to Max and looked around for Poppa. He wasn't there. Finally, my lungs fully filled and some oxygen made it into my brain, clearing away the fog. "My head is throbbing. I was doing that whole talking-to-myself thing that's all the rage. Like how women say something to themselves in the mirror to help them feel empowered."

Max looked at me like I had lost my marbles. I wanted to tell him that he was right. I had lost every bit of sense I'd possessed, because it was right about now that I wished I'd stolen that review and the food. But it was not time to fuss over it now. Now was the time to get the evidence and get Mama off my list of suspects.

"Mama," I mouthed when I realized she'd just become my number one suspect.

"What?" Max asked. "Are you okay?"

"I'm fine. Do you have a report?" I asked, trying to forget all the evidence against Mama and be a lot more objective.

"Yep. It's on the counter." He nodded.

Incomplete thoughts swirled in my head, and my legs felt spongy. Swaying a bit, I leaned up against the counter.

"That's your copy," he said, making me grateful for his words.

"I'm going to head back to the office and go over this. I'll give you a call." I took a deep breath to get enough strength to push myself off the counter and headed out of the morgue.

Later I knew I was going to have to explain my strange actions to Max, but first I had to get to Finn.

When I got back to the Jeep, Duke was busy letting everyone who passed pat his head that was stuck out of the window.

"Finn, where are you?" I asked as soon as he answered his phone.

"I'm on my way back to the office. Toots called to tell me someone with the fake handicap tag was in Dixon's. But by the time I got there, they'd left." He sounded a little frustrated. "Are people that lazy they'd buy fake handicap tags?"

"Did you check with the county clerk's office to make sure there wasn't a special breast cancer drive where they turned the tags pink?" It was a good thought.

"I did. Doolittle Bowman said no," he said. "What about you? Anything back on Frank Von Lee?"

"I was just at Max's and his initial autopsy shows Frank Von Lee was poisoned by a compound called 1080." Gripping the wheel with both hands, I decided to tell him what I was thinking. "And without really digging too deep into suspects, I'm fearing Mama is number one."

"What?" He exaggerated the "wh" out of disbelief.

I drove down the alley and pulled in behind Finn's Charger. I could see his silhouette from the back window.

"I just pulled up behind you." I clicked off the phone. Duke took a leap over me and out the window before I could even open the door.

Finn got out of the car and met me. "What on earth is going on?" There was a tenderness in his expression that in an odd way made me feel somewhat better.

I looked both ways down the alley. "Let's go inside."

Betty was aflutter when we walked in.

"The phone hasn't stopped ringing since the news about Frank Von Lee's death." She jabbed a button and said, "Sheriff's department. Calm down. Calm down. There's not a serial killer on the loose. Yes, Mayor." Betty snapped her fingers at me. "She's right here, Mayor."

I walked over to my desk and threw the file from Max on top. I slumped down in my chair.

"Mayor, line two," Betty said before she answered the next call. Finn also jumped on the phones. "He said that Frank was murdered. Is that true?"

I help up a finger for her to hold on.

"Hello, Chance." I tried to sound as upbeat as I could. "I'm sorry. I just got the report from Max and I haven't read it yet, but..." The mayor informed me that Max was doing his job, keeping him abreast of the situation. "Yes, sir. I'm more than happy to go over the report and come see you. I really don't think there's a need for a council meeting."

"I'm worried that if the rumors are true and your mother is a suspect, you won't be able to investigate without having a biased opinion. Not that I think Viv did it, but it's not ethical." He was right, but I wasn't about to tell him that.

"What rumors?" I asked.

"According to Max's report, he was poisoned. According to your report, there was a chicken pot pie on his desk and it had some bites taken out of it. According to Max's report, there was chicken pot pie in his stomach," Chance said. "It don't take no genius to figure out that Frank was only in town because of your mama's chicken pot pie that she was making for him."

"Kenni, your mama is on line three." Finn put three fingers in the air.

"Mayor, I'll give you a call soon. I've got a call about the case that I need to take," I said.

I clicked the receiver before he could protest and hit the blinking button on line three. I had to give myself some thinking room on what he'd said. I knew he was going to ask me to step down from the case. It was something that anyone would question. But now that the shoe was on my foot, there was no way I wanted to back off the case.

"Mama. What's going on?" I asked.

"There's a matinee at Luke Jones's at two this afternoon. Meet me there. I've got something to tell you about Frank Von Lee." She hung up.

I held the phone up to my ear and let out a few laughs, uh-huhs, and okays pretending it was a no big deal conversation with her.

"Okay. Love you too, Mama." I faked a giggle and hung up.

"What did she do?" Finn asked after he sat in one of the chairs in front of my desk.

"Who?" I asked.

Betty was running around the room doing odds and ends to make it appear as if she wasn't listening, but I could clearly see her eyes snapping in my direction to see what I was doing.

"Your mama." His brow rose.

"Nothing. Why?" I kept it short and sweet. I should've told him that Mama had something to tell me, but I just couldn't. It was my mama.

"Well, first off, you said a few minutes ago that she's our number one suspect and secondly," he exhaled, "you just told her you loved her with a giggle. You never do that."

"Listen." I could feel the frustration that Mama was clearly a suspect ripple deep in my gut. Through gritted teeth, I said, "You and I both know that was pot pie. Plus the note."

"What about it?" he asked.

"Did you read it?" I asked.

"No. I just put it in the evidence bag in case it came back as a homicide." A curious look crossed his face. "What did it say?"

"Go read it while I catch up on the report," I suggested and opened the file.

A few more fielded calls later, a quick review of Max's initial report—poisoning through the food—and Finn was back over to my desk.

"Kenni," his voice was resigned, "this isn't good."

"What's not good is that Katy Lee Hart can place Mom at the inn around Frank's time of death." I pushed the file across my desk to Finn.

He picked it up and opened it.

"What did she say?" He asked.

"Katy Lee owns that Shabby Trends. Every season she has a fashion show for the women in the community and it's hosted at the hotel. She said that

Mama was upset and practically ran into her after Mama had come from the stairwell. What doesn't make sense is why he had the pot pie when he wasn't supposed to have it until the next day," I said.

Finn jumped up and started to write down things on the white board. Unfortunately, he wrote down Mama's name right in the suspect number one block.

He loved that board. It was the first thing he installed after he'd been sworn in as my new deputy. He claims it helped him see holes along with alibis and theories for cases.

"And remember how she took you to lunch, but really went to check out the competition." He reminded me of the gawd-awful event, making it worse by writing it down.

"Okay. Let's do a timeline." I pushed myself back from the desk and got up. I took one of the dry-erase markers and wrote down yesterday's date with a big long line. "We can check dispatch, but we can start here when I went to eat with mama in Clay's Ferry and then the diner to make the red carpet entrance."

"Very good." He nodded.

"Mama was there. She was happy and she talked to Frank. It was around two p.m." I wrote down the time. Underneath the timeline, Finn wrote down Mama's actions. I specifically remember looking up at the clock when Betty had told me not to get too comfortable because Ben had called and wanted me to be at the diner upon Frank's arrival.

"What time did she pick you up to go to Clay's Ferry?" He gnawed on the cap of the pen.

"Around eleven a.m." I watched as he wrote the activities and time.

"What time was the cooking class?" He asked.

"Seven," I said matter-of-factly. "But it's the space in between six and seven p.m. that we need to have her accounted for."

"Why's that?" He asked. "Just so we have clarification and get on the right page here."

"Because Max said that once the poison is in your system, you have about thirty minutes at the most until you start having symptoms." I walked over to the desk and pulled the file closer to me, flipping through to Camille's statement. "Camille states here that he was fine when she first got there, but then became confused, angry, upset, and in pain. That was around six forty-five."

"The records also show that the dispatch call came in around 6:50 and they got in touch with you around seven. Right?" he asked.

"Yes." There was a hesitation in my voice because I was trying to figure out how mama could be put at the scene of the crime with all the driving time she'd been doing.

"You're hesitating." Finn had learned to read me so well.

"If Mama poisoned the pot pie, why? What would've been her motive at that point?" I asked.

"I see where you're going with this." He nodded. "If the pot pie was poisoned and given to him to eat, that would've been premediated and she'd had to have been mad about something with him before he'd even tasted her pot pie."

"And that's not Mama," I said.

"So it's more important than ever that we fill in this time." He made an arrow on the timeline between two p.m. after Mama had dropped me off and six p.m. when mama was last seen at the Tattered Cover Books and Inn. "If she didn't talk or see Frank between these times and their only meeting was with Ben at the diner around two, then she'd really have no motive to kill him. Especially since he wasn't going to try her pot pie until tomorrow."

"Right. All was good in Mama's world. She was very confident that she was going to beat out the barbeque joint in Clay's Ferry after we left." Something else popped into my head. "She made a phone call."

"To who?" Finn asked.

"I'm not sure. She didn't want to tell me. If she won't tell me, I'll pull her phone records." I gnawed on the thought for a minute.

I looked up at the whiteboard. There certainly wasn't enough evidence to arrest Mama or even point the finger at her. In big letters I wrote "Suspect Number Two" with a question mark underneath.

"It looks like we have more digging to do." Finn stood back and tilted his head to the right and left as if the killer's name was going to magically appear. "Did you see or talk to her between the time you left the diner and the time you saw her at the cooking class?"

"Yes, at the diner when Frank got into town. But my dad said that she came home and muttered something about a new recipe. Got a change of clothes and left. After she'd gotten home from the diner, she was working on some different recipes. Not pot pie."

"The next sighting of Viv was by Katy Lee, around dinner time." Finn wrote down the time, place, and people who saw Mama. "Katy said it was around the time Nanette was about to serve supper. She serves around six o'clock, but by the time she made it around to the people who ordered room service and those eating in the restaurant, the time could vary. According to Max, the poison had to be ingested about thirty minutes before the symptoms. The poison doesn't have a taste. Which puts it around six to six fifteen-ish, because Camille got the call around six-thirty." He wrote his words on the board.

"Katy Lee also said that she thought she'd overheard Mama ask Nanette what room Frank Von Lee was in."

I wrote Nanette's name on the board with an arrow under it and wrote "owner of the Tattered Cover Books and Inn" along with the six o'clock supper time.

Both of us sat there in silence looking at the board, our heads shifting side to side as if seeing it from a different angle would give a different perspective.

"I went to see Mama this morning. She's got a black eye." Every word out of my mouth made it worse and worse for her. "You and I both know that it takes about twelve hours for bruises to show up."

"The plate of chicken pot pie and the review were in his room." Finn paced back and forth. "Your mama was nervous about the competition, gave Frank the pot pie, went back to see if he liked it and saw the note. She got angry and they got into a scuffle."

HERE WE WERE, back to trying to make Mama the suspect. Or even just make sense of why she'd kill him.

"That wouldn't make sense." My eyes narrowed as my mind worked overtime trying to take Mama out of the scene of the crime. "If the pot pie was laced with the poison, mama wouldn't've gone back to see if he liked it.

I know mama. She might've lost her mind once she saw the review he'd written. She didn't have motive to put poison in the pot pie."

There were so many unanswered questions that only Mama could answer.

Poppa appeared with a little jig in his step. "I went by your mama's house and looked around for some sodium fluoroacetate."

"What do we know about sodium fluoroacetate?" I asked and walked over to grab the file.

"According to Max's report, the sodium fluoroacetate doesn't have a taste when put into food." Finn made a good point.

"Symptoms are," I read Max's writing to Finn as he wrote them down, "nausea, vomiting, and abdominal pain within one hour of ingestion. Victim had classic signs of sweating and reported to be confused and agitated before the heart attack. All of this goes with Camille's recollection."

Everything was there. What were we missing?

"Heart attack?" Finn asked.

"Yeah." My brows drew together. "I guess I've been so focused on how the poison got into Frank's system that I forgot to tell you that he actually died of a heart attack brought on by the sodium fluoroacetate." I hesitated, but I knew I had to tell Finn everything. "When Mama just called, she told me to meet her at the matinee. She had some information to share about Frank."

"Are you going to try to get her to clarify some things?" Finn watched me intently. My heart sank and it must've shown on my face. "She needs to help herself."

"This afternoon I'm going to go question her. I'll bring her in if I feel like she did it." Only that would mean that she had premeditated Frank's murder, and I knew my mama. She didn't like to get her hands dirty with dirt, much less a murder. "In the meantime, I'm going to head to the diner and question Ben about the meeting they had yesterday when Frank got to town. Maybe he can tell me something about the conversation or why Mama would take Frank the pot pie early." I grabbed the file and stuck it in my police bag. "If she did take him the pot pie."

Both of us stopped talking when Duke jumped up and ran to the door.

"Sorry." Riley Titan, the contractor, stood at the door. "I tried calling, but the lines are busy and I didn't have a cell number."

"No problem." Finn walked over. "Come on in."

"I'm ready to get started." He shoved his hands in his pocket. His eyes shifted around the department.

"Yeah. Great." Finn's voice rose. He pulled his keys out of his pocket and took his house key off the ring. "Here's the key. Help yourself."

"Great," Riley said. "Have a good day."

"Do you think you should've just given him a key?" I asked Finn when he stood up.

"Why not? Ben trusts him. He looks like he does a good job and I just want to get it done." Curiously he looked at me. "You're the first person to tell a stranger how safe it is around Cottonwood and no one ever locks their doors."

"True." I shook my head and rolled my eyes. "You do listen to me."

"Mmmhhmmm." He hummed and bent down to kiss me. "I'm going to follow him out." Finn gestured after Riley. "I thought I'd run and see Dr. Shively to get a formal statement because she called earlier saying she was booked with patients, but would squeeze me in for a few minutes. Now more than ever we need to get her statement."

"Sounds good." I forced a smile, though my mind was numb.

CHAPTER TWELVE

Instead of driving down to Ben's, which was only a short couple of blocks north on Main Street, I decided to take Duke and walk. Walking in the fresh spring air might clear my head and help me start to think logically. Not only had I thought about taking evidence from Frank Von Lee's room where he was murdered, I'd also already convinced myself that Mama was a killer when I knew deep in my bones that she wasn't. She might talk a tough game, but Mama was no different than any other red-blooded woman.

She had feelings. She was just better at shrugging them off and not letting the entire town see.

Duke and I took our time enjoying the spring sunlight on our faces. Why was it that the sun made everything so much better and the warmth put a little giddy-up in my step?

"Kenni! Kenni!" Viola White stood in front of her shop, White's Jewelry, next to Polly Parker. They were trying to open the tripod chalkboard sign. Polly gave it a swift kick and it popped right open.

"Maybe walking wasn't such a good idea," I said to Duke.

Duke trotted on over to Polly and Viola, knowing a good scratch behind the ear was imminent.

"Oh, Kenni." The words were so sympathetic but pretty as they flowed out of Polly Parker's plumped-up lips. Not a normal look for her, but it reminded me of Mama's appearance as of late.

Polly was a petite blonde that worked at the jewelry store a few days a week. She was what I'd call a hillbilly with money. On her daddy's payroll and on the arm of Mayor Ryland—though he was my daddy's age and Polly was a few years younger than me. I had uncovered their affair, which was the hot gossip for a few weeks but had since died down. Now seeing them together was no big deal. I still didn't understand what she saw in him.

"I sure don't think your mama is a killer." Polly drew her left hand up to her chest. On it was the biggest diamond ring that I bet Viola White had ever carried in her shop. "When Chance told me about Frank Von Lee, I had to call all the girls and let them know that we need to rally for Viv."

All the girls? She meant the henny-hens that were my mama's friends and Polly's mama's friends. Apparently, since Polly was dating Mayor Ryland, she'd also taken on the role of pretend wife with his friends.

"Yes." Viola swung the hot pink feather boa around her neck. Duke jumped up and tried to catch the floating feathers that'd wiggled loose from her flinging. "There's no way your mama could hurt a flea. She talks a mean game and she can get stuff done, but murder? Never." She gasped, making her five-foot-four frame seem so much bigger.

A few strands of pearls were wrapped around her wrist and she had a pearl ring on every single finger, though different in sizes and shapes. She was a walking billboard for her shop.

She pushed up her wide-rimmed black glasses with her middle finger before she raked the edges of her short gray hair.

"Who said Mama was a killer?" I asked. If Mama heard the rumors already swirling around, she'd never come out of the house.

"When I found out it was Frank, I knew that your mama had the most to gain or lose from his review. I mean..." Polly's shoulders did a weird wave as she flung that blonde hair of hers behind them. "It doesn't take a cop to put two and two together. If he liked her pot pie, she was going to be famous. If he didn't, she couldn't possibly ever cook again. Not to mention that last night at the end of the Shabby Trends show, I heard through the grapevine that Vivian was seen at the Tattered Cover looking awfully upset." Polly raised a brow. "Suspicious behavior if you ask me."

"Mmhmm." Viola's head nodded up and down. "Plus that." She pointed to the Cottonwood Chronicle box that was chained to the carriage light lamppost in front of her shop.

There were two photos of Mama on the front page. On one side was her coming out of the barbeque shack in Clay's Ferry, and on the other a close-up of Mama with her big shiner around her eye. I ran over and tried to jerk the newspaper container open, but I had to put in two quarters.

"I need fifty cents." I patted around my pockets. Edna Easterly sure did work fast in releasing this paper.

"Hold on." Viola White rushed into the shop.

I bent down to get a look.

"Edna." Disgust came out of my lips. "I can't believe her."

Viola ran over with the two quarters. I took them and pushed them through the slot. The clanking sound of the second quarter let me know I could open the spring door.

I pulled a copy of the paper out and stared at it. Mama wouldn't have let Edna take a photo of her with a black eye.

"How else did she get the black eye?" I swear there was a bit of sarcasm in Polly's voice. "I mean, really?"

"Really, Polly, my mama is not even on my radar." I curled the paper up and stuck it under my arm. "Come on, Duke!" I yelled out of frustration.

When I didn't hear the pitter-patter of his toenails on the concrete sidewalk, I turned around. Polly and Viola had their heads stuck together and were flapping their lips. They stopped when they saw me looking. Both of them shot their hands in the air and gave me the finger wave.

"Duke!" I screamed at my dog when he took off into a full sprint and made it to Ben's before I did. I opened the door of the diner and the bell dinged.

"Wow." My mouth dropped. It appeared as if there was a line for a table. "Business seems to have picked up," I said when I walked up to Ben, who was standing behind the counter.

Through the window I could see Jolee cooking.

"Business has been great. After the news of Frank's death, everyone has wanted to come here and ask questions about it. I only tell them what I know." He swiped the clean rag across the counter and stuffed some singles from a tip in his apron pocket.

"Ben Harrison. You of all people." This was nuts. "You know Mama and she's no killer."

"All I know are the facts." He turned around and threw the rag in the sink behind him before he grabbed a couple paper placemats and napkin-wrapped utensils. "What I know is that Frank Von Lee is dead and your mama was seen leaving the hotel upset. Then this morning she's front and center on the paper with a black eye. It all adds up. Plus I heard about the little fiasco from Clay's Ferry." He threw his hands up in the air. "Yesterday afternoon someone came in and was talking about it."

The kitchen door swung open and Riley Titan walked through.

"Oh. Sorry." He put his hands in the air with a surprised look on his face. "I didn't mean to interrupt. I just need my ladder. I was on my way over to Finn's and realized I left it here."

He looked around. Ben pointed back to the kitchen.

"I found it out here in the corner and had to move it out of the way this morning. I stuck it in the corner of the kitchen," Ben told him.

"Thanks, man." Riley offered a smile and disappeared back through the door. After I heard the back door to the diner shut, I walked over to Ben.

"Seriously, of all my friends," my head tilted to the side and I stared at him, "you're the one who I can't believe is acting this way. And there's no one who said Mama killed someone."

"It doesn't matter. You know gossip around Cottonwood. If they just think that something bad went on around here, they will come for the gossip." He gestured to the full diner. "I need the money."

"Can we talk somewhere a little more private?" I asked when I noticed there wasn't a single spot in the diner without a warm body in it.

"Sure. We can go in my office." He held up a finger for me to hold on and walked over to talk to a couple of the kids on his staff. They made eye contact with me and nodded.

I followed Ben into his office and shut the door behind him.

"Shoot."

"What was said in the meeting yesterday when Frank Von Lee came in?" I asked.

"I greeted him. Like a good gentleman, I introduced Viv and then myself. Both she and I told him how happy we were to hear he was coming and you know," he shrugged, "we took turns kissing his you-know-what."

"How did he react?" I asked.

"He said it was his job and he loved to discover small-town recipes that bring light to the south. Some kind of light," Ben muttered. "Who knew that the expiration of his light would bring in this much publicity?" he asked with a chipper voice.

"Back to the questions." I found it odd that he was so upbeat.

I hated to play hardball, but this was my job and Mama's life was on the line. I couldn't be in denial any longer thinking that I'd made all this up in my head. She definitely was the only suspect and the evidence was just mounting up against her. I'd never had such a clear-cut case. It was almost a little too clear-cut.

"Did he tell you his plans for the evening or what the plan was for today?" I asked.

Out of the corner of my eye, a shadow whisked across the office. My head jerked up and there was Poppa. He was milling around in the office. If he was looking around back there for clues, it saved me time.

"I'm going to look around in the kitchen," Poppa said and ghosted away.

"He said that he'd had a long day of traveling since he only traveled by train and that he wanted to just relax and read." Ben sucked in a deep breath and released it. "I mentioned that Nanette had a great supper, but if he was hungry, he could call over and get something for takeout. He never called."

"Did he eat anything while he was here?" I asked. "Was there anyone else besides Jolee cooking?"

"I offered him a couple of homemade cookies I'd made earlier in the day, but he passed. Jolee is the only one that's been in the kitchen since I fired Chef Mundy. Plus, I'd closed the diner after he left to prepare for today." He shook his head. "Really, I don't think your mama is capable of this, but it's awfully coincidental."

"Do me a favor. Don't give into gossip. Let me see what I can figure out. Let me do my job." I stood up. "I'll get back with you."

We headed out into the kitchen. Jolee pointed to the coffee maker. The steam rolled off of the freshly brewed coffee and the smell made my taste buds water.

"Do you mind if I take a look around?" I asked.

"The place is all yours." Ben poured himself a cup of coffee and one for me as well.

"Thanks," I said and offered a smile.

"I didn't find any sodium fluoroacetate." Poppa stood in the middle of the pristine kitchen. He was as baffled as I was. "If your mama had made a pot pie, then why is that in the trash? She'd never use a frozen dinner."

I looked into the bin. Before I reached in, I took a pair of gloves out of my bag and put them on. I pulled out a cardboard zip tab that you'd find on a premade frozen box. I dug a little deeper in the trash but didn't see a box to go with it.

"Ben?" I called. "Do you use any sort of frozen dinners here?"

"No," Ben said, offended. "Why on earth would you think that?"

"Jolee?" I asked.

"You know better than to ask me something that insulting." She smirked.

"I found this in the trash." I held the long thin piece of cardboard up in the air. I noticed half of a yellow price tag on it that I recognized from Dixon's.

"I have no idea where that came from." Ben turned to head back into the diner, seemingly unaffected by my find.

"How often do you take your trash out?" I asked, pointing to the trash can Poppa found the piece in.

"The ones by the counter are emptied a few times a day." He looked at the one by the pantry. "That one is rarely used because we don't prepare food there. So it might be once a week."

"Once a week." My mind rolled back to the people who'd had access to the kitchen. "Besides you and Jolee, who has been in here?"

"Your mama, me, Chef Mundy..." He stopped when I put my hand up.

"Chef Mundy?" I asked, remembering that the last time I'd seen him, he was wielding a knife at Ben. "Where's he staying?"

"He has a place up in Lexington, but I was paying for him to stay next door." Ben's jaw dropped. "Oh, you don't think?" Ben's brows furrowed.

"I don't discount anyone or any motive." I took another look around until I was satisfied there wasn't anything else to see. "But he was staying at The Tattered Cover Books and Inn?"

"Do you think Mundy poisoned Frank to get back at me?" he asked and looked off into the distance. "I mean, he was right here."

"He was wielding a knife at you," I reminded him. "It's not like that's something you do to someone you care about."

"That's disturbing." Ben leaned back on the counter and crossed his arms. There was a concerned look on his face. "Crap." Ben dragged his hat off of his head and racked his hands through his hair. "I forgot to get his key. I gave him a key to the diner."

"Very disturbing." I patted my leg. "Come on, Duke. Bye, Ben," I said and walked out the back door.

The lid to the dumpster was propped up a little from all the collected trash from the businesses along this particular alley.

"You aren't." Poppa's nose curled.

"I am." I surveyed the dumpster, wondering how I was going to get up in it. I found a sturdy crate and dragged it over to the dumpster.

"This is why you have a deputy," Poppa reminded me as I started to climb in.

"Well, my suspect isn't my deputy's mother. She's mine." I put on another pair of gloves. Duke was busy smelling all the unique smells associated with a dumpster while I took my first step inside.

My feet sank into the bags and the odor was unforgivable. I gulped back a gag and started to sort through the bags. Ben's bags were black, so I grabbed all the black bags I found and threw them out of the dumpster. There were at least eight of them. I put them in a pile and headed on back to the office to get the Jeep to collect them.

The back streets took a little longer than just going down Main Street, but I was in no mood to answer questions swirling around the gossip mill about Mama. Though I did want to know how Edna got that photo.

There was no better time to ask her than on my walk. I dialed her number.

"Hi, Edna." I used my sweet Kenni Lowry voice. "It's Sheriff Lowry."

"Hi there." Her voice wasn't as happy to hear from me as I thought it should be. "I guess you're calling 'bout the article."

"Not so much the article, but the photo and how you got it." It wasn't against the law to take pictures, but there was no way she'd get a good shot of Mama without Mama's permission, and I'd bet my life that she didn't have it.

"I was on a walk and was just snapping pictures of our beautiful city," she lied.

"You mean that you heard about Frank Von Lee and you knew I'd go see my mama. You followed me to my parents' house to get the shot because you knew mama would open the door for me." It all clicked. "Am I right?"

"There's no law against taking photos." She loved to use the law to get her out of sticky situations.

"We do have an unwritten moral law," I reminded her. "Stay away from my investigation."

"You mean to tell me that you are investigating your own mama, not Deputy Vincent?" She was a sneaky one.

"Goodbye, Edna." I clicked off the phone.

CHAPTER THIRTEEN

By the time I'd walked back to the office it was almost time for me to go meet Mama at the matinee.

"People are going crazy around here." Betty told me something I already knew. She'd been fielding calls all morning and avoiding answering any questions that could fuel the gossip more. "And the national news has gotten a hold of the murder too."

"What?" There was something that we didn't need. After all, we'd just gotten through a big scandal from the death of the only famous person from Cottonwood, author Beryle Stone.

"There were a couple of calls on the messaging machine from them celebrity television shows asking about Mr. Von Lee's death. Then a couple follow-up calls after they'd gotten wind that it was a murder." Her right brow cocked, the right corner of her lip following. She finished, "They said they'd be on their way today and wanted to know what time you were holding a press conference."

"Press conference?" I asked.

Press conference? I noodled on the thought and got an immediate stomachache. I ran my hand over my ponytail and knew that I was in no shape to be seen on TV. No doubt they'd tear me to shreds if they did find out that my mama was the reason he was here and that she was really my only suspect at the moment. Though I wasn't discounting Mundy.

"Yep." Betty tapped away on her computer. "That means you better get on over to Tiny Tina's and get your hair done, because they are coming whether you want them to or not."

I looked at my watch. I was already going to be late to meet Mama at the matinee and I had to find out what she was going to tell me about Frank.

"There's no time." The idea of being on camera gnawed at my gut. "I've got to go check out a lead," I lied. I didn't want anyone to find out that I was meeting Mama secretly. "Duke, you stay here." I flipped him a treat and headed out the door.

With Duke left behind at the department, I got into the Jeep, where Poppa was waiting on me.

"Where have you been?" I asked.

"Like you and Finn, busy trying to solve a murder." Poppa was frustrated and I could see why. "And I'm still running off any would-be criminals."

"What?" I jerked and looked at him.

"You think that little snot-nosed brat kids don't try to steal candy at Dixon's or sneak into Luke Jones's to see a movie? You better think again," Poppa scoffed.

"Oh. I thought that you just poofed away and back when I needed you." This whole gig with Poppa was strange.

"I'll always be here when you need me, but Cottonwood still needs me too." Poppa took pride in his new gig and I loved it. "After our earlier conversation, I put some more thought into the situation. I thought I'd keep my ghost eyes and ears open. Found out that I can still scare off any other crimes so you can focus on getting your mama cleared."

"Poppa, the only way we've ever gotten crimes solved, now and before, has been together." I reminded him how we'd always gone back and forth with ideas on different scenarios on how and why a crime was committed.

"I'm just not sure I can hang around and see the evidence pile up on her. I think it's best I continue to keep the rest of the town safe while you focus on finding the real killer." He was dead set on his reasoning and there was no way I was going to change his mind.

This time I could see that the investigation was so close to us that Poppa's objectivity he'd always been proud of was skewed, along with mine.

"I understand that this doesn't look good." I turned the Jeep on and drove down the alley, stopping at the stop sign. "But we have to process all the evidence and prove that Mama didn't kill anyone. You've always told me that solving a crime is like a mystery novel. The clues are there. We just have to pay attention to them to help solve the crime."

He sucked in a deep breath through his nose and let out a long deep exhale out his mouth. I turned out of the alley and then left on Main Street. I had to get to the dumpster behind Ben's and grab those black garbage bags.

"That frozen dinner pull tab really is on my mind. I know that pot pie can be frozen and I wonder who made a frozen dinner at Ben's." I had to get Poppa thinking about the case. It was the only way to get Mama off the suspect list. "Just think about Chef Mundy."

"He had access to the kitchen. He was very vocal about the diner and the noise the construction workers were making. Then he and Ben got into that argument." Poppa was coming around to the sheriff he used to be, putting the what-if scenarios together that made us such a great team. "There was that little moment he had too."

"When?" I asked, pulling up to the edge of the dumpster where I'd thrown the bags out.

"When Frank Von Lee came to the diner to meet with Ben and Viv, no one was in the back of the kitchen. Ben said Mundy still had a key," Poppa said.

"But they would've smelled the pot pie baking." It wouldn't have been possible for Mundy to bake the pot pie then. "Though..." I stopped to gather my thoughts. "Ben did shut down the diner for his and mama's private meeting with Frank so he could get prepared for the real tasting the next day. I'm sure he ran some errands and Mama was who knows where that afternoon, but we do know her whereabouts later that day. I'm going to ask her where she was between the time she left the initial meet and greet with Frank and showed up at Lulu's. Back to Chef Mundy." I put my mind back on him as a possible suspect. "So Mundy could've walked over to the diner, slipped in the back using his key, baked the pot pie, and put the poison in."

"Yeah, but did anyone at the Tattered Book see him?" he asked.

"I don't know yet." I put it on my mental list to check out. "One suspect at a time. Right now meeting Mama to find out her exact whereabouts the entire day is my focus." I smiled and turned the Wagoneer off. "Mama is very sneaky. If she was going to be doing something and not want to get caught, she'd have been a lot more discreet."

"You're right!" Poppa's excitement grew. "I know she didn't do this. We've got to figure out who wants everyone to believe she did."

"Mama is vocal and would be a very easy candidate as a suspect since Frank Von Lee's entire visit was centered around her and that pot pie." I got out of the Jeep and opened the back door.

There was no time to go through the trash since I had to meet Mama, so I threw all the bags into the back of the Jeep.

On the way over to Luke Jones's movie theater, I gave Finn a quick call. When he didn't answer, I left a message letting him know that I might've found some evidence and I'd be sorting it at home. Conveniently I left out the part that it was trash. Smelly trash. Plus I wanted to tell him that I'd found out that Mundy had been staying at The Tattered Cover Books and Inn, which might've put him at the scene of the crime. I was never comfortable leaving messages so detailed on an answering machine, so I left the message very vague.

The smell of warm buttery popcorn floated around me as I got out of the Jeep in front of Luke's house. A much better smell than what was inside the Jeep. We didn't have a movie theater in Cottonwood and it took us about forty-five minutes to get to a larger town if we did want to see a movie, so Luke and Vita Jones turned their basement into a makeshift theater. Granted, the movies were older (practically centuries), but the movie popcorn and candy made up for that.

"Afternoon, Sheriff." Vita Jones greeted me at the door with a big bag of fresh popcorn and a can of Diet Coke. "I figured I'd have it all ready for you when you got here. Your mama is up there sitting on the front couch."

"Thank you, Vita." I looked in the bag.

"Don't worry. I sprinkled some extra M&M's in there." She winked. "Besides, it sounds like you need that extra sugar with a murderer on the loose."

"We're working really hard on bringing some justice for Mr. Von Lee." I offered her a reassuring smile. "Thank you for the extra candy."

"I think your mama just got back from the eye doctor." Vita's brow rose. "She's got on a big pair of dark sunglasses."

"You know Mama," I said. "She's particular about getting wrinkles. Maybe the new spring sunshine is making her squint a little more today."

"That sunshine is welcome from me after the long dark winter we've had." Vita sucked in a deep breath and glanced over my shoulder out the window in the door behind me.

"I agree. Any sunshine is good for me," I agreed. "I'll see you after the movie."

"Groundhog Day. A favorite around here this time of the year." She handed a bag of popcorn to another movie-goer. "We're playing it a little longer this year since the groundhog predicted an early spring."

"I'm glad he did." I headed to the front of the theater.

Luke and Vita had gotten hand-me-down mismatched couches from various citizens of Cottonwood and placed them around the basement for movie-goers. There were different movie posters around the room. Today was a good day for a movie. The screen was pulled down at the front of the room, which was what made it a good day. Sometimes it was finicky and wouldn't cooperate when Luke tried to pull it down. On those days, Luke pinned up a king-sized sheet and played the movie.

Mama was curled in the corner of the couch, butted up to the arm. Her dark glasses still covered her eyes.

"Mama." I held the bag of popcorn out for her to grab a handful.

She waved her hand in the air, a hanky in her grip, declining the tasty treat. She used the corner of it to dab the edge of each eye. I wasn't going to fall for it. She wasn't crying. Mama had pulled the wool over my eyes one too many times.

"Did you see that gawd-awful newspaper?" She sniffed. "I'm going to call Wally Lamb and see what law Edna Easterly has broken because I know you'll tell me to let it go like you always do." She tried her best to mock me with her best follow-up sniff.

I eased down next to her and whispered, because I was well aware of the rubber-necking of the people around us who were trying to get a hint of our conversation. "You should let it go and let me do my job."

"Your job?" Mama squeaked. "You'll have me down there in that jail. In no time my hair will smell like that old fried catfish that Bartley Fry is so proud of."

"If you are guilty of something, then you need to tell me," I encouraged her. "I'm here because you said you had something to tell me."

The lights dimmed and the beginning of Groundhog Day started, and so had the sound of fresh popping popcorn, which let Mama and I talk a little louder than a hushed whisper.

"Go on." Mama threw her arms in front of her with her wrists up. "Cuff me. Arrest your poor ol' mama if you think I killed Frank Von Lee." She jutted them toward me a couple of times with her eyes squeezed shut.

"Mama," I whispered.

Her chin flew in the air; one eye squinted a little behind her sunglasses.

"I see you looking at me. Open your eyes and stop pouting." This was a position I never thought I'd be in.

"Pouting? You've accused me of killing a man. Your mama." She jabbed her chest with her finger. "Ouch." She quickly tried to rub out the hurt she'd caused herself. "I'm your mama. I brought you into this world. I gave you your name. I gave you everything you ever wanted. I paid for your college and now you are using that against me."

"What?" I jerked back.

"You are using the money I spent on your education against me by calling me a killer." She sobbed and threw her nose down into the hanky. "This was your grandfather's hanky."

Our louder-than-whispering conversation had spurred a few shushes from the crowd.

I grabbed Mama by her wrist and dragged her up and out of the basement.

"You mean Poppa?" I asked, dropping her wrist once we'd made it outside.

I'd never heard her call him my "grandfather."

"You know what I mean." She sniffed.

"Mama." I put my arm around her. "Give me something to go against all this evidence mounting up against you." The lines on my forehead wrinkled. I swallowed. Hard. "You went a little nuts in Clay's Ferry. You were seen at the hotel where Frank was staying right before Frank's time of death. Mind you, you were upset. You have a black eye, which makes me wonder whose fist you ran into. You're not your usual self. Give me something. Anything," I begged.

"Fine." All of a sudden the rush of tears dried. She pushed back her hair and jerked her shoulders back. She stood ram-rod straight.

"I wanted to look good. I'm not going to lie. I'd heard about someone doing those Botox parties at the condo complex on the river." I wasn't sure, but I think Mama tried to wiggle her eyes. Her forehead and brows were frozen. "I knew I was going to be doing newspaper interviews, radio interviews, and television interviews after Frank tasted my pot pie."

"Botox party?" I groaned, knowing this was probably something illegal and I'd have to add it to my list of things to look into.

"Yes. You go and pay your twenty-five dollars." She stopped when I put my hand in the air.

"Twenty-five dollars?" She and I both knew that was a red flag.

"Are you going to let me talk or keep interrupting me?" She crossed her arms, her face stern. She continued when I didn't answer. "I went a couple of days ago. I sat in a kitchen chair and they stuck me with needles and put this stuff in my face. I have to say that I was pleased at first. You know that phone call I made after we left Clay's Ferry?" she asked.

I nodded.

"I made an appointment to have more Botox injected. Late yesterday afternoon, I went back to get my eyes done again. The woman said she could make me look better and not blotchy. I was getting Botox around the timeframe you said Frank had passed. Then this showed up." She pointed to her eye. "I got on the internet and Googled. I think I got a bad batch of Botox or got something else."

"Mama, you had the Botox done around six?" This was good, but not perfect. I needed to know if she had given him a pot pie or not.

"That was the second time." She drew in a deep breath through her nose. "I went right after I met Frank because I just wanted to make sure I looked good on the television."

"That explains the eye. What about the food?"

"I have no idea how the food got there. I confess that I had an idea to make ribs like the place we went to eat in Clay's Ferry. I'd even gone as far as to go to Danny Shane's Dairy Barn to get some creamer to make the barbeque sauce thicker and spicier."

"Yes, they did have good ribs." I nodded.

"I didn't give Frank anything. I am guilty of going to the hotel. Nanette gave me his room number. When I went up there, I had planned on asking him if he'd rather have barbeque or the pot pie. He told me that he'd gotten the pot pie I'd sent over and was doing his review and I wasn't going to be happy." She pulled her lips tight. "I didn't take him a pot pie. I told him that I didn't even make the pot pie yet, but he grinned and told me that's what they all say once they get a bad review. I broke into tears and ran off. That's when I rushed back to the Botox party."

"Katy Lee saw you so upset after you'd run out of the stairwell." I made a note to ask Nanette if someone had dropped off a pot pie at the hotel and what the time was to see if it went with the timeline Finn and I had put together.

"Yes. I couldn't tell her that Frank told me he was going to write a bad review. So I did the best I could to keep it together. After I went to get my second injection, I went straight to the cooking class at Lulu's Boutique. In fact, I had a plan to take Frank that pot pie I was going to make in class after we were finished so he could see the first one wasn't mine. I swear." She put her hand up like Scout's honor. "Someone wanted him dead and they blamed it on me. Poor little ol' me." Mama sobbed into the hanky.

"I believe you." I put my hand on her knee.

"You do?" she asked. She looked up at me, her eyes dry as a bone.

CHAPTER FOURTEEN

I strongly suggested that Mama keep a low profile until I got the evidence processed and saw if any more leads came up. Time was not on my side, and I could feel it nipping at my heels like an angry dog. Poppa had disappeared, proving to be no help, angry that the evidence pointed straight at Mama with very little wiggle room.

I found Nanette in her office at The Tattered Cover Books and Inn, sitting behind the computer looking at all the news that'd found its way on the internet about Frank's murder.

"It's everywhere." Nanette's eyes grazed the top of her computer. Her reading glasses sat on the edge of her nose.

Purdy, The Tattered Cover's cat mascot, jumped up on the bookshelf behind Nanette and curled up on a pillow.

"May I?" I picked up one of the cat treats that was sitting on Nanette's desk.

"Sure." Nanette didn't even look up at me. She continued to tap on her computer.

"Here you go, Purdy." I put the treat next to her paw and ran my hand down her fur. She purred and took the treat.

She was a good cat. Nanette had a big sign posted and she told all the guests before they made a reservation that she had a cat. If they were allergic, they shouldn't stay, because Purdy had free reign of the place.

"Kenni, this has to be solved or no one will ever come back to Cottonwood." Nanette got my attention. "The food you found in his room was not from here. He didn't ask for food."

"Exactly how did you know about the food?" I asked since I knew I'd not disclosed any information to the public.

"Well...um...you know. Small town." She meant gossip and someone had let the cat out of the bag. That someone had to be Betty Murphy.

I turned around and looked over her shoulder. She scrolled down a Google page and from the looks of the links the media had published their online news a couple of hours ago.

"Betty," I said into the walkie-talkie and walked around the desk. "Can you please call the Reserve and let them know about Frank Von Lee's murder? Tell them to send some officers down here in case more of the media outlets try to get a scoop on the story. And please stop gossiping about it."

"Now Kenni, when people ask me things, I can't lie. It's not my nature." Betty made an excuse.

"Betty." I paused to make more of a point. "This is a murder investigation. We don't tell anyone anything until we have all the facts and killer in custody." I sucked in a deep breath. "Please make that call."

"Will do, Sheriff." Betty clicked back. "Also, Frank's agent and the Culinary Channel people called to say they were coming. Mayor Ryland has called an emergency council meeting for tonight at seven p.m."

"Thanks, Betty. I probably won't be back at the office this afternoon." I checked the time. It was almost three o'clock now and Mayor Ryland would want some sort of confirmation that our small town was safe and ease the citizens' fears.

"I'll let you know if I hear anything else," Betty said.

I clicked off and scrolled the volume down so I could talk to Nanette.

"This is going to explode all over the media. I mean," fear set on Nanette's face, "this is a big deal when someone famous dies. Remember the media circus from Beryle Stone? No one is ever going to want to stay here again. I'm going to be run out of business." She looked over my shoulder and out into the lobby, where a couple of guests were hanging out. "At least no one's cancelled their room today. We're full, and I feel like I'm going to need the money if we do have a backlash."

"This is why I'm here," I said to Nanette as I sat down in the chair in front of her desk.

It was the perfect opportunity to dig my heels in and ask her questions during her vulnerable state. I dug down in my bag to get my tape recorder and remembered I'd left it at the office, so I grabbed my paper and pen.

"I'm sure you hear that I've got a few leads. I'm asking everyone who was there at the time and wanted to know what you remember. And if you remember seeing mama here around that time."

"I don't recall. I guess I was getting supper ready for the guests." She busied herself with shuffling some papers.

"It's okay. I know that you talked to Mama. I also know that Mama asked you for Frank's room number." I held my pen to the paper.

There was a silence. I waited.

"Nanette." I eased up on the edge of the chair and leaned my arms on her desk. "I know that you don't want to rat on her and that she's my mama, but that doesn't mean I don't want justice brought for Frank's murder. Don't get me wrong, I'm going to try to find out everything I can and hope it doesn't point to Mama, but I'm the sheriff and I have to put all bias aside." She looked at me. "This means that you can tell me everything."

She nodded and took a deep swallow.

"Can you tell me about Vivian Lowry," I decided to use Mama's name to make it seem more professional, "coming in here on the afternoon of Frank Von Lee's murder?"

She nodded again. I took my arms off the desk and sat back a little.

"I'd much rather tell Deputy Finn if you don't mind," Nanette said in a soft voice.

I offered a tucked-in lip smile. Who could blame her? I didn't think about how this was going to make other people feel.

"Kenni!" Poppa appeared at the door. "Come quick!"

"I'll have Finn come by." I stood up, grabbed my bag, and headed out the office door.

Poppa stood at the door. I hurried over and looked out, forcing my mouth to stay shut. There were too many people around for me to risk talking to him.

"Chef Mundy." Poppa nodded toward a small black car. "He was here. He was leaving with a suitcase."

I tried to get the license plate number of the car, but Danny Shane walked past the front door with a ladder in his hands and blocked my view.

Malina Woody was behind the inn's desk. She grew up in Cottonwood and was what you'd call an old maid at the ripe old age of thirty-three. Mama was worried sick I was going to be a Malina Woody. She was a reader. I remembered going to the library when I was younger and seeing her there with her nose stuck in a book. She still walked down the street with a book in her face.

"Malina, y'all having some work done?" Saying her name got her to look up.

"I think we had some gingerbread lattice coming off and a few other things. Mr. Shane's been here the past couple of days fixing it for Nanette," she replied, flipping a page of the book she was reading.

"Did you get your hair highlighted?" I asked, wanting to get a little friendlier.

"I did, and a cut." She smiled and twirled around. Her long stringy brown hair had been cut into an asymmetrical bob that was completely out of her norm. "Do you like?"

"I do like." I really did. Those fancy haircuts weren't for me, nor did it fit my style of just throwing my hair up in a ponytail. I envied how cute she looked. It was a wonder Finn had found me remotely attractive since I rarely fixed my hair or wore makeup.

"I got it done down at Tiny Tina's." She smiled. "The only bad thing about having this kind of cut is that I have to go back every four weeks to trim it up or it won't lay right. Between me and you, I'm going to ask Nanette for a raise."

"Maybe I can help you," I suggested, knowing I probably couldn't and that Nanette really didn't want me around here asking questions.

After all, who wants the sheriff's department in their place of business twenty-four seven? The quicker we get this solved, the quicker she can have the inn back with no interruptions.

"I need a little information, and if you help, I'll be sure to tell Nanette how valuable you really are, because I can tell that you are smart and very observant."

"I was about to go clean room four, so you can follow me up if you'd like." She perked up even more. "Does this have to do with that man who was killed in room three?"

"It sure does. I'd love to follow you up." I leaned back a smidge and looked into Nanette's office. Her head was glued to the computer monitor. The coast was clear.

I waited for Malina at the bottom of the steps and followed her to the second floor where the rooms were.

"Room four, hmm." I played nonchalant. "I thought the inn's rooms were full."

"They are. Well," she stopped at the top of the steps and looked at me, "they were until a couple of minutes ago. This is his room."

"His room?" I asked, probing for some answers.

"That chef that Ben fired was staying here in room four." She pulled a key out of the cleaning bin she'd carried up with her and opened the door. She flipped on the light. "He had an open reservation and had pre-paid for a couple of weeks. He threw his key on the desk and said 'I'm out.'"

"You didn't know he was leaving early?" I asked, following her into the room.

It was a disaster.

"No. He didn't even ask for a refund either." Her brow cocked. "And it looks like he was in a hurry too."

The room was destroyed. The bed sheets were tossed on the floor. The trash can was overflowing. Dirty wet towels were strewn from the bathroom into the suite. The desk had crumpled-up pieces of paper on the top and on the floor around it.

"Malina." I put my hand out when she reached down to get the comforter and the rest of the bed covers off the floor. "I'm going to have to ask you to leave everything here and not touch anything."

"Huh?" Her head jerked back.

"Think about it." I was about to plant a new suspect in her mind, knowing she'd head straight downstairs and gossip a little. The gossip would make its rounds, and by the time it circled Cottonwood, Mama's name would be old hat. "Chef Mundy had a chip on his shoulder from getting fired."

I set my police bag down on the only clear spot on the floor next to the desk.

"Are you saying that he could've killed that fancy food critic? Because he was so nice. I couldn't imagine him wanting to do anything like that. He flirted a little with me." She tilted her head like Duke did when I asked him if he wanted to go for a walk or wanted a treat.

I wanted to pat her on her head and say good girl, but I refrained.

"You are one smart cookie, Kenni-bug." Poppa rocked back on his heels.

"I'm not saying anything," I said to her, because I didn't want her to misquote me, but whatever it was she heard was perfect. "But you might be right. And I can't let any evidence be thrown out or cleaned."

"This is unbelievable." Her voice was hushed. "He didn't seem like a killer when we talked in the kitchen. I mean..." She hesitated before she looked at me with a thin grin. "What can I do to help?"

"Not a thing. You just give me the key and your phone number in case I need to get a statement about your interaction with him, and I'll be sure to tell Nanette," I answered.

I held my hand out. She dropped the key in it. I put it in my pocket and then took out my phone. She rattled off her number and I put it in my contacts before she rushed out of the room and down the hall.

I walked over to the door and peeked around the door jamb, watching Malina's back end disappear down the steps. I pulled my phone out of my pocket and quickly called Betty Murphy at the department.

"Betty, it's Kenni." She did some umm-hmms on the other end. "I need you to get ahold of the judge and get me a search warrant for the entire Tattered Cover Books and Inn. And pronto."

There was a limited amount of time before Nanette got word I was up here going through the room. It was more unflattering news for the inn that she'd not welcome. She would want some sort of documentation allowing me to be in this particular room.

I snapped on some gloves and picked up one of the crumbled pieces of paper off the desk. I ran my hand over it to straighten it out and left it on the desk. I did the same thing to a couple more pieces and noticed the handwriting was the same. I'd have to get a handwriting analysis to see if it was Mundy's, though I suspected it was since all of them were the same writing.

"Chicken pot pie," I read off the top of one, and then the next, and then the next.

One after the other, the text heading read "chicken pot pie." He had been making a recipe and it looked as though each one had a different seasoning.

"He's trying to figure out what your mama puts in her pot pie." Poppa stood in the door of the bathroom. "He's got all sorts of ingredients in here. And there's blood."

"Blood?" I dropped the piece of paper in my hand.

Before I made it to the bathroom, Nanette pushed the door open.

"Kenni!" She stomped. "Do you have a warrant for this room? Because if you don't, I've got someone who needs to stay here."

"It's on the way. And with blood in the tub..." I stood at the bathroom door. There was a deep red blood smear along the bathtub edge. "I'm not moving an inch."

"Blood?" She gasped and drew her hand up to her chest.

"I'm going to need all the paperwork for Mr. Mundy," I informed her and clicked on the walkie-talkie. "Betty, I need you to call Finn and tell him that we have another suspect. Tell him to find out anything and everything he can about Chef Mundy from Ben's."

Nanette went back downstairs. I quickly gathered the papers with the recipes and put them in evidence bags. I swept the room, snapping a bunch of photos.

"You know," Poppa was still studying the blood, "I'm pretty sure the blood on the knives is Mundy's, because that looks like chicken parts in the tub. He seemed to be cutting up the whole, fresh chicken in the tub and probably cut himself on his own knives. But where did he cook the recipes?" He asked a great question. "If he did cook pot pie, then he might've made the one for Frank."

I took the evidence markers and set them around the room while taking photos. I took some swabs of the blood for evidence along with all the ingredients. I went through the trash.

"There's not any sort of frozen dinners in here," I said.

"He's a chef. He wouldn't lower his standards to frozen dinners." Poppa's eyes darted around the room.

"Mundy would have reason to murder Frank," I said to Poppa.

"I was thinking the same thing." Poppa looked out the room door. Apparently, the coast was clear because he kept talking.

I walked over to the door and shut it so no one would think I was talking to myself.

"Jealousy is a very powerful motive." Poppa referred to the second biggest motive for murder.

"You know, he yelled at Ben at the diner the other day saying he couldn't work in such loud conditions, but he was making basic things like biscuits and gravy. He shouldn't have had such a hard time." I looked around the room to make sure I didn't miss anything and picked up the mattress, pillows, and towels. "He might've been working on a pot pie recipe then and Ben didn't know it. He could've tried to take away Mama's thunder and when Ben fired him, he killed Frank out of anger at Ben. Though it looked like Mama did it..."

Poppa smacked his hands together.

"As long as he brought down Ben and the diner, he didn't care who he ran over, including your mama." Poppa's eyes lowered. "He was making the pot pie over here and he served it to Frank."

"Yeah, but if that's the case..." I hated that I always played the devil's advocate to Poppa's ideas. "Why did he leave everything here without trying to clean it up?"

Poppa scratched his chin. "Maybe he saw you downstairs and thought you were there to close in on him."

Nanette came into the room with the paperwork on Mundy I needed.

I grabbed my phone and called Betty.

"Betty, I need you to plug Mundy Brell into the computer databases and see what you turn up."

CHAPTER FIFTEEN

"Where are you?" Finn asked after I'd gotten back in the car and answered his call.

"I'm at the hotel. Where are you?" I asked.

"Chasing dead-end leads on this handicap sticker case." He reminded me that I'd completely forgotten to tell him about Mama's and had even forgotten to ask her about it. "Did you find anything out? Betty called to tell me that I need to check into Mundy."

"Since you are at a dead end, why don't I swing by and get you and Duke. I need to head to the lab in Clay's Ferry." It would be good to have him ride along with me. Not only to tell him the latest news, but just to be with him since we'd not been able to spend any time alone the past couple of days. "I'll tell you everything on our way over there."

"Not the kind of time I really want to spend with you, but I'll take what I can get since I hear tonight we have a town council meeting to go to," he said.

"I'll see y'all in a minute." Literally in a minute, I'd pulled in the alley behind the department where Duke and Finn were waiting.

"Hi." Finn opened the back door of the Wagoneer and let Duke jump in before he got in the passenger seat.

"Hi." I smiled, greeted him back, and leaned over to kiss him. "Pft, pft." I spit when Duke beat Finn to my kiss and stuck his head between us, licking me right in the mouth. "Hi, buddy," I baby talked Duke and rubbed his head.

Finn gave up and leaned back in the seat, tugging his seatbelt on.

On the way to the lab, I told Finn about Nanette and how she only wanted to talk to him.

"Before I'd gone to see her, I went to see Ben." I held the wheel with one hand and pushed Duke back with the other. He finally sat in the backseat. "The diner is hopping. He's got so much business because people are nosy. Then I found a piece of cardboard in the trash."

"I think I found it." Poppa chirped from the back. My eyes drew up to the rearview mirror where I looked back at Poppa. He was sitting right next to Duke with his arm draped around him.

"Go on," Finn encouraged me when I hesitated.

"And I can't help but think it looks like it's off one of those frozen dinners. I got the idea that maybe Mundy, since he still has a key to Ben's, came to the diner and cooked a frozen pot pie, put the poison in it, and gave it to Frank or left it for Frank to let Frank think it was from Mama." It was a stretch, but something to consider. "Not to mention, Ben was paying for Mundy to stay at the hotel while Frank was in town so he could be right there for work."

"Why would Mundy want to kill Frank?" He asked a very good question.

"Tell him about the hotel room." Poppa bounced in the seat. "You can't forget Mundy could've killed Frank out of anger for Ben firing him and wanted to put Ben out of business."

"That's what we need to figure out. You don't know the half of it." We were losing daylight hours. The country road between Clay's Ferry and Cottonwood was winding and trees covered the road like a bridge, only letting the sun through every few feet. "Mundy's room was a bloody mess. He was in the hotel room making food and there were chicken parts all over the bathroom." I pointed to the back of the Wagoneer. "That's why I'm going to see Tom Geary at the lab. I have a bunch of evidence I want tested for sodium fluoroacetate. Grab my bag and get the camera out. You'll see all the photos I took."

"This is why Betty called me to check Mundy out." He was adding everything up in his head.

"Yep." I gripped the wheel and took a sharp right into the driveway of the brown brick building where the lab was located.

Tom Geary was just locking up when we got there.

"Look at that old geezer," Poppa joked and ghosted himself out of the Jeep. "If I was still alive, we'd be doing some good investigating together." Poppa talked to Tom like Tom could hear him.

"Sheriff, what are you doing here?" Tom asked.

"Hi, Tom. This is my deputy, Finn Vincent." The two men shook hands. "I wanted to drop off some items to be tested for sodium fluoroacetate." I stuck my key in the keyhole of the back door of the Wagoneer to pull out the evidence bags from Mundy's hotel room.

"It must be important if you're personally bringing them." He took the bags from me.

"Just like her Poppa." Poppa puffed his chest out.

"You're just like your Poppa." Tom looked at me.

"That's what I hear," I muttered, trying not to look at Poppa "Do you think you can make these a priority?"

"You know it." He looked between me and Finn. "Nice to meet you, Deputy."

"You too." Finn gave the man-nod back.

"I hope he gets those run fast." I put the car back in drive and kept one eye on the road and watched Tom go back into the lab with the other.

It was probably too much to hope for, but I really wished he was going back in there to start the tests, but I knew he had a life just like the rest of us.

"What in the world is that smell?" Finn rolled down his window. The odor from the trashbags in the confined car had finally seeped out and stunk up the car.

Duke stuck his head in from the back and put it out Finn's window.

"Oh!" I started to laugh. "I totally forgot. The frozen dinner I was talking about, well, I found that piece of cardboard in Ben's trash. He said that he takes the trash to the dumpster, so I took all the bags out of the dumpster and put them in the back of the Wagoneer."

"Kenni, you are something else." Finn leaned over and kissed me on the cheek. "Let me guess, we are going to go through them."

"You are so smart." I teased and headed the Jeep back down the winding road into Cottonwood.

"Not that I'm grasping for straws to figure out another suspect, but you have to think it's super weird that Mundy would have all the ingredients in his hotel room that just so happened to be for the recipe Mama was making for Frank." That was just too much of a coincidence to me.

"We need to find the connection," Finn said. "I'm sure like every other business, the chef industry is pretty small once you get into it."

"I think we need to put him on the suspect list too." I gripped the wheel.

I'd always trusted my gut, and it was telling me Mundy knew Frank. But how? It was definitely something I was going to look into, but I first wanted to get the trash out of my car.

"Now what?" Finn looked at the time on his phone. "We don't have a lot of time before the meeting."

"I'm going to take you back to the office to grab your car and go home to go through this trash."

Going into a council meeting armed with as much information as I could was my best shot. And I was hoping that I'd find something going through the trash. It might've been a long shot, but it was worth the effort.

Finn pinched his nose and playfully waved his other hand in front of his face. "Pee-eww. I'll be over to help."

"Thank you." I probably didn't say it to him enough, but I did appreciate all the time and effort he'd put into the duties of the office. "You really are a great sidekick."

"Hey now." Poppa chirped from the back. "I think me and Duke are pretty good too."

My eyes looked into the rearview mirror. I smiled. Finn turned around in the seat and looked into the back of the Wagoneer. Duke was curled up on the backseat asleep.

"What on earth are you smiling at?" Finn asked and turned back around.

"Nothing." I sighed. Eventually I knew I was going to have to tell Finn my little secret about my ghost deputy. I just didn't know when.

CHAPTER SIXTEEN

"And you're going through the trash already?" Finn smiled and plucked the handle of the gate that lead into my backyard open. His perfect teeth glistened in the early evening sun. My heart tumbled inside. "I thought I'd give you a few minutes to get Duke fed and settled, but you just dove right on in."

"I don't let the grass grow under my feet." I held up a piece of half-eaten Derby pie. "Shame." I looked at the pie and frowned. "Someone wasted a great piece of pie."

Duke ran over to Finn with a ball in his mouth. They played a little tug of war until Duke finally let Finn win and dropped it.

"I went to see Nanette on my way over here." He chucked the ball into the far right corner of the yard. Duke took off in a dead sprint.

"Oh yeah?" I looked up at him with my hand dug deep into one of the bags.

"She said that she didn't feel comfortable giving you a statement because she really liked you and your family. She didn't want to be the cause of any bad feelings." He picked up the ball Duke brought back and dropped at his feet.

"I can understand that, but I took an oath to uphold my duties as sheriff no matter what the cost. Including Mama's freedom." As hard as it would be to lock Mama up in jail, a murderer had to be brought to justice. "I'm just looking at all the other possibilities when it comes to strange things like Mundy's hotel room." I did take my responsibilities as the sheriff very seriously and I held the office above my relationships. It was part of the job.

"She confirmed that Viv asked for Frank's room number and that the occupant in room six complained about noise." He took his phone out of his pocket and with the pad of his forefinger scrolled through.

"They did?" I looked up at him.

"Yeah. She took the complaint." He held the phone out. "Here's a photo of the complaint."

I took his phone and read through it.

"It says here that they were in the hallway and that they didn't see Mama go into Frank's room." That was good. "And that Mama kept yelling 'it's not my pot pie.' Which is what Mama told me."

"And the time was around five forty-five. Which tells me that Frank had eaten some of the pot pie because he was already in the middle of writing that review." Finn walked over and pointed to the photo. He smelled so good, which made it difficult to concentrate. "The hotel guest said they'd called down to the office to complain and that's when Malina told them to come down and make a formal statement. As they were going down to the office, they passed someone with a tray and a drink that looked like someone from room service."

"But Nanette doesn't do room service," I noted.

"Right. The person with the drink knocked on Frank's door. They said a couple of words to each other before Frank took the drink, but they couldn't hear what they were saying." Finn had stumbled upon some really good stuff. "This makes me wonder if the empty glass we found on the desk was how he was poisoned and not the pot pie."

"I need to check if those labs from the crime scene are back yet." I'd put the glass in an evidence bag. Actually, I'd bagged everything. "But according to Max, the sodium fluoroacetate was found in the food in Frank's stomach."

Both of us stood there. We really wanted to find a way to prove that Mama wasn't the main suspect.

"After I left the hotel on my way over here, I stopped by the office to see if any of the labs were back and they aren't." Finn's eyes narrowed.

"If we find that frozen dinner box the zipper came from, maybe we can pull prints. I'm looking for the box." My gag reflexes kicked in when I pulled out more half-eaten food. "Thank goodness I have a lot more gloves."

"You are insane." Finn laughed and took a seat next to me. He grabbed a couple of gloves and slipped them on.

"I guess our next step until the labs come in is to talk to Mundy?" Finn asked.

"Yes. First thing in the morning I'm going to look into his past a little deeper," I said.

"Why would Mundy want to kill Frank?" Finn asked.

"I don't know. Maybe their paths crossed. Maybe to hurt Ben's business. Who knows." My body tensed. "Did Frank give him a bad review?"

"That's it!" Poppa appeared in the back of the yard with one of Duke's balls near his feet. Duke was bouncing around, wanting Poppa to throw his ball.

I gulped and prayed Poppa wouldn't throw it. Duke already looked like he had a head worm or something, bouncing and barking at the air—at least from Finn's standpoint.

"You can check out all the reviews Frank did. Anyone could find out where Frank was and kill him. There was no forced entry into the inn's room. Whoever it was, he opened the door. They fed him. He had to trust them enough to eat their food," Poppa said. He kicked the ball with his toe just enough to make Duke lunge for it.

"Is Duke okay?" Finn asked. "He's acting so weird."

"He's fine. Just been cooped up all day." I glanced at Poppa with an uneasy glare. "Another thing. How well did Ben know Mundy? Did Mundy and Frank know each other? Frank did let the killer in. He ate the food. I don't eat anyone's food I don't trust."

"I don't eat anyone's food if I haven't seen their kitchen." He surprised me.

"Really?" My thoughts darted to my kitchen, which happened to be a mess right now. "Speaking of food, I thought that maybe you and I could grab a bite to eat after the meeting."

He grabbed another bag of trash and opened it.

"That was a mess." He set the first bag of trash aside.

"While we look through the trash, we can listen to the first time Camille was interviewed at the scene. Maybe she said something that would point to Mundy as the killer," I suggested, because sometimes we did miss key evidence the first time. I dragged off my gloves and took the tape recorder out of my bag.

I pushed the play button. Camille began to tell her story from the time she was summoned to the Tattered Book and Inn.

We listened to her describe what had happened. "That's when he stood up, grabbed his chest and fell to the ground." She huffed a few times. "I think I'm going to be sick."

"That's when she went to the bathroom and got sick," I told Finn. The recording should've stopped there and gone to his interview with her, but it didn't.

The sound of paper came through the recorder. Finn and I both stopped.

"What's that?" he asked.

"I have no idea. I thought I stopped recording after she went to the bathroom, because I think you came in after that." I stopped talking to him when I heard my voice.

"There is nothing here that says Mama did him in." My voice sounded very nervous. "I shouldn't've ignored her behavior like I did."

There was a long pause before my big mouth started yapping again.

"I can keep the review and shred it. I can flush the pot pie or throw it in my bag. No one will immediately know he was eating it. Though Max will find it in his belly. It'll buy us time to get her a lawyer. A real lawyer, not Wally Lamb."

Shock flew threw me, and with the dirty gloves on, I reached over to grab the tape recorder.

"What was that?" Finn stood up and took the recorder before I could get it.

"It's not what you think." I shook my head and pulled the gloves off my hands. "I was just out of my head. Thinking out loud."

My words sounded really bad. It was when I'd been talking to Poppa after Camille had run to the bathroom. It sounded like I was going to hide all of the evidence against Mama. Very illegal, especially for a sheriff. Something I could go to jail for a long time for.

"You were going to hide evidence?" The look on Finn's face told me that he was upset and in disbelief.

"No." I reached out and put my hand on his arm. He jerked away and stood up.

"It sure sounded like it to me." His lips were open. His chest heaved up and down.

"I thought about it." The words rushed out of my mouth as I defended myself. My integrity. "I didn't do it."

"Thinking about it is almost as bad as actually doing it." His words stung. "What happens next time you think about it and follow through?"

"Are you serious?" My brows crunched as I watched him shove his hands in his pockets, along with the tape recorder.

"I'm dead serious, Kenni. You're the sheriff in this town. You are the accountable one. Maybe you shouldn't be on this case."

There was a look of distrust and disgust on his face I'd never seen.

"You can't see the facts clearly. That's all I'm saying. You've spent the better part of this investigation looking for ways to clear your mama, not trying to find the real killer." His words stung, but he was right. "I'm going to get ready for the meeting. I'll see you there."

He gave me a quick kiss on the top of my head before he left. I could tell he was shocked and upset that I would've even thought about withholding evidence.

"You're human. She's your mama," Poppa reminded me.

CHAPTER SEVENTEEN

"Are you sore at me?" Poppa hung on to the handle grip on the roof of the Jeep as I took the corner of Main and Oak on my way to the council meeting.

Duke's head hung out the window. He gave a few low barks as we passed by people walking on the sidewalk who seemed to be taking advantage of the wonderful spring night.

"What on earth would give you that idea?" I asked Poppa with a sour tone.

"You are driving a little erratically and..."

I interrupted, "You know what? I'm mad at me. I'm mad at me because I know better than to talk to you outside of the confines of my...um...our house."

My nerves felt like a bundle of live wires. Finn thinking I'd withhold evidence really upset me.

"Finn thinks that my morals have been compromised because of the conversation I had with you. I'm mad at myself for letting my guard down." I looked over at Poppa. "At some point I've got to tell Finn that I can see you."

"I'm not so sure that'd be good," Poppa said. "Then he'd really think you couldn't do your job."

"I love that you and I continue to solve crimes, but I can't let Finn think I'd do something illegal," I said.

"You didn't do something illegal. A thought's not illegal, or we'd all be in jail for wishing someone dead," he joked. When I didn't laugh, he said, "You only thought about it. Though Deputy Vincent seems to be taking the moral high ground, the law is based on evidence, not what he believes."

I parked the Jeep behind Jolee's food truck. Duke ran up to her side door and gave a loud bark to let her know he was there, and like every other time, she opened the door with a tasty treat in her hand for him.

"Hey there." She greeted me with a hot cup of coffee. "Things sure have taken a strange turn since I went to help Ben."

"What do you mean?" I took a sip, looking around to make sure no one was around.

"Business has been booming. I told him that I had to do my food truck tonight and left him swamped. He even hired two new bus boys. Can you believe it?" She smiled. "I got my old Ben back."

"That's great." I brought the hot coffee to my lips. It was a much-welcomed salve for my troubled soul.

Out of the corner of my eye, I saw Finn walking into the basement through the door located at the side of Luke's house.

"I have to head up to the mall tomorrow. Do you want to go?" Jolee asked.

"I can't. I've got to check out some leads," I said.

Mundy was on my mind. I needed to get his history and fast. I also hoped Tom Geary would get back to me with some preliminary results from the items from Chef Mundy's room at the inn. "I better get inside." I turned and headed toward the door.

The crowd outside of Luke Jones's house had made its way into the basement. Cottonwood didn't have a traditional town-council room to meet in. Though we had a small courthouse, it was only used for things like car titles and taxes. It just had a small courtroom that wouldn't hold all the citizens that came to the council meetings. Most of the council meetings were about upcoming events and the budgets. Mayor Ryland loved to talk, and people came because they wanted to hear any gossip going on around town.

. . .

"You don't want to go in there." Poppa ghosted next to me and Duke. "They're planning to pull you off the case."

"What?" I jerked around and looked at him. "How could Mayor Ryland do that without telling me?"

"Shhh." Poppa put his finger up to his lips. "You didn't call him back like you said you were going to," Poppa reminded me.

I glared at him, my eyes narrowed. It looks like I made my own bed and now it was time to lie in it, like the old saying went.

"There's not much you can do about it now. You've got to go in there and be smart. Remember not to let your mouth override your tail." He shook that finger at me. "It might not be a bad thing to get pulled."

He was right. I had to go in there levelheaded and listen. Not fly off the handle.

"How so?" I questioned him.

"You could do more snooping around and really dig deep without that uniform on." Poppa did teach me the trick that people talked more when I had on street clothes and not the official sheriff uniform.

The theater had been transformed from full of comfy couches to full of the rickety old fold-out chairs that formed rows facing the front of the room. The movie screen had been rolled up to the ceiling and replaced by a wooden podium where Mayor Ryland would preside over the meeting. Too bad the popcorn machine had been put away. I'd have gotten a bag and thrown pieces at the mayor as he tried to pull me off the case.

Mayor Ryland was bent over by the podium whispering into Finn's ear. His slicked-back salt-and-pepper hair was perfectly coiffed. His jaw tensed underneath his manscaped goatee as he spoke. His eyes swept up past the heads of the citizens sitting in the chairs and focused on me. His lips moved quickly before he stood up and tugged down the edges of his suit coat. Finn took a step back and turned his head, looking straight at me. Our eyes met. He mouthed "I'm sorry."

He closed his eyes and when he opened them, he focused on something else in the room. I sucked in a deep breath, pulled back my shoulders, and took the first step into the lion's den.

Too bad Duke had no idea he was trotting into enemy lines. He accepted every single head pat on our way up the middle aisle to find my seat right next to Finn.

"You aren't going to like what the mayor is going to propose." Finn had enough decency to think he was warning me.

"Finn." I gave one of my best southern grins. Poppa's head popped over Finn's shoulder. He had a big grin on his face too. "I'm not the new face around here. You are. I've seen what Chance does when things don't go his way. I've borne the brunt of his dislike for a few years now, so I'm sure he's going to suggest I be taken off the case."

"Because of your mama." Poppa nodded. He knew what they'd said from his ghostly eavesdropping.

"Because my mama is tied to the investigation," I repeated.

"And because you don't have the right mindset to remain unbiased," Poppa continued.

"Because he thinks I don't have the right mindset to remain unbiased." I kept my eyes on Finn and my peripheral vision on Poppa.

"He also thinks Finn needs to distance himself from you and Finn should run against you for sheriff in next year's election." Poppa's words stung me more than Finn thinking I'd done something to damage the badge I wore so proudly.

"Not to mention," my voice cracked, "he wants you to distance yourself from me personally so you can run against me in the election."

It was no secret that Mayor Ryland wasn't my number-one fan. But I couldn't please everyone.

"Kenni," Finn put his hand on my knee, "I'd never..."

"Order!" Mayor Ryland banged the gavel on the wood podium. "Good citizens of Cottonwood, it's time to bring things to order."

"Kenni," Finn whispered. "You know that'll never happen."

I offered a weak smile. Finn truly was amazing, and even though I was in a tight spot, I knew I was very lucky to have him on my side.

"We called this emergency meeting," Mayor Ryland spoke after the crowd hushed, "because it's come to my attention," he looked directly at Finn, "that Sheriff Lowry is in a very compromising position given the nature of the suspects in our latest murder."

The gasp of the citizens behind me broke the polite silence in the room, forcing Mayor Ryland to bang the gavel again.

Come to his attention? I wiggled my foot around as it dangled from my crossed legs. I tried to remind myself that it was a strange position to be in, but I knew I could keep the case from my personal life. Chance was probably right. The town wouldn't see it that way. It was going to be interesting to see how this all played out.

"I'm sorry, Sheriff." Chance offered an insincere apology. The smirk on his face was all too familiar to me. "We," he gestured to the council members sitting behind him that included Myrna Savage, Peter Parker, Ruby Smith, and Doolittle Bowman, "feel it's best that Deputy Vincent take the lead in the case since your number-one suspect is Vivian Lowry, the sheriff's mother."

"Well!" The scream from the back caused everyone to turn around. "Doesn't that just take the cake!"

Mama stood in the back with her big black shiner on display for everyone to see.

"I didn't kill no one!" She stomped up to the center of the room. I swear I heard people shudder. I know I did. "If you think that, then you can cuff me right now."

She stopped in front of Finn and threw her wrists out in front of her like she'd done to me earlier in the day, almost in the exact same spot in fact. Finn looked between Mama and me.

"Order!" Mayor Ryland banged the gavel and pointed it at her. "You will take a seat before I have Deputy Vincent arrest you for being a public nuisance."

"Arrest me, you big oaf!" Mama had just called the mayor stupid. I braced myself.

"Don't you be calling my fiancé an oaf!" Polly Parker jumped up from the front row.

"Fiancé?" Myrna chimed in. "Did she say fiancé?" she leaned over and asked Doolittle.

Doolittle nodded.

"Err..." Polly's pale face reddened. "Um..." She took a couple of steps back to her seat. Mayor Ryland's chin hung to his chest. "Chance," Polly pleaded in her little girl voice. She didn't care what he thought, because she went right on. "Yes. Chance and I are going to be married." She beamed. Her big white horse teeth appeared as her open-wide grin spread across her face. Her hands were clasped behind her. Her body twisted right and left. "This is our official engagement announcement. Our wedding is going to be the biggest event Cottonwood has ever seen."

Polly looked around the room before she sat back down on the folding chair.

Mama looked at me and I rolled my eyes. It was just like a council meeting to turn to gossip. Edna Easterly pushed off the wall and started snapping photos of the mayor's face and of Polly, whose eyes were glaring at Chance as though they were having a telepathic conversation.

"People, my personal life is of no concern and has no bearing on what the council and I are trying to do tonight." He spoke with an even tone. "Polly Parker is going to be the next first lady of the town. She's right. We are going to have everyone at our wedding."

Polly was all giggles now. She sat up and held her hand in the air, showing off the big diamond I'd seen on her hand the other day. No doubt they'd gotten a discount from White's Jewelry since Polly worked part-time down there for Viola.

"Back to business." Chance tried to get the community to stop congratulating Polly.

I couldn't help but notice Pete Parker's—Polly's father and ex-best friend of the mayor—face. The more his jaw tensed, the redder his face got. It was just hearsay, but I'd heard over a hand of Euchre that after Pete found out about the mayor's and his daughter's secret love shack out in the woods, Pete and Chance had pretty much beat the poo out of each other. Chance had been Polly's godfather, and from what I'd heard, Pete told him that he wasn't no godfather, he was a sick old man that was making his daughter the laughingstock of the town. He'd even tried to get Polly to break it off, but she moved out and into the mayor's house. By the look on Pete's face and the lack of communication with Polly or Chance, I'd say the gossip was pretty close to being true. Unlike Mama killing someone.

"Can I have your attention?" I jumped to the stage and took the gavel from Chance. I gave it a quick couple of bangs. "You don't have to go back to your seats, but I do have something to say."

"You tell them, Kenni." Poppa was nose to nose with Mayor Ryland. "Don't you dare back down from your position while he waltzes in here to take over your office. I'm not so sure that wasn't his plan this whole time."

"There is more than one suspect in the case of Frank Von Lee. I do see how this looks like a conflict of interest for me." I cleared my throat. "I'm more than happy to let Deputy Finn Vincent take the lead on this case and use my expertise about our town and our citizens to help him. There are plenty of other cases I can be working on. Which brings me to a scam going around Cottonwood. There is someone distributing illegal handicap tags. If you or someone you know has a pink handicap tag, please call the sheriff's department. The only way to get a handicap tag is through the county clerk's office at the courthouse."

"Wait." Poppa ghosted over to me. I saw his eyes, large glittering ovals of repudiation. "You can't just lay down like that. You have to be on the case. You have to figure this out. You're the sheriff."

Before I could say anything else, Mayor Ryland jerked the gavel out of my hands and beat it on the podium, making my decision official.

"Kenni." Finn put his hand out to stop me when I stepped down and into the crowd.

"It's okay, Finn." I offered a smile. There was more behind the smile than he knew. Now I felt a little freedom to investigate as I pleased without being watched.

"Come on, Duke." I grabbed Mama by the elbow and dragged her down the aisle alongside me and Duke. She didn't need to be in here running her mouth and getting herself deeper in trouble. I didn't need to stay in there and listen any longer. I'd come to say my piece and now I had a job to do.

"Can you believe about the mayor and Polly getting married?" I shook my head and pulled Mama closer to me. I didn't want to talk about what I had planned to get her off the hook or the other case I was referring to.

"Did you see how she was dressed?" Mama seemed more than happy to get the heat off of her. "I reckon he likes her dressing like a hooker."

I threw my head back and laughed.

"I love you, Mama." I tugged her even closer. "Let's go get a cup of coffee from Ben's."

CHAPTER EIGHTEEN

The next morning I woke up in a foul mood. Not only had Finn tried to call several times, he'd even stopped by. Even though I told him it was okay, it really wasn't. I'd already had my ego bruised and needed to set that aside, but I needed a day to process it. He wasn't as familiar with Cottonwood and he wasn't in the gossip circle like I was, which was going to make it hard for him to get some little tidbits of information that I'd always found helped investigations.

Was he trying to get ahold of me so bad because he wanted to scold me for my words that were just words on the tape recorder? Or was he feeling bad that he'd taken the case right out of my hands and never once tried to protest it? If it was an emergency, dispatch would've called me, so I ignored him.

It wasn't until around three a.m. that I'd finally fallen asleep. Not a peaceful sleep. It was riddled with nightmares that included some weird things like being chased by a big diamond ring that lassoed itself around me. After the ring caught me, Finn was at the ready with a pair of handcuffs and hauled me down to the jail cell, which I had to share with Mama and her striped prison jumpsuit. I finally woke up after Frank Von Lee slid a plate of chicken pot pie between the bars of the jail. He was laughing the whole time, telling Mama and me that it was our turn to eat the poisoned food so we knew exactly how he felt.

That was enough to jar me awake. My phone next to the bed showed that I'd missed a phone call from Betty Murphy. She didn't leave a message. I pulled the covers off and slipped my feet into my slippers and grabbed my sweatshirt.

"Let's go potty," I called to Duke over my shoulder as I tugged my sweatshirt over my head.

On our way down the hall, I called Betty back, flipped on my coffee pot, and let Duke out into the backyard, but not before looking to see if Finn was back there.

"Kenni," Betty whispered in the phone. This wasn't like her.

"Are you at the office?" I asked, wondering why she was so quiet.

"Yes," she answered hesitantly.

"You can talk to me. I'm still the sheriff and will be coming into the office this morning." I took a mug out of the kitchen cabinet and waited for the coffee to brew. "I've got other cases to work."

"I wanted to let you know that I put those seed packets in the planter on your porch where you asked me to put them," she said.

"Are you feeling all right?" I asked her.

"Yes. Finer than frog's hair. Now, go get those seeds and start to water them so they can grow. You have limited time with this one," she said.

"Betty, are you talking in code?" I asked.

"Yep. That's the planter." She could've just said that in the first place. "A little fair warning. The press and media are camped out in the alley in front of the department."

"I'll deal with it when I come in." I groaned, knowing I was going to have to get all gussied up to have my picture taken and be interviewed by the media. "Can you please call Finn and let him know that he needs to be there to answer questions since he's in charge of the case?"

"Sure thing, Kenni." Betty clicked off.

I walked to the front of the house and opened the front door. There was a planter on the small concrete slab full of a dead fern that I'd planted last summer and didn't bother taking out for the winter. It didn't go unnoticed by Mama. Every time she came over, she liked to remind me that there was a dead fern on my front porch.

When I opened the door, there was a corner of paper sticking out from underneath the planter. I looked both ways down Free Row to see if anyone was out before I picked it up, because you never knew who was watching these days and apparently whatever Betty had stuck under the planter was private or secret.

I tipped the planter up on its edge and pulled the folded paper out. When I got back in the kitchen, I put the paper on the table and let Duke in. I poured myself a cup of coffee and sat down, dragging my legs up underneath me.

I opened the paper and flattened it out in front of me. I sipped my coffee and read through all of Mundy's background check. He'd been kicked out of many restaurants. And there was a connection between him and Frank Von Lee. It just so happened that Mundy had been one of Frank's students in a New York culinary class. By the looks of the report, Frank had kicked Mundy out of the class. The last culinary school he'd attended was the one where Ben Harrison had graduated where they'd been classmates.

After Mundy had graduated, he went to work at Le Fork, a nationwide chain that held classes for the common folk like me. He'd worked there until a month ago.

"Where was he between four weeks and a week ago?" Poppa stood by the counter next to the coffee pot. He sniffed the steam. "I sure would love a cup."

"I'm going to have another." I stood up and refilled my cup. "So I guess you're not mad at me anymore."

"I was never mad at you." He looked out the window. "I just don't understand why you gave up so easy."

On my way back to the table to finish reading the paperwork Betty had snuck over, I filled up Duke's bowl with food and grabbed my phone.

"I didn't give up. I'm using my brain." I scrolled through and hit the call button when I found Jolee's name. "I can still look into the murder. Only now all eyes won't be on me." I shrugged and put the phone up to my ear. "I don't have to make official reports unless I find something."

"Which we will." The color came back to Poppa's face. "You're still going to get your mama off the hook."

"Yep. Thanks to Betty." I eased back down into the chair, pulling my legs back up.

"I was going to call you this morning." Jolee answered the phone without saying hello.

"I beat you to the punch." I said. "I've got a quick television press conference this morning."

"Press conference?" She interrupted. "Ooh la la."

"Whatever. Anyways, I wanted to know if the offer still stands to go shopping."

"You mean to tell me that I can drag you forty-five minutes from here into Lexington, shop for a few hours, and then drive forty-five minutes back?" she asked with a hint of caution in her voice. "Because you want to get all dolled up for the TV?"

"No," I said flatly. "I want to go after the press conference."

"Fine. If I have to settle, then you have to buy a cute pair of shoes today," she said, driving a hard bargain.

"Are you serious?" I asked.

"Yes. I'm tired of you thinking that every outfit goes with cowboy boots." She laughed.

"They don't?" I asked, setting her off into a firestorm of how I needed to step up my fashion game. "I'll drive."

"What? You don't want to be seen in the food truck?" she asked.

"I'm sure smelling like food isn't good for my fashion sense either." I took a drink of coffee. "Just joking. I don't mind driving, besides, I want to go to Le Fork."

"Oh, are you planning on cooking a romantic supper for a special someone?" she asked.

"No." I hadn't told Jolee about the latest setback in my relationship with Finn. I looked around for a quick kitchen tool I could purchase there. "I'm thinking about getting a French press."

I hoped my lie wasn't too far-fetched since she knew I loved coffee.

"I can show you the best ones," she squealed.

I probably should've realized anything with food would get her all worked up.

"I'll be over in an hour." I hung up.

"What's on your mind?" Poppa asked.

"It says here that Mundy taught classes there up until a month ago." I tapped the paper. "That's about the time Ben and Mama got word from the Culinary Channel that Frank Von Lee wanted to come try Mama's pot pie for the show. They didn't give Ben a specific date, but you know how fast news spreads."

"Mundy quit his job and came into town to work for Ben while Ben took care of the show gig." Poppa was right on track with what I was thinking.

"I was in the diner the other morning when Mundy was screaming about the construction work and how loud it was. Ben said to Mundy that Mundy jumped at the chance to work for Ben since they knew each other." My brows cocked. I took another sip.

"It would be easy to find out about or get Malina to talk about Frank's arrival. Mundy is smart, so he probably checked the only two places to stay in Cottonwood. Malina probably told him because he flirted with her."

"It doesn't seem like much flirting was needed to get information from her," Poppa said.

"And Mundy's room was right next to Frank's." It was the small details that helped solve a murder.

"Did Malina let Mundy cook in the inn's kitchen?" Poppa asked. "The pot pie that Frank was eating was in a dish, not a cardboard frozen-dinner container."

"So it's safe to say that the container thing is probably not related to the murder?" I stared at Poppa.

"I'd say we go on what we know and keep it in the back of our minds, but not focus so much on it." He slipped away.

It was so amazing how much I'd learned from Poppa when he was living and was still learning from him from the great beyond now.

Here was what I knew. Mama had the most to lose from a bad review, but the evidence pointing at her was just too obvious. Mundy, on the other hand, made himself obvious by fighting with Ben. Which I couldn't help but think was his plan all along so Ben would be out of the kitchen and Mundy would be able to replicate Mama's recipe, once again making Mama look like the killer.

Mundy had the greatest motive. Mama could get over the embarrassment of a bad review. After all, she was a southern woman. But Mundy was a scorned chef with a big ego that couldn't graduate from one of the biggest culinary schools in the United States. I had to believe that followed him to any reputable job at the fancy restaurants where he wanted to be the head chef.

Someone at Le Fork had to know where he was. He'd been employed there the longest. Surely he'd made some friends.

CHAPTER NINETEEN

When Betty said that the media was camped out in the alley in front of the department, I didn't imagine truly camped out. But there were several white vans with television equipment on the top and some big satellites, their station's names printed on the side.

There were at least ten that lined from one end of the alley to the other end. On The Run, Jolee's food truck, was parked in my spot next to the dumpster in front of the department door. I pulled the Wagoneer up to the building and parked tight to Jolee's truck so not to block the alley in case there was an emergency.

"That's the sheriff," I overheard one of the reporters telling her videographer.

With a quick check of the lip gloss I'd put on before I left, I got out of the car.

"Look at you." Jolee grinned. "If only we had different shoes." She jerked a scowl when she noticed I'd put on my cowboy boots.

"At least this is a new shirt." I referred to the brown sheriff's uniform shirt and brown pants. "And the hair is down." I wiggled my brows. "I wasn't going to get caught looking like the last rose of summer."

When Betty had mentioned the media this morning, I had to take that extra time to actually put on makeup and fix my hair.

"Good morning," I greeted the crowd and everyone rushed over. "I'll be more than happy to take a few questions after I give a brief statement."

In the distance, there was a feather swaying in the air and rushing towards the department. It was attached to Edna Easterly's fedora. She scurried to the front of the media with her pen and pad in hand.

"As you know, we are investigating the homicide of Frank Von Lee. We are working on several leads and interviewing several suspects." "Several" was a bit of a stretch when we'd only interviewed Mama. Out of the corner of my eye, I saw Finn's Charger pull up. It was time to include him and the best way to ease into talking to him since our little spat. "I've handed the lead investigation over to Deputy Finn Vincent."

He walked up, not taking his eyes off me.

"Deputy Vincent will be more than happy to answer a few questions." I'd caught him off guard. I glanced over at Jolee and her eyes were big and round, darting between me and Finn.

His eyes softened when he stepped up next to me. He bent down and whispered into my ear, "I'd love to see you tonight."

"I'd love that too." My heart melted.

"Good," he whispered and straightened up. His eyes grazed over the media and he pointed to one of the reporters with her hand up in the air.

"This has really been a bad couple of years for Cottonwood." Her voice boomed above the crowd. "Do you think it's time for a change in the sheriff's department?"

"Change?" Finn asked. I fidgeted next to him.

"The community seems to be under a black cloud of crime. It's strange that crime was rare or actually practically nonexistent until the second year of Sheriff Lowry's term. Do you have anything to say to that?" she asked and held a small tape recorder up in the air.

"Actually, the couple of crimes you are referring to, as well as Mr. Von Lee's murder, are all isolated incidents. There is no crime spree or serial killer in Cottonwood. Cottonwood is safe. Safety is Sheriff Lowry's main concern," Finn stated flatly, not giving the reporter any more time. He pointed to Edna. "Edna."

"Is it true that Sheriff Lowry's mother, Vivian Lowry, is the only suspect in the murder of Mr. Frank Von Lee?" Her brows rose.

"This is an active investigation and right now everyone related to the reasons Mr. Von Lee is in Cottonwood is a suspect." He answered it with such an ease that I even believed him.

"Is the reason Sheriff Lowry is letting you take over the lead because her mother is the number-one suspect?" another reporter shouted from the back.

"There are only two people in our department, Sheriff Lowry and me. The sheriff needs to focus on the entire community, and while this is an isolated event, I'm going to handle it while she takes over all the other aspects of the job." He sure was good with words.

I touched him on the arm because there didn't seem to be any real questions about the case other than about me and my mama.

Finn stepped aside.

"I'd like to thank you for coming out, but we're going to have to ask you to clear the alley. It's not only illegal, but hazardous in case an emergency vehicle needs to drive down." I held my hands in the air. "We will put out a notice of when our next press conference will be. Thank you."

A few more questions were shouted out, but nothing that stopped us from going inside.

Betty's phone lines were lit up and blinking.

"It's going to be a long day of questions." Finn smiled thinly.

"You're going to do just fine." I patted him on the back. "I'll make sure to have a few beers ready for you tonight."

"I'm glad you agreed to see me." His eyes were as sincere as his words. "I've missed seeing you."

"I've missed you too." It was like no one else was in the room, until Jolee interrupted.

"Okay, lovebirds, we've got to go. I've got to get her out of those shoes." She shoved between us.

"Huh?" Finn's brows furrowed.

"I told Jolee that I'd go shopping with her." I left it at that, not wanting to tell him or her my real reason for heading to Le Fork. Maybe I'd have some solid leads for him tonight when he came over.

Within five minutes, Jolee and I were in the Wagoneer and heading the forty-five minutes to Lexington.

"How's things going with you and Ben?" I asked, hoping that things had gotten better.

"He's still a little on edge, but he's letting me have control of the kitchen." She sounded much better than the last time we'd talked about it. "It's the strangest thing. Business has picked up since Frank's death."

"How well did Ben know Mundy?" I snooped.

"He said he didn't know much about him since they'd gone to school. He's just waiting for Mundy to come in and collect a paycheck for the few hours he was there because he said Mundy is hard up for cash." She stared out the window. "Enough about all that stuff. I've got my best friend back for a while."

She turned in her seat to face me.

"It looks like you and Finn are doing okay." I didn't have to look at her to know she was smiling big.

"He's a really good guy." A happy sigh escaped me. "But I'm missing doing my job."

"Nothing a little shopping won't help." She snickered.

It was so nice to spend some time out of the office and have girl time with Jolee. With a little gossip and a lot of laughter, we parked in the mall parking lot in no time. Jolee didn't waste any time we had. She was out of the car and into a boutique before I could get my seatbelt off.

"Isn't this great?" Jolee held a short-sleeved lace shirt up to her chin. "I think this would look great with a pair of jeans or pants. It'd even go with those cowboy boots."

I stared out the window of the shop, across the parking lot and at the Le Fork store.

"Kenni?" Jolee called my name. "Yoo-hoo, Kenni."

"Yes." I flipped around and smiled.

"Did you hear me?" she asked. Her blonde hair was actually fixed today. Normally she had to pull it back or she wore it in a cascading ponytail down her back, or in two with one down each shoulder. She crunched her nose. Her freckles came together, giving her an instant tan. "So?" She held up a top in front of me.

"Yes. It looks good on you." My mind was wondering how I could leave Jolee here and get over to Le Fork to snoop around.

"Not me. You." She shoved the hanger at me. "You didn't really want to come shopping, did you?"

"Of course I did." I held the shirt up to me. "Looks good?"

"Yes." Her voice was flat.

"I'll take it." I held it out to the sales lady.

"You're about as much fun as my mom," Jolee said.

I sat down on the sofa in the fancy boutique. "This just isn't me." I looked around the pink-and-cream-striped wallpapered shop. The chandeliers even had light pink bulbs with tassels dangling from the center of each one. The lighting made every piece of clothing and color look good on anyone. There were high-back chairs and long fabric ottomans positioned around the shop just in case someone was so exhausted walking around looking at the expensive clothes they had to sit and rest

"I like it. I just don't have anywhere to wear that." I pointed to the sales lady who'd walked away with the top.

"Finn." Her brows rose.

"That's not so good." It was time to let her in on what was going on if I was going to get over to Le Fork.

She hesitated. She blinked in bafflement and sat down next to me.

"What on earth happened? What did you do?" she asked, sure that it was my fault.

"Why would you assume that it's me?" I asked.

"Because that man adores you. When he comes to get a coffee or food, he always talks about you." She stared at me. "So what happened?"

"Mama happened." My voice was flat and followed up by a big long sigh. Just as if mama knew I was talking about her, she texted me. I held the phone in the air. "Mama. She must be feeling guilty because she's insisting I come for supper tonight. She's making my favorite."

I tucked my phone back in my pocket.

"At least she's trying." She looked off as though she were remembering something. "I thought she loved him."

"She did, until he got me kicked off her case." I put both of my hands on my knees and stood up. "Let's walk."

She nodded.

"Can you just hold those for a few?" Jolee asked the sales lady before she followed me out of the shop.

The morning had already turned into the afternoon. The outdoor mall was packed. It was one of those places where all the entrances to the stores were accessible from the outside. The parking lot was in the middle. There were little cafés and coffeehouses along with a few restaurants located around the mall.

"Don't these people work?" I had to turn to the side as we started to walk down the sidewalk in order to not get knocked down by a group of laughing women.

"You are so grumpy today." Jolee knew me better than probably anyone. "Spill it."

I pointed to the coffeehouse.

"Yeah, I could use a cup." She shoved past me and went inside.

The coffee smelled fresh and hopefully it would help clear the cobwebs on my feelings about Finn. I felt like my emotions were hindering me from working the case, even though I was off of it.

We ordered a couple of cups and took a seat against the wall at a table for two.

"Can you believe Ben's?" Jolee looked to be making small talk until we got comfortable to discuss why I'd brought her in here.

"The pick-up in business?" I asked.

"You know he was afraid business was going to die, but it's just the opposite." She laughed. "No joke. The news of the famous Frank Von Lee's death has made Ben's famous. Famous," she muttered. "He's making more money than he ever has. At least it looks like it."

"Good for him," I noted.

Both of us took a drink.

"You've been nice enough not to ask about Mayor Ryland, who, by the way, proposed to Polly." I had to get that little bit of gossip in. The look on Jolee's face was priceless. "I'm not upset about Finn taking over. It's probably a good thing. What I'm mad at is that he thinks I was going to hide the evidence against Mama."

There was no reason to tell Jolee about Mundy and my real reason for wanting to come shopping. Mama was no longer a suspect in my eyes, but the more I kept under wraps the better.

"I don't know what evidence you have against her. Why would he think that?" she asked, curling her hands around her mug.

"I taped my conversation with Camille the night of the murder. Some of the evidence points directly at Mama. Frank Von Lee was in the middle of writing his review of Mama's pot pie." I eased back in my chair. "Camille had gotten sick and excused herself to the bathroom. While she was gone I was talking to myself." Jolee looked at me like I was crazy. She'd really think I was a nut job if I told her I was talking to a ghost. "It helps me sort things out in my head to talk out loud. And on the tape I'd mentioned to myself that maybe I should hold on to the evidence until I got Mama a good lawyer."

"You said it out loud?" Her mouth dropped, and her brows creased. "That's stupid."

I could always count on Jolee to be real with me. That was one of the qualities I loved about her.

"Yeah. Well, Camille was so upset about Frank dying that I had Finn go to her office and get her official statement. Long story short…" I held the cup of coffee up to my chin and blew on it before I took a sip. "When we were listening to her statement, the little bit of me talking to myself was on there and I'd forgotten about it."

"And…" She leaned forward.

"And he thinks that morally I've compromised my legal authority, even though I didn't actually do it. I logged the information, I went to talk to Mama, I followed all protocol. Everything found in Frank's room that night pointed to Mama as his killer. You and I both know that she'd take much more pleasure in publicly humiliating Frank than in killing him." I chewed on the inside of my cheek waiting for Jolee's reply.

"Let me get this straight." She sat back. "Though you didn't do anything against your job, Finn is holding this against you morally?"

"We're getting together tonight, but it's kinda a cop thing when your morals are compromised." I shrugged.

"So now that you had nothing to do today, you called me to go shopping?" She was trying to figure out my ulterior motive.

"I shouldn't tell you this, but I'm going to keep investigating." I pointed to the outside. I guessed it was time to come clean. If I couldn't trust my best friend, who could I trust?

"I knew you were coming here and I need to go to Le Fork to get some information about Chef Mundy."

"What about him?" she asked.

"I'm not so sure he didn't set Mama up. In fact, he'd have all the reason to. He knew Frank from culinary school. Frank didn't pass him." I stopped talking when I noticed Jolee's surprised look. "What?"

"It's a big deal not to pass. I should know." She'd gone to culinary school, and she didn't need to remind me how she'd thought Ben was going to offer her a job but didn't. "But what does he have to do with Le Fork?"

"He'd been working there up until four weeks ago. That's when the Culinary Channel announced Frank Von Lee was going to come to Cottonwood." I drank the last bit of coffee in my cup.

"It was about four weeks ago that Ben talked to him. He'd even met with him a couple of times." Her jaw dropped. "Mundy did mention something about the pot pie too. He said that he'd love to have your mama's recipe if it was that good."

"In his room at the Tattered Cover Books and Inn, I found several attempted recipes for Mama's pot pie." I stared at her for a moment, knowing I shouldn't let her in on any more information about the case. But in for a penny, in for a pound. "Frank Von Lee was poisoned. There was a pot pie on his desk and an empty glass. One of them contained sodium fluoroacetate."

"What's that?" she asked, curling her nose.

"It's a fancy term for a poison that has all the side effects Camille reported Frank had before his heart attack. And I want to go see if they know anything over at Le Fork. I want Mundy's address too." I ran the pad of my finger around the edge of my empty cup.

"Then what are we waiting for?" Jolee stood up. "Let's go. I can help."

I smiled. Poppa ghosted into the shop.

"Great!" He bounced. "I knew she'd help you out."

I gulped, trying to stay focused on her.

"I was just over at Le Fork. They're hosting one of their cooking classes.

Maybe one of you can distract them while someone goes into the office to take a look at the files." Poppa had a plan. "I found the employee files in the filing cabinet to the right of the desk. There are rows of filing cabinets that look like a bunch of recipes and orders."

This was information I could use.

"The files look to be alphabetized." Poppa looked disappointed. "I'm sorry I can't just open them and go through them for you. Somethings I can do. Somethings I can't." He held his hands in the air. "Still trying to figure all my new talents out. But have her take some photos with her phone." Poppa disappeared.

"I swear." Jolee stepped into the space where Poppa had just been. "Sometimes I think you've lost your mind."

"What?" I asked.

"I was talking to you and you were staring at me with a blank look on your face. You've been doing that a lot lately." She put her hands on her hips and narrowed her eyes.

"I've got a lot on my mind." I walked past her and out the door. "I was thinking about the office in Le Fork. If they've got a class going, you can take the class and I can look around while you distract them."

"I can't take the class. I know too much." She did have a valid point.

"Okay." We walked through the parking lot, dodging moving cars as we made our way over to Le Fork. "I'll do the class. I need you to listen to me."

She nodded quickly. "This is exciting."

"Focus." I used two fingers, pointing to her eyes and then back to mine. "There's an office in the back. You need to find the employee files that are probably closest to the desk. There are going to be more filing cabinets in the office, but those are going to be invoices, recipes, and other things that we don't need."

She continued to drag her chin up and down. "The files next to the desk."

"Most times the employee files are alphabetized. When you find Mundy's file, don't worry about reading through it. I want you to take your phone and take pictures of every page that you can." I smiled to give her some confidence because there was a hint of reservation on her face. "You can do this."

"Yes. I can." She gave herself her own little pep talk before she walked into the shop and everyone looked at her.

"But don't bring attention to yourself," I muttered, knowing she'd just blown her cover.

CHAPTER TWENTY

"Today we are discussing how to prepare a cake properly." The instructor stood in front of the baking class.

It'd cost me forty dollars to sign up and another sixty to purchase the items I needed to finish the three-course project of learning how to bake a cake. Fortunately for me, I had no idea how to bake a cake, so this was actually interesting to me and took my mind off of Jolee walking around snooping and waiting for the right opportunity to sneak into the back office.

"If you don't mind opening your book to page one, today we'll be going over different pans and different types of icing as well as the icing bags." The instructor went down the row of baking accessories on the table in front of her. "I'll teach you how to attach the tips and couplers to the bags so you can successfully pipe the icing on your cake."

You learn something new every day. I had no idea what those thingies were called. Couplers. I picked up a couple of them and noticed they were different sizes.

The first thing she had us do was mix the cake.

"It's very important that your oven is preheated for at least ten minutes," she said and had each of us preheat the oven we were using.

For the next five minutes she had us beat four eggs, then we added sugar and two teaspoons of vanilla extract. Sifting the dry ingredients was harder than I'd anticipated. Once we added it to the wet ingredients she had us use the whisk as we added milk and butter.

"You are doing a good job." Poppa stood next to me, looking into my bowl of batter. "How do you think Jolee is doing?"

"Jolee," I gasped. I'd completely lost track of time and Jolee.

I looked around and she was standing outside waving her phone at me.

"Are you going to put the batter in the pans?" The instructor had walked over when she noticed I'd become distracted. "You'll need two pans. The batter makes two cakes. Fill each of them halfway. After you do that, you will bake them for about twenty minutes."

"Oh, okay." I picked up the bowl and added the batter to each pan like she'd instructed.

Jolee ran into the room. "What are you doing?" she whispered, leaning her face into mine. "I've got the information. Let's go."

"What about my cakes?" I asked.

"Seriously?" Her eyes popped open, and her mouth fell. "I can bake you a cake." She put the tip of her finger in my batter and stuck it in her mouth before I could bat it away. "Mmm." Her lips flattened together. "Not bad. But I have a better tasting trick." She tugged on my arm. "Let's go."

"But I have twenty minutes and I paid for the class." I was surprised how much I enjoyed the class.

"I've got the information you wanted about you-know-who." She gave me a flat look.

"Another twenty minutes isn't going to clear Mama any quicker nor bring Frank back to the living." I opened the oven and put my two pans in side by side.

"I'm going to get the car." She held her hands out for my keys.

"Fine." I took the towel off my shoulder that I'd been using to clean up batter and threw it on my counter space. "You're going to teach me how to bake a cake?"

"Swear." She criss-crossed her finger over her heart. "Let's go."

I took one last look in the oven at my cakes before I followed out behind her.

"I really enjoyed that," I said once we got back in the Jeep.

"Fine." She huffed. "I got the information you wanted and I guess it's not going anywhere. So I'll go back to the boutique and buy my clothes and you go back and finish your cakes."

It sounded like a plan to me. It'd actually taken my mind off the investigation, but not for long. When I went back to my workstation, no one seemed to have noticed that I'd left. No one except for Poppa. His big nose was stuck in everyone else's batter.

"This just takes the cake," Poppa boasted. "Literally. You're a sheriff, not a baker."

I busied myself by checking the timer, flipping the oven light on and off to see my two cakes, and reading through the manual I'd paid a mint for.

"You're supposed to be trying to get your mama off the hook, not learning how to bake her a cake you can put a file in when she goes to jail." Poppa fumed in front of me.

I shooed him off and jerked the oven door open when the buzzer dinged.

The instructor walked over. She looked at the stick and peel nametag they'd given us. She bent down and looked into the oven.

"Kenni, those look nice and golden on top." Joy bubbled on her face and shone in her eyes. "Class," she smacked her hands together. "I love when a student pays attention. Look at Kenni's cakes. They're a nice golden brown and cooked throughout." She took a toothpick from my workstation and stuck it in the middle. "If it wasn't cooked, there would be some soggy batter on the toothpick."

Other class participants' timers dinged and they were busy checking their cakes.

"Everyone will put their finished cakes on the cake rake. They need to cool for ten minutes." She looked at her watch. "Our time is up for today. I'll see you back here tomorrow where we're going to learn some basic decorating tips."

"Finally." Poppa did a little jig. "Let's get back to Cottonwood where we can help your mama."

Jolee had the Wagoneer pulled up to the curb. I motioned for her to scoot over to the passenger side.

"I enjoyed spying." Jolee rubbed her hands together vigorously. "It was so dangerous."

"Dangerous?" I jerked my head to look at her.

"Well, no, not really, but my adrenaline was running high. It was great," she squealed. "I can see why you love it so much."

I pulled out of the mall parking lot and headed back out of town toward Cottonwood.

"Don't get used to it. This was the only time I'll let you do it. And you can't tell anyone." I pointed my finger at her. "Not even Ben."

"I took some great photos of Mundy's file." She pulled her phone out of her purse. "Here's what they say." She used her finger to swipe the photos.

"Did you get his address?" I asked, knowing that I was going to make an unannounced visit.

"I got that, but the most interesting thing was his background check." She swiped her fingers apart on the screen making the photo bigger. "He was arrested a few years ago for disturbing the peace at the Culinary Institute in New York City. He was arrested in a class where the professor, Frank Von Lee, had used some sort of egg that was endangered. Apparently Mundy is an environmentalist and protested."

"Not much of one since he slaughtered the chicken for the pot pie recipe." I thought about how I could get my hands on Frank Von Lee's class list. It wasn't like I could tell Finn to get one and check out the others in the class.

"I didn't say he wasn't a meat eater, just an environmentalist." Jolee spent the next few minutes scrolling through the phone. "Here is his last known address."

She read it off to me. I wasn't familiar with the area.

"Can you text me the photos?" I asked.

"Sure will." Jolee tapped, swiped, and punched on the phone. A few seconds later my phone chirped with texts one after the other. "There ya go. What's next?"

"I'm going to drop you off at the office and I've got to go to my parents'. I told my mama I'd come for supper. After that, Finn is stopping by for a drink." The Jeep rattled back across the Cottonwood county line. I was really excited for the late-night cocktail. "Have you heard of any sort of Botox ring going around?"

"Kenni, you make it sound like some drug ring." Jolee laughed. She stopped when she saw I wasn't joking.

"Have you seen my mama?" I asked. "Her face is so botched up from a Botox party that I'm not even sure if it's going to go back to normal."

"So she didn't get the black eye from Frank?" Jolee asked.

"You heard she and Frank got into a fight?" I asked.

"You know Cottonwood," she said. "Anyways, you have to be invited to one of those parties, and from what I hear they don't give you much notice."

"If you get invited, will you call me?" I asked.

"Sure. I think Katy Lee had an invite from someone that she sold insurance to. I'll check into it." Her words were music to my ears.

I could get at least one case solved while Finn worked on Mama's. Well, Frank's. I couldn't help but wonder what Finn was doing differently than I'd done. It'd be interesting to see.

I slowed down the Wagoneer when we got into the city limits. In no time we'd gone through the three stoplights in town and turned down the alley behind the department.

Jolee checked her phone.

"We made it back just in time for me to go get the Meals on Wheels." She put her hand on the handle of the door. "Listen, I know that you aren't going back to the office." Her eyes shifted out the window and towards the office door. "I know that if I follow you, which I won't, you're going to go find Mundy."

"What if I am?" I asked.

"Then I'd tell you to be careful." She reached over and we hugged. "I've got a newfound respect for your job since I went undercover." She winked and got out of the car.

"Actually, I only have a few minutes before I told Mama I'd be there. So I'm going to head down to the library and look a little bit more into Frank Von Lee's background. Maybe something will jump out at me." I waved bye and she shut the door.

Before I went into the library I called Finn.

"How's it going?" I asked.

"You know. People calling all day about the investigation. Betty ran Mundy's background," he said. "I went to his house to see him. He said he knew Frank from school but no way did he kill him. He said that he didn't know that Frank was even coming to Ben's when he called Ben for a job."

Right. Liar, I thought.

"Anyways, I'm going to do more digging on him. He's a strange dude," Finn said.

"Are we still on for tonight?" I asked.

"Yes, we are. I can't wait. See you soon." With that we hung up.

Cottonwood's library was located in a small white colonial-style building next to the courthouse. Parking was on the street. The inside of the library smelled exactly as if I'd just opened up a book and stuck my nose inside. That paper smell was always a welcomed scent and brought back fond memories of me getting lost in my fictional worlds when I was a kid and Mama was at her church meetings. Maybe I'd take up more reading since all this time fell into my hands.

There were three rooms to the library: the children's room, the fiction room, and the non-fiction room. It wasn't like they were stuck in the olden times. They had a couple of computers and everything that'd been on microfiche had been digitized into the computer system. That included articles of major magazines. I hoped I could find something, anything on Frank Von Lee.

"Good afternoon, almost evening," Marcy Carver greeted me from behind the reference desk as soon as I walked in. "What are you looking for, Kenni?"

Marcy never aged. It was probably from working in a nice quiet place with no stress, but still, she'd always had the same hairstyle—I'd never seen her without her hair pulled up in a thick top knot on her head. Once I'd asked her about her hair and she told me that if she didn't pull it back, her hair would spring out all over the place. Her dark skin was smooth milk chocolate and her brown eyes were just as lovely as her.

"I've come to get some information on Frank Von Lee." I leaned on the counter. "But tell me, how's your family?"

"Oh, you know. Wade had them grandkids over for the weekend. They wore me out. I was never so happy to get back to the library." She blinked and then focused her eyes on me. "But I've beat you to the punch." She walked over to her desk and picked up a stack of papers and magazines. "I too was curious about our visiting celebrity."

She pushed the pile across the counter.

"Edna Easterly came in here earlier today looking for some articles too, but I knew she'd use them in the Chronicle and I'm a little sore at her for printing that picture of your mama. She knows better, so I didn't give this to her." She cocked her right brow. "She's going to have to go to the city to find any information on him."

"You are a true friend." I reached over the counter and patted her on the arm. "Do you mind if I take these back there and read over them?"

"Not at all." She winked.

I picked up the stack and headed over to one of the empty tables with a computer on it. Marcy had already organized the stack starting with the beginning of Frank Von Lee's career and continuing up until a few weeks ago when it announced he'd made his decision to visit Cottonwood.

There were several articles about his class and how prestigious it was to be accepted into it. There was only one mention of Mundy, and it was just a class roster that accompanied a photo of the seven students Frank had accepted into the class that year.

I TYPED the year of the class into the computer along with Mundy's name as a search tag and a link to a court document came up. I pulled my phone out and scrolled through the photos Jolee had sent me. The court document on the computer matched the court papers in his file. With a few clicks, I logged into the Kentucky police database that was tied into the national law-enforcement database. With Mundy's social security number from the file, I was able to plug that into the database and see that Mundy's record was clean other than the arrest.

I scrolled through the court papers on the police database. It looked like Mundy was kicked out of the class because he had lashed out at Frank. Instead of Frank Von Lee pressing charges for Mundy's assault, Frank took out a restraining order against Mundy. An order was re-filed just a couple of weeks ago for a court date in a month.

"What the hell is that all about?" I whispered, scrolling down a little more to see if there'd been a reason listed for the re-file. "Oh, Mundy, how you lie."

There was no reason listed, but I knew that restraining orders were only re-filed if there was a direct threat. With Frank dead, there was sure a direct threat on his life. I knew this was more incriminating that anything Mama did.

I hit the print button and the printer next to the computer going off was music to my ears. While I waited for it to finish, I wondered about the other people in the class. They'd been witnesses to any sort of disagreement between Mundy and Frank.

Using the mouse, I clicked on the history button on the screen and scrolled to where I'd seen the class list. I double clicked and brought that page back up. I printed it too.

After I made sure the printer had printed the papers I wanted, I clicked out of the computer and made sure I cleared the history so no one could go back through and see what I was looking at, though they'd need my passwords. You could never be too careful.

This was some great evidence that pointed to a tiff between the victim and Mundy that had to be looked into. Was it revenge? I'd think a restraining order wasn't good for a chef's reputation, especially from a famous food critic. But more importantly, I felt like this was the solid evidence to clear Mama as the number one suspect.

The more I dug, the more I read about how Frank Von Lee had really done a number on people's lives. He really wasn't a very nice man, but it still didn't warrant someone killing him. Frank Von Lee either made you rich or poor. Nothing in between. If he came to your restaurant and gave you a great review, you'd made it in the restaurant business. On the other hand, if you got a bad review, from what I read, most of the restaurants went bankrupt. Frank had even been sued by a family by the name of Tooke. It was a big case that was eventually dropped after the owner committed suicide.

My phone rang.

"Mama," I groaned, noticing the little digital time on my phone said I was late.

"Kenni, can you please come over right now?" She sounded desperate.

"Right now?" I asked in my hushed library voice. "Why?"

"I really need you to come now. I don't want to say it over the phone." There was an urgency in her voice that really bothered me.

"I'm on my way," I said and gathered up the papers. I hung up the phone and stuck it back in my pocket as I made my way to the exit. "Thanks, Marcy. You're a gem."

I put her file back on the counter and headed on out of the door.

Downtown Cottonwood had a yawning peace as the late afternoon dragged into the early evening. It was the time of day when everyone had left work to make it home in time for supper and every shop in town closed for the night, except for Ben's, probably where Finn and I would end up later tonight.

The diner was still hopping. I slowed the Jeep down and noticed through the windows of the diner all the tables were filled and Ben was busy taking orders. It looked like his fears had not come to fruition and that made me happy. Soon he and Jolee would be back to normal. Hopefully the case would be solved and peace would return to our small southern town.

I pushed the gas and headed on back down Main Street and turned right on Free Row. Duke had been home and it wasn't fair of me to leave him there when he loved going to my parents' house.

"Let's go, Duke!" I yelled after I opened the door to the house. His back legs flung out from under him when he took the turn at the door too fast, skidding outside. "You're my crazy dog."

He jumped and yelped at the gate, waiting for me to walk over.

"Let's go," I teased my already anxious pup when I opened the gate.

"Hi, Kenni." Mrs. Brown waved from her front porch. Riley Titan was screwing a light bulb in her outside porch lamp. "Have you met Riley? He's very handy."

"Hi, Riley." I greeted them when I walked over. "Yes, Mrs. Brown, I've met Riley."

"Mrs. Brown heard all the banging I'm doing over at Deputy Vincent's house and she asked me to come by and look at her light." He held up the bulb. "Just a bulb out. Easy fix."

"It wasn't the banging that got my attention. It was the yelling." Mrs. Brown's chin dipped.

"Yelling?" I questioned.

"It's nothing." Riley played it off.

"Nothing, my patookie," Mrs. Brown said sternly. "Danny Shane has lost his mind."

"Oh, really. It's no big deal. I'm used to big companies and bullying." Riley shook off Mrs. Brown's comments. "He heard I'd gotten the job offer from Deputy Vincent and he came to bust my chops. It wasn't a big deal."

"It was a big deal," Mrs. Brown protested. "He was going to slug you. Then he saw my wooden rolling pin." She nodded with pride.

"Rolling pin?" I half laughed. Mrs. Brown swinging around a rolling pin was something I'd like to have seen.

"You should've seen her come to my rescue." Riley smiled. Mrs. Brown was smitten with him.

"You didn't need no rescue." Mrs. Brown winked.

"If y'all excuse me. I better get back to work before Deputy Vincent gets home and fires me." Riley waved on his way back down to Finn's house.

"That's strange about Danny," I said. He'd always been a little hotheaded, but he wasn't a bully or a thug. It made me wonder what was going on with him. Maybe a little friendly visit to Danny Shane was on the docket.

Then my mind did that thing. It went to the what-ifs. Not that any evidence pointed to Danny, but what if he was so mad at Ben for losing the job that his revenge was to shut down Ben's? After all, he did say that Ben's had given him food poisoning and he told everyone he knew not to go there. Malina did say that Danny had been at The Tattered Cover Books and Inn for a couple of days fixing things up.

"That's it." I ran my hand down Duke once we said goodbye to Mrs. Brown. "Danny Shane hasn't showed up for jobs. What's going on with him?" I whispered on the way to the Jeep. "Plus he owns those condos where Mama said she got her Botox. Maybe it's time I start investigating that."

CHAPTER TWENTY-ONE

"What do you think your mama wants?" Poppa sat in the front seat and Duke jumped into the back.

"You and I both know that she's got something up her sleeve. I hope she doesn't have a bomb she wants to drop on me about the Botox and stuff. Regardless, I think we need to go see Danny Shane tomorrow before I go back to my baking class."

"I'm not convinced Danny Shane is a murderer, but he'll do anything to keep that family business going. His dad was just like him," Poppa said.

"I'm not saying he's a murderer, I'm just saying he might know more than he's leading on." I continued, "I can just make a courtesy call to him and see what my gut says after I talk to him."

"Remember to always listen to your gut." Poppa ghosted away as I pulled up to my parents' house.

"You are going to have to stay with Mrs. Brown all day tomorrow," I said to Duke. "I've got some investigating to do."

Some familiar cars were lined up on the street. Ones that belonged to Tibbie Bell, Myrna Savage, Viola White, Ruby Smith, Missy Jennings, and the On The Run food truck, which meant that Jolee was there. If it weren't the wrong night, I'd think the Euchre girl's night in was tonight since it was the same gals that played.

The sun was setting and it was getting darker as well as colder. All of the lights were on in Mama's house. I dragged my old sweatshirt out of the back and tugged it on.

"What on earth is she up to?" I asked Duke. I swear he understood me. "Come on, boy." I patted my leg and walked up to the door.

When I opened it, laughter and chatter filtered into the entryway.

"There you are," Mama greeted me with joy. "I thought I heard a car door."

It was a far cry from her attitude since I'd last seen her. She even had her black eye covered with makeup. Though she was still a little puffy, she looked a whole lot better.

"What's going on?" I dragged my hand along Duke as he ran past me into Mama's house.

"I thought that after last night's horrible town council meeting, we'd move our weekly Euchre game up to today. You love Euchre and I think you need a bit of cheering up." She twirled on her gold flats and trotted into the other room.

I wasn't sure if Mama used the excuse to cheer herself up or if she really was trying to cheer me up. Either way, I was glad to get out of my head for a few hours. And the food wouldn't be bad either.

Every week all the girls got together for our Euchre night. Everyone brought a dish, and not just any dish. It was the best they'd make all week. These women took pride in their cooking and if they could outdo each other, they'd do it.

By the sound of my gurgling stomach, tonight was not going to disappoint. Mama's kitchen table was filled with all the southern appetizers.

"Myrna, is this your spicy pimento cheese?" I asked.

I could already taste Myrna's specialty appetizer. I used the fancy spoon in the cheese spread to put some on a couple of toast points.

"Don't forget the asparagus." She grinned. I noticed the wrinkles in her smile line were smooth.

"You look good." I took the tongs and placed a piece of asparagus on top of the pimento cheese. "Are you using a different moisturizer?" I baited her. "This winter my skin took a hit. I've been looking in the beauty aisle at Dixon's for something new."

She licked her lips and hesitated. "You really think I look good?"

"Yes." I nodded.

Come on, Myrna, I thought, tell me about the Botox.

"Or did you get it from Tiny Tina's? I know she's got a new cosmetics line down there." I reached over and put a few fried dill pickles on my plate.

"Well," she leaned into my shoulder and whispered, "there's this new party, kinda like the one that Katy Lee has with that clothing line." She reached over me and took a couple of the shrimp and grits.

"Shabby Trends?" I asked, pretending I didn't know.

"It's not clothes. It's Botox." She smiled and pointed to her lips. "Your mama and I went to get a little for only twenty-five dollars. She had a little reaction, but I didn't." She rolled her eyes Mama's way.

"I saw that she had that black eye." I pretended Mama hadn't said a word to me. "Of course, Edna printed it on the front page of the Chronicle so everyone would assume she and Frank Von Lee had an argument."

"Wasn't that a shame?" Myrna tsked. "Your mama wasn't there when he died, so I don't know why they think she was."

"Myrna, do you know something?" I asked. "It doesn't look good for Mama, and if you do have some information I'd like to know it. Any information can be helpful even if you don't think it could be."

"Your mama was pitching a fit after her eye swelled up and blackened. She was going to go back over there and give them a piece of her mind. Alone," she muttered uneasily. "I told her that there's no way I was going to let her go alone. You know those condos are a little fishy. We went and she demanded her money back. They told her since it was cash only, they didn't offer money back. Then she said that her daughter was the sheriff and she was going to report them. That's when they got a little antsy."

"They did?" I drew back and acted like it was no big deal they were there.

"Her threats worked. They gave her money back and told her to come back and they'd fix the botch." Myrna laughed. "Leave it to your mama to get a bad batch of Botox. Especially when she needed it for Frank Von Lee. Bless her heart." Myrna lovingly glanced at Mama, who was on the other side of the room talking. "Nothing has gone right for her with this Frank thingy. First she wears herself out cooking to make sure each pot pie tastes the same as the next. Then she goes and gets Botox so she can look good, only it's all messed up. Then Poor Frank up and gets himself killed. Poor shame."

"It sure is. Say, do you know the number of the apartment?" I asked.

So as not to seem so interested, I continued to put more food on my plate.

"I thought you'd never ask." She grinned. "You could stand to get those elevens done."

"Elevens?" Never in a million years did I think Myrna Savage would give me beauty tricks.

"These two lines you have between your eyes." She reached up and touched the top of my nose. "They look like an eleven. I had one." She dragged her nail between her brows. "It might cost a little more, but you'll look a lot better. Or," she let out an audible sigh, "you could get bangs. That'd do it too."

"Elevens. Good to know. Thanks." I nodded. "What's the apartment number?"

"Twenty-two. Two, two. Twenty-two." She made sure I remembered. "Tell 'em I sent ya. Maybe they'll give me a discount next time."

"Twenty-two. Got it." I reached over the Crock-Pot. "Y'all have outdone yourselves. Are these Dr. Pepper meatballs?"

"They sure are." Pride showed on her face. She smiled, line-free.

With my plate full and a Diet Coke in my hand, I made my way into Mama's fancy family room where she'd set up the Euchre tables.

Jolee, my partner, was sitting with Ruby Smith and Viola White.

"Any news about you-know-who?" Jolee asked about Mundy.

"No," I said and shuffled the cards, dealing them out to the four of us and waiting to see if any of them wanted me to pick up the red nine on top of the discarded pile of cards.

Each of them knocked their finger on the table. In Euchre talk, they were passing on the nine. I flipped it over and now they had the opportunity to call a trump suit. Each of them passed, but not me. I never passed when I could call a trump, even if I didn't have the highest cards.

"Spades is trump," I called the suit.

For the next half hour, everyone made chitchat without mentioning Frank Von Lee or Mama's involvement. No one made mention of Mama's face or the awful photo Edna had printed. They didn't even mention the Culinary Channel at all.

Until...

"I'm tired of everyone beating around the bush." Viola White's eyes gazed over the top of her cards that she held up in front of her face. She'd opted for a cream turban with her hair tucked up underneath. A necklace with large gold balls the size of eggs wrapped around her neck.

Viola was a substitute. She didn't have a regular partner and tonight she was Ruby Smith's partner. Both old. Both wealthy.

I sucked in a deep breath, waiting for what Viola was going to say and if Mama would end up kicking her out. I threw down the jack of spades, the highest of the round we were playing, hoping to pull out more trump cards. Viola threw a nine of hearts, which told me she had no trump in her hand, while Jolee dropped the queen of spades. Ruby's eyes went back and forth between her cards and the cards played before she finally gave up the jack of clubs, the second highest card in the round.

"And what would that be, Viola?" I asked.

"What on earth do y'all think about Polly Parker marrying Mayor Ryland?" Ruby arranged her cards and rearranged them again.

"Money, honey. Chance Ryland has a boatload." Viola's mouth quirked with humor.

She seemed to have a deep secret about the mayor and his wealth. Of course I couldn't help but wonder what that was.

"If I were Pete Parker, I'd take that girl and give her a good whoopin'. I just can't hold my tongue no more." Viola dragged her long nails down the black feather boa wrapped around her neck, her turquoise rings really standing out against the black. "I know you really like the Parkers, Ruby, but that's ridiculous."

Relief swam through my veins and I eased back in my seat, thankful they didn't bring up Frank, Mama, or me being taken off the case.

"I agree." Ruby took the break to pull out her lipstick and circle her lips with the bright orange color. "There are plenty of women his own age to do that to than that poor girl."

"I can't even imagine what she sees in his wrinkly body," Jolee threw in her two cents.

There was a collective snicker around the table.

"Can you imagine in a few years when her boobs'll still be all perky and up here," Viola flattened her hands under her chin, "and she's pushing him in a wheelchair?"

"Or worse," Ruby's eyes shifted side to side with an evil grin on her face, "her visiting him along with her mama and daddy in a nursing home."

The two women laughed and cackled as I threw more cards, ending the first game in our Euchre round, giving me and Jolee the first win in the set.

"He is very mature looking." I thought it was time to give a little positive spin to it. "She's going to need a caterer." I rose a brow toward Jolee.

She looked at me, but in a through-me kind of way.

"Hmm." Her lips twisted. "That's an idea." The thought brought a smile to her face.

"She works for you, so she's going to need jewelry." I threw the conversation toward Viola White. "You know her wedding will be in all the social papers."

They all knew that when you made it into the societal page of the Chronicle, you were Cottonwood royalty.

"Remember when Tiny Tina's was mentioned in there after that celebrity passed through and stopped to get a quick massage," I said. "She was booked for two years after that."

"You might be onto something." Ruby tapped the edge of her card on the table in front of her before she threw it in the middle to take the next trump. "I wonder if she's going to have an outdoor wedding because I have all those cute chandeliers that can be repurposed into romantic hanging lighting. It's in all the wedding magazines."

"It's settled then." I threw down a trump to get the game finished. They followed suit. "Viola will host an engagement party for Polly. Jolee will do the food. Ruby can bring her chandelier idea. We'll make Polly think it's her idea as we present them to her."

"You're a genius." Ruby reached over and patted my hand. "You are a great sheriff."

"All joking aside," Viola drummed her nails on the table, "I'm not happy Mayor Ryland took you off the case without a full council vote."

"Unfortunately, the law does state that the mayor can govern over the department if there's a conflict." I raked in all the cards and handed them to Jolee so she could shuffle and deal.

"Regardless," Ruby chimed in, "all of us are here for you and if you need anything, you know we'll drop whatever we're doing."

Jolee smiled at me from across the table.

"I'll keep that in mind." I smiled back.

"You know," Jolee shuffled the cards into a bridge, "our sheriff is a mighty good baker. In fact, she's been taking a baking class."

"You never know. I might be trying to get a job down at the bakery if I'm out of work soon," I joked.

"Are you baking a cake for a certain someone?" Ruby asked.

"Oh, spill. How does Finn feel about you not taking lead on the case?" Viola followed up.

"First off, no. I'm learning to bake for me. Secondly, Finn and I both want what's best for Cottonwood." I had to be very political.

"Are you two being nosy?" Mama walked up behind me and put her hands on my shoulders. "I, for one, am thrilled to have this extra time with my baby."

"Me too, Mama." I reached up and patted her on the hand. "Me too."

As much as Mama drove me crazy, I knew she always had my back. Even though she'd rather go to jail over a murder charge than have people find out she had Botox, I was going to have her back. Maybe it was time to get the elevens done.

CHAPTER TWENTY-TWO

It was actually a very nice day, I thought to myself on my way back to the house. It was the first time in a long time that I'd actually taken a few hours to enjoy myself. Even though I wasn't a big shopper, the laughter and storytelling going on between me and Jolee was a lot of fun and the surprise Euchre game mama had thrown together was also enjoyable.

But tonight when Finn stopped by, now that was something I was really looking forward to. Only there was one thing on my list that had to be done: calling the people on Mundy's class list. If I really wanted to give Finn some solid evidence about why I thought Mundy killed Frank, then I needed some eyewitnesses to Frank and Mundy's volatile relationship.

"Boo," Poppa teased as he appeared in the kitchen.

Duke jumped up at the ready to play toss with him. I'd just grabbed a beer and retrieved the papers I'd printed off from the library with Frank's class list.

"What are those?" Poppa asked.

"Names of the students in Frank Von Lee's class." I sat down in a kitchen chair and tapped the papers. "Mundy was in this class."

"He was?" Poppa's ghost somehow kicked the ball Duke had dropped at his feet and Duke shot off down the hall. "That's a connection."

"I found it today." I looked up at him. It started to feel like old times.

At this very table when I was a teenager and even in the academy, Poppa and I use to banter back and forth about his cases. It was something I loved to do.

"Mundy not only got kicked out of Frank's class, Frank had a restraining order against him. Just a few weeks ago, the restraining order was re-filed, which means that Frank had reason to keep Mundy a good distance from him."

"I hope you're going to go and confront Mundy, because if Frank was to show up at the diner and Mundy was there, he'd be in violation of the order." Poppa raised a good point.

"I really don't think it's a coincidence that Mundy called Ben to see if Ben needed help." I recalled how Ben told me that he'd been searching for a chef to help out so he could focus his time on Frank's visit.

"It wasn't like it was a big secret that Frank was coming." Poppa looked over my shoulder and at the paper. "I guess you better use that fancy laptop of yours to look these people up. If we can get even two of them to confirm the tension between teacher and student, it's enough evidence to make Mundy a suspect."

"The restraining order is enough." I dragged my laptop in front of me. I took a big swig of my beer before I got started.

I used the police database to see if any of them had criminal records. It wasn't unusual for chefs to get into some sort of fight in their career and get arrested for something really stupid. Poppa had arrested Ben once. There was a customer who complained and insulted his food. Ben didn't take the criticism very well, and the customer called the sheriff's department. Poppa didn't have a choice but to put Ben in the pokey for a few hours until he calmed down.

"I'm hoping the restraining order wasn't just because Mundy lost his cool." It did tickle my brain that Frank Von Lee would use something so silly to put a restraining order on Mundy, though it did help Mama's case.

With a few keystrokes, I found a couple of the people on Facebook. They were a little older than in their class photo, but it was definitely them. I clicked on the messenger tab and viola. Their phone numbers were right there. "That was easy. Thank goodness for social media."

"Huh?" Poppa's eyes narrowed.

"This is like email." I pointed to the blue messenger box. "Some people actually put their phone numbers in their profile and anyone can call them. This guy," I pointed to the profile photo, "he's this guy." I pointed to the younger version of him in the class photo I'd printed at the library. "And his profile says he's a chef."

"There weren't very many people in the class." Poppa bent down and looked at the class photo.

"It's some sort of exclusive, prestigious class. So Mundy must be good as a chef," I said and typed in the phone number. "Hello, is this Guy Hall?" I questioned when someone answered.

When he confirmed, I continued, "My name is Kenni Lowry. I'm the Sheriff in Cottonwood, Kentucky."

"You mean where Chef Von Lee was killed?" he questioned from the other end of the phone.

"Yes. And we are going through Frank, er, Chef Von Lee's students and we've come across someone you might know from your class."

"You're talking about Mundy, right? What a tool." There was obviously no love lost between them.

"I see that Mundy made an impression on you too."

Duke jumped up from underneath my feet and ran to the back door. Finn was there and waved at me through the screen door. I waved him in.

"He made that impression on everyone," Guy said.

I put my finger up to my mouth when Finn walked in. He had a brown sack with him.

"Dinner," he mouthed and sat it down on the kitchen table.

I pulled the phone away from my ear and pushed the speaker button so Finn could hear.

"Did you actually see any of the tension between Mundy and Frank?" I asked.

"Oh, yeah. Mundy was always telling Chef how he was doing things wrong. Chef was really good at ignoring him until Mundy got in his face about how to make country gravy of all things." Guy laughed.

"Country gravy?" I asked, making sure I'd heard right.

"Yeah. Mundy really thought he was this great southern chef. It wasn't

SIX FEET UNDER

until years later when Chef finally took out a restraining order on Mundy. I was there when it happened." Now he was giving me some good info.

"Where and when was this?" I asked and pushed all the papers I'd printed off from the library towards Finn to help clue him in on what was going on.

"I was taking Chef's master class and Mundy had scored a seat, which I don't know how that happened. Chef told us about the Culinary Channel and how they were giving him his own show about southern foods. Mundy went nuts and that's when the cops were called. The next class Chef told us that he had to put a restraining order on Mundy." There was a pause. Finn and I looked at each other. "Mundy literally went crazy, saying he was the best southern chef and it was a joke."

"Guy, thank you for answering my questions. If I have any more, can I call you back?" I asked with my finger on the end button.

"No problem. I'm more than happy to get that whacko behind bars." The line went dead.

"That was a bit of news." Finn pulled out Chinese containers from the bag.

"Today I went to the library and did a little digging." I gestured to the papers he'd looked over. "This for sure points to Mundy as the killer. Not only does he have a motive of jealousy, but there was a restraining order against him."

Finn looked over the papers and I grabbed a couple of plates and forks. There were some chopsticks, but I'd never learned to use them.

"Ms. Kim threw in some extra fortune cookies." He looked up at me and winked. "She said I was going to need as much good fortune as I could get."

I rolled my eyes. Mrs. Kim was the owner of Kim's Buffet and mother of my friend Gina. She acted like she didn't like me, but deep down I knew she did.

"With all this information, I'm definitely going to tell Mayor Ryland that Vivian Lowry is no longer a suspect. I know we already established that, but it's not official. I want to make it official." Finn scooted his chair next to mine and sat down. He put his arm around me. "I'll do a stakeout at Mundy's and drag him into the department for an interrogation tomorrow."

"That's perfect." I nuzzled my nose in his neck, sitting there in the comfort of his arms. Duke didn't let us sit there for too long before he came over and dropped a ball at Finn's feet.

"Ahem," There was a throat clearing from the corner. Without a shadow of a doubt, Finn was getting a little too close for Poppa's comfort.

CHAPTER TWENTY-THREE

The smell of freshly brewing coffee was the first thing that woke me up. The second thing that woke me up: Mama.

"Good morning, Mama," I answered the phone and looked at the time.

"You're still in bed?" Mama asked.

"It's my day off." Not that I really had a day off, but it was my usual day that I went in late to the office. After last night, I was certain Finn would get Mundy in the office, brought up on charges of murdering Frank Von Lee, and booked.

Though it was only a little past seven a.m., it was past my normal six a.m. wake-up time.

"Fiddle fart! Get up," Mama yelled. "We're celebrating."

I pulled the phone from my ear. Duke looked up from the foot of the bed and then slid his front paws off the edge, followed by his body. He pulled himself into a long stretch and let out a groan before he walked out of the room.

"Did you see the paper?" she asked.

"No. Why? What are we celebrating?" I wondered what'd happened.

"I'm no longer a suspect. Mayor Ryland said in an interview that there's another suspect in the case," she informed me.

"I'm up." I flung the covers off me and swung my feet over the edge. A shiver of cold rushed up through my feet. I pushed myself up to stand. "I can't celebrate. I've got some work to do." I padded my way down to the kitchen and pushed the back door open for Duke to run out to do his morning business.

"You just said that you were off today." She used my words against me. Since when did Mama listen to me? "So get up and let's go get your elevens done."

I put my finger up to my elevens.

"Myrna told you about our conversation?" I asked.

"Yep. And if you're going to arrest them, then I want to be there." Her voice escalated. "They ruined my face."

"You should've known better than to think legitimate Botox would only cost twenty-five dollars." I opened my cabinet and retrieved a coffee cup. "I appreciate all your enthusiasm to shut them down, but I can't drag you along. It's a sheriff's department matter. Don't go back over there. I can't just go in guns blazing. That's not how investigations work."

Though I wished sometimes that they did. Cutting through all the red tape felt like it took way too long at times.

"I really think you should take me. I can be your deputy on this one." Mama was serious. "Deputize me."

Two days ago she wanted me to cuff her and now she wanted me to deputize her. Mama never ceased to shock me.

"Not today, Mama." I wasn't about to put her in the middle of an investigation. "I'll give you a call later."

"But..." Mama faltered. "Grab your umbrella. Rain's a'comin'."

"Bye." I hung up the phone and walked over to let Duke in. "Rain, my hinny," I whispered and shut the door. There wasn't a call for rain in the forecast for a week or so.

I headed back down the hall and into my bedroom. There was no reason to hang around here any longer when I needed to get my day started. I had a to-do list that had Danny Shane's name right at the top. Even though we had good reason to believe Mundy was the killer, I still had unanswered questions about his behavior. Under his name on my list were the condos by the river to check out that Botox ring and then my baking class. Out of all of those things I was surprisingly most excited about the class.

Five minutes later, I'd gotten my shower and pulled on a t-shirt and jeans.

Poppa ghosted into my bedroom. "You need to get down to the department and do a timeline, not only to show that your mama didn't kill Frank, but one for Mundy."

"I'll do that after hours. I want to give Finn time to do his job and check Mundy out. So we are going to unofficially go see Danny Shane this morning." I pulled a sweatshirt out of my drawer and tugged on my cowboy boots. "After that, I've got to head to Le Fork for cake class."

"Cake class?" Poppa obviously didn't like that. "What about the condos? You need to get some kind of justice for your mama's face."

"That's on the list too," I assured him.

He disappeared. I was right behind him after I'd gotten Duke settled and called Mrs. Brown to remind her to check in on him throughout the day.

The sun had faded behind a cloud on my way to the Jeep. I stopped and looked up, giving the air a little sniff. Maybe Mama was right. There was a salty rain smell that was similar to the smell before a big gully washer. I almost walked back inside to grab my rain boots, but the sun peeked out, pushing Mama's observation aside. I was good at believing whatever came from Mama's mouth. She had a way of doing that.

I jumped in my Jeep and headed down Free Row toward the stop sign. The neighborhood was still asleep and all was calm for the time being. At the end of the street I took a left on Main Street going north to visit Danny Shane. The sun hid behind some really dark clouds. I flipped on WCKK just in time to hear the weather update that an unexpected rain shower had begun to move in on Cottonwood but was not expected to last long.

"Spring showers bring May flowers," I repeated Mama's mantra as little dots of sprinkles appeared on the windshield.

That wasn't going to dampen my mood. I couldn't help but smile seeing the line of customers waiting outside to get a seat at Ben's as I drove past. It was about time he did well, even if it was because of a murder. When I was stopped by the stoplight, I loved seeing the Cottonwood Chronicle headline that "Ben's Is Booming" along with a picture of Ben at the stove with a big smile on his face.

Shane's Construction had been around as long as I could remember. The

Shane family ran the business and all three generations had been involved. I'd never ever had a complaint or even heard of any shoddy jobs completed by their company. Something else that I hadn't heard was that Danny had recently taken over the company like Ben had said.

Danny had always been the hardheaded one of his family. He was the only one who really stood up to the mayor and the council when he'd proposed to have the condos built on a plot of land overlooking the Kentucky River. The mayor wanted to keep Cottonwood small, which only hurt our economy where Danny saw the feature and the value of having condos on the river. It not only brought new residents to Cottonwood, but also a community of people who loved the river and started to invest for their retirement here, giving the economy a boost.

The condos where Mama had said she'd gone to get her bad Botox fix. Shane Construction not only built the condos, they still owned the complex plus the land and benefited from the Home Owners Association fee. The thought that he might know about the Botox parties crossed my mind too.

If he did, and if he really did have reason to get back at Ben, then Danny Shane wasn't in his right frame of mind.

"Sheriff." Danny greeted me at the door of the aluminum building that was a temporary office for the new concrete two-story building they'd recently gotten approval from the council to build. "This doesn't look like a personal visit."

He stepped out and greeted me halfway. The cowboy hat was pulled down on his forehead, making a shadow draw down his face. He had his red and black plaid shirt tucked into his tight blue jeans. The sun made his shadow look seven feet tall instead of his six-foot-six frame. A little intimidating.

The grey clouds blanketed the once unblemished grass of the family's three-hundred-acre dairy farm land. The sprinkle that'd fallen on the Jeep on Main Street had finally made its way out to the country. The dry dirt we were standing on would be a big old mud pile soon. Good for muddin' around on four wheelers. I couldn't help but think what Danny's grandfather would say about him digging up their farm and putting that concrete building on it.

His grandfather took pride in their cows. The dairy farm was still on the back one hundred acres and up and running. We were one of few counties that still had milk delivery. And it wasn't cheap to have that fresh milk delivered. Jolee said the cost was nothing compared to the taste that made her recipes so good.

"I've got a couple of questions for you." I slammed the back door of the Wagoneer.

"I'll try to answer them." He strolled a little closer, his boots crunching into the temporary gravel drive.

I glanced up at the sky when I felt a drop of rain. "Looks like a gully washer's coming."

"It'll be good for the crops." He dug his hands into his jean pockets and kept an eye on me.

"How's everything going, Danny?" I asked.

"Construction business has been so busy. It's hard to find good help." He slid his eyes up to the darkening sky. "Do you want to come in out of the rain? I've got some coffee brewing."

"That'd be nice." I offered a smile.

Breaking bread was a great way to ease into a conversation and socialize. In this case coffee was going to have to do.

I headed into the barn, which might seem silly to some. Not around these parts. Most barns on working farms were nicer than the houses the farmers lived in. Same with Danny's. The floor was a nice poured concrete. The stalls were on the right and the offices were on the left. In Danny's case, he had his dairy and construction office in his barn while his employees were in the other building.

"Your mama and them doing all right?" Danny asked, offering the go-ahead to fix my own coffee from the coffee bar in his office.

I grabbed a Styrofoam cup and poured a hot cup of coffee.

"They're fine." I nodded, not sure what to say. "I guess you probably know I'm not here for pleasantries." I used a stirrer to add creamer to my coffee. "I wanted to know what's going on between you and Ben." I turned around to face him.

He was sitting in the chair behind his desk and gestured for me to sit down in the chair in front.

"That so-called job of Ben's was charity."

"Charity?" I asked and blew on the steaming coffee before I took a sip.

"Ben Harrison is having a hard time paying the bills. He came to me with a sad sack story about how he needed to update the restaurant to make it look good for TV. He said that if he won..." Danny shook his head. "He didn't even give credit to your mama." His eyes looked under his brows at me. "Anyways, he said if he won, then he'd get the visibility he'd need to keep the diner open."

"He said that?" I went to Ben's almost daily. Granted, it wasn't packed, but there were always a handful of people in there when I'd go. He never mentioned that he needed money or was having problems.

"Yeah. I was the one who was the sucker and gave him charity. I even donated the damn milk from my dairy cows for the fresh food for the days that critic was coming." The chair squeaked when he leaned back, his coffee mug in his hands. "When I told Ben that we weren't going to use the high-dollar bamboo beams he wanted, he went off his rocker." Danny shook his head. "I had to remind him that I was doing this free of charge. That's when he decided to fire me from a charitable job."

He hesitated and stared at me for a second.

"From what I hear, his diner has been booming since they found that guy dead." He shrugged.

I decided to move on because I was going to have to check out this charity thing he was talking about.

"What about Finn's job?" I asked.

"That was a paying job, but I'm so busy here that I just couldn't hold up to my end of the deal. My guys are swamped. I dropped the ball. We don't usually do residential, so I put him on the back burner." His lips turned down. "I should've told him I couldn't do it, but I hated to turn him down. That good ole southern manners thing."

"I get it." I laughed.

"With a mama like Viv, I know you do." He winked. "I was glad to read in the paper that there's another suspect in the famous guy's death."

"Yeah." I blinked a few times. "No one has been charged yet."

"I know your mama didn't kill that critic. In fact, I'd just left her house with a special order of creamer she'd ordered. I was on my way over to The

Tattered Cover Books and Inn to drop off some fresh milk to that chef Ben had hired."

"You were taking milk to Mundy?" I asked.

"Yep." His lips drew together. He got up and walked over to the filing cabinet. He pulled out a yellow piece of paper. "Your mama showed up here around four. I told her it would take a half hour or so to pull the freshest cream, so we made plans for me to drop it off at her house. I knew I needed to make a drop-off to Mundy and it was on my way."

He shut the file cabinet drawer back and walked over to me with the paper in his hand.

"This is an order form for fresh creamer. We have to log the heifer number, the time of day, and the creaming process. We can't pull too much milk out of our heifers at one time so we can produce the freshest milk, cream, butter," he shrugged, "anything that's made with the milk. Your mama insisted I get her the freshest we had and she'd pay top dollar."

He handed me the order slip.

"Can I get a photo of this?" I asked and pulled out my phone when he nodded. The thought lingered in my head that some people still thought Mama to be a suspect, so I wanted to make it very clear from the timeline that she didn't kill anyone.

"You can see from the timestamp I pulled the cream from the stock at four-thirty, so by the time I got to your mama's house it was around five. She was leaving when I got there. She paid me and I was on my way." He walked back around to his desk and sat down again.

"Do you have the order form from Chef Mundy?" I asked.

"Yeah. He's a strange one. Paid cash. Said he didn't want a receipt with his name or any identifying information." He shrugged and walked back over to the cabinet, pulling out another work order. "Of course, I made an order anyways. We have to for our records."

"Thanks, Danny." I took the paper from him and took a picture of it before I stood up. I pointed to the coffee pot for a refill and he nodded. "I appreciate the information."

"You need to tell that deputy of yours that Riley Titan doesn't have a work permit from the American Builders Association either," he muttered. My eyes narrowed. "Don't get me wrong. We need a residential contractor around here. We had our monthly ABA meeting and when I didn't see him I asked around. The president did a quick search in the ABA database and said he'd never heard of Riley Titan."

"Does he have to be a member in order to do the work?" I had to admit I wasn't very well informed on the laws of construction. Suddenly I remembered Mrs. Brown saying something about Danny trying to beat up Riley.

"He doesn't have to be a member, but it's hard to get a job without good credentials. Maybe not when you're in a hurry like Ben," he said.

"I'll make a note of it. Though I did hear you went to Finn's to sock Riley in his clock." I took a sip of the coffee.

"Are you kidding me?" He rolled his eyes and let out a disgusted humph. "That guy is crazy. I went there to pick up my tools that were left behind. I asked him about his job permit that he needed to file with the city. He shoved me first. Mrs. Brown was being nosy as usual and I just let it go. I'm not the construction police."

"I'll be sure to tell Finn to make sure there's a permit." I still had a question for him. "One more thing." I stopped before I walked out the door and turned around. "Do you know anything about a Botox scheme going down at the condo complex on the river?" I asked.

"What the hell is Botox?" Confusion crossed his face.

"It's something dermatologists or licensed professionals put in women's wrinkles to make them disappear. Mama went to one of the condos and got who-knows-what injected into her face because she wanted to look good on TV. She said she got it from someone living in your condo complex." I still had to follow up on it, even though I wanted to follow up on the Ben lead Danny had just given me.

"I don't know a thing about that kind of stuff, but you'd have to have the condo owner's permission. They own their condo; I just keep up the HOA responsibilities like keeping the landscape nice, the buildings in great working condition, and doing any repairs. " His eyes blazed and rolled over me. "Don't be going and making trouble. I don't feel like going behind you and making any angry residents there happy."

"Thanks for the coffee." I held the cup in the air and headed on out of the barn.

I started up the Jeep and sat there for a second collecting my thoughts.

My stomach growled. I knew what I had to do and I hated it. I hated all of it. I needed to call Finn and let him know what Danny had told me. If he was right, the work Riley was doing might not be legal. I knew how much Finn wanted to get the work finished. With Riley not having the right paperwork, it could set back the addition even longer.

What on earth was he talking about Ben and charity? Jolee and Ben had both mentioned he needed the publicity and that business was down, but was he in dire straits? Though Mundy was now our number one suspect, I couldn't just ignore the strange behavior Ben had displayed, nor the fact that he was all too happy his business had picked up since Frank's death.

My heart sank. Ben and Mundy were friends. Had they staged the fight? The whole thing? Were they in on this together?

"Hey, Betty." I grabbed the walkie-talkie off my passenger seat since I didn't have on my uniform. I decided to go ahead and call in to dispatch to check out what Finn had found out with Mundy. "Is Finn there?" I was sure he'd already dragged Mundy in for questioning this morning.

"No, he ran over to Dixon's because Toots said there were three cars there this morning with those handicap tags," she said.

"Did he bring anyone in for questioning?" I asked.

"Not here he didn't," she said.

"All right. I'll try calling his cell." The only way to know for sure if Ben and Mundy were in cahoots was to pay Chef Mundy a visit. As sheriff, I had no time to play around with fake tags. I might've been removed from the case, but I had to know.

"Kenni." Betty's mom voice came through. "You aren't going to go see Mundy, are you?"

"Maybe," I muttered. "Finn told you about Mundy?"

"He came in here first thing and wrote down all the information on that darn whiteboard. I can read." She laughed. "If I read between the lines, it means that Viv isn't the number one suspect anymore."

"There's nothing wrong with your eyes," I joked. "I'm not sure I can wait until Mayor Ryland decides to give me back the lead. But I'm going to head on over to check out my leads on the Botox scheme. Let Finn know when he gets back."

"Will do, Sheriff." Betty clicked off the walkie-talkie.

CHAPTER TWENTY-FOUR

"I told you that there's something about that chef." Poppa appeared in the passenger seat.

"Just like everything else we know, it's all just talking out loud and trying to fit pieces of a puzzle to make it whole," I reminded him.

"You've got to check out the pieces before you can put them in the puzzle." Poppa's voice held tension. It was his way of telling me to go see Mundy.

"Unfortunately, I have a job to do. I want Finn to succeed, so I'm going to let him take the lead with Mundy. In the meantime, I need to go check out the condos," I reminded him and turned on Poplar Holler Road.

"Then he should be checking out Mundy before he goes on some goofy goose chase about some handicap stickers." Poppa shrugged. "Who cares if people want to park closer? It's not life or death like keeping a killer on the street."

I slid my eyes to the country road ahead of me, biting the edge of my lip. It was time to get to the bottom of the Botox scheme and get them shut down. Then I'd take on Mundy. I was the sheriff in this town and it was about time Mayor Ryland knew it.

"One crime at a time. Botox first. Mundy next." I gave a sideway glance towards Poppa.

"Now we're talking." Poppa bounced in the seat.

I wasn't going to lie. There was a renewed fire in my soul that I'd seemed to have lost over the past twenty-four hours. This was my town. I was in charge and I was going to solve this murder.

The old road ran along the Kentucky River. It was a great place to live if you wanted a relaxing view and to be away from everyone. The condominiums were a sore spot with many locals.

I was one of the people who were pro-condos. I figured it'd be filled with retired folks who'd want a pretty view and an easy rest of their lives in our little town. There'd never been any problems that I remembered and there still weren't. In fact, no one had complained.

I sure would hate to go in there guns a'blazing with no knowledge about the stuff. Nor was I sure that what they were doing was illegal. Today the view of the river was a little more skewed with the rain, but it was still pretty. The limestone walls along the river weren't like anything else. The trees along the riverbank were starting to get their leaves and the grass was starting to grow. The river was a little more churned up than normal, and once it settled the fishermen would be out in full force.

I pulled into one of the guest parking spots and grabbed my phone. Camille Shively would be the best person to ask my many questions.

"Twanda, it's Kenni. Is Camille there?" I asked Twanda Jakes, Camille's receptionist.

"Hi, Kenni. Hold on, I'll see if she's free. We've been slammed with this sudden onset of the flu." She put me on hold and replaced the silence with some rock instrumental that made my toe tap.

"Hey, Kenni. What's going on?" Camille answered.

"I'm not sure if you are aware, but there's been something called a Botox party going on in Cottonwood. I'm not real sure about the medical laws and before I shut it down, is it illegal for the everyday schmo to inject it?" I asked.

"Kenni," she gasped. "I've had so many patients coming in with muscle aches, a few with fever, soreness, runny nose, dizziness, and fatigue. I've been treating them for the flu, but if you say there's someone doing illegal Botox, they could have Botox poisoning

"Poisoning?" My heart sank down into my once tapping toe.

"Yes. Only a medically trained person or a physician who is board certified by the American Board of Plastic Surgery can administer Botox. They'll have a license to prove it too. Kenni…" The pause in her voice sent a shiver down my spine. "This is very serious. I'm going to have to call all the patients who I diagnosed with the flu."

"Can you send a list of those names to the department? I'm going to need them as witnesses after I arrest these people." I stared at the condo complex. "Are these people in danger of dying?"

"If they get enough of it in their system." I could feel the tension in her voice. "Listen, Kenni, I've got to go. Let me know if I can be of more help. I'll have Twanda get those names over to Betty."

She hung up the phone before I could even say goodbye. I looked at the complex and noticed the front of it was all the front doors of each condo. Since I'd never been there, I figured the view was all in the back since that was where the river was and the enticement to buy a condo there.

"This isn't exactly the kind of crime I wanted to help you on." I jumped when Poppa appeared.

"You just scared me to death." I held my heart. "Maybe that's your plan. Be here to take me to the great beyond."

"Don't be ridiculous. I'm obviously here to help you solve Frank Von Lee's murder and here you are doing this Botox thing." He rolled his eyes. "Hurry on in there and get them in jail so we can get to the real crime."

"This is a crime. People could die." I contemplated whether or not to call Finn in case I needed backup. I also wanted to hear his voice and get some information about why Mundy wasn't in the cell at the department.

"I'm going to go on in." He ghosted away.

I scrolled through my phone. The pad of my thumb hovered over the call button. A couple of times I went to push it but pulled back. I didn't need to check up on him. I had to give him the chance to get Mundy.

The sheer thought of seeing him sent electric energy through me. A long deep sigh escaped me. I grabbed my bag from the backseat and pulled my gun out of it along with my handcuffs. My badge was clipped on my visor and I pulled it off and clipped it on the neck of my sweatshirt. When I got out of the Jeep, I stuck my gun in the waistband of my jeans, my phone in one of my back pockets, and my cuffs in the other.

There wasn't any immediate danger so I didn't call Finn. Instead, I set an alarm to signal me not to forget about my cake class. There was no way I was missing out on how to make cute flowers.

The building appeared to have ten condos on each level. If I was right, twenty-two would be on the third floor. Instead of taking the elevator, I decided to take the stairs. Adrenaline was coursing through my veins and jogging up steps would help get that under control.

The stairs were locked off with a keypad next to them. I ran my finger down the names of the residents to see if I recognized any of them. I had nothing.

"That place is crazy in there." Poppa appeared, making me jump again.

"Can't you like ring a bell or something before you show up? I never know when you're going to appear." My words were probably a little harsh, but it was true. He was going to take me back with him if I wasn't careful.

"Ding, ding." Poppa acted like he was tapping a bell. "Is that better?"

"Thank you." I laughed. "I'm trying to figure out who's going to ring me in."

"If you are Kim from Clay's Ferry, you can press number twenty-two." He did his little jig.

"Kim from Clay's Ferry." I grinned. "You saw the client list."

"I did. Your mama's name is on the list on the day of Frank Von Lee's murder like she said. There are two recliners. Two women are injecting the stuff in these women's faces. It's really gross." Poppa made a blech face. "Whaddya say we go and arrest these women so we can get on with the real investigation?"

I dragged my finger down the list of numbers on the intercom and pushed twenty-two.

"Yes," the woman answered through the intercom.

"Kim from Clay's Ferry," I said and turned to Poppa, who was no longer there.

"Come up." The sound of a buzz followed.

I grabbed the door handle and jerked it open. On the way up the two flights, I took two steps at a time. It was the second condo down the hall. I put my ear to the door before I knocked to try and hear if anything was going on. According to Poppa, there were two women in there getting poked and prodded.

"Ding, ding!" Poppa was taking it a little too far now.

I still jumped. "Seriously?"

"I ding, I don't ding. Which is it?" he asked.

"What's going on in there?" I asked in a hushed whisper. I took the clipped badge off my shirt and stuck it on the waistband of my jeans next to my gun. They probably wouldn't be so willing to let me in with a badge.

"From what I gather, the scheme is two women. In the back-right room, there is a lamination machine, a printer, and a computer. They're making the handicap tags in there. They told one of the women that's getting her lips all plumped up that since she's had surgery she can upgrade to the handicap package for another hundred dollars," he said.

"Hundred dollars?" I asked in shock.

"Kim from Clay's Ferry?" The woman jerked the door open and there I was with my mouth hanging open. She jerked her head out the door and looked both ways. "Who were you talking to?"

"Myself." I faked a smile. "I was talking myself into this."

"You need your elevens done bad," she snarled. "I thought you said you wanted your crow's feet, but I think you need a good dose in between them eyes." Her eyes darted around my face. "Or we can do both. It's gonna cost you."

"Can I come in?" I asked.

She dragged the door open and I stepped inside. It was exactly how Poppa had described it. The entire condo was empty except for two chairs and a table. On the table there were some glass bottles, needles, and some rubbing alcohol. There was nothing legal about this. The two women in the chairs were leaned back.

"You're a little early, so you can just stand over there and enjoy the view." She pointed to the windows.

There was an amazing view of both sides of the river. It was still spitting rain and cloudy.

"I'm sorry." I turned around. The woman was bent over the client and using a magnifying glass attached to the chair to get a close-up view of the wrinkles. "Do you have a restroom?"

"Down the hall." She didn't look up. Neither of them did.

I walked down the hall and looked over my shoulder to see if they were watching me. They weren't. The room that Poppa said was the room where they made the handicap hangers was behind a closed door. I walked down the hall to where the bathroom was and slipped my hand around to the door handle. I pushed in the lock and pulled it closed just in case they came looking for me.

I tiptoed back to the shut door where the printing was happening and slowly turned the handle so they wouldn't hear me. After I pushed it open, I put my hand on the other side of the door and slowly turned the knob. It was never a good thing to be caught snooping around. The door gave a slight swoosh when I closed it.

My hand dragged up the wall to find the light switch, exposing the shenanigans. It was exactly what Poppa had said. I took my phone out of my pocket and snapped several photos of all the evidence I was going to need to lock these crazy people up. It already set up to print when I shook the mouse on the mousepad to wake up the sleeping computer. There were already a few tags printed and ready to go. There was a cashbox next to the printer. I opened it and it was filled with twenties and fives. I could hear Myrna now saying how it was twenty-five dollars. This was an all-cash scheme from what I could see. Perfect for not being able to trace it back to them and easy to keep the scheme going from city to city.

After I'd taken enough photos, I scrolled through my contacts to find Danny's number. With my hand over the microphone, when he answered, I said, "Hey, Danny. It's Kenni again. I'm sorry to bug you, but can you tell me who owns number twenty-two in your condo complex?"

"You know what, Kenni, I don't know any of the people who bought condos, but I can tell you that number twenty-two was never purchased, along with number eight. Why? Are you in the market? I can probably give our good sheriff a deal." He was always doing business.

"No one owns it?" I asked.

"No wonder they are going unnoticed." Poppa appeared. "Oh, ding." He laughed.

I glared.

"Thanks, Danny. I'm sorry about earlier. I'm just narrowing things down." I hung up the phone and looked at Poppa. "They are illegally squatting here and doing Botox, plus these." I pointed to the tags.

"Now you go get them." Poppa marched to the door.

"You're right, but first I need to call Betty so she'll be on the ready in case I need some backup." I scrolled down to the dispatch and pushed the call button. I quickly explained to Betty what I was doing and that I'd probably be bringing in two women to stick in the jail, so I'd need her to make a call to the sheriff in Clay's Ferry to let them know to expect a couple of transfers. They had a bigger jail that was equipped for more than one occupant.

I didn't bother trying to be quiet on my way back down the hall. I pulled my badge off my waistband and clipped it back on the neck of my sweatshirt.

"All right. Stop what you're doing." I pulled up my sweatshirt to expose my gun. "You two are under arrest for illegally living here. That's called squatting. Not to mention the illegal making of handicap tags and selling illegal Botox."

"Illegal Botox?" Polly Parker, of all people, flung up from one of the chairs. Her mother was in the other.

Polly's blonde hair was tugged up in a top knot on top of her head. Her face was pale and splotchy, not the normal flawless-looking skin I was used to. Goes to show you what a little makeup could do.

"Step aside, you two." I gestured to the women. "Polly, Mrs. Parker, you stay where you are."

The women were very cooperative. Neither of them said a word to me or each other as I cuffed them wrist to wrist and read them their rights. If I had two sets of cuffs, I'd have cuffed them separately.

"Kenni," Mrs. Parker's southern drawl was a lot deeper than normal, "we wouldn't want it to get out that we were here doing anything illegal. If you know what I mean."

Yeah. I knew what she meant. She knew it was illegal and she didn't want anyone to know that she was an active participant and wanted me to keep my mouth shut.

"Uh-huh," Polly grunted. I wasn't sure, but I don't think she could speak. Her lips were so big and red that her mouth finally matched her horse teeth. Unfortunately, her lips took up her petite face.

"We were getting a little touch up for the engagement photos." Mrs. Parker tried to squint her eyes a couple of times, but when nothing moved she gave up offering a sweet southern bless-your-heart smile that I knew all too well.

"You were here under illegal pretenses, and I just can't think you thought this was all right." I motioned at the needles. "Dr. Shively has several patients that have come down with flu symptoms. When a bad batch of Botox is administered, these symptoms pop up. Not to mention their illegal shenanigans with the pink handicap tags."

"Honey," Mrs. Parker walked over to the women, "how long until I can move my eyes?"

"Mrs. Parker, please make an appointment to go see Dr. Shively and she can give you and Polly all the details." I wouldn't let her speak to the women. "If you and Polly don't mind coming down to the station to give a statement, I'd be mighty grateful."

"Oh, we can't do that, right, Mama?" Polly muttered under her puffy, fluffy lips.

"Right. I told you that we don't want to be associated." Mrs. Parker tugged on Polly. "Let's go."

"I'm sorry, I'm going to have to insist that you come to the department to give a statement." I tried to be nice the first time. They just weren't getting it.

"And what if we don't?" Mrs. Parker pulled her shoulders back. Her eyelids tried to move up and down, but she gave up.

"Then y'all will be sitting in the back of Cowboy's Catfish with these two." The timer on my phone chirped that I had one hour until I had to leave for my cake class. "What's it going to be?"

"If I give a very generous donation to your next campaign, is there any way you can at least not use our names?" she asked.

"I'll not use your names when Edna Easterly comes calling," I agreed.

"Wonderful. We will come down later after we put some frozen peas on our faces and see Dr. Shively." Mrs. Parker tilted her head to the door, signaling for Polly to follow.

"All right, you two, let's go," I instructed them as I dialed in dispatch. "Betty, it's Kenni. I'm bringing in the two women. Call Danny Shane and let him know that he can't touch or even show condo number twenty-two. It's officially a crime scene. Call the Clay's Ferry sheriff and let him know that we've got two transports."

The women cursed and fussed all the way to the Jeep. I uncuffed them, draped the cuffs around the door handle, and cuffed them again. This way I could go grab the evidence that was there. I grabbed my bag that had all the evidence bags and headed back inside. Going up and down the stairs to and from the Jeep was great exercise. I carried the copy machine, all the Botox stuff, and all the handicap tags and put them in the back of the Jeep. After I felt like I'd taken enough photos and all the evidence there was, I decided it was time to take them to jail.

I stuck them in the back and didn't bother turning on the siren. The less attention drawn on me, the better. This way I still had just enough time to get to my class. Later I'd go back to the department after they were transported and write my report, not to mention update Mama's timeline that Poppa wanted me to do so badly.

"I bet your mama ratted on us." One of the women cursed at me from the backseat.

"Actually she didn't." I looked in the rearview mirror at her. "This whole thing would've been over by now if she had."

"So they remember her?" Poppa appeared next to me in the front seat. He was turned around facing the women. "Ask them."

"You do remember my mama then?" I asked.

"What's in it for us if we talk to you?" the other one asked in a curious tone.

"If you cooperate, then I have the authority to ask the judge to go easy on you." It was true.

I played it nonchalant, careful not to lay out all my cards.

"Yeah. I remember her." The first one chimed in but not without getting a hard elbow to her ribs from the other woman. "What? I don't want to go to jail forever."

The Jeep sped down Poplar Holler Road and when I got to the stop sign that led me back into town, I put the gear in park and turned around in my seat.

"Tell me what you know." I looked directly at the one who was ready to talk.

"She came in two days in a row. It's hard to forget someone when they come like that." She smiled. "It wasn't really that that caught my attention because Melanie here was her injector." She nodded toward the other woman. "Anyways, she was upset and she mentioned between her tears that her daughter was the sheriff. Anything doing with the law freaks us out." She gave me a hard look. "That's when I spoke up and told her I'd refund her handicap fee that she paid for the first time she was here if she didn't say anything about her visit to our little party."

"She didn't either. What time was it when she came in the second day?" I can't believe Mama wanted a handicap tag so badly.

"She came around suppertime." She held her free hand in the air and gave the so-so gesture by waving it side to side. "Six-ish."

"My mama was in a bit of a pickle. She's been placed at a homicide scene. Though she's not the number one suspect anymore, it's good to know her whereabouts in case her timeline is questioned." I turned back around and put the gearshift into drive. "Are you willing to go on record with this information?"

"Only if you can help us," Melanie chimed in.

"I'm good for my word." There was a bit of relief that now I had a true timeline and two witnesses for Mama. I only wanted to make sure all my T's were crossed and I's were dotted when it came to Frank and Mama.

"This is good." Poppa rubbed his hands together and bounced a little in his seat. "I'm glad you didn't listen to this old coot." His eyes dipped. "I know I'm here to guide you. I'm sorry for overstepping my boundaries."

Oh, how I wished I could hug a ghost.

CHAPTER TWENTY-FIVE

The Clay's Ferry sheriff's deputy was already at the office by the time I got the two women down there. The deputy waited while I fingerprinted them and took down all their information. I let them know about the process and how they'd be taken to court in the morning for their full charges. They'd have to wait to make their one phone call until they got to Clay's Ferry. I assured them I'd let the judge know about their cooperation, and I was a woman of my word. Even though I had the ledger with Mama's name, I still wanted a written statement. They wrote them while I finished up the transfer paperwork and gave it to the Clay's Ferry deputy.

"Ya know," Melanie said to me before the deputy took them away, "you really should think about getting those elevens filled in." She pointed to the creases between my eyes.

I motioned for the deputy to take them. Betty sat there taking it all in. It was prime gossip for her and she got a front-row seat to all of it.

"Elevens?" Betty asked.

"Don't ask." I rolled my eyes but couldn't help dragging the pad of my finger down the creases. "Give Edna Easterly a call and let her know about this case. It's a scoop she can put in the Chronicle. Tell her that I'll send her the police report tonight." I grabbed the laptop off of my desk. If there was some downtime at the cake class like I'd had at the last class, I'd quickly jot down some of the notes about the case.

On the forty-five minute drive to Lexington, I figured I'd better get in touch with Finn.

"Hey there," he answered.

"You aren't going to believe what just went down." It was strange that he was working one investigation while I was doing another. I knew that his disappointment in my lack of judgement, though it was just temporary, hurt me personally.

This was always my fear in dating him. I had to keep the work stuff separate from the personal stuff. His feelings were just work stuff and I needed to get a little thicker skin in this department of my life. I would apologize to Finn and make it right when I saw him. But for now, I needed to catch him up on the fake handicap investigation.

"Tell me."

"I busted the fake handicap sticker ring. It was two women operating from the condos out on Poplar Holler. They were squatting in a condo there doing illegal tags and Botox." I never would've believed this type of thing would ever go on in Cottonwood.

"Botox?" he asked.

"Yep. That's what Mama had done to her face. Remember when we saw her at Ben's the morning of Frank's death?" I asked.

"Oh man. You did point it out that she looked different," he said.

"That's not all." I took a deep breath. "That's how she got the black eye. She was having a reaction."

"That's so weird the handicap scheme was tied in with that. Toots will be happy that all her handicap parking spaces in front of Dixon's will be open," he joked. "I'm glad they finished out your mama's timeline, but you know that she's not our number-one suspect anymore so you can stop proving it."

"Then we probably should meet up and talk about it."

"How about we get together tonight for dinner at the department and go over things?" His word were music to my ears.

"That sounds so good. Let's meet at the department around seven because I've got to finish a report about those illegal handicap tags."

"Are you sure?" he asked.

"I'm positive. I want you to fill me in on how Frank's case is going," I said.

"Mundy wasn't home when I went over there. I figured I'd hit it again before the end of the day," he said.

We exchanged a few more back and forth comments before we hung up.

The drive to Lexington wasn't so bad after that. I was looking forward to learning how to make flowers for my cake and seeing Finn. It was nice to get a parking spot right in front of Le Fork.

The instructor was putting everyone's covered cakes in front of them. I'd had no idea that it helped to decorate them cold from the fridge. It was so interesting and I'm sure that's why I enjoyed the class. I loved to learn and it also seemed to help me relax, which was something I really needed.

After I peeled off the cling wrap, I noticed my poor cakes had a peak at the top and everyone else had perfectly flat and even cakes. I draped the wrap back over so I didn't have to look at it.

"Today we are going to learn to properly ice a cake by making your very own buttercream icing. We are going to do a stiffening recipe and then we are going to thin it down so it spreads a little easier." The instructor smiled at everyone.

There were ingredients in little bowls at my station. She went through what was in each little bowl. There was shortening, butter flavoring, water, milk, cane sugar, meringue powder (whatever that was), and salt. She instructed us to add the ingredients using a hand mixer, which proved to be a little difficult for me.

"Ding, ding!" Poppa smacked his leg and cackled. "You can handle a gun perfectly but not a mixer?" He bent over in laughter. "You don't take after your mama."

Then a light bulb went off in my head. Was I trying so hard to be accepted by Mama? Or having something that both of us could do together? Everyone knew she wasn't happy with my career choice, and as the years ticked by she wasn't getting any better about it. Just crazier.

I ignored Poppa and firmly grabbed the mixture, determined to get this right. The instructor had already moved on to what she referred to as a cake leveler. Apparently, it was supposed to even out the top of my lopsided cake. I basically used the tool to saw the peak of my cakes off, making them level.

I had no idea so much went into baking a cake. I had a newfound respect for bakers.

The instructor was going so fast. When I looked around, it was only me that was going slow. Everyone else had already gotten an icing bag and attached a tip with a coupler. The only one left for me to pick was the one with the big round hole. We had to make a ring of icing around the top of the cake and fill in the middle with fruit of our choice. Since it was my first cake, I decided to give it to Mama and added strawberries in the middle because they was her favorite.

I put one cake on top of the other and did the same thing, making it a two-layer strawberry cake. Next was the icing part. She asked us to be very generous with the buttercream with her technique of covering the entire cake using the flat end of the spatula to smooth it out. She gave us a short potty break to let our icing set. Some people chose to put a second coat of icing on, but I didn't. She showed us how to use the edge of a knife to go around the sides of the cake to make the ridge pattern. We used another bag of tinted icing to make an icing ring around the cake.

"That's all for today." The instructor untied her apron and put it aside.

"I thought we were learning to do flowers?" I asked.

"That's a little too in depth for a group class, but if you'd like a private lesson, I'm more than happy to do that." She nodded. "You know how to bake and ice your cake now so you can do those at home and come back with them for a lesson in flower making."

"I can do that." It was decided. I'd give Mama this cake and to surprise Finn, I'd give him the one with the flowers. "Yes. I'll do that."

"I'm free in a couple of days," she noted, looking at her calendar that was lying on her workstation. "About the same time?"

"Sure." This made me happy. I knew Mama was not the killer and Finn was no longer disappointed in me.

Life would be perfect after I found Mundy and arrested him for the murder of Frank Von Lee.

CHAPTER TWENTY-SIX

A couple of hours later, I'd dropped off my cake to my parents. They weren't home so I left it there with a note. They were probably out taking a drive or heading out of town for supper. Mama was still laying low and I couldn't wait to get her off the hook.

Duke had been home all day, though Mrs. Brown was letting him out. I decided to pick him up and take him to the department with me. We parked in front of Cowboy's Catfish. The home-cooked fried food smelled good and I was starving.

Bartleby Fry was slinging burgers in the back while talking to the customers through the pass-through. Duke headed straight to the kitchen because he knew Bartleby was always good for a treat. Not just any treat, a real piece of meat, which I rarely gave him at home.

"To what do I owe the pleasure of a front door visit?" Bartleby asked after I'd pushed through the swinging kitchen door.

"I want two fried catfish platters to go," I said, looking at the plated food on the pass-through window, trying not to let the drool run out of my mouth. "Extra tartar sauce and fries, please."

"You got it." He flipped a piece of something to Duke. "I'll bring it over. Coffee or Diet Coke?"

"Both." I winked and headed to the door that was between the restaurant and the department. Duke wasn't going to budge and I knew Bartleby would bring him over with my food.

Betty had left for the day. I flipped on the lights and immediately started to fill out the paperwork on the Botox arrest. My photos from my phone had already synched to the Google photo application we'd started using at the department. Finn had suggested all sorts of new technology that was truly helpful. I attached the photos to the report along with a scanned copy of their statement about Mama. Before I hit send, I read the report carefully.

The clock on the wall told me it was almost time for Finn to meet me here.

"Yep. He'll be here in a minute, so get up and start that timeline." Poppa stood next to the dry-erase board.

"I do want to get some things laid out before he gets here." I looked back at the door of Cowboy's when I could smell the fish frying. It wouldn't be long until he brought the food over.

I hit send on the document to the judge along with the report on the Botox case. I got up and grabbed the black dry-erase marker. I dragged the wet tip of the marker horizontally across the board. I completely filled in Mama's timeline where there were holes. Her whereabouts were all accounted for.

"Okay." Poppa paced back and forth. "Now make a line for Mundy." He pointed. "We know he was at Ben's in the morning when you went with Finn."

I began to fill out Mundy's timeline and put bullet points of his history and why he was our number one suspect.

"Malina saw Mundy at the hotel." I tapped the felt of the marker on the board.

"Don't forget about Danny Shane delivering milk to Mundy at the hotel around five," Poppa reminded me.

"I almost forgot about that!" I snapped my fingers and wrote that down. "What was he doing between five thirty and seven?"

"Forgot about what?" Finn stood at the door of the department with Duke. "Who are you talking to?" he questioned.

"Myself." I reddened. Poppa disappeared. I snapped the lid back on the marker and walked over to Finn. "Duke." My trusty bloodhound ran over, shoving his nose in my pocket where he thought I had a treat.

"Here boy." Finn grabbed a treat off the desk and flipped it towards Duke.

At first I was a little timid about how to approach Finn since there'd been so much tension between us about even the thought of hiding evidence. I put all of that aside and walked over to him. He stared at me the entire time and our eyes never looked away.

"I stopped by the house to see how Riley was doing." He smiled.

"And?" I teased.

"He was doing great." He reached out for my hands. "The new addition is coming along."

"Be sure that his permit is displayed in the window because the Beautification Committee love to drive around and nab people." I'd completely forgotten to tell him about that.

"What do they do?" He laughed.

"It's the law to have a permit, but they get to keep some of the fine the judge will give the contractor. Their part of the fine goes into the committee and they use it to do projects, so they're always on the lookout. They get money anyway they can," I told him.

Those members were ruthless. Once they dinged me for the new fence I'd put up for Duke.

"I missed you today," I whispered and curled up on my tippy toes.

We hugged each other and melted into a warm kiss. The fluttering started in my throat and didn't stop until it reached my toenails.

"I'm sorry I ever had you doubt my moral compass. I'd never ever hold evidence in a case. Even involving my mama." Even though we'd already gotten past it last night, I felt like I needed to say it one last time.

"You shouldn't be sorry. I knew you'd never do anything to jeopardize your career or your mother. It was a knee-jerk reaction on my part." He didn't let me protest. He simply pulled me tighter and kissed me harder.

"Ahem." Bartleby cleared his throat. "Don't mind me. I'm just delivering the best damn fried fish in the state."

I waved my hand in the air but didn't dare pull away from Finn. Bartleby walking in on us wasn't that big of a deal, but a ninety-pound bloodhound was hard to ignore when he pushed his way in between us.

"Are you feeling left out, buddy?" Finn laughed and looked down.

Duke gave a low playful groan followed up by a big yawn. Happy he'd come between us, he sauntered over to his big pillow bed and laid down.

"I'm starving." I rubbed my hands together. "And that food smells so good."

Bartleby had put the two Styrofoam containers on my desk along with two cups of coffee and two fountain drink Diet Cokes.

"Me too." Finn's hand drew down my back. He guided me over to the food.

It was dead silent when we opened the containers and eyed the delicious-looking food. We each took one and dug in.

"I see you've been working on a timeline." Finn smiled. "You thought it was a stupid idea at first."

"I never thought it was stupid. I thought it was a waste of time. But as you can see, I filled in Mama's." My brows rose. "I started Mundy's and was getting ready to start one for Ben."

"I thought you were staying off the case," he reminded me.

"I had to clear Mama. But I can still lend a hand and my two cents. I feel like I need to get in touch with Mundy in order to clear Ben's name." I gnawed on the end of the straw from the Diet Coke and waited for Finn's response.

"Yeah." He took a drink of his Coke. "That thought about Ben crossed my mind only because his business has been so good since all of this. Plus I went down to the bank and found out that they were about to call in his loan because he's not been able to pay full rent." Finn walked over to the white board. He popped the hush puppy in his mouth before he picked up a dry erase marker and wrote Ben's name under the suspect list.

When he swiped a line across Mama's name, it took everything in me not to jump for joy. Instead, I stuffed my face with a big piece of fish dipped in the homemade tater sauce. I chewed with happiness.

"I hate to think that Ben could do something like that, but you have to think about it." Finn started his spiel, "Ben had hired Danny Shane for the construction. When I went to see Danny, he said that Ben fired him after he told Ben that the price was more than he'd thought and Ben was going to have to come up with the extra money before he could finish the job."

Danny had left that part out when I'd gone to see him and he told me was doing the work for free.

"I'm thinking Ben got in the oh-no-what-am-I-going-to-do mode. He got a little crazy and his fuse was short, so when Mundy refused to cook the way Ben wanted him to, he fired him." Finn seemed a little stuck.

I helped him get more stuck.

"Why would Ben kill Frank? That's where I'm stumped." I eyed the board.

"Or we can find Mundy and see what he has to say." Finn cocked a brow. "I went by there again. I wonder if he's on the lam."

"Mundy would have more of a motive than Ben. It would make sense if he thought we were getting hot on his trail, or if he saw the headlines in the Chronicle where Mayor Ryland said we had more than one suspect." I took the marker from Finn and I wrote as I talked. "According to Guy from the Frank's class, Mundy's career almost never happened because he and Frank got into a fight. Mundy got arrested. There's an arrest record. Just by chance Mundy happened to call Ben for a job right in time for Frank's visit to the diner?"

"Very interesting." Finn stepped back and took a long look at the board. "I'll go to Le Fork in the morning and question them."

"Sure, but I've been there and talked to the people who worked there. Same thing. Mundy was a jerk and no one liked him." I walked over to my computer and pulled up a new note to put in Frank's case about the information Jolee had snuck out of Mundy's file, leaving the part out about how I'd gotten the info.

CHAPTER TWENTY-SEVEN

Even with Finn and me spending more time together, I didn't sleep any better. Ben was on my mind and I was sad that he could possibly have killed Frank.

With thoughts of him and trying to figure out a true motive other than money, I tossed and turned all night with images of kissing Finn. We didn't end up leaving the office until well past midnight. It was so cute how he followed me home, even though he had to go that way to go home too. He took it a step further and parked in front of my house, waiting for me to make it inside. Such a southern boyfriend thing to do. He was really fitting in well here.

I flipped over and looked at the clock, turning off my alarm before it even went off. Duke lifted his head as though he was anticipating my next move. He'd even gotten tired of my antsy bed rolling and laid on the floor most of the night. He jumped up when I peeled back the covers.

"Let's go outside." I patted his head and we headed down the hall.

When I let him out, the warmer temperature swooshed in the door even though it was still dark out. I locked the door behind him, flicked on the coffee maker, and padded down the hall to grab my shower.

He'd be out there sniffing around, giving me enough time to get ready.

Five minutes later, I'd showered and thrown on my sheriff's uniform.

Today I opted for a short-sleeved button-up shirt instead of the tee. It was a hair-pulled-up-in-a-ponytail morning. With a swipe of lip gloss and my walkie-talkie strapped on my shoulder, I was ready.

"Betty," I called across the walkie-talkie when I made my way back down the hall into the kitchen.

"Hey, Sheriff. What ya been doing this morning?" Betty asked in an upbeat voice.

The aroma from the coffee smelled so good. I poured a cup and leaned against the counter, staring out into my kitchen. Poppa wasn't here.

"I'm just getting ready to make my rounds." My thoughts turned to Finn. "Do you know where Finn is? I need to talk to him about the Frank Von Lee case." I let go of the button. The entire thing about me knowing where Mundy lived and me not telling him how was weighing on me. That was just another thing I shouldn't keep from him.

"He's not been here yet either. It looks like he's been doing some doodlin' on that white board though." Betty clicked. "And it looks like your mama is off the hook."

"Actually..." I felt flushed. "We started working together again."

Duke scratched the door. I pushed off of the countertop and walked over to let him in. I noticed Mrs. Brown's back floodlight from her porch was already on. Duke walked in, licking his lips.

"Did Mrs. Brown throw you a treat?" I asked the ornery dog.

"Huh?" Betty asked.

"Nothing." My eyes drew up to the clock. "You haven't seen Finn?" I asked again just for good measure because he said that he was going to go to the office first thing and officially call the Mayor to put me back on as lead.

He had to do that to get me officially back on the case. Really it only involved a detailed list of why Mama was no longer a suspect. We agreed that both of us together solving the murder was better than one especially now that we had the Botox and handicap sticker case solved.

"Now that I'm looking around, he might've been here." I could hear her shuffling some papers in the background. "There are a bunch of papers on his desk from the lab."

"Papers?" I asked. "What kind of papers?"

"Oh." Betty's voice escalated. "It's from the lab. And Mundy's name is on it."

"Betty." I grabbed my keys and holster. "I'll be right there."

Duke rushed to the door. He knew the drill. When I grabbed my holster, we were leaving.

"Not this morning, buddy." I bent down and rubbed his head before I gave him a scoop of his kibble, plus a little extra. "Mrs. Brown will let you out."

His ears drew back and his eyes drooped even more than usual. He sat down on his hind legs, pouting.

"You be good. If things go well, this case will be over soon." I tried not to look at him. Whenever he looked like that, it made me feel bad.

The sun was just popping up over the rooves on Free Row. The gate was still a little damp from the dew. Birds were already chirping and playing around. It was a warm welcome that spring was here and the morning chill would soon be replaced by warmer temperatures.

"Mrs. Brown?" I called when I opened the Wagoneer door. She was watching from somewhere over there.

"Morning, Kenni," her voice trilled. "I'm feeding the birds."

"That's so nice of you." I tried to hide my smile. She was so nosy. "I don't see you."

She popped up out of the bush from the corner of her house closest to mine.

"Here I am." Curlers tight around her head, her fist gripped the top of her housecoat.

"You're up awfully early." I glanced over the roof of the Jeep toward Finn's house. His Dodge Charger wasn't there, but it looked like Riley was already there working.

"I was just keeping an eye on the neighborhood." She fiddled with her fingers. "You know, now that you and Finn are living here, there's not much going on. You've cleaned up Free Row."

"Thanks, Mrs. Brown. Do you mind…" I started to say.

"I don't mind having Duke at all. He's good company to me." She finished my sentence. I wasn't sure if that was good or bad. Did I really have her watch him so much that she expected it?

It was still early enough that there was no traffic and all the stoplights were green. It took me a total of five minutes to get to downtown. I passed Cowboy's Catfish and drove up the street to Ben's. Briefly I stopped in front of his diner. There was a faint light coming from the back.

I jerked the Jeep into a spot on the opposite side of street and parked. There was no hesitation. I got out of the Wagoneer and ran across the street. Ben peeked his head out of the kitchen when he heard me knocking. A big smile on his face. Not that of a killer, I thought and smiled back.

"To what do I owe this pleasure?" he asked after he unlocked the door and let me in.

"Coffee." It was all he needed to hear before he waved me back. "I'd love a cup, but this is more of an official stop." Finn should've been here, but I was good at thinking on my toes. I needed to feel Ben out before I got my day started.

"Sure. What can I answer for you?" he asked, not a thought in his head that this official visit had to do with him.

He pointed me to the coffee maker on the kitchen counter as he grabbed a couple of oven mitts and took out some golden brown biscuits.

"Why didn't you tell me about your financial issues?" I busied myself with pouring the coffee and adding a little creamer.

"Here you go." He put a biscuit on the counter next to me. "I'll take a cup."

I handed him mine and looked at him. He gave a flat smile. He lifted the cup to his mouth and took a sip. I got another cup and took the plate with the biscuit and walked over to the preparation island and sat down on the stool.

"You're not my business partner." He leaned back more and crossed his ankles. "It's not something I'm proud of. The rent is going up and I want to purchase the building from the Shane Company, but Danny Shane won't sell."

"Danny Shane owns the building?" Even though I was sheriff, I had no idea who owned what around here. "I assumed you owned it."

"No. So when I told him I needed the repairs done for the show, he was all too willing to do the stuff for free until he got into it and saw that it needed a whole lot more. That's when he told me I had to pay for the work.

There's no way I could afford his price and that's when I hired Riley. He's half the price." He shook his head. "When I confronted Danny about it, he let it slip that he wanted me out to put another shop in town."

"I went to visit Danny Shane and he did say that he was doing the work for free, but he failed to mention he is the landlord or that he wanted you out." That raised suspicion, though not for the murder. He had an alibi. "By the looks of all the lines and the Chronicle, your business has picked up."

"Wait," he stopped me. "Do you think I had anything to do with Frank Von Lee's murder?" His brows furrowed.

"I just have to cross all the T's and dot the I's." I could see by the look on his face that he was hurt and mad. "When I heard you were in a financial bind, it only fit since Frank's reviews could either make or break a place. Bad press like Frank dying can be good press, and your business has picked up."

"Not enough to buy the building, Kenni." He huffed through his nose. "I honestly can't believe that you'd even think I could do something like that. Besides, if anyone has a perfect reason, it's Mundy."

"You mean the fact that Frank was his teacher?" I asked.

"You know about that?" he asked.

"I looked into Mundy and his background. He has the perfect motive. I'm going to head on over to his place this morning and question him." I looked down at the pat of butter that'd melted into a puddle on top of my biscuit.

"You better get a jump on it. He's an early riser and doesn't get home until late." Ben grabbed a Styrofoam cup from the counter and poured a cup of coffee.

"I'm sorry, Ben. It's just that I have to do my job and..." I stood up and picked up the biscuit.

"No need to apologize. I understand. I've got to figure out a way to keep this diner open. I can't rely on famous people dying to keep that door open." He held the cup out in front of him. "Even though Mundy is a jerk and hotheaded, I don't see him as a killer."

"People kill people out of the heat of passion. Almost lose their minds." I took the coffee and offered a grateful smile. I was so glad Ben wasn't sore at me. A lifelong friendship wasn't one to let go of and I was fortunate to have a great friend in him.

"The Culinary Channel is going to do a life story on Frank and they are going to come and do an interview."

"That's great. Maybe that'll bring in business," I said before I exited the kitchen.

"Kenni," he called for me through the pass-through window. "I thought you were off the case. You aren't doing something you shouldn't, are you?"

"Nope." I shook my head. "Mama has a solid alibi and now that she's no longer a suspect, there's no reason I can't continue."

"Good deal." He smiled and nodded before I left.

There was no time to go to the office if Mundy was an early riser. I had to take the opportunity while I felt like I had it. According to the file, Mundy lived on the south side of Lexington, not too far from Le Fork and the shopping strip.

The sunny morning had turned back to grey. It was typical Kentucky spring weather. You never knew what mood Mother Nature was going to be in. A few drops of rain splattered on the windshield. I turned on the wipers.

The entire forty-five-minute drive I rehearsed the typical questions I was going to ask him. I'd even checked the batteries in my tape recorder so I could get the full interview on it. My plan was to be all friendly and tell him I needed him to answer some questions. Maybe throw in the cake-baking class I've been taking from Le Fork and establish a little trust between us.

The apartment complex wasn't the nicest I'd seen in Lexington. The buildings were brown and dull. Mundy lived in building five, apartment nine. There were a couple of unread papers on the doorstep. I gave a hard couple of knocks and backed up. There wasn't anyone around and he didn't answer.

Had he skipped town? I knocked again. The papers certainly appeared to show he'd not been here a couple of days. I knocked again, this time harder and a few more raps.

This time the door cracked open. I took the flashlight from my holster and used the butt to push the door open.

"Mundy?" I called into the apartment. "Mundy?" I asked again, a little louder as I stepped inside.

There wasn't any sort of movement or sound coming from within. I put the flashlight back in the holster and exchanged it for my gun. I held my gun out in front of me just in case he was in there and going to pounce on me.

"Sheriff's department!" I yelled and moved swiftly through the rooms, securing them one by one. There was a kitchen that overlooked a small family room and a bathroom. "Mundy!"

It wasn't like I had jurisdiction over the Fayette county area and he didn't have to give up, but still, words had power. I turned my back toward the family room with my gun pointed down the hall. There were two doors, one on each side.

"Come out, Mundy! I'm here to talk to you about Frank Von Lee's murder!" I swung open the first door down the hallway on the right with the toe of my cowboy boot. My eyes darted around the bedroom before they focused on a pair of feet sticking out from the far side of the bed.

I stuck my gun in my holster on my way over to the body.

"Mundy," I gasped. There was a gun in his limp hand and a bullet wound in his head, or what was left of it. By the looks of it, he'd sat next to his bed and shot himself. There was brain matter splattered everywhere on the ground.

"Yeah. I guess we have our killer." Poppa ghosted next to me.

CHAPTER TWENTY-EIGHT

"Why on earth did you come up here without telling me?" Finn asked, pulling me aside to let the Fayette County sheriff's department do their job.

"I was coming to the office because Betty told me that the evidence from the lab had come in, but I was waylaid by seeing Ben at his diner. I took the opportunity to go in there and question him. He obviously didn't kill Frank. He confirmed that he knew Mundy and Mundy did have the motive. He also told me that Mundy was an early riser so I took the opportunity." My stomach dropped as the coroner took Mundy's body out of the apartment.

I bowed my head and said a silent prayer for him as he went to the great beyond as they passed me.

"I really wished you'd called me." Finn studied me thoughtfully.

"Well, I sorta went ahead and took the lead back," I said and walked out of the apartment to grab my bag.

"You knew more about Mundy than you let on." His eyes clung to mine.

"You know how I said I questioned the employees at Le Fork?" I asked, but didn't wait for his response. "I've been taking this cake-baking class there." I waved my hand. "Actually, I didn't want to take a class, but I had to distract the store so Jolee could sneak back into the office to get a look at Mundy's file."

"Jolee?" He gasped. "You've dragged her into this?"

"I had to clear my mama." I shot him a look. "I couldn't ask you to do it and we certainly had no time to get a warrant from the Fayette County judge. It was easier for me to sign up for a class and have her look."

"How did she know how to find things?" He wasn't going to let it go. It was the cop in him.

We stalked to the Jeep. I opened the door and pulled my bag out.

I couldn't tell him that my ghost grandfather had gone in and done the work for me and I told Jolee exactly where to look.

"I don't know. She's good at snooping, I guess." I shrugged and headed back inside of the apartment.

"Sheriff," the officer called for me. "We found a note." He held out a piece of paper to me. He had on a glove and handed me one to put on.

I put it on and took the note. I quickly read through it. Mundy had admitted to killing Frank Von Lee because Frank had ruined his career from the beginning. He'd even gone into detail on how much he liked Ben and knew Ben was in financial trouble. He knew Frank was going to try to ruin Ben because that was how Frank was. His life's mission to end Frank Von Lee's career had happened and he no longer wanted to feel the sadness Frank had given him, so he decided to end his life.

"I guess we have our killer." I handed the letter to Finn and let him see it.

"I guess we do." He stared at it for a few minutes before he handed it back to the officer.

"Be sure to get all the paperwork to us." I pulled a business card out of my pocket and handed it to the officer before Finn and I left.

"I'm going to go finish up the paperwork at the department." Finn stood next to his Charger. "Now what?

"I think I'll take the day off since you said you were going to finish up the paperwork." It wasn't a bad suggestion, though I had other plans for him that he didn't need to know about yet. "Why don't you come over for supper?"

"Sounds good." He smiled, bending down to give me a kiss. "I can bring over some good Chicago pizza. My sister sent me some." He kissed me again.

The sound of a click drew us apart. Before I could spot Edna Easterly, I saw the familiar feather disappear through the door of Mundy's apartment but quickly fluttered back out when one of the officers ushered her out. The feather darted back and forth as she tried to explain why she should be there.

"Edna Easterly must live by that police scanner," Finn half joked. "I'll see you tonight. Good job, even though you probably could've used some backup."

"You know that I'm used to doing things on my own. But I'll get better." It was true. I still wasn't used to having to call Finn for backup when it was still so new working together.

I let out a small sigh of relief on my way back into town. A sadness draped over me because I'd not seen Poppa again and I knew that he only showed up during the investigation process of a murder or crime. I'd wished I'd known I was going to find Mundy because I'd have told Poppa goodbye until next time.

I headed to the south side of Cottonwood to Dixon's. I was going to make Finn a cake for tonight. It wasn't going to be refrigerated overnight, but I still had time to let it cool. The excitement of baking a cake coursed through me and I picked up all the stuff I needed.

Too bad Toots wasn't working. I was going to tell her that the murder had been solved and telling her meant the word would get around fast.

The sun suddenly came out as I was leaving. My heart lifted and I held the Dixon's paper bag close to me. I couldn't help but smile thinking that Poppa might've had a hand in the sudden shift of weather. At least that made me feel better about not being able to say goodbye to him.

CHAPTER TWENTY-NINE

"Hey, Riley." I greeted him in the new addition he was working on at Finn's. I tapped the toe of my boot on the hardwood floor. "This looks great. You've done a lot over the past couple of days."

I'd gotten home from Dixon's and immediately started my cake. I put it in the oven and decided to go to Finn's and grab the pizza so he could just come straight to my house after he finished up the paperwork.

His addition was coming along nicely. I didn't know much about construction, but the sheer fact that Danny Shane said Riley Titan wasn't certified could've fooled me. The drywall was all screwed in and the drywall tape had been placed for him to slap on some drywall mud. The wood flooring was a nice dark bamboo.

"He's going to love this bigger family room and so is Cosmo." I couldn't help but smile looking at the ornery cat curled up in the sunspot coming from the new bay window in the addition.

Cosmo had come from another murder investigation. We had to find a home for him. Finn's sister had agreed to take him but quickly realized she was allergic to cats once she'd gotten him back to Chicago. Being the sensitive guy Finn was, he couldn't stand the thought that Cosmo might have to go to a shelter, so he adopted him.

"I barely recognize you out of uniform." He looked me up and down with my true fashion sense of my sweatshirt and jeans. Not that his paint-splattered plaid shirt and jeans were any better. "What are you doing here?" he asked.

"Do you have an issue with me being here?" I asked.

Cosmo gave a little meow when I walked over to pet him.

"No. Deputy Vincent just said that I'd be here all day alone because he was going to find that chef that made such a ruckus the day that food critic died." He took the drywall spatula and swiped it overtop the drywall tape going down the seam. "That cat doesn't mind all the beating and banging."

"He's sweet." I pulled my hand back when Cosmo got up and arched his back into a big stretch. "Anyways, you do have the work permit, don't you?"

There was a law that any new addition to a structure had to be approved by the council as well as have a permit posted on the window.

"Do you think that Deputy Vincent would let me in here without one?" he asked over his shoulder as he dragged the spatula full of drywall mud down the tape.

"Of course he wouldn't. I'd gone to see Danny Shane and he mentioned that you weren't a registered contractor," I probed.

I took a step back and looked into the finished part of the house. There was a direct line of vision to the front windows where the permit should be posted.

"Aw, he's sore that I'm taking all the business away from him around here since he's been doing bad work." He dropped the spatula to his side and twisted sixty degrees to look at me. "Word gets around Cottonwood fast."

"It sure does." Out of the corner of my eye, Cosmo jumped down from the window ledge. He pranced into the other room followed up by a few meows, which I knew meant he was hungry.

"Kenni." Poppa appeared. "I'm not getting a good feeling about you being here alone with him."

I gave him a slightly confused look. Why on earth was he here? The murder had been solved. Hadn't it?

"I keep thinking about him." Poppa ghosted next to him. "This job."

I looked around, wondering what Poppa was talking about.

"This was a brand-new addition. Everyone knows that the flooring goes in last." Poppa walked around the perimeter of the room. "Here is drywall mud on the floor. That's one of the reasons the floor goes in last."

"I'm not sure when Finn will be back." Riley threw the spatula in the bucket of drywall mud. His stare was intense. "I'll be sure to tell him that you stopped by."

"I'll call him." I watched his moves. He'd suddenly become uncomfortable. "I've got some new information on the case that gives Chef Mundy an alibi."

"That's good." His eyes narrowed. I could tell he was trying to call my bluff.

"Look there." Poppa pointed to Riley's face. "That's the classic face they teach in the academy."

Reading body language was one of my favorite classes and I did know the look.

"You have to think about all the clues up until now. Everyone knew that Frank Von Lee was coming to town. He suddenly shows up as a contractor and begins to take jobs that can be linked to Frank?" Poppa scratched his chin.

I bit the edge of my lip and looked at Riley, who was staring back at me.

"I'm going to feed Cosmo before I head on out." I gave a slight wave. "Good work. I just might have to hire you." I looked at the floor and noticed more and more dried-up drywall mud.

Out of the corner of my eye, I saw him notice I was looking at the floor. I hurried out of the room. I glanced up to the front of the house. My eyes slid across each window and the front door's window panels to see if there was a posted work permit. There wasn't.

My mind rolled back to the things Poppa had said. Riley showed up at Ben's and put himself in the right place at the right time to talk Ben into hiring him to do that work. Frank was going to be spending a lot of time at the diner. My heart started to beat rapidly when I remembered Riley was at the diner when Mama and Ben had met with Frank alone.

After Frank died, Riley was all of a sudden doing Finn's work, which gives Finn an ear to talk to. Not that Finn would discuss the case, but you never knew what was said over a beer or three.

Then there was the fact that there wasn't a work permit posted at either of the places he'd worked.

Cosmo continually meowed for his food. I slid my glance to the new addition. Riley was still looking at me. I smiled again.

I bent down next to the bag of cat food and pulled out my phone. I quickly scrolled through to Malina's phone number that she'd given me. Quickly I texted her. "Is Riley Titan staying at The Tattered Book Cover and Inn?"

"I don't see a Titan in the register," she texted back.

I used the scoop inside the bag and put two heaping scoops of cat kibble in Cosmo's bowl. While squatted, I glanced over my shoulder through the new door into the addition. Riley's arm was extended in the air, mudding the top of a piece of tape. My eyes drew down the side of his body. His shirt was lifted away from the waist of his jeans. About an inch of his skin was exposed. The metal buckle on his belt caught my attention.

Names on belts as well as needlepoint belts were really popular. Maybe now that Finn and I were on better terms, I'd have a belt or a name plate made for him from Lulu's.

"Kenni." Poppa bent down and looked at the name plate. "That don't say Titan."

I squinted my eyes.

"It says Tooke. T-o-o-k-e," Poppa read off the letters. "Where have I heard that name before?"

Cosmo smacked his bowl. The food flew across the floor. I scrambled around to pick up a few of the pieces so I could buy some time to figure out what to do with this information. While on my knees, I put my hand in the garbage can to drop the kibble and noticed a couple of frozen meal packages.

Tooke. Frozen meals. Things were beginning to add up. My hands shook. I turned back to Cosmo and reached for him. I had to get him and me out of there. He darted off into the new addition.

I stood up and noticed a wallet on the counter.

"Good boy, Cosmo," I said in order not to draw attention to my snooping. I opened the wallet and pulled out the license just enough to see Riley's photo and the name Riley Tooke.

Tooke was the family's name from the newspaper article I'd read at the library after I'd read Frank Von Lee's biography on the Culinary Channel boasting how Frank was harsh in his reviews and this was what made him so sought after. The article said one of the restaurants that Frank Von Lee had given a bad review was a family-owned restaurant by the Tooke family. A shiver rippled through me.

The family that'd gone bankrupt because of Frank. The same family whose father committed suicide over it. Riley's father. This was the perfect motive for Riley to seek revenge.

If I thought back further, Riley had his ear to the ground when I discussed things. He was at Ben's when the fight went down between Ben and Mundy. That would be perfect for him to pin the murder on Mundy, but why Mama?

"Kenni, let's go. He's going to do something," Poppa predicted. "He's part of that Tooke clan. Now, Kenni," Poppa stressed.

I slid the ID back into the wallet and took out my phone. I had to make sure before I accused him. Not that the frozen dinner, name, and lack of construction knowledge wasn't proof enough that something wasn't right.

"What about the name Tooke?" I quickly texted Malina, ignoring Poppa.

"Yes. Riley Tooke. He's in room six. He's a cutie-pa-tooke." She ended her text with a kissy face emoji. "Get it? Pa-tooke? I talked to him while he made his frozen dinners. Why?"

"Cute but deadly," I whispered.

"So you're trying to figure out exactly how I'm part of this whole Frank Von Lee murder," Riley's voice boomed from behind me.

I jumped, wishing I'd had my gun holster on me. I slid my phone back into my pocket but not without hitting the voice recorder button.

"Too late!" Poppa threw his hands in the air. "I don't get it. I've been runnin' all over hell's half-acre to help you and you just don't listen. Why am I here if you aren't going to listen to me?"

"Excuse me?" I tried to play off Riley's words and scooted closer to the garbage can.

"I'm not stupid. Maybe a little careless, and I underestimated the girly sheriff a little, but I can take care of that." Slowly he tapped the head of a hammer in his palm. "I've got a new job pouring concrete. I really don't know much about it, but I'm sure I can practice digging a hole big enough for a dead body and fill that with concrete."

"You could." I shrugged and glanced around to find anything I could to whack him with before he got me. "Or you can just come clean right now. It's completely understandable how much you wanted to get back at him for bankrupting your family business."

"Bankrupting?" He scoffed. "That's just the tip of the iceberg. He gave our family so much stress, I started drinking more and more. I had a wife and a kid on the way. My parents lost everything and had to move in with us." Tears filled his eyes. His nostrils flared. "I wasn't myself. My parents watched as my marriage drowned because of my drinking. My father said it was his fault for contacting that so-called food critic and just when I thought it couldn't get worse, my dad hung himself."

The pain was so vivid in his mind, his body trembled as he fidgeted with the hammer.

"The judge will hear all of this and I'm sure there will be leniency," I sputtered. "You had all the right in the world to do what you did," I lied. It was the only little bit of hope I had that I could get out of here without a hammer to my head.

"You think I believe you?" He cackled, taking a step forward. "You had me. You really had me."

I took a step back.

"I really didn't know that you knew until you looked at the floor. Then I realized you knew the floor was down first. Rookie mistake," he pointed out.

"Not to mention the frozen food container in the garbage. I did find part of one at Ben's. At first I thought it was Chef Mundy's, but no real chef would ever buy, cook, or eat a frozen dinner." The way I saw it, I might as well throw it all out there so if they found my dead body, I'd have taped the conversation, hoping he wouldn't get away with it. "You bought a frozen pot pie, put the poison in it and made Frank believe it was Mama's pot pie. He bought into it and thought mama sent him the sample the night before the actual tasting. He ate it. He died, making mama look like the killer."

"If you can get into the family room, Finn has a gun in the drawer of the side table of the couch." Poppa disappeared.

I started to slowly edge my way around the kitchen.

"The missing permit signs were also a clue that maybe Danny Shane was right about you not having the right credentials. But the big aha moment..." I slipped around the door jamb and ran down the hall to get to the gun as fast as I could.

"Stop!" He was screaming as his footsteps thundered behind me. "I said stop right there or I'll kill you right here!"

"No! Not if I get you first!" I jerked the drawer open. Nothing. "I thought you said the side table!" I screamed at Poppa's shadow. He stood in front of the window and the afternoon sun was streaming in.

"The other side table." Poppa pointed.

The heavy hand of Riley grabbed me and shoved me. As I was going down, I looked over at Poppa. He disappeared, leaving me a good view of the outside world. Mrs. Brown was standing in Finn's yard with her mouth dropped open.

"I know I can't kill you in Finn's house. I'm going to have to take you to the country." Riley was nodding as he played out the scenario in his head. He shook the butt end of the hammer at me as he gripped the head. "You see, now that Mundy is dead and because of the note I planted, Finn thinks the case is closed. He just left before you got here to do the final report. I kinda like it here. Now that my revenge has been taken care of, I'm ready to live my life as Riley Titan."

He grabbed me by the arm. I winced.

"I can't live that life with you around." He flung me in front of him. "Now we're going to go for a little ride."

If I could keep him here for a few more minutes, I knew Mrs. Brown would get me help. At least I prayed she'd get me help.

"Your belt." I huffed and puffed the words out of my mouth, pointing to his belt. "I recalled reading about your family in an article. Before you kill me, I really need to know how you pulled it off."

"That." He laughed and put the handle of the hammer in his back pocket.

He took off his plaid shirt and ripped it apart in long strips that I could only imagine he was going to use to tie my hands. "I've been waiting for an opportunity for Frank to visit a small town to make my move. After I'd gotten my job with Ben, I listened very carefully and found out where Frank was staying. The media didn't report that. I'd only planned to kill him, but your mama, god bless her heart." He put his hand flat on his chest. "That's what you say around here, right?" He winked.

"Right," I answered sarcastically.

"I had no idea I was going to use her as the scapegoat, but it was perfect. Then Chef Mundy was a bonus. He said he wanted to figure out how to make your mama's pot pie. He loved to figure out secret ingredients. I saw him at the grocery store picking up all sorts of stuff. According to that sweet Malina, who is desperate for a man, Mundy had been cooking the whole time he was there using their oven. It was a perfect set up." He ran his hands through his hair before he gestured me to go closer to the door. "I saw your mama take a casserole dish, so I took a dish from the same pattern and put one of the frozen pot pie dinners in it. After I put a little sodium fluoroacetate in it, I left it on the counter with a note for Malina. Of course I didn't put a name on it. Just that it had to be delivered to Frank Von Lee."

He jerked my arm around and grabbed me by my wrists.

"Now, enough talk. I have to get you out of here before Deputy Vincent gets home," he said.

My heart hammered in my chest as I felt the fabric slide along my wrists. It was times like these that the instructors at the academy warned you that you needed to perform the take out moves as easy as you breathed. I wasn't fond of that class and I didn't memorize all the moves, though now I really wished I had.

"Hold it right there, buddy," Betty Murphy threatened Riley Titan, Tooke, or whoever he was, my shotgun pointed straight at him. "Don't make me waste a bullet on you."

Mrs. Brown stood behind her with a wooden rolling pin lifted in the air. "I knew he was too cute for a reason. Makes up for his evil insides."

He took his hands off me and put them in the air. I got up and inched around him, taking the gun from Betty.

"How did you know I was here?" I asked Betty.

"Mrs. Brown called me and I knew I could get here quicker than Finn." Betty and Mrs. Brown high-fived. "He'd made a detour to grab a bite to eat before he came to finish up the paperwork on Mundy."

"Betty, can you run down to my Jeep and grab my police bag?" I asked.

Without a word, she high-tailed it out of Finn's house.

I kept the shotgun on Tooke and pulled my phone out with the other hand. I turned off the voice recording and noticed the time. I was going to be a little late to finish my cake. I messaged the recordings to Finn's phone, and then I called the reserve office telling them to send someone to Free Row and haul the real murderer off to jail.

"You got this until the reserve officer comes?" I asked Betty after I'd securely cuffed Tooke by the hands and feet and noticed the time.

"You're leaving?" she asked with fear in her eyes and took the shotgun when I handed it to her.

"Yep. I have a cake to finish baking and I need to check on it." I brushed my hands together and took one last look at Tooke all cuffed up.

"About that." Mrs. Brown's voice faded away. "There was smoke coming from the backyard and I went over to make sure everything was okay. Your cake."

"Yeah." I lifted my head to listen.

"It's burnt." Mrs. Brown's nose crunched up. "To a crisp. I figured you were down here so that's when I came down to get you. I saw through the window what was going on."

Thank God for nosy neighbors.

CHAPTER THIRTY

"It's not an original Kenni Lowry cake, but I guess it'll do." I forked a big piece of Ben's hot fudge brownie pie with a big scoop of vanilla ice cream and fed it across the table to Finn.

"I still can't believe you're taking a cake-baking class." He smiled and my heart beat double time. He got up from his side of the table and came over to sit in the seat next to me. He slipped his arm around my shoulder, picked up a spoon, and fed me a bite.

"It was for the good of the badge." I winked, tilting my head up to kiss him. I dropped my chin on his shoulder with a sigh of pleasure. "It feels so good to have Frank's death behind us."

"I knew something was wrong when I read Mundy's letter. It didn't seem authentic. I'd even gone back to Ben's on my way back to the office to finish the report and he told me that he never discussed finances with Mundy. He mentioned it in passing to Riley after he and Danny Shane had his blow up. That's what made me head on out to Danny's and talk to him. He told me that he told you Riley didn't have the proper certification. Things started to fit together after that." He scooped another big bite with a lot of fudge. He held it up to my lips and I happily accepted it. "I called dispatch to let Betty know I was going to head home to confront Riley about his work and she didn't answer. I also wanted her to read the rest of the lab results to me. I took it upon myself to call the lab and he told me that Mundy's prints weren't on anything in Frank's evidence. He said all the blood from Mundy's room and knives you'd taken in as evidence only had chicken and his own blood on it. He pulled one print from Frank's room. He ran the print in the database and it belonged to Riley Tooke."

"He had a record?" That was new to me.

"He'd been picked up for shoplifting as a kid and his print was still on file." He took his arm from around me. He leaned against the table and rested on his forearms. "I made a quick call to the reserves and they pulled his name and photo. It was Riley Titan."

"He was smart. He positioned himself everywhere Frank would be and Mundy would be. Even staying in the same inn as both." I couldn't believe that it took us this long to solve it, but Riley was smart.

The bell over the diner door dinged. For a second it dawned on me that maybe it was Poppa with his real ding and not him mocking me. When I turned around, I saw it was the next best thing.

Mama.

"You ain't gonna believe this." She waved a magazine in the air. "I'm famous!"

She smacked the magazine in front of me and Finn opened to the page she wanted me to see. She jabbed it.

"I'm in here." She pointed to one of the photos that Edna had taken of her in the diner that morning before all this mess had happened.

"That's fantastic." I stood up and gave my mama a huge hug.

"Is that it?" Ben walked over and pointed to the magazine.

"It is." Mama took out a piece of paper from her purse. "And I want you to have this."

"What is it?" He opened it. "It's a check." His jaw dropped.

"That should be enough to buy this old run-down building." Mama hugged Ben. "I told the magazine that I knew they were going to make a big documentary on Frank's life and death and if they wanted my interview they had to pay me. Pay me good." She nodded.

. . .

"Mama, you never cease to amaze me." I drew her into a big bear hug. Ben grabbed both of us.

"Now get off me. I've got to show people how famous I am." She pulled away from us and darted over to a group of the Sweet Adelines, bragging on herself.

Ben rushed back to the counter where Jolee was helping him. By the look on her face, they were happy he'd be able to keep the diner.

"Are you okay?" Finn asked.

I looked around the diner. Mama was walking around showing the full diner her famous spread. I could see Jolee and Ben joking around with each other from behind the counter. And a warm arm had slipped around me.

"I'm more than okay." I looked up at my devilishly handsome boyfriend. "Life is just about perfect. Everyone I love is happy and healthy."

"Are you saying you love me?" Finn whispered in my ear. My body tingled.

I gulped. My palms started to sweat and my mouth suddenly went dry.

"Because I love you."

His words were music to my ears.

THE END

If you enjoyed reading this book as much as I enjoyed writing it then be sure to return to the Amazon page and leave a review.

Go to Tonyakappes.com for a full reading order of my novels and while there join my newsletter. You can also find links to Facebook, Instagram and Goodreads.

Join like-minded readers like YOU in the Cozy Krew Facebook Group for dream casting, fan theories, and live Q & A's. It's like a BIG GIANT BOOK CLUB! But if you want to have your own book club, be sure you let me know! I love to send goodies.

DEAD AS A DOORNAIL

A Kenni Lowry Mystery

TONYA KAPPES .COM

Southern Hospitality with a Smidgen of Homicide

Book Five

BY
TONYA KAPPES

DEDICATION

To the Kappes Cozy Krew

CHAPTER ONE

"Hey, Tina," Lucy Ellen Lowell greeted Tina Bowers, owner of Tiny Tina's Salon and Spa, as she shimmied her robust chest in front of the pedicure chair where I was sitting.

Tina was crouched down by my feet, slathering some sort of gritty lotion on my shins. "Hey, Kenni," Lucy Ellen said in a breathy tone.

Lucy's beady green eyes focused on Tina from underneath the wide-brimmed hat on top of her head. Tina's brown eyes were flat as she looked up at me from underneath her brows, not looking at Lucy Ellen at all. Slowly, Tina's jaw moved from side to side with each chew of her gum.

"Tina, you have to do my nails. I have to have them done for the upcoming wedding." Lucy Ellen paused. "I called to make an appointment, but Cheree told me that you weren't taking appointments and I have to get my nails done before Saturday and today is the only day I got open." Lucy Ellen gave Cheree Rath, Tina's employee, an ungrateful raised brow and scowl before she flung her fingers in the air. She was right. Her nails were chipped and in desperate need of painting. "Look here. These are awful. You ain't working, Kenni?" Lucy Ellen continued to show spirit hands, nail side out to Tina.

"I'm actually having a day off." I forced a smile.

It was difficult to take a day off since I was sheriff of our small town of Cottonwood, Kentucky.

"Betty and Finn are holding down the fort," I assured her when I saw from her contorted face that her brain was flipping through names like a Rolodex for who was at the sheriff's department. Betty Murphy was the department dispatch operator and secretary. Finn Vincent was the only sheriff's deputy in the department outside of my four-legged deputy, Duke, my hound dog.

"Finn gave Kenni the gift card. They're an item now." Tina winked. "That's why she's getting extra special love." She kneaded and massaged my calves with her thumbs.

"Sweet." Lucy's face pinched. "Now." Her hands plunged in front of Tina's face. "What about my nails?"

The bell over the salon door dinged.

Everyone in the salon stopped when Polly Parker and four of her friends, along with her mother, nearly fell over themselves as they pushed through the door, giggling.

"We'll be right with you." Cheree said over her shoulder with her fingers stuck in a customer's shampooed hair in the black rinsing sink.

Polly's friends were no doubt here for her wedding that was only five days away, if you included today.

"Go on and pick out some colors if you want color," Tina followed up, ignoring Lucy. "They're here for what's called a preview party."

I smiled and nodded, feeling a wee bit sorry for Tina. Polly was high maintenance even outside of being a bride. I'd imagined she was a bridezilla. Her wedding to Mayor Ryland was the talk of the town. All the small boutiques in town were selling out of dresses and knick-knacks the happy couple registered for. It was actually an event I was looking forward to as well.

"Well?" Lucy Ellen pulled the towel off of the arm of my pedicure chair and wiped the dripping sweat from her brow. I looked between her and Tina.

"Well?" Lucy Ellen asked again and cocked her leg to the side, her curvy bottom following, almost smacking into Jolee Fischer, my best friend, who was sitting in the pedicure chair next to me.

Tina's hands felt like a Brillo Pad as she rapidly rubbed them up and down my legs.

Lucy Ellen pulled her diamond-encrusted gold watch up to her round face and checked out the time. "I've got time now. And..." Her mouth formed an "O" as if she'd just remembered something very important. "Dr. Shively said you could do my toes, but don't put them in the tub since I've been nursing that big bunion and all."

"Lucy, I don't have time today." Tina chomped her gum like a cow chewing the cud as she splashed water on my shins to get the gritty stuff off, not giving even a looksie toward Lucy Ellen.

Cheree put her client under one of those big umbrella hair dryers and plopped herself down in front of Jolee to finish up.

"We are booked solid." Tina took my feet out of the water and patted them dry before picking up a bottle of natural-colored nail polish that I'd picked out, giving the bottle a couple of good whacks against the palm of her hand.

"What do you mean, Tina? I even brought my own flip flops." Lucy Ellen let an exhausted sigh and patted her purse that was slung over her shoulder. "I've been coming here for two years," she cried out. "Today is the only day I've got open before the wedding." Lucy Ellen looked over at Polly. Her eyes squinted and she nodded her head once the fake smile was across her lips. "You've always taken me when I come in."

Lucy Ellen wasn't letting up. She jerked the floppy hat off her head. Her black hair sprang out like coils. Tina choked back a laugh. I kept my eyes on her and didn't dare look at Lucy.

"And my hair needs a treatment awfully bad. And only you can do it, Tina. Only you." Lucy Ellen made a desperate attempt to jam the hair back under the hat, but the hair wasn't having it. With another failed attempt, the hair won and Lucy Ellen shoved the hat underneath her armpit.

"I'm the only one in town," Tina muttered under her breath while she started painting my toes. "That's why I'm her only one." Tina made a good point.

"You can do my hair treatment and let it sit while you paint my toes and then shampoo the treatment out. My hair can air dry while you give me a manicure." Lucy Ellen had it all figured out. "I've got cash."

She reached in her purse and pulled out a fistful of cash.

"Today isn't good. After Kenni and Jolee, we're have Polly's entire wedding party in for a preview look." Tina made it very clear she didn't have time for Lucy Ellen.

Any time I'd ask her about the rocks, she'd swear up one end and down the next that she'd bought the rocks from a beauty supply shop. It was a known fact that Tina Bowers hadn't bought the rocks because I'd received several phone calls from dispatch that Tina was down at the Kentucky River taking rocks off the side of the road when in fact it was against the law to pillage the limestone. Sure as shinola, the rocks under my piggies at the moment were jagged pieces of limestone.

"Preview look?" Lucy's head jerked toward the front of the salon and stared at Polly. "What on earth is that?" Her nose curled. She didn't give Polly a second to respond until she said, "I'm looking forward to seeing the mayor. I've not seen him in months."

"Mmhm." Polly Parker's chin lifted up and down with pride. Her lips parted into a smile that showed off her bright white veneers—a smile that reminded me of a horse's mouth. "Tina is going to paint all my bridesmaids' nails to make sure the color will match their dresses." Polly's shoulders lifted to her ears as her sweet Southern voice escalated. "Each dress is a different color. Gone with the Wind style." She lifted the back of her hand to her forehead as if she were going to faint. "I didn't want any surprises when we come back for the real manicures and pedicures."

Jolee and I looked at each other when Polly said Gone with the Wind and bit back our laughter.

"I've never heard of such a thing." Lucy Ellen tsked. "This is taking too much of Tina's time. Cheree, can't you take Tina's clients? I've got to get my hair and nails done." Lucy Ellen stormed over to Cheree, who was finishing up painting Jolee's toenails.

"I'm sorry, Lucy. We are booked to the gills and we just can't fit you in." Cheree pushed back a stray strand of her long red hair that had found a way out of her low ponytail. Her freckles deepened as the anger swelled up in her. She made it perfectly clear to Lucy, but Lucy Ellen just wasn't having it.

"You can squeeze me into a wee little spot." Lucy Ellen continued to look around the shop. "I've been coming here for two years." She held up two fingers in the air and flip-flopped them around saying it for a second time as if they didn't hear her the first or they didn't realize she'd been coming that long.

"And in those two years," Cheree sounded as if she'd had enough, "you've cancelled at least a dozen times." She looked up over the rim of her glasses from the stool in front of Jolee and stared at Lucy. She had a bottle of open polish in one hand and the nail brush in the other. "Did you ever think of the financial bind you put us in when you don't show up? How are we gonna pay our bills? Did you ever think of that?"

"Then I'll buy the Perfectly Posh." Lucy Ellen picked up the bottle from Tina's nail station and looked at it. "This isn't Perfectly Posh. Where is it?"

She gripped a much lighter pink version in her hand that clearly didn't match her chipped up fingernails.

"You know I don't sell my polish to no one." Tina sprayed down the foot tub and gave it a couple of scrubs to clean it out.

She stood up, tugged the scrunchie from her wrist, and pulled her brown hair in a top knot on her head. She stretched her neck into a slow roll and strolled over to Lucy Ellen like she was gearing up for a confrontation.

"If you ain't gonna do my nails for Polly's wedding, then I'll have someone else do them with your polish," Lucy Ellen said through gritted teeth with another polish in her grips. "You are the only person who knows how to make your own polish that no one else has and I can't have the same polish as the other girls from the Hunt Club at the wedding. I just can't," she cried, clutching the polish to her chest.

Tina plucked the bottle of homemade nail polish right out of Lucy's hand.

"I don't even have any Perfectly Posh made up. Get out of here." Tina's tone meant business. Lucy Ellen slid her eyes past Tina's shoulders and looked at me. I offered a pinched smile.

It was probably time for me to step in even though I wasn't on duty. I went to stand up, but Jolee caught my attention. She shook her head for me to stay out of it.

She whispered, "This is the best part about coming to the beauty shop." Jolee laughed. "All the crazy comes out of people."

The tension crept up my back and into my shoulders. Wasn't this supposed to be a relaxing experience? I thought and continued to look down.

"Well, I never. You'll regret this, Tina Bowers." Lucy Ellen twirled her finger around the shop. "Tiny Tina's will no longer be in business once it gets out in all the gossip circles how you treated me here today." Lucy Ellen brought her hands up to her chest. "I'm sending in a bad review to the Chronicle as soon as I get home."

"Lucy," Cheree called after her before she left, "you might oughta try a wet comb on that cowlick of yours."

Lucy Ellen huffed and puffed before she turned on the balls of her feet and trotted out the door. Bouncy hair and all.

"Good riddance." Tina snapped her fingers and pointed for me to move over to the nail station for my manicure. "She's always sending bad reviews to the Chronicle."

I walked on the heels of my feet, careful not to smear the fresh polish on my toes.

"Geez, I can't believe the gall of that woman." Tina jerked my hand over the puffy brown pillow and adjusted the miniature light over my hand. "Scoot up," she instructed me.

"If she had another wrinkle on that body, she'd be able to screw on that hat," Cheree said under her breath as she finished up painting Jolee's toenails and moved her to a manicure station next to me, sticking Jolee's fingers in a bowl of water for her cuticles to soften.

She walked over to the client under the dryer and felt around her head before she started the dryer back up.

"Lucy's an awful woman. She had the nerve to order from my food truck and bring the food back half eaten with a fly in it saying I cooked the fly in the food when I know good and well the fly flew into her food after she sat down at the picnic table because she'd spent the first few minutes batting them away." Jolee curled her nose. "While stuffing her face the whole time."

Cheree busied herself cleaning out the foot tub where Jolee had been and filled it right back up, motioning for Polly to come on over.

"My mama made me invite her to the wedding. I didn't want to." Polly gave her mom a sideways look. "I didn't want to invite any of them hunting club women, but Mama insisted since I'm gonna be the first lady and all.

Plus, Chance is a member of the club. Not that he goes all that much, but it's good for his position as mayor."

Polly fanned her face with her fingers.

"I sure hope the weather is good next weekend." Polly looked over at her mother.

Paula Parker didn't pay her daughter any attention. She just continued to sit in the plastic chair in the front of the shop flipping through the five-year-old beauty magazines.

"You obviously invited them." Cheree turned the cold water on a little more after Polly sat down and stuck her big toe in and pulled it right back out.

"I told Tibbie Bell to go ahead and invite them all." Polly referred to another friend of mine who was the only wedding planner in Cottonwood. "Chance told me not to worry my pretty little head because this week is their annual gun show, which means the men have taken off work the next couple of weeks to get their cabins ready for the first week of hunting season." Polly sucked in a deep breath and slowly let it out with a humming sound.

"Tibbie told me to breathe when I felt myself getting a little anxious over the wedding. Them women sure do make me anxious." She took another deep breath.

"Now, now." Paula Parker hurried over to Polly and drew her into her arms. "Don't be going and getting yourself all worked up." They hugged for an uncomfortable few seconds.

With a pouty mouth, Polly picked up a bottle of nail polish and looked at the bottom before she set it down and picked up another one. She did the same thing bottle after bottle. All the women in the salon waited to hear what Polly was talking about. It was just how it worked around our small town. Gossip not only bound us together but also tore us apart.

"Lucy Ellen called me about the food." Jolee laughed and threw in her two cents worth of gossip.

"She did what?" Paula Parker's voice escalated. "The nerve," she gasped. "I'm paying you too much money if you ask me," Paula muttered under her breath but loud enough for me to hear.

"Yeah. She wanted to know what we were serving to the guests so she could plan out if she needed to eat before the wedding in case she didn't like the food." Jolee shook her head.

"Maybe you should slip a mickey in her cocktail at the beginning of the wedding so she'll be knocked out." Polly shrugged, half-joking, half-serious.

"Maybe I should slip her more than a mickey," Jolee agreed. "She thinks she can go around and say what she wants with no consequences. She called the fire inspector on me one week, then the health inspector the next. Then she did that article in the newspaper giving my food truck a bad review." Jolee huffed.

I'd thought she'd gotten over that incident, but apparently not.

"To this day, the Hunt Club won't let me park in front of their meetings because of that woman. She's hurting my livelihood." Jolee's foot was shaking up and down. A sure sign she was fired up. "I wish someone would put her in her place."

"I for one am very excited you're catering the wedding." Polly's chin lifted in the air, and in a swift motion, she brought it down to her right shoulder. "Right, Mama?"

"Yes, dear. Anything that comes out of your precious mouth is gold." Paula Parker smiled with pride.

"Kenni," Betty Murphy called over the walkie-talkie that I had in my purse. "Sheriff, are you there?"

I held up a wet fingernail to Tina to hold on and grabbed my purse to take out the walkie-talkie. I still kept my radio on me in case there was a dire emergency.

"I'm here, Betty," I said after I hit the button on the side.

"I hate to bother you on your day off, but we got a complaint from Lucy Ellen Lowell." Everyone's head in the entire salon shot up in the air and looked my way. "She says that she was discriminated against and wants to file a complaint. I told her that Officer Vincent was out on a call and that I'd have him call her back, but she insisted I get in touch with him immediately or she was coming down here and I just don't want to deal with Lucy Ellen Lowell this afternoon."

"Did she tell you that I was at the salon when she came in?" I asked Betty.

"I knew something was up when I told her it was your day off and she muttered something about how she and Darnell had hosted your election fundraiser. I just let that drop. So what do you want me to do?" Betty asked.

"You tell her that you talked to me and that I'll give her a call back." I clicked off and stuck the walkie-talkie back into my purse.

"Maybe I should give her a hair treatment and let the scissors slip." Tina dragged her finger across her neck.

CHAPTER TWO

"Duke," I called from the kitchen when I got home from my so-called spa day at Tiny Tina's. "Duke."

I threw my keys on the kitchen counter and shut the kitchen door. I stood there for a second and let the quiet envelop me until I heard a loud thud, followed by the sound of the pounding of the four large paws of my trusty deputy hound dog.

All the yammering going on down at Tiny Tina's wore me out. I didn't understand how people gossiped day in and day out. All those stories started running together until I'd finally turned it off in my head.

"Hey, you big lug." I bent down and was greeted with the best slobbery kisses. "You ready to go outside?"

He danced toward the kitchen door. I opened it and walked out with him. The fresh air might help clear my head. It was that strange time in between seasons in Kentucky when the weather was hot and humid one day and cold and chilly the next. This afternoon was turning out to be more on the light breezy side that was not quite sweatshirt weather, but not tank top weather either.

"Hey. I saw your Jeep in the driveway." Finn Vincent peered over the gate that led into my backyard.

He let himself in. Before he could say anything else, I pulled him to me with a fistful of his brown deputy sheriff's shirt and laid a big kiss on him.

"You must've missed me." His eyes twinkled, sending my heart all aflutter.

"You must've been waiting by your window waiting for me to pull in," I teased. He lived a couple of houses down from me.

Though he was from the north and not a real southerner, his handsome charm hadn't gone unnoticed by every single girl in Cottonwood when he first came to town. Over the past year, he'd really picked up on the fact that in the south, it's much easier to catch flies with honey instead of vinegar and holding the door open for a woman can go a long way.

"I'm just so glad that you don't like all the girly things, because I just don't know if I could go to Tiny Tina's on a regular basis for nails, hair, and spa days. They curl way more than hair there." I rubbed my head. "My head hurts from all the gossip."

Duke darted from the far corner of the backyard when he saw his ball-throwing buddy. He was always happy to see Finn.

I sat down in a chair on my back porch and enjoyed watching Finn throw the ball to Duke a few times until Duke decided he was going to sniff all the grass along the back side of the fence.

"That bad?" He turned around and looked at me with dipped eyes. "I thought you'd like the gift card."

"I'm very appreciative of the gift card, and it came at a great time since we have the wedding next weekend and I did need my nails done, but I'm amazed at how they can just go from one gossip story to another." Goosebumps prickled my leg as he scooted his chair closer to mine.

"I get enough of their tales at Euchre. These girls do it day in and day out." I left out the part of Lucy Ellen's crazy tirade and how she'd called dispatch since I'd taken care of it. Plus, he'd probably be upset that Betty Murphy had called me on my first day off in months. "How was your day?"

"Made the usual rounds, and I got a call from Bosco Frederick from the Hunt Club. He said something about having a deputy at their annual gun show in a couple of days at The Moose Lodge." There was an amused look on his face.

These were the times that his northern roots stuck out. He didn't understand that guns and knives strapped on the belts of Cottonwood citizens were accessories that completed the look of the locals. If you weren't packing, then we knew you were an out-of-towner.

"The annual gun show." I let out a deep sigh and extended my legs out in front of me. "Polly mentioned that today. I can't believe we're only a couple weeks off from the opening of hunting season." I crossed my forearms across my belly and let the cool breeze float around me. "The Hunt Club wives host this annual show. The men all take the next couple of weeks off to clean and fix up their hunting cabins and deer stands so when the season opens, they're ready to go."

"Annual? How many more guns can people in this town own?" he joked.

"You can never have enough." I winked. "Lucy Ellen and all the women in the Hunt Club are sitting together at the wedding since their husbands are occupied."

"I just don't get all that hunting business. Poor animals." Finn had such a tender heart when it came to animals. He'd even taken in Cosmo, an orange tabby cat that belonged to one of the criminals we'd put behind bars.

"It's just a way of life around here. Plus Lucy's husband is the only person who does taxidermy here in Cottonwood, so she's got to promote her lifestyle." She could've done it a little less conspicuously, but she was harmless and had given Tina and the girls a lot to talk about and entertain me while I'd endured the Kentucky River limestones under my feet.

Duke darted along the fence line up to the gate on the side of the house and followed up with a little bit of barking, then the wagging tail, telling me whoever was walking up the sidewalk on the side of my house was someone he knew.

"There's my grand-doggie." Mama's voice carried into the backyard and made Duke's tail wag faster.

I stood up and walked over, grabbing Duke by the collar.

"Hey, Mama." I stood up. My eyes slid over Mama's shoulder.

She wasn't alone. Polly and Paula Parker were with her. Polly had a hanger in her hand and the white dress bag flowed down with the bottom edges ending in her mama's hand.

"Kenni, can you please chain up that mutt?" Polly's perfect pink-lined lips snarled. "I can't have him ruining this dress." She didn't take her eyes off Duke. He was dancing around in anticipation of the ladies coming in the yard.

I let go of his collar and snapped my fingers for him to lay down. He was a trained dog. Not that he was an official police dog, but I'd had him since he was given to me from my poppa, which was a whole 'nother story all together.

"Polly, he won't hurt you. He's a sweetie." Mama did love Duke.

When I looked at Mama, I saw exactly what I was going to look like later in life. She had shoulder-length brown hair like me. We had the same olive skin tone and if it weren't for a few wrinkles, she'd look my age. Both of us stood five feet, five inches and pretty much had the same body type, though her hips were a little bigger than mine. Only because she'd birthed me, her only child. Trust me when I say that I completely get the only child syndrome.

"Hi, Finn," Polly greeted him, as did Mrs. Parker.

"It's so good to see you in regular clothes." Mama smiled so big, bringing her shoulders up to her ears as she reached out and grabbed my hand to get a gander at the manicure. "I heard you used your gift card from Finn." Mama couldn't stop the big smile when she looked at him.

It wasn't a big secret that Mama had plans for my life other than being the sheriff. She'd planned on the biggest election of my life being voted Debutante of Cottonwood instead of being voted Sheriff.

"You are going to be such a beautiful maid of honor." She let out the biggest happiest sigh that I'd not heard since I let her take me prom-dress shopping back in high school.

"Maid of honor?" My oh-shit meter went off real fast. I started to shake my head as fast as Duke's tail had wagged when I could see what was happening. "I'm sorry," I said. "I thought I heard you say maid of honor."

"Oh, Kendrick Lowry." Polly Parker's chin-length perfectly blonde (though it came from one of Tiny Tina's bottles) hair didn't move as she bounced past Mama. She dragged that dress bag over to me. "I couldn't think of anyone else in my time of need. After all, your job description on the Cottonwood Sheriff's Department website says that the sheriff helps anyone who needs it."

Polly jerked around and handed the hanger off to Mama as she started to unzip the big dress bag.

"My time of need is right now and it's for a beer," I said to Finn and looked back at him. His hand was over his mouth and his eyes were big.

He threw his hands up in the air and stood up.

"I think it's time for me to go." His lips tremored as he tried to not smile. "I'll go grab us some supper from Kim's Buffet and give you a little girl time."

"Girl time!" Mama squealed.

"No!" I gasped and grabbed his hand. "You can't leave me. What kind of boyfriend are you?"

"One that wants to stay your boyfriend. You're gonna need some food." He bent down and kissed my cheek.

"Ta-da!" Polly screamed and pulled the hanger in the air, letting the bag fall on the ground.

"I'm out." Finn pointed his finger toward the gate and walked away, leaving me there with my mouth gaped open.

"I knew you were going to love it." Polly looked between me and the dress, her big horse teeth sparkling. Her head bobbled in delight as she looked at the hunter-green dress that looked like it'd come right off the curtain rods of an old plantation home.

Dr. Bev Houston, the local dentist, should've been arrested for giving Polly Parker those big veneers in that tiny mouth of hers.

"And we can't forget your bonnet." As if they'd rehearsed it, Paula produced a matching green bonnet. If they thought that was going on top of my head, they had another thing coming to them.

"My bonnet?" I took a few steps backward and wagged my finger in front of me.

"Of course, we'd have to get you back down to Tiny Tina's to change out the polish you picked because we are doing Perfectly Posh." Polly gave me instructions like I had no decision in this matter.

"I got Natural Nail." I wiggled my fingers as if this was the worst issue going on here. I was already plum tuckered out and they'd only been here a few minutes. My hands were shaking. I was in a pickle and it wasn't good. Polly Parker and I weren't even friends. "Tina said Natural Nail goes with everything."

"You're right." Polly's eyes squinted as she looked lovingly at my mother as if I were a toddler holding on to my mama's leg. "She doesn't know wedding etiquette at all."

They looked between each other knowingly.

"I didn't see any sort of dress code on your wedding invitation." I brought my hand up to my head and rubbed my temples and forehead.

Jolee and I had a good laugh when the invitations to Polly's wedding came and it looked exactly like something from Gone with the Wind. In fact, all the food Polly had contracted Jolee to cater was deep Southern dishes. But I didn't recall a dress code.

"What is wrong with you?" Mama asked. "I think them stones Tina put in your foot bath have done something to your head."

Mama was so embarrassed by my behavior she turned all of the shades of red on one of those color wheels hanging up in the art room in Cottonwood Elementary School.

"Maid of honor." Polly shook the hanger.

"You're going to be a maid of honor now that my sorority sister from college can't make it." She turned to her mama. "Can you believe that she's not coming because she just had a baby? The nerve of saying yes and then backing out."

It was just like Polly Parker to find fault with a new precious baby. I'd bet my bottom dollar that friend had gotten a gander at this dress and bailed, leaving me in the lurch. Too bad I didn't have a good excuse like a baby.

"I'm...um...I'm..." I couldn't take my eyes off the ugly dress. "I'm not even good friends with you. And I didn't do the website. Betty Murphy did."

I clearly wasn't sure what she wrote on the website. But I would definitely be making some changes.

I snapped my fingers. "What about Toots Buford? She's your best friend and I don't think she's in your wedding party."

"Toots Buford works at Dixon's Foodtown and doesn't have enough money to rub two dimes together, much less buy this three-hundred-dollar dress." She brushed the dress side to side, letting the crinoline crunch to a dramatic halt. "Your mama has not only paid me for your dress, she's even hosting the bridal-party luncheon on Friday that as maid of honor you're supposed to give."

"Well, that ain't gonna happen." The words fell out of mouth. "I've got to work."

"Kendrick Lowry!" Mama cried out and buried her head in her hands. "You sure do know how to embarrass your mama and your family in someone else's time of need." She took her face out of her hands and looked at Polly and Paula. "I raised her better than this. It's living here on Free Row that's done it to her."

Mama's head nodded as she referred to my neighborhood. Free Row was technically Broadway Street, but most of my neighbors were on commodity cheese, food stamps, and any other free things they could get from the government. Not that it was an issue, but they also had broken-down furniture on their front porches and beat-up cars hoisted up on cinder blocks. Not Mama's ideal living arrangements for her one and only child.

Still, it was my poppa's home and he left it to me in his will. I loved it as a young child and I love it as my home now. Especially now that Finn was just a couple of doors down.

"I'm not using bad manners. I'm just saying that years from now you want to look back at your photos with fond memories of each person in your wedding." I thought my reasoning sounded good and I was proud of how I'd just plucked that logic right out of my you-know-what. "Not the memory that I accused you of killing someone a year ago."

It was true. Polly Parker was a suspect in a local murder and I was relentless in proving it. Luckily, I was wrong. I should've known better because Polly Parker would never put her manicure in danger with manual labor like murder.

I watched in horror as Polly's chest started to pop up and down, followed by a turned-down mouth, watering eyes, and a full-out crying hissy fit. And it wasn't pretty. She was not a pretty crier.

"Look what you've done," Paula spouted to me through her gritted teeth.

"Just you wait until the election. I don't care if you're unopposed. I'll write someone in instead of voting for you."

That did it for me.

"Fine. I love the color." I grabbed the dress out from Polly's dainty fingers and held it up to my body. "I love the dress." I couldn't stress it enough. "Perfectly Posh," I wiggled my fingers like spirit fingers, "here I come."

CHAPTER THREE

The moment I agreed to be Polly's maid of honor, I regretted it. Not only was the dress awful, it didn't fit me. I was a solid size eight, sometimes a ten, and it was a four. There was no way I was going to stop going to Ben's Diner for my morning dose of coffee, gravy biscuits, and bacon to fit into the dress, as Polly had suggested with a look of horror on her face when she saw me stuffed into the dress like a summer sausage.

After the wedding brigade left, I wasn't much company. Finn had come back with all of my favorite dishes from Kim's Buffet, but I was in no mood to eat. All the pushing and tugging Mama did to my body to even get me in the dress left me exhausted and mentally drained. Finn went home and I decided to go to bed. Maybe sleeping it off was what I needed.

"Sheriff! Sheriff," the urgent caller's voice jolted me wide awake when I answered the phone at four o'clock the next morning.

"Get over here right away. My wife is dead!" The desperate sound of the man woke me up, but the words "my wife is dead popped me straight out of bed."

Duke leapt off the bed. It wasn't unusual for a small-town sheriff like me to give out their phone number or be listed in the phone book. Small town, small ways.

"Who is this?" I asked, the phone stuck in between my ear and shoulder.

I hopped around on one foot while trying to shove one leg and then the other in my sheriff's pants.

"Oh my God," the man's voice cried. "Lucy!" The sobs from the man dragged out. "Lucy Ellen baby, Lucy Ellen baby. Lucy Ellen baby, wake up."

"Lucy? Sir, I'm gonna need you to calm down. Tell me where you live." The only Lucy Ellen I knew was Lucy Ellen Lowell and she looked perfectly healthy to me at Tiny Tina's yesterday.

"It's Darnell Lowell. I just got home from huntin' and she's...she's...not waking up."

"Darnell, don't move her. I'll be right there." I clicked off my phone and immediately dialed EMT services to get an ambulance over there, which was what Lowell should've done before he called me. But sometimes things were done ass-backward around these parts.

"Let's go, Duke!" I yelled down the hall.

It was too early in the morning to call Mrs. Brown, my next-door neighbor, to take care of him. I shoved some of his kibble in my pants pocket, grabbed a to-go coffee mug, ignoring the fact I was pouring what was left from yesterday morning's coffee pot, and heated it in the microwave. While the coffee warmed, I strapped on my holster around my waist and attached the walkie-talkie on my shoulder.

The last thing I grabbed as I ran out of my house was my bag with all the tools I needed for a crime scene and my Jeep Wagoneer keys. I opened the door to let Duke jump in and tugged the kibble out of my pocket, throwing it on the seat for him to gobble up since I didn't know how long I was going to be at the Lowell house. I stuck my mug in the bean-bag coffee holder that laid across the hump in the floorboard and jabbed my keys in the ignition.

In a fluid motion, I grabbed the old police siren from underneath my seat and licked the suction cup. With my free hand, I manually cranked down the driver's window and stuck the siren up on the roof, skimming the side of it with the pad of my finger to turn on the flashing red light and siren.

With the pedal to the floor and Duke hanging out the passenger window, the Wagoneer rattled down Broadway. Without stopping, I took a right at the end onto Main Street. The Lowells lived out in a subdivision off the bypass and the quickest way to get there was to drive south on Main Street until the flashing light to turn right on the bypass going toward Harrodsburg, another city near Cottonwood. It was a big deal with the input of the bypass around Cottonwood a few years back. The road was built around the outskirts of Cottonwood for unnecessary traffic through Cottonwood.

The houses were ranch style and had been built back in the seventies. Each house had a fairly good amount of property. Just enough to have neighbors, but far away enough to feel like you were in the country with a horse or two or even a nice big garden.

Darnell was pacing back and forth when I pulled up. There were a set of headlights barreling down the drive practically as soon as I got the Jeep in park. It was Finn in his Dodge Charger.

"Kenni." Darnell's face was as white as the inside of a freshly cut turnip. His thick black curly hair sat on top his head. "What am I gonna do?" His eyes searched mine as he wrung his hands. "I swear she's dead. I know how to feel for a pulse. I'm a hunter."

"Hold on. The ambulance will be here shortly." I wanted to offer him some hope. The chill in the night air put a stiffness in my bones as if it knew and was telling me something. "Where is she?"

"Right on in there." His chin fell to his chest as he shook his head. He still had on his camouflage hunting overalls with a lime-green Henley shirt. The members of the Hunt Club had a rule that they had to wear something neon so they wouldn't mistake one another for a deer or whatever it happened to be they were hunting.

Finn walked up with his uniform shirt partially buttoned and his white tee underneath.

"I heard your siren going off, so I jumped up and followed you." Finn was a great deputy. A grateful smile floated across my lips. "What's going on?"

"Darnell, why don't you wait right here while Deputy Vincent and I go in and see what's going on." I nodded and put my hand on his forearm to give him some sort of comfort.

Finn and I walked through the front door. There was a small foyer with what looked like an office to the right. The foyer led into a hallway that if you looked clear down it, you could see the refrigerator. Before you reached the kitchen, there was a step-down family room. And that's where I saw her.

"Lucy Ellen Lowell." I pointed at her feet sticking out from around the corner of the couch.

"Is she dead?" Finn asked as we hurried to her side.

I bent down. Her eyes were glazed over and her skin had already turned blue. I felt for a pulse that clearly wasn't there on her neck and then on her wrist.

"Dead as a doornail." My poppa's ghost stood in the dark corner of the room with his eyes focused on the lifeless body of Lucy Ellen Lowell.

CHAPTER FOUR

My heart pounded and my stomach churned. There was only one reason Poppa would be visiting me from the Great Beyond. That reason was murder, and the only dead person was Lucy Ellen Lowell, which, if you put two and two together, meant she was murdered.

I knew her heart wasn't going to start beating. I knew there wasn't going to be a pulse no matter how many times I checked or where I felt for it. But I couldn't say it out loud. Seeing Poppa's ghost and interacting with him was the only secret I'd kept from Finn. You see, a year or so ago, there'd been little to no crime in Cottonwood, and of course I took pride in thinking that it was because I was such a badass sheriff. Truth be told, my Poppa's ghost had been running off any would-be crime, not only keeping the crime rate low but also keeping me safe. That was good and dandy until two crimes happened at the same time in Cottonwood. Apparently even a ghost can't be in two places at once, and that's when I first saw the ghost of my poppa.

Once those crimes were solved, he'd disappeared. It wasn't until there was yet another murder in Cottonwood and then another that Poppa showed up again. Then I realized that Poppa's ghost only showed up when there'd been a murder in Cottonwood and he was there as my deputy ghost. This was how I knew that Lucy Ellen Lowell was, in fact...murdered.

Again, I reached down with my index finger and middle finger together, acting like I was checking for a pulse. My fingers moved onto her wrist, but the pigment on her face told me she'd been there for a few hours. I tried to calculate the time of death, which I guessed was probably three hours ago, but I'd leave that bit of information for Max Bogus, the coroner, to determine.

"I told you she's a goner." Poppa ghosted himself over to me. "And you've still got this one here?" His head thrust sideways, nodding at Finn.

I bit my lip and kept a poker face, ignoring Poppa. He liked Finn as a deputy, just not as my boyfriend.

"Do you think it was a heart attack?" Finn asked. "Looks like a heart attack. I don't see any wounds or blood. It looks like she fell while doing a crossword puzzle."

I needed to stay calm and not blurt out that Lucy Ellen had been murdered because Finn couldn't see my Poppa. Only Duke and I could see Poppa. Only I could talk to him.

"We still need to process the scene just in case." I knew this was going to make Finn question me and I had to sound calm even with the exploding feeling going off inside me that we had a homicide case on our hands.

I took the toe of my shoe and slid a crossword-puzzle book out from underneath her.

"Pfft. Doing a crossword puzzle." Poppa brushed Finn off. "Someone was crossing her off of this earth. That's what went on here." Poppa stomped around, his eyes darting around the shag carpet that I was sure hadn't been replaced since it was laid.

"Will you go get my bag out of the Wagoneer and make sure Duke's okay?" I asked Finn, who readily agreed.

It'd give me a minute to talk to Sheriff Elmer Sims.

"Hi, Poppa." I smiled so big when we locked eyes. He was the reason I'd gotten into law enforcement and without him, the last few murders in Cottonwood would've taken a lot longer to solve. "I hate that something awful has happened to Lucy, but I do love seeing you."

"Kenni-bug." Hearing my nickname from his lips brought a sense of peace that made me feel like I was going to be able to get down to the nitty gritty of this crime and fast.

"Let's get to work." He vigorously rubbed his hands together.

His broad shoulders dropped from underneath his brown sheriff's uniform that we'd buried him in.

"Lucy Ellen never hurt no one. She might be a little pushy and a bit nosy, but who'd do this to her?" he asked like he used to do when I was a child and he'd be working on a case. It was the beginning of the who, why, and why not game we'd play with one another to help solve the crimes. We were a dynamic duo while he was alive, and even after.

"I don't know. But she did make a few enemies over the last few weeks." I looked down at my hands and at the Natural Nail fingernail color. I couldn't help but recall how she'd acted yesterday when she showed up at Tiny Tina's. "Tina Bowers was one of them. When Tina said she couldn't do her nails, Lucy Ellen had a near fit in the shop. Even called Betty at dispatch to make a complaint."

"That can't be." Poppa squatted down near her torso, where her hands were off to the side. "Her nails look perfect to me."

There was a gun cabinet in the corner full of shotguns and a couple of handguns. Those always got my attention.

"Perfectly Posh," I gasped. My heart sank right into my feet. "Tiny Tina's," I whispered, knowing it was the exact match of Tina Bower's homemade nail polish Lucy Ellen had tried to purchase the day before.

I also knew that Tina didn't sell her nail polish. Which begged the question: how did Lucy's nails get painted the exact same color as Tina's Perfectly Posh? My eyes shifted around the room to see if I could spot a bottle of nail polish. The snap of the closure on my utility belt echoed throughout the quiet house when I took my flashlight out and shined it around the room in the dark crevices. Nothing jumped out at me.

And it didn't help matters that I knew Tina and Lucy Ellen had gotten into it. I shuddered. The image of Tina dragging her finger across her neck was an image I wished I could forget, but her words were the most haunting part.

"Maybe I should give her a hair treatment and let the scissors slip."

"Did you hear me?" Finn broke me out of my thoughts.

"No. No. I'm sorry. I was just thinking." I reached out and took the bag. "What were you saying?"

I unzipped the bag and took out my camera and notepad. I quickly wrote down "Perfectly Posh" and snapped a couple of photos, especially of Lucy's fingernails. I couldn't be 100 percent sure, but I was darn near 95 percent sure that it was the same exact color.

"I said that the EMTs are here and I told them to come on in." His words were barely out of his mouth before they came in. "Why are you taking photos like it's a crime scene?"

"Hey guys," I greeted them. None of us looked wide awake. It had to be around five a.m. by now and dawn was barely sneaking up on the horizon. "Do you think you could be careful? I'm not sure if this is a crime scene or not. I just need confirmation that she's expired."

I'd always hated that word. Expired. Such a sad word.

"We are sure it's a crime scene." Poppa's ghost could get very frustrated with me really fast when he felt like I wasn't listening to him.

I gave him a blank stare. He glared and huffed to the side as the EMTs started to work on Lucy.

"Who were you whispering to when I came back in?" Finn put the palm of his hand on the small of my back. It was nice and comforting.

"Myself. Like always." My standard reply when he'd find me talking to the air, even though I was actually talking to Poppa. "Let's go talk to Darnell," I suggested and headed back down the hallway. "Something doesn't seem right here," I said over my shoulder and walked out of the house.

The fog had rolled in from the Kentucky River and lay across the yard in front of their house. The burnt-orange fall morning told me the sun was peeking out and would soon lift the fog, making it another beautiful fall day in the Bluegrass state.

"Darnell, can you tell me how exactly you found Lucy Ellen?" I asked.

I put down my bag and had my pencil ready to write down what he was telling me.

"I left a couple of days ago with the boys for our annual trip to get my cabin and deer stand ready. Lucy Ellen was upset because she didn't want to go to the mayor's wedding alone. I kissed her goodbye and left. A couple of the guys had gotten some wild hogs, since it's only wild hog season until we can hunt deer. The refrigerator at our hunting cabin was on the fritz so I told them I'd drive them home and see Lucy Ellen 'cause she left a message on my cell all upset over something." His voice cracked as he recalled the last time he'd seen his wife. When he drew his hand up and through his hair, it exposed a handgun tucked in the waistband of his pants.

"Do you have a concealed carry?" I nodded to the gun. I had a rule to keep myself protected before I could protect the rest of Cottonwood.

"Yes, ma'am." He nodded and pulled out his wallet where he kept his certificate.

"What was she upset about? Did she say?" I asked, taking a good look at the paper before I gave it back to him.

"Something about not being ready for the wedding and some appointments getting mixed up with her nails. She was always getting something lifted, tucked, and redone. I could never keep up." His eyes clouded with tears. "Whatever made her happy made me happy. Me and that old gal been married for forty-five years. I was gonna retire soon and we were gonna live the life." His lips pressed together in a duck-bill look.

I offered a weak smile and wrote down what he'd said.

The EMTs came out of the house with an empty gurney and their bags zipped up. They shook their heads.

"We called Max Bogus and let him know. He should be here any minute." One of them referred to the town's coroner and owner of the only funeral home in Cottonwood.

Naturally, it was the next step in the process of removing the body even if it wasn't a crime scene. Cottonwood was so small it only took someone ten minutes to drive across town, and that's if they were driving twenty-five miles an hour and got stopped at all three traffic lights.

"I told her to get her blood pressure checked out. She'd just gone to see Camille down in town for her diabetes." Darnell's eyes were filled with tears. "Do you think she just dropped dead of a heart attack? She always said she wanted to go fast. Did she go fast?"

In the blink of an eye, there was a hearse rolling up the driveway.

It was always hard to see people grieve. In my line of duty, I saw that more than I saw happy tears.

"I'm sorry, Darnell. I can't answer those questions for you right now." I stepped out of the way as Max Bogus rolled the church cart past us and into the house.

CHAPTER FIVE

"Why did you take all that time to process the Lowell house when there wasn't anything to point to a homicide?" Finn plucked the menu from between the salt and pepper shakers after we sat down in our regular table at Ben's Diner.

"Things aren't always as they seem." Poppa sighed and licked his lips when Ben showed up with three coffees. One for Finn and two for me. Ben was good at keeping my caffeine addiction fueled. "He should know that coming from a big-city police department." Poppa scoffed.

Ben pulled a dog treat from his front pocket and gave it to Duke. Duke wagged his tail and happily took a few scratches behind the ears from Ben.

"Here you go." Ben dropped a handful of creamer cups and the Cottonwood Chronicle on the table. He lifted the backward hat off his shaggy head of brown hair just enough to grab the pencil he'd stuck behind his ear. "What'll ya have?"

"The usual?" He looked at me, knowing I wanted some biscuits and gravy.

"With a drizzle of chocolate added." I pulled both cups of steaming coffee to me, cupped the creamers, and dragged those over too.

Duke laid down next to my chair, pushing my feet to the side to make room for him.

"Uh-oh." Ben's brows cocked over his brown eyes. "Bad morning already?" He looked at his bare wrist. "You never have a drizzle of chocolate this early."

"You could say my morning could've started out better." I took a drink of the much-needed cup of joe. "Darnell Lowell found Lucy Ellen deceased this morning."

"That's terrible." Ben's forehead wrinkled. "How?"

"Natural causes" came out of Finn's mouth and "We aren't sure" came out of my mouth at the same time.

"Which is it?" Ben looked between the two of us.

"We aren't sure." I picked up the cup and took a sip.

"I'll have the breakfast hot brown." Finn put the menu back and clasped his hands around his cup of coffee.

I glanced through the paper while Finn and Ben chitchatted about the local high-school football team that was making big state news for the upcoming fall season. Plus the quarterback had some D1 college scouting him over the season.

Just like every other woman in Cottonwood, I flipped to what was known as Page Two. Page Two was really page two, but it had all the social gossip that was going on in Cottonwood and I was sure something about Polly Parker's maid of honor dropping out had to be in there. Boy, was I caught off guard to see a photo of Tina Bowers standing out front of her shop with her hand planted on her hip looking as if she were fussing at someone. On the right corner of the photo was another photo that showed Tina on the side of the road picking up limestones. The headline read "Tiny Tina's Small-Town Fraud," and was written by none other than Lucy Ellen Lowell.

Ben headed back to the kitchen.

"Here is why I think it could be more than just a heart attack." I turned the paper around and pushed it across the table.

Silently I sipped my coffee and watched Finn read. It certainly was the highlight of my morning. I could watch him all day long. I smiled and brought my cup up to my lips.

"Really?" Poppa rolled his eyes. "Leave all the goo-goo-ga-ga for later. We've got to go visit Tina Bowers." He stood behind Finn and pointed to the paper.

"There are always these sorts of crazy reviews in here every week from her. A couple of weeks ago there was one in there about the Pet Patch not carrying some sort of dog food." His lip drew up, his nose curled. "Don't forget about the one she did on Jolee's food truck."

"I agree. But I witnessed an argument between Tina and Lucy Ellen yesterday that's going to be hard to forget now that Lucy Ellen is dead." I dragged my finger across my neck like Tina had done. "Tina did this and said that maybe she should do Lucy's hair and let the scissors slip."

"Why would she say that?" Finn asked. This time he took a little more interest.

"Apparently Lucy Ellen has a bad habit of not showing up or cancelling appointments. She also just strolls into Tiny Tina's when she needs something done and expects them to accommodate her right then." I took another drink of my coffee. I continued, "Yesterday Tina had booked all of Polly Parker's pre-wedding appointments and Lucy Ellen was so mad because Tina and Cheree told her they couldn't fit her in and Cheree told her they didn't have any open appointments this week."

I glanced around the diner, half paying attention as my mind tried to make the jumbled thoughts in my head somewhat organized. The tables were filled and the squeak of the chairs echoed in my head. Ben pushed through the swinging door between the diner and the kitchen with a tray in his hands. He maneuvered his way over to our table and set our food down.

"Doesn't stuff like this happen all the time in those places?" Finn still wasn't buying it. He grabbed the pepper and shook it over his plate. "Gossip. Fights. In ten minutes they're back to being best friends again."

"Y'all need anything else?" Ben asked. "Besides coffee refills?"

"No, I'm good." I picked up the small bowl filled with melted chocolate and poured it over the biscuits instead of using gravy. It was delicious, and I needed some chocolate along with my coffee to think. My eyes zeroed in on my nails and the natural color I'd picked. "Yes," I said to Finn. "But no one usually ends up dead. And Lucy Ellen tried to buy the fingernail polish she wanted painted, but Tina makes her own colors and doesn't sell the polish. That's how Tina has people coming back."

It looked like I was going to have to talk to Tina.

"Maybe she went back there last night." Finn stuck the forkful of food in his mouth.

"Maybe." I shrugged and took a few bites.

I let out a long sigh before taking another drink. I wasn't necessarily frustrated, I just knew that she'd been murdered for the pure fact that Poppa was here and I could see that I was going to have to look into it. "I'm going to have to see what the autopsy says."

I took my phone out of my back pocket and sent Max Bogus a quick text to get me the preliminary autopsy as quickly as possible. My phone rang.

"Oh!" I turned the screen to Finn. "It's Max." I scooted my chair back and hit the talk button before I walked outside and stood on the sidewalk. Poppa and Duke next to me. "Hey, Max. That was quick."

"I got your text and wanted to let you know that Darnell didn't want an autopsy." His words pierced my ears.

"What?" I asked in shock.

"Why would he want to pay for an autopsy when it's pretty certain she died from natural causes?" he said.

"I want an autopsy." I knew that I couldn't order an autopsy if there was no real evidence that pointed to a murder.

"Kenni, I just can't give someone an autopsy because you want it. It's against the law unless you have a reason to think it's a homicide. What's going on?" Max asked with a curious tone.

"Listen, do me a favor." There were some things I wanted to check out before I could point fingers. "Hold off on embalming her until I can get some questions answered."

"He wants her cremated, so that shouldn't be too hard. I can tell him we only cremate certain days. You just let me know how long you need." Max clicked off the phone, letting me know I had a little time to check out what I needed to.

"This might be our hardest one yet." Poppa jumped around like a jumping bean, causing Duke to think he was playing. He barked a few times. "I always loved a good mystery to solve." Poppa rubbed his hands together.

I headed back into the diner. Just as I was about to sit down, my phone rang again. For a hot second I got excited thinking Max had something else

DEAD AS A DOORNAIL

to tell me, but that faded when I saw it was Tibbie Bell, one of my best friends.

Finn laughed when I held the phone out to show him who it was.

"Hi, Tibbie." My tone was flat like my enthusiasm for being in Polly's wedding.

"Kenni, I heard Lucy Ellen Lowell is dead, which puts one of the wedding tables out of whack with an odd number of people and that will just upset Polly, but I'm thinking out loud because that's not any concern of yours." I held the phone away from my ear; she was so loud. "I got a call from Polly. She and I were going over the toast for the wedding."

"I'm assuming you don't mean toast you eat?" I joked.

"In a normal situation with you, I'd think that was funny. In Polly's case, not so funny." Her voice was tight, stressed. "Your toast since you're the maid of honor."

"Tibbie." I was going to keep my mouth shut and put on the ugly dress and do my job, but Polly was overstepping the fake friend thing. "You and I are best friends. I would have a lot to say in a toast about you when you decide to get hitched, but Polly? Come on? Can't someone else in her wedding party do it?"

"Don't you think I suggested that, Kenni?" she asked. "Polly insists that you do it. And..." She took too long of a pause.

"What?" I asked with apprehension.

"First thing tomorrow morning I've got a counseling session for you and Polly with Preacher Bing."

"What?" This was getting ridiculous. "Preacher?"

"It's no different than pre-marriage counseling," she said like she was trying to sell me on the idea.

"I'm not marrying Polly Parker." This whole maid-of-honor thing was a big mistake. Huge. "I'm not coming to no counseling with Polly over a fake friendship."

"Kenni, please. This is a big job for me. If I can pull off a wedding for the Parkers, it'll be great for my portfolio. Just do it for me." Tibbie pulled out the big guns.

"I'll only go if you're going to be there too." It was my one stipulation. I wasn't about to do this alone.

"Yes." Suddenly her voice was much happier. "You're the best, Kenni. Be there at seven a.m. It's the only time Preacher had."

"Bring me a coffee. It's the least you can do." I stared over the table at Finn. He was getting money out of his wallet to pay for the food.

"I'll see you at seven a.m. sharp. Don't forget the dress fitting today." Tibbie hung up.

"Are you okay?" Finn's lips turned down and his eyes dropped to the phone in my hand. He looked back up at me. "You don't look happy."

I took the last piece of biscuit and emerged it into the chocolate sauce, then popped it into my mouth.

"Images of me getting stuffed into that dress is something no one should see." I patted my belly and shook my head, rolling my eyes when Finn looked at me with a question in his big brown eyes.

CHAPTER SIX

To everyone else in our small community, life was hunky dory. The wedding was still the talk of the town and a few grumbles about poor Lucy Ellen and her heart attack was all I'd heard during my rounds. Finn and I had said goodbye and he headed back to the department to look through the fax and phone messages that were left overnight. Then there was Betty Murphy, who fielded all the dispatch calls during the day and did small secretarial jobs for us.

Cottonwood was too small to have more than the three of us on staff and during any normal week, there wasn't a murder and this was our routine. This week would seem normal to them until Poppa and I could prove otherwise.

Secretly, I had no other choice but to start looking at possible suspects and Tina Bowers was first on my list. I sat in the Wagoneer in Tiny Tina's parking lot and waited for Tina to turn the sign on the door to OPEN before I interrupted her morning ritual where she got the shop ready for her clients.

"How are we going to get Max to do some sort of toxicology report?" I asked Poppa.

"I haven't figured that out yet." Poppa and I continued to watch the shop door.

My elbow was propped up on the windowsill and my hand twirled my ponytail, my hairstyle choice for work. It didn't take me long to get ready. With my boyfriend as my coworker, you'd think I'd take a second to get ready by putting on makeup and fixing my hair. But I knew that he'd obviously been attracted to me looking like this, so why alter my appearance? Besides, being sheriff wasn't about being pretty and all girly, though Mama would have me in a pretty gown, heels, and full makeup.

"See what you find out here and then take it from there." He shifted in his seat when Duke jumped to the backseat of the Wagoneer. "What are you trying to accomplish here?"

"I want to see if Tina did Lucy's nails after I left. I know what I heard. There was a roomful of people who could say the exact same thing. I saw what she did with her hand." I slid my finger across my throat. "And then she ends up dead? You and I both know she was murdered. Did Tina do it? She threatened to. But if Tina did do her nails, then maybe she didn't really mean the context of her words and had been just talking."

"You mean gossiping?" Poppa smiled and jerked his head to look at the shop. "What about the other gal in there?"

"Cheree Rath?" Poppa nodded. I said, "I thought about her too. But Lucy Ellen went to Tina. It was Tina that she gave the most grief to." I watched and wondered if Tina Bowers really had it in her to kill someone.

"Not only Tina had a lot to lose from Lucy Ellen going around town and badmouthing everyone. Cheree could lose her job too," Poppa mentioned and adjusted himself in the seat.

"If Tina's business took a nose dive, then there wouldn't be enough customers to have an employee." I looked at Poppa. His brows rose. "Just a thought," I finished.

"One you might want to explore, but I agree that we start with Tina Bowers," he said and pointed to the salon.

Tina flipped the sign on the door to open.

"Let's go," Poppa said before he ghosted out of the Jeep.

I made sure the windows were down, even though it was a cool morning. Duke liked to stick his head out the window.

"Stay," I demanded of Duke and pointed the corner of the Chronicle at him before I shut the door.

"Kenni, what are you doing here so early?" Tina fiddled with a clipboard from behind the counter and stuck it on the ledge where customers signed in when they arrived for their appointments.

"Solving a crime. Geez." Poppa's head popped back. "Why do you think?"

He ghosted around the room, darting from one end to the other.

"Two reasons." I wasn't sure if she'd yet heard about Lucy Ellen since it just happened and I wasn't sure she'd seen the paper. I pulled the tucked paper from underneath my arm and set it on the counter with the review facing her. "Have you seen the paper?"

She picked up the Chronicle and then set it back down.

"She didn't waste no time," Tina said and pushed the paper a little closer to me. I don't care what she thinks. If she thinks..." She stared at me for a second. "What? What's that look on your face?"

"I had a call from Darnell Lowell around four this morning. He found Lucy Ellen dead when he got home." There was no good way to put it.

"Oh no." Her chest deflated and she gave me a blank stare. "That's awful."

"Are you sure you didn't talk to her since she was here yesterday?" I asked.

"What? You think I had something to do with it?" Her eyes lowered. "You've lost your cotton-pickin' mind."

"Has she? Has she really lost her mind?" Poppa got really close to Tina's face and narrowed his eyes. "I'd say she's doing her job." Poppa glared at Tina.

The phone rang and she grabbed it.

"Tiny Tina's." She did a few mm-hms while flipping through the calendar. "I can reschedule you. Oh." Her eyes slid up to me. She grabbed the paper and took another look. "Fine. Don't call me back when you can't get your nails done somewhere else or when you're in a pinch." She didn't hang the phone up, she smacked it down. "I swear, if she were alive, she wouldn't be for long, because I'd kill her."

The phone rang again.

"Tiny Tina's Salon and Spa. Hi-do, shugs." She smacked her hand on the appointment book. "Mm-hm. I'm sorry you've got to cancel. I'm more than happy to reschedule you for later in the day." She grabbed the pencil, eraser side down, and used it in the appointment book. She grabbed the pencil on both ends and broke it in half. "Ugh!" She threw them on the desk after she hung up the phone.

"I'm guessing that was another cancellation due to the newspaper article?" I asked.

"What the hell is going on?" She spit and gnawed on her lip. "That...that..." She stomped out from behind the counter and threw the paper in the trashcan. "That nasty woman."

"Calm down." I tried to distinguish if she was upset about the cancellation or the article or all of it in general. "Can you tell me where you were last night after you closed the shop?"

"Are you kidding me? Are you kidding me?" she asked as if I hadn't heard her the first time. "You think I killed her?"

"No one said she was murdered." I eyed her suspiciously. "The only reason I ask where you were is because I found it so interesting that she came in here and demanded that you paint her nails and do her hair. You turned her away and when I went there this morning, her nails were painted Perfectly Posh."

"Not my Perfectly Posh." She drew her hand up to her chest. "I only have one bottle and don't make more until I'm out."

"What if you run out?" I questioned.

"Then I go right back there and whip more up," she said and gestured to the back room.

Tina darted from her station to Cheree's station, picking through the bottles of nail polish.

"Where in tarnation is it?" Her eyes darted around the room before they settled on mine. "It's not here. She stole it!" Her face grew red as her hand fisted at her side. "She stole it when she was here yesterday and I wasn't looking."

She went from station to station, through every drawer, tearing up the place.

"Listen." I stuck my hand out and tried to stop her. She was frantically looking under, in, and around every nook and cranny in the salon. "If she came back later in the day and you did her nails, it's fine. I just need you to tell me."

"I'm telling you right now that I didn't call her. The last time I saw her was when you saw her." She stomped her foot and pointed down to the floor. "Right here in this very spot."

"Did Cheree have her come back in?" There had to be an answer to this strange situation.

"Not that I know of. Cheree left before I did. It was my late night." She darted off toward the back of the shop. "I'm going to look back here just in case Cheree put it back by the color lab."

"Color lab?" I asked.

"It's where I make my color magic for my polishes like the one Lucy Ellen stole right from underneath my nose!" She hollered before she disappeared through the hippie hanging plastic beads that substituted for a door.

While she looked in the back room, I took a stroll around the salon. The two massaging chairs for the pedicures were clean and ready for the next customer. Between them was a small table with tabloids from two years ago. The cabinet on rolling wheels that Cheree and Tina brought over to finish up the pedicures was tucked neatly behind them.

I rolled it out and looked at the colors on top and the jars with blue cleaner. The pedicure tools were emerged in them. When I didn't see the distinctive nail color, I pulled out the top drawer and found the spongey things they put between toes. The second drawer was the packages of flip-flops they supplied and the third drawer was filled with cotton balls.

After I rolled the pedicure cart back where I'd found it, I walked over to Cheree's nail station. On the right side of the table were the few nail colors that were on display. There was a black folded towel on each side of the table where the customer's hands rested while Cheree filed, trimmed, and painted. On the left side of the table was the acrylic nail light where the customer put her hands in the glowing tube for the nails to dry. I'd never done those; I was more of the naked nail kind of gal, but not Lucy. Her nails were as fake as could be.

In the drawers were new nail files and all the ingredients that were used for the acrylic nails. There wasn't anything different on Tina's side. Then there was the front desk. Besides the register, there was a landline phone, an appointment book, and a fake plant.

In front of the desk were two wire lawn chairs and a small table with more tabloid magazines that were just as old as the ones by the pedicure chairs.

I picked up the cordless phone and almost hit the redial button, but noticed there was a caller ID screen. I used the left arrow to scroll through and there was Lucy's name along with her phone number. Lucy Ellen did say that she'd called earlier that day and the timestamp did go with her story.

"Did the phone ring?" Tina came back in the shop with a fist full of glass polish bottles. "I couldn't find it, but I did have these that I can use in its place until I can make more up."

She held up a bottle with pink polish, but not the exact same color.

"No." I hung the phone back up. "I was looking to see your caller ID."

"Kenni, you're making me feel like I've done something wrong. Is there something you need to tell me?" she asked.

The phone rang.

"Hold that thought." She put her finger with a dagger-like nail up in a hold-on gesture. "Tiny Tina's, best sal-lon and spa in Cottonwood."

Her accent made "salon" sound like two separate words and she did leave out the fact that she was the only salon and spa in Cottonwood so it was automatically the best.

"I heard she died." Tina twisted her piece of gum around her finger and planted her hiney up against the front desk with her back facing the front. "Mm-hm. Heart attack? She came in here yesterday all wound up tight. No wonder." Tina nodded her head like the person on the other end could see her. "Poor girl. From what I heard, she was knock-kneed when she was little and I bet that's what made her crazy as a June bug." She stood silent for a minute. "That was ridiculous. I saw it and I can't believe that after all these years she decided to give me a bad review. And you know, people won't remember her for her. When her name comes up, they'll remember this mean review."

About that time the front door opened and the bell that was bread-tied on the arm of the hardware of the door jingled. The customer sat down in one of the lawn chairs, waiting for Tina to get off the phone.

"Listen, I've got to go, but put me down for some deviled eggs." She stopped talking, then picked right back up. "I am bringing something. I don't care if she didn't like me as of the time of this paper hitting the streets. She was a client of mine for two years. I know her deepest, darkest secrets." Tina hung up.

"Deepest, darkest secrets?" Poppa and I asked at the same time.

"When you sit your tushie in that chair, it's like getting a shot of truth serum," she snarled. "Right now I'm not ready to talk about the dead when her body isn't even cold."

"Something to remember when you drag her in for questioning." Poppa eyed Tina.

"What about deviled eggs?" I asked and decided to let the darkest-secret thing go until Max confirmed that Lucy Ellen was murdered. Then it was fair game to press Tina for answers.

"They're getting together the repast for Lucy Ellen's funeral, though they don't know when Darnell is going to have it." She gave a simple shrug and pulled a black apron off the back of the chair and tied it around her waist. "Hon," she got the customer's attention, "you ready?"

The customer got up and headed on back to the manicure station.

"If you find that bottle of nail polish let me know." I put my hand on the door.

"I'll see you Thursday," she said.

"Thursday?" I turned and questioned with the door partially opened, wondering if the funeral had already been planned.

"Mmm-hmm." She nodded with pinched lips. "Tibbie Bell left a message on the machine and said you're stepping in to be Polly's number one and she's got the sal-lon booked for nails on Thursday."

"Yeah. See you Thursday," I muttered and left the salon with a feeling that I'd be back real soon with more questions.

"Polly," I groaned and remembered the dress fitting Tibbie had scheduled for me. "We've got to get you to the station." I rubbed Duke's head before I shoved him to the backseat of the Jeep.

"Where are we going?" Poppa asked. "Camille Shively's I hope, because you've got to find out about that stuff Darnell was spouting off about Lucy's health and we've got to prove she wasn't sick so we can get him to agree to an autopsy."

"That might be a good angle." I never thought about getting Camille on my side. "I'm not sure how forthcoming she'll be with information regarding Lucy Ellen and I know I won't be able to get a warrant for Lucy's records on a just-because-I-want-to-see excuse to the judge. No judge will give me that warrant."

Camille Shively wasn't one of my friends in school. She was a little younger than me, but old enough to be the new doctor in town now that our former baby doctor was no longer among the living.

"Somehow someway you've got to figure out how we can get an autopsy on that body before Max cremates it. Speaking of the dead." Poppa pointed to my left over to the Old Cemetery, the only graveyard in Cottonwood and his final resting place along with everyone else's. "I better go check up on my friends." Poppa ghosted off just as the first light of the three on Main Street turned red.

CHAPTER SEVEN

Duke jumped up in the front seat and stuck half of his body out the window. His tongue hanging out of his mouth made his slobber fling up on the windshield. I watched as Poppa's ghost crossed Main Street and floated along the old limestone slave wall that surrounded the cemetery. The walls were historically preserved and couldn't be touched. They were built by Irish immigrants and they could be found all over the state of Kentucky.

When the light turned green, we drove south on Main Street. The Sweet Adelines had been busy this morning hanging up new banners on all the dowel rods from the carriage lights that dotted Main Street on both sides. The summer baskets of flowers provided by Myrna Savage's Petal Pushers Florist had been replaced with new baskets filled with mums of a variety of reds, oranges, and yellows. It was the perfect flower choice for the between-seasons décor.

Kentucky in the autumn was a beautiful place; if only the death of Lucy Ellen Lowell wasn't hanging over my head I'd have enjoyed the drive to the office that much more. Normally I'd take a right off of Main and pull down the alley in front of the department, but there was a prime parking spot in front of Cowboy's Catfish Restaurant. I jerked the wheel and pulled right on in.

Cowboy's Catfish had the best catfish and hushpuppies around. And it just so happened that the sheriff's department rented the room behind Cowboy's from owner Bartleby Fry. It was cheaper for Cottonwood to rent the room than building and running our own one-cell facility. The only job hazard was smelling the home-cooked food. Today's special was Kentucky round steak, also known as fried bologna. Duke and I loved nothing better than a piece of fried bologna with mustard between two slices of white bread and a side of Bartleby's sliced potatoes and onions.

"My oh my." I rubbed my belly when I walked into the front door of the restaurant. "Something sure does smell good."

It was good to see all the tables in use and the dining room filled with conversations.

Duke trotted back to the kitchen where he knew he was in for a treat.

"Why is it that you always walk in that front door when I'm cooking up bologna?" Bartleby laughed when I passed him on the way to the department.

"Luck, I guess." I winked and opened the door of the office where Betty Murphy was sitting at her desk talking on the phone. "Come on, Duke." I patted my leg and shut the door after he meandered in. "Oh, stop pouting."

I walked over to Finn's desk and grabbed a dog treat out of the tin sitting there as Betty hung up her call.

"I sure did hate to hear about Lucy Ellen this morning." Betty looked up from filing her nails. "She sure will be missed at bell choir."

"Bell choir?" I asked.

"Yeah." Betty looked up over her glasses. "She's a member of the First Baptist Church bell choir. She's our gyro handbellist."

"Handbellist?" I questioned if that was a word, but went with it anyway. "What is a gyro?"

"It's the vibration of the bell when held in a certain position and gives a different ring than just fluidly ringing the bell. There's so many techniques." Betty held her hand in the air and pretended as if she were ringing her handbell.

"Isn't Blanche Bailey a member of the bell choir?" I asked about the lady who did all the alterations in town and just so happened to be doing my Scarlett O'Hara dress fitting.

I wasn't the best church-going gal in Cottonwood. Making sure that all the fine citizens of our community and their property were safe while they were in church was the great excuse I gave Preacher on why I wasn't able to attend on a regular basis.

"She sure is. She's getting our Christmas Cantata ready." A worried look crossed her face. "Oh dear," her brows furrowed, "I'm not sure who's going to take Lucy's spot since she was our only gyro and the crowd goes nuts over that. And to think the women of the Hunt Club are doing the annual gun show without her."

"I'm sure Blanche will have all of that worked out." I glanced up at the clock over top of the one cell and noticed by the time I got home, grabbed my dress, and got to Blanche's house, it'd be time for my fitting. "Speaking of Blanche, I've got a dress fitting."

"I heard all about you doing that silly maid-of-honor thingy while I was at Lulu's Boutique this morning when I stopped to get breakfast from Jolee's food truck." Betty's face softened into a smile. "Your mama was asking everyone to pray that you'd catch the wedding bouquet."

"That would just make Mama's year, wouldn't it?" I asked.

Out of nowhere, I imagined me standing in that ugly dress watching the bouquet of flowers floating toward me, hitting me in the head and falling to my feet when I refused to catch it.

Right then I vowed not to even participate in the stupid tradition. I'd already compromised my values to be in the wedding (and by agreeing to wear the ugly dress in front of all Cottonwood), but to give an inkling that I was ready to walk down the aisle by catching some silly bouquet that was attached to an old wives' tale? Forget it.

"Do you mind keeping an eye on Duke?" I asked Betty, since he was all curled up and sleeping on his bed near my desk. "I won't be long."

"You know I don't mind." She smiled at him like everyone did when they looked at the big lug. "He keeps me company. And he keeps the best secrets." She winked.

I shook my head, grabbed my bag, and headed back through Cowboy's Catfish, but not without stopping and popping a hushpuppy in my mouth.

"I'll have a plate for y'all in the department when you get back," Bartleby called through the chattering crowd.

I gave him the two-finger toodles on my way out the front door since my mouth was stuffed with the delicious golden crispy ball of dough.

Blanche lived on Second Street. It was only a couple of blocks over from the department. There was a small creek that ran alongside Second Street and all the houses. Each house had a small bridge going over the creek that connected the road and the driveway. It was just another cozy feature of Cottonwood that made the small town so lovely to live in.

I double checked the address Polly Parker had given me because there were several cars in the drive and the last thing I wanted to do was to try a dress on in front of anyone. Being a few minutes early, I'd decided to give Darnell Lowell a quick call and check up on him as well as throw in the question about Lucy's health.

"Hi, Darnell. It's Kenni Lowry." I didn't say Sheriff because I felt that saying my name without the title was a lot less formal. When I didn't have my uniform on, people saw me as a regular person and didn't worry about what they were saying around me. "How are you doing?"

"I'm just not sure what I'm going to do." He didn't sound any better than he had in the wee hours of the morning. "I just feel like she's gone to one of her meetin's this morning and will be home directly."

"Again, I'm so sorry for your loss." I wasn't sure how I was going to get him to even think about an autopsy when he wasn't even accepting that she was gone. "As sheriff, I do need to make sure that you are positive you don't want an autopsy to find out exactly how she died."

"I just figured it was a heart attack. I mean, she'd been going to see Dr. Shively and all. Lucy Ellen said she was seeing stars. Like shooting stars. One of the women down at Tiny Tina's told her that shooting stars meant high blood pressure. Then she came home with some little pills after her doctor's appointment." I could hear an uncertain tone in his voice. Maybe I was getting to him.

"And wouldn't you like to know for sure that Lucy Ellen had high blood pressure and that's what killed her? I mean, I don't want you to beat yourself up over it for years wondering." I crossed my fingers, squeezed my eyes together, and gave a little prayer that he'd change his mind.

"I never thought of it like that." There was a hesitation. "I don't know,

Kenni. I just want to let her rest in peace. We are firm believers that when it's your time to go, it's your time to go."

My phone beeped. I pulled it away from my ear and looked at the screen to see who was calling in.

"Darnell, I've got to go, but you think about it. I just want to make sure that you're doing okay and since you don't have any children, I wanted to offer my suggestion. I'll check in on you later." I didn't wait for his response. I clicked over. "Hey, Max. It doesn't look like I'm going to get Darnell to change his mind about an autopsy."

"Sheriff, it doesn't look like you have to," Max said. "I started inputting all of Lucy's information into the database to register for the death certificate. Lucy Ellen popped up as a certified organ donor. I'm not sure even Darnell knows that."

"And? Are you trying to tell me that you found something out?" I asked.

"All of her organs looked pretty healthy and when I ran the preliminary tests to start to register them…Well." He hesitated. "I'm not sure how you knew, but none of her organs are viable. She's full of poison."

"Poison?" I asked.

Out of the corner of my eye, I could see Poppa appear in the passenger seat.

His round checks were puffing out with a big smile on his face, his comb-over was neatly splayed across the top of his head, and his sheriff uniform was just as pressed and pristine as it was the days he wore it.

"Cyanide, to be exact." Max's words were music to my ears.

"Cyanide?" It was like we were in a repeating game. There was really no reason for me to be shocked, but I was. It was wrapping around me, making me feel like I needed air. Lots of air. I rolled down the window and let the breeze fill the Wagoneer with fresh air as I took a few deep breaths.

"It looks like she died between seven p.m. and four a.m. You've got another homicide on your hands. If you want to stop by, I've got a copy of the organ report. I'm going to call Darnell to let him know that I've turned the case over to you, if that's okay?" Max asked.

"Yeah. Of course it's okay. Listen, I've got to run into Blanche Bailey's and try on a dress for her. I'll stop by after that." I stared at Poppa and slowly shook my head.

Max laughed.

"I heard you're the new maid of honor for the Parker girl's wedding." He laughed harder.

"Word sure does travel fast around here," I noted.

"Yep. And I better get off the phone. Do you want me to call Darnell?" He asked.

"You know what." I hesitated because I should've probably told him, but now Darnell had no choice but to accept the autopsy. It was one last step I had to worry about. "I do want you to call Darnell and tell him that I asked you to call him and we are moving forward with a full autopsy."

"Sounds good. Well, I need to get back to finding out the source of this poisoning. I'll see you soon." Max clicked off the phone.

"Weeee doggie." Poppa smacked his leg. "Go on. Get out of here. We've got a murder to solve."

"I wish I could. I've got to get in there and have Blanche fit me in this dress. It'll give Max time to call Darnell about Lucy." I gnawed on my bottom lip. "And some time for him to process it. Now my questions for him and Tina Bowers are much different."

"Don't forget Jolee Fischer had words with Lucy Ellen too." Poppa knew that Jolee was my friend, but to be fair we questioned anyone and everyone. "Everyone's a suspect until we get the real killer."

I looked down at my phone and used the pad of my thumb to scroll to Finn's name. I hit send.

"Hey there." Finn was always so chipper when I called.

"You won't sound so happy when I tell you that Lucy Ellen Lowell was murdered." I turned the Wagoneer off and reached behind me, dragging that godawful green dress to the front seat. "Max Bogus just called. He said that when he put Lucy's information into the computer to generate the death certificate, she popped up as an organ donor. Long story short, her organs are poisoned with cyanide."

"You called it." Finn didn't seem as surprised as I thought he would. "I don't know how you do it, but you can spot a murdered victim in a second flat upon arrival to a scene."

"Maybe one day I'll tell you my secret," I said, looking over at Poppa.

"No you won't either," Poppa warned.

"What can I do?" he asked.

"I've actually got to go into Blanche Bailey's to try on this maid-of-honor dress for Polly's wedding. After that I'm going to go grab the report from Max and head back to the office to open the official homicide investigation." There were definitely some things he could do that would help. "Max said he was going to call Darnell and turn the case over to us. Do you think you can head back over to the Lowell place and secure the scene? We have to scour that entire house."

I was never so glad that I took photos than I was right now.

"I can do that." He was so agreeable.

"And I also want you to go ask Jolee about her confrontation with Lucy." There was no way I wanted to question Jolee. It was a conflict of interest. "She said something about her and Lucy Ellen having an argument over the food at Polly's wedding or something. I really can't recall because it was when I was at Tiny Tina's and they were all gossiping about everything."

I wished I'd listened better now.

"That's a tough situation to be in with your best friend." He wasn't telling me anything I didn't already know.

"That's why I want you to interview her. Not that I think she did it, but I feel like I need to question everyone who Lucy Ellen had words with." It was only logical.

Back issues of the Cottonwood Chronicle would help me figure out who all those people were since Lucy Ellen was so good at writing negative reviews. The library would have all the back issues.

"Then your best friend is going to hate me. That's the last thing I want as your boyfriend." Him just saying that made me tingly. "I do love you."

"I love you too. So maybe we can get together at your place tonight since we always go to mine." It was a simple suggestion, but I loved his new addition and comfy couch. "A night of Netflix and some snuggling. Of course with Duke and Cosmo." I had to throw in the fur babies.

"Kenni Lowry, you're sweet talking me into going to talk to Jolee." The hint of sexy teasing made me giggle.

"Is it working?" I asked.

"I can't wait. I'll even grab us a couple of plates of food from her food truck." That was a great plan. "I'll text you when I get finished securing the Lowell house."

"Be sure to tell Darnell that we need him to stay somewhere else tonight." I almost forgot that he couldn't be there. Not that the place wasn't probably already tainted from him there, but at least I'd taken some photos. "Talk soon."

"Sounds good." He clicked off before me. I smiled. Suddenly going to try on the nasty green dress in my grip didn't seem so bad knowing that Finn was going to be next to me all night.

"Really? Your mama and daddy were never that goo-goo over each other." Poppa rolled his eyes. "We've got to stay focused. Keep our eye on the prize. The killer. Cottonwood isn't safe."

"First, I've still got to live life, and that includes this dress and my relationship with Finn." My brows rose. "Cottonwood is safe. Lucy Ellen Lowell had a lot more enemies than anyone realized. She made someone mad and that's who's killed her. You and I will figure it out like we always do."

"That's not how we did things when I was sheriff." Poppa was old school and I knew that.

"Poppa, you're here to help me. I'm the sheriff now, and right now we have to let Max do his job and figure out how he thinks she got the poison. There's nothing we can do until her body talks to him. In the meantime, we'll pay Tina another visit."

Poppa must've hated my answer because he ghosted away.

"Oh well." The green dress was flapping in the wind behind me on my way up to Blanche's door. I jumped back when she flung the door open.

"We've been waiting for you," she trilled and swung one arm out. "Tibbie called."

There was an elastic snap attached to her wrist and she wore a bright yellow-and-orange-swirl caftan. Her red hair flowed down her back. Her big brown eyes shone and a smile curled up on the edges of her lips. She took a step back for me to enter.

If there was one thing that Blanche was, it was eccentric. She was in so many women's groups because the word on the street was that the women in Cottonwood liked to know where Blanche was at all times. She was a flirt and she didn't care who she flirted with. The women wanted to keep her close to them.

"Who's been waiting for me?" I asked and stepped into the red walls of her lair.

"The girls from bell choir." She dragged her long fingers down her hair. There was a smirk on her face. She reached out. "I'll take that." She plucked the dress from my hands.

"And why have they been waiting for me?" I asked.

"Do come on in." She walked down the hall and opened a door. "You can go in here and try on the dress. When you are ready, just walk down the hallway and you'll find us."

She hooked the dress on a coat tree inside the room. The room had three sewing machines and all three looked to be in use with something stuck to the needle. There was a rack of clothes and tags with names written on each one. Blanche was a busy woman.

After I'd gotten my sheriff's uniform off, I unzipped the curtain...er...dress and slipped it on. I could barely reach the zipper so I left what I couldn't reach. The murmuring and whispers spilled out and down the hall, leading me right to the women. This room was painted red too. There was a black fireplace that literally hung from the ceiling. It was the strangest thing I'd ever seen. There was a low flame that had to have been set for ambiance. The sweet songs of Frank Sinatra spilled from the ceiling speakers.

On the couch sat Mama, Myrna Savage, Ruby Smith, Viola White, and Dr. Camille Shively with big smiles on their faces.

"Tea?" Blanche dramatically swung her hand across a three-tiered plate filled with cookies and other sweet treats. "Cookie?"

"Well, hello," I said in a flat voice.

Mama jumped up.

"Let me zip you the rest of the way up." She hurried behind me.

"Oh, you look so lovely. Gone with the Wind." Camille's shoulders and edges of her mouth lifted in a delighted gesture before she stuffed a cookie in her mouth.

"Don't you have patients?" I asked, wondering how I was going to slip in some questions about Lucy's health, though it really didn't matter now that her death had gone from natural to homicide. I was still curious.

"I get a lunch." She eased back in the folds of the couch. "Besides, I wouldn't've missed seeing you in that dress for the world after I heard you were filling in."

If I'd not pushed all the air out of my lungs to try and get this dress zipped up, I would've protested.

"If you could just get it over her bottom rib, you can tug real hard." Viola White gave her two cents before she jumped up, pushing her big round black glasses upon the edge of her nose. "Let me try."

"Really?" My brows rose.

"Suck up and in." Viola's head jerked around my right shoulder to look at me so she knew I heard what she said. Her bright red lipstick gave a pop of color to her pasty white skin and short, spikey red hair.

"I'm sucking in the best I can." I filled my lungs again.

She jerked, and red feathers on her vest flew through the air.

"Pfft. Pfft," I blew as the feathers floated down and got close to my mouth.

"Honey, you might be happy it don't fit. I mean, the color." Viola gave up. She came around to look at the front of the dress. Her fingers played with the multi-beaded necklace that draped her neckline under the vest. "I love color. It gives a little life. In fact, color can raise the dead, but this color won't raise no one."

"Mmmhmm." Ruby Smith nodded and agreed. Her lips and hair matched Viola's red feathery vest. Her lips pursed. "Ugly."

"Move it, Viola." Mama practically shoved Viola out of the way. She tugged the dress a little further up on my waist and walked behind me.

"This is my daughter's time to shine in a dress in front of Cottonwood. I'm not giving up that easily." Mama tugged on the zipper and jutted me forward a few times.

"Mama, you're hurting me." I cringed.

"Fashion hurts." Viola White always wore the awfulest-looking get-ups she claimed were high fashion. Since she was the wealthiest woman in Cottonwood, she should know.

Mama whispered something so low I couldn't understand her.

"Huh?" I asked and jerked as the zipper pierced my skin with another jerk.

She mumbled so I still couldn't hear her.

"What?" I asked again.

"Suck in!" she hollered with a follow up of gasps from the peanut gallery. "More!"

"Honey." Blanche tsked, walking slowly around me. Her eyes focused on the dress or maybe the skin that was trying to get stuffed in the dress. My skin. "Looks like someone's gained a little weight." She winked at me. "Happy weight."

I sucked in.

"Try it again, Mama." No way had I gained weight.

When I felt Mama start to tug, I sucked in real deep this time because the look on all of those henny-hen faces was my signal that my not being able to fit into the dress was going to be the hot topic of gossip. Forget about Lucy Ellen Lowell dying. Mama sucked in too and held her breath.

"Nuh-uh." Mama let go, the air leaving her body. "It's not going to zip." There was a bit of disappointment in her tone.

"Yes. Happy fat." Blanche did another walk around me.

This time there was a yellow measuring tape dangling around her neck like a scarf and a pincushion in the shape of a tomato clipped around her wrist with all sorts of pins stuck in it.

"Happy fat?" I wasn't sure, but I think Blanche Bailey just called me fat. "There's no such thing."

Was there? I looked at Camille.

"This is just an old dress that's not the right size." I sucked in so much that I nearly passed out.

"Nope. Not going to zip." Mama's face had a look of concern. "Can you add fabric?" She turned to Blanche.

"Mmmhmm." Blanche nodded and ho-hummed behind pinched lips. "That's happy fat for sure. It's what we get when we are in love. So you must be in love with that handsome Finn Vincent."

"Not that northerner. No way. Ain't that right, Kenni?" Myrna Savage's eyes focused on the dress.

"Love doesn't put fat on you." It was ridiculous. "Right, Camille?"

Camille looked up over her tea cup. She took a quick sip and set it on the saucer on the coffee table in front of her.

"It's not a real term, but I have heard that when we are happy, we tend to gain a little weight, but that's just from some silly study. I didn't read it because you still look good and as your doctor, I'd tell you if I was concerned."

"I'm sure concerned," Mama griped.

"Alright." I turned and headed back down the hall. "I'm out of here."

"Viv! What's wrong with you?" I heard Blanche say to Mama. "She's not only a wonderful woman, but she's an amazing sheriff and girlfriend."

I shut the room door that Blanche used as the dressing room for her sewing business. I turned around, my reflection was staring back at me from the mirrored closet doors. The green dress did nothing for me. I swear the movie version was much more romantic than the real version and surely to goodness Polly Parker didn't think this dress was pretty.

"Easy for you to say. You've got a daughter who's married and gave you grandchildren. I'm beginning to think Kenni is allergic to being a wife. She wants to go around packing a gun all day and chasing bad guys." Mama did the same song and dance with them as she did me.

"She looks great. You're gonna run that girl off one day," Myrna warned. "And you complain that she doesn't stop by and see you all the time. Well, I wouldn't either if you talked about me like that."

I turned around and looked at the backside. There wasn't much more room for the zipper to be zipped. Happy fat? Who ever heard of such a thing?

"Maybe I do, behind your back," Mama teased Myrna.

"Speaking of gossip." Myrna's voice caught my attention. "Can y'all believe that Lucy Ellen is dead?"

"Such a shame, and at a young age." Blanche's voice and footsteps were coming closer to the dressing room. There was a slight knock on the door. "Kenni, can I come in?"

I took one last look in the mirrored closet doors and with a deep sigh, walked over to the door and opened it.

"Come on in," I said flatly. "Happy fat? Really?"

"Honey, it's no big deal. You'll lose it. I see that boy stare at you when I'm at Ben's eating breakfast. You don't even notice me because you're so goo-goo over him." She smiled. There was a twinkle in her eye. "I wish I had that kind of love. All them women think I'm trying to steal their men, but I'm not. I just like a little attention." She winked and planted a hand on each of my shoulders. She turned me around to look in the mirrors. "You know what I see?"

I shook my head and looked at her as she peered over my shoulder.

"I see a strong, independent woman that never let anyone stop her from getting what she wanted. Including Finn Vincent." She grinned ear to ear. "All them single girls out there nearly fell all over each other trying to court him. He only had eyes for you. I could see it. Besides, this dress is ugly and the fabric doesn't give. I have no idea what Polly Parker was thinking."

I laughed and pushed my shoulders back.

"Chance Ryland is no Rhett Butler." Her brows rose and she winked. She patted my shoulders. "Now, let me get this pinned all together and I'll have it ready in no time. And…" She looked me square in the eyes. "Between me and you, that girl Polly had as a maid of honor, I bet she saw this dress and immediately backed out." Her fingernail tapped my chest. "You've got a heart of gold. I know you and Polly aren't friends, but that's your nature. A giving spirit. Don't you listen to your mama."

Blanche Bailey should've been a therapist. I left that room feeling better than I had in years. There wasn't anything stopping me from confronting Mama and the other women as they sipped their teas and gossiped about Lucy.

"We've got it all taken care of," Blanche said and headed back to the chaise lounge in the corner of the family room. Her caftan billowed out around her before she sat down. "Now, what was it you were saying about Lucy Ellen Lowell?"

"Myrna was talking about how Kenni was dispatched to their house this morning when Darnell got home and found her dead of an apparent heart attack." Mama had no problems telling my business. Her mantra was what was mine was hers and what was hers was hers.

My eyes lowered when I looked at Myrna. She turned her face and chin away from my glare. I knew she could see me even from the dimly lit room that was lit up from a dangling light that was red with gold flecks. Blanche Bailey sure did love red.

"I have a po-lice scanner." Myrna crossed her arms. "Ain't nothing illegal about that."

"Camille, Darnell told me that she just came to see you last week. Was she ill? Such a shame," I said, adding the last part for good measure.

I took the tea Blanche had poured for me and sat down in one of the chairs.

"She had claimed she was seeing stars, you know, like from high blood pressure. I gave her a machine to wear and nothing ever registered." She let out a long sigh of sadness. "She was healthy as far as I could tell. Sometimes freak heart attacks happen."

"You didn't give her any meds?" I asked.

"I'd have to look in her chart, but I could've told her to take a vitamin or baby aspirin or something." She shrugged.

"She didn't die of a heart attack." Gingerly, I brought my tea up to my lips and took a sip, enjoying the dropped jaws and popped open eyes staring back at me. These women weren't just part of the bell choir, they were the hiney hens of Cottonwood. What I meant by that: they were the gossip central to all things worth gossiping about. Like my Poppa taught me, there's a little bit of truth in all gossip. If I kept my ear to the rumblings, I just might get some information or leads to check out. Especially about people who had something against Lucy Ellen Lowell. Because any lead right now was a welcomed one.

"She was poisoned. I'm now investigating it as a murder." I set the cup down on the table. "Which reminds me. I've got some people I need to talk to."

"People?" Myrna asked in a silky voice and leaned forward. All the henny-hens, the gossiping women in the room, focused on me. "As in who?" Myrna shifted her legs to the side and took a sip of her tea as if she weren't as interested as she really was.

"People that might've had a beef with her." I shrugged and looked down into my tea while I took a sip so I could let them look between themselves without them thinking I saw them.

"Did you check the men in the hunt club?" Ruby Smith asked.

"What about them?" This was exactly what I wanted to happen when I told them Lucy Ellen had been murdered.

"You know when people walk around the shop, they talk to one another." Ruby was the owner of Ruby's Antiques on Main Street. "If they bring in a big piece like a sideboard or something, they usually bring one of the members of the club because they need help carrying it."

"Did you hear something from one of them?" I asked and took a sip.

"I overheard a couple of them talking about how Lucy Ellen had taken some cash that belonged to the club and Darnell said that he was going to replace it because Lucy Ellen thought it was their money. But you know men." She sighed and raised a sly brow. "The hunt club men." She looked at all the women in the room and they all were nodding and agreeing, which kept the gossip going. "They like to know exactly where their money is going."

"I wonder if that's what Bosco and Darnell got into a fight about?" Viola asked. "That's just hearsay from Alma Frederick when she came in to get that no-good diamond he got her." She rolled her eyes, magnified under those big glasses. She owned White's Jewelry in Main Street across from Ruby's Antiques. "I told Bosco that it might be big, but the quality of the diamond wasn't the best." She laughed. "He said that she'd never know because she only wanted a big one that made all the women in the hunt club jealous."

"Why do you keep that trash in your shop?" Mama asked.

"Because people that can't afford the nicer cuts and quality do like to show off a little. I have to cater to everyone." Viola sucked in a deep breath. "Bosco Frederick can afford a good diamond. After all the crap Alma has put up with all these years."

"What did Alma put up with?" I asked.

Viola looked at me. Her eyes narrowed and glanced over my uniform. Darn. The darn uniform always stopped everyone from talking to me. It was the strangest thing. I could've had that dress on and Viola's lips would've been flapping with information.

"Honey, it's all a little gossip that don't matter a hill of beans. Well, phooey." She scrunched up her nose when she looked at her watch. She sat her tea on the table and grabbed her purse. "I've got to get going."

"I better get back to work too," Camille spoke up and tapped her watch. "My lunch hour is over." She grabbed her purse and hustled down the hallway.

"You call me!" Mama hollered after Camille.

"And I've got flowers for Lucy's service to get ready." Myrna stood up and brushed her hands down her shirt. "I'll talk to you gals later."

My job here was done. I'd put the bug in their ears. They weren't going to go do any work. Camille was going to go back to the office to gossip, while Myrna was probably going to call the people who bought flowers and tell them about the murder. Viola was going to question everyone that came in her jewelry shop about the murder and if they didn't know, she'd be more than happy to claim hearsay so it didn't appear like she was gossiping. I'd given them enough gossip to go forth and do some of my investigation for me.

It'd churn up some details on who just might've fought with Lucy Ellen other than Tina and Jolee.

Why on earth would they really kill her after they'd jokingly threatened her in front of me, the sheriff?

Most of the gossip was a lot of hot air. But my process got down to the truth. I took what was said in the gossip and whittled it down. The truth usually ended up being about half of the gossip. Still, gossip gave me leads and leads led me to questions and questioning people. It was something I'd learned from Poppa.

"I guess I better go. Now that my happy fat will fit into the dress." There wasn't any sort of alarming tone in my voice, just satisfaction that I'd given them the shock of their lives. "Blanche, you're better than any therapist out there."

Mama shot a look at Blanche that was filled with daggers.

"Mama, good to see you." I cordially nodded at both of them.

"Choo, choo." Poppa appeared next to Mama. "You've got the gossip train on a roll. Now we let that get going and sit back to listen in. There's a little truth in each bit of gossip. We've just got to find it."

CHAPTER EIGHT

The morgue was located in the basement of Cottonwood Funeral Home, the only funeral home in our town, and no matter how many bodies I'd seen, it never got any easier standing in the door of the cold institutional-looking room staring at the dead body lying on the stainless-steel table. Especially when you knew the person.

"You gonna pass out?" Max Bogus gestured to the yellow paper gown hanging on the coat rack for me to put on over my clothes.

"Nah." I put my arms through the holes of the yellow gown and wrapped the ties around my waist. I plucked a couple of gloves from the cardboard box and snapped them on my hands. "Anything new?"

"Yeah." He nodded his round face. He stared at me behind his thick-rimmed glasses from over Lucy's body. A scalpel in one hand and a magnifying glass in the other. "You aren't going to believe this."

"Try me." I took my time walking over and stopped a few feet away from the table.

"A large portion of the cyanide is around her fingers, mainly her nail base." He pointed to Lucy's hand with the scalpel. "I scraped a piece of the nail polish off and ran a quick test. Full of the poison."

"You're telling me that Lucy Ellen died from cyanide poisoning in fingernail polish?" I asked, knowing this was the nail in Tina's coffin if that was the case.

"That's exactly what I'm saying." He took a step back and put the items on the rolling tray next to the autopsy table. He took the gloves off, throwing them in the hazardous waste bin along with the yellow gown, and motioned for me to follow him to his office. "Of course, this was a quick preliminary test. I've sent a large sample off to the lab so we can get the breakdowns that I need to finish the report up."

I took off my gloves and gown, putting them on the counter in case I needed to put them back on since they weren't really used and followed him into the office, which was just through another door.

He tucked his blue button-down shirt further into his khaki pants before he sat down in the office chair behind his desk. The room was simple, nothing fancy. He had a desk full of paper piles and a chair in front of his desk, which was where I sat. On the wall were his medical license, business license, and coroner's license. He only had up the necessary items to prove who he was in case he was audited.

Max lived a simple life. He went to work, did his job, and enjoyed his home in the country. There wasn't any romance or social life that I knew of, but then again, I didn't stay in the gossip groups.

"I've seen a lot in my time, but this takes the cake." He opened a file and set it in front of me. He pointed to numbers and graphs that told me about the levels of poison and what they meant.

Of course, the only thing I cared about was the signed autopsy report that stated the cause of death as homicide by poison, because it gave me the go-ahead to start an official investigation.

"If you can find the bottle of nail polish, I bet you'll find the murder weapon." He peeled the glasses off of his face and dropped them on this desk. His elbows rested on the arms of his chair after he eased back and clasped his hands, resting them on his belly. "I never ever thought I'd say nail polish was a murder weapon."

"Unfortunately," it made me sick thinking about it, much less saying it, "Tina Bowers is my number one suspect."

"How did you come to that conclusion?" he asked.

"Yesterday I was at Tiny Tina's cashing in a gift certificate." I left out the details of how Finn had made me take a day off. This was business, not a social call. Nor did he care why I was at Tiny Tina's. "Lucy Ellen came in all upset because Tina wouldn't make her a hair appointment or fit her in for her nails. When she left, Tina said she probably should've cut her hair but let the shears slip across her neck."

"She said that?" His brows furrowed.

"And she did this." I slid my finger across my throat like Tina had done.

"But none of that makes sense." Poppa appeared behind Max. "You don't tell on yourself when you're planning on murdering someone."

"That's strange." Max sat up. "If that's the case, it could be premeditated murder." He reached over and shut the file. "But that's for you to figure out."

It would definitely be premeditated if Tina had gone to the trouble of putting poison in her polish bottle, then calling Lucy Ellen to come back.

"Thanks." I picked the file up. "How did Darnell take it?"

"He's devastated. He's beating himself up for going to the woods because she begged him to go to that wedding. You know how grieving people are. Playing that 'what if' game, trying to change the time they spent with their loved ones the twenty-four hours before death." Max made a great point. Everyone always second guessed themselves when it came to a loved one's death.

"He didn't know she was an organ donor and was real sad she couldn't give life after death."

"That's a shame." I wondered if she'd been able to give her organs if she would've been remembered for that kindness instead of the mean-spirited bad reviews she'd written.

"He wondered if he'd been there whether he could've stopped someone from killing her, but I'm not sure if he couldn't have stopped her from getting her nails done." He sighed.

"I'm not sure anyone was going to stop her yesterday from getting her nails done." It made me wonder if Lucy Ellen had just pushed Tina to her limit after I'd left. Maybe Tina told her to come on in and get her nails done, poisoning her in the process.

Even though Tina had said she didn't see or talk to Lucy Ellen after Lucy Ellen left. Was she covering up what she'd done?

"I'm not sure she had them done so much as did them herself." He picked up his camera from the desk and turned it on. It took a minute for him to scroll through the photos. "Here, this is the right hand. Scroll across five more times to see the photos of all five fingers."

Each photo showed a finger and nail. I wasn't sure what he was pointing out.

"I can tell you don't paint your nails often." He got up and stood over me. He pointed out, "Lucy Ellen Lowell was right-handed." He took the camera from me and showed me another photo. "This is her left hand. They are pretty perfectly polished from her using her right hand."

"She painted her own nails because her left hand painted her right nails and the nail polish is all over her fingers," Poppa chimed in. "Good observation, Max."

I repeated what Poppa had said.

"Exactly. The poison got into her skin. Her toes are pretty perfect, but there's some on the skin around her toes too." Max showed me more Perfectly Posh colored photos.

"Then Tina didn't kill her directly," Poppa observed.

"Tina could still have given her the nail polish with intent for Lucy Ellen to paint her nails with the poisoned polish." The possible scenarios rolled around in my head.

"Tina might say that she didn't kill Lucy Ellen and she didn't know the polish was poisoned. So we need to find the cyanide." Poppa was good at trying to put himself in the mind of the killers.

"Possibly." I nodded.

"Kenni." Max looked over his shoulder. Poppa looked at Max, but Max didn't see Poppa. "Who are you talking to?"

"Myself. Can you give me a sample of the nail polish?" I asked. "I'd like to take it to my lab and have Tom Geary analyze it for the compound. I'd like to know exactly what ingredients she uses. Tina makes her own polish. If this is the polish she makes, it makes even more evidence against her."

"I can do that if you sign it off as evidence in the investigation." He put the camera back on the desk and walked out of the office. "I'll email you the photos."

It didn't take him but a second to snip off Lucy's fingernail into a baggie that I could take to Tom Geary, the owner of the lab I used located in Clay's Ferry, the next town to Cottonwood.

"Here you go." He held it out. "Let me write it in your file and mine, give me a signature, and you're out of here."

"Sounds good," I said and took a nice long look at the fingernail while he got the paperwork completed.

After a few quick strokes of my John Hancock on the papers, I had my evidence and was back out to the Jeep where Poppa was waiting.

"What are you thinking?" he asked.

I turned the engine over and looked around and made sure no one was around to see me talking to myself.

"What you said about it being a premeditated murder is right. I'm not sure Tina has that in her, though anger brings out the worst in people." I looked out over the wheel and put my hand on the gearshift and put it in drive.

"She might if I was right that she didn't technically paint Lucy's nails herself. The evidence is the evidence." He looked down at the baggie in the seat. "Tom Geary is our guy to find out. And where is the bottle of fingernail polish?"

"I don't know." The Wagoneer rattled out of town onto the country road that led to Clay's Ferry. "Tina looked in the back of her shop while I nosed around up front."

"Did she really look in the back or did she get rid of the evidence?" Poppa and I loved to play the back-and-forth what-if game that came along with solving crimes.

"We can look to see if there is a dumpster behind her building, or even search her house." That was a good thought. "Search her house," I said again and nodded.

The late afternoon sun was starting to go down. Daylight savings time really did make the days feel so much shorter with less sun. If I was going to get to the lab before it closed, I better hurry.

I grabbed my phone and called Finn.

"Don't tell me you're cancelling" was how he answered the phone.

"No." I couldn't stop my smile. Poppa grumbled. "I called because Max gave me the report. The poison was put in Lucy's fingernail polish. Max also gave me a fingernail clipping so I can take it to the lab for Tom Geary to analyze. I have to see if this is Tina's homemade polish, because if it is, I'm afraid I'm going to have to haul her in."

"Oh man. This is big." Finn wasn't joking. This was huge. "Right here before the wedding too."

"What does that mean?" I asked.

"When the mayor found out about this being a homicide, he came to Darnell's house while I was securing it. He asked if we could not focus on the investigation so much since it overshadowed his wedding." He paused and I took the moment to speak up.

"Are you kidding me?" I gripped the wheel and pushed the pedal down to go faster. "He's such a jerk. I'm not doing it. I'm going to get to the bottom of this with or without his approval."

Chance Ryland and I had a rocky past. He wasn't a big fan of mine and it was no secret he didn't vote for me. But we could all see who the sheriff was now. I didn't get there by kissing his fanny either.

It was hard to get too upset thinking about Mayor Ryland's arrogance as I drove this stretch of country road. It was easy to get lost in the pops of fall colors and trees that lined the curvy road. The last bit of sun forced its rays through the branches and made little light dots on the pavement.

"He knew you'd say that." Finn laughed. "I told him you were the sheriff and he needed to take it up with you."

"Yeah, I'll take care of him." I was so tired of him and secretly wished someone would run against him, but like me, he was running unopposed this election.

Another four years of him as our mayor was going to be the best lesson in patience. Then I'd also have to deal with Polly Parker and her new title of being his wife. The mayor's wife. I laughed out loud thinking about her wearing a sash around town with a crown on her head. Something I wouldn't put past her.

"What are you laughing at?" Finn asked.

"Nothing." I shook it off. "But I will say that it's strange that the mayor would want us to actually keep the investigation on the down-low or even stop it until after the wedding."

"I said that same thing to him," Finn said. I loved how he and I thought

DEAD AS A DOORNAIL

alike on most instances when it came to cases. "He said that he didn't want anything to overshadow the wedding. He even said something so cold."

"What?" I asked, worry in my head. What if the mayor knew more about Lucy's murder than he wanted to give up? He was a member of the Hunt Club. It was full of the good ole boy mentality and Mayor Ryland definitely had that attitude.

"He said that no matter how quickly we solved it, Lucy Ellen was dead now and would still be dead after the wedding." As Finn said these words, I could actually hear them in Mayor Ryland's voice.

It made me shiver.

"I'm about to turn into the lab. I'll be over after I grab Duke from the department and go home to change." I had to focus on the task at hand and deal with Mayor Ryland later.

"I got Duke a little bit ago. You won't make it by the time Betty leaves and I didn't want to leave him there alone." His kindness made me love him even more. "I'll stop by your house and grab him some food and your clothes if you want."

"That's a plan. I've got a pair of sweatpants on my dresser with a t-shirt. And grab my sweatshirt off the chair." I knew I should probably try to dress in something like jeans and not sweats, but I wanted Finn to love me for me and not my attire. "I'll see you soon."

"Kenni, be prepared to take Jolee's call. She's not happy. I'll tell you about it when you come over." We said our goodbyes and hung up.

"Anything new?" Poppa asked.

"No. I was going to have him look in the dumpster behind Tiny Tina's but decided to wait to see what Tom has to say about the nail polish." There I went again, procrastinating on the investigation when I knew in my gut the polish was going to turn out to be the weapon like Max had concluded.

"You're making sure you're doing it right." Poppa was so good at getting the clues and the evidence before I flew off the handle and went around arresting anyone. "We have to make sure because remember, you're only an election away from being without a job."

I gulped. He was right. There was no job security in being an elected official. I loved my job so it was worth the stress.

The lab was on the edge of Clay's Ferry. It was a small brown brick building. The bell over the door signaled my arrival.

Tom Geary walked into the waiting room where I stood with the baggie. His grey hair was a little thinner since the last time I'd seen him.

"Sheriff, to what do I owe the pleasure?" Tom outstretched his hand and I shook it.

"Pleasure?" I asked. "Even though I do enjoy seeing you, I wish it was under different circumstances."

"I'm assuming what you want me to look at is in that bag?" He looked at the baggie in my hand and nodded.

"It's a fingernail." I held it out for him to take from me. "My victim has been killed by cyanide and it's believed the polish painted on her nails was tainted with it."

"That's awful." His brows furrowed. "Your Poppa and I did a lot of cases with poison put in drinks, but this is a first."

Poppa beamed with pride. He loved being around Tom. They worked a lot of cases together and that's why I still used him. There weren't any labs in Cottonwood and I didn't have time to send it off to the state-run labs, so I continued to have clearance to use Tom's lab when I needed quick results. This was one of those times.

"I remember some of those. Poppa really enjoyed your friendship." I wanted him to know how appreciative we were.

"I was about to go home, but I'll get right on this." He continued to look at the nail.

"I also wanted to know if you could give me a breakdown of the polish. One of my suspects owns a nail salon and she makes her own polish. I just so happened to be there when the owner of the salon said some bad things about the deceased, who was at the time living." It was a lot to take in. Something none of us would even think up, but a cold-blooded killer would. "The deceased even asked for this particular polish and the owner refused to give it to her."

"I see." Tom's lips pressed together in a thin line. His nose flared. "With all my years of working with the police, I shouldn't be surprised by a lot of the outcomes, but this." He shook the baggie. "Sorta sick."

"Thanks, Tom." It was time for me to get back to Cottonwood and put this day behind me.

Once we got back into the Jeep, Poppa was quiet. He stared out the window deep in thought.

"Tell me what's going on up there." The days were getting darker earlier as the seasons started to melt together. It took a lot to stay motivated after sunset when the cold set in. Heading home to Finn keeps me going and staying focused.

"The whole fingernail-polish thing is crazy. Not only does it say that someone is sick, but who would do that to a woman?" he asked. "Another woman." He answered his own question.

"That's what makes Tina look like the killer. She knows about making polish, she makes that particular color, and she did threaten Lucy Ellen." I just felt awful about it. "Why on earth would Tina do something like that? Because of some no-show appointments? Bad reviews? Why would she kill her?"

Sure, when I was there to ask her if she'd seen Lucy Ellen the night before Lucy's death, there were a couple of clients who'd cancelled.

"Was it the reviews that spurred Tina to kill Lucy?"

Poppa's chest heaved up and down as a loud sigh left his body. "What about the other women in the shop when Tina said that? Who was there?"

"There was me, Jolee, and the bridal party, as well as Tina and Cheree." I still wanted to talk to Cheree just to make sure she hadn't talked to Lucy Ellen after she left the shop. "I need to expand my suspect list and go to the library to check out all the reviews Lucy Ellen wrote."

"It's hard to look at our friends and think they can do something so horrific." He had a way of giving me instructions without actually giving them.

"Yes. You're right. I need to go see and talk to everyone who was there that day. Apparently, Jolee isn't happy, and I plan on talking to Cheree tomorrow." I mumbled, "Then there's the Euchre bridal shower tomorrow night where I can feel out Polly and her crew."

"Time and patience will reveal all the clues we need," Poppa agreed. "Keep your eyes and ears open. All them gossiping hens will give you bits and bites of information that you can chew on. Remember, solving a crime is putting a puzzle together. We have the pieces, we just need to fit them together."

CHAPTER NINE

"She wasn't happy." Finn's eyes stared at me. The gold flicker of the candle between us put a sparkle in his eyes. Or maybe it was the look of a satisfied belly from all the pizza we'd just consumed.

Duke lay on the floor underneath the table and Cosmo was curled up in my lap. Finn wasn't a big cat person, so when he took in Cosmo I was completely surprised. Not me. I loved all animals, and Cosmo was a great cat.

No matter how much he told me that my best friend, Jolee Fischer, was mad that I'd sent him to ask her questions about her argument with Lucy Ellen Lowell, I couldn't really raise a care because the way he looked at me overcame any feelings I had about anything going on in my life at this moment. Not even Poppa keeping a close eye on us between his wisps in and out of Finn's house bothered me.

"If she's not guilty, she has no reason to be mad." I shrugged and took a nice long drink of the red wine Finn had grabbed from the Dixon's Foodtown wine aisle, which wasn't much different from Boone's Farm Strawberry wine.

"I think she was more mad that you didn't question her, kinda like girl talk or something." He wiped his mouth and put his napkin on his plate.

He stood up and walked over to his phone that was connected via Bluetooth to his speakers and put on a slow romantic tune. Jokingly, he waltzed over and stuck his hand out. Immediately I put Cosmo on the floor and took Finn's hand. He pulled me up and swept me into his arms.

There were no ballroom dance moves or fancy footwork; it was simply swaying back and forth in the middle of his kitchen until we eventually scooted into the new addition.

"You know you make living here so much easier." His voice was low and seductive as he whispered into my ear.

My hands were snug around his waist. When I looked up, I noticed his calm and steady gaze.

"I am going to use my vacation time during Christmas to go back and visit my parents." Finn's voice was a velvet murmur in my ears.

Finn was from Chicago, where his parents and sister still lived. They were a close family. I'd only met his sister once when he first moved here. She'd come to visit and was actually going to take Cosmo, but fairly quickly found out that she was allergic.

"Christmas?" I asked, trying not to sound like some whiny girl, but I loved Christmas. If there was anyone I wanted to spend it with, it was Finn.

"If we plan now, we can get someone from the state reserve to come for the week and you can go with me." His gaze moved around my face like a soft caress. "I think it's time you met my folks."

"Are you sure?" I stopped the sway. "This is a big step."

Finn had once told me that he never took girls to meet his parents because his mother would hound him about them. I also remembered him saying that if he did take a girl home, it meant that she was probably the one. This sent my spirit soaring.

"There's no one I'd rather spend my Christmas with than all the people I love and want to spend the rest of my life with." He raised his hand and slowly ran the back of his fingers down my cheek.

My chin dipped. He used the pad of his finger to tip my chin back up to look into those eyes that made my toes curl. I quivered at the tender touch of his kiss and knew that calling the state reserve was a priority in the morning. Though Christmas was a few months away, I knew I had to make sure it was a go.

It took everything I had to drag myself two doors down when it was time to go home and get some sleep.

Solving Lucy's murder should've been the main thing on my mind as I tried to go to bed, but it wasn't. My mind exploded with images of a happy Christmas spent in Chicago with Finn and his family, which caused me to lose sleep.

"Sweetly sang the donkey at the break of day!"

That couldn't be the voice of my mama singing to me at six a.m., I thought the next morning. "If you do not hear him this is what he'll say. Heehaw, heehaw, heehaw, heehaw."

The romantic night before with Finn still had my heart in a pitter-patter. I pushed Duke's head off the pillow next to mine and dragged it over my head.

"Sic her, Duke," I instructed my bloodhound. "Right in the jugular."

Mama continued, "You obviously hadn't heard the donkey." She cackled.

"Mama, no one in this room thinks you are funny at six in the morning," I mumbled under the pillow and pressed it tighter to my head as I wished her away.

"Get up. You have one hour until you have to be at the office and you're spending it with me," she proclaimed, swinging my closet door open.

"Remind me to take her spare key away." I reached out from underneath the pillow and ran my hand down Duke's back. I tugged the pillow off my head.

Duke groaned, giving in to her. With both front legs out in front of him, he slipped them off the bed. He stood with his front paws planted on the ground and his butt on the bed, his hind legs dangling off the edge. He and I both watched as Mama went through my closet, pulling out clothes she wanted me to wear for the hour with her.

"I'm going to be spending time with you tonight at Euchre," I said, hoping it was enough together time to suit her.

"This morning, I thought we'd go for breakfast." She pulled out a floral-printed dress and held it out for me to see. "A healthy breakfast since you need to get off a little of that weight."

"If you think I'm fat now, wait until I get back from spending Christmas with Finn's family. I'm going to be explosive," I joked, knowing that it would send her into the looney bin that I wasn't going to be in Cottonwood on December twenty-fifth.

"You're what?" Mama gave me the eye. "Now you quit being ugly and teasing your mama." She held up another dress for me to put on.

I shook my head. Her lips twitched, her nose curled. She stuck it back in the closet and came out with a pair of brown sheriff pants and a long-sleeved uniform shirt. A much better choice, especially since I had to go to work after she lectured me on fitting into that darned dress.

I nodded. She snarled.

"Now get up and get ready." She threw the clothes on the bed. "Come on, Duke. Granny will take you out."

Duke didn't hesitate at the word "out."

"Mama, where are we going?" I asked and dragged myself out of bed and into the bathroom to get my shower. I was going to need a long hot one to get me started on the right foot if I was going anywhere with Mama.

We only had two real breakfast spots to eat at in our small Kentucky town: Ben's Diner and On The Run food truck.

"Paula Parker's house," she hollered down the hall from the kitchen.

"Mama!" I yelled and ripped the shower curtain open. I wrapped my hair in a towel and grabbed my robe, throwing it on my soaking wet body. "What is this? Some kind of intervention? I've already agreed to counseling with Preacher Bing." I walked into the living room.

"For goodness sakes, I know you two are dating, but go get some clothes on." Mama held her hand to her chest like I'd just committed a sin.

Finn stood behind her with a cup of coffee in each hand and the biggest grin on his face. Now that was a face I'd love to see every morning. His smile was infectious and I returned it.

"Good morning." He looked so handsome in his brown sheriff deputy's uniform. "I wanted you to start your day off with a good cup of coffee from Ben's, but I hear your mom is going to take you out for breakfast."

"Thank you." I took the coffee. My body shivered as our fingers touched. He bent down and kissed me. Not nearly like last night, but I didn't care.

"Young love." Mama swooned. "To be your age again." She let out a happy sigh. "Finn," Mama batted her lashes at my beau, "my daughter is really trying to get my goat at this hour of the morning. Isn't she terrible?"

Mama gave me a slight shove toward the hallway. I padded back down to get ready.

"I'm wearing my uniform," I called over my shoulder.

"How awful of her," I heard Finn respond, and then I heard the sound of kibble being poured into Duke's bowl. "What on earth has she done?"

"She's saying that she's going to Chicago for Christmas and I know that's not true. I mean," Mama had on her dramatic Southern voice, "I know that Kenni'd never leave her mama alone on Christmas since she's my only daughter. Could you imagine the pain your mama would feel if you were her only child and she had to wake up on a holiday like Christmas alone?"

I stood with the front of my robe gripped in my hand next to my chest and the water dripping down the sides of my face with my ear up against the crack in my bedroom door. This was a test on just how well Finn could stand up to Mama. A test that I've always feared but never thought would come this soon, or this early, in the morning.

"Please be on your game," I whispered.

"Viv, I did ask Kenni to go to Chicago for Christmas to meet my family. It's only fair that my parents get to enjoy the presence of the fine young woman that you've raised. I want to show her off."

Finn was saying all the right things, if it were any other time of the year that he wanted me to meet his family.

"That just won't do." Mama's sweet Southern voice turned into a sweet Southern strict voice. One I knew all too well. "Your mama is just gonna have to meet her in January. Because we have the big Christmas festival here in Cottonwood and the annual parties of our friends. Kenni will be expected to be in attendance for all of them."

Shortly after she gave Finn a good tongue lashing, I heard the backdoor slam.

"Honey?" Finn called. "I don't think your mama is taking you to breakfast anymore."

About that time my phone chirped a text. I walked over to my bedside table and looked down. It was Mama. She said she'd see me at the Parkers' residence in ten minutes. Too bad Finn didn't make her madder.

CHAPTER TEN

I would've texted Mama back and told her twenty minutes because I wanted to get in a little smooch time with Finn before he headed back to the office, but if I did that she'd have been fit to be tied.

Duke went to the office with Finn and twenty minutes later, Poppa and I pulled up in front of the Parkers' gated mansion. Their massive house wasn't far off the road and it was rumored they'd built it that way on purpose. To show off. It was just like Pete and Paula Parker to do such a thing.

I pushed the button on the intercom and was greeted by one of their hired staff through the black box.

"Kenni Lowry here for breakfast." I looked over at Poppa and rolled my eyes.

They knew I was coming. Why didn't they just leave the gate open?

When the gate did open, I pulled the Wagoneer up and around their circular driveway and parked it right in front of the large lake in the middle of the drive. The four concrete swans as big as my Wagoneer were already spitting water out of their beaks.

There was a woman at the front door with a tray in her hand and she seemed to be awaiting my arrival. On the tray was a green glass of yucky-looking something or another. There was a piece of paper propped up in front of it that read my name.

"I'm assuming this is for me?" My brows rose.

The lady nodded. I could tell she was trying not to smile after I took it off the tray and dumped it over into the Parkers' bushes next to the front porch.

"That was tasty." I smiled and put the glass back on the tray.

I walked into the house. "Sheriff." Paula Parker acted as if she'd not seen me in years. Her nose curled up like it always did and her face squished up like a prune.

I gave her the once-over, noticing her chin-length brown hair looked like she'd just gotten it done by Tina. Her signature pearls were clasped around her neck. I couldn't help but wonder what time the woman had gotten up to get all dolled up for little ole me.

"I don't think this involves me." Poppa fidgeted nervously after he ghosted in and ghosted right back out. "I'll go do some digging around about Lucy. I'll meet you at the Lowell house," he said, reminding me that seeing the crime scene was my number one priority this morning.

I instantly wanted to protest because now I was really alone here and suddenly uncomfortable.

"It's so good to see you this morning, but I can only stay a minute. Duty calls." I tapped the utility belt around my waist with my gun nestled in the holster. "Not to mention I've got an appointment with Preacher Bing."

"Yes. I'm delighted you and Polly are getting along so well." Paula's head tilted to the side, a fake grin on her face. "That's what we wanted to talk to you about, dear." She swung the door open.

In the foyer stood Mama, Polly, Pete Parker, and Mayor Ryland. I glanced back over my shoulder and didn't see anyone else's cars. This was an ambush.

"Won't you come in?" Pete Parker stepped up and gestured toward the fancy parlor room where only the good company was entertained.

"Only if you got something better to drink than that green stuff." I smiled.

"I'm so sorry. She's not a morning person." Mama made all sorts of excuses for what she'd call bad behavior. "Ain't that right, Kendrick."

My ears perked at the sound of my full name as a red alert that Mama wasn't pleased with me.

"You get in here and behave." She jerked me to her like they couldn't see. "You hear me?"

"Are you joking me?" I whispered back as she led me into the room along with everyone else.

Her eyes widened, her lips squeezed together. She was as serious as a witch in a broom factory.

"We won't take up too much of your time." Mayor Chance Ryland raked a few of his fingers through his slicked back salt-and-pepper hair.

Sweet, sweet Polly with her perfectly coiffed blonde hair, black slacks, and white cardigan with her own set of pearls locked around her neck had her hands clasped in front of her, the big diamond ring sparkling as she stood next to her man.

"It's been brought to my and Polly's attention that you are investigating the murder of Lucy Ellen Lowell. As you know, since we did pick you as our maid of honor, we feel like your time for the next couple of days is best spent on making sure Polly's needs are met." His words brought up an anger in me that boiled my insides.

"After all, it's an honor to be maid of honor, especially in the soon-to-be first lady of Cottonwood's wedding." Paula did all the talking for her daughter as Polly stood there with a big (fake) smile on her face. "We don't mind if Deputy Vincent does all the investigative work. It'd be different if you weren't in the wedding. But duties are duties and right now Polly is your duty."

"This is all dandy and good." I took a step back. "But do you hear yourselves?" I looked at each one of them square in the eyes. "You're asking me to give up the safety of all the citizens of Cottonwood for a wedding?"

And I thought I was here to learn how to keep from eating the next couple of days so I wouldn't ruin any wedding photos with my happy fat.

"This is ridiculous." I shook my finger at the mayor. "If this little meeting was to get out to the public, I think everyone would be rather upset with our mayor. Don't you? In fact, didn't you tell Deputy Vincent that you'd like for him to take over the investigation because…" I hesitated for more of an effect and I tapped my finger to my temple. "If I recall correctly, your exact words were, and I quote, 'no matter how quickly we solved it, Lucy Ellen was dead now and would still be dead after the wedding.'"

"Umm." Mayor Ryland shifted side to side.

"I understand that you want to keep everyone in the Hunt Club on your side since you are a member and when election time comes, they do have a lot of influence in Cottonwood. But to use and abuse the power the citizens of Cottonwood have entrusted in you to stop an investigation where there's a murderer on the loose? And all you care about is that your wedding goes off without a hitch?" I didn't have to say much more than that.

The silence that hung in the air was as thick as the spring fog after a midnight storm.

"As mayor I'm not asking anything of you. As Polly's future husband, I'd like to see my bride get everything she'd like." His chin lifted as he sucked in a deep breath through his nose and looked all high-brow down at me. "Of course I don't want a killer on the loose and the citizens are my number one priority."

"Well, technically," Polly laughed, "I'm your number one priority."

I watched with amusement as Mayor Ryland hushed her by waving his hand.

"I thought we were here to talk about the wedding dress?" Mama stepped up. "Not talk about my daughter's job that we elected her to. To honor, protect, and serve. Or how we elected you to run our town."

I looked at Mama. She looked at me.

"I'll be darned." I smiled. "You do have my back."

"Damn right I do. This is a disgrace to not only my daughter's hard work, but to the citizens of our small town, and we are leaving." Mama grabbed me yet again, dragging me out of the room like she dragged me in a few minutes ago.

"Don't worry!" I called out before I slammed the front door behind me. I yelled extra loud so they could hear me. "I'll be at the wedding on time. See y'all then."

Mama stood by the Jeep.

"I'm sorry about that in there. I swear Paula told me that we were going to discuss that gawd-awful dress." She tried to keep a straight face. "It was ugly. And you aren't fat. You are perfect the way you are."

"Thanks, Mama." I hugged her. "But Finn does make me happy. And going to see his family at Christmas is just a week. You get me and him all year long." I pulled back because I wanted to see her face. "I love you and Daddy so much, but I'm going to Chicago with Finn. I'd like to have your blessing, but if you can't give it, I'm sorry."

"No." Mama shook her head. "It's fine. When your daddy and I had only you, we'd actually talked about the possibility of sharing you on the holidays with another family. Talking about it and the real action are completely two different things." She looked away and her eyes shifted back to me. She looked down her nose. "Only this one time though. Next year you're home for Christmas."

"Promise." I made the criss-cross with my finger over my heart and gave her another last hug. "I've got to get over to the church and meet with Polly and Preacher." I rolled my eyes.

"Alrighty. I'll see you tonight at Euchre." She gave me another hug and a peck on the cheek before she and I went our separate ways.

As soon as I got back into the Wagoneer I checked my phone for any messages in hopes Tom Geary had left one. Nothing. I was surprised I hadn't heard from him last night about the polish.

The Cottonwood First Baptist Church was on the south end of town and I took my time driving through town, going in and out of streets to get there. There was no way I wanted to get there before Polly.

The church stood off the road with about an acre between Main Street and the building itself. There was a large staircase that led up to a huge concrete covered porch with five large pillars holding it up. Four large doors were evenly built along the porch that opened up into the vestibule of the church. Preacher Bing stood next to the far-right door greeting the people before service and the far-left door saying goodbye after the service.

Today he was eagerly waiting in his office with Tibbie Bell, the wedding planner, and Polly Parker in the basement of the church.

"I'm sorry." I looked at my watch. "I'm not late, am I?"

"No." Preacher Bing gestured for me to sit down.

His hair was plastered to his head and his bangs hung down on his forehead. He was tall and lanky. He looked like Lurch from the The Addams Family and he always scared me. Today was no different.

"I thought I'd talk to Polly first," Preacher Bing said.

"We were just discussing how you and Polly became friends." Tibbie's brows rose. "Isn't that right, Polly?"

Polly nodded. Her perfect bob swung back and forth, her horse teeth glistened.

"And the big falling out we just had at my parents' house." Polly couldn't just leave well enough alone.

"We didn't have a falling out." I preferred to call it something else. "We had a disagreement because your future husband would like me to turn the other way about Lucy's murder until after your wedding."

"Is that right, Polly?" Preacher Bing turned to Polly.

"Well...um...I..." It was like she'd been caught out in public without makeup on and everyone saw her.

"Don't worry." I knew she'd be all upset if the man of God was disappointed in her. "I'd never compromise the office and Mayor Ryland didn't either after we discussed it. Right, Polly?"

I secretly prayed that I wouldn't be struck dead by lightning from lying and saving Polly's face while in church.

"Right." Polly nodded and the stress fell from her face.

"Fine. We can move on. Now, Kenni, what is your recollection of the first time you met Polly?" Preacher Bing folded his long lean fingers—they had always creeped me out—and tilted his head to the right as if he were really interested.

"Well, we both grew up here so I don't remember the first time I met her." I scooted up on the edge of the chair, hoping it'd be a little more comfortable. "I remember she always had the best of everything. But she's younger than me."

"But he wants to know any fond memories." Tibbie was reaching deep and she knew it.

"When I was on a stakeout a year or so ago, I remember seeing her and the Mayor kissing, proving the rumors true."

"Kenni," Polly gasped.

"I'm sure she meant it was innocent." Tibbie patted Polly's delicate little hand and narrowed her eyes at me as she tried to cover up what I really meant.

"Actually, it was only a rumor at the time, but I was trying to check out Polly's alibi since she was accused of killing poor old Doc Walton." My lips pressed together as I thought of the memory. "Here we are today." I clapped my hands together. "All happy now."

Preacher cleared his throat.

"Do you and Polly have any memories of going to the movies, a fun girls' weekend?" Preacher sat back in his chair.

"No." I shook my head. "Polly had her own set of friends."

Tibbie adjusted herself in her seat in an aggravated sort of way.

"What about the time at bible school when she befriended Toots?" Poppa appeared and came to my rescue.

"I do remember vacation bible school and how sweet it was when she gave Toots Buford her cookies."

The tension melted from the three of them as their shoulders dropped and smiles formed on all of their faces.

"Tell us about that," Preacher encouraged me.

"As you know, Polly was always in the younger group. Toots was new and she definitely didn't come from the same background as Polly. Toots didn't have on the cute matching clothes that included the shoes and a bow in her hair like Polly. Toots seemed really hungry because I remember her gobbling up that cookie and small cup of Kool-Aid they gave us." It was actually a very sad memory. "I remember Toots was sitting by herself and Polly went over there and sat right down next to her at the picnic table."

In some sort of way, I was trying to get Polly to see that I wasn't the right choice and she should ask Toots to be her maid of honor.

"So her kind heart attracted you to become friends with her." Preacher looked happy and satisfied with my answer. "Polly, I think you've picked a maid of honor who truly knows your heart and kindness."

"You mean I'm here because Polly was questioning me taking part?" I give a sideways look to Tibbie. "Because I was under the distinct impression that we were both going to get some sort of counseling."

"Thank you so much for your time, Preacher." Tibbie hopped up and nodded before she rushed us out of there.

"Oh, Kenni." Polly grabbed me into a hug when we stepped out into the hallway. "You are so wonderful for remembering that. I'm so excited to hear your toast talking about my kind and giving heart."

"We need to head on over to the florist." Tibbie lightly touched Polly's elbow.

I snarled at Tibbie. Polly gave me the two-finger wave before giving me the call-you-later gesture.

Next week's wedding couldn't come soon enough. Being in Polly Parker's wedding was proving to be a full-time job. I had to put all that in the back of my head and do my real job. On the way over to the Lowell house, I mentally went over the evidence we had and tried to think of anything that didn't point to Tina.

The polish, the argument, and the negative review on the salon all pointed directly to Tina. There had to be something I was missing.

Duke was on the front porch as if Finn had put him there to be a guard dog. He and Darnell were in a face off.

"Hey, Darnell." I looked between the two as The Good, the Bad, and the Ugly theme song played in my head. "Duke." I patted my leg with my free hand while my other one gripped my bag. "What's going on here?"

Darnell ran his hands through his hair.

"Darnedest thing." He pointed to my trusty sidekick. "I came by to grab some more unders," apparently his word for underwear, "and I couldn't get past this deputy." He snickered a little.

"Duke takes his job very seriously. Says crime scene. Do not enter." I gave a quick head nod. "Come on. I'll let you get your drawers."

Duke had changed his tune when I showed up. He'd always been such a good dog. He'd even taken a bullet for me and the city gave him a medal for it. I swear he knew it because ever since then he'd been even more protective.

"Finn?" I called out once we stepped inside. It was eerie going into the house since the other night. The last time I was here, it was a routine call where we thought Lucy Ellen had died of a heart attack. Well, not me, since Poppa had showed up, but to the rest of the world.

Now it was definitely a crime scene, making it an altogether different feel.

"If I didn't think it wasn't fittin', I'd just have you go get them for me."

Darrell was hesitant to go into the house. "I just don't know what I'm going to do. We didn't have no young'uns or nothing. No family left." His voice trailed off and his eye focused on the spot where he'd found Lucy.

"I know people have been saying it a lot, but you have a lot of friends in the Hunt Club and every one of Lucy's friends." I tried to offer as much of a condolence as I could.

"What's his story?" Poppa appeared and stood in the exact spot of Lucy's body outline. "Where was he again?"

"I know that we talked a little bit about your whereabouts, but do you mind if we talk for a second after you get some clothes?" I asked Darnell.

"Sure, Sheriff." He nodded toward the hall. "Can I grab my stuff now?"

About that time, Finn came into the room.

"Sure. Say, Finn." I smiled, remembering last night and how amazing he was. "Do you mind going back to Darnell's bedroom with him and letting him get some clothes? I want to make sure he doesn't disturb anything, just in case."

"Yes, ma'am." His eyes shifted to Darnell. "Ready, sir?"

Darnell simply nodded and headed on back with Finn, leaving Poppa and me standing there.

"You know he was in the woods." I looked at Poppa.

"Yes, but the husband is always the prime suspect." Poppa had always checked out the next of kin or family members when he investigated a crime. "All t's crossed and i's dotted." Poppa winked.

"I plan on stopping by the gun show too." Thinking about the little show the mayor had put on this morning started to get my blood boiling again. "I want to see how the women reacted to Lucy's death and if there was any tension between them."

While Poppa and I talked, I looked underneath the couch to see if the fingernail polish was there. It was my number one priority to find the polish Lucy Ellen was wearing on her nails.

With no luck, I walked outside to Darnell and Finn. Darnell had gotten his unders.

"Can we talk now?" I asked Darnell. He agreed. "Exactly where were you again the night of Lucy's death?" I didn't want to say murder.

"In the woods with the guys to get our cabins and stands ready. We also have our annual gun show going on, but the wives really like to stay there and take care of it." His eyes were so dark and hollow. He'd really aged in the last twenty-four hours. Grief did that to a person. "Don't take this wrong." He put his hand out in front of him as if it were going to ease the tone of his words. "Most women don't understand guns. They like to take part in the gun show, but as a rule, we like to keep two members of the Hunt Club at the gun show if the others are out hunting so questions can be answered. The women take the money and process the necessary paperwork for a sale."

"Can you tell me who you talked to and everything you did from the time you last saw Lucy Ellen until you found her?"

"Didn't I tell you all this already?" he asked.

"You did, but you've had a day to process what's happened. Research has found that after a period of time, things will start to come back to you that you didn't remember while your body was in a state of shock. You might remember the slightest of things that you think are minor, but in an investigation it could be that one little link we are looking for to help connect evidence." I stopped to make sure he understood me. "So why don't you tell me the last time you saw Lucy Ellen face to face?"

"That morning I was getting my gear ready. My bag packed, food she'd made for me to take. I got my rifles ready. She said something about getting her hair done for the wedding and asked me again." He stopped. His voice cracked. "She begged me to be home for the wedding and I told her no." He buried his head in his hands, overcome with grief.

I reached over and rubbed his back for a little comfort.

"I'm sorry." His lips pushed together, his face squished up. "I just don't know what I'm gonna do."

"One day at a time." I patted and rubbed. "Go on and tell me about what you did after you pulled out of the driveway," I encouraged him.

"Drat." Poppa stomped. "Some kids are in the Dixon's Foodtown about to steal something. I can't have you leaving this interrogation. I've got to go scare them off before Toots Buford calls Betty at dispatch."

I took a deep inhale and let out the big breath to clear my head from Poppa talking to me.

"I'm sorry. I'm just trying to figure out what Lucy's last actions were and it helps if I know where you were and what was going on. If she was upset and all that. Go on," I said again.

"Like I said, I told her I couldn't go to the wedding." He shuffled his feet. "I regret it now. All the men were going to go hunting wild hogs and I had to go. I just couldn't think of them bringing home a hammy and not me. Now I wished I'd just said yes to her. Finn said something about poisoning. What on earth? Do you think maybe she got into something and wasn't murdered?" He teared up again. "The thought of someone wanting my sweet Lucy Ellen dead is beyond me."

I did a little more rubbing and patting. He clearly wasn't ready to talk.

"I don't know. But before I let you go, you did say something about Lucy Ellen complaining about Tina Bower's salon, Tiny Tina's." I wanted to hear it one more time.

"Yeah. She and Tina have this love-hate thing. Tina cuts Lucy's hair too short on purpose, Lucy Ellen claims. Then she got the foot fungus thing and blamed that on Tina. But then they go eat lunch and all that." He sighed. "Women. I just don't understand them. Why? Do you think Tina did this?"

"I don't know. I'm just eliminating everyone at the moment." I wasn't going to show any cards to him. With his arsenal of guns and in his grief, I wasn't sure what Darnell would do when we found out who killed his wife.

"I'm staying out at The Tattered Cover Books and Inn if you need anything else." He gripped the plastic bag. "Please keep me posted."

"I will. I'll definitely be calling with more questions." It was only fair to let him know to expect me to call him. After another day or so, I was sure he'd remember more. "Before I let you go." I paused. "Did you know she was an organ donor?"

"She talked about it, and it was just like her to always give to others." He painted her as a saint.

"What are you thinking?" Finn asked after we heard Darnell's truck door slam and drive off.

"I'm thinking we have to find that bottle of nail polish. I also want Tom Geary to call me with the results of Lucy's fingernail and I certainly am thinking about that ugly dress I have to wear in front of the entire town on Saturday." I laughed.

Finn took me in his arms.

"We'll get to the bottom of this. I'm sorry I've not found anything to help in the investigation. It's like the killer has vanished." He gave me a hug. "I'm going to head on over to Tina's house and see if she'll let me look around. What I find over there will help us decide who we look at next."

"Sounds good." I gave him a kiss through the window of the Jeep after I got in to drive away. "I'm going to stop by the library."

We said our goodbyes and I called Betty at dispatch over the walkie-talkies to see if anything from Dixon's was called in.

"Not a thing going on. Just a lot of calls from the gals about Lucy Ellen and what we're going to do about bell choir at Christmas." She ho-hummed. "You don't want to do bell choir, do you?"

"Betty, I don't know. Let me get through this investigation first, then I'll worry about months from now." Why was it that everyone started to worry about Christmas months in advance?

Even stores were already selling wrapping paper and ornaments.

"Finn's gone to Tina's house to talk to her and I'm going to head on over to the library." I gave Betty the schedule so she'd know where we were in case a call did come in and she'd be able to determine who could get where faster—not that Cottonwood was that big, but I prided myself on the efficiency of a two-officer department.

"Don't eat out for lunch. Your mama brought you a salad and she told me to make sure it was the only thing you eat." Betty snickered on the other end. "Happy fat" was the last thing she said before she clicked off the walkie-talkie.

Suddenly I had a hankering for one of those big pastries and a hot cup of coffee the library offered to their patrons.

CHAPTER ELEVEN

The old white colonial house that was centuries old and stood next to the courthouse had been converted to the Cottonwood Library before I could remember. I'd spent many hours getting lost in different fictitious towns as a child while Mama enjoyed her many group meetings there.

The rush of wind pushed past me when I opened the front door. The smell of paper and old books wrapped around me in a welcoming and comforting hug to my soul. It was such a distinct smell. The kind that immediately brought back those fond memories.

I waved at Marcy Carver, the librarian, when Duke and I walked past the reference desk. She smiled and continued to talk on the phone that was pinned between her ear and shoulder as she typed on the computer keyboard.

The library only had three public rooms. The children's section was probably the most popular, then there was the fiction section that held all of the various genres, and the non-fiction room, which was where I was going to check out the last few weeks of the Cottonwood Chronicle. It'd have been much easier to look up the Chronicle online, if only they put them online as they were published. Unfortunately, Marcy was still in the old-school era and was so very far behind in getting the most recent papers on the internet. Once she told me it was Malina Woody's job since she was the assistant librarian. I'd even gone as far as bringing it up at one of the town-council meetings that Edna Easterly, the owner of the Chronicle and editor-in-chief, should have the equipment to upload the paper, but that failed miserably.

The non-fiction room had a few tables with computers as well as a card catalog for the periodicals. It was also the area where the library had the sweets and coffee bar.

Today was an assortment of cupcakes that definitely didn't come from Dixon's Foodtown. These were fancy. The heavenly smell even made Duke stick his nose up in the air and dance around.

"You can't have any of these." I eyeballed the chocolate on chocolate right off. There was a business card from the Sweet Shop. I took one and put it in the front pocket of my shirt. "This one is perfect."

With a couple pumps of the coffee carafe in a paper cup and the cupcake, I walked over to the card catalog, setting my goodies on top of it.

In order for me to get the back issues, I'd have to write down the exact dates I wanted. I drew my finger down the little drawers and pulled the one with the letter C. The little filing tabs clicked along the top of the drawer as it slid to full extension.

I decided on the last two months' issues. This way I could look up Page Two and see exactly what Lucy Ellen had reviewed. Two months would seem like a long enough period for someone to fester over her words as well as see any potential loss to their business.

There was a basket of scrap paper and tiny pencils, like the ones you'd see at mini-golf, in another basket. I grabbed one of each and wrote down the information from the card catalog.

The squeaky wheels of the book cart screeched from behind me. I turned around when it stopped. Malina was running her finger from one hand down the spines of a row of books and had a book in the other hand.

"Hey, Malina." I held the pieces of paper and noticed her hair was cut shorter. "Where is the Sweet Shop?"

She tucked a piece of her hair behind her ear. She'd gone from long brown hair to a more stylish asymmetrical bob and even added highlights.

"It's a new shop in the strip mall next to Hart's Insurance. They have the neatest desserts." Her smile reached her eyes. "You picked a good one."

"Yeah. It looks so good." I didn't care that I needed to fit into that maid of honor dress. I was going to eat that cupcake for brain power. At least thinking that made me feel better. "I see you're still keeping the new hairdo. It looks good." I smiled.

"THANK YOU, KENNI." She raked the tips of her fingers down the bob. She bent down and patted Duke a couple of times behind his ear.

"Are you still getting it cut at Tiny Tina's?" I asked.

"There's no one else in town." She stood back up, shrugged, and picked up another book off the cart. With the end of the spine, she shoved a space for it on the shelf.

"How's the Tattered Cover?" I asked about the hotel where Darnell Lowell was staying. Malina worked the front desk there part-time.

"It's all good. I'll be picking up more hours during the fall and holiday season, but it's a little slow right now."

Tourists loved to come to Cottonwood during the holiday season since it was on the antique registry. The Christmas Festival also brought in a lot of visitors. Our small town was beautifully decorated, almost dipped in Christmas.

"You said that you still get your hair done at Tiny Tina's. Did you ever see Lucy Ellen Lowell in there?" It might be a long shot, but I thought I'd give it a try.

"Ummm..." She sighed, twisted her lips, and rolled her eyes to the sky. "No," her head shook slowly, "I don't think I ever saw her in there. But I did see your mama in there once or twice getting a pedicure from Cheree. She's just the sweetest. Your mama, that is."

"Isn't she though." I spared Malina the truth about my mama and her role in me being in Polly's wedding. "Anyway," I held the pieces of paper out to her, "can you grab these issues of the Cottonwood Chronicle for me?"

She thumbed through them. "What are you looking for?"

"I'm going to look up all the editorial reviews and comments, along with anything I can pull up about Lucy Ellen Lowell. I know she did a lot of reviews in the paper and it seems like a good place to start to see what people knew about her or who had a tiff with her." I usually wouldn't say so much to Malina, but she was in the public with gossip fluttering around.

"Marcy might know a thing or two." Malina couldn't hide the devious smile on her face. She leaned in and looked up under her brow to see if anyone was around before she said, "Marcy secretly hates—hated—Lucy. Lucy Ellen came in here to use the computer to do her reviews after someone would make her mad. Marcy told her that she was mean and she wasn't going to let her do it anymore. Lucy Ellen told Marcy that she paid taxes and she could use whatever computer she wanted and Marcy couldn't stop her."

"Really?" I never figured I'd put Marcy Carver on a list of persons of interest for murder, but she was definitely going on there for me to talk to.

"It didn't stop Lucy. She marched right on over to that computer." Malina pointed. "Lucy Ellen wasn't smart enough to erase the history off the computer and while she was here, Marcy turned off the internet. When she left Marcy went over to the computer to see what Lucy Ellen had written. Lucy Ellen didn't write a review for the store she'd intended to when she came in. She wrote a bad review about Marcy and how she didn't let people use their tax dollars to use all the library has to offer." Malina laughed. "I've never seen Marcy so mad in her life. She erased the history and the review before she turned the internet back on." She shrugged. "We've learned that if we turn off the internet, Lucy Ellen's review is lost."

"Did Lucy Ellen ever come back in?" I asked.

"Oh, yeah. Only when I was working though." Malina shrugged. "I don't care about other people's business."

Sure you don't, I thought.

"It's a free country and Marcy was right." Malina shook her head. "Lucy Ellen got what she had coming to her."

"Marcy said that? It seems a little harsh to wish death on a few silly reviews," I noted as Malina nodded with pursed lips.

"You'll have to ask her about that." She turned and glanced towards Marcy's office door that was closed. "Anyways, I've got all these issues of the Chronicle on the computer already." She handed the papers back. "I've been trying to get them uploaded the day the paper comes out. Edna is paying me extra to get them up on the new website."

"New website?" I asked.

"Yeah. Edna said there's a big market with online subscription services, which just sends Marcy over the edge." Malina laughed.

"Why is Marcy upset?" I asked.

"Because she says the internet is going to shut down the library and we'll all be out of a job. That's why she doesn't want anything to go online as quickly as I can do it." She leaned around me and looked. She leaned back and whispered, "Between me and you, I'm going to go work for Edna and her online subscriptions. I'm going to be giving my two weeks right before the Parker wedding because Edna wants me to cover and write a story on it since I'm invited."

"Congratulations. I didn't know you wanted to work at a newspaper." I clearly remembered Malina's nose always being stuck in a book.

"I want to be a writer like Beryle Stone." She smiled fondly as she spoke about the only famous (now deceased) citizen of Cottonwood, who was a bestselling author. "Look out, literary world." She brushed her hands in front of her like she was brushing away anything that might get in her way. "Here comes Malina."

"Good luck." I crumpled the papers in my fist and threw them in the wastebasket on my way over to the computer. The cart squeaked out of the non-fiction room with Malina pushing it.

I wondered how Marcy was going to take Malina leaving. It sounded to me like there was some tension between the two librarians' ideas. It was none of my business and I didn't have time to even think about it.

Duke laid down next to the computer table I sat down at to look up the back issues of the paper.

After I logged into the computer, I surfed the web for the Cottonwood Chronicle website. It popped up. In the search box on the left sidebar, I typed in the dates for the last couple months. The articles appeared on the screen with another box overlapping it asking for my subscription information. There were two ways I could do this: I could either get Malina or Marcy to get me the paper copy, or I could easily subscribe through the sheriff's department and have any sort of access I needed from work or home.

I opted for the subscription, which was smart on Edna's part. With the sheriff's credit card information all typed in and my password set, I was in business and flipping the online paper to Page Two, the social page.

There wasn't anything interesting or from Lucy Ellen in the first couple of papers that I looked through, but there was a review in the third paper about six weeks before today's date.

Lucy Ellen had written a review about Pet Patch and in particular shaming Faith Dunaway, the owner, for not carrying a certain cat food. For a minute, I tried to remember if the Lowells had a cat because I hadn't seen one. Regardless, the article said Faith refused to order any in and that she wasn't a very good business owner because she didn't cater to the needs of the citizens of Cottonwood. She also went on to say that Faith wasn't a good citizen of Cottonwood because she didn't believe in hunting and protested many of the Hunt Club's events. There was even a picture of Faith where she'd gone to last year's gun show and threw fake blood on none other than Lucy Ellen Lowell. Edna had gotten a really good shot. Underneath that photo was another one of Faith cleaning out cages at the local SPCA with a snarl on her face. I wasn't sure what it was about, but I was about to find out.

The rest of the papers had the reviews I'd already known about. The one with On the Run food truck and the latest one on Tiny Tina's Salon.

"How are you this morning, Sheriff?" Marcy called on my way past the reference desk.

"Good. I see the children's theater is going well." There was a puppet show going on in the children's room.

"Oh, the kids love it. We're starting to work on the Christmas puppet show for the Christmas benefit. They asked us to join them. I think it's a wonderful idea since parents will open their wallets up to just about anything that supports their children." She clasped her hands in front of her.

"You're getting a jump on things. We haven't even had fall yet." If I didn't know better, I'd think Cottonwood citizens wanted to skip fall and head straight to winter. Not me. I loved fall in Cottonwood.

"It's just around the corner and will be here before you know it. What brings you here?" she asked.

"I needed to look through some of your back issues of the Cottonwood

Chronicle for a little work." Without even telling her what the work was, I knew she already knew.

"I'm assuming you're here to look up the reviews Lucy Ellen Lowell's always done and narrowing down suspects?" she questioned.

"We are looking at all possibilities, yes." I rocked on the heels of my shoes.

"Let me get those for you." She gestured to the room behind the reference desk where they kept the paper copies.

"Malina was very helpful in telling me how they're online now. So I jumped on your computer and even made me an online subscription." As I spoke to her, her neck got red and it crept right on up to cover her entire face.

She cocked a brow. "Is that so?" Her question was followed by a deep inhale and her glare turned toward Malina, who just so happened to be walking by with a fresh load of books to reshelve.

"She mentioned that Lucy Ellen Lowell came in here to do her reviews of shops and her opinions about the people who own them." I said. When I didn't get an immediate response, I asked, "what did you think about that?"

"What? Lucy Ellen's reviews?" She leaned her hip on the edge of the desk. "I thought they were mean spirited if you want to know the truth. When I saw her coming through those doors, I would watch her. She'd sit at one of these desks and gnaw on her bottom lip as she typed away. She'd stop and look up like she was really thinkin'. Then she'd start typing again. Like in a mad rush or something. I know this probably isn't right, but I'd pretend to be re-shelving some books behind her to see exactly what she was doing. If she was writing something that looked like a review to the Chronicle, I'd hurry to my office and turn off the internet."

"Why would you do that?" I asked.

"Because she was mean. Her reviews were only in the Chronicle to hurt people." Marcy looked down at her fingers. "I know it ain't fittin' to say, but if you asked me, she got what she had coming to her."

"Did she ever write a review about the library?" I asked.

Marcy smiled. "About that," her brow rose, "she complained about the internet and I told her that the form was saved and would send to the Chronicle anyways, though I knew it wouldn't. She didn't know better. Last time I caught her doing a review and turned off the internet, she said she was going to write a review about the internet service because she really did believe it was the bad internet here that turned off and not me."

"Some of her reviews obviously got through. How did that happen?" I asked since she said she'd kept a close eye on Lucy Ellen.

"I'm not here twenty-four seven." She let out an exhausted sigh. She slid her gaze over to Malina. "Some people don't care about other's feelings." She returned her stare at me with a blank look on her face.

"You didn't happen to have any ill words with Lucy Ellen, did you?" I asked.

"For heaven's sake, no." She shook her head. "I wasn't about to get in a piss and vinegar fight with her over some reviews or how I felt like she was nasty to people when she didn't get her way. It was best to stay clear of her." She looked back at Malina. "Malina, a word with you."

"Sure." Malina walked over.

"In my office." She jerked her head to the side. "Sheriff, it was good to see you. Bye, Duke." She didn't give me time to say goodbye. She quickly turned on the balls of her feet and stomped back to the office.

As I walked, I thought about the articles. I'd completely forgotten about the call from last year's gun show event. When I went out to see Faith about it, she claimed it was free speech. I'd given her a ticket for disorderly conduct but what had transpired from there, I wasn't sure. But I was about to find out.

"You want to get a treat?" I asked Duke when we got back into the Wagoneer.

He jumped around, panting and wagging his tail.

Pet Patch was the cutest pet store with grooming services. Faith took great care in making sure all animals were welcome there. She didn't sell animals, but she did give out names to reputable breeders of all sorts of different animals. She was the go-to gal for pets in Cottonwood. Duke loved it there. He just didn't like the seasonal baths I brought him in for.

The front door mooed when I opened it, making me giggle. The doorbell wasn't the regular ding; Faith had special ordered one that sounded exactly like a cow.

"Duke!" Faith made it a point to always greet the animals when they walked into her store.

He ran over, knowing exactly what was waiting for him in her pinched fingers.

"I see you brought your mama with you," Faith joked like she always did. She patted Duke as she gave him the treat. "Kenni, I hear you're going to be in the big wedding."

Faith had shoulder-length strawberry blonde hair and sparkling blue eyes. Definitely not the look of a killer. Good cover up though, I thought as I greeted her with a friendly smile.

"I love that bird apron," I said.

She ran her hands down the front of it and they ended up in the front pockets where she took out another treat.

"Can he?" It was nice that she asked before she just did it like the rest of the citizens.

"Absolutely." How could I deny the cute dancing hound?

"We have a special on Duke's food this week plus a manufacturer's coupon." She walked in the direction of the dog food. "It's really a great deal."

"I didn't come here for some, but we can always use a good deal." I followed behind Duke who was close on Faith's heels. "Actually, I came to ask you about your relationship with Lucy Ellen Lowell. I'm sure you've heard she was murdered, and it's my understanding you were a little upset, as you should be, about the mean-spirited review she posted in the Chronicle."

"Mean-spirited?" Faith curled up on her tiptoes and reached up for the bag. I helped get it down. "I think it was downright hateful. I'm sorry she's dead, but it doesn't take away the fact that she was a spoiled brat. What she wanted and didn't get, she made a mess of."

"I went to the library and looked up the review. It said she was mad that you didn't carry a certain cat food. I didn't even know she had a cat." I hoisted the big bag of kibble up on my hip.

"She doesn't. She buys cheap cat food for the shelter. Sometimes I put food on sale right before the expiration date. It started piling up once and I knew she did some volunteer work there. I won't because it's a kill shelter and I can't donate to that. Don't judge me." Faith was aware of how that sounded.

"I'm not judging." Though it was strange that she didn't want to donate food to keep them living instead of the other fate. Still, I was there to gather information, not judge her.

"Lucy Ellen came in and we made an agreement that I'd call her when food was about to expire." It sounded like a good collaboration. But where did it go wrong, I wondered as she continued to talk. "The food I was giving her expired so quickly, I decided not to carry that manufacturer anymore because I was losing money here at my shop. So I discontinued it. A month or so later Lucy Ellen came in. I told her about the food and how I didn't have anything at this particular time."

Faith stopped and gulped.

"She had the nerve to tell me that I was the one killing the cats at the shelter by not giving the food to them at a discount and that was blood on my hands. She ranted on how I didn't really care about animal rights and it was only a ploy for me to get people to come into the shop." Her voice cracked. "Her words are still painful to this day."

"Did it hurt your business?" The malicious words could've played a big part in a motive for Faith to commit murder, but losing money and altering her lifestyle was an even bigger motive.

"That's the funny thing. Business started booming. People were coming in here saying how they knew I was a reputable store because they knew she'd write those nasty reviews out of hate." She coughed up a laugh. "I called her and actually thanked her for the review."

"I bet that didn't go well." My jaw tensed.

"She hung up on me." She rolled her eyes. "Like I said, I hate that she died, but whoever did it was someone who she probably wronged one too many times."

We made our way up to the front of the store where the registers were located.

"Can you tell me where you were the night of her murder?" I asked. Her mouth dropped, her eyes widened. "Just doing this with all the people who got a bad review from her."

"I was actually in Atlanta at the big pet expo. I've got plane tickets, hotel stubs, and even my husband who was with me along with hundreds of other shop owners who can corroborate." She had an alibi and if I did need to look into it I would, but nothing told me she was lying. "Bloomie and I have to keep our grooming licenses up because they expire every year. So while I was there, I did that all over again because I'm almost expired."

"Thanks for being up front and honest." I started to reach for my extra money in my pocket.

"Don't worry about it." She shooed my hand away. "This bag is on me. Does he know?"

"About his appointment on Saturday?" I asked. "No," I mouthed.

She threw her head back and laughed. The alarm over the front door mooed, signaling the arrival of Duke's most favorite dog groomer and Faith's partner, Bloomie Fischer.

"Duke." She bent down and put her arms out. He darted toward her and slid into her lap with his arms and paws extended forward; tail wagging and kisses ensued.

"I can't wait to play with him Saturday," Bloomie whispered over his shoulder.

"We've got to go." I patted my leg. Duke enjoyed one last good scratch from Bloomie. "Alright, Casanova, let's go. See y'all Saturday."

Duke and I walked out very happy customers of Pet Patch. He had a few more treats and I had a free bag of dog food.

Though Faith had some good information on why she and Lucy Ellen had words, it still didn't give me any more information on who killed Lucy.

Going back to the salon to talk to Cheree was my next stop. I checked my phone to see if by chance I'd missed a call from Tom Geary. Nothing. I put my phone on vibrate and put it in my back pocket.

"It's awful about Lucy Ellen Lowell," Cheree whined when she saw me walk in. In one swoop, she pulled her long red hair back and up into a perfect top-knot. "And to think we just saw her."

"We sure did." I looked around. For the late afternoon, I found it odd that there weren't any customers in the joint.

"Who on earth would ever want to hurt her?" she asked in a sweet Southern drawl. She reached into her purse and took out her glasses, nestling those on top of her head too.

"I was hoping you could answer that." I couldn't stop myself from looking at the nail polish bottles in hope the Perfectly Posh would show up.

"What on earth do you mean?" Cheree stopped what she was doing and stared doe-eyed at me.

"I don't come here a lot, but I couldn't help but overhear all the gossip that took place after Lucy Ellen left here."

Cheree looked at me as if she didn't know what I was talking about.

"Oh, come on." Sarcasm dripped from my lips at her ignorance. Was she hiding something? "When Lucy Ellen left here, there was a lot of talk about her and everyone's dislike of her," I said, as if she needed reminding.

"That?" She pish-poshed. "That's all it was. Talk."

I hummed. "Talk? Innocent talk and then she shows up dead?" I shook the bottle of fingernail polish to help mix up the top oily layer with the rest of the polish.

"Lucy Ellen was wearing a color on her nails that looked pretty similar, if not the same as Perfectly Posh," I said, stopping Cheree dead in her tracks. "Cheree?" It wasn't the exact reaction I'd expected, but at least it was something. "Cheree, are you okay?"

My phone vibrated in my pocket. I slipped it out to look and see if it was Tom. When Toots's name popped up, I hit the off button, sending her to voicemail.

"Kenni," Cheree gasped, causing the freckles on her face to widen a smidgen. "That night around eight, I got a call from Art Baskin about our security alarm going off." She tapped the rose gold watch on her wrist. "I'd left here around seven thirty and drove straight to Cowboy's Catfish to get my to-go order. After Bartleby gave me my food, I came back here and that was around eight fifteen-ish."

Art Baskin was the owner of the only security-system provider in town.

"You know it only takes a couple of minutes to get here from there. When I showed up at the shop, Art was waiting in his car. We came in to check it out and there was nothing wrong in here. I turned the alarm off. Art asked if I wanted to call the sheriff, but I said no. I called Tina and told her that I came by and no one was here. I asked her if she wanted me to call you and she said there was no reason to. You know them heathen kids nowadays like to come in and color their hair all sorts of crazy colors. I figured they were trying to steal some color. Nothing looked out of place, but Tina did say the next day that her Perfectly Posh was missing. The last person we saw with it was Lucy Ellen Lowell." Cheree recalled how Lucy Ellen wanted to buy it.

"You didn't see or talk to Lucy Ellen after she left here that afternoon?" I asked.

"Why no, I did not." She said as if I shouldn't ask such a thing, "What are you insinuating?"

"I'm only trying to figure out what Lucy's actions were after she left here. You and I both heard and saw how everyone reacted when she was here." There was no sense in not being up front and honest with her. "You didn't make a police report about the break-in?" I asked.

"Nope." She walked around and plugged in all the styling tools they used on their hair customers. "I didn't see the need to call anyone because there was nothing missing. We have two of everything that is worth anything." She walked around and pointed. "Two hair dryers, two flat-irons, two curling irons, all the nail things, our work stations. If something like a small bottle of nail polish or even hair dye was missing, we'd never really know. I use nail polish and all the hair products when Tina isn't here, like she does when I'm not here. We don't keep records when we finish with a product."

My phone vibrated. I pulled it out.

"Excuse me. I need to take this." It was Tom Geary. "Hello, Tom."

"Sheriff, I'm sorry I couldn't get back with you sooner. I just wanted to make sure and do a little research before I gave you the findings." He was so thorough and I liked that about his lab. "Do you have a second?"

I walked out of Tiny Tina's and got into the Wagoneer so I could grab my notepad and write down what he was telling me.

"I do. Let me grab my pen and paper." I shut the door once I got in.

"I'll be faxing over the report to your office," he informed me. "In the meantime, I felt like I should call you and tell you the results myself."

"That's great." I dragged my bag across the seat of the Jeep and opened it, taking out my pen and paper. "Okay, tell me what you found out."

"The polish base is a clear topcoat that can be broken down into ethyl acetate, butyl acetate, and alcohol." He said words that I had no idea how to spell correctly so I phonetically did the best I could until I could get the report. "It was the color that made me do the longer test that took all night. The color was actually derived from eyeshadow. There was also a lethal dose of cyanide in the small bit of nail that I tested."

"What is your conclusion?" I asked.

"I actually narrowed down the compounds of the eyeshadow to MAC Pink Venus eyeshadow. With the level of cyanide in there if someone had painted even one nail with the lethal polish, they would've died, much less all of her fingernails and toes." It was all I needed to hear in order to march back into Tiny Tina's to see exactly how Tina Bowers made her polish.

"If you wouldn't mind getting that report over to the office ASAP, I'd be eternally grateful." My eyes slid across the seat.

Poppa appeared and stared at me with a dropped jaw and opened eyes.

"Did you say MAC as in the boy's name?" he asked in a whisper.

I nodded.

"I'm faxing it as we speak." Tom said, and I hung up.

"There's a bunch of makeup in the back room of Tiny Tina's that's got the name MAC on them in big bold letters." Poppa looked past my shoulder and out the Jeep window toward Tiny Tina's.

"Looks like we have the ingredients, a motive, and the killer." I gnawed on my lip. I punched the button on the side of the walkie talkie. "Betty?"

"Hey, Kenni," Betty answered as if I were calling to see how she was doing, not as though this was business.

"I need you to get Judge to get me a warrant to search and collect some evidence at Tiny Tina's. I need you to fax it over to the salon. You'll find their fax number over in the Rolodex on my desk. And it needs to be ASAP. Tell Judge that I'm here now and I've got a big lead." I left out the part that the big lead was Poppa's ghost telling me that in the back room was the same makeup brand that Tom Geary had said was one of the main ingredients in the weapon used to kill Lucy.

"Gotcha." Betty clicked off.

Out of the corner of my eye, I saw Tina's old Corolla pull up and her getting out of the car. She tossed her cigarette butt on the pavement and twisted the toe of her shoe in it. With a heavy sigh, I got out of the car.

"Tina," I called before she entered the building.

"Hey, Kenni. Are you ready for your big nail day?" She smiled and used the tips of her fingers to add some volume to her brown hair.

My heart broke in tiny pieces because I knew that smile would falter pretty quickly after we started talking.

"I guess, but that's not why I'm here." I gestured for us to go inside when someone pulled into the parking lot. "Can we go into the back where you make your nail polish? I think you called it the color room the other day."

I thought I'd ask instead of waiting on the warrant.

"Sure." She looked at me with her brown eyes. The smile was gone. She stuck her purse behind the counter. She said to Cheree, "I'm going to talk to Kenni for a minute. I'll be right back."

That was easier than I imagined, I thought when she readily agreed to me going back there.

"That's fine. We had a bunch of cancellations today." Cheree nodded at the door. "I've got one manicure and that's it."

"Great," Tina moaned.

As I looked at Cheree, many questions popped into my head. Before I went to the back room, I just had to know.

"Cheree, you didn't make a police report?" I asked again to make sure I'd heard her correctly before I took Tom's phone call.

"No, I didn't. You can ask Art." She shrugged.

"I will, but in the meantime, why didn't you make a report?" I asked.

"There didn't seem to be anything taken or out of place. Just a break-in, so I didn't see the point in going through the trouble of calling you to make a report. You are a busy woman."

"I appreciate that, but I'm also the law and I take pride in my job." I pointed to the desk. "Do you mind making me a copy of the client lists for the past couple of weeks?"

"Sure." She hurried over to the desk and grabbed the appointment book. "I'll get to it right now." She flung the printer that sat on the front desk next to the phone open and smacked the appointment book on it.

I walked into the back room. It was just a storage room with a steel table in the middle. Tina was standing near the table where she mixed the fingernail polish, but Poppa stood by the makeup on a different table.

"Right here." Poppa pointed to the makeup. "This one is Pink Venus."

I swallowed hard and walked over to Poppa's table, careful not to touch it. I needed to treat this as a crime scene where the weapon was made.

"So you use a clear fingernail polish and add eyeshadow to it to make your signature colors?" I asked. "Where were you between eight p.m. Tuesday night and four a.m. Wednesday morning?"

Tina's head shot up.

"First you send Deputy Vincent to my house, where he found nothing." She glared. "And now you come to my job and question it. What is it that you want from me, Kenni? Are you saying you think I harmed or killed Lucy Ellen Lowell?"

"I want the truth. Simply answer my questions." I rested my hand on my holster. "Do you use this MAC Pink Venus to make your Perfectly Posh nail polish?"

One question at a time.

"Yes." There was a bit of defensiveness in her voice.

"I'm going to go out on a limb and say that you're probably the only person that Lucy Ellen Lowell came to for her manicures. And it just so happens that the day before her murder she came in here and you actually said that maybe you should've cut her hair and had the scissors slip."

"You've got to be joking me." She was getting fidgety and hostile. "It was gossip. That's what we do here. Oh." She twirled around. "I forgot. You don't come to these sort of places. You don't gossip. You're the sheriff."

I detected a hint of sarcasm in her voice.

"I can name five other people here that day that also had a beef with Lucy." She held her hand up in the air and uncurled a finger with each name. "Me, Cheree, Polly, Jolee, and Faith Dunaway."

"Tina, Lucy Ellen Lowell was murdered." I watched her actions.

"It wasn't by my scissors." Her leg jutted out to the side, her hip followed as she planted her hands on her hips. "You can't be back here." She flung her hands in the air just as the ringing phone followed up by the beeping of the fax machine echoed in the air.

"I think you're going to find that the fax coming through is a warrant to not only search the salon but also collect evidence that proves the murder weapon used was Perfectly Posh nail polish laced with cyanide poisoning." I

DEAD AS A DOORNAIL

took a deep breath before I gave the final blow. "Perfectly Posh made with MAC Pink Venus eyeshadow."

"You are seriously accusing me of killing Lucy?" she asked.

"Where were you between eight p.m. to four a.m.?" I asked again out of curiosity because the truth was that the polish could've been poisoned at any time of the day, but just in case I could tie her to the scene, it'd make it a lot more solid.

"I..." She gulped. "I'm not going to answer that. Isn't there a fifth amendment, or is it first? Either way, I'm not answering."

"Ummm...Kenni." Poppa caught my attention. I followed where his eyes were focused. "I think we've got some cyanide."

There was a bottle sitting on the ground. There were no markings on it, but I took Poppa's word for it.

"What are you looking at?" Tina asked.

"What is in the bottle, Tina?" I asked and walked over to it.

"I have no idea. Maybe some sort of chemical." She shrugged, nodded, and harrumphed all at the same time.

"Tina Bowers," I unhooked the cuffs from my utility belt, "you have the right to remain silent. I'm arresting you for the murder of Lucy Ellen Lowell." I continued to read her the Miranda Rights. She interrupted.

"Kenni Lowry, you've lost your marbles." The piss and vinegar started to pour out of her mouth. The cuffs clicked as each tooth on the lock clicked tighter around her wrists. "This beats all I ever seen. Cheree! Cheree, get in here!" She screamed at the top of her lungs.

"What's wrong?" Cheree ran in with a look of fright. There were papers in her hand. She handed them to me.

"That's wrong. Where did that come from?" Tina pointed.

I gave Cheree a chance to look over the poisonous bottle of substance labeled Cyanide.

"Cyanide?" Suddenly it appeared as if she had a quick and disturbing thought. "Tina, you didn't..."

"I ought to smack you silly. Hell no, I didn't." Tina put up a stronger guard now. "Did you? Did you put it here?"

"She could've." Poppa let out an anxious cough. "I mean..."

Before Poppa could say it, Tina finished it, "You've got a beef with her too. It's not just me. After all, you're the one who said we needed to not let her make appointments anymore."

"It was you that said you'd like her dead." Cheree came unglued. "You're the one who complains about her day in and day out. You're the one who does her nails. I never use your homemade fingernail polish. You know I go down to the dollar store and get fifty-cent nail polish. You're the one being the freaky mad scientist."

"Look." Tina pointed at me. "She's trying to turn us against each other. We won't let you pin this on us. We didn't do anything to Lucy Ellen Lowell no matter if we can't tell you how that bottle got there."

"Where were you the night of the murder?" I asked Tina again.

She drew her shoulders back and stuck her chin up in the air. When she curled her lips together and pinched them so tight that the edges turned white, I knew I had my answer. She wasn't going to tell me come hell or high water what she'd been doing when Lucy Ellen was killed and I had no other option.

"Anything you say can and will be used…" I tried to continue the arrest policy when I unfortunately had to use some force. "Tina Bowers, straighten up right this minute," I jerked her wrists closer together as she tried to pull them apart.

Both of us stopped jerking the other. Her hands stopped flailing and there we were, in a stand-off. Only I knew I was going to win.

"Don't make me parade you through the front of the salon acting all nutso. I'm more than happy to take you out the back door," I suggested.

"I've done nothing wrong. I'm going to be using my one phone call now, thank you." Her chin tilted to the side, her eyes drawing down her nose on me.

"You can use the phone once we get to department." I shook my head and pointed to the door. "Go on."

She took in a deep breath, curled her shoulders back, and took the first step out through the beads covering the opening of the storage room.

"Lookie here, y'all." She held her cuffed hands way up over her head as she talked to her clients. "Kenni Lowry. Sheriff Kenni Lowry is crazier'n all get out. Arresting me for killing Lucy Ellen Lowell when I did no such thing."

"Let's go. Cheree, I'll be right back. I'm gonna have to ask all y'all to leave. The salon is shut down until further notice." I had to grab her by the arm and lead her out the door.

"You know what, Kenni," Tina spat. "This is all fine and dandy if I were a criminal. But I'm not and I can't wait for Wally Lamb to tear you a new one."

"Yep, me either." I opened the back of the Wagoneer and stuck her inside. I stood by the door and watched as three women filed out of the salon with half-done nails.

"There goes rent. Right on out the door. In a few minutes, you single-handedly ran me out of business." Tina grunted and moaned. She leaned over to the rolled-down window. "Be sure to write in someone else's name on the election ballot. We can't have a nutso sheriff running around arresting people for no good reason!"

A low deep groan escaped me. "Tina, if you can prove your whereabouts and what you were doing at the time of the estimated death of Lucy, then I'm more than happy to let you go."

Cheree walked over and leaned against the car.

"Now what?" she asked.

"I'm going to go in there and take a few things for evidence and finger-printing. Then, Betty Murphy will call you when we release the salon." It was standard procedure. "If you'll excuse me." I knew this wasn't the last time I was going to talk to Cheree, but I wanted to get Tina out of the environment that was making her nervous and hostile.

I still didn't have a clear-cut answer to where Cheree had been. Granted, she said she called Art Baskin and gotten food. Both of those would be easy enough to check out, but what about all the in-between?

I took a few steps away from the Jeep so I could talk to Betty at dispatch.

"Betty?" I called into the walkie-talkie.

"Go ahead, Sheriff." She was quick.

"Please get the cell ready. I'm bringing in Tina Bowers for more questioning on the murder of Lucy Ellen Lowell." I clicked off.

"Oh my stars." Betty gasped. "Oh my goodness gracious."

"Thanks, Betty." I clicked off again and pulled my cell from my back pocket. I scrolled down to find Finn's contact and hit the green call button.

In the meantime, Cheree was holding a cigarette for Tina to puff on.

"Not in my Jeep!" I snapped my fingers at them, only to receive a glare from Tina.

"Any luck with Cheree?" Finn asked from the other end.

"It just so happens I'm bringing in Tina. Tom called with the report and it should be on the fax machine when we get there. He was able to break down the components of the polish to the exact make of the eyeshadow." I was trying to talk fast so I could hurry back in the Jeep and get to the department and beat the gossip.

"Eyeshadow? I thought it was fingernail polish." Finn was all sorts of confused.

"Meet me at the department and I'll explain all of it to you there. Oh, and I found a bottle of cyanide in the salon."

"I found it." Poppa poked his chest as if Finn could hear him.

"Anyway, I shut down the salon. We need to go through it with a fine-toothed comb. Tina Bowers won't give me a valid alibi. I had no choice." My voice drifted off because the thought of Tina being the killer was unfathomable to me.

But people killed for a lot less. And all the evidence pointing to her was found in her shop. To me that was as good a reason as any to make an arrest, though Wally Lamb might try to prove otherwise.

"He'll meet you there." Cheree had her cell up to her face and was talking to Tina.

"Tell him to bring me something to eat. I'm starving." Tina sat back and suddenly looked very comfortable in the back.

Cheree gave her a hug through the window and walked away. I waited until Cheree was gone before I made sure the Wagoneer's doors were locked and Tina was safe until I went back in and bagged the cyanide bottle, the MAC makeup, and a few of Cheree's bottles. If there were fingerprints on the cyanide bottle, I wanted to have Cheree's in case.

I got in the Jeep and started to pull out of the parking lot, but not without Tina giving me some lip.

"I garonteeeee," her Southern accent had a different take on the word, "you're gonna regret this."

"I hope I do," I muttered and turned toward downtown. "I really hope I do."

CHAPTER TWELVE

"On what basis, Kenni?" Wally Lamb paced back and forth in front of the only cell we had in the department.

Tina was all sprawled out on the small cot eating a catfish special from Cowboy's out of the Styrofoam carryout container, not paying any attention to her lawyer or me.

"Wally, she won't tell me where she was on the night of the murder during the period Max has estimated as time of death. Not that she had to be there, because the murder weapon was the nail polish she made. The ingredients were broken down by Tom Geary's lab over in Clay's Ferry. The report is right here. All the ingredients, including the cyanide, were found in her salon."

After I'd brought Tina back to the department, I sent Finn over to the salon to see if I'd overlooked anything and clear the scene. He took more photos but didn't find anything else.

"Not to mention what she said after Lucy Ellen left her shop the other day in front of me." It was something I just couldn't forget.

Wally stopped and looked at Tina through the bars. He raised his hand and dragged it through his slicked-back blond hair. He let out a deep breath through a small opening in his lips. I couldn't tell if he was frustrated with me or with Tina. Regardless, his stress was showing on his face.

"There are no other suspects?" He finally turned around to me.

"I can't tell you everything. I can say that the evidence is piled against Tina." My eyes shifted between him and Tina.

Betty wasn't fooling anyone. She was acting like she was doing some filing work, but she had one eye on the cabinet and one eye on our conversation.

"Where is this polish that you claim to be the murder weapon?" he asked.

I cringed.

"I don't know." I bit the edge of my lip and prepared myself for his wrath.

"You mean to tell me that you accuse my client of making deadly fingernail polish after she had gossiped in her hair salon, because we know that there's no gossiping going on in a hair salon." He mocked me. "Then you think she polished the deceased's fingernails with it, but you can't find the actual polish to test, just the fingernail of the deceased?"

"The fingernail is really all we need to prove it was tainted. I'd like for your client to hand over the bottle so we can have a murder weapon. If she can provide that, I'm sure we can come up with some sort of deal with the prosecutor." I was laying all my cards out on the table. He and I both knew the fingernail was enough, but I knew the actual bottle the polish came from would help me seal the case.

"Besides, Tina was heard and seen making threats about Lucy," I reminded him.

"So did half the other people in the salon that day according to you and everyone else I interviewed. I also talked to Art Baskin and he said that the alarm would only go off if someone had broken in," he said flatly. "My client was set up and I'm going to prove it. She made a silly gesture. People make veiled threats all the time. It looks like to me that someone has set my client up. You've got the wrong person in custody and I demand you let her go this instant."

"Wally." I sucked in a deep breath. "I'm going to hold her for twenty-four hours."

"Twenty-four hours?" Tina jumped off the cot. "I've got to do your nails and the rest of Polly Parker's bridal party."

Just as if the floodgate opened up, the door of the department flung open.

"I demand you let Tina Bowers go into my custody," Mayor Ryland demanded with Polly Parker at his side.

"Yes!" Tina grasped the bars with her hands and shook them. "Demand it, Mayor."

The scene was spiraling out of control quickly.

"First off, Mayor, I appreciate you and Polly coming down, but this is an open investigation. So you are not welcome. Secondly, I'll let you know how the investigation is going when I'm done here." I wasn't about to let him take charge.

Finn walked in and nervously looked around. His hands were filled with evidence bags.

"Thank God you're here." Polly put her grubby little hands on Finn's arms and brushed down it.

It took everything in my body not to go all girl-crazy on her, but I knew I had to keep myself in check. I seemed to be the only sane one here. But I couldn't guarantee I'd stay that way if she kept putting her fingers on him.

"You've got to knock some sense into your girlfriend. Take control. Be a man," Polly pleaded with him.

"She's the boss. She's the sheriff. She knows what she's doing." Finn stepped away from her and went to his desk. He took out some evidence-processing forms while I continued to try to make order.

"Mayor, I've got this." Wally Lamb knew me and had worked with me many times. He knew that demanding things and trying to make me do something someone else wanted was not only a waste of time, but I'd do the complete opposite.

"But my nails." Polly wasn't budging. "We need Tina to do my bridal party's nails since Cheree can't do all of us."

"I'm sure you'll figure it out." Wally pushed them toward the door.

"Kenni Lowry, you are no longer my maid of honor! I want my dress back!" she hollered at me as the mayor took her out the door kicking and screaming.

I ignored her but walked out after them.

"Mayor, can I speak to you for a second?" I asked.

He looked between me and Polly. He whispered something in her ear. She stomped back toward me.

"I'm going to Cowboy's Catfish to get me a slice of pie." She snarled, her big horse teeth pressed together. Her lip twitched and she glared.

"That sounds so good." I couldn't help myself.

The mayor and I stood in silence until the door had closed fully.

"What is it, Sheriff?" He addressed me with an air about his title.

"It's not gone unnoticed that you're really trying to keep me from solving this case," I stated.

"That's not true," he retorted with his jaw tense.

"You do seem to have a vested interest in keeping me busy. Trying on dresses, doing manicures, seeing Preacher, hosting bridal events when you and I both know that Polly and I are far from being best friends," I stated the facts with a stern stare. "I'm only doing this as a favor to Tibbie and to get her business off the ground." The facts were the facts. "Where were you the night of Lucy's death? To be more specific, Tuesday night eight p.m. through Wednesday morning four a.m."

I felt like I needed to know exactly where he was, even though an alibi wasn't going to clear up who killed Lucy Ellen.

"You've got to be kidding me." He ran his fingers through his slicked back gray hair, loosing up a little of the gel that'd kept it in place.

"I don't joke about murder."

"What evidence would suggest that I have anything to do with Lucy Ellen Lowell's death? Why would I kill anyone, especially her?" His eyes clung to mine, studying my reaction.

"Well, you are a member of the hunt club, where it's been known that Lucy Ellen has caused a few problems. Not to mention she's a bit nosy, which Polly would hate. Then there's the fact that Polly really didn't want to invite Lucy Ellen to your big day. I can only think in fear she'd somehow ruin it. Then there's the election where you have to keep the good ole boys happy so they'll keep you in office and not turn on you right before the election. You wouldn't want to risk a write-in."

"Wednesday night, Polly and I were at a private cake tasting at the Sweet Shop for our wedding cakes. After that, we went to Luke Jones' basement to watch Father of the Bride with Polly's parents." His brows rose. "In honor of our wedding, Luke and Vita are playing Father of the Bride as well as Seven

Brides for Seven Brothers because that happens to be Pete Parker's favorite movie."

"After the movies?" I asked.

He opened his mouth. His tongue played with the back of one of his teeth while his jaw jutted left and right.

"In honor of keeping my bride's reputation intact, I'm assuming you're going to keep this to yourself, but we've already moved into the cabin together." He sucked in a deep breath. "Her parents aren't happy about it because they are old Southern and don't approve of us living together before we got married, so we've kept it very hush-hush."

You could've knocked me over with a feather. How on earth had the henny-hens not gotten wind of this bit of gossip?

"I went home and sent emails for work. You're more than welcome to seize my computer and check out what I was doing online after we'd gotten home. But I can assure you that I didn't kill Lucy Ellen Lowell." He straightened himself with dignity. "Now, if you'll excuse me, I need to get to my bride and you need to get back to Wally Lamb."

Even though Lucy Ellen was killed from the poisoning and Mayor Ryland could've added the poison before that night, I did recall Lucy Ellen saying to Polly that she was looking forward to talking to the mayor at the wedding since they'd not seen each other in months.

"Thank you for answering me honestly." I felt like we'd reached a level of respect that I'd never gotten from the mayor since I took office. "I'm sorry that Polly fired me as maid of honor."

He just nodded and both of us headed back into the department. Betty, Wally, Finn, and Tina watched as Mayor Ryland walked through the department and through the door that lead to Cowboy's Catfish. I turned to face them.

"This turned out good for you. That dress was ugly." Tina shrugged and eased back down on the cot.

CHAPTER THIRTEEN

Tina talked and talked and talked the entire rest of my time at the office. She just talked to hear herself. No wonder she was meant to own a beauty shop and spa. She had to be good at it. Mama always told me that Tina Bowers could talk to a wooden Indian.

By the time I'd gotten Duke dropped off at home and went to Euchre at Tibbie Bell's house, I was plum exhausted.

Tibbie lived on Second Street in a small house on the town branch. All the girls here for Euchre night were all gathered in the dining room where Tibbie set up tables for all the food that everyone brought. I'm talking delicious food too. These ladies took pride in their cooking. It was more like a repass, but no one was dead. I was happy too. I was in the mood for a good home-cooked meal of the semi-formal dinner style that featured collard greens and creamed corn paired with simple desserts like Betty Murphy's rice pudding.

"Kendrick Lowry."

My sudden urge for a big spoonful of the creamed corn went away with the image of an angry Toots Buford, who I could feel staring me down.

"I've called you several times. I left you many messages and you've never called me back." She looked like a puffed-up toad she was so mad. "It dills my pickle that you don't have the gall to call me back. To me, that means that you don't want to discuss the problem at hand."

"And what would that be?" I asked in a calm manner.

"You taking my rightful spot as Polly Parker's maid of honor, that's what." Her right leg flung out to the side and her right hand planted on her waist as she swung her right hip wide. "What do you have to say for yourself?"

"I'm sorry, Toots." I really wanted to tell her to take the job. I didn't want it. "I can't help who Polly picked to be in her wedding. I was just as surprised as you are."

"You are?" She reached around me and took one of the ginger snap cookies.

"Mmm-hmm," I ho-hummed. "If it's any consolation, she already fired me."

"I've been best friends with her since our days at the Toddler Inn preschool." Her brows knitted together. "I taught her how to do her hair and her makeup." She leaned in. "I even taught her how to line her lips so those big veneers of hers wouldn't overtake her wedding photos. And this is the thanks she gives me?"

That tip alone should've given her maid-of-honor status.

"Maybe she's going to call you now," I suggested with a hopeful voice. "I don't know what she's thinking. I'm just doing what Tibbie Bell tells me to do." I offered a sympathetic look.

"Well, I'm hurt to the core. She's pained me. I'm not even sure I'd be her maid of honor if she asked." She jabbed her long pointy fingernail in her own chest. "Painful I tell you." I nodded slowly.

I continued to nod, afraid to say too much in case it got back to Polly or Tibbie. The wrath of them was extra stress I didn't need.

After I filled my plate a couple of times and got the wonky eye from Mama, I headed into the room across from the food where Tibbie had set up the card tables for our Euchre night.

"At least you got to leave for a few minutes," Betty Murphy said about Tina Bowers's non-stop talking at the department.

Betty threw a card off suit, meaning she was out of trump. I didn't know if I would say she was being nice to fill in for Mama's Euchre partner who couldn't make it, or just wanted to come so she could be in on the gossip that was sure to circulate about Lucy Ellen and Tina tonight.

"She wouldn't shut up. Though she did have some really great decorating ideas." Betty offered a wry smile.

"How do you think Finn is doing with her?" I asked, scanning my cards for the right one to play off since Jolee had led off with trump and won the hand. I couldn't leave her there by herself in case she got ill or something, so Finn volunteered to stay the night at the department.

"He was at least nicer to me than you were to Tina, apparently." Jolee's eyes peered over the top of her cards.

"Jolee, are we actually going to even discuss this?" I asked with Mama and Betty looking at me. If there were anyone else other than the four of us at the table, I wouldn't have said anything.

"Excuse us." Jolee laid her cards face down on the table. "We need to go grab a brownie."

"Not Kenni," Mama chirped. "She's got a dress to fit into." She patted her belly. "Happy fat isn't happy in front of hundreds of eyes looking at you in the front of the church."

"Good thing I'm no longer in the wedding." It was with great pleasure I burst her bubble.

"What?" Mama cried out and pushed the chair back.

When she stood up to hurry after Jolee and me, the chair fell backward and smacked on the floor. The other occupants of the four tables stopped and looked at us.

"I can't believe you'd think I'd kill someone. So when Finn showed up and questioned me, I nearly drove the truck into the telephone pole on the way to my next stop." Jolee was hurt. "Besides, I was with Ben all afternoon and all night."

Jolee and Ben Harrison were an item and they were always together.

"What do you mean you aren't in the wedding?" Mama squeezed herself between me and the brownies.

The questions both of them were throwing my way were just a jumble of words in my head. I reached around Mama and took a brownie and stuffed all of it in my mouth.

"Your daughter has ruined my career by arresting Tina. Polly Parker has the power to make me the most sought after wedding planner, but not now." Tibbie had to join in. "You could've arrested Tina after the nail appointments for the wedding."

"That's why Polly fired you as her maid of honor? The case?" Mama's brows furrowed. "The biggest wedding in Cottonwood. You're going to be known for this and it's not good. Couldn't you just take your time for once? It's not like Tina Bowers is going to run out of town or anything."

True, Tina probably wasn't a flight risk.

"Nope. She couldn't leave well enough alone." Tibbie pointed to herself. "Polly is mad at me for suggesting Kenni."

My head jerked to look at her.

"You're the one who told her to ask me?" I'd really thought Mama had arranged it. "I have you to thank for this?"

Jolee took her stab at me.

"At least she didn't accuse y'all of killing Lucy Ellen like she did me." Jolee shoved in her two cents.

"Did you know that she wants to go away for Christmas?" Mama's words stopped Jolee and Tibbie in their tracks. "The whole week."

Mama knew that my friends and I always spent Christmas Eve together to not only exchange gifts, but also to enjoy what we called Friendmas.

Jolee's face went blank. Her eyelashes batted up and down as she blinked in bafflement.

"You could start an argument in an empty house." I grabbed another brownie and stuffed it in my mouth too, making Mama madder and madder. "I'm an adult and can spend Christmas with whoever I want. And I'm not in the wedding because Polly Parker is mad at me for doing my job. So we don't have to worry about happy fat anymore."

I planted a stiff smile on my face and grabbed another brownie.

"As for you," I turned to Jolee, "I couldn't question you about it, because it's a conflict of interest and I wouldn't be a good sheriff if I did ask you questions myself. Of course I don't think you killed anyone. I've got Tina Bowers in the cell right this minute."

I took a quick breath.

"As for you, if you need Polly Parker's wedding to prove to potential clients that you are good at your job, maybe you shouldn't be a wedding planner." I'm sure my words stung Tibbie, but she needed more confidence in herself than that if she was going to be a successful businesswoman.

There were murmurs behind me that caught my attention. Slowly I turned around with half the brownie sticking out of my mouth. The flash of a camera nearly blinded me.

"And that's exactly how it happened." I grabbed the bottle of wine and filled up my glass, Finn's glass, and Tina's glass as I told them why I'd left the Euchre game early. "I got tired of everyone telling me I'm a bad person and now Edna Easterly is going to plaster that photo of me stuffing my face and telling Mama and Jolee off on the front page of the Cottonwood Chronicle."

The two of them laughed.

"I'm certainly glad you came with wine." Tina held up her glass from the other side of the bars. "I'm going to tell you that I didn't lace the fingernail polish with the cyanide and I don't know how it got in there." She held her glass out for a refill. "Have you even thought about the person who set off the alarm?"

"What alarm?" Finn asked.

"Cheree called me around eight thirty and said the shop's alarm was going off and when she went to check it, there wasn't anyone in there and nothing was missing. We get teenagers in there stealing hair color, so we just figured it was a kid."

Finn walked over to his fancy whiteboard and picked up a dry-erase marker.

He made his usual grid with suspects, motives, and evidence.

"Here we go. Craft time," Poppa joked. "I've never seen someone make so many little boxes and stars. Can't he just put it all up here and figure it out?" He pointed to his head.

"Don't put my name in the suspect category," Tina mumbled into her wine glass before taking a gulp. "What part of 'I didn't kill her' are y'all not getting?"

Finn and I looked between each other and her before we both turned back to the board, ignoring her.

"Who else can go up there?" Finn asked and pointed to the suspect column. "If you don't give us an alibi, then you stay our number one."

"What about Jolee Fischer? She said that she'd like to slip her something.

She did it." Tina sounded so upbeat and positive with her thought. "You can't keep me much longer." The wine glass dangled from her fingertips.

"I've got enough evidence collected from your salon to present to a judge to keep you longer if I need to." Finn's brows rose.

Tina's eyes lowered before she sat back down on the cot.

"What about Alma Frederick?" Tina asked.

"What about her?" I asked.

"She thought she was something else since Bosco is the president of the Hunt Club. I do Alma's hair and nails." Tina made it sound like we should know who that was. She harrumphed when she realized we didn't.

"And how is this related to Lucy?" Finn asked.

"Hair." She pointed to her head. "Nails." She dangled one hand out in front of her, dared not to put down the wine glass. "Gossip all together."

"Fine. I'll write down Alma Frederick if you think we need to check her out." He looked at me. I nodded and he wrote down her name.

Tina's face brightened with each letter Finn wrote on the dry-erase board. He moved the marker over to the motive box next to Alma's name.

"Put the squeeze on her, Kenni-bug." Poppa rubbed his hands vigorously. "She's about to break. I can see it in her fidgety hands."

He was right. Tina was starting to pick at her nails, something she'd never do.

"Tell me why Alma should be on this very short list where all the evidence points to you." I picked up a marker.

"I told you I didn't kill her."

"Then tell me where you were the night of the murder. Because it's funny how your lawyer has left you here and hasn't called to check on you or even come down here to get you out." It was almost unnerving how comfortable Tina looked in the cell. "But if you'd prefer to be doing nails and hair in the big house among the real killers and criminals, I guess Cheree will have to hire someone else to buy you out."

"Buy me out?" That got her attention. She stomped over to the bars and stuck her nose through them. "No one is buying me out."

"Answer my question." I slammed the marker on the desk and raised my voice a few more decibels. "You and Lucy Ellen got into a fight. She threatened your business by telling you she was going to write that review. You put poison in the only nail polish she wanted and you let her kill herself unbeknownst to her!" I yelled louder and louder as her jaw got tighter and tenser.

Duke jumped up from his bed and the hair on his spine stood up.

"I was at massage school in Clay's Ferry!" she screamed and quickly shut her mouth. She looked like she surprised herself. She fell against the bars and melted down to the ground. "Are you happy? I'm a fraud. I didn't have a real massage license and I've been going to massage school on my days off and I had a two-day final. That's why I wasn't at the shop that night or the next day until late. I have the certificate and a roomful of people and clients to prove it."

Stunned, I eased down on the edge of my desk. My mouth dropped, my shoulders slumped. Even now that she did have an alibi the night of Lucy's death and the days leading up to it, she could still be held on fraud charges.

"Now let me go. I've got a wedding party to take care of." She stood back up, ran her hands down her shirt and over her hair.

"Not so fast." Finn took over. He could see the shock on my face. "Now we know you're running a fraudulent business. We might be able to help you if you cooperate in this investigation."

"How?" She planted a closed fist on her hip.

"You mentioned Alma Frederick." I gathered my wits about me and pushed myself up to stand. "You tell me everything you know that's not gossip. The truth. I'll check out the truth and if it does check out, then and only then will I think about letting you out of here."

"What about the fraud charges? I have my license now." She chewed on the inside of her jaw.

"I can probably get the judge to be lenient." It wasn't going to be easy since the judge had probably been one of Tina's clients, but I was willing to try.

"Alma and Lucy Ellen hated each other. It's no secret that Darnell wants to be the Hunt Club president." Tina wagged a finger at me. "No different than a sheriff's election to them. Apparently," her voice did an upswing in tone, "Bosco and Darnell are hunting partners. When Darnell and Lucy Ellen were having problems, it tickled Alma pink because she knew the women in the Hunt Club wouldn't vote in a divorced man since their morals are so high brow." She pish-poshed their attitude.

"Darnell and Lucy Ellen were having troubles?" I asked.

Finn was busy making notes on the board while I asked the questions.

"Yes. A year or so ago. According to Alma, they are happy as two love doves now, but Alma and Lucy Ellen compete for the same nail color, same hair color, even same hairstyle." She nodded. "They come in and ask what the other one gets. I'm not going to lie, and I love Jesus. What I do might seem wrong, but I embellish some of their treatments they get."

"What do you mean?" Finn turned around.

"Say Lucy Ellen came in to get a pedicure. Well, I might tell Alma that Lucy Ellen got a pedicure and a hot stone message. Then Alma will top that service for the week," she said.

We looked at her with our jaws dropped.

"What?" she asked as if it were no big deal. "I've got to make a living. I'm upselling. All the big city salons do it."

"I'm not sure, but I don't think she knows what upselling is," I whispered to Finn. "But why would Alma want to kill Lucy?"

"They were in such competition. The last time Alma was in, she asked me about buying the same color nail polish, Perfectly Posh. I told her what I told Lucy. I don't sell it. She told me that Bosco had put her on a beauty budget, which to no end thrilled Lucy." Tina rolled her eyes. "Which made me lose money because Lucy Ellen didn't have to keep up with what Alma was doing. But regardless." She flapped her hand down in front of her. "Alma was none too happy when I wouldn't sell her the bottle. Now it's missing."

Finn and I could see where making a friendly house call to Alma Frederick wouldn't hurt anything.

"Alma knew that Perfectly Posh was Lucy's favorite. She came in and stole it. Put the cyanide in it and gave the fingernail polish to Lucy Ellen as a peace offering." Tina was getting more and more into her idea of Alma being the killer. She scooted herself up to the edge of the cot and stood up. She paced back and forth as the story came to her head, which really wasn't a bad theory. "Not only did Lucy Ellen accept her gift, she painted her nails.

This way, Alma got her revenge without getting her hands dirty. Alma Frederick does not like to get her hands dirty." Tina nodded with satisfaction.

"Can I see you over here for a second, Finn?" I nodded to the corner of the room. This was when I wished we had more than a one-room department.

"What's up?" Finn bent his head toward me after we walked over near his desk, which was at the far side of the room near the back door.

"Alma might be another good lead, but I also heard from Malina that Marcy and Lucy Ellen had words. Apparently, Lucy Ellen was going on and on about how Marcy wasn't letting the citizens use their tax dollars that went toward the library when Marcy refused to let Lucy Ellen use the computers to write her reviews," I whispered so Tina didn't hear. "I questioned Marcy about it, but nothing really came of it."

"What about the polish? When does Tina make the polish?" Poppa asked after he appeared between me and Finn, ignoring the fact that Finn and I were in a conversation.

"The bottle of nail polish is something I really want in my hand," I said. "I know if we can find it, that's our murder weapon."

"How long does nail polish stay good?" Poppa asked another great question. "You need to ask her more questions about the nail polish."

"What was the mayor thing about out there?" Finn asked.

"I think it's strange that the mayor has taken a very vested interest in me not investigating. It's alarming really. Was he hiding something? I just had to know." I tried to stay focused on Finn even though Poppa's observation about the nail polish had my head swirling with thoughts.

"And?" Finn asked, his voice escalated.

"He just wants his wedding to go off without a hitch. That's all. Even though most of these people have alibis, they still could've poisoned the polish and given it to Lucy Ellen and waited until she painted her nails." Something just wasn't right about all of these suspects in my head. I had a nigglin' suspicion I was missing something. Maybe Poppa was right. There was something about the polish.

"You're right. That's why it's so important we continue to track who Lucy Ellen had been in contact with since her last nail appointment." Finn had a terrific thought.

"Tina!" I pushed past Finn. "When was the last time that you did do Lucy's nails?"

"It would be in the appointment book, but about two weeks ago. It was whenever the SPCA was having their big food drive because she's part of that program, though she doesn't have any animals."

"SPCA?" I remembered the review Lucy Ellen had written about the Pet Patch. "Lucy Ellen wrote a bad review about Pet Patch. I did go by and see her. Nothing much to say." I shrugged. "But Lucy Ellen could've made someone at the SPCA mad."

"Faith Dunaway is so good to me and Cosmo." Finn loved his cat so much. "She makes her own catnip." Finn walked over to the white board and wrote "Marcy Carver" and "SPCA."

Just when I thought I was running out of suspects, the list suddenly got a little longer.

"Sweet Marcy Carver?" Tina's mouth dropped.

"Ignore that," I told her and walked up to the cell. "As you know I'm not really up to date on manicures and all things related to girly stuff."

My words made her smile.

"Apparently," she looked at Finn and then looked back at me giving me a wink, "you snagged him and he likes whatever it is that you've got going on." She winked again.

"Focus," I instructed her. "You make the polish as needed. Why?"

"Good work, Kenni-bug." Poppa smacked his hands together and rubbed them vigorously.

"So I won't waste the ingredients." She looked at me as if I should've know that. Then it was as if a light bulb went off in her head. "I make the bottles small because not everyone loves my homemade colors. Lucy Ellen was the only person who loved my Perfectly Posh on a regular basis so I made a small bottle for her. Her bottle is only good for about a week until the ingredients separate." She was getting so excited, that her voice escalated and her chest heaved up and down as she tried to get her train of thought out.

She grabbed the bars with both hands. Her knuckles turned white she was squeezing so hard.

"Whatever polish she used wasn't made by me." Tina smiled so big. Her eyes widened. "I wouldn't have kept her bottle. I hadn't made Polly's bridal shower polish yet. I was going to make it fresh so it looked good."

"Are you saying that you threw out the bottle of Perfectly Posh you used on Lucy Ellen the last time she came in?" Finn asked.

"That's exactly what I'm saying." Tina nodded her head. "In fact, the day she came in demanding me to do her nails, I didn't have any made up. Remember how she kept looking for it while I was doing you?"

"I do," I replied and ignored Poppa who was now in the cell with Tina doing his little happy jig.

"When does your dumpster come?" Finn asked.

"It's long gone by now. That was a couple of weeks ago. And I had no time to make up any nail polish since I've been going back and forth to Clay's Ferry." She let go of the bars and crossed her arms across her chest with a huge grin on her face. "Someone other than me knows how to make my polish."

CHAPTER FOURTEEN

Even though Tina had coughed up her alibi and the fact that she said she hadn't made the polish, it was too late to get the necessary paperwork filed to let her go so late at night. Finn and I decided that he'd stay there to keep an eye on her and I'd go home to get some sleep.

But before I could do that, I headed to Clay's Ferry to drop off the evidence I'd collected at Tiny Tina's.

"Where are we headed?" Poppa asked from the passenger seat.

"Tom Geary's lab." The Wagoneer rattled down the old road toward Clay's Ferry. "The cyanide bottle and the fingernail polish from Cheree's station are my main focus. I want to see if there are fingerprints."

"This was a special circumstances case due to the nature of the murder weapon. Just because everyone seemed to have an alibi didn't mean they didn't premeditate it days or even weeks before." Poppa didn't tell me something I already didn't know. "This might be our toughest case yet."

The anxiety in his words knotted my insides.

When we got to the lab, I knew that Tom had a container in the back of the brick building that led into the building, which was under tight security. The container was for the after-hours evidence that was dropped off. It was big enough for the bottle and the other evidence bags to fit in.

I called and left Tom a voicemail. "Hi, Tom." I didn't worry with calling his after-hours service that would make him come in and process the evidence. "It's Sheriff Lowry from Cottonwood." I told him who I was, though he'd already know. Everything had to be on the up and up and nothing left undone. "I just put a couple of evidence bags in the overnight container. One has a bottle of cyanide that was found at one of the evidence scene locations and the other has some generic fingernail polish that was probably picked up at the dollar store."

I wasn't exactly sure if Cheree had truly picked up the polish there or somewhere else for a dollar, but that didn't matter.

"What I'm looking for are fingerprints. Specifically to see if there are matching prints on either. Give me a call when you get it completed." I hung the phone up and grabbed the bags out of the backseat before I got out and put them in the container.

After I'd gotten home, I spent the better part of the night tossing and turning.

Duke even got so tired of me rolling side to side that he got off the bed and slept on the floor. Not only the fact that Tina had put doubt in my head about her being the killer, but the guilt about Polly Parker and Mama had settled into the bottom of my heart.

It wasn't that I was ruthless or mean—it was the fact that the two of them expected me to do what they wanted me to do. Mama was probably more embarrassed than I was that Polly had dropped me from her wedding.

Instead of waiting for my alarm to go off at six a.m., I decided to get on up. With the coffee pot brewing, Duke let outside, and his bowl filled with kibble, I knew I had to go make amends with Polly. It wasn't until the hot shower was running over me that I got an idea that might make everyone happy. Besides, the annual gun show I needed to check out didn't start until ten and I knew Polly worked for Viola White at White's Jewelers on Fridays. The jewelry store opened at seven, giving me enough time to get ready for my day and be at the shop waiting on Polly before it opened.

White's Jewelers was located on Main Street along with the other boutique shops in Cottonwood. They were all very unique and charming in their own way. It was nice that we had the Sweet Adelines that helped keep everything nice, clean, and in order. The city council also made sure all the shops were tidy and fit the cozy small-town feel that Cottonwood was known for.

Viola White's shop had been a staple since before I was even born. She took pride in her jewelry, which made her business very personal to her and her clients. Viola was getting up in age and she only let Polly Parker work part-time for her to give herself a weekly break. Other than that, Viola was always there. Polly's day was Friday and it being so close to her wedding, a little more than a week away, I was hoping she didn't take off.

The awning over the shop flapped in the cool breeze that shuffled its way down Main Street. The grey awning that had "White's Jewelry" scrolled in calligraphy with two white illustrated diamonds on each side of the name hung evenly over the two large windows that looked right into the shop.

It brightened my day to see Polly Parker in there going through the glass jewelry counters trying on all the fancy rings and holding them out to look at.

"My oh my." Polly Parker's voice dripped of Southern charm when Duke and I walked in. "Look what the cat dragged in so early this morning."

"Polly." I stepped up to the counter. "I know I'm the last person on this earth you want to see, but I've got an idea that might make you happy."

"I've got nothing good to say to you, Kenni Lowry. You have not only stepped on my heart, but you've smashed it into the ground with those boots you wear." Her words made me look down at my feet.

Yeah, so I wore cowboy boots every single day with my uniform. They were comfortable. Duke sniffed my boots as if he knew exactly what she'd said. He looked up at me with those big round brown eyes. I patted his head.

"I'm sorry, Polly. I truly am, but I can't just ignore the law and the crimes committed so I can be your maid of honor." This sure wasn't going as it had in my head while I was in the shower, so I took a deep breath and collected my thoughts. "I have a job to do like you've got a job to do here."

"What is it you want?" Those pretty little blue eyes glared at me before they shifted to Duke as he lay by my feet.

"I know that you're mad because I have Tina Bowers in the county jail and she can't do all the nails of the girls in your bridal party because she's locked up. But she might be out before your nail party tonight. I promise to let you know in a couple of hours." That was the long and short of why she was mad at me. "If what I'm thinking doesn't pan out, what if I let you and your bridal party come down to the department tonight and let Tina do your nails there?"

"Kenni." Polly's voice choked. She brought her hand up to her chest. "You'd do that for little ole me?"

Now she was going to play the poor pitiful Southern belle on me.

"I think it's a way to make you happy and my mama happy. Let's face it." It was time to come clean. "You don't care that Tina Bowers is under arrest for killing someone. You probably only invited her to your wedding because your mama made you." Polly's eyes started to lower. "Don't be going and glaring at me. You know I'm right. You only care that the nails of your wedding party are all done the same and Tina is cheap."

"Yeah, so?" she snarled.

"This way, we both get what we want. You get your nails done. Tina gets paid handsomely by you." I threw that part in because I knew Tina was losing money sitting in jail and I still had my doubts she killed Lucy. "And I'm still your maid of honor."

Duke groaned and rolled to his side.

"Deal." She gave me her word, which was better than a handshake in the South. "Thank goodness, because Mama was going to Blanche's to get fitted for your dress. I was going to have to use my own mama for my maid of honor."

"You should've asked Toots." I gave her another chance to back out of asking me.

"I couldn't ask her. I don't want her to feel obligated to pay that much for a dress when I really want her to enjoy herself." Polly at least looked out for her friend.

"You go on and tell Tibbie that we made up. Then you show up tonight at the department around seven for a nail painting party if you haven't heard from me." It all sounded good until Tina flipped her lid when I got back to the department and told her my idea when Duke and I showed up to relieve Finn since there was still an hour before I had to leave for the gun show and Betty got to work.

"Nail painting party in jail?" She stuck her nose between the bars of the cell.

I thought it was a pretty good idea, however apparently Tina didn't like my thoughts. Finn said he was going to head over to Clay's Ferry to check out Tina's alibi before he went home. I'd expected to hear from him within the hour.

"You agreed to this?" she asked me.

"I came up with the idea." I shrugged, thinking I'd really done something for everyone. "I told her that she had to pay you extra. But this is only if your alibi doesn't pan out."

"No matter what your mama says, you go on and have a great Christmas with that man." Tina winked.

"How did you know about the Christmas thing?" I asked.

"Viv stopped by this morning. She gave Finn all sort of business for asking you to come to meet his parents. It's obvious she thinks you are required to spend every single second of every single holiday, including Arbor Day, here in Cottonwood."

"Mama," I groaned. She was going to mess up anything I had with Finn if I didn't put a stop to her nonsense. I thought she'd come to grips with me going, not the same as okay, but she did seem that she accepted the fact I was going to Chicago.

"Come on, Kenni." Tina waved me over. "Come play cards with me until Finn calls with my alibi."

"I'm not playing cards with you. I'm going to the gun show so I can have a little visit with Alma while you stay here with Betty," I said just as Betty came through the door.

Her pink hair rollers were still in her hair, which wasn't unusual since she believed the longer she left them in, the longer they'd set for her plans later in the day. She had on her usual house dress with her pocketbook hanging from the crook of her arm.

"Tina Bowers." Betty acted surprised. "What on earth?"

"Oh, shut up." Tina snarled. "I know all y'all nosy women on the church telephone list have already tried and hung me for Lucy's murder."

Betty's mouth opened to protest but quickly snapped shut when she realized Tina was right. She scurried over to her desk and put her pocketbook down. She fluffed the pillow in her chair before she sat down. The chair creaked in protest. Though she seemed to be minding her own business, she was doing a busy job of minding mine too.

"I've got an alibi. Go on," she baited Betty, "ask Kenni what my alibi is so you can go and spread it around town."

"You've lost your mind sitting in there all night." Betty rolled her eyes.

Tina motioned for Betty to come closer. "Now, dig down in that pocketbook of yours and get me a piece of gum. You've always got gum when you come see me."

Betty dug deep in her purse and retrieved a piece of crumpled-up gum that'd seen better days. Without even brushing off the specks of God knows what on it, Tina stuck it in her mouth. Betty walked over to Cowboy's.

"So is there anything else you can remember since last night about Alma's relationship with Lucy?" I asked.

"There was something." Tina perked up when she saw Betty bring in a pot of coffee from next door. "Can I get a cup of that coffee? Thank you, Betty. I'm sorry I fussed at you a while ago." She gave a theatrical wink that made me roll my eyes. "As I was sayin', I'd heard that Lucy Ellen got drunk at their last hog boil and Alma found her and Bosco in the barn doing more than talking pig, if you know what I mean."

"Now I heard the complete opposite." Betty couldn't stand it. She had to get her two cents in. She got up and got a cup of the coffee. As she ripped open a few sugar packets and stirred it, she said, "Lucy Ellen told the girls at bell choir that Alma had hit on Darnell. When Darnell rejected her, she went and told Bosco that Darnell hit on her and they got into a big fight and that's why they aren't friends no more."

"I thought they were hunting partners." I glanced over at the whiteboard where we'd written that supposed fact.

"Apparently they don't go to the deer stand the same nights and have switched partners." Betty shrugged.

"Why haven't you told me this information before now?" I asked and wondered who was at the cabin the night of the murder. If Bosco and Darnell didn't go the same time, where was Bosco Frederick that night?

"Because you always tell me the proof is in the evidence and not gossip," Betty jabbed back. "The evidence clearly points right to Tina."

"Gee, thanks, Betty. I have an alibi. Just wait and see when Finn calls." Tina huffed. "When I get out of here, you're gonna regret saying that when you need to get them gnarly corns on your feet sawed down. Besides, Alma was just in the salon to have her nails manicured and painted. She still holds a grudge against Lucy."

"I've told you time and time again that there's some truth in all gossip and you've got to weed it out." Poppa appeared next to the whiteboard. "I'd go see the Fredericks as soon as possible."

The phone rang and Betty quickly answered.

"Hold on." She held it out to me. "It's Officer Vincent."

Tina bounced with anticipation on her toes.

"Hey, Finn. What did you find out?" I asked.

"Tina's alibi holds true. She was doing a massage therapist test up until nine p.m. and after that they went out for a late supper and ended up watching a movie well into the night. Airtight. And her prints haven't been found on the bottle."

"Sounds good." I looked over at Tina, knowing that the alibi wasn't as important since she could've poisoned the fingernail polish at anytime. I really needed to figure out how Lucy Ellen got the polish.

"Well?" she asked.

"You're okay with me going to get some shut eye?" Finn asked. He sounded tired.

"Yeah. Go on home. I'll have Betty call Wally Lamb to pick Tina up." I could hear Tina give a little yelp. "I've got a lot to get done. I'm going to head on over to the gun show at The Moose Lodge to see what's going on there."

We hung up the phone.

"Aren't they gonna have the cutest babies?" Tina asked Betty.

"Her mama already has the names picked out," Betty said. When I gave her a cross look, she followed up by saying, "That's just hearsay and as you can see, hearsay isn't always the truth."

"The truth is what I seek." I grabbed my bag and made sure I had everything I needed. "I'm going to go see Alma Frederick. Be sure to call Tibbie Bell to let her know that you're still going to be at Mama's tonight for the bridal supper."

Mama's bridal supper was the last place I wanted to spend my Friday night. But the way I saw it, in seven days this wedding and hopefully this investigation would both be over and in the rearview mirror of my life.

CHAPTER FIFTEEN

Duke beat me to the Wagoneer. He was ready to go for a ride no matter where we were headed.

"Alright, buddy." I rolled down the windows to let in the fall breeze. "Let's go to a gun show."

There were a couple of cars in the parking lot next to the metal building with big black letters on the side that read "The Moose."

The Moose was a great source of pride in Kentucky. The Moose Lodge was founded in Louisville, Kentucky in the late nineteenth century. It was an organization that gave back to their community. Mostly made of men, but some women. Of course, there was a bar that served super cheap drinks and had a band on the weekends, but as for the giving, they gave so much to Cottonwood. They volunteered in the school system and did many fundraising events for our small town.

There was nothing Mama loved more than a good Moose holiday dance, which was coming up. The Christmas dance was a big deal around here and there was even a Christmas Queen crowned for one of the elder women in the community. It was a sight to see. Truly.

"You coming?" I held the door and looked at Duke.

He jumped over into the driver's seat and hopped out. Soon the parking lot would be full. Everyone loved a good gun show and in the end, it helped them put on the dance, where all the proceeds went to help the needy families in Cottonwood and the local schools.

"Hey there, Sheriff," one of the women at the door greeted me from behind a card table. "We've got all the necessary paperwork to have all the artillery in here."

She flipped open a metal box that had a plastic tray for money. She lifted the tray up and dug through until she found an envelope that had the necessary permits from the clerk's office.

"Here you go." She handed them to me. She pointed to the doors I'd just walked through. "We've got the signs posted as well."

Not that I was there for that, but it sure did give me a good reason to start snooping around for Alma and Bosco Frederick. The gun show was held in the recreation area where there was a big basketball court. Many of the youth used it for the local summer camps and it was perfectly set up today with display cases full of guns, tables, and even a sort of museum that told the history of Cottonwood, hunting, and The Moose's contribution to the community.

"Is your president still Bosco?" I asked.

"It sure is. His wife is right over there." She waved a hand in the air. "Alma! Alllllma!" she hollered and got the attention of a woman with a blonde bob haircut that flipped up at the ends all around her head. The top and sides of her hair were flattened down to her head.

When she walked over, I noticed her polyester brown pants, brown shirt, and white cardigan along with her very sensible brown shoes. She looked like she competed with Lucy. I could definitely see the uptight resemblance.

"Sheriff," Alma greeted me with a grin. She stuck her hand out to shake mine and I couldn't help but notice the big diamond that rested on the top of her ring finger. It had to be the one Viola White had mentioned Bosco had bought Alma.

Alma was a much older lady than Lucy Ellen and I'd put her in her late sixties, if not seventies. The wrinkles on her hand and neck were much more than I'd expected to see. "I'm sure you'll find everything in order. My husband has worked nonstop to get everything together for this year's annual show. Which, as you know, helps fund the Christmas dance."

I couldn't help but notice that her nails weren't painted. Didn't Tina tell me that Alma had just been into the salon to get them manicured?

"Yes. And the department thanks you for your kind service since I know that you do this out of the goodness of your heart." I took out the paperwork and pretended to look through it so she'd buy that I was there for that purpose. "Is your husband here?"

I held the papers toward her and pointed to his signature.

"Heavens to Betsy, no." She giggled like I should know that. "Miss the first two weeks of getting the cabin and stand ready? The weather was perfect for a big hog hunt and he's not about to miss out on that."

"That's right. I'd heard about that from Darnell Lowell." My chin drew down and I shook my head. "Shame about Lucy."

Alma hummed but said nothing more.

"I guess you and Lucy Ellen were friends since everyone here gets along so well." It was a simple statement that made her react with a big inhale that caught my attention. Maybe there was something to this gossip Tina and Betty had talked about.

Like Poppa always said, when it came to gossip and fact, there's some truth in between the two somewhere; you've just got to pick it apart and find it.

"I wouldn't call us friends." Her words had a bit of a sour bite to them.

"Really?" My head shifted to the side. "I'd heard y'all were pretty good friends since your husbands shared a deer stand together."

"Just because they share a deer stand doesn't mean they share everything. And they stopped sharing recently," she said, giving Duke a pat on the head. She was as calm as a millpond.

Duke found her boring after a couple of sniffs and took off toward another woman who offered a much better scratch behind the ear than Alma did.

I was getting the sense that she knew I wasn't there for the permit anymore.

"Of course, we were Ladies of the Moose together and had some of the same friends, but outside of that we weren't as tight as some would think." Her chest lifted along with the tip of her chin. "I feel terrible about what happened, but I'm sure Darnell feels worse."

"Yes. He's devastated. I'm sad to think that he and your husband aren't best friends, because he could use a friend right now. He is already very lonely." It was a mere suggestion to see if there were any sort of reaction to hint toward what Betty had said about Alma and Darnell having an affair.

"Jail will do that to you..." Her voice trailed off.

"Jail?" I asked.

"Isn't Darnell in jail?" she asked. When I looked at her funny, she said, "For killing Lucy."

"Why on earth would you think that?" I asked.

"Oh dear." She waved her hand toward me and got a bit teary eyed. "I'd heard Darnell and Lucy Ellen were having a big fight about the wedding."

The wedding. My jaw clenched just thinking about it.

"Yes. He said that she wanted him to go, but he told her no because he wanted to go hunting."

My lips pinched together and flattened out across my face. "Who told you that?"

"Bosco. He said that it was all the talk at the cabin that night. So when he went home, we figured they got into a fight." She shrugged. "It's still a tragedy."

"What about their relationship?" I asked and wondered if Bosco had told her all that when in reality he was at the Lowell house pursuing an affair with Lucy. But how would he have poisoned her with the polish?

"Why are you asking me?" she questioned. "How would I know?"

"I was thinking that maybe you and Darnell might've been a little more than just acquaintances." There. I said it. I practically accused the woman of having an affair.

"I see the sheriff has a very active imagination along with the rest of Lucy's friends. And they're supposed to be church women. They're the worst." She looked me square in the face with a dead-eyed stare. "I think it's time for me to go work on my display. If you or the department are in the market for some real guns," her eyes drew down my uniform and stopped at my holster, "y'all should come on over to my booth and buy some. Of course, it all goes to a good cause, just like we all here at the Moose do for our small town. I'll be here all day long. Not going nowhere."

"And we appreciate all the lodge does. My mama and daddy wouldn't miss the Christmas dance for nothin'." I tipped my head and excused myself. I patted my thigh. "Here, Duke," I called.

Stares and whispers greeted my back when I walked out the door. I'd done what I wanted to do there: put a bug in the ear of the Hunt Club women where I knew the gossip would trickle around.

When we got back into the Jeep, there was a text from Tibbie. Not only had she thanked me for making amends with Polly, she told me to go back to Blanche's for a final fitting so Blanche would have a week to get my dress fixed. Then she texted she'd see me tonight at Mama's.

"You should be sleeping," I said to Finn when he called on my way to Blanche's.

"I can't sleep. I can't stop thinking about this case." The determination in his tone told me to not even try to get him to rest. "I really want to go back to the Lowell house and check out everything again."

"I haven't been there to clear it, so why don't we meet up there after I go for my final dress fitting?" I asked.

"Sounds good."

"And I also wanted to know if you wanted to go to the woods tonight." I had an idea.

"Huh?" The city slicker was stumped.

"I think we need to go out and take a look around those hunting woods, maybe check up on Bosco Frederick and see if all those rumors about him and Lucy Ellen were true." If Bosco wasn't coming home, I was going to go to him. I quickly filled Finn in on what I'd heard about Bosco's meandering ways.

"Are you buying into all that cheating stuff?" he asked.

"I went to see Alma and she was very uncomfortable with me asking questions. She mentioned that Bosco had told her about the fight between Lucy Ellen and Darnell. He said Darnell had mentioned it but in another breath said they weren't friends. Why would Darnell tell Bosco something so personal?" I asked. "She also said Darnell was gone from the cabin and fighting with Bosco, but Darnell told us he was at the cabin. I'm wondering if the truth about Bosco and Lucy's affair was about to come out."

"And it was Bosco who wasn't at the cabin and Lucy Ellen told him about the fight between her and Darnell." Finn read my mind.

"That's what I'm thinking." I agreed.

"No wonder you two make such a good team." Poppa sat in the front seat with a big grin on his face. "He's not so bad, I guess."

CHAPTER SIXTEEN

"Blanche?" I'd knocked on the door a couple of times and no one answered. "You stay," I called back to Duke, whose head was stuck out the window enjoying the cooler weather.

I walked around the side of the house when I heard some music. "Blanche?" I called in the direction of the vegetable garden that looked like it'd seen better days.

"Kenni, honey." Blanche stood up with a fistful of weeds in both hands. She dropped them and made her way toward me. "Do you think I'll ever get this garden winterized?"

"I know you can." There wasn't a single doubt in my mind that whatever Blanche set her mind to, she did.

"Every year I say that I'm not going to do another garden, but then I forget." She tapped her finger to her temple. "Maybe I just need a swift kick in the you-know-what when it comes spring and planting a garden."

She curled her fingers in the crook of my arm and we started walking toward the house.

"I hear you're back in the wedding party." She squeezed her fingers and used her other hand to pat my arm. "If we ever get this girl married off, we'll be doing good. But I fear she's taking this First Lady of Cottonwood thing too far."

She opened the screen door that led into her porch. The dress rack with all the wedding party dresses that was in the bedroom had been moved here.

"How so?" I asked and stepped inside.

"She's now wanting to be introduced by Preacher Bing as the Mayor and First Lady." Blanche tsked and walked over to the rack, pulling out the green dress. "This sure is ugly."

"It's her dream to have a Gone with the Wind theme." I bit my lip to stop any sort of gossip about Polly's wedding. The last thing I needed was to get kicked out again. "I just wish I'd gotten that dress instead."

The red one on the hanger was much more flattering.

"How's it going, sweetie?" she asked out of concern.

"Mama and I still haven't talked much about Christmas and I figure it's a couple of months away, so I'll let her let the idea sink in her head for a few weeks and then I'll just tell her that I've got my plane ticket and I'm going." It sounded so simple and easy, but the thought made me nearly sick to my stomach. Mama was never easy.

"Your mama will come around." She took the green dress off the hanger. "I've pinned and added some material here." She patted her hips as if that's where the happy fat had decided it was happiest. "And a little here." She patted her stomach.

"If I wanted to get insulted, I'd have called Mama," I joked and took the dress she was thrusting toward me.

"You can just throw it on right here." She twisted around. "No one is around. Besides, I want to hear all about Lucy Ellen while it's just me and you."

"There's not much to tell." I knew I had to keep most of the investigation close to the vest. I slipped the dress over my head and slipped out of my clothes, letting the big ole dress cover me. "I'm still trying to follow leads and talk to people who didn't think the best of her."

"Have you checked out them women at the Hunt Club?" She cocked a brow and gestured for me to turn around. She zipped the dress up. "They're all swappin' husbands and cheating and stuff." Her shoulders jerked when she let out a laugh. "They all worry about me stealing their men, when it's right underneath their noses."

Did Blanche know something that might be a lead?

"I thought the same thing and stopped by the gun show on my way over. Of course the women were all sad about Lucy, which is natural," I added just for empathy's sake.

"Yeah, right." The sarcasm was apparent in Blanche's tone. "They don't care about each other. I do all their alterations."

"Really?" I asked. "And?"

Blanche's eyes shifted sideways to look at me, but her face stayed turned to the dress. She gave a slight smile.

"And they have all their private functions at that cabin that's situated in the middle of all them deer stands. From what I heard, Art Baskin and Danny Shane not only built it for the club, but they put in security cameras in case someone came in and trashed the place. Darnell and Bosco were fighting over who was going to pay for their share. Darnell claimed he did all the taxidermy for cheap where Bosco did nothing." She let out a deep breath. "Now, that's just what I heard while I was pinning up Danny's wife's dress for the wedding."

She referred to Art Baskin, the owner of the only security system store in Cottonwood, and Danny Shane, owner of Shane Construction.

"She told you this?" I asked but didn't make eye contact.

It was an unwritten law that if there was some knowledge, in this case gossip, being spread, eye contact while telling the tale made it more solid. And no one in Cottonwood would ever get caught gossiping. Right.

"Sheila Shane was on the phone and I can't help but overhear things." She brushed her hands along the fabric around my waistline and down my hips. She took a step back. Her head tilted to the left and to the right as if she were getting perspective of her handiwork and how it fit me. "And there was some talk that they'd never know the truth behind the fight between Darnell and Bosco because the only witness was now dead."

"Lucy?" I questioned.

"Honey, it looks so good now." She drew up her chin up to my face, her eyes followed. She gave a sweet smile that told me she wasn't going to confirm my question, but I knew I was right.

"Well, I better get going." I turned back around to let her unzip me. "I left Duke in the car. He's probably ready to get going."

"The dress looks so much better." She bent down and picked my clothes up off the floor since the dress and crinoline made it hard for me to even move. "Now, you take it home and next week a couple of days before the wedding, I'm gonna have you try it on again before I quickly sew it in place."

I slipped my jeans up my legs and took the dress up over my head to put my sheriff's shirt back on.

"What do I owe you?" I asked.

"Just find out who killed Lucy Ellen Lowell. Not that she and I were best friends, but she does deserve to rest in peace." She patted my hand. "You come back and tell me what happens with your mama and Christmas." She winked and walked me outside of her house, making her way back to her garden.

I hurried to the car with the dress draped over my forearm.

"Good boy," I said to Duke and shoved the dress behind me in the backseat. I patted Duke's head and he gave me a couple of good kisses. "We've got to go make a stop to see Bosco Frederick."

"That's what I'm talking about." Poppa appeared in the front seat of the Jeep.

Duke jumped to the back.

"Duke." I reached around and tugged on the dress but Duke didn't budge. "Can you get off?"

"He ain't gonna hurt that ugly thing." Poppa's nose curled.

"I guess you're right." I turned the engine over and pulled down Second Street.

The dress was the last thing on my mind now that it fit. It was Blanche's story that had me raring to go. I drew out on my cell and called Art Baskin. He'd worked with me on a couple cases before and I wanted to get his take on what Blanche had told me about the argument between Bosco and Darnell.

"Hi there," I said when someone answered the phone of Art's office. "This is Sheriff Kenni Lowry and I wanted to speak to Art."

"He's not here right now. Actually, he won't be here for a few days. He's gone hunting." The lady told me. "But I'll leave a message for him if he calls in."

"That'd be great. Thanks." I hung up. I scrolled through my phone. I'd called Danny Shane a couple times about his construction business as well as his dairy farm. "Hello, this is Sheriff Kenni Lowry. Can I please speak to Danny?"

"I'm sorry. He's on vacation this week." His secretary was a lot more discreet than Art's. "I'll tell him you called, unless this is an emergency? Then I can put you through to Sandy."

"No thanks. I'll just wait to talk to Danny." I clicked off my phone.

"We are on our way to Darnell's." I tapped the wheel in anticipation for the stoplight to change so I could turn left out of Second Street and then take a right on Main. "But first I want to drop Duke off at the department."

The thought of the murder sprinkled goosebumps along my neck.

"The question I keep going back to is who is framing Tina." I looked over at Poppa. His stare were haunting.

The next hour I spent going through the Lowell house with permission of Darnell. I picked up couch cushions, went through Lucy's car and all of the beds and drawers, plus the basement, and literally found nothing. Finn was right. It was as if the killer and any sort of crime had vanished. I'd even looked for the bottle of pills Darnell told me Lucy Ellen had been taking since Camille didn't seem to know when I asked her about it at Blanche's house. Camille said that Lucy Ellen didn't have high blood pressure or any other illness. What was she taking?

I flipped on the light to Darnell's work building, which was just a detached garage behind their house. The beady eyes of mounted deer heads, bucks, raccoons, and other critters with their mouths open, teeth showing, stared back at me. It was an unsettling feeling being here and knowing they'd met their demise from someone actually stalking and hunting them, sort of like the person who wanted Lucy Ellen dead.

I stepped inside to take a look around. Not that I thought Darnell had even thought to kill his wife, much less put cyanide in her fingernail polish, but just like Poppa said, no stone unturned until we find the killer.

The unsnapping of my flashlight holder echoed through the garage as I curled up on my tiptoes to shine the light into the animals' mouths in case something was hidden.

"The killer doesn't want to be found out." Poppa scared me out of my skin.

I jumped around with a tight grip on the handle of the black flashlight.

"Poppa! What happened to letting me know you were coming?" I asked.

"We've gone over this," he said flatly. "I've shown up unannounced and this is how you react. I've shown up announced and this is how you react. It seems to me that it's you who needs to be more observant."

"Whatever." I eyeballed him. "You never told me what happened at Dixon's."

"Just a bunch of rowdy preteen boys that needed a little scaring. If they don't get scared now, they will be the next criminals." He laughed. "I'm kinda liking this ghost thing. I untied one of the boy's shoes and stepped on the shoelace with one foot and did the same to the boy standing next to him. When I sent the candy flying off the shelf, they looked at each other and tried to take off running. Then tripped all over one another because I was standing on some shoelaces."

This was a different side of Poppa that he rarely showed. When he was living, he was so focused on the job and not living life. Being a ghost brought out the playful side in him and I enjoyed seeing it.

"Heathens," he spat, and both of us laughed.

There were a few of those cardboard boxes that stored printer paper with "photos" written in Sharpie stored on one of the wire shelves.

"Yeah. There's a lot of heathens around here lately." I slid the lid off and started going through the memories Darnell was holding onto.

There were photos as far back as their wedding. Lucy Ellen sure did make a beautiful bride. Looking at her made me think of Polly. I really should be much more involved and nicer than I'd been. After all, it was her big day.

The beach pictures of her and Darnell were sweet. They were smiling and laughing. Though they never had children, they did look like they really enjoyed themselves.

"Whoa, look at that." Poppa was looking over my shoulder. "They sure were good friends."

Darnell and Bosco were in some hunting photos holding their trophies up by the antlers.

"And vacations?" he asked when I continued to thumb through more photos of Lucy, Darnell, Bosco and Alma together on what looked like a cruise, at casinos, and on the beach.

"And look at this one." I held up one where Lucy Ellen was sitting on Darnell's lap and Alma was glaring at them. Bosco must've taken it. "And this one."

There were several photos where Alma was not the happy one in the photos.

"And she told me they weren't friends." I let out a long deep breath. "I've got to go see Bosco Frederick. I wonder if he's at home."

"Only one way to find out." Poppa was thinking what I was thinking.

"With Alma at the gun show, maybe he's home, so we'll check there first." I stuck a couple of the photos in my pocket and put the lid back on the box before I slid it back into place on the wire rack. "If he's not there, we might have to go to the woods." I looked over at Duke. "I'm going to take you to the department first."

Within a couple of minutes, we'd pulled in front of Cowboy's Catfish in the open parking space, which was rare, so I took it.

Laughter spilling out of The Tattered Cover Books and Inn caught my attention. Darnell had said he was staying there and a quick stop in to ask him about the photos wouldn't hurt. I needed to get down to the truth about the friendship Alma and Lucy Ellen had and why Alma was going to great lengths to cover it up.

Duke and I trotted across the street like a game of Frogger. The Tattered Cover Books and Inn, Tattered Cover for short, was one of two places to stay while visiting Cottonwood. The other was The Inn and it was located near the river. So you could choose to enjoy the downtown shops and eateries if you stayed at The Tattered Cover or the beautiful Kentucky scenery and landscape the country had to offer at The Inn.

"You stay out here," I instructed Duke. He wasn't very fond of cats and Purdy was the mascot of the hotel.

Nanette was sitting with Darnell in what I called the refreshment room, to the right as soon as you walked through the front door. Nanette was the owner and operator of the hotel and she took great pride in offering refreshments and cold iced tea to her inn guests.

"Lucy Ellen did love cats." Darnell rubbed down Purdy, the feline curled up on his lap.

"You know if there's anything I can do to make your stay more comfortable, you just have to blink. Not even ask." Nanette stood up. She gave me a sympathetic smile when she noticed I'd walked into the room.

"Hi, Kenni." When she said my name, Darnell looked up. The sudden jerk must've scared Purdy because she bolted off his lap.

"Hello, Nanette." I gestured to Darnell. "I wanted to come by and ask Darnell a few questions. Do you mind leaving us alone for a minute?" I asked.

"Sure." Nanette nodded and walked backward toward the hallway. "I can even shut the double doors so no one else will interrupt you."

She moved back a couple of the wing-backed chairs that helped keep the doors propped open and quietly shut the doors behind her.

"Do you have any news?" Darnell asked.

"Nothing yet, but I wanted to know about these." I pulled the photos out for him to look at.

He cracked a weak smile and gave a slight nod of his head.

"Those were the days." He flipped through them again before handing them back to me. "The four of us were good friends in our younger days. Me and Bosco used to be hunting partners, but Alma put an end to that."

"How?" I asked.

"She started to do some really weird things, like sabotage things Lucy Ellen would do for the club. The members of the club, we like to get together. Lucy Ellen had prepared all the meat for one of them get-togethers and it was all the meat from our freezer. Alma ended up bringing Bosco's meat." He looked down at his hand and twirled his wedding band.

"I don't understand."

"It's a big deal to have your meat featured at a cookout and all your buddies eat it. Lucy Ellen loved to prepare my meats in a fancy marinade and sauce. Bosco didn't let Alma prepare his meat. But Alma couldn't stand that my meat was going to be featured and when she pulled out their meat, Lucy Ellen lost it. She didn't understand why Alma would do such a thing when there was an unwritten rule."

"I see." I eased up to the edge of the chair. "Are you okay?"

His hands were shaking, he looked up with wet eyes, his lips curled in, his chest jerked as he tried to fight back tears.

"I never thought of Alma hurting my Lucy Ellen until now." His voice cracked. "Do you think she did it?"

"I'm not sure. But I'm looking at everyone." I patted his leg. "Did you know of any other tension between the two women?"

"That was the beginning of this crazy notion that Lucy Ellen had to compete with Alma. Lucy Ellen started doing weird shopping and wanting all sorts of crazy things done to her body like..." He started to tap his head.

"Botox?" I asked.

"Yes. Lucy Ellen said she talked to Camille about it. I told her no. That she was beautiful the way she was and she said that she didn't want to look older than she was. I told her she was acting nuts." He gulped.

"I talked to Camille and she didn't say anything about Botox, but she did say that Lucy Ellen didn't have high blood pressure or any other illness. You said..." I took my notebook out of the front pocket of my shirt and started to flip through it. "Where is it?"

I continued to flip until I got to the page.

"Here." I read off my notes from the initial investigation. "You said that she was taking a pill. Do you know what pill that was?"

"No clue." He shrugged.

"I couldn't find any pills at the house and Camille said it could be a vitamin. Did she take vitamins?" I asked.

"I'm not sure. She took care of any medical things. If I got a cold, she took care of me and I swallowed whatever she gave me."

I smiled at his words.

"Who's going to take care of me now?" He put his head into his hands and began to sob. "Who would do this?"

"I'm not sure." I rubbed his back and sat with him for a few minutes until his crying stopped.

"I'm sorry. I know I shouldn't be crying like a baby, but me and Lucy, we don't have no kids and no family here. My brother down in Tulsa said I could come live with him and his family, but that's just not home." He wiped his face with the sleeve of his shirt. "I've got an appointment with Max today to make arrangements for the funeral."

I wanted to tell him to steer clear of next weekend's Parker wedding, but I figured Max would know all of that.

"I've taken up enough of your time. If you remember anything specific about Alma and Lucy, let me know." I stood up. "One more question. What did Bosco think of all this nonsense between your wives?"

"He said that we couldn't be partners anymore. He said that Alma continued to ask him to find out what Lucy Ellen was doing or where she was during the day, clubs she was in outside of the Hunt Club. It was weird, so he said that it was best we didn't hang out anymore because it drove his wife crazy and she was driving him crazy." He sniffed.

"Thanks, Darnell. I'll be in touch." I opened the double doors and waved to Nanette on my way out of the hotel.

"Good boy." I patted Duke on the head. He'd stayed exactly where I told him to. He was such a good boy.

We crossed the street and headed on back to Cowboy's Catfish.

The restaurant was busy and so was the staff. Duke and I headed on back to the office, though Duke did make a small detour to the many outstretched hands that summoned him over for a pat. He was a sucker for those fingers.

"Thank gawd you're back." Tina jumped up from the cot and stuck the center of her face in between the bars. "I've got to get a shower before tonight. I've got an alibi. This is ridiculous."

"Kenni, she's driving me crazy." Betty raised her hand in the air, extended her fingers, and make the talking gesture.

I looked between them. Betty's face was pinched and stressed.

"Wally hasn't come to get her yet?" I asked.

"Nope," Betty griped.

"I was going to leave Duke here, but I guess he can go with me. I can drop Tina off." I knew it was unconventional and her lawyer should come get her, but Cottonwood and our department was unconventional.

"Great. And," she handed me a piece of paper, "call your mama."

I tucked the piece of paper in my back pocket and walked over to the cell. I twisted the handle.

"You mean to tell me this wasn't locked?" Tina stepped out.

"Nah." I put my hand on my utility belt. "Betty, can you pull up Bosco Frederick's address?"

"I know where they live." Tina sucked in a deep breath. "Freedom sure does smell good."

"You know how to get there?" I asked.

"I had to go out there once when Alma had the Hunt Club ladies over for a spa day. I'm not gonna say it's far, but I had to grease the wagon twice before I hit the main road." Her lips duck-billed.

"That far?" My shoulders slumped. I wished I would've let Wally get her now because I didn't want her to talk my ear off.

She nodded.

"I've got plenty of time to show you." She smiled, knowing it was some good gossip.

"Did you get a lead?" Betty asked. She leaned in. Her face didn't look so stressed as she craned her neck to listen.

"Let's go. But you're staying in the car." I warned Tina and jerked my head to the side. "Come on, Duke."

Betty flipped him a treat on our way out.

"Why you going to see Bosco? And is that your dress for Polly's wedding back there?" Tina yammered on and on before I could even answer one question.

"It's not any of your business why I'm going to see him. You're going to just sit there and not say a word." I headed on out of town.

Duke continued to try and push his way up to Tina's seat.

"He's alright, really." Tina lifted her hand and patted him. She tried to be nice, but after the fifth time she pushed him back. "He just wants to give me some lovin'."

"Duke, back." My voice was a little more forceful and he knew I meant it.

I glanced in the rearview mirror. Duke was sitting on the dress and Poppa was right next to him.

Tina was right. It was a far piece out to the Frederick house. The only good thing about driving this far was how Mother Nature had painted the landscape with her beautiful foliage. The stone slave walls hugged the road on each side and the leaves were losing their green touches to early signs of vibrant oranges, reds, and golds.

"How did your visit to the Moose go?" Tina asked, knowing I'd gone there to check on her story.

"I saw Alma and she claims that she and the Lowells were never good friends. Especially her and Lucy." The Jeep curved the country road like a glove.

"She's lying. At least they were friends until all the cheating occurred," she protested.

"Do you know for sure if they cheated?" I asked.

"Not for sure, but I do know they were friends. Good friends. When I came out here to do the spa day for the women, Lucy Ellen insisted that she pay for it. Which she did. She and Alma did that back-and-forth no-I'll-pay or at-least-let-me-pay-half conversation until Lucy Ellen finally gave in and let Alma pay for it. Granted, Lucy Ellen bragged on how much money she and Darnell have and I don't think that sat well with Alma." Her jaw dropped. "You know what?" she gasped. "It was then that the two started competing for spa treatments. Lucy Ellen did back down to a couple of times a month and then she'd miss appointments or cancel them all together."

"When was this again?" I asked.

"During the summer. I can go back through my calendar at the shop and give you an exact date." She continued to give me directions by finger pointing to turn here and yonder until we made it.

The Fredericks' house sat on a bit of land going east out of town into the deep country. The view was unbelievable.

"I thought you said they didn't have as much money as the Lowells?" I knew this was a million-dollar view.

"I didn't say that. I said that Lucy Ellen said that to me when she'd come into the spa. If you ask me, I think it was the other way around and Lucy Ellen only bragged to make it look like they had money." She continued to stare out the window. "I thought you said you talked to Alma this morning."

"I did, why?" I asked.

"Why on earth would she come back here if she was going to spend the day at the Moose?" she asked.

"Where is she?" I looked out the windshield expecting to see Alma.

"I guess inside, but that's her car and Bosco's truck." She brought my attention to the two vehicles parked on the side of the house.

"You stay here." I looked at her and Duke. "I'll leave the windows down for air."

Poppa walked next to me as we made our way up the front steps of the cabin and onto the covered porch. Being nosy, I walked to the right side of the porch and noticed it wrapped all the way around. Poppa had already disappeared. On my way back to the front door to ring the doorbell, Poppa appeared. His face was faded even more than his normal ghost self.

"What's wrong?" I asked him.

"Kenni, call for backup. They're dead." His words sent a shockwave through me.

CHAPTER SEVENTEEN

"Betty." My voice cracked when I spoke into the walkie-talkie, "I...um..."
"Y'alright, Kenni?" Betty had a habit of stringing her words together.

I cleared my throat and took a deep breath to gather my wits as I stared at Bosco Frederick lying with his legs half in the house and his torso half out of the house. His was staring toward the sky, his arms cast straight out to his side and a bullet hole right in between his eyes.

I took a step over him, being careful not to disturb anything.

"I'm going to need a backup squad at the Frederick home immediately." I clicked off and rolled the volume of my walkie-talkie down in case there was someone still there.

I flicked the snap of my holster, drawing out my gun. With my arms at full extension, I looked around, pointing the gun in every direction.

"Alma?" I called out her name when I noticed she was slumped over the table. "Alma? Sheriff's office. Come out if anyone is in here!" I screamed a couple of times in different directions.

The faint sound of sirens echoed through the open door.

"Sheriff's office!" I yelled again and stepped over to look at Alma.

My body stiffened. Her nails were painted Perfectly Posh. But I clearly remembered she wasn't wearing it earlier today.

I quickly did a sweep of the house and cleared it before Finn entered.

"Oh my God." His chest was heaving up and down. It was so hard for me not to lose myself into the warmth of his arms to let him assure me that everything was going to be okay. "Are you okay?"

"Yeah. I'm fine. Alma's nails are painted Perfectly Posh." I looked over his shoulder and stared at her. "Are they still wet?"

From where the light was shining in, the nails were still wet.

"She's not been dead long," I said.

"Bosco is still warm. I didn't feel a pulse, but I still called in an ambulance, just in case." Finn strapped his gun back in his utility belt and I followed suit.

Both of us worked like finely oiled machines until the EMTs got there. We secured the perimeter of the crime scene. We took photos and marked the gun that was next to Bosco's hand. It appeared to be a suicide. Only I wasn't sure how Alma got the polish or where the polish was. It appeared to be missing like it had been at Lucy's house.

"Kenni, you better get in here," Finn hollered for me as I bagged up the gun and the EMTs pronounced both Alma and Bosco dead.

"What?" I walked into the room they used as an office.

"Looks like a note was left on his computer." His gloved hand pointed to the computer screen in Bosco's office.

I leaned over to look at the screen.

"Lucy Ellen and I were having an affair. I'm not proud of myself and have tried to stop it for several months now. Lucy Ellen was going to tell Darnell and even write one of those articles in the Chronicle like she always does. It would be too much for my Alma to take. In fear she'd leave me a lonely old man, I broke into Tiny Tina's salon."

I looked over my shoulder at Finn and sucked in a deep breath before I turned back round to continue reading.

"I knew exactly what nail polish Lucy Ellen loved because she'd complained about Tina refusing to do her nails. That night I left the camp in the woods and decided to poison the nail polish. I took it to her house that night because I knew Darnell was at the cabin and cleaning it. So I knew he wouldn't be home," my voice cracked as I read his sickening letter, "and I told her that I'd talked Tina into letting me buy the polish. She still said that she was going to reveal the affair even though I'd given her the polish as a peace offering, and that she was looking forward to typing the words to the Chronicle with her nails painted pink."

"This is awful." Finn shook his head from behind me and ran his hand down his face.

I swallowed hard and continued, "I left the cyanide at Tina's salon to plant the evidence. Then I went back to Lucy's and she'd already painted her nails and had died. I took the polish and put it in my hunting bag to get rid of when I went back to the cabin. This morning while I was in the shower, Alma came home from the Moose, cleaned out my hunting bag, and found the polish. She painted her nails with it since she'd been competing with Lucy Ellen on her spa days. When I got dressed I found Alma dead from the poisonous polish. That's how I've decided to take my own life. I just can't bear to live without the women I love."

"Where's the polish?" I asked and took the vibrating phone out of my pocket. It was Tom Geary.

"Still haven't found it." Finn hit a few buttons on the keyboard to save the screen and turned the machine off. "I'll pack up the computer after I print off this note."

"I never saw this coming." I shook my head and put the phone up to my ear. "Hi, Tom. Do you have any information?"

"There are some disjointed prints on the cap of the cyanide bottle where the ridges of the cap had cut off some of the print. I can tell you that the prints on the fingernail polish aren't a match."

He confirmed that neither Tina's or Cheree's prints were on the bottle, making me think they really didn't have anything to do with Lucy's murder. "I put the jagged print in the database and there's nothing that's coming up."

This only made me wonder if Bosco was telling the truth. I'd never heard of Bosco getting in trouble with the law to see if we had fingerprints on file, but that'd be easy enough to find out.

"Did you send the report over?" I asked.

"I called you first, but I'll fax it right now. Anything else I can do for you?" he asked.

"Get Bosco's prints over to Tom." Poppa bounced on his toes. "If he truly did use the cyanide, then his prints would be on it. I arrested Bosco years ago for public intoxication and I fingerprinted him."

"I'm going to call over to dispatch and see if Betty Murphy can pull another set of prints and fax them to you." We clicked off the phone and instead of calling Betty on the walkie-talkie, I decided to call her.

"Kenni, what's going on over there?" Betty wanted firsthand knowledge.

"The Fredericks are dead. It looks like an apparent murder-suicide, but I'm not convinced." There was just a tug in my gut. "I need you to look up Bosco Frederick and get the fingerprints on file." I looked at Poppa, who nodded. "If I remember correctly, I do believe he was arrested years ago for public intoxication and he was printed. Can you send those prints to Tom Geary's lab?"

"I've got it covered." The phone line went dead.

"Kenni! Kenni!" A blood-curdling scream came from outside.

Finn and I took off running out of the cabin.

"Duke!" Tina yelled from the Jeep. She pointed to the side of the house. "He jumped out and is going nuts over there digging."

Duke was going to town with his nose stuck deep in the earth and his paws kicking up the wet dirt behind him.

"Duke!" I called. He looked up at me with a dumbfounded look on his face, his nose muddy, and his paws covered in it. "Drop it," I instructed him when I noticed something sticking out of his mouth.

Finn and I walked over to Duke, where he'd laid down with the item between his two front paws.

My mouth dried, my heart beat rapidly.

"The polish." Shock came out of Finn's mouth.

"The murder weapon." I sighed. "Duke, come." I patted my hand on my leg for him to come with me to the Jeep to get him away from the polish.

He darted back to the Wagoneer and took a leap back into the backseat.

"No!" I yelled, remembering the dress in the back and now his muddy paws were all over it.

"Don't worry. Maybe he'll make it prettier with the mud. It's so ugly it'd make a freight train take a dirt road." Tina's brow furrowed. "My polish. How on earth did it get here?"

"Bosco left a note saying he was having an affair with Lucy. Lucy Ellen was going to tell everyone about it and he couldn't let her do it." I gave her a quick recap of how he was the one who broke into the salon and how Alma got ahold of the polish.

Tina sat there in shock. Her eyes continued to take big long blinks.

"She going to be okay?" Finn asked.

"I think she might be in shock." I clicked on my walkie-talkie. "Betty," I called.

"Yes, Sheriff," she immediately answered.

"Can you call Max and tell him he needs to come to the Frederick home to pick up the bodies?"

"I'll call him." Her voice didn't hold the boisterous tone it had before.

While I was talking to Betty, Finn walked Tina back to the Wagoneer to sit down and gather her wits and called Wally Lamb to come pick her up. I secured the crime scene and took a lot more photos until I heard Wally pull up. Duke jumped out and lay next to the front tire.

"It was awful." Tina took Wally's cheap hanky out of the pocket of his polyester suit coat—I was sure it came from the local Walmart—and dabbed the corners of her eyes. "Like my daddy would say, I'm tougher than the backend of a shootin' gallery, but being behind bars about did me in."

"Now, now," Wally consoled her. "We'll get you home in no time."

Wally turned to me.

"Sheriff, we're just so happy that you finally brought the killer to justice. At least now that this case is over, my client can get back to her normal life, though a bit embarrassed, and the mayor will be happy because his bride will be happy." Wally Lamb escorted Tina to his car.

Wally didn't waste much time giving me the look. He got in and zoomed down the Fredericks' driveway, nearly running Max Bogus's hearse off the road. Duke jogged next to his car, barking the entire time.

I stood there with Poppa by my side and watched as the hearse swerved and maneuvered back on the driveway.

"What are you still doing here?" I asked Poppa, who usually quickly disappeared as soon as a case was solved.

"I fear this isn't over." His words were bone-chilling. "I did my normal routine that I've always done after we solve a murder, but this time it didn't work. I walk into the fog and put the murder to rest, then I go around town scaring people away while keeping a close eye on you, but this time when I walked into the fog, it fell around my feet. It was the darnedest thing."

I tried to choke down a swallow to help bring some color back to my flushed face before Max got out of the car.

"Think about this." Poppa noodled an idea. "That letter from Bosco was written on a computer. Not handwritten and not saved. It was just too much explanation for me to even think it was from a distraught man. So he wrote the letter after he'd just found the love of his life dead, took the nail polish and buried it, all before he shot himself?"

"Why would he bury the nail polish?" I asked out loud.

"Good question. I was thinking the same thing." Finn startled me from behind. "Are you doing that whole talking to yourself thing again?"

"Yeah." I couldn't help but smile when I saw him. "I can't shake the notion that this isn't what it seems. It's all too perfectly packaged."

"And why bury the nail polish?" Finn asked my question.

Max Bogus got out of the hearse with a look of piss and vinegar.

"Wally Lamb is crazy." Max shook his fist. "Did you see that he almost ran me off the road?" Max looked back toward the driveway, but Wally was long gone.

"I did," I said and turned to go back into the house.

"Murder-suicide?" Max asked.

The three of us took the steps and stopped shy of the door.

"That's what I thought when I first showed up. But I'm not so sure the facts will show that." I knew that Max had an obligation to do autopsies on both bodies since it was the law in Kentucky with a murder-suicide and since Bosco appeared to be Lucy's killer.

"I'm not saying Bosco didn't do it, but I agree with the sheriff. It wasn't as smooth as he made it seem in that letter," Finn told Max. He handed Max a piece of paper with the suicide note printed on it.

"I'm not sure what I'm going to find, but it appears that Bosco came in and found Alma dead from the polish he'd poisoned and killed himself." Max handed the letter back to Finn. "Only forensics will tell us the truth and that could take a few weeks."

We didn't have a few weeks. Cottonwood was already crazy with next weekend's wedding and this only added on the stress.

"Besides the whole cheating thing, which in itself is a huge motive to kill your spouse." Finn was right. Cheating was the third leading motive in murder cases.

"Duke." When I said his name out loud, I remembered how in the car on the way over he'd continued to try and smell Tina's fingers.

He jumped up and ran over to me. His tail was wagging so fast. I bent down to pet him. Finn took a treat from his pocket and fed it to Duke. Finn was so thoughtful when it came to Duke.

"He was acting so odd on our way over here. He was trying to smell Tina's hands and fingers. I kept pushing him back because I thought he wanted to be scratched. I told him to stay in the Jeep when I got out, but he didn't. Next thing I know, he'd dug up the nail polish. Why did he want to smell Tina's fingers? How did he know to dig up the polish?"

"Maybe he picked up on the scent at the shop when you went to see Tina or he's been to Tiny Tina's with you and picked up on the scent there?" Finn questioned.

"You're probably right. He knew the smell and when his keen nose picked it up, he dug it up." I gave Duke a good rub along the head and neck. "Good boy. Good boy."

There were just some things Duke did that I couldn't explain and this was one of them.

"Yep, I got you one fine dog." Poppa proudly rocked back and forth on his heels.

"All I can do is let the autopsy speak for itself." Max headed on inside to take a look at what he had to deal with.

It was unusual to have to take two bodies at once to the morgue, but luckily his hearse could fit two church carts side by side.

While we let Max do his thing, Finn and I stood outside and pondered on what had just happened.

"This really doesn't make sense," I said to Finn. "I went to the gun show and talked to Alma."

"And?"

"Alma was there setting up for the show. I talked to her about Lucy Ellen and she believed Darnell was in jail for killing Lucy Ellen and she even acted as though they weren't friends. When I went back to the Lowells' I found photos of the couples on vacations and having dinners, and not just local." I pulled the photos out of my pocket. "I also went to see Darnell. He said that they'd always done things together, but Alma got jealous of Lucy. Or was it the other way around?" I thought for a second. "Maybe both were jealous of each other. Anyway, Darnell said that Lucy Ellen wanted to get Botox and all sorts of stuff done to compete with Alma."

"If you ask me, no amount of work was going to help Alma." Poppa was never one to shy away from the truth about anyone's appearance. "This morning she looked tired." He started flapping his hands. "I don't know much about women's nail polish, but I remember your mama flailing her hands around after she painted them when she was a kid. She claimed it took so long for them to dry." Poppa was good. He might not have realized he was onto something.

"And her nails." I smacked my hands together. "Alma's nails weren't painted this morning and she came home to paint them when it takes at least twenty minutes to be good and dry. But she was supposed to be at the gun show all day. She told me she would be. Plus Tina said that Alma didn't get the same nail polish because she didn't like Perfectly Posh. Alma only wanted the same treatments. So why would she paint her own nails Perfectly Posh when she didn't like the color?"

I opened and held the door for Max as he wheeled the first body out in a gray body bag.

"Maybe she found out about the affair and wanted to have her nails painted like Lucy Ellen when Bosco came home." Finn's eyes focused on the body bag. He grabbed the end and helped Max down the steps.

"Hmm. If the prints come back and Bosco isn't the killer, it looks like someone from the Hunt Club wants to silence anyone and everyone." Poppa sucked in a deep breath. As he exhaled, the air came out in long stream of fog. "Kenni, have you ever been to the huntin' cabins the Hunt Club uses?"

"No, but I think there's no better time to check it out," I muttered under my breath.

After Max cleared the bodies, it was time for Finn and me to get down to the nitty gritty and really look around.

"Are we still going out to the woods tonight?" Finn asked.

"Before I close this case by naming Bosco the murderer, I just want to check out the cabins and interview a few of the men that were there that night to see if Bosco said anything to anyone, or at least find out how he acted." It was going to be very interesting to see Finn in that environment.

"What time did you want to go?" he asked.

"Mama's big bridal supper is tonight." It reminded me that one week from tonight, I was going to have to give my first of two toasts. The first being the rehearsal dinner, the second was the wedding the very next day. "I'll make an appearance and then we'll go."

"Appearance?" He laughed and shook his head. "Your mama is really going to hate me."

"Nah." I winked.

One of the reserve officers took the computer back to the office so Betty could set it up. It was in those types of things Betty was worth her weight in gold. Since she loved to snoop and be nosy, combing through a computer was her thing. I think she really took pride in knowing the technology, which was sort of surprising since she was much older than the average techie. I wasn't techy, and since we kept it in house, if something did get out, I knew the source. Betty knew that too, which kept her from gossiping.

One thing I did know now was that I needed to stop by Camille Shively's office.

The waiting room was typical. The walls were painted gray, and the carpet was gray with small white diamond shapes scattered about, and chairs lined the walls. There was a television hanging on the wall that played one of those twenty-four-hour news stations and a rack filled with all sorts of magazines was underneath that.

"Kenni, come on back." Camille stuck her head out the receptionist window and pointed to a door.

When I opened it, she was on the other side waiting for me. I followed her down a couple of halls until we made it to her office.

"What's up?" she asked. "Are you here about that whole happy fat thing? Because you don't have anything to worry about. Honestly, I had to talk your mom off the ledge about you dying from diabetes or heart disease."

"No. I'm here to ask you a few more questions about Lucy." I bit back anything snide I wanted to say about Mama. I knew her heart was in the right place, but once she got a topic in her head, she beat it like a dead horse.

"I told you everything the other day at Blanche's house." She walked around her desk and sat in the chair.

I remained standing and walked around as I talked.

"We have a confession." I looked at her fancy degrees framed on the wall.

"That's wonderful." Her voice rose. "Polly will be so relieved and happy that you can take the next week to really focus on her wedding and your big toast."

The big toast made me cringe.

"I need to tidy up a few loose ends." I turned around and noticed a picture of Camille all pretty on her graduation day. A big smile on her face. No wrinkles. Nothing. Perfect.

"Who killed Lucy?" There was concern in her voice.

"Bosco Frederick." I looked at Camille. Her brows formed a V. "Apparently, Lucy Ellen and Alma were jealous of each other. Long story short, Lucy Ellen was on a mission to look younger. She'd been taking some pills. Darnell thought they were for her blood pressure. Do you happen to know what those pills were?"

Camille pushed her chair back from her desk and eased her head back and looked up at the ceiling.

"Oh my God. Why didn't I think of that?" she asked herself. "Kenni, remember you asked me about the blood pressure?"

"Yes." I took a seat in a chair.

"Well, she told me she was seeing stars and getting light-headed. I asked her if she'd been eating enough because she'd lost some weight. She assured me she was. There was no reason to not believe her. She'd always been a good patient. I got her initial blood test back. Nothing of huge concern, but I called to let her know we'd keep an eye on it. I don't think I got the long blood test results back yet." She clicked on her computer for a couple of minutes. "I think she might've been taking weight-loss pills." She picked up the phone. "Suzie, can you bring me Lucy Ellen Lowell's file please?"

"What did you find on your computer?"

"I logged into our system. Her blood results came back last night and I've yet to check my emails today. She tested positive for amphetamine. It's in diet pills." She eased back in her chair. "I told her not to take them. I wonder who she was getting them from."

"Darnell said she was thinking about Botox too." I took out my notebook and began writing down what Camille was telling me.

"What does all this have to do with her death?" Camille asked.

Her office door opened and Suzie, her nurse, walked over and handed Camille the file.

"I have to make complete reports and fill in all the holes." That was true, but Poppa was still lingering and I knew I had to figure out real fast who this killer really was.

"Here I made a note that she asked about wrinkle creams and Botox. We talked about the cost and she said something about Darnell not wanting her to spend money on those things because they were about to retire." She shut the file. "That was about all. But the diet pills she asked for are expensive, so if she was on them, which I believe she was, she was paying a pretty penny."

"Expensive." Poppa waltzed in out of thin air.

I looked at my watch. I still had time to make it to the bank. There was someone there I needed to see.

"Thanks for your time." I stood up. "I'll see you in a week at the wedding."

"I can't wait to see that dress on you." She scrunched up her pretty little nose.

"What are you thinking?" Poppa asked when we got back into the Jeep and headed to the bank.

"Hi, Kenni." Vernon Bishop came out of his fancy bank president office and greeted me. "What are you doing here?" He looked around like there was some trouble.

"Just here on a little business having to do with my investigation concerning Lucy Ellen Lowell." I nodded toward his office. "Can you talk in your office?"

He readily agreed. "I'm not sure how I can help, but I'll try."

He wore a nice three-piece pinstriped suit. His grey hair was neatly combed to the side. He wore the perfect amount of gel in his hair as well as cologne. He was much younger than he looked. He was about fifteen years older than me. His wife, Lynn, was a nice woman. She stayed home and cared for their three children who were scattered in ages.

They had a modest house in a typical neighborhood, but always looked well put together.

"Your mama has already got us working on the Christmas benefit." He smiled and offered me a seat and a sucker. I took both.

"I'm sure she does." I snapped the plastic wrapper off the sucker.

"I also heard you won't be here for the Christmas festivities." I nearly choked on the sucker. "I'm sorry. Did I misunderstand your mama?"

"You're right. I plan on going to visit Officer Vincent's family in Chicago, but I sure wish Mama would stop telling people." I bit the sucker off the stick. I was never able to really lick them down to the nub.

"We sure will miss your light-up Christmas sweater." He laughed.

If he only knew that Mama made me wear that darned thing every year to the Christmas tree lighting and the fights we'd have about it.

"Thank you. But I'm short on time." I tapped my watch. "Bosco Frederick has—"

"Died," he finished my sentence. "Small town."

"Yes. News does travel fast around here. Anyway, I wanted to see if you can tell me a little bit about Bosco's account."

"You know we freeze the account since we are a small bank and a small community." Vernon explained to me how most big banks didn't put holds on accounts, but since Cottonwood was a small town and somehow dishonest people trolled the obituaries, Cottonwood First National put holds on accounts until estates were settled.

"That's all fine and good, but I need to specifically know if there was any sort of payment made to Art Baskin or Danny Shane."

He hesitated.

"You and I both know that I can get a warrant if necessary, but why don't we save the tax-payers money and just answer my question," I said, laying out the fact. Sometimes I found it was better to be upfront instead of beating around the bush.

"Bosco never came in, but I know about it because Darnell Lowell came in. He wanted to look at his 401(k). He mumbled something about not being able to retire and owing money to someone, but he was so antsy, I couldn't understand a word he mouthed." He clicked around on his computer. "He came in earlier asking about how much he had in his savings because of funeral costs for Lucy. He's sad. Very sad." Vernon's eyes grazed the top of his computer and he stared at me. "He seemed surprised when I told him that Lucy Ellen had cleared out that account a few weeks ago."

"She did?" I remembered the wad of cash she had in her hand at Tiny Tina's. "Did she say why she was withdrawing it?"

"She said that she was getting some work done." He shrugged.

"Like Botox? Diet pills? Did she mention any of that?"

"Diet pills?" He looked at me like every other man when I mentioned it. "I assumed she meant home remodel or something."

"No." I shook my head as I realized that poor Lucy Ellen was fighting so many inner demons.

"What does all this have to do with her death?" he asked.

"I'm not sure." I tapped the edge of his desk with my fingers. "Thank you for your time. I've got to run."

"See you at the big wedding!" he yelled after me. "I hear you're in it."

I nodded and waved. Mama. She sure didn't know how to keep her mouth shut.

Even though I knew I should go home and get ready for not only Mama's shindig, but also the night at the cabin with Finn as we snooped around, but I had to go to the SPCA to see for myself that someone there wasn't bent out of shape over Lucy.

The sun was still out due to daylight savings time and the days were getting longer. It made me feel like I could get more accomplished in the day and since the sun was still up, so was the homestretch of this murder investigation. The trees were just starting to lose their full green leaves that were fed rich limestone soil through their trunks. The famous Kentucky bluegrass was starting to die along the old Military Pike Road that lead all the way out into the country where the shelter sat on fifteen acres of donated land.

The shelter did a lot of fundraisers and donation drives where they did really well. It didn't surprise me because the true heart of Cottonwood citizens showed when it came to the animals and in tough times in the community.

"Hi there," a young man greeted me when I stepped inside. He stood about five foot eight with a pageboy haircut, bangs dangled down into his eyes. "What can I do for you, Sheriff?"

He flung his head to the side, sending the bangs along with it and his brown eyes drew to my badge that was pinned on the brown shirt.

"I wanted to ask some questions about Lucy Ellen Lowell. A volunteer here." I made sure I continued to watch his face for any sort of discomfort while talking about her. Body language said a lot with words.

"We sure were sorry to hear about her death." His lips turned down. The frown reached his eyes. "She knew exactly how to get things we needed."

"What do you mean?" I asked.

"If the animals needed something and we didn't have it in the budget, she'd go out and get someone in the community to donate it or give a hefty dollar donation. She really helped us out." He let out a long sigh. "I'm afraid I'll never be able to find anyone like her that I can count on to get things done."

"That's nice to hear about her because I've heard some nasty things about her not getting along with people." I offered a slight smile. "Can you tell me if she had any problems with people here?"

"Not a one that I know of. She was always so giving of her time. She couldn't offer much financial assistance, but she did get people to donate. It was her way of being able to give back to the animals." As he finished talking, a girl walked through the door.

"Are you talking about Lucy?" She asked and tugged her blonde hair onto a ponytail using the rubber band around her wrist.

"I am." I took interest in what her take on Lucy Ellen would be. "Did you know Lucy?"

"Oh yeah. Everyone knew her. She was great. We all loved her. She did so much for the shelter that no one else has ever done."

"The shelter is about the only place in Cottonwood that she didn't write a review for." I pulled one of my business cards out of my front pocket. "If you remember anything or anyone that might've wanted to harm her in anyway, please don't hesitate to call. Anything." I wanted to make sure there wasn't anything that was too small to report.

CHAPTER EIGHTEEN

"Do you think Lucy Ellen wanted to keep herself looking young because she really loved Bosco and wanted to leave Darnell for him?" Finn asked me.

I'd put on a one-piece denim jumpsuit with a pair of wedged sandals that Tibbie had dropped off from her Shabby Trends clothing line for me to wear to the big bridal dinner. While I stood in the bathroom in front of the mirror, Finn sat on the edge of the tub talking to me about the case.

"I don't know. I just know that Lucy Ellen had been spending all sorts of money when I know Darnell was planning on retiring." I brushed some lip gloss over my lips and rubbed them together.

"Do you think Darnell did it?" Finn asked.

"I've gone over and over the possibilities. I still want to talk to the other guys tonight about what they've seen or heard." I ran the brush through my hair one more time. "I can't explain it. It's like. . ."

He interrupted me, "I know. Woman's intuition. Remember, I've got a sister and a mother." He smiled and moseyed closer up behind me.

That's wasn't why. Poppa was why, but I couldn't tell him, so I let him just go with the intuition thing.

"Yep. I can't explain it." My eyes and jaw softened looking at him through the mirror. "It seems like an awfully complicated way to kill someone. To go through the motions of figuring out what Lucy Ellen wanted most that day, the nail polish, then researching that cyanide. It just seems like it's a crime that was very thought out."

"And Bosco couldn't do that?" he asked.

"I don't know." I gnawed on my bottom lip, scraping off some of the lip gloss.

"One thing I do know." He snuggled me, wrapping his arms around my waist. "You look beautiful."

"You don't think I have happy fat?" I asked.

He pulled away.

"Happy fat?" His face contorted. "What is that?"

"Nothing." I brushed it off. If I started to think about it now, I'd be mad at Mama all over again before I even made it to the dinner. "I've got to go make my appearance so we can go to the woods."

Duke left with Finn as I headed out to Mama's house. Duke and Cosmo would keep him company while he got ready the equipment we needed for our date night in the woods. Not that it really was a date night, but I thought it might be a little romantic under the big late summer moon. And the thought of a chilly night and needing a little snuggling wasn't such a bad thought either.

By the time I got to Mama's, I'd already dreamed up a romantic night instead of an investigation.

"You've got it bad, Kenni-bug." Poppa appeared just as I turned onto the street of my childhood home.

"I do. I can completely see myself with Finn Vincent for the rest of my life." I gulped. It was strange hearing myself say that when I really never took the time to figure out what I wanted out of life. "I've always been so happy being the sheriff here, having my girlfriends, my family, but somehow Finn makes it all complete."

"Being away for Christmas isn't weighing heavy on you? Because you love Christmas and you'd never miss the Christmas Festival."

"You're right. I do love it and I want to share that with Finn, but it's strange. It's like I've put my own needs and wants aside because I want Finn to be happy." My lips quivered as I tried to keep a big smile from emerging. "I can't believe that I'm actually happy to put someone else's needs before mine."

Not that I never did that before, but most times I put others before me because it was the good Southern girl thing to do.

"Oh no. You've really got it bad." Poppa's eyes teared up. "I bet you're gonna marry that boy one day."

"Why are you sad? You should be so happy that he loves me so much." I put the Wagoneer in park when I pulled up in front of my childhood red brick home.

"Because I'm not sure how you're going to feel about keeping me a secret. There should be no secrets in a marriage. Or a relationship that's heading that way." He brought up my worst fears about my relationship.

"I've thought about telling him, but every time I get ready to or think about it, something comes up and I just can't." I took notice of all the cars already at Mama's.

The days were getting shorter and the darkness was starting to blanket Cottonwood. Goosebumps pricked my skin. I wanted to blame it on the temperature dropping, but I knew it was from the thought of losing Finn when or if I told him about Poppa.

"I wonder if you told anyone about me how it would impact us." He looked at me. His eyes were hollow. "Would you still need me as your backup if he knew? Would I just go away?"

"I'm not willing to find out just yet." I closed my eyes to stop from crying at the thought and ruining my fresh face of makeup I'd taken the time to do for Mama's sake.

When I opened them, Poppa was gone. I took a second to collect my thoughts and get my emotions in check. I tugged the rearview mirror toward me and reapplied some lip gloss.

"I'm just going to meet his parents. It's not like he's asking me to marry him," I told my reflection, giving myself a good reason to keep my Poppa a secret a little longer.

"And to think she gave me a bad review before someone knocked her off" was the first thing I heard as soon as I walked through Mama's front door. "And to think they used my nail polish."

The warmth of comfort swirled around me as the familiar smells rushed over me. Home. There was nothing like it. I stood in the foyer and looked left into the fancy living room that was completely furnished from Goodlett's Furniture store, a locally owned business. The living room was rarely used. I took a couple of steps and entered the hallway. To the right were the three bedrooms, two on one side and one on the other, plus a bathroom at the end. To the left was the entrance to the family room and the kitchen along with an eating nook, laundry room, another full bathroom, and the door to the garage.

It wasn't a big house, but it was a comfy warm house my mama poured her heart and soul into because she loved to entertain. Many of those times, as a child, I escaped to my poppa's house.

The weather was so nice Mama had opened her windows and the door leading out to the back patio. The two nail stations were set up in the family room and the food and entertainment were on the patio.

"It was awful." Tina was hunched over her manicure table doing a hand of one of Polly's bridesmaids who was from out of town. "Jail is not for gals like us."

I cleared my throat. Cheree jerked around from her manicure table and Mama, who was her client, looked up at me, as well as Tina and the gal in front of her.

"Kenni!" Mama wiggled her fingers toward me. "You're a bit late, but you're here."

"It's about time." Tibbie walked in with a glass of champagne with a cherry floating in it. "Polly has been freaking out."

"I had to work." I gave Tina a sideways smile.

"Oh, we heard." Mama drew back with an audible gasp. "Tina told us about Bosco Frederick killing Alma and Lucy. Just awful."

"And with my polish." Tina nodded.

"Shame, shame," Tibbie said, then took a sip. "Let's get you a drink."

"I'm not drinking tonight." I walked out to the patio with her and realized I didn't recognize any of the girls in Polly's wedding. "I've got to skip out early. Work calls."

"Nuh-uh. No way." Tibbie's eyes grew big. "You promised."

"I said I'd be here and here I am. I've got some things I need to check out with Lucy's case and it has to be tonight." Mama had done a fantastic job with the shower.

"Yay." Polly tapped her fingers together with a fake greeting when she saw me walk out the door. She grinned, winked, and gave me the finger wave from afar as she talked to someone on the other side of the patio. She had on a white dress that was fluffed way out with crinoline and a white wide-brimmed hat with a big silk bow tied under her chin.

There was a banner that read "Fiddle Dee Dee" strung over a snack table that held a tiny replica of Tara the mansion along with little figurines of Scarlett and Rhett. The cookies were in the shape of a woman's dress like Scarlett had and some cookies were decorated like hand fans. A little over the top, but adorable no less.

On The Run food truck was pulled up in Mama's backyard. Jolee had strung twinkly lights that hung over some café tables and chairs. Jolee was serving mason jars layered with BBQ beans, cole slaw and smoked BBQ chicken, shrimp and grits on toast, red velvet cupcakes with cream cheese icing, Southern pralines, mint julep cookies, cheese straws, watermelon, and peach tea punch. Everything I loved.

I reached for a piece of the shrimp and grits toast. Tibbie smacked my hand away.

"Ouch." I jerked away.

"The watermelon is for you." She jutted her finger out and gave me a grin.

"I swear. I hate all y'all." I rolled my eyes, knowing she was talking about that happy fat thing. "I'm not hungry."

"Fine." She turned around to look back at the party and I grabbed a mint julep cookie, stuffing it into mouth right as she turned back to me. "Kenni!"

"I am hungry," I muttered through the sweet treat as I chewed.

"Anyway, here is the game we are going to play. Do you think you can at least be here for that since you came up with it?" She handed me a piece of paper that I had clearly not come up with. "Polly or Scarlett" written in fancy script on the top. "Go with it. Polly thinks you came up with this game and she needs to feel loved by you."

"Really?" I asked with sarcasm. "Only for you will I go along with this."

There were a series of question with their names listed next to it and the guests had to circle which one was Polly and which one was Scarlett.

"Her favorite color is pink?" I asked, knowing Polly was wanting to get Perfectly Posh on her nails. "Really?"

"It's a game. Besides, you've solved the murder. And a week before the wedding. Polly and the mayor are so happy. Me too." There was excitement spewing from her. "I'm so happy you figured it out."

"Yeah. Me too." I swallowed the last of the cookie. The women's intuition Finn talked about earlier kicked in and I couldn't accept the fact that Bosco did it. It wasn't just the fact that Poppa was still here—it was the evidence that was just too perfect. "Excuse me."

"Where are you going?" There was a worried tone and look on her face.

"Inside." And then out the door, but I didn't say that.

I'd made my appearance. Polly had seen me and I'd get my nails done later.

"Okay. I'll see you in a minute." She handed me a piece of paper. "Here's your toast."

"You hold on to that for me." I headed on inside and bent down to Mama while she was getting the second coat of her nails painted. "Mama, I've got to go. Emergency."

"Kendrick," she scolded and jerked around.

"No, no, no, no." Tina wouldn't let go of Mama's hand. "You're going to smear."

"Kenni, no." Mama warned again. "You aren't doing this right now. You call Finn."

"Mama, my toast is written on a piece of paper that Tibbie has. You're so good at speaking in public." I waved bye and headed down the hall, getting myself safely out of the house only because Tina had a hold on Mama where she couldn't budge.

The temperature had dropped some more after the few minutes I'd been there. I even turned the heat on in the Jeep once I got in to take the chill out of the air.

"You ready?" I asked Finn when he answered his phone.

"That didn't take long."

"Mama was sitting in the nail chair and I figured it was a good time to skedaddle." It was all sorts of wrong and Mama was going to be really mad, but I had a job and it was an important one. "For some reason, I really feel that there's an urgency to us getting to the woods."

"Well, I'm ready. How far away are you?" he asked.

"I'm turning down Free Row now. I need to put on some jeans and grab a sweatshirt."

"Meet me in your driveway?" he asked. "I'll bring Duke back."

"Yep. We can take the Jeep." We said goodbye and hung up.

I hurried into the house and threw on my clothes, pulled my hair up into a ponytail, strapped my police utility belt around my waist under my sweatshirt, and grabbed my police bag from the table just in time to open the back door for Duke to run in.

I made sure he had some kibble and fresh water before I walked out the door where Finn was already in the front seat of the Wagoneer, Poppa right behind him in the backseat.

"If you hurry, you'll be able to talk to Danny and Art," Poppa said. "I went to the woods while you were stuffing your face with that cookie and they're all sitting around a fire discussing how they're going to come home since they've got to go to Lucy Ellen's layout at the funeral home tomorrow to pay their respects before Darnell moves out of town."

"Moving out of town?" I said.

"Who's moving out of town?" Finn asked with a funny look.

"Finn." I turned in my seat to him. "Do you think maybe Darnell Lowell killed Lucy?"

CHAPTER NINETEEN

"Darnell?" He eased back into the seat. "I guess I never really suspected him."

"And that was his plan." I started to remember a bunch of little things about the investigation.

"Go on, Kenni, play the what-if game with him like you did me." Poppa encouraged me this time instead of discouraging me.

"You know I love my poppa a lot and I learned so much from hanging around the department from him." I gripped the wheel as we made our way out on Cottonwood Station Road, the curvy road that took us deep into the woods where the turn-off was for the hunting grounds the Hunt Club used. "Anyway, you and I can talk through clues using your whiteboard, but maybe now you and I can play the game that Poppa and I used to play."

"What's that?"

"The what-if game. With Darnell, I mean." There was a brief silence. "Like this. What if Darnell had an affair with Alma and Lucy Ellen found out, threatening to expose him because Lucy Ellen knew it would make Alma look bad to everyone, making her the ultimate winner in their little jealousy fight?"

Finn looked at me and teetered his head back and forth as if he were noodling the idea.

"What if Darnell killed Lucy Ellen using her favorite polish because she couldn't get it from Tina? He broke into Tiny Tina's. He somehow left the cabin unseen and then after Lucy Ellen was dead, he took the fingernail polish and hid it in the cabin.

"Bosco found it and put it in his hunting bag since he knew Alma would like it. Then Alma went home to question Bosco after I went to see her and she found the polish in his bag like the suicide note said, but the note was written by Darnell," I said, playing the what if game.

This was how Poppa and I used to work on his crimes when he was sheriff. It helped us think outside the box and maybe come up with some new leads to look into.

"Or Darnell was having an affair with Alma and he gave her the nail polish so she'd die too. He waited for Bosco to come home and he killed him, making it look like a murder-suicide, and wrote the confession about Lucy." Finn was good at this game.

"But why did he kill Lucy? Was she threatening to expose the affair? Was there an affair?" I threw out questions.

"There might be something in the timeline of that night and when Bosco was at the cabin compared to Darnell." Finn stared out the window.

"I guess we'll know here shortly." I turned the Jeep up the dirt road that took us back five miles until we got to the clearing where the Hunt Club members parked before they used their four-wheelers or hiked back.

"Kenni." He reached over and put his hand on my shoulder. "Thank you for sharing the game with me. I know your poppa stays on your mind a lot and I'm honored you opened up to me."

I choked back my emotions. This was not the time to be emotional. There was one thing I knew. I knew I loved Finn and I was going to have to start sharing all of my life, not just parts of it, with him if I truly did see myself with him for the rest of my life.

"We're here." I shoved the gearshift into park.

"Where are the cabins?" His head twisted around and looked at all the parked cars.

"Back that way." I pointed into complete darkness. "I hope you brought your flashlight."

We got out and unsnapped our flashlights from our utility belts. I gave

Finn one of the reflective jackets I'd stuck back in the Jeep to put on so the guys wouldn't think we were some sort of game to shoot. I led the way. I'd been to the cabins many times in my life.

The night sky had fallen and it always seemed darker in the country. Even in the small town of Cottonwood, the little bit of light didn't make the darkness seem so black. In the country, you could see miles and miles of stars in the sky. If you stood still long enough and with a tiny bit of luck, you'd catch a shooting star.

We were silent most of the walk and about fifteen minutes later, there was an orange glow from afar.

"Sheriff here!" I yelled into the dark. "Danny Shane! Art Baskin!" I yelled out, knowing that I'd recognized their cars when I'd pulled up to park. "Sheriff Lowry here!"

"Sheriff?" The familiar voice of Art echoed into the night. "Is that you?"

"Yes! Deputy Vincent and I are here." I didn't have to yell as I got closer and closer.

There were six men around the fire when we walked up. Everyone greeted us, but there was a lingering curiosity in the air.

"We were just discussing going home tonight because we really need to support Darnell at Lucy's funeral tomorrow." Danny said, followed up by echoes of agreement.

"Tomorrow?" I asked. I'd not heard anything about a funeral.

"He said with her body being part of the investigation, he was going to have a small memorial before he headed out of town," another one of the men said.

"Out of town?" I questioned.

"He said something about moving to his brother's down in..." he paused.

"Tulsa?" I asked.

"Yep." He snapped his fingers and pointed to me. "That's right. He said that he's decided to move to Tulsa for his retirement. I told him I'd pack up his stuff and bring it to him."

"What are you doing here, Sheriff?" Art Baskin asked.

"I'm here to actually talk to all y'all." I made eye contact with each of them. The fire flickered and sent an orange glow around the group. "I'm sorry for the loss of your president Bosco Frederick."

"Yeah, crazy stuff. I just can't believe he'd do something like that." One of the guys shuffled around. "Poor Darnell. He's not only lost his wife but also his best friend."

"Best friend?" At first I thought the guy meant Lucy, but I realized he was talking about Bosco. "I was under the assumption their friendship was over."

"Oh yeah. Bosco ended their friendship earlier in the summer. They'd been friends for over forty years. But Lucy Ellen started to get a little whacko over Alma and obsessed with all the success Bosco was having with the Jarrett company," Danny said before taking a swig of his bottle of beer.

"Jarrett as in the rifle company?" Finn asked.

"Yeah. He sent in a shot of a ten-point buck he caught last fall to the company using one of their rifles. They contacted him and did a big spread in their magazine," Art said and took the bottle of whiskey being passed around. He took a drink and passed it to Finn. "The article got picked up by many more hunting magazines and they did a big photoshoot with him and Alma. Bosco was so knowledgeable about hunting and guns they started paying him to write articles for them. It was good money too."

"Were Bosco and Lucy Ellen having an affair?" I asked.

"Hell no," a few of them men said collectively.

"What about Darnell and Alma?" I asked.

"Never. Darnell and Lucy Ellen were having financial problems, but nothing such as cheating." Art looked at Danny. "Lucy Ellen was caught taking money from the fund. We didn't press charges, and that's when Bosco had asked me and Danny to come down here and put in a few Lift cameras."

"Those cameras hunters put in the woods on trees and stuff. They're disguised and designed to work in any condition." Finn was surprising me for a city boy. "I saw something about that on the local public television station."

"They're pretty neat, but expensive." Art nodded.

"Do you have the footage for the camera?" I asked.

"Cameras. There's several. But yes, I have the technology to bring it up on my phone." Art pulled out his phone from this camouflaged jacket.

He used his finger, tapping his phone a few times before having everyone pass the phone down to me.

"Those are six cameras and you can click on the one you want to watch or watch all them at once," he said.

"Can we go back to the night Lucy Ellen was killed?" I asked.

"Yep. Just hit the three bars in the right corner and adjust the calendar to when you want. Technology is crazy nowadays." He wasn't lying.

"Do you mind showing Finn all of Darnell's stuff you've bagged as well as the cabin he and Bosco shared?" I asked.

The next hour or so, I played with his phone and went back to the times Max had narrowed down Bosco's time of death. My eyes might've been tired, but I didn't see anyone leave the camp the entire time. Which made me believe that if Bosco didn't kill himself or his wife, whoever did this had nothing to do with the hunt club.

While I watched the camera footage, Finn got a lesson in hunting and a tour of the cabins. The only thing that bothered me was the fact that Darnell and Lucy Ellen had been having financial issues.

"Did you find anything?" I walked over to Finn.

"Nothing with Bosco." He took an envelope out of his back pocket. "I did find this in the cabin. It's a letter from the bank saying their account was overdrawn by one thousand dollars."

"Bosco's account?" I couldn't read it in the dark.

"No. It's addressed to Lucy Ellen and Darnell Lowell." He leaned in. "Do you think Darnell killed Lucy Ellen over money?"

Our eyes met. We stared at each other for a second before I decided it was time to wrap this up.

"Did any of you see Bosco or Darnell leave the night Lucy Ellen was murdered?" I asked and handed Art his phone back.

All of them shook their heads and a few of them yawned. It was getting late.

"Gentlemen." I walked around and gave each one a firm handshake. "Thank you for your information. Again, we are sorry for your loss."

"Can you send us a copy of the camera tape that the sheriff watched?" Finn was so good at collecting evidence.

"Sure will." Art nodded.

The flashlight showed us the way back along with a few lingering lightning bugs. In a couple of weeks, those cute fireflies would be long gone and not show up again until next summer.

"It's sad that Lucy, Bosco, and Alma will never see another firefly." My words disappeared into darkness and broke the silence on our walk back. My phone rang out and nearly scared me to death. "It's Max."

We stopped shy of the clearing where the cars were parked.

"What's going on, Max?" I noticed the time was well into the night.

"Some of the forensics came back, and I'm sorry to tell you that there's no way Bosco Frederick killed himself. From the path of the bullet, I can tell it wasn't from close range, nor was it from his gun." Max only confirmed what I was thinking.

"Thanks, Max. Can you send over what you've got so far?" I asked.

"What's up?" Finn asked on our way across the clearing to get back in the Wagoneer.

"He just confirmed that Bosco didn't pull the trigger. He was shot from afar." My mind went back through the crime scene.

The pictures in my head clicked between the kitchen table where Alma was found with wet nails and where Bosco was found lying halfway out the back door with the gun stuck in his hand. "Duke digging up the fingernail polish," I said.

"Are you doing that whole talking to yourself thing?" Finn questioned me as I started up the Jeep.

"Darnell and Alma were having an affair. She knew he killed Lucy, but she was still in competition with Lucy Ellen even after Lucy's death. He gave her the polish." My words trailed off. Then I looked up. "He killed Alma because she was going to come forward that he killed Lucy Ellen."

"And Bosco came home early from hunting, catching them off guard. Darnell keeps a gun on him with his conceal and carry. He pulled his gun and shot him, while Alma was sitting at the table dying," Finn suggested.

"On his way out, he buried the nail polish. Duke has been to the salon with me and he's been scratched on the head by Tina so much that he knew to find the familiar scent." I gulped and picked up my phone.

It was nearly midnight.

"I think Darnell killed Lucy Ellen because of money," Finn hit a nerve in my intuition, making me stiff.

"I went to the bank and Vernon told me Darnell had come in to check on his retirement account, but after Lucy Ellen died, he came in to get some money out of their savings to pay for a funeral for her. Vernon said Darnell was shocked to learn that Lucy Ellen had cleaned out that account a few weeks prior." I took a left off the dirt road and headed straight down Cottonwood Station Road.

Finn took out the envelope and opened it.

"This is dated a week ago." Finn continued to read. It had to be the account Vernon was talking about.

"I think our version of mine and my poppa's what-if game is turning into what happened." I looked at the big moon hanging overhead, hoping Darnell was looking at it because it was the last night that he'd be standing under it as a free man.

CHAPTER TWENTY

The Wagoneer was the most uncomfortable place to try and sleep or at least rest my eyes. After the late night in the woods and after I'd dropped Finn off, I just couldn't sleep. I'd even stayed outside throwing Duke his ball into the fresh night air.

The thoughts about Darnell killing Lucy Ellen and the Fredericks made so much sense. The conversations I had with him over the past four or five days continued to haunt me. The things he'd say about how much he loved her and how was he going to survive without her made me think it was all a ploy for me to feel sorry for him. It scared me when I found out from the guys that he was going to skip town, so I decided I was going to do a stakeout.

Duke was my sidekick and we'd sat out in front of Darnell's house all night long. There was a U-Haul parked out front and a few lights on in the house. I'm not sure when he turned them off because I did doze off and got a crick in my neck.

Duke perked up and so did I when I saw his front door open.

"I dare you to get in that truck and take off," I warned him under my breath.

He walked straight past the truck and headed right to me. His eyes bore into the Jeep. I almost reached in the back to grab my rifle off the backseat because I was stupid enough to have left my utility belt at home.

"Sheriff." He handed me the cup of coffee in his hand. "Thought I'd bring you a cup of coffee. You deserve it after sitting here all night long."

"That obvious?" I shook my head in fear he'd poisoned the cup like he did the fingernail polish.

"I figured it was a matter of time before you thought I killed Lucy. Especially since there was tension between me and Bosco." He took a drink of the coffee, making me regret not taking it.

"So you don't mind if I call Deputy Vincent here to sit with you while I check a few things out?" I knew I wanted to go to the bank when they opened at nine this morning to check out his 401(k) and see if he'd cashed it in.

"Not at all." He held up the cup again. "You sure you don't want me to get you another cup while you wait?"

"No thank you." I was suspicious of how nice he was being.

As he walked away, I called Finn.

"Good morning." His voice made my heart skip a beat. "Want to come down for a cup of coffee?"

"I'm sorta not home." I knew he was going to be mad on a boyfriend level that I'd been on a stakeout, but happy that I'd thought of it on a professional level.

"You what?" His words were drawn out after I'd told him what I'd done and why I'd done it. "I'll be right there."

And he was. In no time I was on my way to the bank, only I knew they wouldn't let me in. Duke had his appointment with Bloomie at ten and I knew they opened up around seven thirty on Saturday. I'm sure Faith wouldn't mind if I dropped him off and then went to the bank.

Duke hopped out of the Jeep and ran straight up to Pet Patch's door. When he heard the moo come from the bell, he howled. I heard Faith laugh from the back.

"Hey, Kenni." She waved to me with a pair of shears in her hand. "Back here in the grooming department. Come on back."

Duke darted around the shop looking for Bloomie and decided Faith was good enough for right now. With another good scratch, he headed back into the shop.

"I'm a little early," I said.

"That's fine. Duke's a good boy. He'll just hang out in here with me and Bobo." She pointed to the mini-poodle and walked over to the counter. She opened the cabinet. "Just the regular wash, flea bath, and dry?"

My eyes focused on the contents of the cabinet.

"Is that fingernail polish?" Poppa appeared next to Faith. "I swear that's the same fingernail polish that Tina Bowers makes."

"Kenni?" Faith called my name. "Are you okay?"

"I'm fine." I snapped out of the stare and watched as she opened the polish and started to paint Bobo's fingernails. "I didn't realize you painted dog nails."

I walked over to the framed license on the wall. There was one for her and one for Bloomie. The dates caught my attention.

"Didn't you say that your license was expiring soon and you just went to the pet expo to renew it?" I recalled what she'd told me when I asked her about Lucy. "It looks like Bloomie's was just renewed and you did yours a couple months ago."

When I heard the glass of the nail polish knock against the steel counter Bobo was standing on, I turned around.

"I think I'd like to see those airline tickets with your name on it." I watched her reaction with a keen eye.

"I...um..." She hem-hawed around for a second and then opened a drawer up. "It's in here somewhere." She shuffled papers and reshuffled them. When she looked up at me, her face was as white as I thought a ghost's face would be. But not Poppa's.

I knew right then and there that she was the killer. I felt for my holster and realized for the second time this morning that I'd left my holster at home. "Why did you kill her? Why did you kill Alma and Bosco?"

I kept my eyes on her hand as she slid it across the table and grabbed the shears, the very pointy shears.

She brought her hands to her sides.

"Do you know how hard it is to make a go of a business in a small town? When someone like Lucy Ellen Lowell decides to get mad, she takes out her anger on me and my business. I had to listen to whispers and deal with people staring at me. People who bought animal products from me started going to Dixon's Foodtown to purchase items." Nervously, she took the shears and dragged them back and forth at her thigh, cutting her khaki pants and drawing blood. "The last time I'd gone to Tiny Tina's, Alma Frederick was in there. She apologized to me for Lucy's behavior and she told me how they'd stopped being friends. When I went to the Chamber of Commerce meeting last month, I overheard Vernon say that Lucy Ellen Lowell was spending money like crazy."

She lifted the scissors up to Bobo. My immediate reaction was to pummel her to the ground, but without my own weapon I stayed still.

"Don't hurt Bobo." My voice was stern.

"Idiot. I'm grooming him." She cut a big chunk of fur and it floated to the counter. She cut another chunk.

"Why did you kill them?" I asked in a very calm voice.

"When you came around here the other day questioning my whereabouts, I knew you weren't on the trail of Darnell. I'd planned it so well. But you were so stupid. I can't believe I voted for you." She snarled. "I knew I had to kill Alma too. With all the rumors going around, I knew if I killed her it would appear that the rumors about Darnell and her were true. It was her husband that I didn't expect to come home." She took a step back from the grooming table and pointed the sheers at me. "I don't even know if Tina remembers telling me how to make polish because it's been so long ago. Years in fact. When I told her I was painting my clients nails, she gave me her little tip on making nail polish. It was perfect for me and easy to break into her shop and make the nail polish. After I put just enough cyanide in my Perfectly Posh, conveniently I left the bottle in Tiny Tina's. There's so much junk back there, I knew she wouldn't notice an extra bottle, much less the cyanide bottle." There was a very satisfied smile growing across her face.

I heard Duke's nails clicking on the tile floor of the shop getting closer and closer.

"Ah, Duke." Her eyes lowered as she looked towards the sound of the clicking. "I never figured he'd find the polish I'd buried at the Fredericks. He's a hell of a lot smarter than you."

"Here boy." Poppa came in ahead of him and called for him. Duke was the only one other than me that could see my Poppa. "Get it!"

"Glad I got this little guy." She bent down and lifted up the hem of her pant leg, exposing a small handgun. She unclipped it out of the ankle strap and when she stood up, she put the gun on the counter with her hand positioned perfectly for firing.

Duke walked in. His nose went straight up in the air and I could tell his eyes focused on that nail polish next to Bobo. My instinct kicked in and so did Duke's. Both of us lunged at the same time. He went for the nail polish and I went for gun.

Faith scattered after it too, but I grabbed it before she got it, and Duke grabbed the polish. Poor Bobo was yipping and yelping, shaking in fear.

"Hold it right there!" I yelled and pointed Faith's gun at her. "Don't you move a muscle because I have no problem putting a bullet in your leg, arm, or chest."

Duke looked between Faith and me. He dropped the bottle and stiffened, giving Faith a low growl.

"Good boy. Good boy." Poppa danced around behind Faith.

Little did she realize that Duke was growling at Poppa to play with him even though he looked like he was going to attack her.

"I'm not going anywhere." Faith dropped her head and began to sob.

ONE WEEK LATER... Wedding Day

The week leading up to Polly's wedding was one filled with forgiveness and fluff. The forgiveness was between Tina Bowers and me. By all rights, she'd been a fraud for many years under the fake certificate that said she was a massage therapist. Like I told her I would, I went before the judge with her charges. Luckily, she was only given a hefty fine and had to prove that she was now a legal therapist. Unfortunately, the judge also took away the shop's certification to do massages for one year, but she could still do manicures and pedicures. On the upside, she wasn't going to the state pen.

Then there was Darnell. He was sad and lonely. He'd not only filled Lucy's big shoes at the SPCA, he ended up adopting a dog that seemed to keep him busy. He named her Lucy. He even stepped in to fill the open president's position at the Hunt Club. He was going to be okay after all.

We'd all gone to Faith's sentencing, where it was decided she'd spend the rest of her life in the state penitentiary for the murders of Lucy Ellen Lowell, Alma Frederick, and Bosco Frederick. She said at the sentencing that she'd done all of Cottonwood a favor by getting rid of Lucy Ellen and that we should thank her. I thanked the judge for locking her up.

Another person I had to make amends with was Mama. She'd worked so hard to have such a nice bridal supper for Polly the night I'd skipped out. This week nothing made Mama more happy than going with me to my final fitting at Blanche's, a girl's day at Tiny Tina's getting the manicure I'd missed the night of her house, and fixing supper for me and Finn a couple of nights that included things that didn't feed my happy fat.

Finally, I made amends with Polly Parker. With the murders solved, I made sure that I was at her disposal all week long. I took every single phone call from Tibbie and every text message from Polly.

Even the frantic one the afternoon of the wedding.

"You've got to get over here right now." Polly was crying on the other end of the line.

"On my way." I groaned and got up from the couch.

It was so hot today, the squirrels were putting suntan lotion on their nuts, as my poppa would say if he were here. He'd not been around all week, which told me he still was only my guardian ghost during an active murder investigation.

"Duke, you've got to stay here all night."

His head twisted left and right like he understood before he laid back down. It was even too hot for him to go out and run for his ball.

"I'll leave extra kibble and water," I called behind me when I walked down the hall to get the maid of honor's dress and bonnet. Everyone was going to the wedding or I'd have gotten Mrs. Brown, my neighbor, to watch him. Or Jolee, or Finn, or even Mama. I was a little thankful for the bonnet. My honey brown hair was stick straight, but something about high humidity really put a crazy wave in it. And it wasn't pretty like those beach waves those crazy tools did to the girl's hair in those infomercials.

With my outfit for the wedding in my hand, I grabbed the little cosmetic bag filled with what little makeup I used, headed out the door, and a few minutes later pulled up to the back parking lot at the Cottonwood First Baptist Church.

"Thank God you're here." Tibbie Bell was sprawled out on a folding chair with her legs straight out in front of her and one of the wedding favor fans in her hand, vigorously waving it over her face. "I can't take another minute in this hot weather."

"This should go into your party-planning book." I couldn't help but notice she was glistening with sweat.

"What would that be, Kenni?" she asked with a sarcastic tone.

"Keep in mind the crazy weather in between seasons in Cottonwood." I couldn't help but smile knowing Polly had driven her over the edge. "I think a few years ago it was snowing on this exact same date."

"Kenni, this is no time to talk about the past. It's the here and now, and right now I think I want to string up our bride by her bra straps." She fanned quicker.

"Oh no. What does she want you to do now? Sue Mother Nature?" I joked.

"Not funny." She pointed the fan to the church. "Go on. Go in there and take a look."

I shrugged and headed inside with the hanger flung over my shoulder. It was going to be a little uncomfortable with that big dress on in this heat, but I was bound and determined not to complain and keep the peace between me and Polly, at least until tomorrow.

"Kenni." Polly's shrill voice stabbed my ears. "Look at this." She pointed to what I assumed was her cake. "The air conditioning is broken and the cake is melting. Look at the bride." She pointed to the sugary figure on top that was distorted. "That's supposed to be me."

She broke out in tears.

I reached out with a reluctant pat on her back.

"Look at my hair." Her words seethed with anger. "It's falling out. All the Scarlett curls are falling out and Tina Bowers has no idea how to fix it. And this makeup." There was a visible line that ran along her jaw. "It's melting off my face. I hate the weather here!"

She stomped toward the door that led out to where Tibbie was still fanning herself and smacked them open.

"Tibbie Bell! You're fired!" Polly screamed and headed back inside, disappearing into a room. She slammed the door.

Tibbie held up her hand and gave Polly a not-so-nice gesture and continued to fan herself.

There was only one person that could handle this, and it wasn't me.

Toots Buford didn't waste any time driving to the church from the time I called her. When I saw her 1965 pink VW bug pull into the church parking lot, the stress melted off of me.

"Where is she?" Toots hurried in with all sorts of bags hooked on her arms.

"She's right in there. Toots." I stopped her before she hurried in to rescue her best friend. I draped the maid of honor dress over her shoulder. "I think this is for you. Consider it my wedding gift to Polly."

Toots's bright red lips, that matched her bright red hair, drew up into a huge smile. She sent an air kiss my way before she disappeared into the dressing room to put her magical touch on her best friend.

"Move over," I instructed Mama once the organist started to play the song the bridesmaids were walking down the aisle to.

She looked at me with a horrified look on her face.

"Don't worry," I whispered and made her scooch some more to make room for Finn. "Polly exchanged me for Toots. It's all good."

Mama wasn't about to throw a hissy fit right there in front of everyone. She and Daddy scooted down, making enough room for me and Finn.

I had to admit the wedding was beautiful, especially now that I didn't have to wear the green hoop dress. Preacher Bing had used the church's emergency fund to call a heating and air conditioning contractor from Clay's Ferry to fix the HVAC unit. Needless to say, there was nothing wrong with it. The weather had been so chilly last week, Preacher Bing had forgotten he'd turned off the air conditioning and when the HVAC mechanic flipped it back on, Preacher Bing simply said a prayer and asked me to keep it between us. The rest of the wedding went off without a hitch.

The reception was everything Polly Parker Ryland wanted. It was Gone with the Wind on steroids. The entire inside of the reception hall looked like the movie set of Polly's favorite movie, down to the green velvet curtains.

"I still can't believe you are taking my baby to Chicago for Christmas." Mama cried in her cocktail at the reception.

"Ignore her," I instructed Finn. "Don't look at her."

"Kenni, why do you have to be so disrespectful?" she asked.

"Ladies, all the single ladies," the smarmy voice of the DJ called out. "It's that special time of throwing the bouquet."

"Get up there right now." Mama pointed to the front where Polly was twirling her bouquet around her head. "You're already breaking my heart about Christmas. Just act like you want me to be happy."

"Fine." I rolled my eyes and pushed back my chair.

As soon as I stood up, it was just like the other wedding when I planned in my head how I'd keep my hands to my side and not participate. The bouquet went flying in the air. The single ladies in front of Polly stopped jumping when they realized the flowers had passed over their head and they turned around, watching as it went into a free fall, hitting me smack dab in the forehead and falling on the floor next to my feet.

"Your parents are going to love my Kendrick." Mama's voice oozed with happiness.

The End

If you enjoyed reading this book as much as I enjoyed writing it then be sure to return to the Amazon page and leave a review.

Go to Tonyakappes.com for a full reading order of my novels and while there join my newsletter. You can also find links to Facebook, Instagram and Goodreads.

Join like-minded readers like YOU in the Cozy Krew Facebook Group for dream casting, fan theories, and live Q & A's. It's like a BIG GIANT BOOK CLUB! But if you want to have your own book club, be sure you let me know! I love to send goodies.

TANGLED UP IN TINSEL

A Kenni Lowry Mystery

TONYA KAPPES
.COM

Southern Hospitality
with a Smidgen
of Homicide

Book Six

BY
TONYA KAPPES

DEDICATION

To all the friends that I consider my family
　　even though we aren't blood!
　　Thank you for your continued support,
　　unconditional love, and friendship.

CHAPTER ONE

"Let's get this Christmas season kicked off!" The sound of a scratching record rose about the sounds of whistle calls and festive cheers from inside of the Hunt Club's annual Christmas Cantata. "I'm DJ Nelly. I'm excited to be the DJ at the annual Hunt Club Christmas Cantata. I'm ready to ring in the holiday season with y'all with this little ditty to start us off," DJ Nelly said into the microphone, the black headset perched on top of her head.

You better watch out, you better not cry. The music was barely heard over the residents of Cottonwood singing along as they formed a circle in the middle of the makeshift dance floor at The Moose Lodge.

DJ Nelly from WCKK, the only radio station in Cottonwood, had more than just the regular DJ happy-go-lucky voice, she had the spirit of Christmas coursing through her veins. It was strange seeing her in person and at this hour of the night, not that it was extremely late. It was eight p.m. and on a usual night all of our small town of Cottonwood would be tucked in. Especially on this cold winter night. The fact that DJ Nelly was a morning DJ, who played toe-tapping music to get me through my morning rounds, was messing with my head.

"Here you go." Finn Vincent walked up with a couple of bourbon and cokes to start off the festive occasion. The perfect set of white teeth underneath his mesmerizing smile sent my heart into a tailspin. "I'm looking forward to my first Cottonwood Christmas Cantata," he said as his eyes captured mine.

"Cheers." He held up his plastic cup to mine.

"Merry soon-to-be Christmas." I winked as we clinked our plastic cups together before we took a drink.

The strobe lights twirled and flashed with bright colors to the beat of the Christmas tunes DJ Nelly was spinning.

"I didn't realize so many kids would be here." He nodded towards the dance floor at the jumping teenagers who were singing at the top of their lungs.

"Santa Clause is Coming to Town."

I didn't blame them. Vivid memories of me doing the same thing were at the forefront of my mind. I was excited to show Finn all the wonderful traditions Cottonwood had to offer now that he wasn't just my deputy, who should love all things Cottonwood since he too served the amazing small town, but also my boyfriend. The only difference between then and now: Cottonwood had grown. Cottonwood had grown over the past year and it was practically impossible to know everyone like I used to. As the sheriff of Cottonwood, I wanted to know everyone who lived here.

"I thought those two weren't supposed to be dating?" Finn pointed at the two heads stuck together at one of the long banquet tables, which was covered with a table cloth that looked like Santa had thrown up on with all the symbols of Christmas.

"Leighann Graves and Manuel Liberty," I mused, noticing that Leighann looked a lot more grown up than the last time I'd seen her. Then, she'd come head-to-head with my five foot five inch frame. Now she appeared to have grown taller and more mature.

Leighann's long red hair was tied up in a ponytail with what looked to be silver tinsel that was used to decorate a Christmas tree. Every time Manuel swung her around, she threw her head back and let out a great peal of laughter that echoed all over the room. Seeing her happy did make me smile.

"Leighann is now eighteen." I took another sip of my drink. "Since she turned eighteen, I don't think we've gotten any calls from her parents."

"I'm talking about her parents, not her." Finn brought the cup up to his mouth and took a sip. "Look at Sean."

He gestured to one of the tables across the room where Sean and Jilly Graves were seated, alone, and furthest away from their daughter. By the looks of disgust on their faces, neither Sean or Jilly appeared to be happy that Leighann and Manuel were still an item.

Sean had his arms folded across his chest. Jilly's face was set, her mouth was clamped, and her eyes were fixed on the young couple. Across the way, I saw Juanita Liberty with her other two sons at a table about as far away from the Graves as you could get.

"Last time I spoke with Sean, he said they were going to try and get along." I straightened up and sighed loudly before I took another drink to try to chase away the stress of the job for just one night. "He said that Leighann was legally an adult now so there's really nothing they can do."

Leighann Graves graduated last year from Cottonwood High School. She wasn't one to conform to her parent's rules and when she didn't, they'd called me, Sheriff Kendrick Lowry, to go out and find her.

I wasn't sure what they expected me to do. It wasn't like the young couple was breaking the law. Plus, Manuel worked for Sean. It wasn't technically trespassing like Sean would tell me. I did the best I could to try to talk to the young kids, but that's about all I could do.

"Look at Juanita." I pointed her out to Finn.

Finn started laughing.

"What?" I asked.

"We are always so busy assessing people and their body language that we just can't enjoy a night off." He shook his head and reached over to hold my hand.

"Job hazard." I winked. "But look at them. Both families have that disgusted look on their faces."

"Why don't they like him again?" Finn asked.

We watched as the love birds got up from their seats and moseyed up to the refreshment table.

Manuel took a couple of plastic glasses full of the best darn punch around from one of the Sweet Adelines and handed it to Leighann. You know that delicious punch, the kind that's made from Neapolitan ice cream with a ton of Spirit cola poured over top of it? The sweet and tart was the perfect combination.

It was a bonus if you got a little bit of ice cream in the cup too. Plus, the Sweet Adelines were serving it from a real glass punch bowl and not just a plastic one, making it taste even better.

"I think it was because she kept running away from home to stay with Manuel, plus her sneaking out at night didn't help." I couldn't help but smile when I noticed my mama, Vivian Lowry, hand Manuel a napkin and gesture for him to use it on the little bit of punch Leighann had spilled on her chin.

Mama was always mothering someone, and, in this instance, Southern manners went a long way in her book. Manuel was getting a dose of Mama's class in Southern manners about right now. I also couldn't help but notice Sean Graves shake his head and lean over to say something to Jilly before they both got up and walked towards the exit.

"They aren't staying long." Finn had truly gotten to be just like one of us.

It took a few months for him to understand our unspoken rules of family and friends and gossip. This was just ideal gossip between me and him.

"By the looks of Leighann and Manuel, Sean and Jilly better get used to seeing them together. Time sure hasn't stopped the chemistry between them," I said after Manuel had pulled Leighann in for a kiss.

Out of the corner of my eye, I happened to notice my Mama walk out from behind the refreshment table, collect my daddy and head right towards me and Finn.

"Over here," I called and waved my hands in the air, acting as if I was inviting them over and not waiting on her to barge in like she always did. "Where have y'all been? Do you know how hard it is to save these seats?" I asked, even though I'd seen her through the dim lights doing her duty to her Auxiliary Women's club list of volunteering.

Another one of Mama's Southern rules in life was to volunteer anywhere you could. She was on every committee she could fit into one day.

"You know your mama." Dad rolled his eyes so hard, it made his nose curl. "First, she tried on several different outfits. Then when we got here, she took on more jobs than she'd signed up for and one of them was pouring out the punch."

"Why?" I looked at Mama. "It's the Moose Lodge. It's the Hunt Club not the Sweet Adelines putting it on. You need to enjoy yourself every once in a while."

"I wasn't sure if they'd made all their money to put on the annual dance, so I was just helping out where needed." Her Southern drawl not only drew out her words to make them longer syllables, but it drew her hand up to her chest and she lightly tapped the pearl necklace around her neck.

Earlier in the year the Hunt Club puts on their annual gun show where they rent this space from the Moose and sell guns. The proceeds go to put on this annual Christmas dance where all those proceeds go towards the schools and library of Cottonwood.

"I mighswell tell you." Mama's lips pursed as her words ran together. These are words that you never wanted to hear from Mama. They had a deeper meaning when they came from her.

"Tell me what?" I encouraged her with a deep-knotted fear that I was going to regret it.

"I'm running for Snow Queen," she proclaimed with pride. A squeal of joy broke from her lips.

"You're what?" My jaw dropped.

Finn lifted his hand to his mouth in an effort to try and cover up the smile on his face.

"The fame of being on the Culinary Channel has gone to her head and now thinks she needs to run for Snow Queen." Daddy didn't sound as enthusiastic about it as Mama did.

"Shush that up," Mama scolded him. "You turn that frown upside down because people will see that you're not happy for me. That's negative."

My eyes darted between my parents. No way, shape or form was daddy going to win this battle. Yet another defeat.

Daddy took my plastic cup and downed what I had left in my drink. "Come on, Finn." Dad nudged his head towards the cash bar. "I'll buy you a drink. I'm gonna need a double."

Mama had a big ole smile on her face and graciously nodded at everyone walking by.

"What's wrong with your hand?" I asked when I noticed she did some sort of flicking motion when someone walked by and said hello to her. "I'm sure Dr. Shively is here somewhere and can take a look at that for you." I twisted around in my seat to see if I could find Camille Shively, the only doctor in Cottonwood and who could give Mama something for her twitching hand.

"Obviously you haven't been watching any of those public broadcasting shows about the Queen and how they wave to their people." She did it again. "I'm practicing. If I win, I'll be in all the parades. These will be my people." She gestured to the room. "I'm hoping to get one of the car dealerships to sponsor me and I can sit on the back of the seat of a convertible."

"You've lost your mind." I shook my head.

"What?" She drew back. "I know it's winter, but convertible cars have heat. Besides, I've been eyeballing this fur down at Lulu's Boutique and it'd go perfect with my hair coloring." She sniffled and lifted the side of her finger under her nose. "What else do I have to look forward to this Christmas?" Her voice took a sharp turn from upbeat to tearful with a few extra sniffs to drive her point home.

"Here we go," I grumbled under my held breath and drank what little cocktail was left in my cup.

Now it was my turn for a good Southern scolding. My Mama was going to tell me which way was up and right now I was on the top of that list.

"You bet, here we go," she mocked me and shook her finger. "How do you think your father feels about you leaving us on Christmas? You're our only child. And you decide that you're going to leave us without a Christmas after all we've done for you. After all these years?"

She was so mad, she could've started a fight in an empty house.

"I guess you wouldn't know how your father feels because you're still not married and I've got no grandchildren. Thank God for that. Hallelujah!" She threw her hands in the air. "Because it's bad enough you're leaving us alone for Christmas. If we had grandchildren and you took the pleasure of spending Christmas morning with them away from you, you mightswell stick me in a nursing home and never come see me."

"Don't worry. I'll come see you once a year." I teased "Or at least make sure the girls who work there will wipe your mouth after you eat."

I patted her hand. She jerked it away from me, apparently still not amused with my jokes.

"Mama, you've pushed me to get a boyfriend. Now that Finn and I are dating, you're mad." It was a lose-lose situation with Mama if things didn't go her way.

Mama and I had the typical Southern mother/daughter relationship. It was a love/hate relationship that no matter what, in a time of need we were there for each other one-hundred percent. The problem was, she had an image of what my relationship should look like in her head, not what was real in the world.

"Yes. But I never said that you going away for Christmas was part of it. We like Finn. He's the hunkiest male in Cottonwood." Her words describing Finn made me feel icky inside because they shouldn't be coming from my mother.

No denying she was right. He was heaven on earth and his tall, muscular six-foot frame was that of an angel. There was only one downfall. His northern accent threw me off sometimes, but he was starting to get a bit of a twang. Around here, we called it hillbilly.

"You know that we have traditions here. Them yankies don't." Mama's face drew into a pucker.

"Mama," I scolded her. "You can't be calling people from Chicago yankies. He's a northerner."

"Northerner, yankie what's the difference?" she spat in protest.

"The difference is, Finn Vincent is my boyfriend and he loves his family just as much as I love my family. That means that we have to visit them too. We live here, and I see you practically every day," I reminded her. "Besides, you were okay with it a few weeks ago."

She stuck her pointer finger up in the air.

"Christmas is once a year." She jutted that finger towards me. "Once a year," she emphasized. "A few weeks ago was just that. Now that we are down to the nitty-gritty of Christmas Day, I thought you'd've come to your senses by now and decided to stay here."

If this would've been ten years ago when I was a teenager, I'd've tried to snap that finger off her hand.

"You two look like you're having an intense conversation," Finn said and sat down in the chair between me and Mama.

He had two drinks in his hand and he slid one to me. Daddy sat on the other side of Mama. She grabbed the wine out of his hand before his hind-end hit the chair.

"I'm gonna need the full bottle," she said in a sarcastic tone.

"It's from a box," Daddy corrected her.

"What?" Her face contorted.

"The wine." Daddy's head nodded towards her glass. "It's not from a bottle. It's from a box up there."

"Good Gawd." Mama curled her lips with icy contempt. "Lord, help me. What is this world coming to?"

I shook my head and widened my eyes to let Finn know that what Mama and I had been discussing wasn't a topic that we should be talking about. Mama had made it very clear over the past few months of her disapproval for me leaving Cottonwood during the big traditional festivities. I was going to miss being here for them since I'd not missed one since birth, but it wasn't fair to Finn. One thing I've learned since dating Finn was the fact that he too had family, a big family, and they loved Christmas just as much as we did.

"Why don't we work on your waltz since I know you're going to win and have to do it in front of the entire town the night of the tree lighting?" Finn put his hand to Mama.

She giggled in a school girl way that made me roll my eyes before she took his hand. He guided her to her feet and she tucked her hand into his elbow, letting him lead her. She did that whole Queen wave, hand twitching gesture the whole way to the dance floor.

"She's lost her mind," I leaned over to my dad and whispered.

"She's alright. She's just trying to keep her mind occupied with you going out of town." Dad dropped his head and looked at his glass of wine.

He wasn't all too thrilled about me leaving for Christmas, but he'd at least accepted it.

"You know." Dad leaned back in his chair. "I remember what it was like to leave my family for the first time at Christmas when I was dating Viv." He glanced out at the dance floor.

Mama was having too good of a time while Finn waltzed her around the plywood floor to "Have Yourself a Merry Little Christmas".

"I remember how sad my own mom was, but when I left for good and moved here, that was a whole different story." Dad had uprooted his life to move to Cottonwood and it was a story he rarely told. "The look in my mama's eye is the same look in your mama's eyes. It's just a change. Viv will get used to it, but in the meantime, if she wants to be in the Snow Queen pageant to occupy her time and it makes her happy." He smiled. "Then I support her."

I reached over and took my dad's hand.

"It's only one Christmas," I assured him and gave his hand a squeeze. "I'm actually looking forward to it." I drew my hand back and wrapped it around my plastic cup. I'd only met his sister and I was looking forward to meeting the rest of his family. "He's looking forward to me meeting them."

"Honey, your Mama is worried that you're going to go up there, love it and never come back." Dad patted me on the arm. "By the way you look at that boy, I'm a little worried too."

"There's nothing to worry about." I gulped and suddenly came to the realization that the thought of ever living outside of Cottonwood never crossed my mind.

"If Finn doesn't want to live in Cottonwood his entire life, it's an issue." Dad's words didn't comfort me any.

I dragged the cup to my mouth as I watched Finn spin Mama in one direction. On the outskirt of the spin, Mama did that hand-ticking wave thing to whoever was watching and when Finn pulled her back in, she carefully placed her hand on his shoulder like she'd already had the Snow Queen crown on her head.

"Do we know who else is in the running for queen?" I asked because I silently wanted to offer up a little pray for their safety.

"No. And God bless their hearts who do run against her." Daddy took a big swig of his cocktail and planted a big smile on his face when he saw Mama coming back. "She has practice this week at the fairgrounds. Then we'll know who her competition will be."

Once Mama gets something in her head, she doesn't stop at any expense to get it. It was all part of our Southern upbringing. I wasn't too off that mark myself. Ever heard of the apple doesn't fall too far from the tree? Well, Mama was the tree and I was the apple. Only I hid my crazy better than she did.

Mama wanted me to go to college and find me a nice man to bring home to Cottonwood where I'd be in her clubs and volunteer alongside of her, but when I told her I was going to the police academy to follow in the footsteps of her dad, my Poppa, Elmer Sims, she threw a hissy fit bigger than a toddler wanting a piece of candy they couldn't have that was dangling in front of them.

"That was fun." Mama winked at Finn. I glared at her. It was one thing for her to like my boyfriend, but to blatantly flirt with him was another. And he knew it, egging her on every time.

"My pleasure." Finn kissed the top of the hand that she'd offered him.

He was good at manipulating her like putty in his fingers. It was only him that talked some sense into her when she'd stomped around for a few days insisting I was trying to kill her by not being here for Christmas. But now, it seemed she'd gotten back on the pity wagon about it.

"Now what about you?" He turned to me with an outstretched hand. "A dance around the floor?"

Before I could even answer, there was a big ruckus going on over at the snack table near the punch bowls. Manuel and a girl that wasn't Leighann were screaming at each other at the top of their lungs. Manuel grabbed Leighann by the arm and jerked her back from the girl after Leighann started screaming at her too. Finn sprinted across the room, breaking up the three in the heated argument.

"Man, you better tell her to lay off," Manuel threatened.

"Just stop it!" Leighann screamed at Manuel and then looked at the girl. "You've always been jealous of me," she said through gritted teeth. "Get out of my life! Forever!"

"No problem. You're dead to me!" The girl turned on the balls of her feet and swung around.

"What's going on?" I asked after I moseyed on over, not in too big of a hurry because Finn seemed to have it under control.

"Nothing." Manuel jerked free of Finn and tugged down on the hem of his shirt. His muscular arms flexed without him even trying. "I told you that you need to keep better friends." His mustache quivered, and he pointed to Leighann. She was visibly upset.

Angela Durst had come to Leighann's side and pulled out a Kleenex from the pocket of her Christmas vest. Angela was Sean Graves's secretary at the towing company. She'd seen Leighann grow up.

Leighann wiped her eyes while Angela rubbed Leighann's long red hair down her back. Beka, Angela's daughter walked up and asked Manuel what was going on. He didn't answer her.

"It's nothing, sheriff." Leighann gave a fake smile. "Merry Christmas."

Manuel grabbed Leighann's hand. "Let's get out of here, babe."

"Don't babe me." She jerked away but followed him anyways. "You've run off every single friend I've ever had."

"You need better friends," he said back to her.

"Are you two okay?" I asked again before they darted out the door. They didn't bother answering me.

Finn and I looked at each other.

"Do you think they're okay?" He asked me.

"I'm sure they'll be fine." Angela shrugged. "They've had worse fights than this."

"It's getting colder out there. I think the big winter storm is going to be moving in quicker than they predicted. Get this," DJ Nelly's excitement blurted out of the speakers and interrupted our conversation with Angela. "We just might have a white Christmas."

The cheers from the crowd were catching on and soon everyone in the room was singing "I'm Dreaming of a White Christmas". Even me.

"No, no, no." Finn shook his head. "No white Christmas here."

"It's beautiful when it snows in Cottonwood." I smiled with fond memories of sledding and how they had horse drawn carriages for the tree lighting ceremony.

"Not if we can't get out of here on that big bird to go see my folks." Finn's face grew stern.

"Don't worry." I brushed off the white Christmas and any notion the airport in Lexington would close down. "What does a DJ know about weather? She barely knows what today's hits are, much less how to predict snow." I laughed and tugged him out on the dancefloor.

I didn't dare say it, but it would be my luck that we'd get this big storm and here I'd be.

CHAPTER TWO

"Gone away is the blue bird, here to stay is the new bird. We sing a love song as we go along. Walking in a winter wonderland." I couldn't stop my finger from tapping on the steering wheel of my old Wagoneer as it rattled down Free Row–what I lovingly called Broadway Street–where I lived.

Free Row was the nickname mainly because the residents that lived on Free Row lived off the commodity cheese and other perks the government gives them.

"Walking in a winter wonderland," I sang along to the catchy tune as I began my morning route around Cottonwood to make sure everyone and everything was alright with the world. At least in our little part of the world.

The Wagoneer came to a halt at the stop sign at the intersection of Broadway and Main Street.

"Can you believe it, Duke?" I rubbed down my old hound dog and gently nudged his back end towards the seat so I could see if any cars were coming down Main Street before I turned left. "Just a few more days until we go to Chicago."

Duke wagged his tail and stuck his head out the window into the bitter cold winter jet stream that'd decided to blanket the entire state. His droopy brown eyes had a little sparkle in them as his long tan ears flapped into the wind.

"Well, until I go to Chicago," I whispered because I didn't want him to hear me since he was going to have to stay with Joelle Fischer, my best friend.

Though he wouldn't mind since she owned a food truck and he loved riding with her. Free food, who wouldn't?

"Good morning, Cottonwood. Remember last night at the Hunt Club's annual Christmas dance where I announced the weather alert?" DJ Nelly chimed in after the song with her perky voice. "Well, batten down the hatches, get those winter gloves, hats and snow boots out because I'm coming at y'all with a wee-bit of advice since a blizzard is coming. If y'all are anywhere near the Dixon's Food Town, I suggest you stop on in and get a loaf of bread and some milk. From what I hear, they've got a new shipment overnight and it won't last long. Y'all, we ain't gonna escape this winter blizzard heading straight for us in a few days. Stock up now and don't wait."

"Seriously?" I shook my head and pulled the Jeep out on Main Street and headed north towards downtown. "Every year they say the big blizzard is coming and we get a dusting of snow. A dusting, just like powdered sugar that Ben's Diner puts on the waffles." My mouth started to water. "Man, waffles sound good about right now," I talked to Duke like he was going to answer me. "Ain't that right, Duke?"

Rowl, rowl. His feet danced on the seat to get a little more balance to avoid smacking into the dashboard when I turned the wheel.

"And while you're there, be sure to grab a shovel and some salt. Excuse me for yawning, y'all kept me out a little too late last night. You're listening to WCKK for all your Christmas tunes." DJ Nelly clicked off and so did I.

"If she thinks that a little snow is going to stop me from going to Chicago and spend Christmas with Finn and his family, she's got another thing coming and I don't want to listen." I gripped the wheel and looked up. "So, if you can hear me," I should've summoned the big guy in the sky, but I didn't. I summoned the other big guy in the sky that I personally knew and that had come to visit me a time or two in the afterlife, Elmer Sims, my Poppa. "Not that I want you to come because of a murder, but I'd like to go meet Finn's family. So why not grant me this one wish and stop any snow coming." I looked at Duke. "That should do it."

I was confident that there wasn't going to be any snow. There couldn't. Not after all the planning Finn and I had done to go to great lengths to make it happen over the past few months. Being sheriff of Cottonwood and Finley Vincent being my only deputy made it hard for both of us to take a day off, much less a few days off.

The Wagoneer headed up Main Street and I couldn't help but slow down to look at the carriage lights that dotted each side of the street. The Beautification committee had not only hung beautiful and full poinsettias on the rods next to the hung "Christmas in Cottonwood" banners, they also strung white twinkling lights up the poles. It was strange to imagine myself not waking up on Christmas morning, heading down to Ben's Diner and serving food to the homeless or taking food to the shelter.

The stop light turned yellow, slowing me down to a stop at the intersection of Chestnut Street and Main Street. To the left of me was Cowboy's Catfish, where the city rented the back portion of the restaurant for the sheriff's department. It wasn't a conventional copshop, but nothing in our small town was conventional. White's Jewelry was next to Cowboy's, next to that was Tattered Cover Books and Inn, the only place to stay downtown. Beyond that was Ben's Diner. All of their display windows were decorated with Christmas decorations and lights. The Tattered Cover had green wreaths with big red bows on each window of the three-story brick building.

A smile grew on my face when I imagined what would happen if there was a big snow storm. Downtown would look amazing and much like a winter wonderland you'd see in a fancy winter painting of a quaint small town.

Across the street there was Ruby's Antiques, that brought visitors from all over the state for Ruby Smith's delicious treasures. Kim's Buffet, a local family-owned Chinese restaurant, was next to Ruby's. Along with the radio station where DJ Nelly was all too happy giving the news of the upcoming weather I refused to even speak of.

I forced the images of the weather report to the back of my head. I'd heard Chicago was amazing this time of the year. Finn had mentioned something about going to see The Nutcracker and I really wanted to go.

Finn was from Chicago and had been a deputy with the Kentucky State Reserve. He'd worked a homicide with me here in Cottonwood and we just so happened to have an opening for a deputy. A few short months later, we were working side by side and we couldn't deny the chemistry between us much longer, so we started dating. In the spring, he'd asked me to go to Chicago for Christmas to meet his family. It was a no-brainer. Now that it was a few days away, no way was an over-exaggerated weather forecast nor excited DJ on the radio going to stop our trip.

It'd taken a few steps, along with a couple of headaches and campaign promises, to get City Council to approve the request for us to leave and for the State Reserve to send us an officer to fill in for us since it was Christmas. Now...getting my Mama to accept me not being here was an act of congress that still hasn't gotten full approval.

A big sigh escaped me, and I gripped the wheel a little tighter.

The warm glow of the carriage lights caught the Christmas wreaths in an angelic way. All the quaint shops were closed this early in the morning, but not Ben's Diner. When I drove by, I could see the regulars were already lined up like soldiers bellied up to the counter. Ben's baseball cap was turned around backwards like he'd always wore it. His mouth was already flapping while he went down the counter filling up all of the coffee mugs.

"I sure would like a cup of his coffee," I said to Duke and picked up my thermos I'd filled up with my coffee from home.

The old bean bag coffee holder slid off the floorboard hump when I got my coffee. I should've probably invested in a real cup holder for the old Wagoneer, but I couldn't bring myself to do it. This old Jeep was my Poppa's and many memories of me playing with the bean bag coffee holder were fond ones for me.

"It's not going to snow," I repeated to myself before I turned right into the Pump and Munch on the corner of East Oak and Main Street.

The Pump and Munch was the only gas station in downtown Cottonwood. There was a small market attached to the garage with two big steel doors and small windows across the top. Luke Jones was already hunkered under the hood of a car and looked up when my tires ran over the tube that dinged the bell inside.

He gave a slight wave to let me know he'd seen me and I waved back. Luke believed in the old way of things and coming out to pump the gas himself.

When I saw him coming out the door, I pulled down my visor and took out the gas card that belonged to the sheriff's department.

"Mornin', Sheriff." Luke wiped his hands down the blue cover-alls he was wearing, which didn't make any sense because it appeared they were just as dirty as his hands. "You fillin' up to get the Jeep ready for the storm of the century?" he asked as we both saw his breath.

"Storm of the century?" I asked and pushed Duke away from my lap. He couldn't contain himself to his side of the front seat when my window was rolled down. "Just a little dusting."

Luke's arm plunged inside of the window as he reached across me to pat Duke. A stream of bitter air came with it.

"That's what all them meteorologist are calling it. Saying it's just like the blizzard of 1977." His chin lifted up and then down. "The way I figure it, I'm gonna be busy. People gonna come in here today to get gas for all their cars and generators." He pointed over to the side of his garage. "I've got plenty of gas cans on hand to sell. You need one?"

"Mark my word," I smiled and shook my head, "There's not going to be a storm of the century. Maybe a few flakes here and there, but they're always wrong."

"The Farmer's Almanac said so too." Luke's brows furrowed. He put his hands together and blew in them before he briskly rubbed them together. "Don't you got one?"

"Of course, I do." I took in a deep breath. "Doesn't everyone in Cottonwood?" I questioned under my breath.

Everyone in my small Southern town lived and died by the Farmer's Almanac. If you didn't get your seeds or crops planted by the time the black ink on the pages said, your crops weren't going to grow. But who was I to question it? I wasn't a farmer. Just a girl in love that wasn't going to let a few snowflakes keep her from meeting who could potentially be her future in-laws.

Just the thought of it made my stomach flip-flop and heart flutter.

"Filler' up?" He asked.

"Please," I said and rubbed my hands together. "And not because of the storm. I just need gas."

There was no denying that the temps were prime for a blizzard, but the sun was out and there was no way Poppa was going to let this happen. I looked up to the sky and said a little pray in my head.

"You're all set." He tapped the window sill. "What night are you and the gals coming by for White Christmas this week?"

Luke Jones and his wife, Vita, also owned the only community movie theater in Cottonwood. It was run in the basement of their house. They had popcorn, sweet treats, and drinks to purchase. He had a big pull-down screen that sometimes worked and sometimes didn't. On the days that it didn't want to pull down, he used a sheet screen that was actually three king sheets that Vita sewed together. Every year he ran the old movie, White Christmas, for three or four nights during the Christmas season. My best friends, Jolee Fischer and Tibbie Bell, and I had a yearly habit of making a girls' night out during Christmas that included our annual viewing of White Christmas at Luke's.

"Actually, I won't be coming. Finn invited me to Chicago to meet his family during the days you're showing the movie." The smile on my face got so big, I blushed. "We are going up a few days before Christmas so I'm going to miss all the fun festivities at the fairgrounds and everything." I planted a frown on my face for effect.

"Kenni," Luke gasped, his eyes grew big. "I knew you were going out of town, but this'll be the first time that I can remember where you weren't in front row with a big popcorn sprinkled with chocolate and big coke."

"I know." I shrugged. "I'll have to start a new tradition with a New Year's movie."

"Who's going to run our town?" The line between his brows deepened.

"The state reserve is sending someone to run the joint. I don't anticipate anything going wrong," I said. "He'll be in the office today. So be nice if you see a stranger meandering around our parts."

It wasn't unusual for the town folk to give the riot act to any stranger in town that appeared to be gawking or a little too nosy. Gossip spread around our small town like wild fire and if I could make the temporary deputy comfortable before he got here, I was going to try. The last thing I needed when I was in Chicago was to get a call from Betty saying the people ran him out of town.

"What about the big blizzard? What if someone is trapped? Needs rescuing?" He asked.

It took everything in my power not to roll my eyes.

"Luke, mark my words, there's not going to be a big blizzard. They haven't gotten the weather right in years. Everything is going to be fine. I promise," I assured him, then crossed my heart and jerked the gear shift into drive. "Duke and I are off to do the rounds."

"Tell everyone you know to grab some milk, just in case. I've stocked up if Dixon's is out." He tapped the side of my Jeep before I took off.

There was no denying that it was going to be strange not being in Cottonwood during Christmas. I'd never not been here during Christmas. Even when I went off the college and joined the police academy, I came home every year. Change was good. At least that's what I was telling myself.

"Kenni, Kenni." Betty Murphy's voice came across the walkie-talkie loud and clear.

While I held on the steering wheel with one hand, I used the other to turn down the volume on the walkie-talkie strapped to my shoulder. It was the old way of communication, which Finn had tried desperately to get us to change, but it worked.

Like my Poppa always said, why try to fix something that's not broken?

"Go ahead," I said after I clicked the button on the side and crossed over York Street.

"Jilly Graves needs you to come to their house right away. Leighann didn't come home last night and it's not like her to do that." Betty Murphy was my dispatch operator at the department.

"Not like her to do that," I said sarcastically and looked over at Duke. "It was totally like her to not come home."

I reached up and clicked the button on the walkie-talkie.

"How long has Leighann been gone?" I asked, doing my civic duty.

"Since she left the Hunt Club dance last night." Betty clicked off.

"It's not even been twelve hours," I said to Duke. Leighann Graves had been giving her family fits for years by sneaking out. "She's probably at Manuel's after they made up from last night." I remembered how they'd gotten into that little tiff.

Duke's big brown eyes looked at me. His tongue was sticking out with a drip of slobber while he panted.

"Are you at the department?" I asked Betty when I noticed the hands of the manual old-time clock on the dash said it was still thirty minutes until she was due to the office to start her job as dispatcher.

"Well, Jilly knew I wasn't in the office yet and so she called me at home. I rushed right on in here so I could get ahold of you." Betty was talking so fast, she was out of breath. "I knew you were probably off doing your rounds, and I would've called Finn, but he started his shift down at the Dixon's Foodtown ringing the bell for the kettle foundation this morning. You know, the thing you volunteered him for."

This was the time of year that I knew if the department didn't volunteer for anything, it'd come back and bite me in the you-know-what when it was election time. Sheriff was an elected position and it was hell enough trying to get the residents to vote in a female, hard enough now that I was here and under a microscope. Luckily, we'd just gotten through an election and I was safe for another four years.

"Alrighty. I'll run on over to the Graves's house, though I don't classify Leighann as missing and you know that until she's missing for a couple of days, we don't usually take report. She's an adult too." I figured it was another one of Sean Graves's ways of trying to keep control of his daughter.

Graves Towing and the Graves's house was on the north side of town past Lulu's Boutique. It wasn't like it took me long to get from the south edge of town to the north edge. Driving under a few stop lights and I had made it. Since I was already heading north on Main Street, it'd be quick.

Sean Graves was a third-generation family business owner and had kept up the company. The white clapboard farmhouse on the family farm was surrounded by black Kentucky post fencing. He took pride on how nice and neat he kept the property, as he should be. It was a beautiful farm.

The tow lot was full of cars that he'd repossessed or even took in as a junk, even sold some of the parts to customers. Behind a chain-link fence was the ever-mounting pile of a junk yard.

I drove up the driveway and around the back of the big farmhouse where the entrance was to their home. Their business was located behind the house and that's where you could see the generations of the Graves's hard work.

Sean and Jilly had lived off the property in a small home in town while Leighann was in school, but over the past few months, they'd moved back to the farm and focused more on the business. Especially since Leighann had decided not to go to college and to continue to work with the family business instead. At least that's what the word around town was. By that, I mean gossip.

The Sheriff's department used Graves's Towing a lot. We had no other choice. I didn't mind going out there to ease their minds. After all, they'd hung signs on their fence and voted for me in both elections.

Colored Christmas lights were strung across the gutters of their house. The few bushes on each side of the front door had those nets that were made out of white Christmas lights. They had a blow-up famous cartoon character in their front yard with a beer in his hand and a Santa hat on his head. That didn't shock me. It was a pretty typical characterization of Sean Graves. One of the good ole boys in Cottonwood.

I just shook my head and put the Jeep in park.

"Come on," I said to Duke and patted my leg. It wasn't unusual for him to be with me. My deputy and protector. He'd even received a medal for saving my life once and taking a bullet for me.

Duke jumped out my side and ran up to the bushes, leaving his mark on each one. I grabbed my police bag and shut the door. My bag was everything I needed when I went on a call or an investigation. No matter what type of call it was. It was easier to grab the whole thing than to get the notebook and pencil out.

"I'm guessing by the lack of the sheriff's light, my Leighann's disappearance isn't that important." Sean Graves stood at the door with bags under his eyes. He must've been watching for me.

"If there was someone out on the roads this early, I'd've used it, but I was lucky enough the roads were clear." I wasn't going to use the siren. I was positive that Leighann had just pulled one of her tricks again. "Which got me here quicker."

"Get on in here." He opened the door wide. When I took a step in, I could see Jilly sitting on the couch next to the stocked-up fire in the wood burning stove. There was a kettle on top with steam rolling out from the spout.

"Sheriff, would you like a cup of coffee?" She asked. There was a bit of fear in her that I'd not seen before when Leighann would disappear.

"That'd be great." I pointed to the chair. "May I?"

"Of course. Sean, go get Kenni a mug out of the cupboard. Can I get something for Duke?" She asked.

"No. He's fine." I pointed to the ground for Duke to take his command.

"Go on, Sean." Jilly shooed him to get me that coffee.

When I sat down, Duke laid down next to my feet. On the opposite side, I sat my bag down and unzipped it, taking out the notepad and paper.

While Jilly made sure I was comfortable, and Sean got my coffee, I wrote down the date, time and purpose of the visit so I could transfer my notes into the computer when I got back into the office.

"I got a call from Betty saying that Leighann is missing." I took the cup and nodded a thank you. "Why do you think this is different than any other time?" I asked.

"This." Jilly held up a cell phone. "This is Leighann's. You and I both know that these kids today don't put their phones down. Especially her. She's on this thing twenty-four seven."

"I was beginning to think it'd attached to her skin she never puts it down." Sean offered me creamer and I held my hand up declining.

I sat the coffee on the small table next to me and took a vested interest because they did have a point, though I wasn't thoroughly convinced Leighann was actually missing.

"We all know that the past is a proven history that Leighann has left here before." I reminded them of all the calls before Leighann was of legal age.

"Yes. But like I said, this is her phone and she never left without it in the past." Jilly eased herself to sit on the edge of the couch. Her hands clasped and tucked in between her knees.

"Is the phone still in your name? Do you pay the bill?" I asked and both of them nodded.

"Is it possible that she and Manuel got a phone in her name?" I asked again. "Maybe cutting some ties with you guys now that she's legally able to leave?"

"No. Both of their phones are owned by the company. We've accepted that she's out of high school and an adult. She's going to keep dating that boy no matter what we say." Sean seethed. Apparently, no matter what he told me, he'd not accepted their relationship and maybe not at any age.

Jilly leaned over and touched him to calm him down.

"We are open to the fact that she loves him, and we will train him and her to take over our business when we retire," Jilly said. "Just like your parents did for us."

"I want better for her." Sean jerked away from Jilly and stood up. He ran his hand through his hair and paced back and forth. "You and I have a hard enough time making ends meet. What's going to happen when we retire? They aren't as hardworking as us."

"This is the problem." Jilly's voice rose and octave. "You don't give them a chance to even try to grow up."

"Back to the cell phone." I had to reel them in. "Have you talked to Manuel this morning? Is she with him?"

"No. I mean yes." He waved his hand in the air. "She's not with him. And yes, we've talked to him. That's what worries me." Jilly said, "Sean and I left the dance last night before they did."

That I remembered.

"Manuel said there was some sort of argument. She and Manuel were leaving. She'd met him at the dance because he was on a call for us to pull in a repo. When they were leaving the dance, she threw the phone at him as she yelled that she didn't want him to call her and jumped in her car. She took off. He said he drove off after her, but she was going so fast that he couldn't keep up with her." A look of worry set deep in Jilly's eyes.

"He hasn't seen her since?" I asked.

"No. And that's not like her. You know just as much as we do the trouble we've had keeping her away from him even when they did fight. And they've had some doozies." Jilly looked at Sean. "That's why we tried to discourage them from dating. They have these big, blow up fights that are bad now. I can only imagine what would happen if they got married."

"Has Manuel ever hit Leighann?" I asked only because I wanted to get a complete picture of the type of relationship they'd had.

"We don't know. Leighann would never confess to anything. She says that they love each other so much that they fight." She scoffed, "Who ever heard alike?"

"Do you believe him when he says he's not seen her?" I questioned, keeping in mind that their opinion of him was a bit skewed.

"We don't know what to believe. After she graduated, we sat down with her and told her that we approved of her relationship. She didn't have to go to college and she could learn the business. She was pleased with that. When she and Manuel started working together every day, side by side, we noticed she'd gotten a little more distanced from him. Last year, she'd jump in the cab of the tow truck and go all day long when she was off a day from school. Now we have to beg her to go help him." Sean's lips pulled in and snugged up against his teeth. "I feel like something is wrong. I don't know if he had anything to do with it, but I can't find her. After he showed up here with this phone and said she never came to his house, he got worried and came here to see if she'd come home."

"We checked her phone. There's no unusual activity or calls and even her text messages are fine." Jilly sucked in a deep breath.

"Can I take her phone with me?" I asked. They readily handed it over to me. "If we can't find Leighann, which I'm sure we will, I can subpoena the records of the phone. Last ping. Those types of things. Is there any particular place she goes when she's upset or angry that you might know about?"

"She and Manuel liked to go down to the river over at Chimney Rock, but I drove over there this morning after Manuel had come by. Granted, it was dark out, but I didn't see her car." Sean frowned. "I asked Manuel about Chimney Rock and he said that he didn't have plans to go there with her either."

"I'll go speak to Manuel. I also witnessed that argument last night. I even talked to them. There were a few other kids standing around. I'll go see the other kids involved. In the meantime," I put my note pad and Leighann's phone back in my bag. I pushed myself up to stand. Duke jumped up and trotted over to their door. "If you do hear from her, please call my cell immediately."

I took a business card with my cell phone printed on it and handed it to Sean.

"Thank you, Kenni." Sean walked me to the door. "If anyone can talk to Manuel and figure out what he might be hiding, it's you."

"I'll be in touch." I nodded and patted my leg for Duke to follow.

"You've got my cell number, right?" He questioned as I walked towards my Jeep.

"I sure do." I opened the door and Duke jumped in.

"Good. That big winter storm is coming, and I imagine I'll be out in it pulling out idiots who get out in that stuff. Do you have an emergency kit in your Jeep?" He asked and walked up to the driver's door.

"I've got what I need," I assured him.

"Everyone needs an emergency kit in their car at all times. I made sure Jilly has one and Leighann has one in her car. So if Leighann's in some sort of emergency right now," his voice cracked, "I know she's got food, water and first aid kit." He sniffed. "I even got her a kit from Lulu's boutique with her initials on it." He let out a little laugh. "Leighann is so girly. She loves all that initial stuff."

"I'm sure we'll find her," I assured him. My words met his blank face.

"Nonetheless, be careful in the storm." He slammed the door.

"There's not going to be a winter storm," I confidently yelled back to their front door.

CHAPTER THREE

If I was going to drive out to the Liberty house, I figured I was going to need to get a fresh, hot coffee because just like Manuel, his mother wasn't one to mess with. Juanita Liberty let people know that Manuel was to go to college on a football scholarship. She didn't hold back when Manuel had told them he wasn't going to go to college, turning down the scholarship and staying in Cottonwood. It was a dispatch call that I dreaded and could still feel that sick gut feeling.

The call had actually come from Jonathan, Manuel's brother. Juanita had gotten Manuel in a choke hold, demanding she wasn't going to let go until he signed the scholarship, but Manuel insisted he wasn't going. It took a while for me to pry her hands from around the poor kid, but it did end peacefully.

Heading south, on my way back into town, I took a right next to Lulu's Boutique. Duke danced back and forth between the front seat and back seat of the Wagoneer in delight.

The boutique was a really old, small, yellow clapboard house that Lulu McClain had turned into a cozy knick-knack shop that sold local arts, candles, some clothing items and accessories for the home. In the back she'd host different arts and crafts for the various groups, like knitting, pottery, crocheting, and whatever else the Auxilary Women could find to fill their days and nights.

It wasn't the boutique that Duke was so excited to see, it was Jolee Fischer's food truck, On the Run. Jolee pulled the truck up to the curb next to Lulu's every morning so she could caffeinate all the Cottonwood people who got up early. The food she cooked and served was straight home-cookin' that made our mouths water. Duke was a recipient of some of her treats and his tail nearly knocked me over as he jumped out of the Jeep after I opened the door. This was why I knew he'd be just fine while I was gone to Chicago.

It was too cold to eat outside, and Jolee knew when she opened the food truck that everyone needed a place to commune if they wanted to. Lulu and Jolee had made an agreement that Lulu would open the craft room in the back of the boutique for people to eat and enjoy. Cottonwood was about community and being together.

"Kenni, really?" Lulu came out of nowhere and wiped her hand across the front pocket of my brown sheriff's jacket. "You could use a little monogram on this to make it pop a little. Or make it a little more feminine."

She pulled away and her fingernails racked the edge of her short, twiggy styled black hair. There was some jingling going on under the faux fur coat she had snuggled around her. No doubt the jingling was the armful of bangles she had from her wrist to her elbow.

"Lulu, it's monogramed with the sheriff's symbol." My eyes lowered, "Have you been talking to Mama?" I asked.

"Have I?" She squealed with delight. "I just have to show you that fur coat she's going to look fabulous in when she's sitting on the back of a fancy car in a parade."

"Lulu, you aren't feeding Mama a line of bullarky about this silly notion of her wanting to run for Snow Queen, are you?" I gave her a sideways look.

"Well, she mentioned something about you going to Chicago and she's got to have something to fill up her broken heart. But I did tell her that you'd be a beautiful bride. If you insist on going, we would like you to have something come out of it. After all," She cozied up to me, "a fall wedding in Cottonwood is beautiful." Her nails dug into me.

"You and my Mama can get any notion of me getting engaged while I'm in Chicago out of your head." Though the image of me being Finn's bride might've popped in my head a time or two, it wasn't something I figured on right now.

Come on? What girl didn't start dreaming of her wedding at age three? Lulu let out a long sigh.

"Fancy nails you got there." I pulled her hand away from my arm and noticed the red and gold tips with a smidgen of glitter on them. "Shimmery."

"Oh honey, I'm one of Tina Bower's Guinea pigs down at Tiny Tina's." She curled her nose. "All that shines makes my heart sing."

"It's cold. I'm going to grab a coffee." I patted her on the back. "You're dressed for Antarctica."

"I'm getting out all my furs due to the storm of the century coming." She shimmied proudly and ran her hand down the front of her coat with a twinkle in her eye. "Not just your Mama wants one of my fine furs."

"Don't tell me that you're believing this weather forecast?" I questioned because Lulu McClain was one that didn't let anyone pull the wool over her eyes. "Of all people in this town, I didn't figure you'd fall for it."

"Honey," her Southern accent made her response so much more charming, "I'll give it to you that the weather people on the television are probably about ninety-nine percent wrong, but I do believe with the way the clouds are shifting and the wind is breezing, they might've gotten that one percent right this time." She shivered and wiggled her shoulders. "Can't you feel it?"

"Nope. Not one bit." I shrugged and wasn't about to give into the fact that she had her faith in the one percent.

"Put your nose in the air and smell it." She jutted her chin out and up, taking the biggest inhale. "Agggghhhhhh," she released it. "I can smell it and I can see it." She dragged her hands out in front of her. "The freshly fallen snow that blankets Cottonwood in all its sparkling splendor. The real thick snow that the kiddos can pack into the tallest snowmen you've ever seen." She elbowed me. "We haven't had a snow like that since you were a youngin'."

"I remember." It wasn't a fond memory either. "Mama decided she needed to go to Dixon's Foodtown when Daddy told her not to. She threw me in the back of the family station wagon and backed out of the driveway and before she even got going the wagon slid back and hit a fire hydrant."

Lulu's brows furrowed.

"That's when Graves's Tow company came and got us out. I can hear daddy now," I continued in my best dad voice, "'Viv, I told you not to go out in this stuff, but you had to be nosy.' Mama said, 'no I wanted to get bread.' Dad said back to her that she was wanting to make sure she wasn't missing out on any gossip in the baking aisle. Then they fought over the big bill from Graves's towing. Right here at Christmas time." I shook my head. "I'm hoping the weather is still ninety-nine percent wrong."

"We'll see," Lulu ho-hummed and gave me a wink as she walked away.

The line to the front of On the Run food truck was about five people deep. Each one greeted me with the typical nod and "mornin' sheriff". Of course, I was kind and asked how they were doing. Before I knew it, I'd gotten caught up on their lives and I made sure to ask them if they'd seen Leighann Graves. No one had and before you knew it, I was up to the front of the line where Jolee had my coffee poured and ready to go.

"You haven't seen Leighann Graves around have you?" I asked.

Not that I'd expected Jolee to say yes or even that Leighann had stopped by the food truck. No stone unturned was the motto I liked to live by and you just never knew.

"I haven't. I don't even remember her ever coming here, but not that she wouldn't today. It's been a weird morning." Jolee leaned over and out the window of the food truck. She turned her head right and left. "None of my regulars are here. I swear it's this whole snow thing. Damn storm of the century."

"There's not going to be a storm." I looked at her up under my brows. "You're my best friend. You can at least agree with me."

"Unn-hun, no way." She shook her head. "You're trying to bail out on our annual White Christmas girl's night. I don't want you leaving me for Christmas. Who cares about you leaving your Mama behind. It's me you're leaving behind."

"Whatever. You've got Ben," I said.

She wasn't fooling me any, though she'd never bailed on a girlfriend night since she started dating Ben Harrison.

"Anyways, if you see Leighann let me know. She didn't come home last night after she got into that fight with Manuel at the dance. She'll turn up." I was sure of it.

"I'm sure she will." Jolee's eyes moved past me and onto the next customer.

"Let's go, Duke," I called after my trusty sidekick.

There was just something about going to see someone early in the morning. It always felt like an intrusion. Was I waking them up? Catching them at a bad time? Were they going to work? Still in their pjs?"

As the sheriff, I had to put those feelings and silly notions aside and rely on intuition when I got there. I'd have Duke and my other trusty sidekick, my pistol.

The Libertys lived on the outskirts of the south side of town. I had to take interstate sixty-eight and take a left on Keene Road. Not that Keene was a bad area to live in, it was just a small community that stuck together. They were a tight-knit group of neighbors. The houses needed a lot of work, but they didn't care. Most days you'd drive through Keene and everyone would be outside talking to the neighbors.

The Libertys' home was a small brick home with a poured concrete front porch slab. The Christmas lights hung around the door were barren and missing a couple of twinkles every couple of bulbs. The doorbell hung out from the brick and barely hung on by the wires that attached it. I knocked a few times since getting electrocuted wasn't on my Christmas list.

"What you want?" Juanita Liberty stood at the door. Her massive head of black hair was piled up on the top of her head and falling down on the sides. There were bags underneath her eyes.

"Sheriff," Manual pushed past his Mama and out the front door. Beka Durst, Angela's daughter was standing in the background with Juanita's other son, Jonathan. Manuel tugged on his Cottonwood high school sweat shirt. "Did you go look for Leighann?"

"Leighann?" Juanita's nose turned up like she smelled a fart. "What's she done now? Not that getting you to quit football and stay in this godforsaken town your whole life after I uprooted our family to give you a better life was enough."

"Leighann Graves?" Beka asked with a concerned look. "Is she okay?"

"Who cares?" Juanita said over her shoulder.

"Don't mind her." Manual pulled the door shut behind him with Juanita still fussing about how much she disliked Leighann to Beka and Jonathon.

This was the exact reason I didn't want to come here this morning, but I was elected to do a job.

"I'm guessing you haven't seen her?" I asked. By the looks of him, he'd been up all night.

"No. And it's unlike her when we have a fight for her not to come running back or at least give me more of a piece of her mind until we make up." He blinked his big brown eyes. His lips turned down. "I love her, sheriff, I do."

"I'm not sure what your fight was about last night, but publicly fighting or fighting at all wasn't the brightest idea." It was my opportunity to mother him a smidgen since it appeared his mother hadn't. "What was the fight about?" I asked.

"Just stuff. Mean girl stuff." He shrugged.

"Your Mama really doesn't like Leighann?" I asked and nodded towards the only front window where Juanita was watching us and yammering on a mile a minute about what I could guess was still Leighann.

"She's mad that I've decided to stay here in Cottonwood and not go play college football, but that's not Leighann's fault. Leighann told me to go. Encouraged me. But I just don't want to. Even her parents have finally gotten to the point where they can tolerate me." He gave a weak smile. "Now this," he swallowed hard and choked back the lump that seemed to have gotten in his throat.

"Do you have any idea where she might've gone?" I gave suggestions only to get head shakes. "Friends? Old flame? Family member?"

"None of those that I know of. I went through her phone before I gave it to her parents to see if she got any calls, but she didn't. No messages. Me and her are inseparable." He let out a long sigh.

"What about Chimney Rock?" I asked, wondering if she were sitting down there right now with her heat on, Christmas tunes cranked and just waiting them out for a few hours.

"No. We always made plans to go down there, but not during the winter and certainly not with this big blizzard coming." His words made me glare at him.

There's not going to be a blizzard, were the words that formed a bitter taste in my mouth, but instead of saying them out loud, I said, "Sean did say that she'd stopped going on tow runs with you." Not that I suspected he knew where she was, but it would give an indication if she was mad and staying away for a little. "And it's not unlike her to not to come home."

"When she didn't come home, she was with me." He was getting fidgety. "We'd tell them if she wasn't coming home so they wouldn't worry, even though we didn't have to anymore since she is an adult."

"There wasn't a place that the two of you went that you're not remembering?" I asked.

"No. No. No." He looked down and shuffled his feet. "As for work, just recently she started to say that it wasn't good for us to work together all the time. I didn't know what that meant. She said something about how she didn't want us to be like her parents. I didn't know what that meant either. I figured her parents got in a fight and her mom said something about putting up with Sean all her life, like she always throws that in his face and Leighann would open up when she was ready to." He paused, "Maybe she's getting sick of me," his voice cracked.

"If you remember anything or any place she might've gone, please call me. Or stop by the station." I suggested.

He clearly needed someone to lean on, but I wasn't a therapist. I barely got my own relationship going a year or so ago, no way could I help out anyone else.

"You better be careful out there, Sheriff," he said. "The news just said that storm of the century is headed right towards us."

"I'll be fine," I smiled but silently cursed the weather person, "I can guarantee that storm will shift right before it's due to hit and we won't see nary a flake."

"Huh." Manuel scratched his head. "You're the authority, I guess you should know."

"Let me know if you hear from Leighann." I tugged the Wagoneer door open a little harder than normal. The last time I had to do that was when my Poppa had come to get me during that snow storm Lulu had mentioned earlier.

Poppa told me to tug because the chill lingering in the air made the old

Wagoneer door stick a little. He also told me that's how he knew the storm was coming.

"Good boy," I ran my hand down Duke because he stayed on his side of the Jeep when I got in and didn't try to jump out.

I looked up to the sky. My jaw tensed.

"Okay," I said my prayer out loud, "Poppa, if you can hear me, right now is the time." Most times, I'd summon him when I was trying to solve a murder and he'd conveniently disappear. This time I needed that storm to shift. "Blow on that storm. Don't let that storm hit here."

Duke leaned over and gave me a big lick across my cheek, bringing me back to my senses.

"You're right." I laughed. "I'm acting nuts. There's not a storm coming," I assured myself.

If only I believed myself.

CHAPTER FOUR

"Something smells good today." I stepped into Cowboy's Catfish after parking the Wagoneer in front of the restaurant on Main Street. "I could smell it as soon as I got out of my car." I patted my stomach.

"Mornin' Sheriff," Bartleby Fry, owner of Cowboy's Catfish, was busy wiping off one of the tables next to the door. "That'll be the special this mornin'. Kentucky round steak and scrambled eggs." He threw the damp cloth over his shoulder and reached down to pat Duke. "I've got you something special."

"Just a nibble," I warned Bartleby. "We are both getting fat with all this cooking." I patted my stomach and teased on my way back to the department. Though I do love me some Kentucky round steak and eggs, which was just a fancy name for fried bologna. "You send Duke back to the department when he starts to get on your nerves."

The back room in Cowboy's Catfish restaurant was where the Cottonwood Sheriff's department was located. To some that might be strange, but not for a small town in Kentucky. After all, we had a movie theatre in Luke Jones's basement along with the town hall meetings. Our entire town seemed weird, but it was quaint to us.

"Good morning," I chirped when I walked into the office with my cup of coffee in one hand and my bag in the other.

There was a man lounging in Finn's chair. He looked super comfortable all leaned back with his hands folded together across his belly.

"Hi there," I greeted him personally.

"Sheriff Kenni Lowry, State Reserve Office Scott Lee." Betty Murphy tugged one of her pink curlers out of her hair.

"Sheriff?" Scott looked funny at me. It was the whole girl sheriff thing that threw men off.

"Nice to meet you Officer Lee. We are grateful you're here." I shook his hand. "I'm really excited to get some much-needed time off."

"I'm happy to be here." He pulled off his big round State Reserve hat that looked a little like the Boris Badenov, in Rocky and Bullwinkle. "I'm ready to serve the people of Cottonwood, which I hear is about to be under a few feet of snow."

"Shhhh," Betty looked at him and slowly shook her head. "Don't mention snow in front of her," Betty warned him.

"Right!" I snapped my fingers at Betty. "You know why? There's not going to be any snow." I assured him. "If there was any chance of that, then I wouldn't need you because I'd be snowed in from my trip and that's not going to happen." I looked at Betty. Her lips were tucked in between her teeth. "Right, Betty?"

"Right, Sheriff." She smiled and nodded. The remaining curlers flipped and flopped with each nod.

"What did you find out about Leighann Graves?" Betty asked.

"I found out that she didn't come home, and Juanita Liberty hates her as much as the Graves hate her boy." I sat my bag on my desk and took a long drink of coffee before I walked over to the closet next to our only cell in the room. "What size are you, Scott?"

"Medium shirt, size thirty-one thirty-two pants," he said and walked over to me.

"I'm sure she's mad. We can put an APB out on her car. I got her license plate number written down on my notepad." I handed Scott his Cottonwood Sheriff's uniform to use while he was there. "I know it's not as flattering as your reserve blues, but brown is all we got and stands for a lot around here."

"No problem." He looked around. "The restroom to change?"

"Right on through the door." I gestured towards the restaurant. "We use the same bathroom as the restaurant."

There was a perplexed look on his face. He didn't say a word.

"Give me the juice on Leighann Graves," Betty begged and jumped right on in after the door shut behind Scott. "Don't leave a single thing out."

She rested the back end of her house dress on the edge of her desk. Heaven help us if Betty Murphy ever came to the office in the sheriff uniforms we've given her.

"There's nothing more than I told you. The people that Leighann hangs around haven't heard from her. I did get her cell phone and I'm going to sit down here and go through it. In the meantime," I unzipped my bag and took out my notebook. "Take this license number and run it. Put out an APB. See if she's been stopped by any neighboring towns and go ahead and put out a statewide Amber alert on her. Call the hospitals. You know the drill." I scribbled the number down.

"You do think she's missing?" Betty took the sticky note from me.

"Why do you think that?" I asked.

"This is against your twenty-four-hour rule." She stared at me from over top of her glasses.

"I just want to make sure everything is nice and tidy before I head out of town next week. That means Leighann Graves at home in her bed when Santa comes to town," I assured her.

Not that Leighann was a child. She was eighteen and she could do whatever darn well she pleased, but this wasn't normal circumstances. I was going to Chicago. A rare occasion for a sheriff in a department of three employees to take off and I'd been planning it for months. A snippy, mad teenager in love wasn't going to ruin my plans.

"Sheriff's department." I grabbed the phone before Betty could because I wanted her to get that alert out. "This is the sheriff," I assured the person on the other end of the line.

"Kenni, it's Doolittle Bowman. I was pulling my boat out of the river because you know that big storm is about to hit and it's not good for a boat to be in frozen water and under snow," she said.

Doolittle Bowman was head of the town council.

If there was a complaint in town or a business mishap, people called and filed those complaints with Doolittle. She also led the town meetings in Luke's basement. She took pride in banging her gavel.

"What is it that you called about, Doolittle?" I asked, trying to figure out what she wanted.

"I was pulling out my boat and saw what looks like one of them Toyota four-doors sticking ass-end out of the water. I think that's strange." She wasn't one to worry about how she said things or even offended people.

"That is odd." I grabbed a pen and the sticky note. "Where was this?" I asked.

"Down at the Chimney Rock boat dock right where you put in and pull out." She referred to the public boat ramp that local boaters used to put their boats in the Kentucky River, which bordered Cottonwood.

"I'm on my way." I hung up the phone. "What did I write down about Leighann's make and model of the car?" I held my breath hoping it wasn't Leighann's car.

"Nissan or something." After those words left her mouth, my heart went back to beating since Doolittle said it was a Toyota. "Who was that?"

"It was Doolittle. She said that there's a car submerged in the river." I grabbed my cell phone. "Do you mind giving Scott a tour of the place?"

"What's there to tour?" She pointed. "That's your desk." She patted her desk. "This is mine." She pointed again. "That over there is Finn's desk."

"You know what I mean." I glared at her. "All the papers he'll need if he gets called out and how to work the fax. The schedule we keep. Like check the messages in the morning. Call to see if there were any dispatches overnight."

Since it was a two man...errr...one man, one woman's office, and Betty on dispatch during the day, we didn't have a night dispatch. Unless you counted all the residents calling my cell phone, we used Clay's Ferry, the neighboring town's, dispatch service.

CLAY'S FERRY was a little bigger than Cottonwood, so they had a much larger department. We traded off favors every once in a while, and I offered my services where I could. It was the neighborly thing to do.

"Take care of Duke for me," I called out on my way back through the restaurant where Duke was still sitting patiently next to Bartleby while he cooked over the hot grill.

Once I got into the Jeep and headed east of town on Sulphur Well Road towards the river, I grabbed my cell and told my phone to call Sean Graves. I was going to need a tow truck and maybe some work would be something he needed to get out of his house.

"Did you find her?" Sean answered the phone without even saying hello.

"I was hoping I'd call and she was home." I was having an inner struggle on whether to ask him to come or get the tow company from Clay's Ferry to meet me there. I pulled to a stop at the four-way stop sign where I needed to take a right on the curvy country road leading me straight to the boat dock. Cell service was spotty.

"No. Not a word." His voice faded off. "I'm trying to work, but I just can't concentrate. Did you talk to Manuel?"

"Yes. He hasn't seen her nor has his family," I said. "I've got a job if you're up to it. Might be good for you to get out of the house."

I would let him to decide. When he gave me the go-ahead, I proceeded and told him to meet me at Chimney Rock put in. He said he was on his way and it'd be a much-needed distraction for him.

"Chimney Rock?" He questioned with a nervous tone. "Do you think?"

"Doolittle didn't describe Leighann's car," I said and tried to give him some peace of mind. "I just thought maybe I'd call you and get you out of the house."

"I forgot how cold these winter storms make these doors stick." My Poppa's ghost sat in the passenger seat, vigorously rubbing his hands together.

I slammed the breaks of the Wagoneer, bringing it to a screeching halt.

CHAPTER FIVE

"I'm guessing you aren't here to tell me that you've taken care of my little request about the storm of the century?" I asked and tried to hide my fear I was feeling inside my gut.

Seeing Poppa's ghost was no big deal, I'd gotten used to it. The reason I was nervous about seeing his ghost was the fear. The only time the ghost of my Poppa came to see me was when there was a murder in Cottonwood. Something I'd come to realize after the first murder that'd happened in Cottonwood during my second year of my elected four-year term.

Long story short, my Poppa and I figured out that he was my ghost deputy during a major crime. All the years before, his ghost was running around scaring off any would-be criminals which made Cottonwood crime free under my watch, until there just so happened to be two crimes going on at once. Ghost or not, he couldn't be in two places at once. Here he was.

"Nope. Not here for the weather." Slowly he shook his head. "Trust me when I'm going to tell you that it got on my nerves listening to you beg me to change Mother Nature's mind. She's just like any other woman. When her mind is set, it's set."

His words or presences didn't bring me any comfort at this particular time.

I gulped. I shook my hands in the air to keep them from tremoring before I grabbed the steering wheel. I wasn't sure how long I was there, but I know it was long enough for Sean Graves to pull up to the four-way stop, beep, and startle me.

I glanced in the rear-view and saw his face, then I slid my gaze over to Poppa. His chin drew an imaginary line up and then down. I closed my eyes, took a deep breath and reminded myself that I had a job to do and remain calm.

I jumped when there was a knock on my driver's side window.

"You okay? Do I need to tow you?" Sean tried to joke, though I knew his heart was worried, and soon to be broken.

I manually rolled the window down.

"Actually," I was taken off guard with the sudden puffs of air smoke coming from my mouth as the air mingled with my words. "I don't need you after all. False alarm. No car."

No way was I going to take the chance that the car was Leighann's and Doolittle didn't know what she was talking about. Who didn't know the Toyota symbol verses a Nissan?

Sean looked at me. His jaw tensed. It was as if he could read my mind. He stormed back to his tow truck. I jumped out of the Jeep and put my hands out in front of me as he barreled the big truck around my Jeep and towards me.

"Sean. Don't go. Sean. Do not go." I begged him as he went around me, not giving two-cents if he was going to hit me.

When I realized he wasn't going to stop, I jumped back into the Wagoneer.

"Damn, damn, damn." I reached under the seat and pulled out the old red police beacon. I licked the suction cup and stuck my hand out the window, sticking the siren on top of the roof. My finger glided over the switch and turned on the siren.

The red siren circled in the air, giving its shadow to the empty-leaved trees that lined the old road. I passed the tow truck once I'd caught up with him. There was no way I was going to let him get there before me.

"Tell me," I urged my Poppa. "Tell me what's going on."

"I think you already know why I'm here. I done told you it wasn't about the weather." He wasn't one to mix words when it came to official sheriff business. When I glanced over at him as I drove on the straightaway before I took the sharp curve, his eyes were dark, struck with fear. "I hate to see the demise of any young person."

My eyes filled with tears as I tried to focus back on the road. I reached up to my walkie-talkie and pushed in the button.

"Betty, can you send Deputy Lee to Chimney Rock." I knew I couldn't send for Finn. At least not until his volunteer shift at Dixon's Foodtown was over. There wasn't nothing wrong with throwing Scott right on into the frying pan.

"Sure. Is everything alright?" she asked back.

"I don't think so. I think we've found Leighann Graves's car," I said. The words left a chilly trail up my spine.

I knew it wasn't just the car that was found since Poppa was here, but I couldn't let the cat out of the bag until the facts were presented.

See, only me, Duke and Poppa knew about Poppa. Not even Finn. Though it was getting harder and harder to hide how it was that I knew clues before those clues were even discovered. That didn't matter now. What mattered now was figuring out who did this to Leighann Graves.

"Oh Gawd, Kenni," Betty's voice quivered. "Do you think she's...um..."

"I don't know if she's in there or not." That wasn't a lie. The fact was that Poppa was here which meant Leighann had been murdered. The bigger question was where was her body? "I'll let you know as soon as we get the car pulled out of the water."

"You don't sound so confident." Betty couldn't have been more correct.

"I called Sean Graves to come pull the car out before I realized who the car belonged to," my voice trailed off when I saw Doolittle Bowman in the distance next to her big Dually truck and her boat hitched up to the back. "I'll call you back. Send Max," I reiterated before I got off the phone.

"Well," Poppa rubbed his hands together, "Let's get to it."

Poppa loved a good crime to solve. He was the reason I went into the academy. I'd spent many days and nights in this same Wagoneer riding around with him on calls. Murders were rare in Cottonwood, so it was mainly neighborly disputes over religion or opinions. Poppa would tell these people the same thing, "opinions are like assholes. Everybody has one. Just respect each other."

I wish it was as easy as that nowadays.

"Doolittle," I greeted her when I got out of the car.

"Sheriff," She pushed her glasses back up on the bridge of her nose. The knit stocking cap was tugged over her short hair. "Right on over there."

Without me having to even look, I knew Sean had pulled up when I heard a door slam followed up by stomping footsteps.

The gravel from the boat ramp spit up under my brown sheriff shoes with each hurried step. On each side of the ramp was a wooded area with tall trees that were barren of their leaves. The Kentucky Bluegrass had long gone into hibernation and would soon flourish in the spring as the limestone underneath warmed the earth's surface.

I walked into the wooded area to get down to the river bank a little more. By the looks of the river banks, it appeared the small SUV had drifted to the right once it went into the river and dragged down the banks. It also looked as though it went top heavy as it dragged along the shoreline, getting the nose stuck in the mud underneath the water. The only thing visible was the back window and tail lights and the fact it was red. The license plate was the exact match to Leighann's that Jilly and Sean had given me earlier.

"Oh my god, my baby!" Sean screamed and ran past me, confirming my worst fears. It was definitely Leighann's car.

"Sean!" I screamed at the top of my lungs before he could do anything stupid. I grabbed his arm and dug my nails into it. "Don't!"

"Get my baby out of there," he seethed through his gritted teeth. His finger jutted towards the river.

Out of the corner of my eye, I saw Poppa walk down into the water and disappear.

"We don't know she's in there. It could just be her car," I said in a steady voice. I tried to talk to him calmly so he'd settle down a little bit, though I knew it was probably hoping for too much. "If there's some evidence in the car or on the car and you jump in, I won't be able to use it to help find her."

"You think there's hope?" His eyes burned with tears.

"I think you need to let me do my job." I let go of him when I felt like he was a little more together. "Now, if you don't think you can pull..." I stopped and had to keep my composure when Poppa came out of the water. His face said it all. "Listen," I tried to turn Sean around so he'd stop staring at the backend of the car. "I'm going to call S&S Auto from Clay's Ferry."

"Why would you do that when I'm right here and can get it out?" He got unglued and started to pace back and forth.

"Because of this." I pointed out his behavior. "You are rightfully so upset. I need this to be pulled out with no emotions attached to it whatsoever. That means you need to let me do my job and what I think is best. And." I gave him a firm look and took a deep breath. "And, if she is in there, I can't have the scene tainted until it's processed."

About that time, Scott pulled up in his car and got out.

"Who the hell is that?" Sean asked with disgust.

"This is Officer Lee, Scott Lee. He's with the state reserve and will be here during Christmas." I knew Sean wasn't comprehending anything I was saying, but I had to go through the motions. "He's going to talk to you while I make that call to S&S."

Sean nodded and sat down on the cold earth.

"Why don't you come sit in my car," Scott suggested to Sean. "I've got a nice hot cup of coffee from Cowboy's Catfish you can sip on to keep you warm until we get this all straightened out."

"I'll be a yellow-bellied-sap-sucker," Poppa eyeballed Scott and repeated one of his favorite phrases that meant he was in shock. "This here feller is a perfect fit for your department. He knows how to talk to everyone."

I ignored Poppa until I took a few steps towards the car and away from the other people so I could ask him some questions.

"What did you see in the car?" I asked under my breath.

"She's in there. Or someone is in there. Long hair floating around the face." The edges of Poppa's lips turned down. "I'm figuring it's the Graves girl."

I gulped. The stinging pain of tears crept up in the back of my nose and rested in my tear ducts as I tried to keep them from coming out.

"Kenni!" I jerked around when I heard Finn's voice. He hurried towards me. Poppa disappeared. "Why didn't you call me? I had to find out from Toots Buford at Dixon's when she came in for her shift. She asked me what happened because she heard it on police scanner."

"That's exactly how they all found out." I gestured to all the cars that were showing up and parking along the outskirts of the Chimney Rock boat dock.

"Doesn't take long around here." Finn's brows rose when he looked over at Scott and Sean. "Is it the Graves's girl car?"

"Afraid so." I put my finger up and clicked the walkie-talkie.

"Go ahead, Sheriff," Betty's voice rang out in the quiet and echoed off the cliffs that surrounded the river. I rolled the volume down.

"Betty, can you call S&S Auto in Clay's Ferry to come here?" It wasn't necessarily a question, but she agreed and clicked off. "I had no clue it was her when I asked Sean to come pull it out. I figured it would be good for him to work and get Leighann off his mind."

"Let's hope she's not in there." Finn looked at me through some very optimistic eyes. "What? You look funny. You think she's in there, don't you?"

"It doesn't look good. That's all," I stated. "No one has seen her. She's not tried to get to her phone."

Over the next twenty minutes as we waited on the tow company to get there, more and more citizens showed up. Most of them were out of their cars and had gathered at the top of the ramp. Sean had gotten out of the car and joined them. I left it up to him to give them any updates he found necessary.

Finn and I both got out the police tape and began to mark off the property where we felt was enough to preserve any sort of evidence. I made sure it was far away from the view of the car because I didn't want the public to see us tow it out.

We still needed to scour the ground. I was praying for us to find something, but I didn't know what. I'd gotten the camera out of my bag and took photos of the ramp, though Doolittle Bowman's pull out had brought a lot of the lake water with it, washing away any evidence left from Leighann's car.

The wind had picked up and I zipped up my coat.

"Looks like it's moving in." Poppa bounced on his toes and looked up to the sky. "Wee-doggie it's gonna be a good one."

"Do you see something?" Finn asked.

In a normal relationship, I'd been thrilled my boyfriend was watching my every move, but with my Poppa's ghost here, I had to be more diligent of my reaction to him.

"Nothing." I stuck my hands in my pockets. "It's getting windy." I glared at Poppa, giving him the unspoken gesture to skit out of here. "I'm not sure if it's the cold chill sending shivers up my legs or what we might find in that car."

"Sheriff, do you have a statement for the Cottonwood Chronicle?" Edna Easterly asked with her handheld tape recorder held over the police tape.

The brown fedora was perched on top of her head. The feather waving in the gust of wind. The index card that had REPORTER written in Sharpie was barely dangling on the hat. She had on her fishing vest with all the pockets over top of her winter coat. She filled the pockets with all her reporter stuff.

"People want to know if it's Leighann Graves and if it is, is it foul play?" She yelled out questions. "Is her own dad going to pull out her car? I heard from an unnamed source that she and Manuel Liberty were in a fight last night. Do you think he did something to her? You were seen at the Liberty house this morning, why were you there?"

"Hi, Edna." I could feel the tension starting to build above my brows. I rubbed my forehead on my way over to talk to her. "There's no comment because we know nothing. When there is something to tell, I'll give you the information. But for now, you need to move along."

The yellow lights of the tow truck from S&S Auto were seen well before the truck. There was a big wreath on the front of the truck grill and a small light up Christmas tree dangling from the rear-view mirror. The sharp reality that life and holidays still continued even in the depth of pain and sorrow hit my gut and I suddenly felt sick just thinking about what was going to take place in a few short minutes after the SUV was pulled from the river. Finn helped direct the driver after he'd talked to him about where the car was.

Edna Easterly didn't give two hoots about space or even what I'd said. She was snapping photos and asking the tow-truck driver all sorts of questions. Finn backed Edna away.

The big burly man with a curly mullet that I'd dealt with before got out of the tow truck after he drove down to where I was waiting for him. He wore a pair of blue mechanic overalls that were exactly what I'd seen him in before.

"Sheriff," He eyed me, not making the same mistake he'd done when he met me a year ago by brushing me off since I was a girl. "Looks like we got us an SUV to pull out."

"It appears that way." I wasn't one for small talk. I just wanted to get the car out of the river and get on with this investigation of the homicide.

"He's so country he thinks a seven-course meal is a possum and a six-pack." Poppa joked about the truck driver but I didn't laugh like I normally would. All eyes were on me and my every single move, facial movement and breath. "Kenni-Bug," Poppa noticed my solemn attitude. "Honey, this is going to be hard, but it's part of your job. You've got to spit-shine that star these citizens voted you in to wear and get a stiff upper lip. They need your strength. The strength you innately have in you."

I gulped, holding back the tears, and rubbed my finger over my five-point star. I drew on my inner guidance to get the energy and courage I needed when I heard the tow truck start to rev up to get a little closer to the edge of the water. I made sure my face was stern as I watched the man pull on a pair of waders and boots. He got into the water with big chains over his shoulder. He hooked them up to the hitch of Leighann's car.

When he got out, he took off the waders and boots and flipped the switch on the truck. The buzz of the chains clinking together made my heart beat faster and faster as they jerked up the end of Leighann's car up and out of the water. The water-logged SUV was dragged up to the ramp, spewing out water.

Sean Graves took a few steps forward, only to be greeted by the stiff arm of Scott. I couldn't help but notice Finn's face when Scott did something that normally Finn would do. There was a sense that Finn was glad he wasn't the one trying to stop Sean Graves.

"Let's take a look inside," I whispered to Finn and took the first step forward with him following behind me.

There was mud so thick that it covered the hood and the doors. I slipped on a pair of gloves and so did Finn. It was crucial to preserve anything we could. Though Finn didn't realize how crucial.

I ran my finger down along the creases of the driver's side door before I opened it.

"Empty." My brows furrowed.

"Thank, God," Finn's breath he'd been holding let out a long audible sigh.

The windows of the SUV were also covered in mud and though the sun had come out, it was still dark in the SUV. I unsnapped the flashlight from my holster and shined in the back. My heart fell to my feet when I saw Leighann in the very back. It was her beautiful red hair with the shimmery flecks of the silver tinsel that I'd noticed in her hair at the dance that told me it was her.

I pulled out of the SUV and handed Finn my flashlight.

"What is it, Kenni?" I heard Sean scream out my name from behind me. "Is she in there? God don't tell me she's in there!"

There was something about facing a father to tell him that his daughter was dead that didn't make me like my job.

When I turned around to look at him, it only took a split-second eye contact to take the man to his knees.

CHAPTER SIX

"Do you promise you're going to find out what happened? How am I going to tell Jilly?" Sean ran his hands through his hair and wiped them over his mouth. Sean Graves begged and pleaded with me, "Promise me, Sheriff."

"I promise I'm going to try and figure out what happened." I knew it was going to be hard and any crime was a lot like a puzzle. There were pieces that fit here and there, it was trying to figure out where those pieces went that took the longest.

"I can't understand it. She was such a good driver." His nostrils rose and fell with each hard breath he took. "How am I going to tell Jilly?" His face crunched together, his lips rolled underneath his teeth, his jaw set and tears welled up in his eyes. He dragged the sleeve of his jacket across his eyes, blinking several times to keep the tears at bay.

It took about thirty minutes for Finn and Scott to clear the scene of the residents that'd come down to see what was going on. It took a whole lot longer to get Sean Graves to let Scott take him home. Took me even longer to gather my wits about me. Leighann Graves was the youngest homicide I'd ever had and I wanted to scream from the top of my lungs. Who on earth ended this young life too soon? Only, I knew I couldn't. I couldn't even tell my deputy that she was murdered.

We didn't touch the body until Max Bogus, the owner of the only funeral home in Cottonwood and our town's coroner, got there. There were steps that needed to be taken and I was going to make sure this one was by the books.

"How do you know some of these things?" Finn asked with a perplexed look.

"What things?" I asked back and tried not to get lost into his big brown eyes.

"You really thought she was in there, like you knew. You sure you're not one of them voodoo women?" He joked while we waited for Max to get Leighann's body on the church cart.

Max wore his typical khakis with a button-down shirt. This time he had on a V-neck sweater, probably due to the cold weather, and a heavy coat. His black rimmed glasses fogged with each breath he took.

"I guess it was just all the lack of contact Leighann had given over the past few hours." Lines creased in my forehead as my brows dipped. "It was like her to run off from her parents' house, but not like her to disappear completely."

I hated myself for lying to him. But I wasn't sure how he'd take it if I said that my Poppa, the ghost, told me. That's just something I wasn't sure even how to go about telling him. Nor did I want him to think I was nuts and dump me. Just not on my Christmas list this year.

Max motioned for us to come over. His round face was tense.

"Well?" I asked wondering what he saw.

"Nothing that's really apparent. I'm going to take her to the morgue to run some quick tests like drugs and alcohol to see if she was drunk driving or high, but on the outside, she's in perfect condition." He pinched his lips together.

"You don't think it's a homicide?" Finn asked.

"It's strange that she was in the back. Though she could've floated back there if she didn't have her seatbelt on, I'm guessing. But how did her keys get in her pocket?" He used the end of his pen to pick up a set of keys that were resting next to her hand on the gurney. "I checked the ignition and there were no keys in it. Plus, the SUV is in park."

I looked down at the ground so they couldn't see the relief on my face.

The keys in her pocket and car in park was just more evidence it was a homicide and the less I had to prove what I'd been calling my hunch...which was Poppa.

"We are going to be busy this Christmas." Poppa did a jig. "Selfishly, I was afraid I wouldn't get to wish you a Merry Christmas, but now I can sing to you!" He was giddy with delight. "Oh, you better watch out." Poppa's mouth formed a dramatic "O." "You better not cry."

I walked a few steps to get away from him. I knew he was sad about Leighann. There just comes a time after you see so many homicides that you have initial emotions, then you realize it's part of the job and it's like your heart gets hard. Or maybe it was the way your body and mind coped with the idea of death. Poppa had told me many times that I'd get used to seeing dead bodies, and the feelings would change over time.

Right now, Poppa wasn't being insensitive, he was just living what he'd always told me. He loved Christmas and he always made sure it was special for me, his only grandchild. Right now wasn't the time to discuss it, though I was happy to see him too. Not under these circumstances. Unfortunately, these were the only circumstances under which we were able to see each other.

"That is odd." Finn shook his head and ran his hand down his head, resting it on the back of his neck. It appeared to him now that some foul play had happened. "And it looks like the right rear panel of the car is gone."

"By goodness," I gasped, "You're right."

We spent the next hour or so combing the area for that panel or anyplace that appeared the car had hit for the panel to be knocked off. We used the chains from the tow truck to drag the area where he'd pulled the car from the water, but there wasn't anything in there.

"This is really strange," I said to my Poppa when I got into the Wagoneer and he was sitting in the passenger seat. I drove up and down the road very slow, scouring each side of the road to see if there was any sort of object she could've hit or even if the panel was on the side of the road somewhere. Anything that looked like it could've been hit with the car. "What are you thinking?"

"I was thinking that she was coming down the road and maybe a deer or something crossed in front of her car. She slammed on the breaks, sending her into a tailspin." Poppa retold stories I'd heard all over Cottonwood as a kid where someone's car got destroyed by a deer.

"That could be a possibility if her keys weren't in her pocket and not in the ignition." When I checked out the back of the car, it wasn't wet, and it was too cold out for the back to have dried that quickly. "And how does that explain how the car got in park and in the river?"

The thought of it made chills crawl up my spine and down my arm, forcing me to grip the wheel as I turned back towards the boat dock where Finn continued to look into the woods for anything.

"That's how we know it was a homicide. And we both know that foul play is here." He gestured between us. "This means that me and you need to play our little game."

The little game he was referring to was the back and forth we loved to do when I was a little girl and now that I was sheriff. In fact, every time he did ghost himself, we'd play the game and it helped get more clues for me to look into.

I got out of the Jeep and slammed the door.

"You're right. I've got to go see the Graves again. Not to mention Manuel and his mother." I sighed.

"I hope you're going to take a look at Juanita Liberty since she wasn't fond of the girl," Poppa said with a troubled face.

"She sure didn't make any bones about it," I added. "Not that she was going to admit that she killed Leighann."

There was a history between the Graves's and the Liberty's where neither family were happy with their child dating the other. Both claimed they wanted better for their children. Many times over the past year when Leighann was underage, I was called out to the Graves's house or the Liberty house due to Sean Graves's claiming Manuel had been trespassing or they were fighting.

"When I've been to the Liberty house to talk to Manuel and Juanita was there, she made it clear that she was just as unhappy as Sean Graves with the two dating." I gnawed on the inside of my cheek and turned the Wagoneer around to head back to the crime scene. "She certainly didn't say she wanted the girl dead."

"She didn't say she didn't. She just made it apparent she didn't like her."

Poppa frowned. "Not that Viv would kill anyone, but she's not happy with Finn for taking you away in a few days. Juanita is a Mama bear like Viv."

"She did say that she wanted better for Manuel than working at a tow company. He did have a future in a football career." I signed. "If Juanita got rid of Leighann, maybe Manuel would rethink his future."

"And gives her a motive to kill Leighann." Poppa's words made me get a queasy stomach.

"I'll have Finn bring her into the department. I don't want to question her at home," I said and watched Finn walking towards my Jeep as we pulled back into Chimney Rock. "She's a single mom with those other two young boys."

Manuel had two younger brothers. One was in high school and the other was much younger and I wanted to say he was in elementary school.

"Who are you talking to?" Finn glanced around the inside of my Jeep.

"I wasn't talking." I tried to play it off.

"There was condensation coming from your mouth as you spoke." His face grew serious, his jaw tensed.

"I guess I was just going over things in my head and didn't realize I was saying it out loud." I smiled to hide the crazy I was feeling by trying to keep him and Poppa's conversations separate.

"You're going to have to tell him sooner or later. I'd prefer sooner so he'll high-tail it out of here and leave you alone. You can't be a good sheriff and be all goo-goo-eyed over this northern." Poppa snarled, putting up his dukes like he was going to pop Finn in the nose. "Taking you away from your Mama during Christmas. What was he thinking?" Poppa spit. "He wasn't thinking, that's what happened. He wasn't thinking of you and your family like he should be if his intentions are true."

"I don't have time for this," I muttered under my breath.

"Time for what?" Finn's head jerked up.

"This...murder." I stomped to cover my slip up. I cozied up to Finn and gave him a kiss on the cheek. "We are getting ready to go to visit your family. Which I can't wait for." I gave him an extra little squeeze when I wrapped my arms around him. "The last thing we need is an investigation hanging over our head during Christmas."

"Then it means that we're going to be stuck side by side for the next few days to get it solved." He smiled, those perfect teeth appeared and sent my heart into fluttering overdrive.

Those were teeth you didn't get around here from the dentist. It was one of Finn's best qualities besides his perfect parted short brown hair.

"Not on my dime you won't, buck-o!" Poppa yelled in Finn's ear.

Finn blinked his eyes and pulled his finger up to his ear, the one Poppa yelled in, and gave it a vigorous shake.

"Dang." He jerked. "There's a loud ringing in my ear."

"I'm sure it'll go away soon." I gave Poppa the stink eye. "Probably stress," I said to Finn.

"Fine. But when you summon me, I might not come." He ghosted away, but I knew better. There wasn't anything Poppa loved more than a good case. This was the makings of a good one because there were some strange clues that needed to be answered, like where was her back-side panel?

"What are you thinking up there in that noggin?" Finn was catching on to the Southern slang.

"After we get done here, I'm going to have you go get Juanita Liberty and bring her down to the department." I looked up and caught an unexpected look on his face. "Yeah. When I went by there this morning, she didn't have anything nice to say about Leighann. Plus all the history between the two women. With Leighann gone, I think she'll be happy."

"Happy? That's a morbid thing to say." Finn's brows furrowed.

"She wants more for Manuel than Cottonwood." I looked at Scott when he walked up.

"Didn't he have a big future in football?" Scott asked.

"He did and that's what Juanita is upset about. He didn't take the scholarship for college and she's upset about it." I looked up and noticed the clouds were taking on a gray color.

"Don't step on a mama's toes." Finn shrugged.

"A Southern mama's toes at that." Scott nodded. "They will go through hell or high water to see to it that their baby gets their due."

"Mmhmmmm," I ho-hummed in agreement.

Finn's gaze arched slowly back and forth between me and Scott like he was trying to decipher the conversation between us.

"It's Southern talk," I noted. "Finn's from Chicago."

"Oh." Scott's mouth formed an O, his chin lifted up. "We were sayin' that his Mama would do anything to..."

"Yeah. I get it." Finn glowered and turned away.

Scott and I stood there in silence as we watched Finn walk back down to where they'd pulled the SUV out of the water. He used the bottom of his boot to brush on top of the grass and his flashlight to focus on the ground as if he were looking for more clues or evidence.

"What's up with him?" Scott asked.

"He's a very good deputy. Very by the book." I noted and tried not to get the vibe that Finn wasn't too interested in Scott or his help. "If you don't mind, why don't you head back to the department and get the paperwork started for the case. Let's treat it like a homicide until Max tells us otherwise."

"No problem." Scott glanced at Finn before he gave me the nod and headed out.

"What was that about?" I asked Finn when I walked down to talk to him.

"It's weird seeing another person on the team. Not that we couldn't use it right now, but I felt like an outsider." Finn smiled. "Stupid really."

"I'm sorry I made you feel that way. I never intended it." Softly, I touched his arm. "I think it's super cute that you still try to figure out what we're saying."

"I think it's more of my jealousy that you communicate with him in a different language or something." Finn smiled. "That's all."

"I'll communicate with him in any way as long as we can get this murder solved before we leave for Chicago." I turned it around to a positive, so any sort of negative feelings Finn was having wouldn't hurt the momentum of the investigation.

"Where do we start?" Finn rubbed his hands together.

"We need to find that side panel, we need to figure out who Leighann and Manuel were fighting with last night and we need to know what they were fighting about." Everything I was saying was just the basics that'd help put any sort of pieces together.

"You don't think the panel is somewhere in the water?" He asked a really good question.

"I don't because the back of the SUV isn't wet. It appears the front end went in, stuck in the mud and sort of drifted a few feet from the put in. I don't think the side panel fell off when it went into the water. What did it hit to make it fall off?" So many questions were stabbing me.

Solving a murder was like a giant puzzle. It was up to me and the deputies to put those pieces together. Unfortunately, the pieces didn't always fit together in a nice little way and hopefully Leighann's body and a few answered questions were going to get it completed.

"Juanita is your first thought?" Finn asked.

"She'd be the one with the highest priority of motive since Leighann is the one who had the most influence on Manuel and his life. The Graves told me this morning that they'd accepted the relationship," I noted.

"You believe them even after the look on their faces from the dance last night?" Finn folded and crossed his arms across his chest.

"They'd given Leighann a job and Manuel still had his job, so I do believe they've accepted it. Not that it means they still didn't want better for Leighann, but to kill their own daughter?" I questioned. I just couldn't go there at this time. I inhaled deeply, "I don't think they were so mad to kill their own flesh and blood."

"I agree with you, but what happened to no stone unturned?" His features hardened as he threw my own mantra back at me.

"That's why we are going to question everyone. Including the Graves again." My eyebrows dipped in a frown. "While you go get Juanita, I think I'll stop by the Graves's. Check on them and maybe ask a few questions now that it's turned from finding her to finding out what happened to her. I'm sure the entire Auxiliary Women's club is there with food and people stopping by."

When someone died in Cottonwood, the entire town rallied around each other. Immediately, the Auxiliary Women's club would get to work in the kitchen, taking many dishes to the family.

"I'll give you about an hour and continue to just comb the area while you do that. I'll pick up Juanita on my way back." His gaze softened.

After we said our goodbyes, I got into the Wagoneer and headed back to the Graves's house.

Their driveway was already filled with cars from Cottonwood citizens there to give their condolences. This was when it was really great to be from a small town. There might've been a lot of gossip, but whenever there was a tragedy, we put our differences aside and pulled together to help the family and community get through it. Though Leighann was an adult, she was still just a child and there was something wrong about the death of a child before the parents.

Instead of knocking, I just let myself in. The family room was filled. Mayor Chance Ryland and his new bride, Polly, were sitting in chairs that were in front of the couch, talking to Jilly and Sean. No doubt they were telling them that the department, me, was going to do everything in our power to get to the bottom of what happened.

I headed back to the kitchen to find Viola White, Ruby Smith, and Mama logging all the food that was being delivered to the house. They would write down who brought what food and would label the dish they'd brought it in. This whole food repass thing was also sort of a competition between the women on who got the most compliments. I knew it was a messed-up theory, but that's how the pride of these Southern women worked.

"The broccoli salad is from Bev Tisdale." Mama lifted the lid and her nose turned up. "We can just throw that one away. I can smell the store-bought ingredients."

"Sounds good to me." Viola grabbed the tin and tossed it in the black garbage bag in her other hand. "What about what Polly brought?"

Mama lifted the foil off the plate that Polly must've brought as a good gesture.

"Ugh. I can't even make it out." Mama didn't bother putting the tin foil back on it. "Pitch it. What's wrong with people?"

I could spot Mama's famous chicken pot pie from anywhere. And she sure did love to boast about it since it was now on the menu at Ben's Diner and featured on the Culinary Channel. I was proud of her too. But the other women were green with envy.

"Kenni," Mama's voice rose when she saw me. She rushed over with her hands out in front of her. Viola and Ruby rushed over too, their ears on full alert. "Everyone wanted me to call you and ask you what happened, but I knew you'd be busy."

"Tell us." Viola held out a piece of her homemade potato candy that she knew I couldn't resist. It was a Southern classic favorite and her homemade peanut butter was to die for. "Here." She stuck the napkin in my hand.

"There's not much to tell." I took a bite of the candy and was thankful when Myrna Savage came into the kitchen with an armful of flowers.

"Help me," she squealed when she noticed the women were standing there looking at me. "I've got a van full of flowers."

Myrna Savage was the owner of Petal Pushers, the only florist in town.

I grabbed one of the vases out of her hand and stuck it on the window sill next to a prescription bottle of Ambien that belonged to Sean. Poor guy probably had a hard time sleeping, I waved my concern for him away.

"Come on, Viv." Myrna grabbed Mama by the sleeve. "I need your help."

Mama would normally protest but under the circumstances, she bit her lip and hurried out the door beside Viola and Ruby.

"Honey, how are you?" Myrna asked and pulled a piece of baby's breath out of her black hair.

"I'm alright. It's a shame to see a young person come to their demise before they should," I said and glanced over her shoulder at the medication bottle on the kitchen window sill.

"Honey, I wholeheartedly believe that when it's your time, it's your time." She nodded her head and in her own way, I knew she was trying to come to grips with it herself. "Jilly is a strong woman. I'm not so sure that Sean's interior is as tough as his exterior, but he's gonna need a lot of help. I done told Dr. Shively that she's gonna have to give him something." She continued to nod, "if you know what I mean."

"My goodness," Mama fanned her hand in front of her face when she walked into the kitchen with a couple flower arrangements. "I used to love flowers, but now the smell reminds me of a funeral home."

I didn't let the women continue to fuss and argue over where to put the flowers. I took it upon myself to take them from Mama and put them on the window sill right next to the prescription bottle. Upon further inspection of the label, it appeared Sean Graves's prescription was written by Dr. Camille Shively.

I headed back into the family room. The room was filled with low murmurs and everyone seemed to be facing the Graves, who were sitting on the couch with Mayor Ryland and Polly next to them. In the chairs next to fireplace was Angela Durst, the secretary for Graves's Towing. Her daughter, Beka, was in the chair next to her. Both of them looked up at me with turned down mouths. Angela blinked a couple of knowing blinks. There were a few Baptist nods from other people who were there to give their condolences.

"Mayor, Polly." I greeted them and set any difference the three of us had aside. It wasn't a secret that we butted heads a few times over the course of my terms. "Sean, Jilly, can I talk to you?"

I saw Polly shift in her chair and straighten up as though she were getting herself ready to hear something.

"In private?" I asked.

"Of course." Jilly jumped up and tugged on Sean's shirt. "We can go into the office."

The office was in the other side of the old house and I'd been in there a few times. Including the time I'd caught Leighann and Manuel in there being a little more intimate than her parents probably wanted her to be. Actually, not probably, I knew for certain they didn't want Leighann near Manuel.

From the photos of Leighann and Manuel that were framed in the office that weren't there before, it sure looked like those times had changed.

After they shut the office door to give us some privacy, Sean started in with the questions.

"What happened? There had to be foul play." He insisted. Jilly did her best to calm him down, but he kept saying that she'd never take her own life.

"She did say she was going to a few times," Jilly's voice cracked.

Was it possible that Poppa was here during a situation where they did take their own lives? It's something we'd never come across and he certainly wasn't around right now to hear this.

"That's enough, Jilly." Sean's jaw tensed, and he glared at his wife. "Our daughter didn't do this to herself."

"There's not much I can tell you about any preliminary reports from Max," I referred to the coroner, "But I can tell you that her car keys were in her pocket, the shift was in park and there were no visible signs of a homicide."

"You." Jilly jumped up and shook a finger at Sean. Her face was lit on fire.

"You did this to our daughter. She told you that you were the one who'd make her take her life and now she has."

"Jilly, Sean." I had to calm them down. "A death is very hard. I'm sure the death of a child is something that is unfathomable. But right now, I need you two to help me figure out exactly what happened. And being at each other's throats isn't going to get us anywhere."

Jilly sat back down and planted her hands between her knees.

"Kenni is right." Sean did the right thing by going over to his wife, bending down and taking her into his arms.

"We don't know if there's foul play or not. But we do know that it's awfully strange for her to drive off the boat ramp, put her car in park and put her keys in her pocket." I wanted to try and give them some information that would trigger anything. "When we did a little more investigation on the car after it was pulled out, we noticed the right back panel was missing."

By the look on Sean's face, I could tell he didn't know.

"Did Leighann have an accident that day?" I asked.

"No." Sean shook his head. "In fact, she was washing her car because she'd said that she saw on the weather channel a snow storm coming. She put a sealer on it to keep off the snow and the salt that would get on her car while it was bad out."

"Did she act funny? Or talk to anybody that day? Anybody?" I asked.

"Rachel Palmer came by, but she always comes over." Jilly shrugged and wiped her eyes with her hands.

"She did before she went off to college. It's not like they've been great friends since they graduated." Sean corrected his wife.

"Did you hear anything they were saying?" I asked and wrote down Rachel's name. I knew her parents from church. Nice people.

"I watched from the office window out there, but then we got a call about a tow and I went ahead and dispatched it out to Manuel because I really think it's important," Jilly swallowed hard, "was important that Leighann kept in touch with her friends outside of Manuel."

"I see that y'all seem to have accepted Manuel and Leighann's relationship." I picked up one of the frames off the credenza.

"This was where Leighann worked on paperwork and we let her make it her own." Jilly's lips turned into a little smile. "She was excited to have her own space. I even took her to the Dollar Shop in Clay's Ferry to get her frames for cheap. The first thing she did was go down to Dixon's Foodtown and use their photo machine where you can hook up your cell phone and get the pictures right off of it."

"It wasn't that we didn't want her to date him. But like Jilly said, we felt like she was losing her friends. She spent so much time with him and she had a scholarship to go to the community college, but she didn't want to do that." There was disappointment on his face. "Maybe if we made her go, we wouldn't be here right now."

"Some kids don't go to college now, Sean." Jilly sucked in a deep breath. The frustration was visible. Her lips tightened. "We told her she didn't have to. Maybe next year. We thought that once she saw how hard it was to have a full-time job, she'd rethink the whole college thing."

"What do you know about Manuel's college?" I asked.

"You know he was such a good football player. It's true. They met here. He's a good worker. But when I saw him and Leighann kissing a couple years ago, I lost it. I made sure he was busy when Leighann was here. I gave her extra money, so she didn't have to come to work. I tried so hard to keep them apart," Sean said.

"They were just kids." Jilly tried to soften Sean's words for him. This was something she'd often do in public. "We thought it would end."

"We thought wrong. After a few months of that is when Leighann started acting up and sneaking off. She was saying how much she loved him, and no one was going to keep them apart. I didn't know who he was coming in here and messing up our lives that we had planned out." Sean appeared to be as mad today as he was the first time I'd gotten a call from him about putting the boy in jail.

"I've reminded Sean how many times that we were no different." There Jilly went again making him look better.

"Times were different then, Jillian." That's the first time I'd ever heard him call her by her full name. "Prices were cheaper. We got this from my family. Leighann was throwing her life away on a boy."

Jilly buried her head in her hands. "She'll never know what it's like to hold her own baby. We will never be grandparents," she screamed towards Sean. "I swear if she took her own life...but you said she was in the back."

She looked at her husband. He nodded. "She always wore her seatbelt. There was never a time she didn't. It's me that forgets, and she wouldn't even start the car until everyone had a seatbelt on."

"This doesn't appear to be getting you anywhere," Poppa ghosted himself next to the desk. "What was the relationship between Sean and Leighann like recently?"

"What was your relationship with Leighann over the past six months since she didn't go off to college?" I asked.

"I told her that if she didn't go to college that she was going to pay for her own cell phone, get on the company's payroll, pay her own insurance on that SUV and health." He appeared to have realized how bad that sounded because he looked down.

"And she had to pay rent." Jilly looked up at me. "He told her that she had to pay rent on her own bedroom."

"I was trying to scare her into going to college. It's no different than what the experts tell you to do." He ran his hand through his hair.

"Did she have the money to do those things?" I asked.

"She worked all the time. She'd do dispatch at night, but if it was a call that was an emergency, like a car wreck that needed us, either me or Manuel would come out," Sean said.

"Tell her." Jilly growled. "Tell her how you packed up Leighann's clothes and told her to move in with Manuel until she paid her rent."

"Is that true?" I was beginning to see a side of Sean Graves that I didn't think he wanted me to see. A side that maybe said he and his daughter weren't on the best terms.

"I'm ashamed now, but yes. She and Manuel lived out of the SUV for a while. I guess they were taking spit baths in the employee sink or something because I'd gotten a phone call from Juanita," He referred to Manual's mother, "and she told me that she wasn't letting my daughter live in that house because she ruined her son's life."

"That's when Sean told her that her son ruined our daughter's life and squashed her dreams. It was a mess." Jilly's brows furrowed, the crease between them deepened. "Juanita's other son came over here with a gun and knives strapped to him saying that Sean better not disrespect their Mama again."

I made sure I'd gotten everything they were saying on the notepad. It was enough evidence, if true, to think that one of the Liberty's had done something to Leighann. They were big boys and very protective of family. Though I couldn't rule out Sean. "Did you ever hit your daughter?" I asked. Before he could protest, because he was revving up, I followed up by saying, "I understand how heated things can get as a teen. I've been there with my parents. If you did do something, I understand, but I'm gonna need you to tell me now. Not in a few days from now when I've spent all this time looking for someone who killed her. If you did hurt your daughter, I know you didn't mean to, but..."

"You hold it right there, Sheriff." He pointed his finger at me and took a step forward.

"Whoa, diggity-dog," Poppa ghosted between us. "You move one more step towards my Kenni-Bug and I'll put a haunting on you that would scare them zombies in that tv show."

"Please remove your finger from my face," I said in a stern and steady voice.

He dropped his hand.

"If you think I hurt Leighann in anyway physically, you are wrong. I'll take a lie detector test right here, right now." His eyes didn't move. "I might've disapproved of her boyfriend, but I'd never hurt her."

"Have you ever laid a hand on Leighann?" I asked because he truly didn't answer the question. His dancing around it would suffice some, but not me.

"Sean," Jilly stood back up and placed her hand on her husband's back. "He can get a little upset at times."

His shoulders started to jump up and down. His chin fell to his chest. Her words were ringing true with him.

"At times he could get a little out of control. He can break things and he can yell really loud. He's even back handed me and Leighann a time or two." She rubbed his back vigorously. "But he is a good, hardworking man. He's been a wonderful provider. He makes sure we have everything we want. He puts food on the table and we've never been in debt. I'm confident that he didn't hurt our daughter."

"Your daughter is dead," I reminded her. She might've been making herself and Sean feel good with her excuses of why he was such a jack-donkey, but I just couldn't let it go.

"You nasty sonofa..." Poppa's words strung together. He could never stand for a man hitting a woman.

"This is the time to come clean with anything you need to tell me, because her body will reveal the answers. If her body tells me that someone hurt her, you're the first person I'm going to come after." It wasn't a threat, it was the gods to honest truth. "I saw you and Jilly at the dance last night. I saw the two of you get up and walk out without saying good bye to Leighann and you looked upset."

"I didn't hurt Leighann." His chin drew back up and he locked eyes with me. "Like I said, I'm more than happy to go down to the department and take a lie detector test."

CHAPTER SEVEN

"He's the only hell his Mama raised." Poppa was spittin' mad when we got back into the Jeep. "Sean Graves is a tricky man."

I'd left out the office door and walked around to my Jeep because I was so thrown back by how volatile Sean's relationship was with the women in his life that I just couldn't force myself to make small talk with the town folk there to support him without me saying something about his true character.

"I'm guessing you know something about him?" I asked.

It was kinda good that Poppa was the sheriff before me because he knew the parents and grandparents of people my age.

"You know how he bugs you about Leighann and Manuel? Well, Jilly's parents did the same thing about him. When I was in your shoes, they told me he hit her, but she'd never fess up to it when I'd go to her house and question her." He drummed his fingers along the window sill of the passenger side door. "She had some sort of home economics scholarship to a higher learning school and if I remember correctly, she didn't go because of Sean. Her grandfather didn't go to the wedding. It was small. I remember I was down at the Moose having a drink when he came in. He put down the awfulest sight of clear you ever saw." Poppa shook his head in disgust. "He said how much he wanted more for his granddaughter than the old Graves family."

"What did he mean?" I asked.

"Honey, them Graves are as rough as the Libertys." His eyes lowered, and he slowly turned his head to look out the window. "It sure is gonna look so pretty around here when that snow comes."

He changed the subject to yet another subject I didn't want to discuss.

"There's not going to be any snow," I informed him. "Because you are going to go up there and plead with the big guy."

"Kenni-Bug, that's up to Mother Nature and trust me when I say that she's one stubborn brood." He threw his head back and laughed.

"Snow or not, killer caught or not, I'm going to Chicago with Finn." I flipped the turn signal on right and turned south on Main Street. "We need to get back to the department. Finn is bringing in Juanita Liberty. We can ask her about them boys of hers going to the Graves with their weapons. You let me do that talking and you just ghost yourself on over into a corner," I warned Poppa when I parked the car in the alley behind the department.

Juanita and Betty were talking about some sort of recipe when I walked in. Juanita's face stared me down as I made my way over to them.

"Go on," Juanita didn't even let me get my coat off before she started to hound me. "Ask me what you want. I've got stuff to do tonight."

"Juanita," I looked her square in the face.

"Kenni-Bug," Poppa whispered in my ear. "Breathe in Jesus, breathe out peace." It was his way of telling me not to lose my cool.

I adjusted my thoughts and took the tape recorder out of the top drawer of my desk. I pushed record and sat it on the edge of the desk closest to Juanita. There wasn't a word I wanted to miss.

"Juanita." I planted my hands on the desk and leaned over her way as she sat in the chair. "I've got a dead girl on my hands. It appears to be awfully suspicious. It happens to be about a young woman you didn't care for. I've got a few questions for you and it might take me a few minutes or up to hours. It all depends on how much you cooperate."

"If you're wondering if I've got an alibi or hurt Leighann Graves in anyway, I didn't and I do have an alibi. I was with my boys last night at the dance and then at home." She looked at her watch. "Which is where I need to be right now. You can ask any of my boys."

I slid my gaze over her shoulder at Scott. He was writing something down, which I assumed was some of her statement.

"About those boys." I decided not to press her too much on where she was and who she was with last night until I got the particulars about the autopsy from Max Bogus. "Tell me about the time they showed up at the Graves's house with guns," I told her.

Sometimes it was best not to give the whole hand, but to give just enough of a push or poke in hopes it would prompt her to do something that'd lead me to a clue or lead in the case. Besides, I wasn't so sure she had anything to do with Leighann's death.

SHE EASED BACK in the chair as her head slowly tilted to the other side of her shoulders. Her mouth slightly opened, and I could see her tongue fiddling with her back teeth.

"Sean Graves had said some not so nice things about their mama." She slid her body up to the edge of the chair, leaned in towards me, and stared me square in the eyes. "When you heard people talking about your mama's recent situation, didn't that burn you up?" She asked. "Didn't that make you want to draw your pistol on them to shut their mouths? Just because my boys took up for me, doesn't mean I killed no one. Just like your Mama didn't kill no one."

"Did I say you killed someone?" I asked.

"You didn't have to. Don't mistake my accent or my living arrangements for stupidity. I'm far from ignorant and I know what's going on here." She looked around. "My son's girlfriend is dead. Apparently murdered, or you wouldn't be here snooping around. Me and Leighann didn't get along. She kept my boy from making it big in life and for what? A tow company?" Her shoulders jerked as she let out a chuckle. "Honestly, I don't know what he likes about working there. I've been on some late-night runs with him when he had to take the overnight shift and got paid minimum wage. I swear. He should've taken that scholarship. His future would've been so much better. But, just because that's my opinion and I didn't like how she has a hold on my boy, doesn't mean I wanted her dead."

"Did you hear that?" Poppa ghosted next to me. "She said has a hold on my boy. Present tense. She didn't do it."

One little hint we learned in the academy was not only to watch people's body language when you were interrogating them but to listen carefully to their words.

"If it's all the same to you, I'd like to talk to your children. What is a good time to come out to your house?" I asked and ignored Poppa who was now pacing in front of the desk between me and Juanita.

"We've got barely little time since the tree lot is going full blast for the high school football team. You're more than welcome to come by there. Plus, we could use an extra set of hands. I'll let you talk to Jonathon because he's old enough to know what's going on, but my little one is off limits. He's too young to even understand what's going on." She put her hands on her knees and pushed up to stand. "Will that be all?"

"Thank you for coming in." I didn't bother getting up. I just leaned back in my chair and stared at the blank white board.

"Oh dear," Betty groaned. "Remember last year's tree lot?"

"What happened last year?" There was a bit of a worried tone to Finn's question.

"Yeah?" Scott followed up.

"Go on, Kenni, you tell them." Betty's brows rose.

"I think you're better than me at telling it." I shrugged and got up to walk over to the white board.

"Well, last year we got a call from Sean Graves about Leighann and Manuel. It was an all-out brawl." As Betty told the story, I wrote Leighann Graves name in the middle of white board.

Just like we'd been doing since Finn insisted on us using one, I made a big circle around her name and drew out line extensions from it.

On one I wrote Juanita Liberty, another I wrote Manuel Liberty, another I wrote Sean Graves and the last one I wrote girl at the party, who we'd yet to identify.

"Manuel was playing Santa for the little children and Leighann was in an elf suit." Betty rolled her eyes and shook her head at the same time. "Sean had gone to drag Leighann home, like some daddy caveman, but not without him and Manuel getting into a fuss. All sorts of kids were crying.

Sean'd pulled Manuel's Santa beard off. It was a mess. Trees were falling over, and the strung lights had been jerked down from them fussin' and fightin'. It was like one of them crazy reality television shows where all them women catfight and all."

"What is your reasoning for putting Sean up there?" Scott asked.

"According to him and Jilly, the relationship with Sean and Leighann hasn't been any less than rocky and volatile at times. Maybe she and Sean got into an argument, nothing new, but this time it was the straw that broke the camel's back."

"Don't you know," Betty looked over at Scott and eased herself up out of her chair. "What's always done in the dark always finds its way to the light. That's what my mama, and her mama, and her mama used to say."

"It rings true every time." Poppa nodded and agreed right along with Betty. "Now put on there about Manuel looking at the phone and all."

"Oh, good one," I said and totally forgotten Manuel had said that.

"Good one?" Finn eyeballed me.

"I just remembered something, and I was saying it to myself." I sucked in a deep breath and got composure before I wrote down what Poppa had reminded me about. "When I was visiting with Manuel. He said that he'd gone through Leighann's phone before he gave it to the Graves. There could've been something on there erased. I think we need to get a subpoena to the cell phone service to retrieve any information we can."

"I can do that. I've had plenty of work with those things at the reserve," Scott spoke up and started to write down something in his notebook.

"Betty," I stopped Betty, who was preparing to go for the night. "Did you set Scott up on the database with a password so he can just go into the file and pull up Leighann's case?"

"I sure did," she said and pulled on her coat. "You good?" She asked Scott.

While they finalized some things, Duke woke up from his nap after he heard his name and stretched out on his dog bed.

When he noticed it was me, he pushed his paws forward and stuck his butt up in the air, doing a real downward dog position like those crazy pretzel ladies in those yoga classes do. His mouth gaped open into a big yawn before he got up on all fours and trotted over to me.

"Any news from Max?" I asked Betty and took a treat from the treat jar that Finn had on his desk for Duke. I flipped him a treat and gave him a good scrub on the head.

"Are you kidding me? You'd be the first after me to hear," she tsked. "I'm giving you fair warning, this is all the talk around town and when you get to the church, I'm sure you'll get asked a lot of questions."

"I think I can handle them." I was pretty confident I could, but I still appreciated Betty's concern, even though I knew there was a deeper meaning behind it.

"Are you sure you don't want to tell me anything, so I can help keep the buzzards back?" She gave it another good old college try.

"I'm positive. Thank you for your quick work today. I truly appreciate it." It was my way of kicking her out without telling her to get out.

"Alrighty then. If you don't need me." She pushed her pocketbook in the bend of her elbow and bent her arm up. "I've called Clay's Ferry Dispatch to take over."

"Thanks, Betty. I'll see you soon." I walked over and held the door open for her. "Stay," I instructed Duke when he stuck his nose out of the door to get a smell of the fresh air.

"Before I go." She put her hand on the door to stop it from shutting. "I'm heading on down to Dixon's. I had Toots Buford hold me back some bread. Do you want me to pick you up something before the big storm?"

"Nope." My lips parted to say something else, but I slammed by mouth shut, followed by the shutting door. "If I hear one more person say they believe this storm of the century is really coming, I'm might go into a tizzy."

"It's supposed," Scott started to say.

"Aaaa," I wiggled my finger. "Don't speak it out into the world."

"What are you talking about?" Finn asked and walked over to the white board. He picked up the blue marker and took the top off.

"You know all that new age mumbo-jumbo about think positive thoughts and it'll come true." I watched both of them nod at me but not without looking as if they thought I'd lost my mind. "Anyways, I'm positive the storm is going to scoot down a skoosh and hit Tennessee really hard or move up a smidgen and hit Ohio, bypassing all of Kentucky."

"It clearly looks like..." Scott started again before I put my palm flat out in front of him.

"Not another word about the weather while you are in my department because we've got to focus on solving what happened to Leighann Graves." I sucked in air to fill my lungs and slowly let it out. A relaxation tip that Tina Bowers had given me a few months ago when she said I needed to get rid of stress.

"Then let's get started." Finn and Scott gave each other a strange look but I chose to ignore it because it wasn't worth getting into. "What's your thoughts?"

"My thoughts are that she was placed in her car after she'd passed out or died. Something. Her Mama insists that she always wore her seat belt." I talked as Finn wrote under Leighann's name. Duke realized we weren't leaving and he got back in his bed for another nap. "The keys were in her pocket."

"Did she have a reason to end her life?" Scott asked.

"That's what I was saying before." I hated for this motive to leave my mouth, but I couldn't help but remember that in the academy they always said that more times than not, people were murdered by the hands of a loved one. "Leighann had a very rocky relationship with her dad."

He moved his hand over to the motives section under Sean's name.

"Jilly confessed that Sean did use some physical attempts to get his point across." I didn't want to say it. It was so hard for me to wrap my brain around.

"He was an abuser." Scott did a much better job getting it out. "Jerk."

I proceeded to read off my notes, so my words wouldn't be biased. The internal feeling I was feeling for Sean Graves was not kind. I wanted to make sure this investigation went by the book and me not be accused of harboring hard feelings towards him.

"You mean to tell me that he admitted to striking his daughter?" Finn asked. "I'd never thought it."

"Me either, but I could tell something was off. I mean all those times we went there. Manuel once said to me that he had to get her out of the house. That stuck with me. I wonder if that's what he was talking about." I had to see Manuel again.

I would question him when I went back out to question Juanita.

"I want you to put Manuel's brother on the list too. Jonathon did pull that gun on Sean." I didn't like hearing how he'd used a gun to get a point across and I'd make sure he had gun permits.

Most of the residents of Cottonwood packed heat. That wasn't an issue at all, it was the ones that didn't have the right permits that bothered me most.

I wrapped up the information I'd gotten from the Sean and Jilly and that included the confrontation with the Graves.

"This is like modern day Hatfield and McCoys." Scott rubbed his hands together. "Dude, why didn't you tell me this was the good stuff instead of how we sit around the reserve."

"You never asked," Finn replied.

It never dawned on me that the two of them knew each other until this exact moment.

"You two know each other. Huh." I felt my jaw drop and my eyes lower before I quickly brought them back to their normal position.

"We would pass each other in the halls but never worked a case until now." Scott was a lot more excited than Finn.

"Glad you are here. We expect you'll be just fine while we are gone." I turned back to Finn and smiled. This had been a long time coming and I couldn't wait to meet his family.

"We ready to go?" Scott jumped to his feet.

"Whoa, buddy." Finn put the top back on the marker. "It doesn't work that way around here."

"Right. First, we have to get the report back from Max that proves Leighann's murder is a homicide. If the report comes back, which I expect that it will, then we go and start asking questions." It was the small-town way of policing. It took Finn a lot of months to figure that out when he was hired to be my deputy. I too believed in my gut and followed my instinct, but since my Poppa was here, I really trusted my gut.

"On my rounds in the morning, I'll go back the funeral home and see if Max has anything unless he calls first." Sometimes he did call first, but I'd yet to hear from him. "Depending on if he has any new information will determine my day and who I see. For now, I've got to get to the church and Finn's got to get Duke home."

"What do I need to do?" Scott asked.

"I'm guessing you can go on back to the hotel." I knew we'd put him up at the Tattered Book and Inn down the street. "Or you can go help us set up."

"I think I'll grab a to-go dinner from Bartleby and go get some sleep." He pushed himself up to standing. "I'll be here in the morning."

"Thanks for all your help today. You got thrown into the fire and I really appreciate you taking care of Sean." It was hard for me to even think we were so nice to him now, but I stood by the innocent until proven guilty.

He was guilty of that since he admitted to it and that didn't make me happy.

"No problem. I kinda wish I wasn't so nice now." He only said what we were all thinking.

While he got his stuff together, Finn and I both cleaned up our desks and did a few here and there chores to tidy up the place to get ready for tomorrow.

"Do you really think Sean did it?" Finn asked as soon as Scott closed the door between the department and the restaurant.

I walked over and locked the door.

"I think the families had a feud between them and given time, I'm not so sure Leighann and Manuel would've stuck it out." I walked up to him and put my arms around him.

"Do you think she was tired of being in the middle? She was tired of trying to figure out where she was going to rest her head next?" He looked down at me. "She put the SUV in neutral. Once the car was somewhat submerged in the front, she put the car in park and took out the keys." He acted out the movie playing in his head. "Then she climbed in the back of the SUV in a little bit of a panic because she realized what she was doing wasn't right and climbed to get out and stuck the keys in her pocket, it was the point of no return and she drowned."

"You big dummy." Poppa appeared. "No. That's not what happened." He put his hands under each armpit and started to walk around like a chicken, flapping his elbows in and out. "He's lost his mind. We hear you cluckin' boy, but we can't find your nest."

Poppa walked around Finn and me in circles, clucking and doing his chicken dance. My nose started to flare like it did when I tried not to laugh out loud. My lips pinched in between my teeth, but I let go on his last cluck and busted out laughing, taking a step backwards.

"Kenni, honey?" Finn cautiously asked. "Are you okay?"

"Don't you honey, my Kenni-Bug." Poppa's clucking and chicken dance had stopped, and I got my composure together.

"Finley Vincent." I forced myself not to laugh. "It'll be our luck if this darn weather system does dump on us." I turned it around to make him think I was laughing like a crazy person.

"Now you've got that stinkin' thinkin'." Finn used my own phrase on me. "Where's my little optimistic girlfriend?"

"I guess I've heard everyone that I've encountered today say something about this snow and it's starting to sink in my soul." Now I was back to thinking about that dumb weather forecast.

"We will be able to drive to the airport and get on that big bird that'll take us all the way to Midway Airport." He was good at trying to reassure me. "They won't ground the planes."

"You are my hero." I curled up on my toes and took his promise with a sealed kiss.

My phone chirped from my back pocket and I grabbed it. It was a text from Max Bogus.

"It's Max." I showed my phone to Finn. "He's got a preliminary report ready."

"Let's go." Finn read my mind. He patted his leg. "Let's go, Duke."

CHAPTER EIGHT

"Is Max working late?" Finn asked when we turned down Main Street towards the one-stop shop funeral home.

"I recon." As sad as it was, death still came without being murdered and from what I'd heard last night, the grim reaper had come to take a few of our elder citizens during the holiday. "Seems that he's all full up with funerals, so he must be doing the autopsy when he has moments throughout his day."

Finn stared out the window. He had his left hand planted over Duke's body. My goofy dog had positioned himself between the front and back seat of the Jeep.

Finn put his hand on my shoulder. "You're going to love my family. They are already going to love you. My sister has told them all about you."

"I'm excited too." I sucked in a deep breath and tried to ignore that I suddenly realized I wasn't going to be home for the tree lighting. My stomach started to hurt.

"Feeling sick?" Poppa appeared in the back seat of the Jeep. Duke squirmed his way back next to poppa. He wagged his tail with glee. "Home sick?"

My eyes slid to the rear-view mirror and I stared at my Poppa. His eyes were soft. He always knew when I wasn't feeling well, even emotionally.

"What's wrong, boy?" Finn turned around in the seat and snapped his fingers for Duke to come so he could pat him. When he continued to bounce on Poppa's lap, Finn looked all sorts of confused. "Is he feeling okay?"

"He's fine. I swear he does weird stuff like that all the time in here and at the house." I watched in the rear-view mirror as Poppa pat on and scrubbed up under Duke's chest, sending the dog into a full-on howl. "Maybe he sees my Poppa's ghost or something."

Poppa's head jerked up and he looked at me in anticipation that I was going to tell Finn our little secret.

"I've heard dogs and kids can see things we can't. I'm not sure I can get behind that concept or not." Finn shrugged it off, letting me know that he wasn't quite ready for my secret life. I swallowed the lump in my throat, wondering if he'd ever be ready.

POPPA'S SHOULDERS SLUMPED, and I peeled my eyes away from the mirror.

"I believe in spirits." It was a topic we'd never brought up. "I think..."

"Alright. Seriously? Right before we go into a funeral home full of dead bodies. I'm getting the heebie-jeebies just thinking about it." Finn grabbed his thermal mug out of the bean bag coffee holder and flipped the lid to take a drink. "You bringing this up now is just going to make me more on edge."

He reached up and turned the knob on the radio to make it a little louder.

"Good morning, Cottonwood. DJ Nelly coming at you this morning with some sweet sounds of this time of the year. The hustle and bustle can bring out the worst in us, so be sure to be kind. After all, Christmas is only a few days away and it looks like it's gonna be white." DJ Nelly had to've planned playing "White Christmas".

I hit the off button on the radio.

"You don't love 'White Christmas'?" Finn looked at me. "You sure are getting cranky. Are you sure you want to go to Chicago? Because you don't have to."

"No. I'm fine." I shook my head. "It's just that I don't want to jinx our trip and all this talk of snow and all the memories of how much fun a white

Christmas around really is," I shook it off. "It's all just getting to me. That's all."

I put the shift into park after I pulled up behind Max's hearse.

"Kenni," Finn put his hand on my leg. "Really, honey. If you want to stay here, we can."

I bit the inside of my jaw so I wouldn't say anything.

"I know you want to go to Chicago. But I also know you love tradition. I truly think it's born and bred in you Southern women." His gaze softened and he smiled, making my insides explode with how lucky I was to have him in my life.

"Puh-leeeeeese," Poppa's sarcasm dripped. "I used that old song and dance on your granny."

"You were saying?" I asked and ignored Poppa.

"Why don't we have a nice romantic dinner tomorrow night and you tell me all about the traditions you love. This year you can experience my traditions. Then next year, me and you decide on what traditions we want together." His words were so sweet and kind, my heart fluttered.

"That sounds really good, but I've got my weekly Euchre night with the girls. They're already mad I'm not doing our annual White Christmas movie. If I skip out on Euchre night, I might not have any friends when we get back from Chicago," I said.

"Okay. That's fine." He got out of the car. "Let's get this over with."

"Does that mean he's going to be around for a while?" Poppa asked.

"I hope so," I said back to Poppa before I got out of the Jeep with my bag in one hand and Duke trotting alongside of me.

"Right there." Poppa pointed to one of the windows of the outside of the funeral home.

"Yes. Right there you laid in corpse." It was something that I wrestled with every time I came to see Max, even on unrelated issues.

"You know that every Sims before me was right there in that window. You'll be there too." He tapped his temple. "Do you think if you asked Max, he'd agree to put a plaque up underneath that window with our name on it?"

"I don't think so. All the Harrisons have laid there, not to mention the Ramseys and Browns." It wasn't like we were special. "When there's no other competition in town and there's only a couple of windows where the casket will go, it's not that special." I muttered with my head looking down at the ground so Finn would think I was talking to Duke.

"Hhmmm." Poppa stood outside the window and looked at it like a shrine. Duke sat down next to Poppa.

The two-story brick home had been an old house that'd been transformed into the only funeral home in Cottonwood. There were two large, ceiling to floor windows in the front and our family had always been laid out in that one particular window.

"We better get in there because I'm limited on time." I tapped my watch.

"Come on, Duke," I called when I got to the steps. He wasn't budging from sitting next to Poppa in front of that darn window. It looked as if Duke was paying some freaky homage to that window. "Come on," I called a little bit louder and clapped my hands together.

"Woooooo." Finn wiggled his fingers at me and did some sort of ghost call. "Maybe he sees one of them spirits you believe in."

"Stop it." I smacked his fingers away in a joking manner. He stepped inside the funeral home and I left Duke outside. It wasn't like he was going to go anywhere. Everyone around town knew Duke and he would find his way around the town or sit on the porch to wait for me.

We headed inside, and a chill swept over me. No matter how many times I'd come in here, and the fact that I actually had a relationship with a ghost, this place still gave me the heebie-jeebies. Going to the morgue wasn't at the top of the list of things I liked to do as Sheriff.

The morgue was in the basement. The upstairs of the funeral home was worlds different than the morgue. The funeral home had warm carpeting, richly painted walls, antique furniture and the large crown molding. The morgue had concrete floors, swinging metal doors and steel tables. The entire thing was just one big, cold room.

I looked through the small port window in the swinging doors that stood between me and Max. He was standing over Leighann's body.

I tapped my fingernail on the glass. Max's head jerked up and when he noticed me, he waved us in.

There was no denying that there was something so strange and eerie when you were in the presences of the deceased all laid out in their Sunday best clothes.

Finn's shoulders shook, and he did a little jump in the air when we passed the first room on the left.

The sound of a drill and clink of metal told me that Max was hard at work.

"Are you going to be okay?" I asked Finn before we stepped into the room where I could see Max from the little port-hole window in the door.

"I'm fine." Finn's man-ego appeared, which was rare. "I saw Leighann yesterday. Like all the others."

Seeing a dead body at the scene was much different than on the table at the coroner's office, cracked wide open and with all sorts of tubes draining all that fluid.

"Good evening, Max," I said and pushed into the door with Finn behind me. I plucked a couple of gloves from the box and snapped them on my hands. I held the box out to Finn for him to get some. "Finn?" I waved a hand in front of his blank face. "You're white as a ghost."

I took a quick look around to see if Poppa was there and Finn had seen him.

"Finn!" Max dropped one of his metal instruments on the tray next to him and ran over, catching Finn right before his head smacked the floor. "Finn?"

Max shook him by the shoulders.

"I'm guessing he's still not used to being in a morgue," Max said with a bit of entertainment.

"Remember the reserve officers are pampered men of the law," I joked and grabbed the smelling salt for Max to crack open and swipe under Finn's nose. "Here," I took off my jacket, though I knew Max kept the temps in here nearly freezing, but poor Finn needed a pillow. "Wad this up and put it under his head. He'll be fine."

About that time something beeped. It was like a cow poker to Max's back-end, and he jumped. He almost dropped Finn's head on my flat coat.

"I've been waiting for this report." He scurried over to the fax machine. "I contacted Tom Geary last night and wanted to get his take on it."

"On what?" I asked and walked over to Leighann.

Finn had gotten to his feet and was drinking a glass of water Max had gotten for him.

Outside of the V cut Max had performed on her and the tubes draining out of her, she looked like she'd been sleeping. Her long red hair had dried since she had been pulled out of the river. It laid around her in long waves. The kind of waves women paid a lot of money to get from a fancy salon. I rested my hand on her hand that was lying at her side and said a little pray to myself. I noticed a small heart tattoo on the fatty part of the underside of her thumb.

"Leighann," I said as if she could hear me, which she might. I looked over at Poppa. "I'm going to find out exactly what happened." I promised the young girl then and there. "I want you to know that no daughter deserved the treatment you received."

I felt it necessary to apologize for her parents. If I'd know about how Sean treated her and Jilly, I'd probably have been more on Leighann's side during all the calls Sean had placed to the department to bring his daughter home and runaways she'd attempted. I'd certainly have arrested Sean for some sort of domestic violence abuse.

I even found myself mad at Jilly for not stepping up to the plate and being a mother to the poor girl.

"Thank you, Tom." Max gripped the faxed papers and shook them in the air. "When I did the preliminary toxicology report on Leighann, there were some traces of Ambien in her system." He pulled out his file and opened it, pointing to all sorts of numbers on a grid that I didn't even understand.

Tom Geary was the owner of a lab in Clay's Ferry that I used in the department when I needed something fast.

"Sleeping pills?" I asked, not real sure. I continued to flip through the file to see the notes he'd made in the sidebars.

"Yes. Just a trace. Tom has some real sophisticated equipment that would help detect just exactly how much." He took the papers off the fax machine and muttered Tom's report under his breath. "Yep. I knew it."

"Did Tom confirm?" I wondered.

"He did. Which doesn't necessarily point to a homicide, but the amount in her system is just enough to put her in a deep sleep and if she was underwater, she wouldn't wake up." His eyes bore into my soul.

"Are you saying she didn't take them?" I asked and looked over at Finn. The color had come back into his face.

"I'm saying that the time of death doesn't coordinate with how long her body has been under the water." He beat around the bush.

"She was given the medication before her car went into the river," Poppa appeared next to Finn and he stood over him. "This boy needs to toughen up."

"Someone gave her the medication. When she had no control over her body, they put her in the SUV and somehow got it into the water." I was playing the game with Poppa without Max understanding what I was doing.

"Someone did give it to her, but how did they get the car in park? The SUV can roll if the keys aren't in it, but how did they get the car in park? Was someone in the car with her?" Poppa posed questions that were so hard to answer.

"Who could lift her into an SUV?" I asked.

"These are questions you're going to have to find the answers to." Max made another copy of Tom's report and stuck it in the file labeled "Sheriff's File" along with the case number of Leighann Graves. "The water in her lung tissue and the time release of the sleeping pills don't coordinate. There was some time in between."

"It's hard for me to forget the prescription bottle of Ambien for Sean Graves on their kitchen window sill." There was a light of uneasiness that passed between me and Max.

"Sean can be a bear. I know that. You know that he hangs out with me and some of the guys and plays cards, but I don't think he could kill that little girl of his. She gave him fits, but he loved her," Max said.

"He also hit his wife and daughter. Not only that, he also kicked his daughter out of the house, and she had to live in her SUV and got food from the food shelter at church." It almost made me sick that Max was almost making Sean Graves out to be a great man.

"He never said anything about all that." Max handed me the file. "I'm not saying he didn't give some of his sleeping pills to her either or that he did, but I am saying that it appears she had some sleeping pills. Now, whether she took them herself I can't tell you that, but I do know it's enough that if she was in a bathtub and went under, she'd not wake up."

I wasn't asking Max to do my job. I knew that he could only give me the facts based on what Leighann's body was telling him. It was now on my hands to take what her body had said along with the evidence I was collecting to arrest a suspect.

"Now, I don't know about what you found in the SUV, but I'm positive she didn't have time to put the keys in her pocket from the time of death to the length of time she was in the water."

"She was murdered," I said it out loud and declared it right there.

"I'll be out here." Finn got our attention and he pushed out the door.

"I'm sorry this has happened right here at Christmas. It seems the holiday season doesn't stop death from coming. I'm so busy, I feel like a spec of water in a hot skillet." Max untied the white apron from around his waist and threw it in the clothing basket and motioned for me to come to his office.

"I'd heard last night that you were full." I waited for him to get the paperwork together that I had to sign off on.

"Yep. Alright. I'm going to say this was a homicide because I just can't make the timeline work." He turned the piece of paper towards me and pushed it across the desk. "Sign right here."

I took one of the many pens from his pen cup and signed exactly where he told me to.

"I'll keep you posted if I find out anything else." Max stood up. There was a frown on his face. I could tell he was hurting because he trusted Sean just like the rest of us even though Sean hadn't been found guilty of anything.

"Looks like we've got us a killer and we better get jingling if we are going to figure it out before Christmas." I grabbed Finn's hand and dragged him out of the funeral home.

CHAPTER NINE

"Now where are we going?" Finn held onto the handle of the passenger side door when I peeled the Wagoneer off the curb after slamming the gearshift in DRIVE.

"According to Tom Geary's report." I tapped the copy of Max Bogus's report he'd put in the file he'd given me about Leighann Graves. "Leighann had Ambien in her system."

"So, she took a sleeping pill?" He asked with a peculiar look on his face.

"I don't know, but I think her car will have more evidence we can pull from and that's why I'm going to drive on out to Clay's Ferry to S&S Auto. Read the file to me." I knew we were racing against time because it was pretty darn close to any business closing up for the night.

Clay's Ferry was about twenty minutes away. The curvy roads were hard to navigate during a bright sunny day, much less a dark winter's evening with the temperature dropping rapidly. I gripped the wheel and listened to Finn read the initial report and Tom Geary's report sent by fax to Max.

"Max says here that the Ambien had been in her system and her nervous system long enough that she wouldn't be able to unbuckle her seatbelt, drive into the water, put the car in park and put the keys in her pocket. The timeline of the effects of the drug in Leighann's system doesn't add up. This is where he concludes it's a homicide." Finn closed the file and I could feel his stare.

"This is why I couldn't let Sean take her SUV to Graves Towing. We need to go over her car with a fine-tooth comb." There had to be some clues. "I doubt we'll get any prints off of it since the mud would act as sandpaper."

"When I initially looked at the car, I didn't see anything in there. There wasn't a purse, jacket or nothing. I've never seen a teenager's car so clean." Finn made a good point. "I thought it was strange and I did note it in the report."

"What about an emergency kit?" I asked. "Vividly I remember that Sean had mentioned that Leighann had an emergency kit in her car that included food, water and first aid when I went to their house on the initial phone call when they reported her missing."

"One with her initials on it, too." Poppa chimed in after he reappeared in the Jeep.

"You'd know it because it had her initials on it," I said.

"Not that an emergency kit that's monogramed should surprise me around here, but it does. Still. I didn't find anything in her car. Nothing." He shook his head. "I even looked under the seats." He reached over and flipped the heat up a notch. "It's getting colder. It does feel like snow weather."

"Don't even start with that," I warned. "I'm in no mood to hear about this ridiculous notion there's a blizzard coming."

"Wow, someone's on edge. I'd heard the holidays bring it out in everyone." He joked but I didn't laugh. "Listen," he reached over and put his hand on my shoulder. "This is just a job. We can't live every second and have every conversation built around the job, Kenni. We have to have a life outside of the office."

"We do. It's just that right now, we need to get to Leighann's car and figure out something." It was hard for me to put the job as second in my life. I'd never done or known anything in my adult life other than being the badge. It'd been a challenge for me to have a life outside of the office when I clearly wasn't used to it.

"I'm not saying we don't go and check out the car. It's pretty dark and it's not like the killer left a calling card. Really, this can wait until the morning." He was right, but I didn't care.

"Yep. See here." Poppa ghosted between us and he jabbed his finger in Finn's chest. Finn drew his hand up and rubbed the spot. "My Kenni-Bug is the sheriff. She calls the shots. You take them, Buddy."

"All I'm saying is that while it's fresh in our minds, we need to go look at the SUV. We have flashlights." I put the turn signal on when I got to the chain link fencing that was built around S&S Auto.

It was a first-class junk yard, tow company and impound lot. They had their cars stacked up in neat heaps and in rows of repose. The office hours posted reminded me that they closed at five p.m., something I'd forgotten.

"Says they're closed," Finn mentioned. "Like I said, we can come back tomorrow."

"Not closed if I see a light on." I noticed dots of lights coming out of a closed window blind from the far end of the building. I grabbed my bag and got out. "Somebody has got to be in there."

Instead of knocking on the door of the office, I walked up to the window and knocked on it. Two of the blinds snapped open and two beady eyes stared at me. I recognized those eyes as the secretary who gave me a hard way to go last time I needed a car out of their lot.

I gave her a minute to walk down to the door after she'd shut the blinds.

"You again." The woman's happiness to see me was apparent in her tone. "I'm assuming you're here for the girl's SUV?"

"Actually, I just need to look at it." I stared at her baby blue cardigan that was tucked down into the waist of her brown pleated pants. She still had the same chin length bob that looked more like a football helmet than style. "It's part of evidence and no one is going to move that car until I clear it."

"I'm in here finishing up the paperwork. If I can get ahold of Frank, I'll see what I can do." She started to pull the door shut. "And only because I feel bad about that girl and would like to get a murderer behind bars."

Finn looked down and scratched his head. His eyes peered at me from under his brows. "Why do you think this is a murder?" He asked her.

"Because the last time she was here," she flung a finger at me, "it was a murder. By the way she's acting and by the late hour of the night, it's gotta be a murder." She turned and went back into the office, shutting the door to keep us out in the cold.

There was a slight grin on his face.

"You sure did get her britches in a tangle last time we were here." He laughed.

"Look at him." Poppa pointed out. "He's pickin' up on our sayings."

That was two compliments for Finn tonight from Poppa in a Poppa kinda way. The funeral home window thing and now the Southern slang.

"You are a something else, Finn Vincent." I couldn't help but laugh back, then I got all serious again. "We are going to quickly just check out a few things. I'd like to get a good look to make sure there's no first aid kit in there with Leighann's initials. Or if the entire emergency kit is gone."

"Why does that seem so important to you?" He asked.

"The side panel of the car is gone. Did she take the emergency kit out at some point after she hit or was hit by whatever? Use it?" Then it dawned on me. My jaw dropped. "What if someone slipped her the pill and knew she'd drive somewhere, become unconscious and wreck?"

"She did wreck but didn't die." Finn looked out as though he were trying to piece the incident together.

"We need to determine how fast the car was going because if that's true, Max said that she didn't have any physical signs," I threw that out there because we had to put the facts with our theories so they would be a complete puzzle of what exactly happened.

"Do you think that someone followed her and finished off the job?" Finn asked.

"Exactly." Poppa clapped his hands and did a jig. "We need to find out where that panel has disappeared to. That is going to be the second crime scene in this murder."

"What's the first?" I asked.

"Wherever she was when someone slipped her the pill." Poppa's words left chills down my legs.

"What's first?" Finn asked with furrowed brows.

"Wherever the person slipped her the pill." I repeated Poppa and looked at Finn with furrowed brows. "I mean," I gulped and caught myself. "I think the scene we investigated at the river is the third crime scene. The first is the pill. The second is wherever that side panel is and the third is the river."

"We need to find that side panel." Finn ran his hands through his hair. He let out a long-exhausted sigh that hit the condensation of the cold air and a stream of smoke trailed. "You need a vacation. You say things out of nowhere like you're having your own little conversation. After we take a look at the SUV, if Frank is here, why don't you go home and go to sleep. Skip feeding the needy at church."

"Yes. A murder stresses me out, but I'm not skipping church tonight. It makes me feel good." I turned and gave Poppa the stare down. He was as sneaky as a pickpocket.

"I guess Frank is here," Finn said and pointed at the locked gate leading into the impound lot. The lights had turned on and Frank was standing there in the same outfit I'd seen him in every time I'd interacted with the man.

"Evening, Sheriff. Deputy." Frank unlocked the gate. "I've only got about fifteen minutes until I've got to scat. Wife duties and all."

"Thank you, Frank." It felt good to call him by his real name since I'd never known it. "It'll just take a few minutes tonight. Can't see much in the dark and we just wanted to check something out."

"No problem." He held the clipboard out for me to sign. I was glad to see they kept records because people were dishonest, and a killer would have no problem jumping this fence to mess with the evidence. "I'll tell you that whoever knocked this car's side panel off has to have some red on it." He took me around to the missing side panel of the car. "Right here's some strange marks. I noticed it when I was doing the checklist we have to do after we pick up a car to make sure the owner can't come back and say we did the damage."

Finn and I both unclipped our flashlights from the utility belt at the same time. I took a good look at the marks and made a note to take some photos of it when I got the camera out of my bag.

"I'll take the driver's side and you take the passenger side." I dragged the light from the front bumper, along the side, and ended at the back bumper. There didn't appear to be anything that struck me as unusual. I opened up the driver's side door and shined the light at the dashboard. There was a dried water line but nothing else. The floorboard was clean, and the driver's seat was too. A little too clean for me.

I reached into my bag and grabbed a pair of gloves and some fingerprint dusting powder to coat the seatbelt release button with.

"You're dusting for prints tonight?" Finn asked.

"Listen, if our theory about someone slipping Leighann a pill and hoping she'd wreck is true, they had to have gotten her out of her seatbelt. And a killer in a crime of heat, which appears to be what this is, doesn't think things through enough that they would put on gloves." I snapped gloves on my hands.

"It's also freezing out and it was the night she was found." Which was his way of saying the killer might've had on gloves.

"Exhaust all possibilities." I didn't have a good response for him. "I'm going to dust."

He eased back around to his side of the SUV but not without taking a pair of gloves from my bag.

"I'm going to look under all the seats really good now," he said while I brushed on the dust and let it settle. "You know that I can actually put my whole body into the space between the steering wheel and the seat."

This struck me as odd because Leighann and I were pretty much the same height and build. If I were driving or she were driving, the seat wouldn't've been back this far.

"What did you say?" Finn leaned into the passenger side front door and shined his flashlight in my face.

"Look." I got into the seat and extended my arms and feet out in front of me. Neither of them touched the wheel or the pedals. "The last person in this car was a good four to five inches taller than Leighann."

"Good work. Now you're using your noggin.'" Poppa grinned from ear-to-ear in the back. "Which means that someone drove this car into the river, but how did they get out in time, turn the car off and put the keys in Leighann's pocket?"

"What am I missing?" I gnawed on the situation.

"I'm going to go look around." Poppa ghosted away.

"I hope you find something," I whispered under my breath.

"We are missing this side panel and where this murder started," Finn said with a long sigh.

"Did you see any emergency kit?" I asked and got back out of the car.

I reached down into my bag and got my camera out so I could take pictures of the seat and took my measuring tape out for some accurate measurements.

"There's nothing in here." Finn walked around and took the gloves off. "What about any fingerprints?" He leaned into the passenger side when I moved to write down the measurements.

"See any?" I asked.

"No. I'm afraid the grit in the river water must've acted like sandpaper like we thought." The glow of his flashlight circled inside of the SUV before he twisted around and shined it in my face.

"At least we got some information about how tall the killer might be." I looked at Finn's chilled eyes.

"What if she took the pills and was awake just enough to undo her seatbelt, push her seat back, drive the car enough in the water to carry it and pass out. Then she drowned." Finn was looking at all angles which he should've. But I was looking at my facts.

Poppa.

CHAPTER TEN

"I'm so glad you were still able to come." Preacher Bobby had greeted me at the doors of the undercroft.

"I don't leave for Chicago for a few days. I'd never miss this," I assured him and tried to switch hats from sheriff to volunteer. More times than not, this was a difficult task for me.

"I'm talking about taking time out of the investigation for Leighann Graves." His chin fell to his chest. "Bless her young soul."

My eyes darted back and forth wondering if I was supposed to let out a big amen, hallelujah, or a nod. I chose none of those and pinched a smile when he looked back up.

"I went by to see the Graves and they sure are having a real hard time and questioning God." Preacher Bobby rocked back on those black, preacher, thick-sole shoes and folded his hands in front of him. "I know I'm getting ahead of myself by a couple of weeks, but I sure do hope to see you more during Sunday service. It's been brought to my attention that you won't be at the annual tree lighting, caroling, and sleigh rides this year." He lifted his hands in the air and whispered something as he looked up to the sky.

"I'm super excited about Finn's parents' tradition on Christmas eve.

They go to a bar and tie one on before Santa comes." I winked, elbowed him and walked in the undercroft.

"Oh Kendrick Lowry, I never can tell when you're pulling my leg." He laughed behind me. "I'll see you in the new year," he called out.

I stuck my hand in the air and wiggled my finger as I continued to walk through the undercroft and followed the sounds of the bell choir.

"I'm not joking about this one," I confirmed about the Vincent's bar tradition.

Finn did tell me that they all went to a local pub, put down a couple of pints before they came home to do a sort of white elephant exchange. It was pretty exciting to get to see a new tradition.

There were a few minutes between the time I got there and the time the doors opened for supper, so I headed up the back steps of the undercroft to the foyer of the church that led into the sanctuary. The three Christmas trees lit up on the stage in front of where the congregation sits literally took my breath away. The trees were so full this year and I wondered where they'd purchased them. It kinda made me envious that I didn't get a tree, though I wasn't leaving until the day before Christmas Eve. Maybe I'd rethink getting one. At least I could enjoy it while I was here.

The poinsettia plants were strategically placed around the steps leading up to the stage where the bells were set up going down the center. The bell choir, which consisted of most of the Sweet Adeline's, was very special to Cottonwood and the church. There were bells of different shapes and sizes, each one of them making a different tone when played. Mama stood behind Lynn Bishop and appeared to be instructing her on how to handle the bell.

Lynn was the newest addition to the choir and I wasn't sure why she was holding Mama's bell. It was a job that Mama took very seriously.

"I'll never get tired of listening to the sweet sounds of those bells." Poppa appeared next to me, making me jump.

I glanced around to see if anyone saw me.

"Oh, I forgot." He made the motion that he had an imagery bell in his hand. "Ding, ding." He let out his boisterous laugh that was one thing I truly missed.

He was being a smart-alec. I'd once asked him to try and somehow announce himself before he just appeared because it freaked me out. Then he decided it was best to ding himself in like Clarence from the movie It's a Wonderful Life.

"You are far from an angel," I joked back to him underneath my breath. To me he was the only angel, but I didn't tell him that. His head was already big enough.

"Why doesn't your Mama have on her white gloves?" He asked a very good question.

The bells were very sensitive and had to be tuned every year. It was something that was set in the budget of the church because they had to be sent off for tuning. Each member of the bell choir had to wear gloves to be able to handle them with care. Mama was a stickler. Her gloves were washed after every practice and performance and to see her up there without the gloves and standing behind Lynn made me very curious.

"I swear it's you going away for Christmas that's put her in a funk and she just can't get out of it. I hope you're happy." Poppa ghosted up to Mama after he'd decided to skin me a new one.

When he placed a hand on her shoulder, I saw her look up and smile. I wasn't sure if she felt him or it was the sweet sounds of the bells, but I took much more comfort in thinking she felt her father's presence.

She looked over at me and had that wonderful grin on her face. I returned it. She walked down the steps with her Southern ease and grace.

"Are you getting in your concert since you won't be here to hear the real thing?" She asked, referring to the Christmas tree lighting ceremony that ended with a bell choir performance and good food. "It's going to be real pretty too at the fairgrounds." She nodded.

This year the tree lighting and festivities, like Mama's pageant, were going to be the same night down at the fairgrounds.

"I'm here to do volunteering for the food shelter tonight and I couldn't stand not to come up here and watch you when I heard the bells." It was a very fond memory of my Mama dragging me to bell choir practice with her when I was a child.

It was the traditions that we Southern women loved the most and it was starting to sink in my gut that I was going to miss out on that, but quickly turned that thought into Finn and his family traditions. What was one year? No big deal. At least that's what I told myself.

"Your Poppa loved to hear the bell choir." She shivered. "I swear every time I pick up that bell, I feel him."

"Why aren't you playing your bells?" I questioned and ignored the fact that Poppa was still standing there and how much so Mama was right.

"I can't be crowned Snow Queen and come play the bells in the same night." She did that wave thing with her hand. I pushed it down. "My nails have got to have plenty of time to dry before I take the crown...er...participate in Snow Queen. Those gloves fit so tight, I just can't risk it."

"That's disturbing." I sucked in a deep breath.

"Anyways, since I'll be moving around the tree lighting talking to everyone, I figured I better step down this year and let Lynn get the hang of it." She looked up at Lynn and squinted when she planted a fake smile across her face. "Bless her pea-pickin' heart. She just ain't got no rhythm."

"At least she's trying." I assured her. "And you've got a few days until the event, so I'm sure she'll be practicing until then."

"Hhmmm." Mama rolled her eyes. "I'm not so sure about that. Them youngins' of hers are so excited about Christmas, she said they haven't slept a wink. Of course, Vernon's not. He told her that he was the one who had to go to work in the morning and how she got to stay at home and take a nap." Mama's nostrils flared. "You know what I'da told your daddy if he said that to me?"

"No, and I don't want to know." My dad was a saint and I just knew there was a crown filled with jewels in heaven with his name on it because Vivian Sims Lowry was one hard woman to deal with.

"I'm gonna tell you anyways, because this is a life lesson for you." She poked me in the arm with her finger nail. I rubbed out the pain and prepared myself to just let whatever it was she had to say roll right on over me.

"Mama, you stop that carryin' on, you hear me?" I swallowed. "Daddy never had the nerve to try and tell you what to do."

"That's because I laid down the law when we were dating." She gave me the good ole, hard Baptist nod. "With you going away and all for Christmas, you apparently haven't laid down the law with Finn."

"Mama, that's enough," I warned. "Or I'll be gone every year at Christmas."

"You're gonna miss me when I'm dead and gone." Her eyes snapped at me. "And regret doing me this way."

"I love you and you know that." I gave her a hug even though she was pouting. "Anyways, I better let you get back to your teaching."

"Toodles." Mama waved and headed back up to the stage. She did a few nods and smiles at Lynn before I headed back down to the undercroft where all the volunteers had started to gather around who else...Betty Murphy.

Out of the corner of her eye, Betty noticed I'd come into the room and she quickly straightened up and shut her mouth.

Everyone turned to see me and scattered in all sorts of directions. I swear it was the uniform. If I'd put on street clothes, they would've stood there and gossiped just like they do when we have our weekly Euchre girl's night out. It was the same when I went to talk to someone about a case. I guarantee that if I went to see Juanita Liberty tomorrow without the uniform on, she'd be a lot more forthcoming and it was truly something for me to think about.

"I'm thinking y'all weren't talking about the upcoming weather?" I asked Betty.

"Heck no. You know what we were talking about. I told you about it before I left work." She and I both walked over to get the tablecloths, so we could put them on each table. It was sorta our job each year. For some reason, they'd stuck us on the committee that set the tables and cleaned up. I'd much rather been serving the food, but that job was given to the women of the church who do a little ministering to the homeless.

"Did you hear anything I should know about?" I asked, referring to any gossip.

"Well, I'd heard, hearsay," hearsay was a nice way of saying gossip. "Angela Durst had taken Leighann under her wings over the last couple of months. In fact, when Leighann and Manuel had come in here to get a warm meal a few weeks ago, Angela was curious to why they were there and Leighann told her everything about how her daddy had kicked them out. Sean Graves abused her. Now everyone in here thinks he's a killer."

"Is that right?" I asked and tugged on the edge of my side of the table cloth while she tugged on her side before we slipped it on the first table.

"Mmmhhh," she ho-hummed. "What do you think about that?" Her jaw dropped. "You already knew about that, didn't you?"

I tapped my five-star sheriff's badge on my pocket.

"I wasn't elected for my good looks," I joked because I never wore my hair out of my ponytail or wore makeup during the day.

"My stars." She gasped. "Are you telling me that when I go to work in the mornin', Sean Graves is going to be sitting in our cell?"

"Did I say that?" I asked. "Now that's how rumors get started."

"You didn't say it and I've worked with you long enough to read you a little better than you want me to." Her face shifted to the side and she looked over at me out of the corner of her eye.

"I can't believe that Angela Durst didn't know about it since she's Sean's secretary and all," I said knowing that I really needed to put Angela at the top of my list to talk to.

"What if Angela said something to Sean that next day and he laid into Leighann for saying something about their home life?" Poppa appeared next to us.

I avoided his stare since I knew everyone was looking at me. I had to play it cool.

"You and I both know that something fishy happened." She grabbed another table cloth and handed an edge to me.

Over the next few minutes we did our little ritual of putting on the table cloths together. It wasn't until we went our separate ways where she did the napkins while I did the cups that I got lost into my train of thought.

Poppa followed me around, giving little tidbits of information and how I needed to question anyone and everyone.

"While you and Finn were playing detective, I went down to the river." Apparently, that's where Poppa ghosted off to while I was at S&S Auto. "I walked along the banks."

"Walked?" I questioned him and looked down at his feet. "More like swept?"

"It is quicker," he assured me. "You know that Sterling Stinnett has a lot of stuff down there."

"It's cold out. He's got to be staying at the shelter." I'd bent down and acted like I was picking something off the floor, so no one would hear or see me talking to what they'd think was myself. "I hate to admit it, but it's too cold out there for a frog, much less a person."

"Sterling still goes and checks on his stuff. I saw him. He might've heard something." Poppa wagged his thick finger at me. "No stone unturned. Haven't I told you that before?"

"On more than one occasion." I stood back up and looked over at Betty. "I learned that motto from you," I said to him with some pride.

Had Angela really taken in Leighann? I wondered why Manuel didn't follow suit. Where was that car panel? I couldn't help but wonder what that fight was about this time last night at the Christmas dance.

These were all sorts of questions that I needed answered and the only way to do it was to go and talk to Angela. Making another little visit to Manuel wouldn't hurt either.

As if God himself gave me a sign, because we were in his holy house, Sterling Stinnett was the first to walk into the undercroft doors. His eyes met mine and I could tell he had something to say.

"Give me an extra helping of mashed potatoes," I told Viola White who was on mashed potato duty.

"As long as you vote for me for Snow Queen." Her eyes drew down her nose. Her hand lifted to pat the fur stole neatly draped over her shoulders. The circular diamond pin held the ends together.

"It's for Sterling," I said flatly and looked at her fur. "Now don't you go playing Mama's games," I warned her in a loud voice so Mama would hear. "Nothing good can come from that."

"Hush your mouth, Kendrick Lowry." Mama took a spoonful of green beans and put them on my plate. "You can vote for Viola. It's not going to help her none."

"Mmhhhmmm," Viola's lips pinched. "We'll see."

"What's that supposed to mean?" Mama dropped the serving spoon in the tray of green beans. "You better back up your words, Viola White."

"Ain't we pickin' our peaches before they're all fuzzed up?" Viola was getting all sorts of sassy with Mama. She scooped up another spoon of mashed potatoes and served them on top of the others she put on my plate.

"Ladies, this is no way for a future Snow Queen to act. Especially in the

Lord's house." I simply used their guilt techniques on them. "God don't like ugly."

"You sure are right." Mama's shoulders straightened. She picked up the serving spoon and went back to the line that'd now formed out the door.

Two things Southern women loved: God and food. We were right here amongst both and I used them against the pair who took their heritage more than most.

I turned around with my tray to see if I could find Sterling.

I didn't have to look around too much. Sterling was already through the line and sitting alone at a table up front.

"Hey, Sterling," I greeted him and sat down, putting the plate on the table.

"Sheriff." He nodded and sopped up what was left of the gravy with his biscuit. "Getting cold out there."

"It sure is." I pushed my plate towards him.

His face jerked upwards.

"I'm not hungry," I said building up to my questioning. "I've got this murder investigation on my mind and just not able to really eat."

I never understood why Sterling had chosen to live the life he did. He was talented in many construction type jobs and never was at a lack of job offers. He just chose to not have a house or any sort of living quarters. As long as he wasn't a menace to Cottonwood, he didn't bother me any.

"I know that you're the unofficial eyes and ears of Cottonwood and you've really given me some great information over the years in a lot of my investigations." I wanted to stroke his ego a little while he stuffed his face. It was true. He blended in so much that he'd become part of the landscape. People never really noticed he was around.

"I'd heard you found that girl down at the river." He folded the turkey slice in half and stuffed it in his mouth.

"I'm thinking it was right around where you hang out. Though I know it was cold that night and I'm sure you weren't there, but if you did hear something that I might need to know, you know where to find me." I stood up. "I hope you have a very Merry Christmas."

"Sheriff," Sterling called after me. He waved me over. "I did hear something that night but I didn't go check it out because I heard tires."

"You heard tires?" I asked.

"You know that hairpin turn about a mile before Chimney Rock put in?" He asked. I nodded. "I heard a crash. No squealing tires or nothing. But there was another car behind it that stopped."

"Did you see it?" I asked.

"No. I just heard it and didn't bother going to check it out when I heard the other car. I'm assuming they were there to help." His bushy brows furrowed.

"Help? Yeah, help kill," Poppa chimed in.

"Did you hear any voice?" I asked.

"No. Just tires of another car. A door slammed a few times and drove off again. I went back to getting some stuff together because it was the first night the shelter opened. But it didn't open until eleven thirty." He gave me a time.

"Eleven thirty." Poppa noodle the time as well as I did.

"Eleven thirty," I repeated.

"It was about fifteen minutes later that the tow truck came." He stopped me in my tracks.

"Did you say tow truck?" Poppa and I asked at the exact same time.

"I know it was a tow truck because the rotating round lights was exactly what I needed to help find some of the items I wanted to take with me while I stayed in the shelter." He'd just given us a major clue.

"Did you see them?" I asked.

"No, I told you that I was getting my stuff together." He dragged the small plate with a piece of pie closer to him.

"Manuel, Jilly, and Sean drive the two trucks," Poppa named off my list of suspects.

"Thanks, Sterling. If you hear or remember anything else, can you call me?" I asked.

"Sure thing, Sheriff." He forked the pie and stuffed it in his mouth.

"Someone used the tow truck to toss her SUV in the river," Poppa said as his ghost kept up with me while I hurried around and picked up used paper plates and napkins.

My duty was clean up. Clean up more ways than one. I had a murder to clean up and it took everything I had not to run out of there and force my way into Graves Towing, giving Sean Graves a piece of my mind.

The more I cleaned, the more my mind wandered over the clues.

He had the bottle of Ambien. No matter how much he said he'd accepted Leighann and Manuel's relationship, he still loathed them together and it was apparent on his face when I'd seen him that night at the dance. Then there was his abusive side that I'd uncovered while talking to him and Jilly. He knew all of Leighann and Manuel's hook up places, Chimney Rock being one of them. He and Jilly left before Leighann. Leighann had plenty of time to make it home, talk to her parents, get slipped an Ambien before she was going to Chimney Rock to meet Manuel. Her father followed her and when she fell asleep at the wheel, he towed her car into the river and that's why the seat was set back, Leighann unbuckled, with the keys in her pocket.

But did Sean Graves really kill his own daughter? If he didn't, who lured her there?

CHAPTER ELEVEN

I barely felt like I'd slept when the alarm went off. Duke jumped off the bed, which meant he wasn't going to last through a snooze, so I rolled over and sat up in bed. The first thing on my mind was Leighann Graves and what I had to do today.

The warmth of my slippers felt so good as I padded out of my bedroom and down the hall towards the back door where Duke was eagerly paw dancing to be let out. This was the usual activity after he'd spent some time with Finn, alone, the night before. Finn wasn't aware of a treat limit and gave Duke a fistful of doggie biscuits.

I flipped on the coffee pot and unlocked the door, pushing open the screen door that stood between Duke and my fenced-in back yard. He darted out, yelping his way back to the fence where he smelled whatever critters had gotten into the yard while he was sleeping. He didn't care that the temperature had dropped a good twenty degrees overnight.

I shook my head and checked the coffee pot on my way back to the bathroom to start my hot shower. Duke took just enough time to smell and do his business while I got my shower.

While the hot water felt good, it still wasn't enough to make me feel confident that Sean Graves was who had killed Leighann. The muffles and rumblings I'd heard around town, Sean Graves was already tried and arrested, and it wasn't a big secret he was known as a hard man.

It amazed me how something like news of a break-up took precedent over an abusive man, which would be this case. Because I'd never heard until this week that Sean was abusive.

The clues surely did point to him. I didn't have enough concrete evidence to arrest him. No judge or prosecutor would take a case on hearsay, gossip, and a bottle of Ambien. Not even the knowledge that he abused Leighann and Jilly, even that didn't make him a killer. Especially since Jilly or Leighann never filed a complaint.

I had to go see Rachel Palmer, Leighann's friend, while she was home from college. Heading to the tree lot to interview Juanita's boys was also on my list. The number one thing on my list was to check out the hair-pin curve Sterling Stinnett had told me about. There was no sense in wasting my time searching the area he was talking about without him. Having him there would shave off some time.

I'd decided to go with the street clothes today because I really was going to use my theory on Juanita and her boys to see if I could get some information out of them.

"Hello?" Finn's voice echoed down my hall while I was in my room getting ready. His voiced was followed up with Duke's nails tapping on the hardwood floor coming towards me.

"Hi," I stuck my wet head out the door and looked down the hall at Finn. "I'm going to throw my hair up in a ponytail. Fix yourself a cup of coffee."

My house on Free Row was small. It was a basic ranch with the family room in the front, kitchen in the back, small hall with two bedrooms and a bath. Off the kitchen was a small slab porch where I had a couple of chairs and premade fire pit. The chain link fence was great for Duke and Mrs. Brown, my neighbor, was nosy. It was a typical small-town neighborhood. Perfect for me since I'd spent a lot of my childhood here since it was my Poppa's house.

"No snow yet." Finn handed me a cup of steaming coffee and we clinked them together.

"No mentioning the 'S' word." I wasn't going to say or even think about snow until after we were on the big plane to Chicago. I'd welcome the snow there.

"Deal." He smiled and gave me a kiss on the head. "But you could use a little Christmas cheer around here."

"I was thinking about a Christmas tree since I do need to go to the Christmas lot today." I took a nice long sip of coffee and stared at him from underneath my brow. "I miss not having it in front of the window this year. It was fun to come home to."

"Just because we won't be here for Christmas eve and day, doesn't mean you can't celebrate while we are here. It's still the season." He always made so much sense. "Maybe after your Euchre girl's night out, I can walk over and we can decorate it."

"I'm a lucky girl." I walked over and gave him a sweet good morning kiss. "I guess I hate to get Mama's hopes up so when she does barge in here, she'd get the impression that I'd decided not to go to Chicago. I'll think about the tree."

She always came unannounced, which was typical of how a small town operates.

"Okay. Any word overnight or was everything quiet?" He asked.

"Not a word." I set my cup down and strapped my holster on underneath the grey sweatshirt I'd decided to wear with my jeans and duck boots. "Last night Sterling Stinnett told me that the night Leighann died, he heard a car crash about a mile away from Chimney Rock. That's just the beginning." My brows rose. "He also said that he heard another car come up right behind the crash. After a while, he saw swirling orange lights like a tow truck."

"You're just telling me this?" He looked at me with hawk eyes. "Let's go."

"Whoa. You just got here." I had to remind myself that we were having a friendly conversation and he wasn't trying to be my boss, which was difficult for me. "I think we need to pick up Sterling this morning from the shelter and take him to where he heard the sound. If it was Leighann, maybe the back panel is there."

"The tow truck? Sean?" Finn's jaw tensed. "I swear. If he hurt his daughter." He shook his head and stopped himself.

"I'm disturbed by the fight between the Graves and Libertys. Even if they didn't have anything to do with Leighann's death, they need to be reminded that gun slinging isn't on the up and up with the law. Which is why I still want to stop by the tree lot."

"I'm coming with you today since we've got Scott at the department." Finn grabbed two of my thermal mugs out of the cabinet and filled them up.

"You're going to have to go change because..." I opened the cabinet underneath my sink to fill Duke's bowl with kibble.

"Your theory." Finn laughed and headed to the back door. He grabbed my keys. "I'll meet you in the Jeep. I'll start it up. It's freezing out."

While Duke ate up his food, I gathered the rest of my stuff and even stuck a uniform in my bag just in case I decided to change while at the office today. With me wearing street clothes, I didn't have to come home and change before Euchre tonight. I could work right up until it was time to go. Plus, there was food at Euchre because all the Sweet Adelines brought their best recipes.

"Did he say it was freezing out?" I questioned, eyeballing the grey sky that was starting to waken the day. "Not today," I said out loud to ward off any bad weather. "We've got a murder to solve."

I grabbed my bag and locked the back door, whistling for Duke to follow me out the gate.

"That didn't take long." I jumped into the driver's seat when I noticed Finn was already in the Jeep. He only lived a couple of doors down which made it nice for long date nights.

"I kept on the same pants but threw on a sweater." He unzipped his coat and showed me the black V-neck he'd chosen. "I hope your theory about how wearing street clothes is less intimidating than my gun because I can tell you that a gun speaks for itself."

"I'VE GOT MY GUN, it's the badge that scares them." I put the shift in reverse and then drive to head towards the south end of town where the shelter was located.

It was on the same road that we took to get to the fairgrounds, but it was still too early to go there. Not much was open in Cottonwood at seven a.m.

"You stay," I instructed Duke after we pulled into the shelter house and parked. "Ready?"

"I sure am." Finn opened his door and got out. I grabbed one of those peel off sheriff stickers I gave to children and stuck it in my back pocket against my phone.

The inside of the shelter house had a desk in the middle when you walked in. It was an old school that'd been converted into a men's and women's shelter. It was also a place where the child services and handicap services had started to work out of. The second floor was where the social security administration worked out of and I recognized a few of my neighbors.

"Hey there, Merv." I greeted the older man at the counter. He'd been a junk man as long as I'd been alive. He drove an old, beat up truck that was loaded to the gills with junk. It was probably a hazard to drive behind him not only because the stuff could fall right off and make you crash, but also because of the fact that he drove so slow that it took three times as long to drive down Main Street as normal. Either way, he was safe and warm here.

"Sheriff." He nodded. "What can I do you for?"

"Are you working the desk this morning?" I asked.

"Yes, ma'am." His chin drew a line up and down.

"Is Sterling Stinnett still here?" I asked.

"Is he in trouble?" He asked with a curious look on his face.

"Sterling? Absolutely not." I smiled.

"Then he's here. I'll go round him up." Merv got up from the chair and scooted his feet along the old school tile floor on his way back through the men's swinging door.

Finn and I stood silent while we waited, giving each other a look every time the door opened, and it wasn't Sterling. Finally, Merv and Sterling walked out.

"Sheriff." Sterling looked as if he'd just woken up. His disheveled hair still looked the same, but his eyes were tired. "Is something wrong?"

"Actually, do you remember when you helped me out at Viola White's Jewelry store a year ago?" I pulled out the sticker from my pocket. "I need you again."

A year or so ago, Sterling had stood in front of the jewelry store because it was just me and Betty holding down the fort. All he really had to do was to make sure no one would enter the store and trust me, Sterling was a little scary to most people who didn't know his good heart, so he was perfect to stand there for an hour.

"Are you kidding?" His eyes grew wide open as they locked on the sticker.

"May I do the honor?" I peeled the sticker off the backing and held it out to him.

"Yes, ma'am." He nodded and stuck his chest out real far. I patted the sticker right over his heart on his jacket.

"Afterwards, we are taking you out to breakfast at Ben's." I winked and gestured for him to follow us.

"Where we going?" he asked when we got into the Jeep. Duke jumped all around him and nudged Sterling's hand.

"Last night at the church you told me that you heard a car crash on the hairpin turn about a mile from Chimney Rock. I want you to show me where you think that crash occurred." I adjusted my rear-view mirror to look at him as I turned the Jeep towards the old river road.

He did the usual way everyone told directions.

"Take a left over the rickety bridge, at the wooden cross go right, go left at the fork, when you pass the old red barn with the chipped-up fence line, you're going to veer right. The hairpin curve is yonder." He pointed into the front seat.

Above the trees on the horizon rose a blurred and blood-red sun. The trickle of the dawn danced along the bare limbs of the winter trees and over the river.

"I'm going to pull along the side and put my flashers on so if there is something here, we don't disturb the evidence." I veered off the main part of the road and hugged the edge of the grass as close as I could, so I wouldn't get into the grass.

"You'd think there'd be some tire tracks." Finn looked out the window.

"Like I said, I heard a crash but no screeching tires," Sterling said before he got out of the car. "Just beyond that tree line yonder is where I set up camp. It's for that reason only." He pointed to the painted sky.

"It's beautiful." Finn's eyes had a look of awe as he turned his head from right to left, taking in all the amazing wonder. "We just don't have this type of sky in Chicago. I don't know if I'll take this for granted."

"I'm glad, but right now, we are here for the sound Sterling heard." I had to bring them back to the moment.

"If you thinks that's pretty, you should come stay at my camp sometimes when it gets pretty. Some people don't understand why I like to live out here. I don't understand why they want to stay cooped up inside when all the beauty is here." Sterling made perfect sense and that really made me respect him.

Finn looked at me and smiled. I smiled back.

We all took time to scour the area. The grass had become stiff from the cold weather. There didn't appear to be any car tracks. None of the tree trunks seemed to be disturbed or scratched as if a car had swung around and hit them.

"Hello!" I'd lifted my chin and hollered out into the quiet morning air.

Hello, ello, llo, ooo, the echo of my voice came back to me.

"Hi," Sterling said back to me.

"If there was a crash, it might've echoed," Finn said, knowing exactly what I was doing.

"That means that it could be a little more this way." I pointed and walked a little further down. "Or even this way." I pointed behind me. "Either way, we know it's somewhere close if Sterling saw the lights of a tow truck."

"I'll go this way." Finn proceeded to walk opposite of me.

"Or over here." Poppa's ghost appeared across the road where the tree line was much closer to the road. "Because I think this here is a back panel."

I took off running across the road, not playing it off cool at all.

"Finn! Here!" I yelled making it half-way across.

He bolted towards me.

"It's definitely Leighann's side panel." Poppa stood with his hands down to his side.

The piece of plastic laid upside down and appeared to be the exact same color and shape as what was missing from Leighann's SUV.

"How on earth did you see this from over there?" Finn ran his hands through his hair before he bent down to look at it.

"I've got pretty good eyes." I gulped and sucked in a deep breath before I walked a little further away from the piece of car. "Here are some tracks."

There were tracks that showed tires had gone off the road and the back tire swiveled knocking into a tree, but not enough to make much damage to the tree.

"She wasn't going very fast." Poppa looked back towards the hairpin curve.

"She was either passed out or passing out. Let her foot up off the gas and didn't make the turn. The car probably wasn't going very fast. Just enough to smack the tree, knock off the panel." I pointed out.

"The echo must've made it sound much worse to Sterling than it really was," Finn made a good point.

I took my phone out of my pocket and noticed the time. Betty should be in the dispatch and I quickly dialed the office.

"Sheriff's department," she answered.

"Betty, it's Kenni." I'd left the walkie-talkie at home so she didn't know it was going to be me.

"Mornin'. Where are you?" She asked.

"I'm out at Leighann's crash site. I'll fill you in on the details later. Is Deputy Scott there?" I asked.

"He is," she answered.

"Can you tell him to come back out here? I'd like him to tape off the crime scene while Finn and I go check out some other leads." It was nice having another set of hands so Finn and I could keep our heads together to keep working.

"Will do." She clicked off.

While we waited for Scott to get there, I took pictures and picked up the panel for the evidence. I also gave S&S Auto a call.

"S&S Auto." The secretary answered.

"Hi there, this is Sheriff Lowry from Cottonwood." I was met with silence. "I wanted to know if you could tell me if your tow company had a call about eleven thirty p.m. to Cottonwood about three nights ago?"

"Is this about that SUV you had Frank tow?" She asked. Though I knew it was more out of curiosity, I figured I'd be nice and see if she'd give me the information instead of me having to get a subpoena.

"Yes. I found that side panel that's missing and someone told me they saw a tow truck here and I wanted to check with you before I check with tows around here." The sound of a car about to go around the curve caught my attention.

"We didn't. The only call we've gotten from Cottonwood this week was from you," she said through background noise of ruffling papers. "I hope that helps."

"More than you know." I clicked off and put my phone back into my pocket. "She said no," I said to Finn as we walked towards Scott's car.

"Are you thinking what I'm thinking?" Finn choked out the words that were swirling in my thoughts.

"Yes. That sonofabit..." Poppa started to go off on Sean Graves, but I gave him the look.

"I'm sickened at the thought. But we need more than just this." It wasn't enough. I knew it in my gut that something wasn't right.

In the beginning of me seeing Poppa, it was enough that I found the killer and he'd disappear back to wherever he'd been in the afterlife. The past few times, he'd sorta hung around until the killer was behind bars.

After Finn and Scott had a brief discussion about how we liked the crime scene to get taped off and how we liked the evidence bagged if he found some, we were back in the Jeep with Sterling and Duke on our way back to town.

"I'm starving." Sterling rubbed his hands together and down Duke. "It's so cold out there."

"It sure is." I flipped on the radio to keep me from discussing the situation with Finn. It was official sheriff business and it wasn't appropriate to talk in front of Sterling.

"Brrrr, it's cold out there." DJ Nelly's voice made my skin crawl. "The temperatures are dropping and making it ripe for the blizzard that's still set to move in a few days before Christmas. I hear that Dixon's Foodtown just got a new supply of shovels and sleds. Something for everyone." She laughed like she was taunting me through the radio. "Be sure you're ready for the storm of the century. Remember you can tune in here for all the storm updates while singing to your favorite carols on WCKK, Cottonwood's only radio station,"

"She just gets on your nerves, doesn't she?" Finn asked with a coy look across his face. He busted out laughing and bee-bopped his head when "Frosty the Snowman" came on and poked me with his finger in my rib making me laugh.

"No. It's just that it's my luck that this storm will happen. Trust me." I gripped the wheel and turned into the open parking space on Main Street right in front of Ben's Diner. "If we didn't have a big trip planned, there wouldn't be nary a snowflake."

"It's gonna snow," Sterling said as matter-of-factly as anyone could. "I've lived most my life outside and in many winters. The air feels different." He continued to talk and talk about the air as we sat down in one of the diner's tables near the front window.

"Flip your cups," Ben Harrison, owner of the diner that was his namesake, instructed with a pot of coffee in his hand. Not just any pot like those black plastic ones, it was the glass carafe that sat in the coffee pot itself. It was full to the brim.

"Keep it coming." Sterling nodded and licked his lips. "It's on the sheriff today."

"Is that right?" Ben grinned, showing off those cute dimples.

"Mmmhhhh. Sterling has been a big help this morning." I nudged Finn who'd sat down next to me. "Ain't that right, Finn?"

"Sure is," Finn confirmed.

Ben pulled the pencil out from behind his ear.

"Do you know what you want?" He asked.

"I want you to put in an order of a big heat wave." I joked and turned when I heard the bell over the diner door ring.

"He makes a lot of things around here, but no way in hell is he going to cook up some warm weather." Ruby Smith's orange-lined lips were flapping, and she rubbed her elbow. "My elbow can tell weather better than any meteorologist and I'm telling you right here and right now, there's a blizzard a-coming."

"You heard it here first." Ben pointed to Ruby, who'd already moseyed on by and continued to rub her elbow up to the counter where she eased down into a stool. "Now, what do y'all want?"

"I'm gonna eat four pancakes, side of bacon, couple of biscuits and some fried eggs." Sterling truly didn't hold back.

"I'll have that too if it's on Kenni," Finn said with a twinkle in his eye.

"Make it three. When in Rome." I smiled.

CHAPTER TWELVE

"This seems to turn our plans around today." Finn clicked his seatbelt in place after we'd taken Sterling back to the shelter, so he could get on with his day with his full belly.

"When is he going to learn that in the south, you're supposed to respect your elders? And by right," Poppa was perched on the edge of the backseat with his head stuck up between me and Finn like Duke did. "This is my Jeep and if you're driving, which I love, then I should be right up front."

My eyes stayed focused on the street, but my mind drifted off to how I was going to handle Sean Graves when I did announce he was our number one suspect.

"Do you want me to get Sean Graves and bring him in?" Finn asked like he was reading my mind.

"He does seem like the obvious suspect," Poppa said. "In case he lost his temper and maybe hurt the girl. Does he have a spare key to her SUV?"

"You know," I couldn't believe that I didn't think of that. "I do want you to go out and interview them. I want them interviewed separately." I wasn't sure if Jilly would be able to talk freely with Sean there. "You know what," I changed my mind. "Why don't you go out and interview them. I'll get Jilly alone at some point within the next day or two, but I really want to go to see Rachel Palmer."

"Sounds good." Finn shook his head. "I hate to say it, but since Sean admitted to hitting his wife and daughter, I see him in a different mirror. One that's not favorable."

"Darn right it's not favorable. Favorable? What kinda word is that?" Poppa spat. "Is that one of them northern words?" Poppa exaggerated northern so he'd get his point across that he listened to me earlier.

"I really wished I'd known this last year when we continued to take Leighann back to her house." I'd never regretted anything in my line of duty since I'd been sheriff, not even when I'd accused or arrested someone wrongly, but this time, I wasn't sure how I was going to forgive myself if Sean did kill Leighann.

Continuously, I took her back to her parents. I put her back in the danger she was apparently trying to get out of but didn't have the self-confidence to tell me. There was no sense in beating myself up about it. The only thing I could do was to get her murder solved and put whoever did it in jail for a long time. Even if it was Sean Graves.

When I'd dropped Finn off at the station, I stopped in real fast to update the white board.

I used the dry eraser to wipe off girl from dance and replaced it with Rachel's name. Not that she was a suspect, but she was one I wanted to question.

"Can you get me the address for the Palmer girl?" I tapped the tip of the dry-erase marker on the board.

"I sure can." Betty quickly flipped through her rolodex on her desk.

She loved to use that old thing and refused to even think about using the computer. Just like I wasn't about to go to a more modern way of communicating to Betty. The walkie-talkie system worked well and it was one of the things I didn't let Finn change when he wanted to bring the department up to the technology standards.

Next to Juanita's name, I wrote down the feud details between them and the Graves. Under Sean's name, I wrote down Sterling's information about the tow truck as well as the prescription medication. Under Leighann's name at the top, I made bullet points and wrote down the basics from Max's report.

Betty would gasp with each stroke of my marker since I'd not fully told her the details.

"Just terrible," she tsked and tried to act as though she wasn't paying too much attention. "Here you go." She handed me a piece of paper with the Palmers' address. I stuck it in my pocket.

"I'm heading out to the tree lot first. If you need me, just call me because I don't have my walkie-talkie with me." I gestured to Duke, he was cuddled up on his dog bed. "Do you mind?"

"Of course, I don't." Betty went back to filing and I headed out.

On my way out to the fairground, I took the opportunity to give the Palmer girl a call.

"Hi there, this is Sheriff Lowry and I'm looking for Rachel," I said to the woman who answered the other end of the phone.

"This is Cara, Rachel's mom. Is she in trouble?" There was a nervousness to her voice.

"No, ma'am." I put her at ease right off the bat. "I was going to stop by and talk to her about Leighann Graves."

"Poor Jilly," Cara's tone turned from fright to empathy. "I just can't believe it. When I told Rachel this morning, she was stunned."

"I'd witnessed Rachel and Leighann in a little argument the other night, and I'd like to talk to her about it." Even though I knew I didn't need Cara's permission to talk to her daughter since Rachel was eighteen, I still had enough respect that it was necessary on my part.

"Rachel had nothing to do with Leighann's death," Cara made sure I understood that. "She was at home with me and her father after the dance. She told us about the fight."

"I just want to talk to her. Is she home?" I asked, wondering if I was going to have to change my plans this morning and stop by there first, then the fairgrounds.

"She's not here right now, but do we need a lawyer?" She asked with concern.

"I'm just going to ask her about Leighann and what she was like since they were best friends. Can you tell me when she'll be home?" I asked.

"She's volunteering for her old cheerleading team at the tree lot at the fairgrounds," she told me.

"Oh, I'm on my way there now. I'm going to ask her a few questions, but if you'd like to be present, I'll wait," I gave her the option.

"I'm fine with it as long as you don't think Rachel had anything to do with Leighann's death because she didn't."

"I have a few more questions." I wasn't about to back myself into the corner. I would have no idea until I talked to the girl if she led me to believe that she had anything to do with Leighann's murder. The only thing I knew was that there was a fight and I wanted to exhaust all possibilities of other killers before I arrested Sean Graves. I wouldn't know that until I talked to her.

The fairground was deep in the country off Poplar Hollow Road. We had our annual summer fair there when the carnival came to town. The 4-H club used it for their cattle shows as well, and the Boy and Girl Scouts used it for their camping excursions. There were barns and stalls used for any sort of livestock and there was even a stage under covering where the annual Miss Cottonwood Beauty Pageant was held during the summer.

It was also used for the local Farmer's Market as well as the tree lot for the Cottonwood High School, which made me believe that there was no better time to check out what the team thought of Manuel. Just out of curiosity, of course.

I was actually surprised to see that there were a lot of vendors set up under the big tent already.

The church choir members stood next to the concrete fire pit with their red cloaks and mittens, both lined in white fur. They were in harmony and peered down at their song books.

It appeared Cottonwood was going all out for this Christmas season. Figured, since I wasn't going to be here.

"One, two, three." There was a voice over the loud speaker. I turned to see a man with a microphone in his hand directing something going on with the stage. "One, two, three. Step to the right. Wave. Step to the left. Wave. And don't forget to smile, ladies. And bow at the end of the runway. Make your Southern mamas proud."

"My Southern Mama has been dead for years." I heard a familiar voice followed up by some snickers. Just as I walked in view of the tent, Viola

White bent down to the ground in a curtsey. The red feather boa around her neck shed small little feathers as she struggled to get back up.

"I'm not going to be able to get back up and throw kisses to all my loyal supporters." She finally got up and stuck her hand on her hip. She wore a bright yellow turban on the top of her head that perfectly matched the color of her wrap that was loosely draped around her shoulders. Barely sticking out from underneath the layers of feather boa was a gold necklace with balls the size of baseballs that had to've been hurting her neck. It made my neck hurt just looking at it.

"Get off the stage, Viola! Let the Snow Queen have her rehearsal." Mama stepped up the side stairs, stage right. "One, two, three, one, two, three," she repeated like a little girl that was in dance class as her legs glided like she was ice skating.

It was very odd and looked very strange. I stood behind a pole that'd been wrapped with garland and so many Christmas ornaments that no one was going to see me.

"Wave and bow." She abruptly stopped. "Is it wave and bow or bow and wave?" Mama put her hand over her eyes so she could shield them from the lights that were shining on the stage.

"It's step to the left and wave, then step to the right." The man showed Mama.

"I know. You don't have to show me. I was a debutant." She sucked in a deep breath and stuck out her chest. "Move to the right. Wave," she whispered and did that darn hand thing she'd been doing.

"Wait!" The man yelled. "What is this?" The man snarled and did the strange wave. "This is not appropriate."

"It's the Queen's wave and I'm going to do whatever I want." Mama was getting upset.

I closed my eyes and took a gulp in hopes I wasn't going to have to step in because this man clearly had no idea who Vivian Lowry was and she by no means had any problem letting him know.

"I'm not sure," The man started to say before I stepped out from behind the pole.

"Good early afternoon," I smiled at him. "Hello, Mama." I waved. "You're looking mighty good up there."

"Shep, that's my daughter, Kendrick Lowry. Sheriff Lowry of Cottonwood." Mama hated the fact I was sheriff but was more than happy to use the title when she felt like it was going to get her something.

"I just stopped by to make sure everything was okay out here," I said.

"We are fine. I was just showing Shep my wave like the Queen." She continued to walk the front of the stage. "Elbow, wrist, elbow, wrist and then the wave."

"She's got it down pat doesn't she?" I asked Shep. What kind of name was Shep? "She's been practicing a long time."

By the look of the light bulb going off in his head, I could see he knew that I was just telling him that it was better to let her go than to correct her.

"I'm sure you've got your hands full with all these women." I turned my attention to him while Mama continued to do her ice skating moves and weird waves.

"Only with your Mama and Viola White. Those two might have a fist fight." He shrugged. "I'm not sure I'd stop it either. I've never seen two women their ages wanting so badly to be crowned queen."

"I'm taking it that you aren't from here or the South?" I asked.

"Neither, honey." His nose snarled. "I'm doing this as a favor for the county pageant officials. Unfortunately, they decided to send me to nowhere Kentucky."

"I'm sure you'll find our little slice of nowhere to be quite charming if you'll let it. How long are you in town for?" I asked and noticed Jolee's food truck pulling into the fairgrounds.

"Only until after the pageant. I'm leaving that night on a red-eye back to California so I can be home with my loved ones for Christmas."

"That's nice. Well, if you do need anything, you give me a holler." I pulled a business card from my back pocket since I was in street clothes.

"Holler?" He asked sarcastically. "As in a yee-haw kinda Kentucky thing?"

"Just a word of advice, Shep," I leaned in real close and said real stern, "Around here, we take our little hillbilly world to heart."

He drew back as if I offended him.

"You are referring to us as hillbillies," I made no room for him to correct me. "And by no means take our accents as ignorance. We are very kind and smart people. If you just stay focused on why you are here and maybe take whatever stick is stuck up your you-know-what, you might find that you'll enjoy our little town here in Kentucky."

At this point, I'd had my fill of Mr. Shep and I would let him deal with the arguing that Mama and Viola seemed to be involved in on stage left as I dismissed myself and made my way back to the far end of the fairground where I could see rows of trees all tied up to different tomato stakes. Above the trees there were strung twinkling Christmas lights that outlined the entire tree lot.

On the side of the lot, I could see Darnell's truck pulled up with the lift gate down. There were a few boys hauling freshly cut trees out of the back of it. Kenneth Chalk, the football coach, had his whistle in his mouth and was directing the boys where to go with the firs.

"You're like a drill sergeant," I joked when Coach came to greet me after he saw me walking up.

"Gotta be strict with these young men or they jump out of line real quick." He put his hand out for me to shake. "Sheriff, how are you?" A knit stocking hat covered up his bald head.

"You know. Same old, same old." I tucked my hands in the pocket of my jacket. "It could be a little warmer though."

"Oh no," he shook his head. "Perfect for a white Christmas."

"You and I both know that weather around here changes with the wind." I hated to see everyone get their hopes up about this big snow storm that never was going to happen.

"Even so, you better pick you out a nice tree to look at over the next week or so because if we do get that big snow storm, you won't be leaving your house for days." His brows furrowed. "I guess you might somehow since you're the sheriff and could get some calls."

"I'm not going to need a big tree this year. I'm actually going to take a little vacation." I watched the boys to see if I recognized them from the dance.

"Vacation? At Christmas?" He acted as if it was the strangest thing he'd ever heard. "I thought your Mama was in the running for Snow Queen."

"I'm going to go meet Finn's family in Chicago. I guess I'm going to miss the big crowning." The girl I'd seen arguing with Manuel had walked up to one of the boys hauling trees out of Coach's truck. It wasn't polite to walk away from Coach, so I watched her every move.

"That'll break your mama's heart. That's none of my business. But she'll make it everyone's business." A hint of a smile made the corner of his lip turn up.

"I'm actually here to see you." I watched the girl hastily talking to the boy. He jerked his arm away from her and she stormed off into the tree lot, leaving him to do his job. "I wanted to know if you knew of anything strange with one of your old and current players."

"You're referring to the Libertys." He rolled his eyes. "At least Sean Graves isn't here this year to ruin our fundraiser. Is this about the Graves girl?" He asked. "I sure hated to hear that she was found in the river. Do you think an animal ran out in front of her?"

"I'm not sure, but I'd love to get your take on the Liberty home situation," I said.

"You asking about Manuel turning down his college opportunity?" He asked, and I nodded. "Well, if he were my boy, I'd made him take it, but his mam doesn't have no control over those boys."

"What do you mean?" I asked.

"Them two boys of hers run around all night. Take Jonathon for instance. He's a good player and he might be better than Manuel, but he can't keep up with his grades or keep his head on straight. I went to Juanita and told her but she's so distraught over Manuel and the Graves girl, she didn't want to discuss either of her other two boys." He leaned in. "Over the past couple of days, I've never seen the woman so happy. She's been here volunteering and singing. She don't care one bit that her boy is trying to mend a broken heart over his girlfriend's death. Beats me." He shrugged.

"Your Mama makes the best fruit cakes." He pointed to his truck. Mama must've been up to her tricks of giving out her famous sweets for a vote for Snow Queen. "She brought me one this morning. Good woman your Mama is. Anyways, for your sake, I hope you get out of here in time for your vacation. You sure do deserve it." His eyes softened. "Now what about that sheriff's department donation this year?"

During the year, the sheriff's department, the three of us (Me, Finn and Betty), always put our spare change in a big ole glass whiskey jar that sat on the ground. At the end of each year we liked to pick a charity to donate the saved money to, and generally we had around five hundred dollars which wasn't bad for some change.

"You know, I need to check with Betty Murphy on that."

He dragged his stocking cap off his head and rubbed it.

"Alright. You stop on down to the department and pick up your annual donation," I told him and took my hands out of my pocket.

I rubbed them vigorously. I swore the air was even ten degrees colder since I'd been standing here.

"Is that the Palmer girl over there with Beka Durst?" I questioned the coach since I knew he knew all the kids in school while I took my phone out of my back pocket and quickly texted Betty to write a check out to Cottonwood High School for our annual donation.

"Yeah. She came back this year to help with the lot while home from college. She's a sweet girl." He pinched his lips. "I'm not sure what happened, but she and the Graves girl used to be real close."

"I'd heard that. It was great talking with you. Good luck." I gestured to the trees. "I'm gonna pick me out one before I get out of here."

The carolers had moved around while I'd been shooting the breeze with Coach. At least during our conversation, I'd found out that Juanita had almost completely taken over as the head volunteer over the past couple of days.

I watched Mama as she walked over to the food truck, this time with a big sash diagonal across her body that read "Snow Princess" in gold glitter.

I hurried inside of the trees before Mama could see me because if she did get a minute to corner me, she'd asked all about the Graves and I wasn't prepared to make a statement just yet.

The young girl I wanted to talk to was out sitting at the card table with Beka. A metal money box that I'd seen at many of the gates of the Cottonwood High School home football games was on top of the table.

"Hi, Beka," I greeted her. "How's your Mama doing?"

"She's fine," she answered. Her hair was pulled up in a high ponytail like the other little cheerleaders running around. "She's busy running the tow company while the Graves take off a few days. You know, for the memorial and all." She looked at Rachel and frowned.

"Are you going to the memorial?" Rachel asked Beka.

"If mom gets the work done. She's got to log the mileage on the tows and keep them filled with gas, which takes up a lot of time."

Mileage? Her word circled my brain when it flicked my gut.

"You're thinking now." Poppa ghosted next to a small fir tree that stood up next to the girl's table. "This is perfect for your house this year. Plus, I know mileage could tell if one of the Graves's tow trucks was used the night of Leighann's murder." Poppa's thoughts were all over the place.

He took the words right out of my mouth, on both, and I tucked that thought in the back of my head.

"She's doing a good thing." I confirmed. I turned my eyes upon the girl with her. "Are you Rachel Palmer?" I asked the girl.

"Yes." She looked at Beka and they both shrugged at each other.

"I'm Sheriff Lowry and I wanted to know if I could talk to you about Leighann Graves." Both girls' eyes grew big.

"Sure." She and Beka could pass as twins. Both had on the varsity letter jacket that had "cheerleader" sewn on the back. "I'll be right back."

I couldn't help but notice Beka grab her phone and start texting. I was sure she was letting all the kids in high school know I was going to talk to Rachel.

They even had on the same eye shadow, lipstick and hair pulled back as tight as bark on a tree in a high ponytail.

"Would you like a hot chocolate?" I asked after we walked out of the tree lot and I noticed Mama was no long at the food truck. One of Jolee Fischer's homemade fudgy hot chocolates with mini-marshmallows sounded really good about right now.

"I'd love one if you're paying because I have no cash whatsoever. If I didn't have to work this stupid tree lot for the team, I'd be home in my warm bed. Poor college kid." Rachel Palmer was no different than Leighann Graves. No wonder they were friends.

"I THOUGHT YOU WERE VOLUNTEERING?" I asked.

"I am, but Coach usually gives out a little gift card at the end. I sure could use it," she said.

"Sheriff," Jolee's eyes skimmed over me and focused on the girl. "Hi, Rachel. I'm sorry to hear about Leighann."

"Yeah, me too," The girl replied. "I'll have a hot chocolate on her."

"Okay." Jolee's eyes got big and when she directed her attention to me, I nodded. "Two?"

"Two and extra marshmallows." I held my fingers in the air. "Why don't we go sit under the shelter where they are holding the Snow Queen pageant?"

Rachel shrugged.

"Do you mind bringing us the drinks?" I asked Jolee.

"Nope. It'll be a second. My fudge is in the oven." She looked behind me. "Can I help you?" she asked the next person in line behind me and Rachel.

We headed over to the shelter where there were picnic tables in the back. The front was already filled with folding chairs in anticipation of the tree lighting.

"There's the tree." Rachel pointed to the truck hauling a hitched trailer with a big pine tree on it. "We also get to decorate it."

"The team?" I asked, and we sat down on the very far right picnic table closest to the food truck.

"Yeah. Leighann loved doing that when we were cheerleaders." She gave a slight grin as if she was having the memory play in her head. Her arms propped up on the table.

"I saw the two of you arguing at the Hunt Club dance." She stared at me with blank eyes as I talked. "Can you tell me about it?"

"I'm so upset that she's dead, but she's the one who changed everything." Rachel sat back and put her hands in the letter jacket front pockets.

"How so?" I asked.

"She and I were going to go to Bluegrass College together last year. We had it all planned out. The sorority we were going to join. The dorm where we were going to live. Matching bedding and all the fun monogramed stuff. Then," she rolled her eyes, "Manuel Liberty got buff and decided he could be the football star and steal her heart." Her words held a real bitter tone.

"Is that a problem?" I asked.

"It is when my boyfriend was the head football star and supposed to get a full scholarship to Bluegrass College. Then Bluegrass College decided to look at Manuel instead. That became a real problem. Neither of our boyfriends could stand the other. It didn't help that Manuel is a bit of a bully." She rambled on and stopped when Jolee walked over with the steaming cups of hot chocolate.

"Here you go." She sat down a baggie full of marshmallows. "Extra goodness."

"Thanks," I said and handed Rachel the bag first. Jolee walked back to her truck. "What does this have to do with you and Leighann?"

"She decided that she wanted to go with Manuel since she started dating him." Slowly she stirred the hot chocolate with the wooden stir and blew on the steamy goodness.

"Both decided not to go to college. Why?" I asked about the new name she threw in.

"Whatever Manuel wanted, Leighann wanted too." She said it in that duh kind of way that made me thank god I wasn't a teenager. She pulled out her phone. "How long is this little talk of ours going to take? Beka needs me."

"You and Beka close?" I asked.

"We're friends. I didn't hang with her much in high school since she's a year younger." She threw some more marshmallows in the cup.

"It looks like there's a lot of boys that can help her manage." I wanted to ask her some more questions. "Can you tell me what you and Leighann were arguing about at the dance?"

"Last year when she worked up the nerve to tell her parents, who by the way are head cases," she put her hands in the air to get her point across, "that she wasn't going to college. She was going to take a gap year. That's when I realized she was leaving me high and dry to go to Bluegrass by myself. It was too late to get a roommate at that point, so I had to go with an unknown. The worst."

"What was the fight about the other night?" I couldn't understand how she could lose me so fast. I'd ask her a question and she'd circle it back to nothing I needed to know.

"I'm trying to forget about that. Especially since it was the last time I'd talked to her," Rachel's voice cracked. "I ran into Leighann in the bathroom and when I ignored her, she got up in my business. I told her I had nothing to say to her since she ruined our plans. When I left the bathroom and saw her and Manuel making out by the punch bowl, I about barfed." Her head was moving back and forth as she told the story as if she were right back in the situation. "I marched right back up to her and told her that I actually wanted to thank her for dumping me because I'd met a bunch of new friends and she didn't have any because Manuel made sure she didn't." She shrugged and pressed her lips together, which evidently had a direct line to quirk her right brow, because she did this a lot when she talked. "I regret it."

"You had no way of knowing that she was going to pass away." I wanted to offer some sort of comfort, though I still had more questions. "He made her stop having friends?" I asked to clarify my thoughts. Before now, I thought Leighann had chosen to dump her friends.

"He's a loser. After they started dating, she'd cancel our plans because Manuel didn't want her to go or didn't think she should do whatever it was we were going to do. I can't believe she wasted what time on earth she had with him. I can't even believe I was friends with her. When friends make promises, they keep them." She brought her hand up to her head to push back a stray piece of hair that'd fallen out of the ponytail, exposing a tattoo heart on the fatty part of her thumb. Just like the one Leighann had.

"Tell me about your tattoo." I pointed to her hand.

"It was a big mistake I'd made with Leighann. Now," she spoke softly and ran her finger over it. "I will treasure it because we got it when we were the best of friends and before all this happened." She gulped. "'Friends forever tattoos' was what we called them." She rubbed the tattoo like she was trying to rub it away. "After she ended our friendship, I wanted to get it removed. Actually," She folded her hands between her knees, "Manuel is the one who ended our friendship."

"Clearly, you're still very hurt by it." I watched her body language as she struggled with being upset and trying to hide it.

"How do you think you'd feel after you made all these plans and suddenly they were changed?" She asked. "While I was at school, I'd forgotten all about her. Now that I'd seen her and now that she's dead, it's all come back." She stood up. "I'm super sad she's dead because I'll never ever get to make it right with her. I'm not sure I can live with that."

"After your fight at the Christmas Cantata, where did you go?" I asked.

"That's a whole nuther thing. I went home." Her country accent deepened. "If I'd known my parents made me have a curfew when I came home after having freedom while away at college, I might not've come home for Christmas."

"What time is your curfew?" I asked.

"Midnight," she replied with a sarcastic tone. "Ridiculous. Like I'm some baby. Even Beka's curfew is later and she's still in high school."

"Before you go, how is your roommate in college now?" I asked.

"Great." She frowned. "I'm not sure I'd have so many new friends if Leighann had gone with me. She's a one-friend person and with my new roommate, we joined a sorority and we've met all sorts of people not from around here."

"I'm glad you're enjoying it. Bye, Rachel." I waved, knowing in my heart that she didn't kill Leighann even though I knew I'd be able to confirm where she was by tracking her phone that never left her hand and talking with her parents.

The tree fit the perfect length of the roof of the Wagoneer. Not too tall and not too short. Perfect for a little Christmas cheer while I was here. It was tied down nicely by Jonathon Liberty and Beka Durst.

"Thanks." I gave them both a couple of ones for a tip. "It's not much, but it's something."

"Man, every little bit helps with college." Jonathon seemed grateful and stuck it in his pocket.

"I've been saving up for some new lipstick for my Mama for Christmas. This helps." Beka stuck it in her pocket and walked away.

"Jonathan, I wanted to talk to you," I said.

"Yeah. My mom told me you were going to question me about when we went all loaded up on old man Graves. We didn't have any bullets." He tried not to grin as he told the story. "That man is a jerk. I swear it was the guns that made him change his mind about my bro and Leighann."

"How so?" I asked, restraining from reprimanding him.

"That's the same week that Leighann told them she wasn't going to college and she and Manuel had decided to stay in Cottonwood." His eyes slid over to his mama's. She was standing with a customer but looking at us. "Mom was so mad though."

Jonathon gnawed on the side of his cheek as though he was trying to hold back something.

"Jonathan." I reached out and touched his arm to bring him back to the present. "If there's something you need to tell me, it's safe with me."

"My mom will kill me, but I know that you think she's a suspect. Far from it." He looked down at his feet and pushed around some dirt with the toe of his boot. "Truth is, my mom has Crohn's and she's not getting better. She only wanted what's best for us. Since Manuel is the oldest, he took it upon himself not to go to college and work, so he can provide."

He bit back the emotions I could see swelling up inside of him.

"Mom was mad and blamed Leighann for it. But in reality, it's her sickness that kept him here," his voice cracked.

One after the other, little town secrets were coming to light. First, Sean Graves being an abuser and now Juanita Liberty's illness. Now I wasn't so sure she didn't kill Leighann.

"Where were you the night of Leighann's murder?" I asked him.

"At home. Mom had a little set back that day. I had to take care of the kids while Manuel went to meet Leighann at the dance. When he got home around eleven, he said I could go on out, but I was slap worn out. Mom had finally fallen asleep." He shoved his hands in his pocket. "I'm no cop or nothing, but I know Leighann didn't get along with Sean at all."

"Thanks. I might stop by and talk to your other brothers." I gave him a little warning just in case I wanted to check out all the stories. "And another thing, your brother looks up to you and gun slinging is no way to teach him a lesson."

"That's what my mom said. She was fit to be tied after Sean Graves called her. All the business about 'we are better than them' and all that." He looked over at his mom. "She's a good woman. She's done the best she could with us unruly boys. Leighann was strong like Mom, but Mom was upset about Manuel's decision and I think it was easier for her to blame Leighann and not herself. She didn't want the world to know she was sick. Just her and Dr. Shively."

"If there's anything you boys need, or even your mama, you can always call me." I wanted him to know that I was there to help in any way.

He simply nodded and walked away.

CHAPTER THIRTEEN

"She's got Crohn's?" Finn hung the silver tinsel around the back side of the tree and I took it from him to carry it around to the front, then back again. "That doesn't make her innocent."

"I think that if she's in pain and in bed like Jonathon said, then she couldn't physically have taken all the steps and moved Leighann around like a rag doll."

"I bet deep down she knew that Manuel stayed because of her." Finn made a good point.

We did the tinsel wrap around the small tree until there was none left.

"Why didn't Leighann tell her parents that's why he stayed?" I asked.

"True. Maybe they'd been more sympathetic to the situation." Finn shrugged.

"I also talked to Rachel Palmer, Leighann's best friend. She claimed she had a curfew and was at home that night, but I'd talked to her mom before I talked to her. She too confirmed Rachel was home."

"What was their deal the other night?" He asked and walked out from behind the tree.

"It seemed all like immature teenage angst junk that just escalated. Rachel and Leighann were best friends. When Leighann and Manuel started dating, it appeared the friendship started to go south. Leighann stopped hanging around her friends." I opened the ornament box and started to hang the ornaments on the tree. "Then Leighann had skipped out on them going away to college together and even rooming together. Rachel still harbors bad feelings of betrayal."

"Oh no." Finn bent down and looked over the ornaments. "Are you and your friends hanging out less because of us?"

"Don't be ridiculous." I pushed him on the ground and snuggled up to him while we looked at all the colored lights we'd put on the tree first.

Duke bounced around us. He gave a few woofs thinking we were playing with him when I was trying to break the sudden mood from happily putting up a Christmas tree to talking about the murder.

"My Poppa used to put his tree in this same spot." I rested on my elbow and hip. "He would love it. All these colored lights."

"It's beautiful, just like you." Finn reached over and tucked a strand of hair behind my ear.

"You aren't even looking at the tree," I said.

"I'm looking at you. Tell me something else about your Christmas past." His encouraging me only opened up the flood gates.

"Well, when I as a little girl and we did get all this snow every year, he would get a real sled and some of his friends' horses to pull us in sleigh rides." The memories were so vivid in my head, just like it was yesterday. "He'd have hot chocolate on the sled and warm quilt blankets. He'd have them take us down to the courthouse lawn where they had the big Christmas tree. This was way before the fairgrounds had the tree lighting event."

"That was one time only?" Finn asked and snuggled up close behind me, resting his chin in-between my ear and shoulder.

"It was a couple of times but then the weather started to get warmer and warmer, so we would just drive down to the tree lighting." I tried to swallow the big lump in my throat because talking about it made me realize that this was the first year that I'd not been here when they did light up the tree. "Just like this year with me going with you. Things change."

"Are you trying to convince me that you're not going to miss out on the tradition or convince yourself that it's going to be okay?" He asked.

"Because if you aren't okay with it, I don't mind going to Chicago by myself. You can meet my parents anytime."

"No." I jiggled my body around to face him. "Don't be ridiculous. This just can't be a take and no give relationship." Though I suddenly wanted to burst into tears. I had to get up and stop talking about it. "And if I don't want my friends to dump me, then I've got to get to Euchre."

"I'll clean up here, feed Duke and head on home." He reached up and extended his hand for me to help him up, only his real ploy was to tug me down into his arms for some more snuggles before I really had to go.

This week's Euchre night was at Tibbie Bells's house. We had decided she had the best house out of all of us and she didn't have a boyfriend, children or pets to worry with.

Tibbie lived right off Main Street on what we referred to as the Town Branch. There was a small water brook, or branch, that ran the length of the street. Every house had a small concrete bridge that gapped the street to the driveway. The houses were old like most of the houses in Cottonwood and so were the bridges. Most of the time the small creek was dried up and not much water flowed these days, but it was still some history and part of my childhood that made Cottonwood the cozy, Southern town all of us loved.

The room on the left was where Tibbie had all the tables for the Sweet Adelines to put their food. I'd like to say it was the best part of the night, but it wasn't. The best part was the hissy fits and fights that the Euchre tournament brought out in everyone. This was especially good since there'd be a lot of talk about Leighann's death. This was when Poppa always told me to keep my ear to the ground because somewhere in all that gossip there was some truth.

Still, I grabbed a plate at the end of one table and perused all the finger foods that I'd call my supper.

"Good gracious, didn't I see you in that outfit today?" Betty asked as she slid up to the right side of me.

"What was all this nonsense I heard down at the jewelry store that you were using Sterling as a deputy?" Viola White eyeballed me as she came up on the left of me. "Now, I might be old and halfway senile, but I do know that my good earned tax dollars do not pay for Sterling."

"You got two things right," Mama said and snuck up behind me. "You are old and senile."

"Oh shut up, Viv. You ain't too far behind and with zero grandchildren I might add." Viola's eye drew up and down me. "If you don't get that baby factory kicked in gear, you'll have to shut down production."

"My production is just fine, thank you. Ain't that right, Camille?" I asked Camille Shively, the only doctor in Cottonwood when she walked into the room.

"I'm pleading the fifth. I knew not to come tonight. Nothing ever goes well at these events." Camille picked up a meatball and popped it into her mouth. "Mmmm, good."

"It's a shame about that Graves girl." Myrna Savage walked in with a big container of poinsettias. "That's for you, honey. Merry Christmas," she said to Tibbie and handed them to her.

"Why thank you. They are lovely." Tibbie took a few cheery steps across the room and replaced the Dixon Foodtown flowers with the poinsettias, though I didn't know why she just didn't put them somewhere else since Myrna Savage also supplied the grocer with fresh flowers from her greenhouse.

"Anyways, about that Graves girl." Myrna sashayed though the crowd of beady little eyes that suddenly focused on me. "You know anything yet?"

"Now, now, Myrna," I wagged a finger. "You know I can't give out any official details."

I moved on down the line and filled my plate with Christmas bark, fancy holiday cookies and a couple of slices of pie, skipping the hanky-panky and any sort of meat dish that might be healthier than the sweet treats I'd opted for.

"The Christmas Cantata turned out nice." I saddled up to Tibbie in the other room where she was finishing setting up the four-person-each card tables where we'd start our Euchre games. "You did another fine job."

"Thanks." Her hazel eyes had a twinkle in them. "I really enjoy my job," she said and referred to her event planning occupation. Her long brown hair was normally parted down the middle, but tonight she wore it in a deep side part and fishtail braid down the side of her head. "Are you all ready for your big trip?"

"I am. That doesn't mean I won't miss y'all." I reached over and squeezed her arm.

I had to throw it in there since I was going to miss our annual movie night that Jolee had already scolded me for, but I certainly didn't want me and my friends to end up like Leighann and Rachel. Though I'd hoped we were much wiser since we were older.

"This is exciting though." Her shoulders rose up with excitement. "You're going to go to Chicago for the first time and it's going to be so romantic. What if the snowstorm hits there instead and when you wake up on Christmas, it'll be a white one just like the movie."

"If it is, I sure don't see Finn singing 'Snow'." I laughed.

"You could sing 'White Christmas'." She laughed. "But knowing Finn, I don't think so."

"Are you going to Leighann's memorial tomorrow afternoon?" Tibbie asked.

"Tomorrow?" I halted with shock.

Neither myself nor Max had cleared Leighann's body to be handed over to the family.

"By the way you are acting, I'd take it as a no." She peered at me. "You seem a little shocked."

"I'd not heard about it and since I've not cleared her body to the family, it's a bit shocking." I wondered what'd transpired.

"It's a memorial. They said they weren't having a body. The church phone line is abuzz with food for it." Tibbie nodded. "I have no idea how I got in charge of the phone line, but now I wished I'd turned it down. But you know if I'd done that, my mom would've died of embarrassment." She nudged me. "You know we good Southern daughters always make our mamas proud." She winked.

The phone line was technically a gossip hot line. In between there was some sort of organization on who was bringing what to a funeral or memorial or even the birth of a baby.

"They are going to bury her in a private funeral later." Tibbie's brow rose as her chin lifted up and then down.

"Very interesting," I muttered and walked into the other room to join the other card players.

The room had started to fill with the girls and they were already taking their seats with their partners. Jolee and I had to play Mama and Viola White, which was going to be interesting to say the least since they had this little competition thing going with Snow Queen. Sometimes it drove me nuts how competitive Mama really was.

Camille Shively had walked into the room and while Tibbie continued to set multiple card decks down along with pens and paper, I took the moment to see exactly what the good doctor knew.

"Kenni, you know that I can't tell you what's in a patient's file." She always used the client privilege law on me.

"I just want to know how long Sean Graves has been on Ambien. And what stage of Crohn's disease Juanita Liberty is in. That's all. Don't make me go to a judge and get a subpoena when you can just tell me." It was a little dance she and I did that made things so interesting between us.

It wasn't like Camille and I were best friends or even good friends when we were growing up. She was the young pretty girl with beautiful black hair that only movie stars could afford, only hers was real and not from a bottle down at Tiny Tina's. She had the perfect skin and black eyes. She was like a real-life Snow White.

She was real smart too. She'd decided to become a doctor and move back to Cottonwood because our doctor at the time was knocking on death's door and she knew eventually she'd have the market, kinda like Max Bogus in the death industry.

"Why don't you stop by my office tomorrow and bring me the filled-out paper work that you'd submit to the judge. It's a lot more private there." She twisted her head around. "Everyone will suddenly know everything if we talk here."

"I'll be by around lunch," I told her because I had to go talk to Angela Durst, the Graves' secretary.

The games got underway and Mama was the dealer.

"Cut the cards?" She asked, holding the deck out. I knocked on it to pass. The knocking was an enduring Euchre term.

"I'm not cutting my luck. I need all the luck I can get," I said.

"Speaking of luck, how unlucky was it that poor Leighann got luck of the draw with Sean?" Viola snarled over the cards. "I'd like to beat that man."

"You and the rest of Cottonwood," Mama nodded and dealt two cards to everyone and then three to finish out, so we could start the hand. "I remember when they signed the adoption papers."

"Adoption papers?" My head jerked up.

"Don't you know?" Mama asked and all of us passed on the trump card she'd flipped over on the throwaway deck. All of us passed again before she called hearts as trump. "I'll go it alone," she proclaimed and shoved the throwaway deck over to Viola.

"I hope you play this hand better than you're playing your cards at the pageant," Viola whispered under her voice. "But I trust my partner."

Mama eyed Viola before she slid her gaze to the cards fanned in her hands. She led with the Jack of Hearts as she drew out the hearts in mine and Jolee's hands.

"I don't know what, Mama? Concentrate," I encouraged her.

"I am concentrating," she snipped back.

"I mean on the story." My last nerve was tickling my anger that I felt welling up in me. "Don't I know what?" I asked again.

"Leighann isn't Sean's daughter. He adopted her when he and Jilly got married. She was just a tiny tot and cute as a button," Mama dragged off topic.

Jolee and I threw our cards in the middle when we realized that Mama was going to take every card trick with her hearts and win four points.

"You're telling me that Sean Graves isn't Leighann Graves biological father?" I sat there dumbfounded.

"That's probably why he felt like it was okay to be mean to the girl," Viola said with a stern-faced expression.

I didn't know how I made it through the rest of the Euchre tournament. We'd even turned out the nightly winner. With this new information that'd come to light about Leighann being adopted, it put the desperate father, Sean Graves, in a completely different light.

CHAPTER FOURTEEN

"How did you not know about this and live here all your life?" Finn asked over a cup of steaming coffee as both of us stared across the diner table at each other the next morning.

"I was a kid myself when this happened." I really had tried to think back to when I was a kid to remember. "I would've been around twelve years old when that happened. I was riding around with Poppa and playing records, not wondering what was going on with people I went to church with. It wasn't like they just showed up in Cottonwood one day. They both lived here."

"Who is the dad?" Finn asked.

"I have no idea. I even asked around at Euchre and Mama said that was one of the biggest mysteries in Cottonwood." I held the cup of coffee up to my lips and took a sip. "Now that I think back in the investigation since her death, he's never called Leighann his daughter."

"What about before she was killed and all those times he'd called about Manuel?" He eased back and let Ben put a biscuits and gravy plate down in front of him and one in front of me.

"Are you talking about the Graves?" Ben sat down in the empty seat next to me. "I was going to tell you that something strange happened the week before Leighann died."

"What?" I asked. Then I put my hand up. "Is this on record?"

"Sure." He nodded.

"What happened?" I asked and pinched off a piece of my biscuit, giving it to Duke.

"That local slimeball lawyer, Wally Lamb, was in here with Jilly Graves. They were sitting right over there in that corner table away from everyone." He pointed to the far corner opposite us next to the kitchen. "I offered them a table up front since the kitchen can be loud."

"They didn't want anyone to hear them." Poppa ghosted in the seat next to Finn. My lashes lowered, and I glared at him. "Oh, ding, ding." He winked.

"Then she left and Leighann came in." Ben looked over his shoulder when another early customer came through the door. "I'll be right with you." They made eye contact. The customer walked up to the counter. He continued, "Leighann was crying saying that her mom deserved better and hoped that her mom could get half of the business. That's when I heard something about divorce. Leighann really brought on the tears after Manuel and Juanita came in."

"Divorce?" Finn, me and Poppa all asked at the same time.

"Now, I don't know for sure, but Jolee told me that Sean was an abuser and it dawned on me what'd taken place right over there and it's something I just can't swallow without reporting it." Ben stood up and topped off our coffee mugs before he left to go take care of the other customers.

"The kitchen was covering up their voices so no one could hear them." I was getting really good at repeating Poppa and his observations.

"Right." Finn snapped his fingers. "Maybe she was telling him something about the abuse and trying to stop it."

"Maybe Sean didn't know that she was thinking about divorce and Leighann confronted him about it, and out of anger—resentment maybe—took out Leighann and planned to do away with Jilly. But Jilly called us about Leighann's disappearance before he could hurt her." It was a far-fetched idea and plan, but it gave us more clues to go on. Not to mention made Sean Graves more of a suspect.

"Every other time they've called about Leighann with Manuel, wasn't it Sean that did the calling not Jilly?" Finn asked.

"Yes. This time it was her. But we need to double check." I pointed to our plates. "We better eat so it doesn't get cold and we can get out of here."

For the next ten minutes, there might've been silence between us but I could tell that his mind was going as fast as mine on conspiracies and why Sean Graves would kill Leighann.

Before we even realized, we were down the street at the department looking up old files and records from when Sean Graves had called the department about Manuel. Duke had climbed in his bed and curled into a tight ball. He liked cold weather but not the bitter and depressing cold that'd hung over the entire town of Cottonwood.

"There are fifteen times in the past two years." I kept my finger on the last one. "The last time he'd called was right before she'd turned eighteen."

"Then it appeared that he'd just washed his hands of her." Finn brushed his hands together. "No longer responsible for her."

"That's why he made it easier to toss her out of the house," Scott spoke up from the makeshift desk he'd made near the fax machine.

"That's not entirely true." I glanced up at the clock. It was nearing eight a.m. "I'm going to go see Angela Durst, the secretary of Graves Towing. I'd heard she'd taken in Leighann when Sean kicked her out."

"This is all very interesting." Scott had a perplexed look on his face.

"Oh my God," I gasped. My eyes shot over to Poppa. "Sean did say that he went to Chimney Rock that night to see if Leighann and Manuel were there."

"Covering his tracks." Poppa's eyes lowered. "If I was alive, I'd give him a good ole one-two." Poppa jabbed the air with his best boxing moves.

The door opened, and Betty walked in.

"Weee-doggy." She gave a shimmy-shake. "I wish that storm would blow in and get it over with. I'm so tired of hearing the news and radio about it. It's cold as a gravestone out there."

We all snickered, and she looked up.

"What? What are y'all staring at? Did something happen?" She dragged her pocket book from her elbow and sat it down on her desk before she peeled off her coat and flung it on the back of her chair.

"Betty," I stood up and patted my leg. "Get the cell ready. We might have a customer by the end of the day."

"Really?" She gasped in delight.

It wasn't every day, heck wasn't every week that we got to use the only cell in the room and I could feel it. I was getting close to solving this murder.

"Finn, do you mind checking up on the report of Leighann's phone records? Scott, can you check with the forensics on the side panel to make sure it was a match?" I asked and gathered my bag and patted my leg for Duke to come. "I've got to go get some answers from the eyes and ears of Graves Towing: Angela Durst."

"Don't forget about what you told me about Camille Shively," Finn reminded me how I'd told him over coffee that Camille told me to bring the subpoenaed paperwork and she'd take a look at it and possibly give me what I needed without actually going through a judge.

The Wagoneer took much longer to heat up than normal. I kept sliding the old knob to the right to see if it'd go any further.

"It's an old Jeep. You've got to be tender and gentle with her." Poppa patted the dashboard, just like he used to when I was a kid. "It's not a modern-day fancy car."

"Now that we are alone." I stopped the Jeep at the stop light and zipped up my coat. "What is your take on the new light of things?"

"I think that Sean looks very suspicious. I'm not sure what killing Leighann would do for him." Poppa brought in the logical side of things. "Did she have something on him other than he hated Manuel? After this divorce or whatever Ben had witnessed, was there going to be some sort of information? Why would he drug her first and not her mama? That's not logical at all."

"I'm not sure, but you can bet your bottom dollar we are going to find out," I said in a hushed whisper on our way back out to Graves Towing.

"The sky sure looks grey." Poppa looked out window. "Do you remember when it snowed a lot when you were a kid and I'd gotten that sled?"

"Best memory of winter I've got." I blinked back a tear and looked over at him, but he'd ghosted away.

Poppa was never one for sentimental feelings. He was a tough old geezer and that's what made him a great sheriff. There was a legacy I had to hold up to and I prayed I was doing so, even in the midst of a murder.

The tow company sign was flashing on and a little bit in me wished Sean had closed the company, but a business was a business.

"Hi-do, Kenni," Angela Durst greeted me from her desk. "If you're here to see Jilly or Sean, they are gone to the funeral home. They are having a quick memorial tonight and tomorrow is going to be the funeral without the body since...well, you know the circumstances."

Max wasn't releasing Leighann's body until all the facts were presented for a final report and I'd gotten it. We didn't want to just turn the body over and maybe miss something. It was a little early for the Graves to have decided to do something. It'd only been a couple of days.

"No. I came here to see you." I took a couple of steps closer to her desk. "I know you practically run the place."

"I wouldn't say that." She blushed. "But you're right. I'm not sure what I can do for you though. Does this have to do with Leighann?"

"I'd heard that you took Leighann in when Sean kicked her out. Is that right?" I asked.

"Let's just say that now I wished I'd done more." Tears lined her lids. "She was such a sweet girl. She was young and in love."

"Can you tell me about your relationship with her? A confidant? A friend?" I asked. "Beka her friend?"

"I guess you could say that she and Beka were friends. I mean," she shrugged, "Beka grew up here next to me when I worked and she and Leighann played a lot together. She's the one who told me that she'd overheard Sean kick Leighann out."

"What did she overhear?" I asked.

"She can tell you herself." Angela pushed her chair back from her desk and got up. "She's in the back filing some paperwork."

While she headed down the hall to get Beka, I noticed the shelving behind her desk. They were black binders that were labeled on the spine with dates. I walked over and dragged my finger down them, pulling the latest one out. When I flipped it open, it was a mileage spreadsheet with the vin number of the tow truck and the date.

"Hi, Beka." I replaced the binder when I heard them walk back in. "I guess I should've asked you at the tree lot about your relationship with Leighann."

She looked at her mom with a confused and scared look on her face.

"It's okay. She's going to figure out who did this to Leighann. You need to tell her about what Leighann told you about Sean." Her mom encouraged her. "And what you overheard."

"I'm accusing no one of hurting her." Beka wanted to clarify with me.

"I'm not saying you are. I'm just trying to figure out her last days." I offered a sympathetic smile.

"I was filing some stuff for them because they pay me under the table and I'm saving..." she stopped in mid-sentence, "I didn't mean to say pay me under the table."

"Honey, Kenni isn't the IRS." Angela laughed. "We told her not to tell anyone we were paying her cash to work here without filling out a W-2 form. She's saving to join a sorority because we heard they can be very expensive."

"Good for you. I'm glad you're getting paid under the table. I had a job like that when I was your age. If you can believe it, it was to help my Poppa who was sheriff at the time." I was trying hard to help her feel less scared because I could see her hands trembling.

"Go on, Beka," Angela encouraged her.

"Anyways, I guess that Sean was mad about her and Manuel going over the data on their personal time. He'd turned off their data and when Leighann had stayed at home, she couldn't text Manuel in the night. Since his mama's been sick, Manuel didn't want to talk to wake her." Beka cleared her throat. "The next day after school, she told me about it and that her dad told her that day that if she wanted full data then she needed to move out or pay them rent."

"What day was this?" I asked.

"It was the last day of school before Christmas break last week." As she talked, I made notes in my notebook. I was going to tape her but I figured she'd really freak at that. "I told my mom that we couldn't let Leighann live in her car."

"What made you think she was going to live in her car?" I questioned.

"Because she said that Juanita had told Manuel she couldn't live there." Beka looked down at her fingers. She picked at her hangnails. "Leighann said that she and Manuel didn't have a lot of money. She didn't say why, but Jonathon told me that every cent Manuel made went to the family."

"All of this is just awful." Angela's voice cracked. "I didn't want to overstep my bounds, but I went to Jilly. That's when she told me Sean had been abusive and that she'd talked to a lawyer."

"What did she want with a lawyer?" The obvious was divorce, but what about the business?

"She didn't say divorce, but she did say that she wanted to know the particulars of business and what her role would be if they did get a divorce." Her eyes dipped with sadness.

Heaviness settled in my chest. The temperature in the room seemed to have dropped ten degrees with the goosebumps that collected on my arms.

"How did you know Jilly went to see a lawyer?" I asked.

"You don't work with men that drive tow trucks as one of only two women without the two of you becoming friends. It's been a hard road on Jilly. She came to my house and noticed Leighann's car there. I had to tell her that Leighann had been staying the night with me because I loved Leighann too and I couldn't imagine putting Beka out." Angela sucked in a deep breath.

"Do you think that Sean found out about Jilly talking to a lawyer?" I asked. "It wasn't like she didn't cover up meeting with Wally Lamb at Ben's Diner."

"She didn't seem to think Sean knew because Sean never goes into town unless he's got a tow job." She shook her head.

"Is that all?" Beka asked. "I'd like to finish so I can get to the tree lot."

"Yeah, I hear Coach gives you gift certificates." I wanted to break the tension Beka was probably feeling from being asked questions by the sheriff. It could be a little intimidating.

"Aren't you forgetting to tell Sheriff Lowry something?" Angela didn't let her off that easy. "This is very important, Beka. It's okay."

"I'd overheard Leighann screaming at Sean saying that she was going to find her real father. Then he told her that she was trash just like her real dad and she was ungrateful. They got into a big fight, that's when I snuck away so they wouldn't see me," her voice trailed off.

"Thank you, Beka. I know this was very hard, but you are doing a good thing for Leighann. You were a good friend to her." My greatest fear about Sean was starting to come to light and it appeared he was more of a suspect than he was this morning.

"Is that all?" Angela asked.

"What about those files? Do you keep a log when all the trucks go out, even at night?" I asked.

"I sure do. If there's a service call say in the middle of the night, there is a log in the trucks and the drivers will bring that in to me to log. It's all for tax purposes and liability. Every tow has to be accountable," she said.

"Can you tell me if there was a tow on the night of Leighann's murder?" I asked.

"Sure, but I don't think there was." She walked over to her desk and flipped through the binder. "I just logged in yesterday's." She dragged her finger down one of the pages and shook her head. "Mmm...nope." Her lips pinched, she looked up at me.

"Do you have a running total on a spreadsheet for all the trucks in use?" I asked.

"Of course," she confirmed and pulled another paper off her desk. "Here are the trucks we've been using this month. We rotate trucks since we have to keep them serviced. These five are the ones we are using now. Especially since the blizzard is coming and they've got the winterized package on them."

I didn't know or care to know what the winterized package was, because I refused to believe there was going to be a winter blizzard.

"Can I go take a look at the trucks and compare the mileage to make sure they match?" I asked.

If my theory about someone, whether it was Sean Graves or not, drugged Leighann and after she'd crashed, they'd towed her car to the boat dock, and it went right along with what Stinnett had seen, then one of these trucks had to have been used.

"No problem." She walked over to what I thought was an electrical box and opened it. "I've got to grab the keys. We don't have any on tow right now, so we are good."

She plucked five sets of keys from the box and brought them over to me with the piece of paper.

"The vin number for the trucks are right here on the spread sheet. It coordinates with the number here on the key chain. You'll find the match on the outside right bumper of the truck." She handed them to me.

"Thanks. I really appreciate this." I was so glad she didn't pull that warrant crap on me. "I'll be back shortly."

The trucks were lined up facing the drive, ready to go at the call. I looked at the bumper first and then got the keys. The first three matched the mileage and I was getting a little bit discouraged until I got into the fourth tow truck and the mileage didn't match. My hands shook and my throat dried.

"Back here, Kenni-Bug." I heard Poppa call to me from outside the truck.

I got out of the tow truck and saw Poppa pointing to the back where the chains would've wrapped around the car it was towing. There was red chipped paint on them.

"That's those strange marks." Poppa nodded.

I walked over to my Jeep and grabbed my camera out of my bag. After I turned it on, I flipped through to the photos I'd taken at S&S Auto. Frank had pointed out to me the chipped off paint before I could even investigate it since he had to fill out the information on the cars they tow so there's no damage made by them.

"Just what I thought." Poppa stood over my shoulder and looked at the camera as I compared the marks side-by-side.

"I just can't believe it." I dragged my phone out of my pocket and dialed Finn.

"Any news?" Finn asked.

"Yeah. I'm going to bring in Sean Graves after he gets back from the memorial, but I'm going to go ahead and tape off the house and business." I swallowed, hard. "I think we have crime scene one."

"We sure do." Poppa ghosted into the house and would get started on looking around.

"Do you want some help?" Finn asked.

"If you don't mind sending Scott out to Chimney Rock and log the miles from there to Graves Towing, that'd be great." I gave Finn a quick explanation. "I'll also let him take over and I'll finish up talking to Dr. Shively before

I bring him in. I'm going to send Angela Durst and her daughter on home." There was a sick feeling in my stomach.

"My news isn't any better." There was little hope in Finn's voice. "Leighann's phone records came back and there wasn't anything out of the ordinary."

"Nothing seems to surprise me anymore." My head started to hurt thinking about what was going to happen in Cottonwood once everyone heard that Sean Graves was our number one suspect.

It was also so easy nowadays to try and convict someone before they were really in front of a jury, but the evidence was so strong against Sean Graves that I too had even had him locked up in a state penitentiary for murder.

"If we can get this behind us, we can take the next week off for some much-needed time." Finn's words comforted me before we said our goodbyes, it was the grey clouds that appeared to be moving in that worried me.

CHAPTER FIFTEEN

Angela Durst had already left before Scott had gotten there. I'd kept my mouth shut so she wouldn't go and squeal to anyone at the memorial since she and Beka were headed there after work. Scott recorded the exact mileage the tow truck was over and not been reported.

"If Sean Graves didn't drive this truck out to the river, I don't know who did." There was a grave look on Scott's face.

"It makes me sick." I shook my head and grabbed the big round keychain out of my bag.

Scott and I had used the bump key to jimmy the lock to the house and the shop since they were combined.

Scott had taped off the property while I headed in to see what Poppa had found.

"Those are Leighann's journals. They date back years and years of abuse from Sean." Poppa had discovered multiple notebooks in Leighann's childhood home. "She knew from a long time ago that she was adopted."

"This was a shocker to me. It had to be the best kept secret in Cottonwood," I said of the unusual nature of it.

"Secrets always make their way out of the woodwork." Poppa had told me that several times but this time he was spot on. "Leighann and Sean were on thin ice."

"The night of the Christmas Cantata, he was aggravated with her because she was there with Manuel having a good time. She didn't even let it bother her that she was having these issues." I started to play the back and forth game we loved to play.

"When she got home, they ended up having another fight and she brought up the fact he wasn't her father." Poppa paced back and forth as the scene unfolded before us.

"She continued to threaten him about how he wasn't her father and he felt she was ungrateful, using his medication to poison her." I wasn't really sure how that fit in, but I threw it in there.

"How did he get her to drive to Chimney Rock?" Poppa asked a question I'd yet to even mull over since I'd seen the whole mileage thing.

"He told her that Manuel had called," I said not so convinced that's how it happened. "He knew she'd jump in her car to go after Manuel and just to be sure he followed her."

"There's only one way to find out." Poppa was right. "Bring him in."

"Not without crossing all my I's and T's just yet. I've got some time to get over to Dr. Shively's to talk to her before they get back from the funeral home." I pulled my phone out of my pocket. "Just for good measure, I'll call Max Bogus to give me a heads up when it's over and they're leaving. I'll come back here to get him."

"You leaving the new kid here?" Poppa asked.

"I sure am." I headed on back out of the house and gave Scott some specific instructions on what I wanted bagged up. The journals and the pills for sure.

I gripped the Wagoneer's steering wheel when I pushed the pedal all the way to the floor. Rarely did I ever go over the speed limit and when I did, it was with my siren on. I had some ground to cover before Leighann's memorial was over. Max told me that the memorial was going well and he'd call me when Sean and Jilly were about to leave. There were some kids Leighann had gone to high school with and the line was longer than they'd anticipated even though there was no body to see.

Since it was already in the middle of the day, I'd hoped people might've cancelled any appointments they'd had with Camille Shively and she'd have an open window to discuss Sean Graves and the prescription. In light of the current evidence against Sean, I still wanted to talk to her about Juanita Liberty's Crohn's condition.

The waiting room was empty like I'd hoped. I walked up to the receptionist window.

"Sheriff." Her eyes drew down my nose. "I'm assuming you're here on official business."

"That's right. Camille is expecting me." I stood there gripping my bag and watched her rush off.

I turned around and faced the small brown leather loveseats and perfectly matched end tables. Framed photos of Camille in her graduation cap and gown decorated with all sorts of colored cords hung on the walls. They represented just how smart she was in her class. The all-important piece of paper that told us she that she was in fact a doctor was proudly displayed.

The doctor's office was already an unnerving place to be when you had an appointment and I could tell that Camille had taken great lengths to make the office homier to help get rid of the white coat syndrome.

The water feature in the corner tickled a soothing sound. I couldn't help but wonder if Camille had strategically placed it there since it was the latest rage in battling anxiety. I could tell her that it wasn't working for me. The more I thought about Sean Graves and what I was about to arrest him for was stress beyond the normal. Stress came with the job, but when a father figure was accused of such a horrific crime, the level of anxiety was almost unbearable.

Before I could even sit down, Camille was at the door in her doctor's whites, looking very much like the girl next door that made her clients feel comfortable with her. Her long black hair was pulled into a low ponytail at the nape of her neck. Her pale face softened as she smiled.

"Kenni." She held the waiting room door for me. "Let's go back to my office."

"Thanks for seeing me." I unzipped my bag and had the papers that she'd requested all ready for her. "Here's the request for subpoena."

"I can tell you that Sean Graves isn't a man that appears to be anxious or even unstable. He's got some anger issues that we are working through, but if you think he killed his daughter, I'm going to strongly tell you that in my professional opinion, he did not." Camille didn't even give me a chance to ask her any questions before she started right on in as though she'd already rehearsed it.

"Professional opinion? Pweft." Poppa appeared next to Camille, blowing her off. "She needs to stick to doctoring and not policing."

"He'd been having some trouble sleeping the past couple of weeks because he and Jilly are having some issues coming to agreement with how to handle Leighann's decisions as an adult, but now they have a whole set of different issues they are going to have to face," she said.

"He's got a lot of issues, lady." Poppa rocked back on his heels. "You need to give her something to chew on."

"I appreciate your professional opinion, but the evidence speaks for itself and right now it's screaming that Sean Graves murdered his stepdaughter." My words caught me off-guard. I'd never called Leighann his step-daughter and it did make the awful crime more realistic and believable rather than calling her his daughter. "Her car was towed into the river. She was floating in the back and the keys were in her pocket. The mileage log on his tow truck just so happens to be the exact mileage from his shop to the river."

"Weee-dogggy." Poppa smacked his knee in delight. "Look at that shocked look on her face."

I literally had to suck in a deep breath to keep from saying too much. So I went in for the kill.

"I'm going to need copies of all of your records on Sean Grave as well as the prescriptions because Leighann was given Ambien before she was murdered," my words were met with the good doctor's jaw dropping.

"I'm..." she stammered, "I...um..." She looked away and cleared her throat. "I had no idea. He seemed genuinely concerned about Leighann's future."

"It appears that Juanita Liberty was the same way. And I'd like to know about her Crohn's disease." I watched Camille write on a piece of paper. "I know that I have to have all my I's and T's crossed with solid evidence that Sean Graves had anything to do with Leighann's murder. From what I've heard, Juanita is battling Crohn's disease. She felt the same way about Leighann as Sean did Manuel. She too had motive to kill Leighann, but she was at home ill the night of Leighann's murder, so technically she's not a suspect. But I'd like to know if she's as bad off as they say."

"I'm assuming you'd get a warrant for that too." Camille pushed a button on her phone and called for the secretary. "She does have Crohn's. We are working with a specialist on various treatments but until it's under control with all the new meds, then I'd say she's a little touch and go. We've been treating it for years, but now we are having to use some experimental things."

The secretary walked over to Camille and took the sticky note she'd written on.

"I need all the files copied," she looked up at the secretary under raised brows. The secretary hurried out.

"I'm sorry to hear that. She's got a few young children." My heart ached for Manuel.

I couldn't imagine what was going through his young mind and sympathized with how he was going to have to take care of his mother once her disease progressed.

My phone chirped a text. I dragged it out of my pocket and read it from Max.

"Did Juanita happen to take Ambien?" I asked just to make sure.

"No. She's already tired enough without needing a sleep aid," she confirmed.

"I've got to go." I stood up. "Do you think she's done with the copies?"

"She should be." Camille stood up too. "I'm sorry about my thoughts about Sean. I guess it goes to prove that you don't know someone by what they tell you."

"He's not tried and convicted yet." I reminded her and left the office, grabbing the files from the secretary on my way out.

"Good boy," I pat Duke on the head when I got back into the Jeep.

"What are you waiting on?" Poppa tapped the dashboard with his fingers. "Get a move on it. We've got an arrest to make."

I took a couple of deep breaths before I turned the engine over.

"Well? What are you waiting for?" Poppa asked. He hit the dash a little harder this time. "Go!"

"Poppa, weren't you the one who told me that I better make sure because I just can't go off and accuse people of crimes they didn't commit?" I asked.

"Yes, I did, Kenni-Bug." His chin lifted up and then down in a definitive yes. "What more evidence do you need? He has a prescription of Ambien. He has a history of abusing the poor girl. His tow truck matches up to what happened to the SUV in the river. He flew off the handle when she told him she was going to find her real father. He also had to've found out that Jilly was going to leave him. That does a lot to a man."

"You're right. We can't make the evidence up. These are all facts and it all points to Leighann's death." A lump so dry formed in my throat and I could barely swallow to make it wet.

Instead of fighting the fear inside, I simply put the Jeep in drive and headed right on back to Graves Towing to do one of the hardest arrests I've ever had to do.

CHAPTER SIXTEEN

"Kenni, won't you come in?" Jilly held the door open for me to enter. "I appreciate that, but I'm here to see Sean." My face set stern, my eyes had a softness to them as they looked at the wife and mother who was about to lose everything. My heart ached for her, but I had a job to do and bringing Leighann's killer to justice was my only concern.

"Kenni. Honey." Sean walked up and stood over her shoulder. "Is everything okay?"

"Can I see you outside?" I questioned.

"It's awful cold and we really just want to get some rest. If you've got some information, come on in and we can talk over coffee." Jilly still continued to try to get me inside. "The Sweet Adelines left so much coffee cake and we've got to eat it."

"I think she wants to talk to me." Sean moved past Jilly and stepped outside. It was easy enough for me to size him up when my head came up to his chin.

"Yep. About the same distance from the pedals in Leighann's car to the seat." Poppa had noticed what I'd noticed. "Oh, Kenni-Bug." The tone in his voice didn't make me feel any better. "You've got your work cut out for you."

"You got the killer, didn't you?" Sean looked down at me.

"Yes," I choked out and then cleared my throat. "Sean Graves," My chin lifted into the air, my voice loud and clear, I said, "You are under arrest for the murder of Leighann Graves."

"What?" He drew back. I stood firm. "You've lost your mind!" His boisterous voice blew past me and it was so powerful, it almost knocked me over.

"Anything you say can and will be used against you." I reached around my utility belt and unclipped my cuffs.

"I'm not going," he protested and chuckled. "You're crazy."

"Sean? Kenni?" Jilly stood at the door. The cup of coffee she had in her hands shattered on the front porch when she dropped it. "No, Sean, no," she pleaded and shook her head. The tears began to flood down her face. "Not my baby. You killed my baby?"

"No." He pointed to Jilly and then pointed to me. "You are wrong. Very wrong."

"I'm taking you down to the department." I reached for his wrist. "If I'm wrong, we can sort it out down there."

"We are going to sort this out," he demanded. "Jilly, woman, get yourself together. You hear me?" He hollered.

"You've man-handled her long enough." I clipped the cuffs on him a little tighter than I'd normally done. "I can't wait to see you behind bars."

"Kenni, stay calm. Just do your job." Poppa ghosted past me towards the Jeep. "Get him in the Wagoneer and let's do the job."

"Jilly, call Wally Lamb!" He had one good scream before I shoved him in the back seat of the Wagoneer.

I'd like to say there was complete silence or even some sort of sadness on the way back into town, but he was just piss and vinegar the entire way.

"You think you're going to get re-elected, you're crazy. I don't care who I have to throw money towards to beat you right out of office, but I'll donate today." He spewed hate words the whole way there. "Too bad you're not like Elmer."

"Sean, I'm telling you to stop talking," I warned him.

"Are you going to take my right to talk away too?" He asked sarcastically.

I gripped the wheel so hard that by the time I'd parked the Jeep in the alley behind the department, my fingers were numb and tingling.

TANGLED UP IN TINSEL

"Finn," I called after I'd beeped in my walkie-talkie. "Can you come get Sean out of my Jeep?"

He didn't even answer back. He bolted out the door. When I got out, our eyes met. There was an unspoken word between us. He knew he had to give me a few minutes to collect myself and I knew it too.

"Betty, I'm going to go to the bathroom and get a coffee. Please make Sean comfortable." I didn't look at her. I unzipped my coat and hung it up on the coat tree.

"Wally Lamb is on his way," Betty warned as I pushed through the door between the department and Cowboy's Catfish. "And your mama dropped off a casserole for you to take to Manuel Liberty. She said something about how he's grieving too."

The bathroom light flickered above my head as I stood at the sink, grasping the edges. My stomach hurt, and I felt like I was going to be sick. I just couldn't believe that Sean Graves had been given the precious gift of having a wonderful daughter and took her life.

"Over what?" I looked hard into my own eyes in the mirror. "What did you kill her over?" I asked myself like I was going to ask him.

Only the hint of tears burned the top of my nose. I knew I had get a grip before I could go in there and interrogate him when Wally Lamb got there.

I turned on the cold-water knob and let it run for a few minutes to get good and cold. I bent my head overtop the sink and used my hands to splash water on my face.

"Ding, ding," Poppa pretend to ring the bell. He pinched a faint smile. "These are the tough times," he reminded me. "You've got to remember all the good. All the donations you do during the year. All the volunteer hours. The citizens who drop by and bring you pies just to thank you. The sticker badges you put in the smallest hands of Cottonwood that look up to you and when they grow up they want to be sheriff. Those are the events you have to remember to get you through the bad times like this one."

"Sean Graves?" I still questioned with disbelief. "It's so unthinkable. All the times I went to bat for him and all the times we used his towing company." I shook my head and used my sleeve to wipe off any left-over water.

"You and I both know that people lose their minds and do things that are out of their character, but now that the spotlight has been bright on Sean

Graves, I think you know deep down that he didn't lose his mind." Poppa jabbed his finger towards my heart. "He's been down-right ornery for a while, only behind closed doors."

I wiped my face one more time and shook my head.

"You're right." I sucked in a deep breath. "I really wish you were here."

"I am here. Right here next to you," he assured me.

"Will you make sure I ask the appropriate questions?" I knew when I proceeded with Wally Lamb there as I questioned Sean, Wally would try and turn every question into a debate.

"I'll be right there." He nodded.

There was a sense of light that passed between us that gave me a confidence that I'd dug down deep to get. I was ready to bring Leighann's killer to justice.

CHAPTER SEVENTEEN

"Sheriff Lowry, I think you've gone on an all-out hunting spree since you're trying to bolt out of town with your boyfriend." Wally Lamb slid his shifty eyes toward Deputy Finn Vincent. "You haven't even taken the time to properly investigate this case in the last what," he see-sawed his hand, "forty-eight hours, seventy-two hours?"

He drew back, duck-billed his lips and gave me a geesh look.

"Am I right or am I right?" He asked and sauntered over to the cell. "I'm going to have to ask you to let my client go. Now, open the cell."

"Listen here," Finn took a step forward.

"I've got it." I shot Finn a look. "I'm just waiting for Mr. Lamb to finish before I tell him how this is going to go."

"Is that right?" Wally Lamb asked and folded his arms across his chest over his fancy suit.

"That's right. I've arrested your client and if you'd like to stay for some questioning, you may do so per the law." I grabbed a tape recorder out of my desk drawer. "This is my domain. I was elected by our peers and citizens to do a job. I'm going to do that job whether you, Mr. Lamb, like it or not."

"Fine. Proceed," he said with a smirk. "Don't worry," he assured Sean.

"If I was alive, I'd show that boy how to treat a woman and use good manners." Poppa huffed and puffed.

"Scott, can you pull the desk closer to Mr. Graves?" I didn't want it all to be so formal, but Wally left me with no choice. Finn helped him with the desk and finished up by putting the chairs next to the cell.

"Please state your full name," I told Sean after I'd pushed record.

"Sean Howard Graves," he said loud and clear.

"I think we can lose the formalities," I paused to receive an agreement from him. "Can you tell me how it came to be that you adopted Leighann?"

"About eighteen years ago, Jilly had come to town looking for a job. She had an infant daughter. My daddy had an opening in the office and he gave her a job. Over the course of a few years, I'd grown fond of her and Leighann. She'd bring her to the office and my family tended to the baby like she was our own." He took a gulp. "I fell in love with them. When I asked her to marry me, I swear it was the happiest day of my mom's life. She and my dad were so happy."

"I wish I could say that he's putting on an act, but I clearly remember how much they loved her and Leighann. They were happy." Poppa had softened on me.

"Yep, sounds like a killer to me." Wally threw his hands up in the air.

I shot him a look. He turned away from me.

"How long have you been taking Ambien?" I asked.

"Recently after Leighann and I had gotten into a fight and she said she was going to move out, I couldn't sleep because I wasn't sure where she was, and I knew I had to let her fly in order to let her survive." He looked down at his hands as he clasped them together. "I knew where she was the whole time. I would follow her around in my car so I knew she was okay. I even knew that Angela Durst had taken her in. I was waiting her out."

"What about the night of the dance? I saw the look on your face when you saw her and Manuel cozied up next to the punch bowl. You didn't look happy." This was the beginning of the end from what I could tell.

"Leighann had come over to the table upset because Rachel had made fun of her for staying in Cottonwood. I was mad because this was the exact reason I wanted her to go to college and get an education. People made fun of me all my life for taking over my parents' tow company. Even though they need me, they still turn their noses down. I couldn't imagine a world where Leighann would live and her peers treat her badly," his voice trailed off.

"That does make sense," Poppa said and made me wonder whose side he was on. What happened to him telling me that he'd have my back when I was in the bathroom?

"When Leighann got home, you and she had a fight. She said she was going to find out who her real dad was and you got mad, slipped her one or two of your sleeping pills before you let her get into her car and drive off." My voice escalated before I went in for the kill, "When you realized she didn't die in the crash, you drove your tow truck, put her car in the river after you'd unbuckled her and put her keys in her pocket."

"Are you crazy?" He jumped up and squeezed his face in between the bars.

"Sheriff, you have a very active imagination." Wally clapped his hands. "I'm gonna have to give you an award for a big imagination."

"How do you explain the fact that her car seat was pushed back to the exact height you'd be sitting down or the exact distance you've got between the pedals on your personal tow truck to the seat? It's the exact same measurements." I opened the folder and took out the photos and the measurements from both. "And how do you explain this?"

"What is that?" Wally picked up the photo I'd taken from the mileage log and the photo of the odometer from his tow truck.

"Mr. Graves's tow truck that he uses wasn't logged properly. The missing miles is the exact mileage it takes from his shop to Chimney Rock and back." I smacked my hand on the desk.

"Wally? Aren't you going to stop her?" Sean protested, shaking the bars.

"Sean Graves, you got mad at Leighann for wanting to search for her father. You got mad at Jilly for filing for divorce and you were seeking revenge. Jilly even said you two'd not been sleeping in the same bed. You killed Leighann Graves and you just need to save the poor citizens our tax dollars and just admit it." I didn't let up.

"Bravo!" Wally Lamb clapped and laughed. "Like I said, you have a very active imagination. Now, if you don't mind. I think Betty said we've got a bond hearing."

Betty sat bug-eyed and speechless at her desk with her mouth dropped wide open. Slowly she nodded. Her mouth closed, opened, closed and popped open again.

"That's it?" Sean looked between me and Wally Lamb. "You're not going to say anything?"

"I've got plenty to say. Before the judge." Wally tipped his head. "See you in a couple of hours."

There was complete silence until Wally Lamb walked out of the door.

"That's it?" Sean shoved off the bars. "What kind of coo-coo lawyer is he?"

"He's right." I walked back over to the cell. "The judge will give you a bond and Wally will bond you out. Then he'll start to put together a case for you."

Not that I wanted to let Sean know anything, but he did still have rights.

"Kenni, do you honestly think I killed Leighann?" He eased down on the cot. "The night she went missing, I told you that I went to Chimney Rock to look for her. I didn't go that night. I jumped into my tow that morning after Manuel came by saying she wasn't with him. I'd completely forgotten to put the mileage in the log." He bent over and rested his forearms on his thighs. "Jilly and I had been going to marriage counseling. She met with Wally Lamb at Ben's Diner to tell him that we were staying together and not going through the divorce."

"That's good to hear." Poppa was a sucker. He ghosted himself next to Sean on the cot. "Poor Jilly has been through enough."

It took everything in my person not to just fly off the handle at Poppa, but I couldn't risk everyone seeing me and thinking I was the unhinged person in the room.

"We left the dance and that night I slept in our marital bed. You can ask Jilly. I didn't move until Manuel knocked on the door. I didn't kill Leighann. I loved her. I raised her. And I'm not proud of the wrongful things I've done to my wife and daughter, but I am seeking help for that." He wiped his hand across his face and dropped his chin to his chest. "I love my girls."

"He didn't do it." Poppa hopped up. "Go back and talk to the Liberty boy." Poppa tapped his temple. "Something ain't right. Something's off."

CHAPTER EIGHTEEN

"Sheriff, what are you doing here?"

I was surprised to see Beka Durst answer the Liberty's front door. By the look on her face, she was as surprised as me.

"What are you doing here?" I asked her back.

"I'm waiting on the Libertys to get back from the memorial. I told them I'd hang out here." She shrugged.

"I'm shocked you're not at the memorial," I said and wondered why the Libertys were still at the memorial when Sean and Jilly had gone home and I'd arrested him.

"I'm not really good with all that dead stuff. I mean, I loved Leighann and all, but it wasn't like we were great friends." Her eyes slid down to the casserole carrier.

"I'm dropping off one of Mama's chicken pot pies." I held the handles of Mama's casserole carrier that she made during a craft night at Lulu's boutique. "Do you mind if I put it in the kitchen?" I asked because if I didn't take it out of the carrier and bring it back to Mama, she'd freak out.

"Not at all. They've been getting a bunch of food." She walked away from the door and I walked in. "Everyone feels bad for Manuel. It wasn't like they were married or anything."

"Are you friends with Jonathan?" I asked, knowing that she was a senior and so was Jonathan, figuring they were in class together. Plus, I'd seen them at the tree farm.

"Ummm." She shrugged again on the way to the kitchen. "Not really. I was more friends with Manuel than Jonathan. That is, before he started dating Leighann."

Okay, I wondered to myself, did she have a thing for Manuel? I let the thoughts swirl around in my head like they were marinating while I sat the casserole carrier on the kitchen table and took out the foil pan with Mama's chicken pot pie in it. There was book bag next to a monogrammed purse with Beka's initials on it. Upon deeper inspection, something else in her bag caught my eye.

"It's great that you're here for Manuel," I said, stopping Beka in her tracks. "Is that your purse?"

"Mmmhmmmm," she hummed. "Juanita got it for me from Lulu's Boutique. I mean, Mrs. Liberty."

"I really like it." I picked it up to disguise that I wanted to knock over the bag and see if I saw what I thought I saw. "I'm so sorry," I gasped for effect when the bag went tumbling to the ground when I picked up the purse. All the contents fell out, even the emergency kit with Leighann's initials on it.

She scurried over and tried to grab all the contents and throw it back in the bag. I snatched the first aid kit from her.

"Who knows, maybe the two of you can date now that Leighann is out of the way." I held up the kit in front of her face.

My body language reading skills kicked in, but so did Poppa's commentary.

"Did you see that?" Poppa appeared next to Beka. "Her jaw. It tensed. And..." he pointed at her. "Her chest is rising."

"His mother would like that," she said in a low voice as she stood up. "Juanita didn't like Leighann. Neither did Manuel's brothers. She really didn't deserve him."

"That's why you killed her, so you could date him." The pieces were falling into place, though when I sized her up, she wasn't as tall as my calculation from where the seat in Leighann's SUV had been moved. "You had access to Graves Towing and the Ambien prescribed to Leighann's dad."

"I don't mean no disrespect." Beka opened a counter drawer and shuffled through it like she was looking for something. "I don't think you understand the connection me and Manuel had before Leighann came along."

"Why don't we head on down to the station and sort this out?" Now I wished I'd had on my uniform or at least my gun strapped on my utility belt instead of in my bag, which did me no good since I left it in the Wagoneer.

"No, I can't do that." Her eyes darted around the room. "I mean," her head twitched, "you obviously know."

"What do I know?" I questioned so she'd calm down. She looked like a cat in a roomful of rocking chairs.

"You know I killed her." Her shaky hand outstretched in front of her as she pointed at me.

"I'm not sure of it. And if you did, I'm sure we can work this out." I took a step towards her. "I get it. You were, are, in love with Manuel. Trust me." I put my hand in the air when I noticed she shuffled to the opposite side of me. I wanted to gain her trust. "If someone tried to take Finn away from me." I shook my head. "I don't know what I'd do."

"She wasn't taking him from me. I was taking back what's mine. What we used to have before she flaunted herself at him at the towing company after he'd found out his mama was sick." She started to cry. "Juanita had told me that she wished he'd dated me. All those times Sean kept Leighann away from Manuel, Manuel came to me." Beka's nose flared as the words came out of her gritted teeth. "He told me that we could go off to college and forget this town. I had it all planned out."

"Did the two of you date?" I asked, trying to bide the time for her to get comfortable with me.

"No, but we would've if it weren't for her. I'd given her a few months to show her nasty side to him. When she decided not to go to college, I knew that I had to get a plan to set him free. If she wasn't around, we could get out of Cottonwood and begin our lives."

She walked over to the window to look out.

It was a perfect opportunity to slip my phone out of my pocket and quickly hit Finn's phone number. "Manuel and his family will be back soon. I need to be sure I'm here for him and continue my plan."

"He's going to need you." I'd slipped the phone with the speaker side up in my front pocket. "The Sweet Adelines will probably be stopping by soon."

"Those nosy old coots." Beka rolled her eyes.

"They are, but they have a good heart, just like you." I tried to soften my facial features, so she'd start to trust me, but the fact I was the law wasn't helping none. "I just don't understand how you did it."

"Leighann was upset and I texted her to meet me at her house. I'd gotten my mom's keys to the towing company and knew if I could get in there, I'd be able to get Sean's sleeping pills." She smiled, her eyes narrowed, and it made me sick to my stomach. "Kids nowadays are soft. You know? They like to take the easy way out. I knew if it came out that Sean was abusive, and she and Manuel were having problems, then it was a no brainer to look like she'd hurt herself."

"So, she slipped her a mickey, huh." Poppa swept up next to her and got real close. "How did she get the car in the lake?" Poppa asked.

"Exactly how did the SUV get into the water?" I asked.

"I'd seen her throw her phone at Manuel when she got mad and left the Moose. I knew she didn't have it on her. I asked Manuel to get her a fountain Cherry Coke from Ben's since it was her favorite and when she came to his house, she'd be all goo-goo eyed. Little did they know that I'd been to Ben's earlier with my mom and gotten a Cherry Coke fountain drink with no ice to-go. Cherry Coke was Leighann's favorite. When she showed up to meet me at her house, I'd already slipped a couple of the sleeping pills in her drink." There was a certain look of pride on her face as if she'd completely gotten away with it.

"After we talked, I pretended to get a text on my cell and told her it was Manuel. He said that if I'd seen her to tell her to go to Chimney Rock like they used to when they were younger. It was their secret rendezvous place." She crossed her hands to her heart. "It was a perfect place for her to die and now we can have our own rendezvous spot."

"She drove there?" I still hadn't connected how the back-side panel had been found so far down the road.

"I didn't realize how fast the sleeping pill was going to work. My plan changed after I followed behind her to Chimney Rock. She fell asleep at the wheel and when the car went around one of the curves, it went off the road and bumped a tree just enough for the panel to fall off." She rolled her eyes. "Her stupid car was stuck."

"Did that kill her?" I asked.

"No," she said abruptly. "If it had, I'd've left her there. But I had to make sure she was good and dead. That's when I decided that I was going to have to put her in the river. I drove back to her house and used my mom's keys to get into the tow company where I got keys to one of the tow trucks. It actually turned out better than my original plan because I loaded her car up on the tow and then just backed up on the boat ramp and dumped the entire car in the river."

"That's why the car seat was moved so far back because this here nut job is taller than Leighann." Poppa was standing next to her sizing her up. "You can take her. She's a pipsqueak."

"You moved her out of the driver's seat?" I asked, hoping all the details were going on the recorder of the phone.

"I shoved her after I got the car towed to the boat dock." Beka tsked.

"What is it with these young kids today? Just want what they want and take it," Poppa said with a disgusted tone.

"How did the keys get in her pocket?" I asked.

"That was a bit of a rookie move on my end," she said non-chalantly like we were just two buddies having an afternoon sweet tea. "Before I went to get the tow truck, I turned off the car so no one would see the exhaust because it's so cold with that storm coming."

"There's not going to be a storm!" My voice escalated. I was sick and tired of hearing this junk about the storm. Apparently, my voice scared her and she ran past me, shoving me to the side.

"Don't make me do this!" I yelled, running after her.

It was the worst thing in the world to get into a pursuit and with a kid.

Before she'd made it to the front door, I leapt into the air and tackled her to the ground.

She was sobbing, but I had to hold her like a tied hog or she'd run again. I flipped her over to her front and with my knee jammed deep in her back, I realized I didn't have my cuffs. Quickly I looked around and saw the coat tree. I jerked a belt from one of the coats and used it to wrap around her tiny wrists.

She was just a kid. Too bad, she had her whole life in front of her until this crime of passion over took her sense of emotions.

"Beka Durst, I'm arresting you for the murder of Leighann Graves. Do you understand me?" I asked her. There was nothing but sobs escaping her limp body. "You have the right to remain silent, though I've got it all on my phone. Anything you say can and will certainly be used against you in the court of law." I jerked her up to stand and continued reading her the Miranda rights. I grabbed my phone off the floor on our way out.

With one hand, I gripped her arm and the other had my phone.

"Did you get all that?" I asked Finn.

"I'm on my way to the Libertys' right now." He clicked off and I slipped the phone back in my pocket.

We headed out of the Libertys' front door just as Manuel and his family were piling out of the family van.

"Now, I've got to get you down to the station." I opened the back door of the Wagoneer and helped her inside.

"It's only because I love you Manuel Liberty!" She screamed before I slammed the door, not caring a bit if the glass window smacked her in the nose. "I'd do anything for you!"

"What's going on here?" Juanita Liberty strutted up to the Jeep with all her sons in tow.

"We have a confession. Leighann Graves was murdered by Beka Durst because she was jealous of their relationship and is in love with your son." My eyes slid past her shoulder and caught Manuel's face. "I'm sorry, you'll have to wait outside until Deputy Vincent comes to clear the scene."

Manuel's eyes slowly closed shut as his chin fell to his chest.

"Good work, Sheriff," was all that Juanita Liberty could muster up before she gestured for her boys to wait by the car.

"Manuel! Manuel!" Beka's voice was distorted by the glass between her and the world as she desperately tried to get Manuel to look at her when he walked by. "Tell him how much I love him, Juanita!"

I looked around for Poppa as I walked in front of the Jeep to get inside and haul her down to the one department cell, but he wasn't around.

"Silent night, holy night," the radio played when I started up the Jeep.

"Turn this crap off," Beka said snidely.

I turned it up and smiled.

"This is for you, Poppa." I sucked in a deep breath and put the gear shift in drive.

CHAPTER NINETEEN

"You let my baby go, Kenni Lowry!" Angela Durst had run into the sheriff's department with Wally Lamb on her heels.

"Let me take care of this because it seems that our good sheriff here is going to arrest everyone in Cottonwood for Leighann's death." Wally stuck his arm out, stopping Angela from going after me. Or it appeared she was gunning for me. "Kenni, um, Sheriff, on what grounds do you believe you can arrest my client?"

"On the grounds that she is in love with Manuel Liberty and out of a crime of passion she killed Leighann Graves to get her out of the way so she, herself, could live happily ever after with Manuel." I stated the obvious.

"Not to mention that she confessed and happened to have the missing contents from Leighann's car in her possession," Scott finished up.

"She's a minor and I want her out of that jail cell right now," Wally Lamb said with a stern voice. "And Sean too."

"I have no clue what's going on." Sean sat stunned on the edge of the cot.

"Beka confessed to killing Leighann. She's got all the details." I grabbed the cell keys out of my drawer and went over to unlock it. Scott stepped in and took Sean by the arm. "Sean, you can come out."

"Thank God." He stood up and turned to face Beka. "After everything I did for you and your mother, you killed my daughter?"

"Beka, you tell her right now the truth." Angela rushed over to the cell and gripped the bars, staring at the young girl who had replaced Sean on the cot. "Beka, I know you didn't do this. You were home." Angela's jaw dropped, and she swiveled around on the balls of her feet. "She was at home watching a movie with me. She went to the dance but had to be home by curfew."

"Mama, hush. I did it. I drugged and killed Leighann." She bolted off the cot and stood ramrod straight with her fists to her side. "I killed her! I killed her!"

"She didn't kill no one." Poppa appeared cross-legged on the cot, nearly making me faint.

Why was Poppa back? What in the world was going on? Had I just hauled in a teenager for a murder she'd not committed? What was I thinking?

"Wait." I stopped them from talking and that included Poppa. I had to have a clear head. "You said that you texted Leighann to meet you at her house." I recalled what she'd said about how she lured Leighann that night. "But Manuel had her phone, so how did she get your text?"

"Shut up! I did it!" She screamed through gritted teeth.

"Give me a minute with her, please." I put my hand out to everyone.

"Is she covering up for something Manuel had done?" Poppa stared at Beka who was suddenly on the floor in fetal position, repeating that she'd killed her over and over.

"Beka." I unlocked the cell and bent down next to her. "This is a very nice jail cell, but if you killed Leighann, I promise that you won't be in a prison anywhere near this nice. Your entire life will be over."

I stroked her hair and tried to comfort her while she sobbed on the floor.

"Love is a very crazy and real thing. Especially at your age. I understand that you are in love with Manuel, but if you are covering up for him for something he's done, that's not love on his part." I continued to talk softly with her and let everyone around me drown out. "You have your entire life ahead of you. Don't you want to join Rachel at State and be in her sorority? Remember all the fun she was telling you about when you two were working the tree lot? If you go to jail, you won't ever go to college. You won't ever have another boyfriend or even get married. Your life will be over. And for what? Manuel will still carry on."

She pushed herself up to sit side-legged on her hip.

"What about a sick person in jail? Will they get medical help then go home?" She questioned with big tears in her eyes.

"Juanita Liberty. Ummm-mmmm," Poppa's lips were pressed together. "She killed that girl. I know it."

"Yes. Like Juanita Liberty?" I asked Beka. "If Juanita killed Leighann, she'd get some medical treatment for her Crohn's and be released." She nodded.

Out of the corner of my eye, I saw Poppa ghost right on up through the ceiling. My heart fell.

"I didn't know she did it until I found Leighann's emergency kit in their house. Juanita walked in and saw me holding it. She's the one who told me how much she loved me and wanted me to be married to Manuel. She said that if it came down to it and I took the fall, I would get off because I'm a minor. No one was going to send a kid to jail. That's what she said." Beka wiped the tears from her eyes. "She said that since she had Crohn's and in the last stages, that she didn't care if she went to jail because she'd die knowing Leighann couldn't hurt her son's future anymore. But if I took the fall..." Her voice trailed off. Angela rushed to the cell bars. Beka looked up at her. "I'm sorry, Mama. I thought I was doing the right thing."

"Beka, honey, she used your lack of knowledge about the disease to get you to take the fall for her dirty work. She's not dying." Her mama tried to tell her daughter how Juanita had manipulated her.

There was some scurrying behind me and I knew it was Scott rushing out the door to bring Juanita Liberty to justice.

"It's going to be okay." I stood up and let Angela come into the cell to console her daughter while I called Finn.

"I'm about all done here," he answered the phone.

"Don't leave. Deputy Lee is on his way over there. Don't say anything until you talk to him when he gets there, but Juanita Liberty is the real killer." My words were met with silence. "Are you there?"

"Yeah. We'll bring her in." He clicked off.

Beka had retracted what she told me and actually had told me the truth, which wasn't far from what she'd confessed. In fact, Juanita had faked sicker than what she was and knew that her son and Leighann had a fight. She also knew that her son would stop at nothing for Leighann and if she ended Leighann's life, she'd be giving Manuel his life back.

"Juanita saw it as a win-win situation. The disease is progressing and she knew that if she was dead and gone, Manuel would marry Leighann and it'd be Leighann that'd move into her house and finish raising Manuel's brothers while Manuel worked. It was a life she didn't want for her boys. In the end, Juanita Liberty couldn't find it within herself to forgive Leighann for helping Manuel make the decision not to go to college, when in fact, it was her sickness that made Manuel's decision easy." I told Mama over supper that night after we'd gotten Juanita placed into custody.

"Juanita had only confessed to Beka after Beka had found Leighann's emergency kit in the Liberty house while visiting. In some sort of sick way, Juanita had told Beka that if need be, Beka should confess to killing Leighann so Juanita could spend what time she had on the earth with her boys. She also gave Beka the permission to live in her house, happily ever after with Manuel," Finn finished up the story while I continued to eat Mama's chicken pot pie that she'd made for me as a special I'm-sorry-for-being-so-crabby-about-Christmas make up.

"Juanita Liberty is really that ill?" Mama asked.

"Yeah, she was hauling them trees like a champion the other day," My dad chimed in between bites.

"Not really. She only told her family that because she needed an excuse to kill Leighann. She had tricked Leighann into talking with her by telling her that Manuel was really upset and she wanted to make amends with her so they could move on." The sadness of it all made a lump in my throat. "Can you imagine the excitement Leighann felt when she thought Manuel's mother had finally come around and their life was going to be happy?"

"Why was Leighann driving?" Mama asked.

"Juanita had originally thought she was just going to shoot Leighann, but when she saw the sleeping pills, she'd made Leighann some water to sip because she was so upset. Then proceeded to tell Leighann that Manuel had made a special night for them down at Chimney Rock boat ramp. Alluding to the fact Manuel had gotten Leighann an engagement ring for Christmas." Finn shrugged. "Leighann jumped in her car and headed that way thinking Manuel was there waiting for her with an engagement ring."

"She followed Leighann to make sure she'd wreck and die, but when Leighann survived the wreck, she remembered seeing the keys to the tow trucks, so Juanita took Leighann's keys back to the tow company, let herself in and took the keys along with Sean's truck so she could easily slip the SUV into the river and bye-bye Leighann." I let out a big long sigh. "Another sick thing she did was take everything out of the Leighann's car because she didn't want anything in there to help Leighann if she woke up."

Everyone looked at me with shocked expressions on their faces.

"Why on earth would Beka try to say that she did it?" Mama asked.

"Beka thought that since she was a minor, that she'd not go to jail if she took the fall and her and Manuel could be happy together."

"I heard her mama is getting her some counseling," Mama chimed in.

"That's good. She needs it." I was happy to hear that.

"That seems like a lot of work to go through because you simply didn't like someone." My dad pushed back from the table.

"You'd be surprised." Finn tweaked a grin. "I've seen so many crimes of passion killings that nothing surprises me now."

"This might surprise you." Dad gave Mama the look. It wasn't a look that he gave often, but when he did, you knew he meant business.

"What?" My eyes shifted between him and Mama.

"I want to say," ahem, Mama cleared her throat. "I'm sorry for the way I've acted over the past few months. It was immature and childish to think my one and only daughter would never leave me on Christmas."

"Vivian," My dad's voice boomed over the table.

"I'm getting there," she told my dad. "Finn, you are a very nice young man. If Kendrick is dating someone and has to visit his family, I couldn't think of a nicer boy we'd like to have her date. With that, I'm asking for your forgiveness."

"Oh, Mama," I gasped and jumped up, running around the family table to give her a hug. "This makes it so much easier on me. Thank you."

"I love you and I want you to go and have a wonderful time." She returned the hug and held it for a long time.

Deep in my soul, I knew everything was going to be okay and the excitement was building up.

"Don't forget to come pick me up," I reminded her that she was going to pick me up in a couple of days to take me to the airport.

CHAPTER TWENTY

"Get up, get up!" Mama ripped my warm covers right off me. "We're going to be late."

Beep, beep, beep.

My alarm sounded just in the knick of time. I was happy to see that Mama was there on time to take me and Finn to the airport. And she was in a very good mood, which made me much happier. Duke was snuggled up next to me. The excitement of leaving to meet Finn's parents was building up in my stomach. I was surprised at the little giggle that escaped my body.

"I have to admit that when the weathermen get it wrong," DJ Nelly chirped through my alarm clock radio, "they get it wrong. But not this winter wonderland."

"Winter wonderland?" My head jerked to the side and I bolted out of bed.

"Stay safe out there and bundle up if you're headed out to the fair grounds." The radio played "Let It Snow".

"No. No. No," I begged and ran across my cold bedroom floor, jerking open my curtains. "No." My heart sank into my gut when the thick blanket of snow made me realize my worst nightmare.

"Honey, don't forget to make your bed. You never know if the fire department is called and they have to come in while we're gone to the pageant since you can't get to Chicago because the airport is closed."

No wonder she was so chipper. She'd gotten her way. Vivian Lowry had gotten her way, again.

"Come on, Duke," my voice was flat. My phone was on the counter in the kitchen and I wondered what Finn thought.

The murmur down the hall told me she wasn't alone. I grabbed my robe off the chair and threw it on, tying it as I walked down the hall.

"Ah oh, you look mad. When you get mad, you get ugly." Mama had on a full face of makeup and bright red lipstick. "God don't like ugly, Kendrick."

"I'm sorry." Finn stood up from the chair at the table and put his arms out. "Last night you fell asleep and it'd started to snow. I knew it was going to come pouring down overnight. So I went ahead and called the airport to exchange our tickets for after the new year."

"It's all worked out." Mama clasped her hands together.

I melted into Finn's arms and cried not only for me and him, but all the pain and suffering Cottonwood had felt for the loss of Leighann Graves, plus the fact I didn't get to say goodbye to Poppa. I'd been keeping it all inside.

"I'll just be going. Your daddy is waiting for me in the car," Mama whispered. "I'll see you at the pageant."

I felt Finn give a nod and heard the door open, the click of Duke's nails across the kitchen linoleum floor, and the door shut.

"Is she gone?" I asked.

"Yes." Finn took his finger and lifted my chin up so our eyes met. "It's no big deal."

"It is a big deal. I really wanted to meet your family." I took a step back and wiped my face. "I needed to get out of Cottonwood and let this whole Leighann thing get behind me." I gestured between us. "We need to get out of Cottonwood and take a break."

"AND WE WILL." He walked over to the coffee pot and poured a couple of cups. "I promise. Besides, I'm looking forwards to watching your mom do that wave thing on stage this morning."

"I'm going to get a kick out of her trying to keep that crown on her head when she's serving the annual Christmas lunch at the undercroft." Both of us laughed. "You get Duke in and feed him while I go get ready."

While getting ready, I'd gotten to the point where I'd accepted the fact the plans had changed back to my old plans. There was some joy knowing that Finn was going to get to experience Christmas with me and my family along with the great town we protected. When Vivian Lowry was involved it was an experience like no other.

Keeping with the spirit, I turned up the radio and listened to DJ Nelly play the Christmas music while I got ready. With my jeans tucked into my snow boots, I headed down the hall. There was a note on the table alongside my coat that said to come outside when I was finished getting ready.

I locked the back door, figuring Duke was with Finn because he wasn't darting around the snow in the backyard and walked through the gate up to the front of my house.

"Merry Christmas." Finn was standing up in a red sleigh that was attached to two horses and a driver. Poppa was sitting next to the driver in his most glorious of ghost forms with Duke sitting next to him.

"Ding, ding," Poppa said and grinned from ear-to-ear, making fun of me. "What's that saying about when you hear a bell ring an angel gets his wings?"

Ding, ding, ding.

The driver tugged on the string that was attached to a bell on the sleigh.

"Merry Christmas, Kenni-Bug," Poppa waved and disappeared.

"Merry Christmas, Poppa," I whispered looking up into the sky as the big snowflakes tumbled to the ground.

"Ready?" Finn put his hand out. "I wanted you to have that experience you had with your Poppa the first time they had the Christmas Festival at the fairgrounds. I can't drive or even ride a horse, so this'll have to do."

He stuck his hand out and helped me into the sled.

"You did good, Finn Vincent." I wrapped my arms around him and kissed him before the driver said it was time to go.

The wind whipped around us when the driver had the horses go.

"He did do good, Kenni-Bug," the wind whispered in my air. I tugged open the quilts sitting between me and Finn, snuggling up underneath.

The lights that were strung between the carriage lights along Main Street twinkled even more against the white background. The spirit of Christmas began to fill every part of my being with each sound of the horses' hooves hitting the impacted snow.

"Is it how you remember it?" Finn whispered as we made our way onto the fairgrounds.

"Even better." I snuggled closer. "Better than I remembered."

The tent was filled with a standing crowd. The sled had come to a halt and I took a moment to look around.

There were many fire pits going with people standing around and listening to the carolers sing as they passed. Cottonwood was welcoming Christmas and all it had to offer. No amount of snow could dampen the spirit of this small town.

"May I?" Finn held his hand out. Duke jumped out before me. "We don't want to miss our front row seats."

"What is up your sleeve?" I asked.

"You aren't very good with surprises." He was right. I think that's why I was so good at being a sheriff. I liked to keep the peace, know what was going on and no surprises.

I took his hand and got out of the carriage. We held hands and walked up to the fairgrounds' metal building that was used for the crafts during the summer and the display of pies during the pie competition. He opened the door and Jolee was just inside. Duke jumped and danced around her until she bent down.

"There you are. The show is about to start," Jolee said and gave Duke some good scratches.

I glanced up and the entire inside looked like the basement of Luke Jones's movie theater basement. There was a sheet hung up and just enough chairs for me and my girlfriends.

"Enjoy your annual White Christmas movie," Finn whispered in my ear.

"You did all this?" I asked in disbelief.

"He sure did. In a few short hours too." Luke nodded and handed me a big bag of popcorn that was littered with melting chocolate chips on the top. "Jolee has your Diet drink waiting for you too." Jolee waved from the front.

"Thank you." I turned around to look at Finn. There were tears in my eyes. "No one has ever done something so nice for me."

"No one has ever loved you as much as I love you." He bent down. Our lips met in a soft and warm kiss. "Go have fun. I'll be hanging outside."

"You've got you a good one right there." Jolee slipped her arm into mine and we walked up to the seats.

"Yeah." I sighed. "He's a good one."

The entire time "White Christmas" played, and Bing Crosby danced alongside Rosemary Clooney, I watched my friends. Then I wondered what I'd be doing if I was in Chicago with Finn's family. No matter what I'd been doing there, fun or not, I'm sure I'd been thinking about what my friends and family were doing here. I wasn't sure what next year would bring, but I did know that right now, I was truly grateful for the blizzard. This was exactly where I was supposed to be.

Just like Finn said, he was outside waiting for me and Duke.

"Let's go under the tent." He nodded towards the big crowd, hoots and hollers and some whistling. "It looks like we just got here in time."

Duke trotted beside us, sniffing everyone's feet and dangling gloved hands.

Finn pointed to the stage.

"And the winner of this year's is..." Edna Easterly slowly ripped open the red envelope and peeked inside. Mama stood up on the stage in a long red cape with white trim. She and Viola White were holding hands like you'd see on the Miss America pageant.

"Lord help us all if Mama wins," I curled up on my toes and whispered in Finn's ear. He smiled.

"Viola White!" Edna Easterly screamed in the microphone.

Mama had already begun her walk and wave, for sure thinking she'd won the title. Viola practically shoved Mama out of the way and stepped right on up to get that crown from Mayor Ryland and batch of flowers from Myrna Savage.

Mama was a pitiful sight as the disbelief showed on her face. True Southern Mama style, she drew back her shoulders, planted a smile on them bright lips and began to clap. When Viola caught wind of Mama, she started to really prance around the stage and blow kisses.

"Ah oh," Finn said in a scared voice. "Is this going to be a good Christmas?"

"Mama is going to be a sour puss all day," I said as we made our way over towards the edge of the stage where all the contestants were walking off. Duke had already beat us up to the front.

"I swear you paid them off," Mama scoffed.

"I did not." Viola gripped the bouquet of flowers. "They know a real beauty when they see one. Inside and out." She poked herself in the chest.

"Now y'all stop your bickering." I shook my head and realized that no amount of spirit that Christmas brought would bring these two to ever see eye-to-eye.

Just then snowflakes had started to fall from the sky. They were even bigger than before. My insides tickled, and I looked up into the falling flakes.

Ding, ding, the faint sound of a bell jingled from above.

"Merry Christmas, Poppa," I whispered knowing Poppa had gotten his angel wings.

"Merry Christmas to you too." Finn pulled me in for a Christmas kiss that was better than any present or trip he could've ever given me.

THE END

Don't miss a beat! Continue your visit in Cottonwood with Diggin' Up Dirt, the next book in the Kenni Lowry Mystery series is now available on Amazon or FREE in Kindle Unlimited.

Keep reading for a sneak peek of the next book in the series. Diggin' Up Dirt is now available to purchase on Amazon or read for FREE in Kindle Unlimited.

Chapter One of Book Seven
Diggin' Up Dirt

"That youngin' is meaner than a rattlesnake. Givin' Woody's boy and Woody a fit all these years and the state pen let him out on good behavior." Mama elbowed me in the back of the Cottonwood Funeral Home. She nodded towards Woody's grandson, Rich Moss. "Done gone and put his daddy in the grave. Wouldn't doubt it if he put Woody there too."

"Mama," I scolded her, though I had heard that Lenora and Woody's only child had died of alcoholism years ago. "Don't be speaking like that in front of the dead," I warned and looked around to make sure no one else heard her. "Don't be throwing that bad juju on me." Chills ran up my spine and down my arms. "See what you did?" I lifted my prickly arm up to her face.

"Don't be looking at me in that tone." Mama's right brow rose, in her forewarned you're-never-too-old-for-a-scolding Mama way.

"Ah oh." Myrna Savage, owner of Petal Pushers Florist, scurried past with an open heart-shaped mold of white roses and white carnations. You know, one of them that's laid at the gravesite. "Someone is walking on someone's grave." Her brows lifted when she noticed me rubbing the goosebumps away.

"Hhhmmmm," Mama's lips pinched, her nose curled. "Who sent those?"

"Lulu McClain." Myrna shrugged and headed straight up the middle row where Woody Moss laid in corpse, a polite, Southern way of saying "dead". "Vivian, you sure are slacking."

Mama watched in jealous silence as Myrna shimmied past the mourners and placed Lulu's wreath at the foot of Woody's casket.

"Which one did you send?" I asked, knowing the bigger the flower arrangement, the higher up in the social ladder you'd be that week.

"It doesn't matter," she quipped. "Where is your father? I'd like to get a seat up in the front before Preacher Bing starts the service."

"I'm sure he'll be here soon." I sucked in a deep breath and wondered the exact same thing about Finn Vincent, my boyfriend.

The sound of curtains opening just behind the casket caught my and Mama's attention.

SNEAK PEEK OF DIGGIN' UP DIRT

"Well if I ain't seen it all," Mama gasped.

"What on earth is it?" I asked about the big window behind the curtains, which had a car pulled up to it looking right at Woody Moss.

"Max Bogus has gone on and put a drive-up window in the funeral home." A look of disgust drew across her face. "Next thing you know, he'll have the corpse sitting up, arm attached to a string like a puppet and waving somehow."

I wasn't sure whether to laugh or groan. It was the strangest thing I'd ever seen, especially when a bus from the Cottonwood Acres Rehabilitation Center pulled up and flung open the van door. The rehab center was more than just for therapies, it also had a small emergency room on one side. We didn't have a hospital in Cottonwood and Dr. Camille Shively wasn't open 24/7. We needed something for quick emergencies so that we don't have to drive forty-five minutes to Clay's Ferry or a bigger city close to Cottonwood.

"Well, I'll be damned," Mama spat with disbelief.

"Now, Mama." I patted her arm to get her to calm down. "Woody died in the rehab center and probably made some new, elderly friends that wanted to pay their respects."

It was like a train wreck. Mama and me couldn't stop gawking at the blue-hairs, the elderly, as they took a gander at Woody in his casket through the window.

"I'm telling you right now, hand to God," Mama said and flung her hand up in the air, "If you let them do that to me, I swear I'll haunt you the rest of your life."

"Just like Poppa?" I asked.

"Huh?" She jerked around and looked at me.

"Joking," I said, a flat out lie.

My Poppa, Mama's dad and retired sheriff of Cottonwood, hadn't necessarily been haunting me, but since I took over as sheriff, Poppa was my guardian angel deputy from the great beyond. Poppa only showed up when there were murders in Cottonwood and I was happy to report he wasn't here today so that meant not only that Woody wasn't murdered, but no one else in Cottonwood was either and all was well in our little town.

"If you'll excuse me, I'd like to go give my condolences to the family," I finished my sentence and wanted to get away before Mama realized what I'd said and questioned me further.

No one knew about me having the ability to see and visit with Poppa except Duke. Duke was my hound dog and I was sure he wasn't going to say anything to anyone.

Mama didn't say a word, so either she was still stewing over the fact that Lulu McLain was about to replace her on the top rung of the social status or that Daddy was late. Mama didn't like to be late and that rule included Daddy, who she claimed was a direct reflection on her as well.

I didn't want my relationship with Finn to be like that, so I took a deep breath and knew he'd get there when he could make it. After all, he was holding down the sheriff's department while I'd taken the time to come here early and shake a few hands.

As the sheriff of Cottonwood, I had to attend every funeral, birth, baptism, and whatever else appealed to a family. It was, after all, those times that the good citizens of Cottonwood would remember when it was time for me to run for re-election in a couple of years. Little did I realize that my saturated childhood of "yes, ma'ams" and "no, sirs" along with the bit of Jesus that Mama beat into my head would all come in handy when running for an election around here.

Or maybe it was all the lessons, Lordy the lessons—piano lessons, tap lessons, modeling lessons, clogging lessons and handwriting lessons to mention a few—that added to the lunacy of my life that made me want to follow in the footsteps of my Poppa and not become a debutant, which was the very thing Mama was trying to make out of me by doing all them darned lessons.

The funeral home was packed, which made sense because funerals, weddings, and births were a big deal around these Kentucky parts. Woody Moss's funeral would be front page news on the Cottonwood Chronicle and talk of the town down at Ben's Diner. That's just how it was.

"Hi, do." I nodded and shook hands as I weaved in and out of the crowd, making my way back to the room where Woody's family had gathered.

Even though I knew some of them people didn't vote for me, I always remembered what Poppa would say to me during his election years – "Don't cost a nickel to be polite."

Having good manners and giving social grace was just a way of life around here. I was sure that was why there were so many people at funerals whether you knew them or not.

There was a line of folks giving their condolences and telling stories they had with Woody. I couldn't offer any of those. He was an elderly man I really didn't know other than when I talked with him about my Poppa's reign as sheriff. Everyone loved Poppa. I made my way to the back of the family room and stood in line with my hands folded in front of me.

"I told you I did the best I could." I couldn't help but overhear a young woman with shoulder length blonde hair, fair skin, and the brightest of red lipstick on her lips talking to the man Mama pointed out as Woody's grandson, Rich.

"If I find out that your best wasn't good enough, they'll be hell to pay," Rich said to her through gritted teeth as she jerked her arm out of his grip.

"Is everything okay here?" Not that I wanted to butt my head into someone's business, but if I noticed it was a little more physical than an average conversation, I'd stick my nose into it.

"What's it to you?" Rich snarled.

"I might not have my plain brown uniform on," I pulled back the blue blazer I was wearing and exposed my five-point star sheriff's pin clipped to the waist of my blue skirt. "But I'm Sheriff Kenni Lowry and I sure hope nothing is going to get ugly while we are all paying our respects for you grandfather." I took it a step further. "Especially since I understand you were let out of prison early for good behavior. What I just heard didn't sound like good behavior."

"I'm fine." The girl shook her head and turned, going back out of the room.

"Is she fine?" I didn't take my eyes off of Rich Moss.

He stood about five feet nine. Thick as a tree trunk and the blackest eyes I'd ever seen. He had olive skin and a five o'clock black shadow that seemed to be going on ten o'clock but wasn't yet a full beard. He was shiny bald on top and had a tattoo that went from ear to ear around the back of his head.

"She walked out without a limp, didn't she?" His cold words were like an ice cube dripping along my spine.

"I don't expect to have any trouble out of you while you're in town, right." It wasn't a real question. It was a threat, so he'd know that type of activity wasn't welcomed here.

"Yes. Sheriff woman." His lips curled up at the edges with a hint of laughter in his voice.

"Sheriff Lowry," I corrected him and turned around when I felt someone come up behind me.

"There you are," Finn said and smiled. "I saw Vivian and she's not in a good mood. She's trying to get Myrna to go back to Petal Pushers and make a bigger flower arrangement." He laughed and suddenly stopped when he noticed I'd not tried to grin. "What's wrong?"

"I'd like you to meet," I started to introduce him to Rich Moss, but Rich was gone. "Never mind." I shook my head and glanced around the room, not seeing him anywhere. "Did you get your parents settled?"

"You are going to have to brace yourself," Finn warned with a slight smile, guiding me out of the room. "They drove their RV and parked it right in front of Mrs. Brown's house."

"Oh no," I groaned, looking up at my six-foot-tall boyfriend, and knowing that she would be calling as soon as she saw it.

Mrs. Brown was the neighbor between my house and Finn's house.

"I already went to see her and told her they'd only be here for a few days so they can meet you." He melted my heart right there in the funeral home. His big brown eyes had a spark in them like a little boy that'd gotten exactly what he'd wanted.

Finn had wanted to me to meet his parents, who lived in Chicago, for a year or so now. We'd even made huge plans to be there over Christmas until the biggest blizzard to ever hit Kentucky blew in the day we were supposed to board the plane. Now, Mama was thrilled to death that it'd snowed to high-heaven because that meant we were stuck with her for Christmas.

"Where are they now?" I asked about his parents and pointed to a couple of seats near the front of the casket.

"They are at my house visiting with Cosmo." He put his arm around me. Cosmo was a cat that'd he'd taken in after the owner had gone to jail when we'd arrested her for murder. See, he had a huge heart and I loved him for that. "Really, waiting until they meet you tonight."

"I hope Mama acts her best." The thought of Mama hosting Finn's parents made me anxious.

I pointed to the empty seats next to us since Preacher Bing had taken his spot at the podium. I'd have to give my condolences to Woody's family a little later.

After the funeral, I made a quick exit out of the funeral home and let Finn do the repass, the after-funeral home festivities.

Howllll, howwwwwl.

Duke was happy to see me when I'd gotten back into the old Jeep Wagoneer after the funeral. Rarely did I ever go anywhere without him. He was known as my deputy dog. He'd even been given an award for actually taking a bullet for me once.

"I know, Duke," I confirmed how good the fresh air felt and smelt with the wind whipping in through the windows. Not to mention how good it felt to get the stink off of me from all the flowers at the funeral home.

There was no way to describe just how much I hated the smell of flowers at a funeral home, so much so that I'd changed my will to include no flowers at my own funeral. They reminded me of death. My Poppa's funeral was filled with flowers and that was a horrible time for me. The memory was still unsettling.

Duke's long bloodhound ears flopped in delight outside the window. His tail, that I was sure had a string to his heart, wagged in delight. There was nothing like when summer was right around the corner in Cottonwood.

"What a day for a funeral." The sun was hanging bright in the early afternoon. The only real thing I had to do was meet my friends at my house so they could help get me all prettied up to meet Finn's parents. That wasn't until late this afternoon.

Before I could turn the Wagoneer north of town after I'd pulled left on Main Street, Mama was calling.

"Before you start lecturing me," I answered the phone because I knew she was mad that I'd sent Finn to the repass after the funeral instead of me. "I have to get all gussied up for tonight when you meet Finn's family."

That would get her attention.

"You know I love when you actually dress in something pretty, but you've got to get over to Woody Moss's house," there was a bit of panic in her voice. "His house has been ransacked. Like someone has broken in and stolen stuff."

"Be there in a minute." I tried to tell her.

"You know, I bet that Rich did it. He was in jail. And I bet he'd steal a wreath off his Meemaw's grave." Mama had decided to throw her two cents in.

"Mama, I'm on my way." I clicked off the phone instead of listening to her theories, though they probably weren't too far-fetched. But there was no way I was going to tell her that.

I jerked the wheel to turn the Wagoneer around, all while grabbing the old-time beacon siren from under my seat and licking the suction cup before smacking it on the roof.

Rowl, rowl, Duke howled along with the siren. One of his all-time favorite things to do.

"Hold on, buddy," I warned and pushed the pedal to ground. "Who on earth would target the house of a dead man?" I'd heard of criminals perusing the newspaper to see who was dead and break into their house, but not on the day of the funeral.

"Rich Moss."

I was certain.

Don't miss a beat! Continue your visit in Cottonwood with Diggin' Up Dirt, the next book in the Kenni Lowry Mystery series is now available on Amazon or FREE in Kindle Unlimited.

If you enjoyed reading this book as much as I enjoyed writing it then be sure to return to the Amazon page and leave a review.

Go to Tonyakappes.com for a full reading order of my novels and while there join my newsletter. You can also find links to Facebook, Instagram and Goodreads.

Join like-minded readers like YOU in the Cozy Krew Facebook Group for dream casting, fan theories, and live Q & A's. It's like a BIG GIANT BOOK CLUB! But if you want to have your own book club, be sure you let me know! I love to send goodies.

Also By Tonya Kappes

A Camper and Criminals Cozy Mystery
BEACHES, BUNGALOWS, & BURGLARIES
DESERTS, DRIVERS, & DERELICTS
FORESTS, FISHING, & FORGERY
CHRISTMAS, CRIMINALS, & CAMPERS
MOTORHOMES, MAPS, & MURDER
CANYONS, CARAVANS, & CADAVERS
HITCHES, HIDEOUTS, & HOMICIDE
ASSAILANTS, ASPHALT, & ALIBIS
VALLEYS, VEHICLES & VICTIMS
SUNSETS, SABBATICAL, & SCANDAL
TENTS, TRAILS, & TURMOIL
KICKBACKS, KAYAKS, & KIDNAPPING
GEAR, GRILLS, & GUNS
EGGNOG, EXTORTION, & EVERGREENS
ROPES, RIDDLES, & ROBBERIES
PADDLERS, PROMISES, & POISON
INSECTS, IVY, & INVESTIGATIONS
OUTDOORS, OARS, & OATHS
WILDLIFE, WARRANTS, & WEAPONS
BLOSSOMS, BARBEQUE, & BLACKMAIL
LANTERNS, LAKES, & LARCENY
JACKETS, JACK-O-LANTERN, & JUSTICE
SANTA, SUNRISES, & SUSPICIONS
VISTAS, VICES, & VALENTINES
ADVENTURE, ABDUCTION, & ARREST
RANGERS, RV'S, & REVENGE
CAMPFIRES, COURAGE, & CONVICTS
TRAPPING, TURKEYS, & THANKSGIVING
GIFTS, GLAMPING, & GLOCKS
ZONING, ZEALOTS, & ZIPLINES
HAMMOCKS, HANDGUNS, & HEARSAY

ALSO BY TONYA KAPPES

Kenni Lowry Mystery Series
FIXIN' TO DIE
SOUTHERN FRIED
AX TO GRIND
SIX FEET UNDER
DEAD AS A DOORNAIL
TANGLED UP IN TINSEL
DIGGIN' UP DIRT
BLOWIN' UP A MURDER

Killer Coffee Mystery Series
SCENE OF THE GRIND
MOCHA AND MURDER
FRESHLY GROUND MURDER
COLD BLOODED BREW
DECAFFEINATED SCANDAL
A KILLER LATTE
HOLIDAY ROAST MORTEM
DEAD TO THE LAST DROP
A CHARMING BLEND NOVELLA (CROSSOVER WITH MAGICAL CURES MYSTERY)
FROTHY FOUL PLAY
SPOONFUL OF MURDER
BARISTA BUMP-OFF
CAPPUCCINO CRIMINAL

Holiday Cozy Mystery
FOUR LEAF FELONY
MOTHER'S DAY MURDER
A HALLOWEEN HOMICIDE
NEW YEAR NUISANCE
CHOCOLATE BUNNY BETRAYAL
APRIL FOOL'S ALIBI
FATHER'S DAY MURDER
THANKSGIVING TREACHERY

ALSO BY TONYA KAPPES

SANTA CLAUSE SURPRISE

Mail Carrier Cozy Mystery
STAMPED OUT
ADDRESS FOR MURDER
ALL SHE WROTE
RETURN TO SENDER
FIRST CLASS KILLER
POST MORTEM
DEADLY DELIVERY
RED LETTER SLAY

Magical Cures Mystery Series
A CHARMING CRIME
A CHARMING CURE
A CHARMING POTION (novella)
A CHARMING WISH
A CHARMING SPELL
A CHARMING MAGIC
A CHARMING SECRET
A CHARMING CHRISTMAS (novella)
A CHARMING FATALITY
A CHARMING DEATH (novella)
A CHARMING GHOST
A CHARMING HEX
A CHARMING VOODOO
A CHARMING CORPSE
A CHARMING MISFORTUNE
A CHARMING BLEND (CROSSOVER WITH A KILLER COFFEE COZY)
A CHARMING DECEPTION

A Southern Magical Bakery Cozy Mystery Serial
A SOUTHERN MAGICAL BAKERY

A Ghostly Southern Mystery Series

ALSO BY TONYA KAPPES

A GHOSTLY UNDERTAKING
A GHOSTLY GRAVE
A GHOSTLY DEMISE
A GHOSTLY MURDER
A GHOSTLY REUNION
A GHOSTLY MORTALITY
A GHOSTLY SECRET
A GHOSTLY SUSPECT

A Southern Cake Baker Series
(WRITTEN UNDER MAYEE BELL)
CAKE AND PUNISHMENT
BATTER OFF DEAD

Spies and Spells Mystery Series
SPIES AND SPELLS
BETTING OFF DEAD
GET WITCH or DIE TRYING

A Laurel London Mystery Series
CHECKERED CRIME
CHECKERED PAST
CHECKERED THIEF

A Divorced Diva Beading Mystery Series
A BEAD OF DOUBT SHORT STORY
STRUNG OUT TO DIE
CRIMPED TO DEATH

Olivia Davis Paranormal Mystery Series
SPLITSVILLE.COM
COLOR ME LOVE (novella)
COLOR ME A CRIME

Grandberry Falls Books

ALSO BY TONYA KAPPES

THE LADYBUG JINX
HAPPY NEW LIFE
A SUPERSTITIOUS CHRISTMAS
NEVER TELL YOUR DREAMS

About Tonya

Tonya has written over 100 novels, all of which have graced numerous bestseller lists, including the USA Today. Best known for stories charged with emotion and humor and filled with flawed characters, her novels have garnered reader praise and glowing critical reviews. She lives with her husband and a very spoiled rescue cat named Ro. Tonya grew up in the small southern Kentucky town of Nicholasville. Now that her four boys are grown men, Tonya writes full-time in her camper she calls her SHAMPER (she-camper).

Learn more about her be sure to check out her website tonyakappes.com. Find her on Facebook, Twitter, BookBub, and Instagram

Sign up to receive her newsletter, where you'll get free books, exclusive bonus content, and news of her releases and sales.

If you liked this book, please take a few minutes to leave a review now! Authors (Tonya included) really appreciate this, and it helps draw more readers to books they might like. Thanks!

Cover artist: Mariah Sinclair: The Cover Vault

This book is a work of fiction. The characters, incidents, and dialogue are drawn from the author's imagination and are not to be construed as real. Any resemblance to actual events or persons, living or dead, is entirely coincidental.

Copyright © 2021 by Tonya Kappes. All rights reserved. Printed in the United States of America. No part of this book may be used or reproduced in any manner whatsoever without written permission except in the case of brief quotations embodied in critical articles and reviews. For information email Tonyakappes@tonyakappes.com

Made in United States
Orlando, FL
18 March 2025